Order of the Dragon—Book One

A Novel of the House of Basarab

LISA J. YARDE

Cover design by Mirella Patzer.

ISBN (Print only): 978-1939138248

Acknowledgments

This novel, while a work of fiction, would have been impossible to complete without four years of intensive research. Thanks to the popularity of Bram Stoker's *Dracula* novel, the truth about the Dracula family of late medieval Romania cannot escape legends about the undead.

I could never have finished this story without the timely publication of Dr. A. K. Brackob's *Dracul: Of the Father-The Untold Story of Vlad Dracul* (2021). Critical information also came from over a hundred publications, including the following sources:

The Dracula Family and their Relatives

Dracula by Matei Cazacu (2011).

Dracula's Bloodline: A Florescu Family Saga by Radu R. Florescu and Matei Cazacu (2013).

Mircea the Old: Father of Wallachia, Grandfather of Dracula by A. K. Brackob (2020).

The Hungarian Royal Court and Warfare

Barbara of Cilli (1392-1451): A Hungarian, Holy Roman and Bohemian Queen by Daniela Dvořáková (2011).

The Hussite Wars (1419-36) by Stephen Turnbull (2004).

The Laws of the Medieval Kingdom of Hungary (Online Decreta Regni Mediaevalis Hungariae) by János M. Bak (2019).

The Raven and the Ring-The Life and Times of John Hunyadi by Paul Pulitzer (1988).

Medieval Eastern Europe

At Europe's Borders: Medieval Towns in the Romanian Principalities by Laurenţiu Rădvan (2010).

Byzantium between the Ottomans and the Latins: Politics and Society in the Late Empire by Nevra Necipoğlu (2009).

From Nicopolis to Mohács: A History of Ottoman-Hungarian Warfare, 1389-1526 by Tamás Pálosfalvi (2018).

The End of Byzantium by Jonathan Harris (2010).

Medieval Ottoman Turks

A Military History of the Ottomans by Meset Uyar and Edward J. Erickson (2009).

Armies of the Ottoman Turks 1300-1774 by David Nicolle (1983).

Ransom Slavery Along the Ottoman Borders (Early Fifteenth-Eighteenth Centuries) by Géza Dávid and Pál Fodor (2007).

The Sons of Bayezid: Empire Building and Representation in the Ottoman Civil War of 1402-1413 by Dimitris J. Kastritsis (2007).

I am grateful to the members of the HisFictCrit group and the Chapter-by-Chapter Critique Group for Novelists, who helped refine the manuscript in its early stages. Special thanks to Anita Davison, Mirella Patzer, Diane Parkinson, Maggie Andersen, Susan Cook, Lori Higgins, Julie Howard, Philip MH, Karen McCullough, Kayli McIlrath, Rosemary Morris, Jennifer Pittam, the late Katherine Pym, Randy Reimer, and Maria York. I owe an enormous debt of thanks to Mirella Patzer and Susan Wands for helping me to complete the novel.

PREFACE

About the Order of the Dragon – Book One

What should you understand about the fifteenth-century world of Vlad Dracul and its inhabitants before reading this novel? Vlad Dracul has been confused at times with his more infamous namesake son, Vlad Dracula, immortalized in fiction as a vampire. The father was a legend too. A warrior for God and a leader of men. Europe's kings, princes, emperors, and despots alternately admired and mistrusted him. The Ottoman Turks, his most formidable foes, not only limited the boundaries of Christianity; a kinship tie he shared with the Turks set him on the path of destiny.

Vlad Dracul's birthplace was Wallachia, not Romania, which did not exist as the name of a country until 1866. In Hungary, he lived in the cosmopolitan capital of Buda, or modern-day Budapest. The Hungarian town of Pozsony rather than Bratislava in today's Slovakia, and the region of Styria instead of southeast Austria were familiar to him. His native Wallachian tongue was not the only one he understood. His mother taught him Hungarian. He spoke Latin, German, Greek, Italian, and the Old Slavonic language, which united the Orthodox Christian faith. He knew the Serbian name Đurađ rather than George, and the Polish name Jadwiga instead of Hedwig. The Roma, known as Gypsies, lived as slaves throughout medieval Wallachian society, including the courts where the family of Vlad Dracul reigned.

The bonds of blood and brotherhood influenced his fate. A lover and a husband, he became associated with many women. The most prominent were Călţuna and Cneajna; the latter's name is correctly pronounced as "Nahj-na." Both females, from diverse backgrounds, cherished him and his children. The dates of all the historical events of his time, including battles and sieges, and celestial phenomena mentioned in the novel took place following the Julian calendar. The modern method of marking events did not occur until more than a century after him.

Above all, dear reader, you should know that in the epoch of Vlad Dracul, belief in the existence of ghosts, revenants, vampires, werewolves, shapeshifters, and witches prevailed.

A Prince in Exile

1408-1410

CHAPTER 1

The Dragon's Breath

"Love is the crowning grace of humanity, the holiest right of the soul, the golden link which binds us to duty and truth, the redeeming principle that chiefly reconciles the heart to life, and is prophetic of eternal good."-Petrarch (1304-1374 AD), Italian Renaissance poet and humanist.

In the year of our Lord 1408. North of Milcov, Buzău district, Principality of Wallachia (modern-day Milcovul, eastern Romania), and *Argeş, capital of the Principality of Wallachia* (modern-day Curtea de Argeş, eastern Romania)

Hand in hand, the twin siblings Vlad and Arina fled northeastward over the craggy terrain of Wallachia. Most foreigners called their birthplace the Transalpine area or "the land across the mountains." Thick patches of mist obscured the slick ground. A poor omen for what might be an ill-starred venture.

Twice Arina almost skidded in the rain-soaked muck, but always, Vlad sensed her peril. He aided and reassured her.

Despite the encroaching darkness, the route to safety beckoned. Behind them, only doom and a fate worse than death existed now. Neither of them could ever return to their childhood home, the Wallachian capital at Argeş.

She asked, "How far are we, brother, from there?"

Not far enough, he thought, and urged her along. She huffed and climbed with him.

Toothed peaks atop the Carpathian Mountains pierced the night sky. Vlad guessed another three days of travel lay ahead, though on foot. A slow and perilous journey of fourteen leagues so far. Halfway from home, the dense forest canopy of the Argeş River Valley became their first offer of shelter and respite. It did not last long. They could not linger. The guards of the ruling prince, his halberdiers, would be in relentless pursuit of them.

They had endured scattered downpours each day. The Argeş River even overflowed its banks and almost thwarted what should have been an easy crossing. Their stolen horses foundered amid steep rocks. They left the animals behind. It seemed the Devil himself sought their ruin, or so their lone guide had said at the previous day's end.

Marko the Gypsy slave trudged on ahead of them with shaggy dark brown hair atop his head, bowed beneath a stiff spring breeze. He kept a firm grip on the staff in his meaty hand. Not once did he stop. The slave's footfalls squelched in the mire of damp and rotting leaves, a steady and somewhat reassuring rhythm. As the land rose higher and higher, he and his faithful pair of wolfhounds huffed in unison, their breaths issuing in swirls of white smoke.

He never asked the purpose of their flight or probed why Vlad chose him as their sole protector. Since leaving home, they avoided the region of Rucăr, veered away from the Wallachian border town of Bran, and kept far from taking the Bran Pass near the Kronstadt area into Transilvania, "the land beyond the forest." Marko seemed unfazed as the route drew them ever closer to the Principality of Moldavia, along the eastern range of the Carpathian Mountains.

Gypsy slaves knew better than to ask questions. Marko understood they needed him to help forage and hunt when stolen provisions ran out, and to guide and guard them. The sole truth he required.

Vlad tugged his sister's hand when she slowed again. "Come on. We don't want to lose Marko and the dogs in this haze."

Arina whimpered. "Can't you ask him to slow down or stop?"

He glanced over his shoulder. She lifted the trailing edge of her fleece-lined cloak. Gold shimmered as a thick rope necklace bulged over the top of her ankle-length boot, where it grazed her gown's hem trimmed with rabbit fur. He crouched and yanked her down. In an instant, he regretted it, his touch more forcefully than intended. She gasped and clutched at his forearm. Her nails clenched his sleeves.

"I'm sorry," he murmured without looking up.

He put the bauble back into the leather footwear, tucking it around her hose dyed indigo. A single, russet-hued braid, the length and thickness of his sword arm, fell into view. She wore no veil, as did all unmarried females. Despite a commonly held belief among their people that deemed the dark reddish-brown color of her curls unlucky. The sign of evil.

Vlad never overheard anyone who dared say so within their ruling prince's hearing or his. As her twin, he would have pummeled the speaker.

She touched the forelock of his coal-black hair and smiled. "Dearest brother. Mother said I came from her body before you did, but you're always protective of me."

I will never fail you, he vowed inwardly. Her smile widened in wistful regard for him.

His gaze followed the length of her slim hand to the delicate wrist. The top of her short, doeskin glove turned aside, revealing blue veins beneath pallid skin and the contour of a jutting bone. A fragile creature, she could never survive the fate the ruler Mircea the Great intended for her. Vlad must protect her at all costs.

He reminded Arina, "Trouble stalks us. The prince's halberdiers."

"They'll continue the search even on a night such as this?" She pushed back her hood and swept aside the long braid. Stiff breezes billowed folds of black cloth around her head.

Her agate-tinged eyes, which reminded him of dew-coated green mosses at twilight, scanned the sky. Her angular face evoked the image of fairies from childish imagination. An idea she dispelled as she snorted and batted away the tiny insects encircling their heads.

Vlad would have laughed, but when she glared at him next, he bit his lower lip. There could be no secrets between them.

"You know they'll never stop, sister. Neither can we."

His stare flitted to Marko. Damn, if the man had not lengthened the distance between them. Twigs snapped as the Gypsy ascended the sloping ridge toward the higher and drier ground, over which they must move faster.

"Come along, Rina, hurry," Vlad said.

"Oh, I am!" She whined as he hauled her along. "The treasures I've stuffed into my boots and sewn between the folds of my garments—"

"They weigh you down," he finished for her.

Their grandmother, Dowager Princess Ana-Călina, must have been furious when she learned about the missing jewels. *Perhaps she'll forgive the theft of them one day*, he reflected.

The sensation of rueful mirth stirred a smile from him. He even heard mild laughter.

She won't, Vlad. Grandmother will say we lacked cause to take her fine stones.

The words echoed in his mind. As if Arina had said them aloud.

After he looked askance, her lips twitched as she added, "You know I'm right."

As he also recognized, his sister perceived every belief in his head or word he might have spoken before he uttered one. He possessed the same ability to know her mind and moods. A strange connection in an existence rarely spent apart from their days in the womb. Even a shared cradle. Some eerie sense bound them. Vlad never knew what to make of it, but he held one certainty. No one else could learn the truth.

They might have gone about their lives without direct speech to each other. Whole conversations once took place in their heads until they reached the age of four. Their parents had questioned the nursemaids about why the twins laughed and smiled together but never talked openly.

At six, they had even tested whether distance would affect their link. Once Vlad hid in the stable while she sat indoors with their elder sister and mother at embroidery. He smiled now, recalling how Arina had communicated her loathing of the task along their bond. Even her disdain radiated to him as if he stood in the same room she then occupied.

"It's a tiresome skill," she muttered beside him while she took nimble steps between brambles. "I would rather pray to God or read the Bible than stitch."

"Nuns might do needlework, sister. Who else cares for their vestments, but them?"

An uncanny flare of heat buffeted him before she snorted and trudged on. When roused, her aggravation blazed hot as his. Like dragon flame.

One week before fleeing their home, they undertook dutiful practice in speaking aloud always, lest Marko found their interaction odd. The superstitious world where they lived would have deemed them unnatural and termed them the devil's children. Or did worse.

"We'll need everything you carry at our destination." He returned to the discussion of the trinkets. "To ensure a nunnery will accept you with little question."

"There may be some query. What about your fate, Vlad?"

He could not answer, not when he no longer knew. Once, a knighthood might have been his. Maybe other possibilities. None now, after this flight from the Princely Court.

Arina insisted, "A cloistered life is all I have wanted. For you, there must be more."

In his wildest daydreams, he once yearned for such. Now, that could never be, not after having stolen away from Argeş in the dead of night.

A flurry of thoughts rushed to him along their inward connection, but he forestalled her words by saying, "God alone will decide my future, Rina."

Shrouds of mist thickened and swirled around them. He realized they were losing sight of the Gypsy. "We'll worry about the future in Moldavia after we've crossed its border. First, let's catch up with Marko and his dogs."

More than wolves and bears roam Wallachian forests at night, he recollected.

Arina's nails raked his wrist as she clutched at him harder. In his mind, he apologized for frightening her with careless consideration.

They followed Marko until the trio reached a clearing at last. A menacing growl from somewhere in the woodland made their footfalls cease. Marko's dogs stiffened and the kennel master sniffed the wind.

"What is it, Vlad?" Arina whimpered.

In their childhood, Dowager Princess Ana-Călina told tales, passed down to her as a girl, of firedrakes hiding in the mist-filled caverns.

Grandmother never said they lived in the forests. Vlad could not allay the rampant thought.

An acrid scent like smoke rose along the slope. He turned at the same time as Marko warned, "*Domnule,* they've found us."

Vivid proof from torchlight shone among the trees below, scattered across a wide swath, drawing closer to them.

Vlad tugged Arina despite her tearful protest. "Don't falter. Marko, are there caves nearby where we may hide?"

"Above the ridge, there are many, *Domnule*."

"We'll make for one. By God's grace, we won't stumble upon an animal's den."

They darted through the clearing. Vlad's breath billowed in the cool night air. Dark brambles pulled at his calves encased in green woolen hose.

Let me go. Arina's plea filled his head. "Let them take me. You and Marko must escape." *You know there is no life for him back in the capital now.*

"Be quiet, Rina," he insisted. "Worry about yourself. Mother told us your betrothed is cruel. He killed a brother in their struggle for the throne. Will he have any regard for you?"

He wants the marital union and the prospects of gold and fighting men that come with it, Vlad. The man won't harm me. I'll convince him to let me keep the Christian religion.

Rina, do you think life as a heathen Turk's bride is the only outcome awaiting you back in Argeş? We've defied Wallachia's ruling prince! If we return, he'll mete out a brutal punishment.

Vlad dragged her along toward the edge of the clearing. Trees and larger bushes grew there. The gaps between them offered concealment. The ridge must lie behind the woodland. If they could only reach the crest and the caverns.

"*Domnule,* stop!"

The baritone voice was so close behind them. The snorts of horses made Arina cry out, but Vlad surged forward. A bolt whizzed in the darkness and found the trailing edge of his black mantle. As he pushed on, the material made a satisfying rip.

Another bolt felled Marko's closest companion. The bitch best favored in the hunt. Her yowl vied with her master's own. He fell to his knees and gripped her fur.

Vlad climbed again, even as Arina struggled in his grip.

"Marko, get up! Wait, brother. They'll kill him."

No, sister. I care not one whit for any other life, even the Gypsy's, more than yours.

"Eh, my boy. The next one will pierce Princess Arina's foot. As loath as I am to harm her, your mother's healing arts would ensure the wound doesn't fester and scar. You know my skill and may believe the third bolt from my crossbow won't delay the wedding. I adore your sister as you do, but I have the prince's orders."

Vlad whirled and met their pursuer. "Staico! You're a good dog, always at hand and ready to do the ruling prince's bidding. Do you hope for some show of gratitude this time?"

He eyed the burly man. The only uncle Vlad knew from boyhood. A bastard, though not baseborn. He maneuvered a sturdy Carpathian pony toward them, always with a surprising deftness in handling the reins. Only three fingers remained on his mangled right hand; the thumb and index finger severed at the base, lost to Turks. He rested the other unblemished hand atop the crossbow nestled on his lap.

Behind him, his Gypsies held their torches aloft, trained the same weapons as his on the ground, and kept the rest of their dogs at bay. They surrounded Marko.

The royal halberdiers hung back as if they wanted no part in the events to come. Absent their true master, the Wallachian sovereign, they followed Staico's command. The wind stirred the bristles of his hoary-gray hair, reminiscent of a porcupine's quills. Staico, a lord revered among the peasants.

"Why did you do this, *Domnule*?" Staico asked. "Steal away with the princess in the middle of the night, eh? You've jeopardized the Turkish alliance. Your father will not forgive you for forfeiting the life of his best Gypsy kennel master. How could you?"

Arina trembled and blubbered, burying her tear-stained face in Vlad's shoulder. He shook also but glared up at their father's most stalwart supporter.

"What would you have done instead, uncle? Do I already know?"

Staico averted his gaze and bowed his head. Even then, Vlad would not relent.

"I can guess you would've let the prince sacrifice Arina like he did our sister Anna. A grand prize, wed to an enemy of Christendom this time."

"God's grace, you're a boy of fourteen. Arina is moments older. What could children know about Wallachia's troubles? Your father understands. It's a blessing he rules and not you, impetuous whelp. Arina must become a peace-weaver. Like her mother and sister."

Vlad bridled most at being called a child. He had not felt like one for some time.

"Three weeks ago, you told our mother the prince's daughters have special places in your heart, because you'd never make another bastard like yourself."

Staico raised his head. The hard glint more often found in his half-brother's eyes shimmered like obsidian. "I thought Princess Mara and I were alone outside the chapel when I said that."

"If you loved Anna and Arina; if you mourned Anna after she and her little babe died in her childbed, how do you think I feel now that Arina faces the same fate?"

"It may not go the same way as with your eldest sister. Nothing is certain in life, eh?"

"Here's what I know, uncle. The Turk, the enemy of Christendom, wants money for his wars with his brothers. She's the means to get what he craves."

"Her union would also be a boon to our people, my boy, or do you ignore the most important truth that guides your father's choice in allowing the marriage?"

"As for the sovereign prince of Wallachia, if peace came at the price of his daughter, he would only wish he'd fathered thousands more like her."

"He loves his children better than his countrymen."

"They think he's a warrior for God against the Turks. He's afraid, like everyone else."

"You don't have the good sense of fear, eh, my boy?"

"My love for Arina is greater." Vlad gathered her closer to him. "She is my twin. My last sister. The only one among five remaining siblings who matters most to me."

Her copious tears cleaved a ruthless path like the rushing waters of the Argeş River through his heart.

"Princess Mara spent more time with you and your little brother than her husband permitted her with their elder sons." Staico shook his head. "You alone inherited her ability to feel things keenly. She's taught you too much about love. What do you intend now, eh?"

Vlad kissed his sister's forehead, released her, and set her apart from him.

She scrabbled at his sword arm. "Brother, don't. Please."

He warded her off. "I must, Arina."

Her ensuing silent plea almost ensnared him. He shook his head and cast aside the intrusions into his mind, unwelcome for the first time. The act took all his concentration, but finally, her attempts ceased. The bleak silence that followed struck him as odd at first.

He required clear thought as he untied the strings of his mantle. The material slid off his thin shoulders, revealing a close-fitting, short, quilted doublet or jacket of velvet lined with linen. Dark blue and silver patterned sleeves, each slashed from shoulder to elbow exposed the white tunic under the jacket, laced up to its high collar.

From his leather belt, he drew the sword buckled there. Its theft must have infuriated Prince Mircea more than his mother after she realized her jewels were gone.

Staico remained atop his mount. "*Domnule*?"

"We were never so formal before. Call me 'my lord' again, and I'll run you through."

"You may try, my boy. We are of the House of Basarab, but we will not fight and kill tonight. Fondness will stay your foolhardy hand but mark me. Love will be your downfall."

Vlad chuckled. "May it strengthen my limbs. It's better to feel love than to be a cold monster like the ruling prince."

"You are a poor judge of your father's sentiments."

"His brutal, murderous history already suggests what men of the House of Basarab may do to each other: absent love, given motives and the means."

Staico shook his head. "The prince would strike you if he heard that lie."

"I'm not frightened of him, and even less of you. You've trained my sword arm well."

"Give up this fight. Don't start what you cannot finish."

"Dismount and test me. See what I've learned by your good hand, war master."

"Your father would no more thank me if I maimed you in this foolish endeavor than if I had lost you in the forests and failed him."

"Your elder brother, yet he will hate you until his end, Staico."

"I know."

"He'll never reward you with his trust or affection. You're the proof of a mistake his father made. A mere cast-off he kept at court for your skilled sword hand. Use it now."

Staico laughed and muttered, "You mimic the insults I've endured from your grandmother. I'd sooner see all my fingers cut away than strike a sword blow at you, my boy. I will save you from your recklessness and the prince's ire."

"It can't be more bitter than what I have felt for him most of my life." Vlad raised the sword as his uncle taught and readied for a downward attack.

Staico patted the stallion's neck and nudged him forward. Vlad moved in unison with the mount and stayed out of reach of the animal's forelegs, lest the pony reared and kicked him in the chest. A Gypsy child died like that once, in the courtyard of Vlad's home.

"I'm no dance master, my boy. You weave and waver after such a bold challenge?"

"I don't want to topple you too soon, old man."

Despite the taunt, Staico kept coming while Vlad maintained his distance, watching for an attack. Soon, he realized his uncle had maneuvered him in a half-circular path through the brush. He stood downwind with the halberdiers behind him.

They never contented themselves with idleness for long.

Staico gave no signal, so they must have planned the attack. Three of the warriors grabbed Vlad's arms and tugged him backward. A fourth, clad in silvery armor and chain mail like his companions, wrenched the ruling prince's sword away. Despite Vlad's struggle, none of Mircea the Great's men dared hurt him. No, they sought his subjugation alone.

"You still have much to learn, my boy." His uncle approached again, the tiller of the crossbow in a firm grip. "About dance, as a cultured prince should, but also warfare and life. It is not always the greatest fighter who survives. To win any contest, a warrior or a prince must develop good tactics. Learn about and develop good strategies." Staico steadied the skittish animal and halted near Vlad, who kicked out in wild fury.

"I'll hate you forever, Staico! Nevermore shall I call you kin."

"I understand. Come tomorrow, you'll despise me even more for this." Staico raised his arm and brought the butt of his weapon crashing down on Vlad's head.

Vlad, wake up. Dearest brother, you must. Please. Arina's words became a litany.

Slung over the back of a Carpathian pony like the deer their father hunted, and covered in a blanket, Vlad lifted his throbbing head. A wave of dizziness followed.

Easy now, Arina urged. *Give yourself time and attune your senses.*

He followed her advice and regretted it as his perception reawakened. The stink of the horse's flanks filled his nostrils. Flies buzzed in a drone he found irritating. The glare of sunlight gave him a headache. The blood surged through his limbs. His fingertips prickled like many sharp stabs from needle points. A taste of copper saturated his mouth, tongue slick and somewhat swollen.

The Gypsies sprinted ahead to the capital. At Staico's urging, the return home took half the time in which Vlad and Arina had reached the slopes above the Argeş River Valley. Their father, the ruling prince, relied on men of endurance in his ranks of halberdiers, who covered enormous distances and the roughest terrain with speed. Gypsies outmatched them.

Their swiftness heralded Vlad's misery. Although worried about his sister more than himself, dismay at Staico's behavior bedeviled him. His uncle had actually hit him. He also could not believe how much the blow still hurt.

You knew better than to try Staico, Vlad. Riding apace with him, Arina sighed. "I'm glad you're awake at last."

"I'm not happy to greet the day." *The pain is awful and gained us nothing*, he thought. Gusts of wind took black streaks of his hair and slapped them against his cheeks, harsh like a leather whip.

We should not have fled at all. Truly, there is no place he could not have found us. Resignation bowed Arina's shoulders. "I will plead with our father for your sake, Vlad. Say I forced you to help me."

"He would know the lie as soon as he hears it, Rina. The burden must fall on me."

"This was your rash idea, in its entirety?" Staico snorted as he interrupted them from his riding position ahead of Vlad. "I thought a female voice planted the seed that bore bitter fruit in your mind. Who suggested your ill-fated escape? Princess Mara or the Dowager?"

Vlad gazed at Arina. *Don't give proof of Staico's assumptions*, he warned her inwardly.

By God's Grace, she closed her gaping mouth and looked ahead.

"Both of you are quiet now, eh? So silent, always. Good. You have much to consider. Spare a thought for Marko, while you can. His fate is your doing."

Arina's chin dipped. A heavy sigh rippled through Vlad. With his hands and feet bound tight together by two ropes, he could not have escaped the sight of the Gypsy's butchered body dragged behind his mount.

Marko's kindred and friends of old had stabbed their chieftain's son deep in the chest with curved blades the length of a man's arm. His dogs died by the crossbow beside him. Such loyal beasts, raised as pups and fed by his hands alone, would never have answered another. With great solemnity, the Gypsies had carried the prone forms down the slopes. Marko's end, meted out by those closest to him, restored their clan's honor.

By custom, his actions, even undertaken at Vlad's command, amounted to a crime. At a minimum, the ruling prince could have ordered the soles of his feet flayed. He might have been sold as a galley slave, rowing under the lash. Better a quick death than that fate.

"A waste of a good kennel master and fine hunting dogs." Staico's words echoed the progression of Vlad's guilty musings.

He even wondered if his tongue had slipped, giving voice to such thoughts. An irritating lump had remained lodged in his throat since Marko's death.

He grumbled, "Don't speak to me, Staico. You're no longer an uncle of mine."

"That's fair. Your father has never viewed me as a true brother." Staico swung in the saddle toward Arina. "I'll seek his mercy for you, princess. Once we arrive, go to your mother's side. Stay far from the sight of your father, eh? Give the rage in his lion's heart time to cool. The Princely Court's black cellars are no place for a tender maid like you."

"Thank you for your care, uncle. What about my dearest brother here?"

"I cannot alter the ruling prince's judgment. Besides, Vlad admitted his fault to me."

Seething, Vlad yelled, "Which you shall profess on my behalf, Staico. Christ's blood! Marko should have kenneled you with the rest of the pack."

"Recall, Vlad, you didn't wish to hear this lowly dog's words. Save your breath for your father. You'll need his mercy, not mine, at the Princely Court."

Staico's horse cantered alongside the Argeş River's east bank, Prince Mircea's sword slapping against his thigh. He drew them ever homeward.

Arina peered at Vlad. *Don't stay angry with our uncle forever because of me.*

He sighed. *Would that I could. He does not bear responsibility for what happened to Marko. I do. My plan entrapped him.*

Further regret mired him over boys his age, Marko's twin sons, Tobar and Yoska. Orphans now. Honor demanded Vlad provide for them and secure their futures. Yet, he could not guess his own. Not when a certain wrath awaited him.

Could a father slaughter his son? Did his child's life mean more than that of a full-blood brother? The turbulent past of the House of Basarab warned of doom.

One of the Gypsies blew a hunting horn and signaled their arrival. They left the mist behind them at the base of the valley's slopes, but Wallachians were a superstitious people. They did not trust any figures emerging from the fog, where shapeshifters and demonic creatures took form.

Arina lifted her pointed chin and stared straight on. Vlad closed his eyes and blotted out the sight of his birthplace. He needed no view of the familiar walls of red stone and bricks, built seventy years ago after a Hungarian invasion of old Basarab's principality, to herald his homecoming. The cacophony of German traders, likely from the city of Hermannstadt in Transilvania, and Eastern Orthodox pilgrims bound for Saint Nicolae's church reminded Vlad of how close he came to a reckoning.

As he expected, gasps and inquiries echoed from onlookers. His uncle spared his humiliation in the streets with the blanket strewn over his form but could and would never have saved him from Mircea the Great.

After Vlad entered the stockade, he peered out. Behind a stout wooden palisade, the princely fortress' graying walls shone in the sunlight. More halberdiers and other soldiers thronged the courtyard. As did a score of Gypsy slaves, distinguishable by their plain dress and leather collars around their necks. Marko's wives and children numbered among them.

Vlad's guts roiled. The doors swung back, and three figures emerged on the gray-green portico of the Princely Court at Argeş.

The Dowager, Princess Ana-Călina, dressed all in black as befitted a widow. Her billowing veil barely concealed the edges of blood-red hair streaked with molten silver. Her gaze swung between her grandchildren and the bastard who approached the portico, carrying the ruling prince's sword. Spittle retched from her mouth and soon landed near Staico, but he ignored it and kneeled in the dirt, the sword's hilt in his grip. Vlad could not tell if the Dowager's fury lay with his uncle or her grandchildren.

A gold circlet for his crown, Prince Mircea folded lean arms across his chest, covered in green wool and several gleaming necklaces. Each hung with crucifixes in a gaudy display from a man of dubious conviction about God's power and certain judgment.

The foulest accusations about him came to Vlad's mind. *Usurper. Kin-slayer.* A red haze shrouded his view of the parent he despised.

Stop, it's not the time for the blood fever, Arina warned him. *Your anger won't help us.*

Wallachia's ruler did not spare a look at the half-brother abased before him. Instead, he turned a stoic stare on the woman weeping at his side. A white-gloved hand covered her mouth, as if she held back screams. Vlad's mother, Princess Mara, shuddered and pressed against the stone balustrade. She sought no comfort from her husband, but then, she knew better than most that he gave none to anyone.

He bypassed Staico and went down to the clearing where the arrivals waited. With a wordless beckon, he summoned the halberdiers. Soon their captain stood a pace behind him, and the royal bodyguards formed a half circle within the treeless courtyard, standing apart from the Gypsy slaves.

Vlad awaited the sovereign's next utterance. It would not include a grant of mercy.

"Princess Arina, come to me now," the man said.

Fat tears slid down Arina's cheeks. She pushed back the hood of her mantle and dismounted, unattended. She walked the well-worn path across the courtyard.

Vlad held his breath until she bowed before their father.

"*Domnule*." Her voice shook while she pronounced 'my lord' as their parent expected from all his children, especially while spectators watched.

He grasped his daughter's chin and raised her. Arina gasped, deeming his touch rougher than she would have liked. Vlad knew by instinct.

A head taller than her, their father looked into her eyes. Whatever he saw there made his hand fall. Perhaps her tears, which he hated most, as with all signs of love.

He said to her, "Your return is all that matters. You shall be the bride of the most biddable Turkish claimant. Make him happy and guarantee peace for our people. Before this winter, I shall conclude the negotiations. You will get married next year. Now, go to your mother."

"As you wish, *Domnule*."

First, she looked over her shoulder at Vlad. Her stare reflected his turmoil and regret. *We tried, dear brother, but it is over.*

Sweet girl. She sought only to placate him. He rebelled against the effort. *We can try again. I will never give up on your freedom, Rina.*

"Daughter," Mircea the Great warned.

All sentiments disappeared behind her lowered gaze. In the connection of her mind to Vlad, a void fell like a cloak, darker than the one he wore.

He blinked. *Rina? Don't shield your thoughts from me.* No answer, not even a feeling came to him. She kept him at bay, as he'd done the night before. Their bond shuttered.

She raced up the steps to their mother. They never embraced in public, but Princess Mara gave Arina's fingers a furtive touch the ruling prince could not have seen. Vlad did.

Prince Mircea acknowledged his half-brother at last. "Staico, come."

The stockier, younger man rose. His elder half-brother snatched the sword without a word of thanks and turned his back to the courtyard.

His voice boomed. "I am Mircea the Great, son of Radu, of the House of Basarab. My word is law once given. Staico, take the boy Vlad to the place of exile I have chosen. He'll travel under my writ of *salvus conductus* so none may harm him."

Although Princess Mara and Arina screamed in unison, the ruler's voice rose above theirs. "He must remain there until I send for him. Hear me. Until I send for him. Go now. Do not return before my summons may arrive, Staico. Or your fate will be far worse than his."

Vlad hung his head, although the blood-rushing sensation blurred his vision. He closed his eyes as if to blot out the ensuing hurt.

What did Prince Mircea's guarantee of safe conduct matter, when the person who most reviled Vlad's existence awaited him in exile? A bully who possessed everything Vlad ever wanted, including the approval of their father and a share of his power.

CHAPTER 2

Into the Pit

"Have courage, or cunning, when you face your enemy."-Publilius Syrus (circa 85-43 BC), Latin writer.

IN THE YEAR OF OUR Lord 1409. Târgoviște, Dâmbovița district, Principality of Wallachia (modern-day Târgoviște, eastern Romania)

Warm wetness splashed on Vlad's face and stirred him from the previous night's fitful sleep. Ghostly apparitions haunted the southern Princely Court and always tormented him. Their icy fingers pulled at his clothing. They cackled in the shadows while he trembled with fright. Thanks in part to them, he could get no rest during the night or day.

He came fully awake and spluttered immediately. Bitter, yellow urine seeped into his mouth and splattered his tunic. He retched and rolled away on his side atop a bed of stable straw. Laughter and taunts filled his ears, as did the snorts of horses.

"Thought to hide from me here, brother? I'll always find you whenever you try. You'll never be rid of me, sniveling cur."

A steady stream of piss soaked the back of Vlad's sleeping tunic and ceased only when his tormentor stopped speaking. He spat once more, before his glare met eyes quite unlike his own.

Only Vlad, the third son, and Arina, the second daughter, inherited the agate hue of their mother's stare. Everyone else possessed the dark brown, almost black bleakness of their father's gaze. Including Vlad's hated eldest brother, Mihail, the prince of Târgoviște. The chosen heir. A man aged twenty-seven, twelve years older than Vlad, but still given to childish ways. Mihail laughed again now, with lanky arms akimbo and large feet splayed.

Vlad could have taken him down. He did so before, the first time more than a year ago, after he arrived in Târgoviște. Mihail's features, drawn and pallid, became monstrous before he backhanded Vlad into the muddy waters of the Ialomița River. Vlad sprang up and drove both fists into his brother's belly until Mihail crumpled. Vlad would have ripped the man's innards out with his bare hands if he could have. Staico's intervention forced them apart.

From that moment, Mihail never appeared without the boyars' sons who stood behind him in the stable now. Great brutes in manhood like their companion, who would happily pummel Vlad into a bloody pulp for the pleasure of their prince.

Again, the history of the House of Basarab repeated itself. Brother fought brother in a vengeful cycle Vlad could not escape.

His tunic clung to him as he rose and wiped his face. His fingers ran over the prickly bristles sprouting from his cheeks. He closed his callused hand into a tight fist.

"Don't you both have anything better to do?"

Vlad and Mihail looked toward the stable door at the same time.

Staico leaned against a wooden post. A baleful, gray-eyed look from him swept over them before he moved across the dank straw. Only then did Vlad notice the two Gypsy boys, Tobar and Yoska, his charges. The sons of Marko, orphaned by Vlad's folly. Had they witnessed Mihail's cruelty and fetched Staico to the stable?

Their uncle halted between Mihail and Vlad. Staico sniffed and scrunched up his lined face further. "At least, your brother didn't shove you into the pen of pig shit this time."

Mihail giggled, almost as if a girl, but Vlad's forehead throbbed. "No. That was last week."

"You snivel about it still, little Vlad," Mihail mocked him. "How can you be a son when you whine like a daughter? Shall I have my friends geld you and make it official?"

"Be quiet!" Staico interrupted. "A messenger has come with news from your mother."

Mihail's sneer faded in an instant. "Why didn't anyone inform me sooner?"

Staico shrugged. "I just did. If you'd stood in the courtyard, you might have seen the herald. I gave him money and sent him on his way. Before he left, he gave me this."

Between the three fingers on his mutilated hand, Staico held the edge of a roll of parchment, the red wax privy seal of the House of Basarab broken. The symbol of the lion rampant encircled with the regal title, '*Io* Mircea Great Voivode,' had severed unevenly.

"You opened a royal communication before I could read it?" Mihail demanded.

An irreverent rumble of laughter filled Staico's throat. "No matter how you or your father treat me, I'm a hereditary prince of the land with a boyar's daughter for a mother."

Mihail snatched the missive. His lips pressed together in a thin seam.

Vlad ached for knowledge of the letter's contents. His mother remained absent from his sight for more than a year. Mihail read in silence and kept his brother in suspenseful longing. When Vlad could not take it any longer, Mihail regarded him, tapping the length of thin parchment against a slim thigh covered in yellow silk hose.

Deep-rooted terror roiled Vlad's gut. Princess Mara had never written during his exile. She did so now, meaning substantial cause drove her. Perhaps she sent bad news about Arina?

Won't you tell me anything? Please, Vlad begged her inwardly. The detachment between them didn't matter. *Arina, I'm still here. I'll always be here for you. Answer me!*

Only a dim blackness suffused their bond. Yet, he took it as proof that their uncommon link could not sever easily. Shielding their feelings required great concentration for each of them. Whenever faint tinges of misery or fear afflicted him at odd times, he knew she struggled with her emotions. In those moments, he answered with reassurance and love, filling him up. Her mind stayed closed off to him, all thoughts hidden.

The marriage might have occurred already, as their father had promised. Was Arina far off at her husband's side? Had the Muhammadan prince prevailed over his brothers, claimed their warrior father's throne in Turkish-controlled Adrianople, and gotten his new wife with child? A son who might one day fight the heirs of his Wallachian relations. Strangers to him.

Such a terrible fate; the true disaster that brother and sister once hoped to avert. A horrid future where Arina's and Vlad's eventual offspring might meet in a deadly clash of swords.

A larger concern loomed in his mind. What if Arina died in childbirth instead, like their oldest sister, Anna? How could Vlad bear the loss of another beloved sibling?

Surely, Mihail knew the truth about their sister. He received dispatches from the northern capital at least twice a month. Prince Mircea would have told Mihail if Arina's circumstances altered, but he said nothing about her to torment Vlad.

With a loud exhalation, he released the breath he did not realize he had held. He uncurled his fist, held out both palms, and cleared his throat before humbling himself. "Mihail, please, I'm asking you for a measure of tolerance. As my full-blood brother, let me—"

Mihail ripped the sheet of parchment right down the center. He quartered their mother's letter and tore it up again. Small pieces fluttered to the stable floor like flower petals. The prince of Târgoviște brushed his hands together before he smirked.

The blood fever colored Vlad's view, flushed in a red haze. He charged toward Mihail but slammed into their uncle's broad chest. Built like a bear, Staico gripped him.

No matter how Vlad twisted, he could not escape. "Let go of me. Bastard."

Staico yelled, "Mihail, the princess of Argeş is coming in a day for you and your brother. Shouldn't you prepare a feast and send out escorts to meet her on the road?"

Mihail snapped an order at the boyars' sons. They left the stable with him.

After Staico would not relent, Vlad butted the man's bare chin repeatedly. His fury swelled like an inferno as Staico's hold only increased. Vlad cursed and flailed.

His uncle spoke to Tobar and Yoska in their Romany tongue. "Until your master has calmed himself, leave us, *čhave*." He insisted on calling the Gypsies 'children,' although they were the same age as Vlad, bigger and taller. "Bar the stable doors behind you. Oof! Wait beside them. I'll knock when we're ready, oof, to come out."

The words, punctuated by rushes of air timed with each blow Staico received, gave Vlad some satisfaction. He envisaged smashing against the larger man's aquiline nose, breaking it until it looked even uglier and crooked. The blood would spurt.

As Vlad aimed, Staico's arms fell away before he drew back. Vlad hurtled a few steps until he righted himself. He yelled a loud curse. The horses kicked their wooden stalls.

He rounded on Staico. "You did that on purpose."

"Maybe. When we are alone, I can always help you see reason."

"What did Mother say? Why is she coming here? Is Arina dead?"

You cannot be. I would feel it. Why will you not answer, sister?

"Princess Mara's words were, 'My warring sons should prepare for my arrival, at the command of their father.' That's all, my boy."

"That's all?" Vlad repeated.

"Why should there be more?" Staico frowned and eyed him as if he had no more sense than the jesters at both Princely Courts. "Letters and heralds can go astray, thanks to those devious scouts of the Ottoman Turks. Your parent knew not to say anything else."

Vlad nibbled at his lower lip. "What if she brings other bad news?"

"You can't hide in here, that's for sure. If I tell Tobar and Yoska to open the stable doors, will you go to the river and bathe? You stink. They will accompany you for safety."

"I don't need them."

Staico scowled. "Your mouth and wet tunic say otherwise. I'll bring fresh garments."

Reeking and cold, Vlad nodded and said, "Your aid changes nothing between us. I will never trust or rely on you as I once did, as an uncle."

"That's why you've spurned every offer to stay at the inn with me in town. Mihail's torment will continue. I can't help you if he won't let me live in this fortress."

"Our ancestors built it. Father consigned me here. Mihail will suffer me, as I must him."

"Will you tell your mother about what you've endured at his hands?"

Vlad shook his head. "She's not the one I must convince to end my exile."

"Go bathe." Staico rubbed at the corners of his eyes. "Your stench makes them water."

Vlad stomped and kicked the pieces of torn parchment as he went.

Later in the shadows of the red brick palace, he ate and shared a meal with his two Gypsies. A kitchen maid, who often pretended she did not see him sneaking through the doorway, left a basket for him daily. He crammed fresh bread and cheese into his mouth and ate a third of the pigeon pie, bacon with pears, and thick slices of venison. He wished for ale or wine, instead of a beaker of water. All the flagons were in the dining hall where Mihail and his courtiers feasted. Vlad would never join them again after what they had done to him.

His brother once ordered a meal of roast dog served to him last Easter. He ate some of the flesh before braying laughs warned him off. The kitchen maid confessed the rest later, while she cried. She loved that animal. Vlad held and comforted her afterward. In return, she offered a kiss and her buxom body. Greater pleasure than food.

AS THE AUTUMNAL NIGHT fell, Vlad went down to the cells after telling Tobar and Yoska of his intention to hide from Mihail there. Built for storage and occasional prisoners, each cavernous dusty room showed its age. He found a spot behind old crates, the odor of mold and decay rife. His stomach growled as he sat alone picking cobwebs from his doublet.

He did not know the hour when he drifted asleep or why he came awake. His stare scanned the darkness, and a breath escaped him. Not wispy and white. Nor did a chill course through his body. An otherwise sure sign of the presence of restless spirits.

Something squeaked and bit into his right ear. He yelped and jerked upright. The light cast by a lone torch revealed scattered rats. Meat scraps fell from his clothes and sprinkled on the floor. From the stair-lined end of the room, masculine laughter rumbled before it faded.

Vlad fled the underground cells and went outdoors. Soldiers gathered in the courtyard around the fires. His ear burned as if inflamed. When he fingered it, blood dotted his thumb. Tobar and Yoska occupied the shadows of the stables, where he found and roused them.

"I'm leaving," he muttered. "I can't stay, no matter what the ruling prince ordered."

Tobar rolled over, dark brown hair like Marko's own, falling over his gray eyes. Yoska brushed aside wheat-colored strands around his beefy face. Both gaped at Vlad. "*Domnule*?"

"I'm not finding Staico to tell him why." Vlad's chest heaved, weighted with frustration at the unfairness of his abuse by Mihail. "I trust you'll let him know I'm gone, my last command. I won't forget you. You've each been as good and loyal as your father, Marko."

"We'll come," they said in unison. Both youths stood and rested their hands on bone handle knives with thick blades.

Vlad shook his head. "You'll be blamed for running with me. Punished as slaves."

Tobar and Yoska looked at each other before saying, "We don't care."

This uncanny habit they possessed of speaking at the same time unnerved Vlad. Their stubbornness also filled him with gratitude. He needed their help to evade the guards. A palisade surrounded the fortress at Târgoviște, bounded by angled wooden stakes as a deterrent to invaders. The gate with an hourly patrol provided the only means of egress.

Vlad's stare shifted between the twins. "How do we leave?" He noticed a few guardsmen studying them.

"Through the stables," Tobar said.

Yoska nodded. "We went that way this morning when *Domnule* needed help."

"Through the stables?" A frown made Vlad's forehead pulse. "You must show me."

They did. At the end of the stalls, which abutted the palisade's southern wall, piled mounds of straw hid a tunnel.

"We go to your uncle first?" Tobar asked.

Vlad shook his head. "No! I've told you no already."

The Gypsies asked no further questions. Yoska slipped into the hole in the earth first.

The doors of the stable creaked. A gruff voice echoed. "They went in here, captain, and still haven't come out. Yes, we'll search for them at once."

Vlad crawled into the dirt tunnel, with Tobar following. They crept through the loamy earth. A light flared behind them. Vlad worried if the warriors came down dressed in armor, they would scrape against the walls and collapse them.

A muddied Yoska waited for them at the exit. Vlad brushed at the dirt coating his blue velvet doublet, which worsened the stains. Scanning the darkness, he and his companions found two horses tied up under a wooden shelter next to some boyar's enameled-roof townhouse. Vlad hated the noblemen's sons who caroused with Mihail each day. By extension, he disdained their fathers and held no qualms about stealing their mounts.

Moonlight shone through the trees where the trio escaped the town. Despite the savagery of multiple Turkish attacks over the years, broken sections in the perimeter defenses remained near the western forests. They soon rode uphill, covered with the horse blankets the boyar left for his animals. Though early autumn, the nights were wintry cold.

Vlad urged his horse onward with no destination or actual intent. Another night in Mihail's court might have driven him mad.

Although certain the conditions of his exile would never change, a doubt perturbed him. Flight from his brother's torment was the act of a coward. No one had ever accused him of cravenness before. His mother never raised him to be so. What would she say when she arrived and found him gone?

Rain poured fat droplets as heavy as last summer's ripened berries. The water pelted him without mercy. Mist rose from the ground. His horse slowed and found its footing when they reached a clearing. Vlad dragged the woolen cover over his head. He looked back at the Gypsies, forced to share a blanket and mount. He glimpsed only the whites of their eyes.

His stomach soured. Princess Mara would be worried and disappointed. The latter bothered him the most. With Arina gone from his life, his mother's opinion mattered more.

"I have to go back," he said. He realized his companions could not have heard him. He yelled over his shoulder, "We must return!"

Something rustled in the brush ahead. The rain turned the forest detritus into mush, and Vlad's horse skidded. He calmed the mount and scrutinized the darkness. The wind tugged the blanket from his shoulders. His fingers, the cut on his ear, and the tip of his nose burned.

He lowered his head again and maneuvered the horse. His mount skittered and danced across the ground. Vlad peered into their surroundings and saw nothing.

A burly shape lumbered into view as the full moon's light filtered through the canopy. Tobar and Yoska gasped beside Vlad. He had not even realized the Gypsies drew up next to him. They brandished their arm-length weapons, while Vlad cursed at not having tucked an eating knife under his leather belt.

Dark fur covered the animal's heavy body. A bear with small ears spaced wide on its thick head. When the lightning flashed, it lumbered closer and huffed, scarred face and short, stocky neck low to the ground. A growl rumbled before it bared sharp, yellowed teeth.

"An old male," Tobar whispered in Vlad's ear.

"Do we turn the horses?"

Tobar shook his head. "He's trying to get enough food before winter comes. If he can keep pace with horses in these woods, he can bring one of us down with it."

While he spoke, Yoska slid backward. Vlad dared not look for him and risk losing sight of the bear as it huffed again. White steam billowed from its nostrils.

Soon, something behind Vlad cracked, startling the horses and their riders further. The bear growled once more.

Yoska re-emerged between the two mounts. His leather belt now secured the handle of his knife to a fallen branch longer than his body.

He shoved a similar piece of stout wood at Tobar on horseback. "Tie the knife to it."

Tobar nodded and muttered, "*Domnule*, we'll drive the stakes into the ground when the bear attacks. The knives will do the rest."

Before he could finish securing his blade, the bear raked the ground and charged at them. Yoska yelled and brandished his makeshift spear. The animal swiped at the tip of the knife with its paw and groaned, but it also kept coming.

Tobar thrust his readied weapon and the bear batted at it. Almost knocked it from his hold. The Gypsy boy angled the length of the wood.

The brothers stood together against the beast. It shifted to the side as they moved with it and continued their threats. The growls increased as the animal's agitation grew. It couldn't draw any closer because of the knives' sharp edges, but clearly, it wouldn't let an opportunity for a meal get away.

The bear roared and reared, dwarfing them. Vlad shuddered and shied his horse away.

The motion caught his attacker's attention. The bear fell on its forelegs and ran at him. Vlad's mount reared in fright, whinnying as he fought for control of it. The other horse fled.

Tobar and Yoska leaped atop the bear's back. As one, they drove their blades forward, Tobar's once into the animal's neck and Yoska's into the skull, twice. The beast crashed in its death throes, tearing through the brush. Tobar stabbed underneath into the throat.

Dawn broke soon afterward and showed the trio the full size of the monstrosity they had killed. Longer and larger than any of them.

Vlad swallowed and dismounted. He turned to his companions, who expelled ragged breaths and draped an arm over each other's shoulder. Their bond stirred his heart, as did their courage and determination to ensure his survival.

He said, "I don't care what I must do or how long it takes, but I'll see you freed."

Although Vlad regretted leaving the carcass, they did not have time to skin it. The other horse nosed the ground in the next clearing. In the day's brilliant first light, Vlad rode back to Târgoviște with his faithful companions.

VLAD AND THE GYPSY twins re-entered the town by the same earlier route. Daylight glinted off frost-coated vineyards covering the surrounding hills. By the time they reached the gates of the fortress, they found them open.

At the center of the courtyard, amid royal halberdiers in silvery armor, Princess Mara glared up at Staico and jabbed her forefinger at his leather cuirass. He stood with arms folded.

"Get after him, Staico. My husband gave our son over to you and you will find him! Mircea's wrath won't compare to mine if you don't bring my dear son back to me. Today!"

He looked past her slim shoulder. "As you wish, *Doamnă*." Although he addressed her as 'my lady,' as befitted her rank, his thick eyebrows waggled. He pointed to Vlad. She followed the gesture and turned.

Her moss-tinged stare, a mirror of Vlad's own, narrowed and her lips thinned.

He never felt more ashamed in her presence. Not even a speck of travel dust dotted her ebony mantle. The collar met the edge of her white linen veil secured by a braided gold fillet.

She demanded, "Where have you been?" She glanced at the Gypsies, filthy like him, their improvised weapons smeared with the bear's blood. "Do I even wish to know?"

He opened his mouth, but she raised her hand, cutting him off. "Not one word. You will clean yourself up and meet me in the throne room at noon. Whatever folly you undertook before my arrival, I don't doubt your brother's involvement. I will speak with Mihail alone after he meets with his boyars. Do not keep me waiting, my Vlad."

She turned her back on him and led her escort of halberdiers inside the fortress.

Vlad bathed. Staico laid out fresh clothes in a small room assigned to Vlad, with only a chest and a bed, which he had not used in ten months. Mihail snuck inside at odd hours to plague him. The ghosts bothered him, too. Mihail had made clear his resentment of allotting the space for Vlad. Before his arrival, the space had served as the dressing room of Târgoviște's prince, next to Mihail's chamber.

Staico brushed Vlad's shoulder-length, black hair away from his face before scrutinizing the cut on his ear, sighing, and departing.

With an exhalation of shaky breath, Vlad laid his palm flat against the black brick wall. He must have pressed too hard because a section of it opened with a creak. Not brick after all, but wood painted to match the surrounding wall. A door between this and Mihail's room.

Vlad's hands fisted at his side. "No wonder he always caught me unawares here."

He pushed the panel. A tapestry hung behind it, but he shoved aside the wall-hanging, determined to confront his sibling. The room was empty but for the large bed with its thick coverlet stitched with the family's coats of arms, a desk and chair, woven carpets, chests, and more tapestries hung between the three windows.

Vlad noticed a door opposite the exit and rattled the handle. A groaning creak preceded the sensation of cool air billowing his silk sleeves. Stone-carved steps descended into the darkness. On an impulse, he took the route. An unnatural chill ensued. His fingers brushed over chinks in the cold masonry. At the base of the stairs, he found another door. Shouldering it, he discovered crates behind it in the cellar where he had tried to sleep the previous night. So, that was how Mihail and his friends found him.

Perhaps there were no uneasy spirits at Târgoviște either. Only young men who plied cruel tricks.

Church bells pealed during the hour. Vlad left the cellar by its customary exit and went to the throne room. Halberdiers stood outside its closed doors, made of heavy oak, with their long pikes crossed, barring entry, even for him.

A loud conversation occurring inside the chamber drifted beyond the wooden entryway.

"You are a man. He is still a boy! If the pair of you weren't my sons, I'd have you both locked together in a dark cell below until you learned to rely on each other."

"He's a coward, Mother. He ran. My soldiers told me so. They saw him crawl through a tunnel in the stable. It's filled in now. He can't escape again—"

"An act, which your behavior inspired. You dared set food for rats on my child's body?"

"I'm your son as well!"

"Then behave like one! A true prince of Târgoviște."

Their mother's voice fell. Vlad drew back before she pushed at the double doors. She snapped at the halberdiers. "Oh, stand aside!"

She looked resplendent in a bright blue and gold gown, having removed her black mantle. She clasped her hands. "I was about to send one of these louts here to find you, my Vlad. No more running."

"I never wanted to leave, Mother, but Mihail has made my exile impossible."

"I have not!" His brother shouted. "I've only teased you occasionally."

"You are both mewling kittens instead of a mighty lion's cubs." Their mother glared in turns at them before she waved Vlad inside.

The murkiness of the throne room reminded him of the cellar below. He trudged toward his brother, seated beneath the only painted window, while their parent fell into step with him. They rounded a pit, where a fire crackled each day and night, no matter the season. Vlad once overheard his brother joking with friends; the ever-present heat ensured the boyar council never lingered too long during their summer meetings.

Mihail slunk lower atop the throne as Princess Mara came up the three steps of the dais to him. "I want you to promise you'll stop tormenting Vlad."

She turned to him. "I want you to render the respect owed to your brother, as your future reigning prince of Wallachia."

The siblings stared at each other until she threw up her slim hands. "It's not impossible. You will do it before we return to Argeş, in time for Arina's nuptials."

Vlad grasped their mother's long fingers, tipped with talons. "She's unwed?"

Instead of answering him directly, she pulled away and peered down at Mihail. He sank so low on the throne, only his lean legs kept him from sliding off the edge.

"You've never told him about Arina, not once in his six seasons here? I knew I'd raised hard sons. Each could succeed his father and hold this land. I also knew why Mircea favored you. You're as vicious as he can be. Perhaps even crueler, if possible."

Surprised at her acknowledgment of her husband's ways, Vlad listened in silence.

"Get out of my sight." She leaned closer to Mihail. "I'm claiming the quarters of the prince of Târgoviște and will take my meals alone in that room. Send my two grandsons to me. It's been five years since I saw your children. I don't want to see you again until we leave here."

He blinked twice. "You're dismissing me? From my throne room?"

"You may be your father's favorite." She straightened. "His heir. However, he is still the ruling prince of ALL Wallachia. Get off Mircea's throne! You're not fit to rule in his stead."

Mihail's cheeks reddened, but perhaps more so because Vlad witnessed the censure. He would never forget the moment. Neither would his elder brother. Mihail rose, adjusted his cloak, and left without another word. He stumbled near the door, which only Vlad saw.

He faced their mother. "Thank you."

"A show of gratitude?" Her scowl turned on him. "For what? Rescuing you? I knew Târgoviște would be a trial, but I never expected you to flee from a challenge. Is this all you have learned since you and Arina absconded? How to run away and return defeated?"

He backed away from the dais, but she followed.

"The only reason your sister has not already married is that her betrothed is still at war with his brothers. They've kept him from our Black Sea coastal lands in Dobrogea and prevented negotiations of the marriage settlement between him and your father. Until now."

She raised her tiny fists and pounded his red damask doublet. "It was bad when you left with Arina, but even worse, you let Staico return with her. Why didn't you flee where the wretched Turks and your father could never find her? Why did you fail, Vlad?"

His mother sobbed and he held her close, even while she took to bashing his back. She cried out and gripped him at the waist. "God forgive me, please! Would that my last girl had died rather than face marriage with a heathen."

"Mother, I swear, we tried our best," he whispered. "The halberdiers were better. Too fast for us. The prince wishes for my return so he can gloat and show me how he thinks he's subdued the deceitful Turks, offering them a bride as a bribe to stop their attacks. Their leader wants our fighters and our land. He doesn't care about my sister."

Rina, I am coming to you. Don't despair further. Despite the absence of her thoughts in his head, he did not doubt she heard him.

Their mother withdrew and wiped her eyes. "The Ottoman prince will have all he desires. He comes to us at Argeş with a host of Turkmen, Serbians under the rule of Stefan Lazarević, and Bulgarian forces. Your people, Wallachians, will join them. Battling for the enemies of Christendom. Arina won't contemplate escape this time."

"You knew we'd run," he accused her. "You didn't order it, but you approved."

"I did not know!" Her agate eyes glowed like hot jewels. "Now you'll face more peril."

"Prince Mircea has called me home to punish me further?"

"No. You won't be there for long, my Vlad." She sat on the edge of the dais.

"What do you mean?" He joined her on the topmost step below the throne.

"Your father doesn't want you at Argeş, where you two would only quarrel daily. I agree with him." Her sigh echoed in the room. "You'll never learn to be a man here, not with Mihail's example. Mircea is sending you to another royal court, I know not where, to join the retinue of some prince or king. Even the Byzantine Empire is an option."

Vlad leaned back and swept a hand up his forehead. There were only two reasons a man surrendered his children to another. Young boys with no training served as pageboys or squires before seeking knighthood.

Older youths, like him, sent to the household of a father's overlord became hostages, guarantors of loyalty or compliance.

His thoughts crashed together like the wild waves of the Black Sea. Whatever fate held for him; another permanent exile loomed. He rested a palm on the seat of the throne.

Princess Mara craned her slender neck and looked at his fingertips, caressing the smooth, velvet cushion, until he removed his hand.

"I know you covet it." She gave him a slight smile. "All the sons of a Wallachian prince are eligible heirs, even bastards, if the boyar council offers support. The noblemen are loyal to Mircea. They've accepted Mihail as his co-ruler and eventual successor. You're the third son. Before you could ever ascend, two others have an older claim."

"I don't need the reminder, Mother," he exclaimed.

"See that you do not." She kissed his cheek and rose beside him. "Think no more of the throne. Prepare yourself for a reunion with your father." She clasped her hands and left him.

He stared into the fire pit. His gaze strayed to the throne again. The center of his forehead pulsed.

Why couldn't he be the prince of Târgoviște instead of Mihail? Their mother spoke the truth. His brother was not fit to rule. Another must take his place.

CHAPTER 3

Lionhearted

"You have power over your mind, not outside events. Realize this, and you will find strength."-Marcus Aurelius (121-180 AD), Emperor of Rome.

IN THE YEAR OF OUR Lord 1409-1410. Argeş, capital of the Principality of Wallachia (modern-day Curtea de Argeş, eastern Romania)

Eighteen months after leaving his birthplace, Vlad stood in its courtyard again. His family gathered in the shadows of the enamel-roofed portico north of the enclosure. He waited on horseback while cool winds swirled, an unusually quiet Staico beside him. His mother greeted her husband and Vlad's grandmother, while each of his siblings bowed. Mihail had left his two spoiled sons behind with governesses at Târgovişte.

Vlad fixed his stare on Arina, but his sister ignored him. She stood so small beside their grandmother, the Dowager. Subdued. Had his twin's eyes and hair dulled? She wore a silken, high-collared, belted gown in a scrolling leaf pattern, the same dark green color and style as their grandmother's broadcloth dress. Arina's cheeks seemed hollower than the Dowager's above the raised neckline.

Will you share nothing with me, Rina, not even after a year and a half? He wondered, *are you angry with me because we could not flee Argeş, or because I've stayed away so long?*

His attention shifted once his mother addressed Prince Mircea again. The formality with which they often talked, and the stiffness of their interaction made it hard to fathom how they had created six children. Recalling a final tryst with the kitchen maid before leaving Târgovişte one week ago, Vlad could never imagine his parents in the throes of lust.

At a summons, Mihail bowed before their father again and looked over his shoulder at Vlad, saying something. His lips twisted in a sneer while the elder man chuckled in response.

Already wary and disgusted, Vlad looked away from the hated sight of the pair. The noonday sun barely penetrated a haze of gloomy midafternoon clouds, heralding a storm. Shades undulated across the low grass, fortress, and outbuildings.

"Your father summons you," Staico said, drawing Vlad from his reverie.

He glanced again and saw the ruling prince's beckoning hand fall away. Vlad gave the reins of his horse to Staico and dismounted.

"Will you take the mare to the stables for me?"

"You know I will, Vlad. Your father and family can have no further need for me."

Staico raised a hand in salute before he urged his horse to the royal stable. He grasped the reins of the mounts that Vlad, his brother, and his mother rode to Argeş. Afterward, Staico would eat with the Gypsies in his preferred custom.

Vlad trudged toward the fortress. The world around him shrunk to the rustle of his ankle-length boots in the grass, and the shadow bands weaving before his eyes. He climbed the steps to the portico. Little Alex's face brightened. He flashed a gap-toothed grin. Three years younger than Vlad, he stood at the same height.

"*Domnule.*" At the top of the stairs, Vlad bowed. Years of resentment simmered in the ensuing silence. Staico behaved more like a father than the one who stood in front of him.

"Humph. As I foretold, *Doamnă*. Stubborn as ever. No matter the changes you've heralded." Her husband's scowl knitted profuse, dark-russet brows. He peered at Vlad's mother, who made no reply. "You're still angry, boy. Does the duration of your absence at Târgoviște bother you or merely that I commanded it? Or because your mother fetched you and Mihail to me now? All three, I would surmise."

Vlad stared straight ahead and kept his mouth closed.

"*Doamnă*, I warned you. Our son still hasn't learned the lesson I wished to impart."

Always the term, *Doamnă,* 'my lady,' rather than addressing Vlad's mother by her name. What affection could ever exist between such a man and any other?

Vlad tried to tamp down the rage roiling in his gut. He failed. His fingers curled.

"What lesson was that, *Domnule*? How did you plan to teach me anything from afar?"

Prince Mircea's brows flared, as if surprised by the tenor of his voice. Vlad's mother gasped and stared hard at him before she glanced at her husband.

"We'll speak later, boy. Alone. I've awaited your arrival long enough. To the great hall!"

The man turned away. Mihail fell into step beside him. Their mother and the Dowager followed, with Arina between them.

Vlad stared hard at their backs before he tousled Alex's black curls. "I'm glad to see you again, little one." His youngest brother frowned and batted his hand away.

"What about me?" Their elder brother Radu laughed in a thick, throaty noise, reminding Vlad of the eight-year gap between them. "Vlad, you're no taller than Alex now."

Up ahead, their mother called, "Come, my sons. I'm sure we're all hungry."

In the great hall, a feast awaited the family, as did the nobles of the principality. They stood before long benches, applauding and hailing the House of Basarab.

Mircea the Great led his relations to the trestle tables set on the wide dais. By rote, they took their usual places. With their parents at the center, Mihail, Radu, Vlad, and Alexandru pulled out chairs to the left. Their grandmother and sole sister sat on Princess Mara's right. One seat remained vacant for Anna, who had been dead for several years.

Vlad leaned forward and looked down the long row as Arina slid into her chair. For the first time, she met his regard. She placed her napkin on her lap and stared at an empty plate. Before his exile, she would have flashed him an impish grin.

What did Prince Mircea do to you after I left Argeş? Vlad stared at his sister so intently that their mother's regard swung between them before she shook her head.

The feast lasted well into the afternoon. When their ruling prince rose, everyone else did the same, although he waved them back to their seats. He strode half the length of the trestle tables and soon stood beside Vlad, who swallowed the last of the goulash, the meaty soup a staple of the region.

"You will come with me, boy."

Vlad rose, aware of how his female family members and older brothers watched him. He followed their father. They took three passages, lined with household guards, and went through one of the double doors into a spartan room where the boyar council met each day.

The windowless space had a few lit torches and one chair, meant for the sovereign, with lion's claws carved on the armrests. A chill seeped through chinks in the rough stone masonry. No tapestries hung on the walls, as in the great hall. Nothing offered comfort.

The ruler gestured to the seat. Despite his surprise, Vlad settled on the hard oak and sat in silence while Prince Mircea paced before him. White smoke billowed from their nostrils.

Vlad wished he would speak and be done with it. Why draw out this confrontation with the son he despised?

"You asked earlier about the lesson I tried to teach by sending you to Târgovişte," the man began before he stopped crisscrossing the brick floor.

Vlad shared an expectant look with him as he resumed his strides.

"I wished you to learn about surviving adversity. Life does not bend to our will. We must fight. Struggles teach a man tolerance and his limits. Show him why the way of pride is foolishness. You hate your eldest brother. Perhaps with good reason, given what your mother has relayed. You would have stayed weak if you never fought him."

Shaking his head, Vlad couldn't believe what he was hearing. Not one word of sympathy, even now, from the one who had fathered him.

He dared ask, "Then you approve of all the things Mihail did to me, *Domnule*?"

"I did not grant you leave to speak! Of course, I like nothing that happened. Mihail took his fun too far, what with the rats lately and the dog meat at Easter. Tell me, how much of it filled your gullet before you knew?"

"Two bites, *Domnule*, after which the laughter started. I knew something was wrong and vomited on the floor, which amused Mihail and his friends more."

"Afterward, you fled, and never ate in the great hall of Târgovişte again."

Vlad nodded, although no question underlay the tone.

"You'll soon learn another important lesson." Prince Mircea halted with hands clasped. He peered down at Vlad, his dark gaze narrowed. "You can't always run. A life of cowardice will not be yours."

Vlad snorted. How dare the man lecture him about craven behavior?

"Isn't it also ignoble to buy peace from the Ottoman Turks, *Domnule,* with Arina's life?" This time, he did not care if he had permission to talk.

Mircea the Great seemed uncaring too, as he leaned closer. "A wise man would recognize the necessity. You are neither wise nor a man."

Vlad huffed and peered up at him.

"I support this Turkic prince, Vlad, our inborn enemy, against his brothers because their disunity keeps them killing each other, not us. He is the youngest among his siblings. He'll do anything to keep me as an ally. One day he will look upon his firstborn son, a child with a Wallachian grandfather, and remember my help."

"And if he dies before then, *Domnule*?"

"Then I'll aid another Ottoman prince. I don't care which, so long as they quarrel. I'm doing all I can to save our country by pitting our enemies against each other."

Vlad recognized the wisdom of encouraging Turkic internecine warfare. What about Arina's wishes or the feelings of anyone else, including Vlad? Should he try reasoning with Prince Mircea, as Staico often wished he would?

"*Domnule*, I have no right to question you," he began. "Yet, how can you imperil my sister's future, even for your people's sake? What if she becomes a pawn in the Turks' struggles? You must not let Arina go to those ungodly, warmongering people."

"They believe in a God, the same as you and me. Your ignorance is troublesome, but that will change after your sister weds. She will be a peace-weaver, and the Ottoman Turks shall strike at us no more."

"What have they done to you, *Domnule*? All my life, I've heard the stories of your heroism from my mother and grandmother. Your survival in the battle of Nicopolis two years after my birth. You once fought our enemy. Now you cower and sacrifice your last daughter."

"Never question my bravery!" Mircea the Great whirled and grabbed the collar of Vlad's silk doublet hard until the material tore. His rage evoked the image of the lion rampant etched on his signet ring. "There is a time for swords. Another for diplomacy. I've relied on both in my twenty-nine-year reign. Do you know how I've maintained rule over Wallachia?"

Vlad swallowed. There were two stories about the man's rise and political power.

"Mother said you allied with Zsigmond of the House of Luxembourg, the Hungarian king." He chose the cautionary answer. "You became his vassal three years ago."

Prince Mircea released him. "You wonder how I, as an Eastern Orthodox adherent, could have submitted to a Catholic king as overlord?"

Vlad nodded. Two centuries after the Catholics sacked the great city of Constantinople, the memory of their treachery lingered throughout eastern Europe. Born and raised in the Orthodox faith, the Basarab family never trusted the papacy or Catholicism's followers.

"King Zsigmond and I recognized a common enemy, boy. The nations bordering enemy lands in the east needed alliances with the western kingdoms. Do you know when the Turks last penetrated the heart of Wallachia?"

"Two years before my birth. My tutor told me. When your elder brother Prince Dan marched an army south to the former Bulgarian city of Vidin, under the Turks' rule."

"Did your teacher also say their sultan launched a reprisal with forty-thousand men? I commanded a quarter of his number. Afterward, he put a usurper on my throne for twenty-six months. The Ottoman ruler who defeated me was also the father of the man who will marry your sister. Still doubt my plan for Arina, boy?"

Vlad did not but rebelled inwardly against their parent's lack of regard for her wishes.

Prince Mircea heaved a heavy sigh and strode back and forth across the room again. "I've pledged myself to the ruler Zsigmond in Hungary. I must show my continued loyalty as a vassal. While Arina buys us peace with the sultan, you'll ensure the king's protection."

"How? By what means?"

"After your sister's wedding, Staico will escort you to Buda Castle in Hungary, where you'll serve the court of King Zsigmond well."

Despite his mother's warning, the decree shocked Vlad. "In what capacity will I do so?"

"Do what the king tells you, boy. That is all you must know."

"Why would you send me to the Hungarian capital when you've called it 'the devil's pit' long before you chose vassalage?" Vlad shook his head. "Did I mishear you?"

Mircea the Great laughed and startled him. He gripped the lion armrests and winced.

"You did not, boy. It seems you need that lesson about adversity."

Vlad sat back in dismay. He would become a king's hostage. What else could he be? If a parent failed duties to his overlord, a son's life could be forfeited.

"You and your sister surprised me a year ago. I knew you would flee the court with her. Having heard all your earlier objections to Arina's marital union, I assumed, when you ran with her, you might do so in the days before the nuptials. Once final preparations distracted your family. Too impetuous. You must learn patience, boy."

Vlad hated the taunt, as much as the idea that Prince Mircea had expected his folly.

"Once my uncle Dan left Argeş, how long did you wait before taking his throne? Are the rumors I've heard from childhood true? Had you plotted for more than a year with Dan's disloyal boyars to ensure the Turks killed him in Bulgaria?"

The moment he uttered the fateful words, the man dragged him out of the chair.

"What did you dare say to me? Are you accusing me of fratricide?"

He never answered. A savage cuff to the face felled him and he stumbled, barely avoiding the chair arm. Relentless blows pummeled his belly and face.

The fighting spirit born of Mihail's torments ensured Vlad defended against and answered each wallop. Until his mother came in and grabbed her husband's arm. She flung her body between him and Vlad.

"Great God, what are you doing to him? Would you kill our child?"

"I swear the boy's the devil." Prince Mircea wrenched himself away from them.

"If so, you sired him. We created him in our bed. Look at how you've hurt our son!"

Blood dripped from Vlad's throbbing nose and seeped into his mouth. It tasted no better than Mihail's piss. Hurting everywhere, Vlad rose at his mother's urging.

"I asked the household guards where you were," she said, "because the Dowager wants to see you in the chapel, my Vlad."

He swiped his hand over his mouth and staggered to his feet.

"My mother can wait, *Doamnă*. I'm not done with him."

"Oh, yes, you are!" His mother sat on the floor and cupped her forehead. "Vlad, go from the council chamber and close the door behind you. Leave the *Domnule* and me alone."

His vision swam at the first step. Determined that neither parent would know how much the beating affected him, he stumbled forward. Though his strength ebbed, he opened and closed the double doors. The voices behind him drifted.

"Good Lord, Mircea. This is a fine mess you've made of things."

"Don't blame me, Mara. Your son provoked me."

"My son, is it? Let me see the cut over your eye, dearest love. Don't smear the blood!"

Vlad had never heard them address each other by their personal names before, much less offer endearments. He turned and peeked through the slight gap between the doors.

His mother had tugged her husband beside her and removed her veil. Golden curls fell over one of her shoulders as she dabbed at a vicious wound with the hem of the blue material until he flinched.

The sight pleased Vlad. Blood trickled from the same spot on his brow to his cheek.

"Oh, my love. You'll have bruises later. Vlad will too."

"He deserves them. The boy vexes me."

"Why did you two attack each other?"

Vlad prepared himself to hear only lies.

"The boy repeated the story my enemies and others have often told, about how I must have arranged Dan's murder in Vidin. My brother and I were rivals once, as you know."

"I remember how you wept after you received the news of his assassination. There would never be reconciliation between siblings. That fact pained you the most."

"I don't care if others think I killed Dan. I wish my third son thought better of me."

Vlad covered a gasp with a hand over his mouth. The man cared about his beliefs?

"He's hurt you." Mara grasped her husband's bearded cheek and turned his face to hers.

Mircea grimaced and fingered his jaw. "Nothing you can't mend. The aches will ease with your good poultices, which you'll prepare for both of us."

"I will do so, but you know I didn't mean bodily aches, my dear."

"It seems our son's learned how words can wound."

"Where do you suppose he gained that understanding?" He pulled away, but she clasped under his chin and thumbed his silvery russet beard again. "You're not an easy man to love. You've earned a reputation for cruelty and stubbornness. A certain temper, which you've passed on to our sons. Forgive. Vlad isn't aware of how the past has grieved you."

"Let's not speak of it now. I wish to forget in your kind care."

"Would that you could, my dearest husband. We've fought so hard for our children's futures. Vlad doesn't understand the sacrifice you must make. I pray he'll never bear the same burden as a father. Would it shatter your heart to show him a little love before he leaves his home forever? Love's not a weakness, Mircea."

"You know why I cannot hold the same view, sweet Mara. I showed too much love for a child of ours once. I can't feel it all again. It causes only pain in the end. And an ending always comes too soon. In the meantime, I do what I must for our family and country. Come, I need your care and don't want the children to see me. They'll glimpse Vlad's face soon enough."

VLAD WALKED THROUGH the fortress with his head bowed until he came outdoors and sighted the chapel. Several guardsmen looked at him and pointed. He dismissed them from his mind.

Instead, he pondered Prince Mircea's words. What child of his had he ever loved?

Within moments, Vlad stood at the opened chapel doors. Inside, near the nave, the Dowager appeared next to a strange man. A reddish-brown pelt of shaggy hair fell on either side of his narrow features, aligned with the edges of a thin mustache and the tops of his beard. The pale gray wolf's skin draped across his shoulders gave him a feral look.

Vlad's grandmother smiled at the man. He bent and kissed her fingertips. He straightened and held out the stem of a white flower before he pulled his slim hand back. He must have realized Vlad had watched him. His lips thinned, pulled back in a snarl.

Princess Ana-Călina beckoned Vlad. As he approached, she said to the stranger, "Go to the house of your dear father. We shall speak later, Vlậcsan."

"As you wish, *Doamnă*."

Vlad shared a sharp look with this Vlậcsan as they bypassed each other.

The Dowager averted questions as she tucked the flower into the wrist of her garment and held out a crinkled, timeworn hand. "I see you and your father argued, my Vlad."

"Neither of us won, Grandmother."

"When a parent quarrels with a child, both lose." She fingered his swollen face. "In the year that yours and Arina's births occurred, the court astronomer warned a great fire-breathing beast would consume the House of Basarab. Later in the summer, we heard from western travelers that a celestial dragon had swallowed the sun for hours. After your exile, the same phenomena occurred in some German cities, Nürnberg among them."

Puzzled at first, he asked, "A dragon swallowed the sun? You mean an eclipse occurred?"

"As a child, when such things ensued, my parents said demonic beasts and shapeshifters ate the sun. The village priests made baleful noises. They burned a huge cross in the marketplace's central square to ward off the evil. When your father or Mihail have roused your fury, your skin, the blood beneath it boils hotter than those flames in my reminiscence."

"Arina calls it the blood fever. It's frightened her since childhood. She said my skin burned as if I would burst ablaze. She always tried to cool my anger with her smile."

The Dowager nodded before the chestnut centers of her eyes almost disappeared between slits. "You never listened even when I last warned you about your father."

He sputtered, "Grandmother, I—"

"Be silent!" She sighed and ran her fingertips over gray-flecked reddish brows. "Over a year ago, I told you to flee north with your sister. What was my advice back then?"

He swallowed and worked his aching jaw before summoning her words from memory. "Don't rouse the prince's suspicions or his ire. My lion son would tear you apart."

"Humph. You listened, but not very well. Arina won't talk about the aftermath of your return. Your exile has since altered her; the sweet smiles went away with you."

The corners of his eyes prickled, but he wouldn't weep like a babe before the Dowager about the changes in his sister. A deep and painful wound of the heart and mind.

He said, "We fled Argeş in the hour of the wolf under the new moon's light. Marko the Gypsy protected us. We moved northeast, away from the Argeş River, and avoided Rucăr, the fortresses of Bran, and then Kronstadt in Transilvania. The western bank of the Siret River is near the remnants of Milcov. We saw some ruins that the Mongols left of that city. As we climbed the hollow hills around Milcov, Staico found us."

"Staico." She spat the name. "Bastard! Only a loyal dog of your father."

"I said the same." And regretted it often since then.

She grunted as he added, "Prince Mircea told me he knew I planned to run with Arina."

"My wily son expected the possibility. Nothing more." The Dowager tapped her curved nail against her lips. Her hand fell. "Why did you take my jewels?"

"Forgive me, please. I guessed we would need bribes at the convent in Moldavia."

While his grandmother gaped at him, Vlad recognized his error.

"You assumed I entrusted two royal children to the care of a Gypsy slave without having considered your safety and future? My Vlad. I may have expected too much of you at fourteen. The stars have charted another destiny for you and Arina. As for concerns about the past?

Best forgotten now. Find your mother, my boy. Mend under her healing touch."

"She's seen me already. The fight stopped after she found us."

"She's with your father? Wait here a little longer. At the sight of you, Mircea's guilt and regret would only agitate him, make him even more disagreeable."

"Guilt? Regret?" Vlad didn't think the Dowager knew what she said.

"Don't look at me as if my mind has gone addled. Your father will be sorry."

"He won't be. He never thinks he's done anything wrong."

"Oh, he knows he has in a long lifetime. He bears the sorrow of his choices each day."

"What choices? Before I left him, he and Mother were talking. He said there was a child whom he loved too much. I suppose that's Mihail, since he's so spoiled."

"You would be wrong." While Vlad's grandmother spoke, she looked up at a mural painted high on the wall and smiled at the image of her beloved husband in ceremonial robes and his crown. "Come with me to the doors, my boy. The autumnal temperature makes my bones ache, but also serves as a reminder. Life is not finished with me."

As they walked, she resumed the conversation. "There was once another little prince, the elder twin of Mihail."

Vlad halted briefly. "I never knew Mother bore other twins. What happened?"

"Her firstborn was beautiful. Possessed the flowing black hair you, Mihail, Anna, and Alex inherited from my husband. When their child was two, Mircea and Mara took him and Mihail to the bank of the Ialomiţa River at Târgovişte, on a late winter's day. They didn't realize how much the ice had thinned under the snow cover. Their first boy escaped his father's hold, fell in, and drowned. Mircea keened for his little prince. Even I could not comfort him."

At the chapel door, Vlad blinked back tears. His grandmother wiped her wet eyes.

"Once Mara birthed you, Mircea gave you that boy's name," she added. "Mara screamed at my son for a month and called him cruel. The eclipse last year reminded me of the court astronomer's prediction when you and Arina were born. Never fear the return of the celestial dragon if you should ever encounter it. A herald of great change for you."

"For better or for worse?"

"Only time will tell, my Vlad."

"Did your son intend to alter me in Târgoviște?" The Dowager made no reply, so he continued, "His firstborn was Vlad, too? Why did Fa...call me the same name?"

His grandmother grinned at the slip of his tongue while he looked away. He hated himself for having even thought of the word. Father.

"Mircea did it for the love of an innocent boy, denied his future." The Dowager surprised him by offering no witty remark. "My child held on to hope that another son of his might grow to manhood. As a result, your parent also tolerates Mihail's behavior. Now you know why."

"He doesn't love me." Vlad sniffled as tears threatened again. "He's never said it."

His grandmother enfolded him in her spindly arms. His body quaked.

"Oh, my woefully ignorant grandchild. In fifty-six years of life, my son has lost his primary heir and a daughter. When we received word of Anna's death in Serbia, Mircea wept even more for her than for his first boy. He once said, 'This is an unnatural world, where parents bury their children.' I thought he'd will himself into the grave. He fought against infinite grief each day after Anna's loss for the sake of his remaining children, who occupy the beating heart in his chest. A lion's heart."

THE AUTUMN SEASON CAME and went too soon, in Vlad's opinion. Light winter snow heralded the Ottoman prince, introduced to the Wallachian court as Mûsâ Çelebi.

One look at the olive-skinned Turk with golden-brown eyes beneath the ruby-fringed cloth on his head, and Vlad feared for his sister's future. There was something grim about the prince's mouth. He spoke Latin better than most Christians, but never smiled or laughed, even among the small delegation at his side. He would not appear without a man called Bedreddin, whose pleasant mien contrasted with the visage of the dour prince.

"Why are they always together?" Vlad asked his elder brother Radu as they ate with the Ottomans in the great hall. "Is Bedreddin the head of the prince's bodyguards?"

"How would I know?" Radu shrugged and speared another roasted pigeon. "Why does their closeness matter to you? They'll soon be gone from our lives."

"Yes, taking our sister with them." Unlike Radu, Vlad perceived they would remain under constant threat from the barbarous Turks.

Their father's guests dined with them daily. Vlad wondered if the Turks knew the boyars cursed them in the Wallachian dialect, even loud enough for Prince Mircea to overhear and scowl at his nobles. Their wives, daughters, and all the women of the Princely Court ate their meals elsewhere.

Vlad once heard their father telling Mihail, "In their custom, men and women who are strangers don't share meals. I won't disrespect their rituals."

Vlad barely spoke with their parent now, unless good manners required it. Arina became a rare sight. She kept to their mother's side during wedding preparations. Mircea the Great argued about the marital arrangements for a proposed Turkic, rather than a Christian wedding rite. Vlad understood this when he chanced upon the Turkish prince, who hailed the Wallachian co-rulers outside the throne room.

"*Salvete*," the Turk greeted them in Latin. "We must insist the nuptial union occurs according to the laws of my land. It is as much for my bride's protection as it is my wish. I cannot take part in a Christian ceremony."

"Then you insult my Christian sister," Mihail interjected.

"I do not intend any offense," Mûsâ Çelebi replied. "Our laws ensure that even with her religious faith, your sister will be treated the same as any wife of an Ottoman ruler. My ancestors who married Christians; including my great-grandfather who wed a Byzantine princess, my grandfather who took a Bulgarian for his third wife, and my father, married to a Serbian woman; all of them honored their brides. I will do the same. Respect my wishes."

He gave a curt nod. His constant companion said, "The peace of God be with you."

Mûsâ Çelebi and Bedreddin withdrew with the rest of their entourage into the courtyard and rode their horses to the encampment outside Argeş.

On the last day of the year, Arina married the prince at a Turkish ceremony. They stood together in the palace courtyard, with her under a heavily brocaded veil and white furs to ward off the cold. Beneath an open-air tent, while snow flurries swirled, Mûsâ Çelebi's aide Bedreddin said marital vows in Latin on behalf of his master.

Vlad's father spoke the ritual words in his daughter's place. "I consent, I consent, I consent." Afterward, he sealed the nuptial pact with the lion rampant on his signet ring.

Vlad stood behind his mother and watched with the rest of their family. "If you receive word from Arina, will you write to me about her?"

"I will not, my Vlad," Mara replied. "My daughter's future is her own. Besides, a boy concerns himself with the past. You travel to Hungary to become a man. To seize the destiny, none may deny you."

CHAPTER 4

Dawn over the City of Jeweled Eyes

"Circumstances don't make the man, they only reveal him to himself."-Epictetus (circa 50-circa 135 AD), Greek Stoic philosopher.

IN THE YEAR OF OUR Lord 1410. Hermannstadt, Transilvania (modern-day Sibiu, Romania)

The morning after the wedding, once Arina departed at the side of her new husband, Vlad also mounted his horse. He set out, northbound with his escorts, including Marko the Gypsy's boys. Alongside them rode Staico with his thirty Gypsy slaves and their dogs, all protected by Wallachia's royal halberdiers.

During the winter journey of untold weeks, Vlad often shivered beneath his hooded, fur-lined mantle. Frigid air had rolled down from Transilvania's Făgăraş Mountains in the northeast. Prince Mircea had held the hereditary duchy of the Făgăraş region alongside another place called Amlaş for forty years. A grant from Vlad's great uncle and namesake. Frost gripped the snowfields of the Turnu Roşu Pass, which the travelers took toward their western destination.

At the base of an escarpment, through gaps between withered sagebrush and oak and linden trees, Vlad spied the sheen of the frozen Olt River. A ribbon gleaming in the last hours of sunlight, the waterway guided them along a narrow gorge. The night would cover them in darkness soon. Staico led them, the royal halberdiers having parted with them on the border with Transilvania.

Tobar and Yoska rode on either side of Vlad in the tapered defile. While he held no doubts about the bravery of Staico's Gypsies, more closely packed bodies would have also offered respite from the cold.

The Roma people in heavy furs led well-muscled, iron-shod horses and hunting dogs across the wintry landscape. Each morning, a third of the men scouted ahead for heavy snow, rockfall, and dangerous crevasses. They took leaf fodder in baskets made of birch bark and lined icy tracks in advance. Snow buried much of their efforts except in patches.

The scouts reported no sightings of any persons, none so foolish as to cross the Turnu Roșu Pass during midwinter. Before their leave-taking from the capital, Vlad had hoped his mother would plead for some delay until spring, once the land thawed.

She never did. Instead, knowing that Arina's wedding arrangements were complete, their mother prepared him for his journey. It could take months, depending on the severity of the season. Well-stocked with salted and dried meats and oats carried on the backs of pack horses, no one would starve outside the hunt. The wood-corked skins belonged to Staico who liked his ale brewed by monks at Vodița Monastery.

Vlad wore a dual pair of woolen hose, his feet stuffed into leather-soled boots, greased daily with sheep tallow and beeswax. His footwear was one size too big for him. Larger boots allowed for stuffed straw and layers of socks, made of wool stitched by his mother's hands. Like the felted gloves he wore, trimmed with fox fur. A woolen hat covered his hair and ears, as did the hooded mantle worn over the woven tunics. Still, the chill seeped into his bones, and he dusted and shook off the snowfall throughout the day.

"A boy concerns himself with the past." His mother's words became a temporary distraction. How could he avoid the intrusion of the past and everything dear to him?

Cold, bereft, and mired in his thoughts, he considered the loved ones left behind in Wallachia. His mother and grandmother, and his brothers;

little Alex with his impish grins and Radu. Both were irreverent unless it came to the family's safety and defense.

What did the future hold for Vlad without them? Bleak fears about Arina's fate. He mulled over their final goodbye at regular intervals. Only a silent wave before her chin dipped and she rode south with the Turkic prince. She never looked back even though Vlad quietly willed it. He accepted the truth. He would never see her or hear her thoughts or sense her feelings again. Their bond was sundered by her choice.

The finality of their last farewell stunned him into the silence he maintained along the journey north. He spoke only if Staico queried him in their encampment at mealtimes. The older Gypsies talked among themselves and did not openly acknowledge his moods.

A fact that made the elder of the Gypsy twins' behavior strange. From time to time along the snow-covered track, Tobar would lean forward in the saddle, as if he wanted to say something, and eye Vlad. He could not understand why.

By the fifth instance, Vlad raised his head and met the slave's frown. Was Tobar angry because he and his twin did not have the freedom Vlad promised on an impulse? He never asked Prince Mircea, who held their lives.

How could he tell the Gypsy boys about his failure? He warred with himself. Did slaves need an explanation? In his heart, he knew he should say something.

Tobar forestalled him. "Is *Domnule* cold? Your teeth are making noise."

The description of his incessant chattering might have amused Vlad if the next breath had not drawn the frigid air deep into his chest. He coughed and spluttered.

Tobar undid the leather sash at his waist and removed his matted outer fur, revealing another pelt stitched up with leather. Probably the hides of some wolves by the size and tincture. The Gypsy boy flung the black animal skin over Vlad, who could have gagged once the unwashed garment covered him. Instead, gratitude for its warmth filled him.

Some talk began among the clansmen nearby. "The young prince did not ask." Or, "Foolish child. Willful, like his father Marko. May end up dead like him, too." Conversation spread and disagreements reared.

"Stifle this racket at once!" Staico slowed his Carpathian pony and wheeled it around. His gray gaze swept over the men before returning to Vlad.

"It's better, yes? Are you warmer, *čhave*?" He spoke Romany, so all might understand. The gravelly tone uttered in a foreign tongue, with which Staico called Vlad his nephew, reminded him he would never be without family in exile.

"Yes," he replied. Even the chattering of his teeth quickly subsided.

"Good." Staico addressed the Gypsies. "He, not his father, is your prince now. Recognize his needs, see to his comfort, and protect him. From this day until the last, you are bound to his service forever."

The riders resumed the journey and finally stopped within the shade of a tree line. The fires of their encampment turned aside the eerie oak and beech forest's dimness. Stone ramparts and billowing smoke rose from the outskirts of a nearby town. Hillside vineyards lay dormant under layers of frost.

A third of the Gypsies, including the twins, tended the horses. Others searched for silver fir branches, which they heaped on the campsite, averting exposure on the cold ground. The last third of the men skinned small rabbits from the morning hunt alongside Staico.

Vlad's uncle gestured north with the carved handle of his knife. "Hermannstadt, the city of eyes. Do you know why it has that name, Vlad?"

"No, but I expect you want to tell me." When no immediate answer followed, he scowled at his uncle, who shrugged.

"I don't know either, my boy. I thought that maybe your mother said something. She rode through the town on her way to wed."

He shook his head at the insufferable man.

"Are we going to bypass Hermannstadt as well, Staico? We've paid the road tolls, but avoided every township and castle, even the monasteries between Argeş and the region of Tălmaciu, only three leagues south of here."

Silence met his words, disrupted only by the work chatter of the Gypsies.

"Did your half-brother tell you to do this, to keep to ourselves?" Vlad rubbed his hands together as the sensation returned to his fingertips, warmed by the campfire.

"No. My common sense warned me I should not betray the presence of Mircea the Great's son, even among a company of fierce Gypsies. Your father could have enemies here."

"I've seen little outside of Wallachia before now. Arina and I didn't run this far north."

"I remember."

"You would." Vlad frowned again. "I may never come this way after today." Not if Prince Mircea sent him as a hostage. Would he don shackles while he served at Buda Castle?

His uncle finished skinning the third rabbit before sitting back on his haunches. "I suppose you may visit Hermannstadt if you like. It's a major trade area and the location of nearly twenty guild halls. A Saxon place by heritage. You've seen German traders before, but never known their overt influence upon a town. Don't stray there, Vlad. We'll want to be on the road before tomorrow evening."

After the camp's members ate and settled in at twilight, Vlad bedded down beneath the canopy of shimmering stars, devoid of any cloud cover. The wind moaned and ripped at the trees. One dog who took a liking to Yoska lay between the twins, near Vlad where it nosed his hand. The scent of the rabbit lingered. He rubbed the hound's head.

His mind drifted. Did Arina share his vision of the violet-streaked night?

He reached out to her thoughts with his, despite the shroud of silence she imposed. As he promised during the flight from Argeş, he would never give up on her.

This is the furthest I've ever been from home. From you. Already, I've seen so much that is different, yet familiar. You may have done the same. Wherever you are, Rina, I hope you can reflect on all you've encountered and take some joy in it.

"Your thoughts wander again," their uncle commented, despite the thick forearm shielding his eyes. "Your interest in Hermannstadt made me think you held some concern for your present circumstances and the future."

"How could you ever guess what I'm thinking?"

"I know you, boy."

Vlad sighed. "What do you want me to say? Shall I forget how Arina treated me?"

"She did as your father taught and saved her heart from pain. She aided you, too."

"How so? She was distant from me."

"She was saying goodbye, Vlad, forcing you both to accept the inevitable." Staico farted and then rolled on his side toward the blackthorn bushes. "The princess is infinitely stronger than you realize. You are too. All your father's children must be. Sleep now."

Vlad did so at some uncertain hour, but in the languor between sleep and wakefulness, a soft sob echoed in his mind. *Brother.*

A TORTUROUS VISION haunted Vlad that night. A woman cackled and woke him fitfully. A frightful bitter cold encased his body. As his lids lifted, a ghostly white apparition swirled above him. Hair billowing in a wild cascade around cadaverous features. Something talon-like raked his cheek. His heart pitched in terror, and he opened his mouth. The image vanished. He closed his eyes and dreamed no more.

Dawn arrived sooner than he expected. He came awake again, as the breeze rustled his hair, and took in the golden pink hues of the sky. He slept bundled in the odious fur, but the ferocious night wind must have turned aside the pelt. Or had something else done so? He shook his head, recalling the nightmare. Perhaps he had only imagined the strange visage, just as he thought Arina had called to him before he drifted asleep.

His uncle's Gypsies spat and pissed wherever they stood. Staico waited atop a bluff and watched something with intent interest. Vlad joined him.

"Eh, nephew, what's that scratch on your face?" Staico fingered Vlad's cheek. A streak of blood trailed along the thumb.

Vlad swallowed and shook his head. "I must've done that in my sleep." He hoped.

Below their position, a young girl on horseback raced up the hillside from the town. Sunlit hair streamed out beneath a white veil. Perspiration bathed her mount, with its dark brown and white irregular patches, and feathered forelegs reminding Vlad of the Gypsies' horses. Was she a clan member?

Her brocaded blue mantle embroidered with gold tassels made for a fool's belief on his part. Her uneasy grip on the galloping animal's reins imperiled her. She was screaming for the horse to stop. How did such an inexperienced rider come to be atop a wild mount?

"We must help," Vlad urged, as her horse neared the summit.

Over his shoulder, Staico yelled for his and Vlad's ponies. With the tree line on his right and the river valley below on the left, perhaps he thought there would be nowhere else for the girl's horse to go except between them.

"I pray you know what you're doing," Vlad whispered as he mounted.

"When I say wave your arms, do so," Staico ordered, his leather saddle creaking. "Christ's bones. He's already seen you. Wave your arms, Vlad, wave him off!"

Although he felt foolish, Vlad did as his uncle said. Before the oncoming animal turned, he glimpsed the girl's tear-streaked face. Jewel-like eyes smoldered with green fire.

"Good, boy! Now, don't move. I have him." As Staico kneed his horse and sped toward the other, it craned its muscular neck in his direction. The female's face reddened as Staico's mount bore down on hers. When it appeared both animals would have collided, he circled her, sped up, and reached out for her reins. The riders were side by side as Staico slowed. At last, the spooked horse cantered beside the Carpathian pony.

Vlad released a pent-up breath. The girl still appeared terrified and prepared to scream again, because his uncle said, "Don't! You'll only frighten him."

"Me? Scare this beast of my brother's choosing?" The husky response startled Vlad. Not a girl's voice, but that of a young woman. Her small frame evoked his mother's image. Golden hair as well. The similarities stopped there. She exceeded Mara's beauty and made him next consider shameful, carnal thoughts.

While their mounts stopped, huffed, and snorted in unison, Staico clambered down. He kept a firm grip on both reins.

Vlad rode to them and said, "My lady, we have water, or ale, if you prefer."

"I wish for nothing except to show my gratitude." She dismounted without aid. Her emerald-eyed stare swept over Vlad before she gave him her back.

"You saved my life," she said to Staico. "I'm truly grateful. My youngest brother thought this unruly creature was already tame and invited me along for a ride. When it bolted, he slid off the pony's back, with me left holding fast to the reins."

"A foolish business, if you'll excuse my candor, my lady. You and your sibling should be more careful. Our Gypsies there have some rope. We can lead your horse into town."

She drew back a few paces and smacked into Vlad. She whirled, her mouth gaping as if having forgotten he stood there. "Forgive me..." her voice faltered, "but I would prefer not." She cleared her throat. "You've aided me, but I can't rely on strangers to this land."

Staico grinned. "How do you know we don't live in Transilvania?"

"Not even the most stupid of Transilvanians would spend a night in Dumbrava Forest. When my grandmother was a girl, the townspeople hung a witch from an elm tree here. Her ghost roams at night, seeking vengeance."

Vlad swallowed. He put a hand to his cheek again, crusted with blood. The skin itched.

While Staico's belly quaked with laughter, the woman slipped her horse's reins from his grasp. "Besides, my father doesn't know my brother and I took this wretch from the stables. I'd prefer Father never knew."

"Then you should have said so first, my lady." Vlad's uncle sobered a little. "Not offered some fanciful tale meant to frighten children like my nephew here."

She peeked at Vlad and his breath caught in his throat. He forgot to scowl at his uncle for referring to him as a child. The woman's beauty astonished him.

"I'll walk the pony down into the valley to Hermannstadt myself," she said.

Staico's brows flared. "Without an escort?"

"I needed none to reach you."

"Is the choice wise," Vlad persisted, "given the animal's nature?"

She ignored him and tugged her mount. "It's market day. Already, Hermannstadt has stirred. No one there will allow him to harm me. I thank you again, strangers. Go with God."

As Vlad watched her retreating figure, his uncle said, "I suppose there's no way we'll avoid entering the town now."

HERMANNSTADT'S MERCHANTS greeted buyers under light snow dotting their stalls. Carts lined the thoroughfare along the central square, like the layout of the market in Târgoviște.

Townspeople haggled over linen and woolen cloth at the drapers, visited the ale brewers, drank hot mulled wine, and struggled to keep sight of their children. The smoky scent of garlic-fried sausages vied with human sweat and the stink of livestock. Peddlers carried their wares in giant baskets under their arms or atop their heads. They spoke some languages Vlad knew; his native Wallachian dialect, his mother's Hungarian tongue, and the German of Transilvania's majority Saxon populace, as expected. Even Romany.

Rather than draw attention to their large company, Vlad and his uncle had left the Gypsies on the outskirts of Dumbrava Forest. Staico stayed close, glaring at loose women who enticed them with a flash of shapely calves and pink breasts, and muttering threats whenever someone in the crowd barely jostled them.

"They're impossible to avoid in such a place," Vlad reminded him, but he merely shrugged and grimaced at another passerby.

Vlad scanned several female faces but found only disappointment. The young woman at the edge of Dumbrava Forest had become another distant, if not much more pleasant, dream. He could not find her in the packed square. Its occupants stood shoulder to shoulder. His heart sank like a stone as he recalled she never said her name or asked his.

He and his uncle walked in the shadows of the half-timbered guild halls. Each building rose two or three levels above them, dwarfing the square and shielding the marketgoers from the chill. Two small glass windows on each floor faced the street. His uncle grasped his elbow and pointed to the pitched roofs of each guild hall. The rounded and elongated dormers with squares at the centers evoked the iris of an eye. Afterward, everywhere Vlad looked, they seemed to follow him.

If he and the woman encountered each other again in this city of eyes, would she have some better regard for him?

"Do you suspect she was a horse thief?" Vlad asked his uncle.

"Who do you mean?" After Staico laughed at his scowl, the man added, "You think it?"

"I did not say so."

"Why else would you ask?"

A miracle play performed on a cart distracted Vlad. Puppeteers reenacted how the venerated Saint Gheorghe, whom Eastern Orthodox Wallachians called Sângiorz, saved a princess from the monster that terrorized her father's villagers.

Along with the audience, Vlad and Staico booed and shooed away a vain minstrel who brayed nearby. The pair did not pay attention for long, given the incessant clanging from blacksmiths' stalls. They moved on after the sword pierced the monster.

"When my countrymen acknowledge the saint's day four months from now," Vlad observed, "for the first time, I won't be among them."

"You may celebrate Sângiorz's Day in the manner of your choosing. The future is of lesser concern; I must have something in my stomach now. Let's buy some of that mead."

To Vlad's relief, they did more than drink. The mead washed down smoked sausages stuffed with apples, trenchers of beans and fried bacon, chicken pies saturated with yellow saffron, and salted, baked pastries shaped into a knot, which the baker called pretzels. As they strolled beneath the eaves of the guild halls at midday, breezes rustled. The knotted shape of the pretzels worked in iron, swung from metal hooks outside the bakers' guilds.

Vlad sampled varieties of the local honey before he returned to the pretzel baker and called for three dozen pastries, which he would return for in midafternoon. Heavy growls and snarls alerted him before he turned to the sight of men leading a lumbering chained bear and dogs toward a pit.

From the leather purse affixed to his sword belt, Staico finished counting out the coins and gave half of them to the female beside the baker before he grumbled, "I assure you, Vlad, the Gypsies have hunted fine fare since the morning. They won't be hungry upon our return."

Vlad ignored his words and grasped his arm, pulling him away when he would have viewed the bear baiting. "When we rejoin them, I must make amends to Tobar and Yoska."

"With pretzels?"

"No, fool man. The night I left Târgoviște, the twins saved me from a bear. On an impulse, I vowed to free them from the ruling prince, but never talked with him."

"You had no right to offer them liberty. Their lives aren't yours."

"I know, but how may I explain the matter to them? People speak ill of Gypsies, but clan members are dutiful and hold each other to their oaths...."

Vlad trailed off and halted as his gaze, at last, rested on the woman they had met earlier.

Her simple attire puzzled him. A sheepskin vest worn over a linen shirt paired with the wide skirt and two narrow *catrințe;* fringed aprons of flax or hemp, dyed black and red. Common dress among the lower classes. Her waist-length yellow hair hung in two thick plaits. No less beautiful, though, with her flushed cheeks aglow. She placed handfuls of vegetables and dried fruits from a peddler's cart into the wide basket balanced against her slim hip.

"She's a servant," Vlad muttered.

His uncle's chortle rumbled in his ear. "What a curious estimation. Does the possibility diminish her appeal? You seemed so enthralled at the first sight of her."

Meanwhile, she smiled and gave the peddler some coins before the boom of a man's voice summoned her. "Come, daughter!"

Like a child, she skipped across the narrow cobblestone street. An overstuffed wagon waited at the bottom of an incline. She clambered aboard and spoke to the enormous man who held the reins. His great belly rumbled underneath the folds of what must have been some richer man's cast-off mantle, as he laughed and urged on a pair of horses.

"I must see where they will go, Staico."

"No, Vlad! Leave the young woman be."

He had already started following the cart.

His uncle's stream of curses preceded booted footfalls. "Do you know why you and your father have exchanged angry words so often?"

"No, but I presume you shall tell me."

"It's because you're both stubborn as goats."

Vlad smothered his laughter beneath Tobar's wolf-skin and tracked the wagon from the market square through several thoroughfares, going north across sloping land into the upper town. They passed under the shade of a white tower before the wagon slowed outside a boyar's estate, nestled against a pond. The house's tiled roof bore the same type of dormers Vlad glimpsed atop the guild halls.

He and Staico hid in the corner of another building at the bottom of the street.

The woman helped her parent dismount. Other females in similar garments came out and aided boys who awaited the cart. Was the man the chief cook of a nobleman?

Vlad's confusion increased as the woman's father cast off his threadbare mantle. Beneath it, he wore a doublet topped with a gold brooch that closed at the neckline. The glimmer of the metal vied with the sheen of lustrous tresses falling on either side of his puffed face. He kissed the cheeks of the daughter with whom he shared nothing more than their hair color before going up the front steps to the house.

Why did the man choose the outward appearance of the lower classes?

"To avoid robbers. See his purse? Twice the size of mine."

Vlad frowned, not realizing he had uttered the question aloud. The woman directed those who offloaded her father's goods. The servants went through a wooden gate and disappeared behind the house.

"So, she's his bastard," Vlad concluded. The possibility vexed him, but why should it? After he left Hermannstadt, he would never see her again.

"Is she, Vlad? Does that matter more than when you thought her a servant?"

The last kitchen maid took the vegetable and fruit basket. A boy led the horses through the gate, presumably to the stables. Vlad turned away.

"Have you seen enough, stranger?"

He looked over his shoulder to where his quarry leaned against the house's fence. She glared in his direction with her arms crossed over a small bosom.

"You may as well show yourself fully," she called out. "Otherwise, you would have walked all this way from the marketplace for nothing."

"I believe I did." He stepped out from the shadow of the adjacent building.

Her laughter pealed in the almost empty street. "You were so eager before now. What were you seeking?" She moved to him.

"A better understanding of you. I've failed utterly. You're a puzzle. A noblewoman who rode an untamed horse without her father's permission met us on a hill at dawn. Then, disguised as one of the poor, she bought goods at the market."

"Even the poor must eat." She guffawed. "Wouldn't you agree?"

"I do," he sputtered. "Who are you? I demand to know."

Her resultant smile mocked him. "And who are you to command me?"

"I am Prince Vlad of Wallachia, third son of Mircea the Great of the House of Basarab and Mara of the House of Tolmay in Hungary." As an afterthought, he tilted his head toward her. "My father is a vassal of the king of Hungary, Zsigmond of the House of Luxembourg. I'm journeying to his court to serve as a royal attendant."

With a slight giggle, she only clasped her hands behind her. She remained unimpressed.

Had her father never taught his bastard the courtesy owed to a Wallachian prince? Vlad's stomach plummeted, but the sensation agitated him further. None of this would matter after he left Hermannstadt.

"You've claimed a princely father and a noble heritage, but who are you without this illustrious heritage?"

How dare she question a prince of legitimate blood? He bowed, although she did not deserve any civility. "Someone who shall trouble you no further. I bid you a good day."

He forced his shoulders back and marched to the market.

Staico kept his mouth shut for the duration of the afternoon. He paid for the three sacks of warm pretzels and hefted them. They departed Hermannstadt before evening fell. The Gypsies awaited their return.

"We must leave at once," Vlad commanded his uncle. "I never want to see this accursed forest or that town again."

Staico finished tying the sacks to the saddle horns of the three Gypsy chieftains among them. He merely nodded to Vlad.

They rode off under an orange sunset, putting some distance between them and Hermannstadt long before nightfall. Vlad's mood never improved. Once they camped in the woodland's shade, he bedded down earlier than anyone else did, having refused the evening meal or another pretzel.

Staico frowned at him like some recalcitrant child. He did not care and rolled away from the fire's brilliance. Sleep did not come easily. When it did, jeweled eyes haunted his dreams.

CHAPTER 5

On Raven's Wings

"Thief knows thief and wolf knows wolf."-Ancient Greek proverb.

IN THE YEAR OF OUR Lord 1410. Hunyadvár, Transilvania (modern-day Hunedoara, Romania)

As their ponies walked a well-worn track through the forests south of the Carpathian Mountains, Staico's men passed around his skins of ale. His head bowed over some parchment, his gloved fingers traced a list of places with notations recorded beside them, all written in Hungarian.

Riding beside his uncle, Vlad cleared his throat, starting a conversation for the first time in two days. "Where does Mother's itinerary place us?"

"So, you've decided not to sulk anymore, eh?" Staico grunted without lifting his gaze.

Vlad could not deny the accusation. His behavior after they left Hermannstadt was more like that of a toddling child. He always bristled whenever Staico reminded him of his age. If he wanted to prove his uncle wrong, he must do better.

He answered, "It was foolish of me to let revelations about the woman in Hermannstadt be a bother. She is best forgotten as with all past concerns."

If only he could convince himself to feel that way about Arina's marriage, too.

Staico met Vlad's stare. "The past does not define one person or dictate the future. You can always choose another, better path in life. You understand?"

Sudden, unfathomable tears came to Vlad's eyes. He burrowed further beneath the stinking wolf-skin.

Staico reached out and touched his shoulder with the three fingers of his mangled hand. As a little child, Vlad would have shied away from the gesture in revulsion. Now he sniffled and looked at his uncle.

With a frown, Staico asked, "Did you not take my meaning?"

Vlad perceived the intent behind the words well enough. His stomach soured before he admitted, "There are times I wish you had sired me. Often, you've offered wisdom while your half-brother meted out cruelty and neglect. His halberdiers abandoned us along the border with Transilvania, rather than ensuring my safe arrival at Buda Castle."

Staico withdrew his touch and patted his mount instead. Quietude ensued and time slowed. From somewhere among the trees, an owl hooted. With each passing moment, Vlad swallowed and waited for some acknowledgment from his uncle.

Unable to bear the tension, he asked, "Do you fault me for saying how I feel?"

"Never repeat those words." Staico straightened in the saddle and did not regard him.

"But you've been more of a parent to me than—"

"Cease, Vlad! Mircea the Great wanted the halberdiers at your side until we reached Buda Castle. I reminded him royal troops outside Wallachian borders would invite undue scrutiny. The letter of *salvus conductus*, which carries your father's privy seal, shall suffice. If we meet trouble on the road, we have the Gypsies."

Vlad swallowed, but the lump in his throat did not ease.

"If you wanted to prove you understood what I'd said earlier, you've failed," Staico added. "Your father is as he is. Accept it. Only a child wishes for what is futile. A man assesses his circumstances and makes the most of them."

Tears prickling again, Vlad hung his head. He gave what he believed might be the highest compliment to his uncle, but Staico rejected it.

"My half-brother has always had everything I ever wanted, Vlad. First, our father's full love and acceptance. The distinction between me and my legitimate siblings became clear to his household and courtiers. I never complained when they whispered 'bastard' out of his earshot. Still a child, I vowed no offspring of mine would suffer the ignominy. Later, as a man, I did not think marital happiness would be likely."

Vlad sniffled. "I've heard you lived like the monks at Vodiţa who brewed your ale."

"Your father made the claim." Staico gave a low, rueful chuckle. "He thought he offered an insult. He never knew the dual reasons for my vow of celibacy. For one day in spring, I lost my heart to a woman whom I could never marry. A golden-haired beauty recently arrived at the Princely Court. Destined for a union with the half-brother who despised me."

A gasp escaped Vlad. As Staico eyed him again, he searched his uncle's craggy visage.

"I've kept my feelings hidden for thirty years." Staico continued, "Don't think less of me for revealing them now. I've never shamed your mother, nor would I. She does not know my sentiments. She will not while I draw breath upon this earth."

Vlad could not believe it. Princess Mara held Staico's heart all this time. He recalled their close interactions, including the last at Târgovişte, where she upbraided Staico over him when she thought he was missing still. Not once did his uncle ever show her anything but the respect she deserved as the ruling prince's wife, despite having loved her for years.

An owl hooted again and drew Vlad back to the present, where his uncle said, "Don't wish for the impossible. That path leads to heartbreak and regret. Relinquish the past with your father. I have. Find joy in the future that you will build with a wife and children at your side. Be a devoted and tolerant parent. Impart the lessons you will undertake."

"I'll never forget your teachings." Despite the prevailing chill, Vlad extended his forearm from beneath the wolf-skin. His uncle's grim visage softened before he made the same gesture. The pair grasped each other at the elbow.

After they drew apart, Staico's throat bobbed. He returned full attention to the itinerary on his lap. "We've gone north from Hermannstadt and now travel in the shadow of the Western Carpathians. If there is no snow, we should reach Hunyadvár tonight. We'll pay the toll in the morning and move on."

"Did Mother note anything special about this castle or its master?"

"Why? Did she have much to say about the others? She wrote here that Hunyadvár is on a hill and within a day's ride of the star-shaped, white fortress of Bălgrad, which we left this morning. She was right. I judge the distance to be about fourteen leagues between the castle and Bălgrad, given the markers we've encountered on the road. We should see Hunyadvár soon, rising above the trees and the Zlasti River."

Vlad leaned aside and scrutinized the document, the thirty-year-old words etched above his uncle's three fingers. "Mother used the number of days she traveled as an indicator of the distance between all these places where we have now ventured. She journeyed from Hungary in the spring."

"Therefore, it's better to rely on leagues...." Staico's voice faded. He rolled up the supple parchment before returning it to his saddlebag. "A more accurate means, *čhavo*, of determining the length of any trip. Especially into the unknown."

Around them, the easy banter between the Gypsies ended in an abrupt and tense silence. Vlad glanced behind him. No more ale drinking, either. Tobar and Yoska quieted too, after trading banter all day about their individual skills with weapons.

Vlad nudged the horse closer to his uncle's mount and whispered, "Why did you switch to speaking Romany?"

"We're being watched from the trees. Don't look up," Staico murmured.

Even if he did, the glare of sunset would have blinded Vlad. When the owl hooted again, he cocked his head. Someone was mimicking the sound. A likely warning to others in their company, so they might know the position of the Wallachians.

His heart thrummed. If bandits hid among the canopies, surely, there could not be enough to take on thirty-two Gypsies, including the twins, and Staico, a battle-tested man over fifty years old.

Vlad asked, "What makes you think those who watch us won't understand Romany?"

"I'm hoping they don't," his uncle replied. "That pelt you're wearing won't turn aside arrows. Not if a skilled archer attacks. My men will protect you, but that'll also draw attention, making it clear you're a prize for bandits. You've got a sword in its scabbard against your hip. Can you draw it without betraying your movements?"

"Yes, but...." He gaped at his uncle. "You would let me fight?"

"You will do so when you must, but don't be eager, *čhavo*. Killing for true, for the first time, differs from stabbing a straw man or pig carcass."

"You've trained me for combat since I was seven years old."

"With wooden and then blunted swords."

"The crossbow Radu gave me is tied to the saddlebag." He shot Staico a grin. "I'm almost as good with it as a sword."

"You'll take too long with the windlass. Show me your youthful bravado at another time." Staico pointed ahead. "Look to the next rise. Hunyadvár."

The last embers of a burnished copper sunset blazed atop the high roof of one rounded tower. They must reach the fortification soon.

With the stillness around them came the unmistakable sound of water rushing nearby. Would they have to cross a bridge? Could they do so before the bandits struck? Would the castle's occupants offer shelter or turn them away?

Momentary panic almost overwhelmed Vlad. He fought for each calming breath. His uncle relied on the Gypsies with faith. Vlad trusted him more than he would ever admit. Still, what if something went wrong?

"Shouldn't we hurry, Staico?"

While he spoke, twilight fell in a gray hue, tinged with orange.

"No, *čhavo*. The time for that is long past. If we speed up now, they'll know we're on to them. They're counting on us not reaching the castle before dusk sets in. We also don't know who or what awaits us at Hunyadvár."

Staico's fingers disappeared beneath the outer woolen cloak, his movements deft before he nodded. "We're going to need your sword, my boy."

Vlad drew cold air into his lungs. His hand closed on the pommel in time.

On either side of them, bandits dropped from the trees. Vlad did a quick count. Four men were on his left and five were on Staico's right. Two others held on to the ropes they used for their quick descents. All eleven brandished weapons. They lacked chain mail chest coverings and helmets but carried mostly short swords and one-handed axes. Two sets of bows and quivers of arrows among them.

A man, older and stocky like Staico, wielded the lone spiked club with rusted tips. With an ominous sneer on his lips, the bandit rushed at Vlad and aimed his brutish bludgeon.

Vlad threw back the pelt and drew the sword from its scabbard. His opponent swung his weapon while Vlad slashed with the blade. The robber arced his body. The sword cut through nothing but air.

"Get off the horse before he pulls you down and bashes open your skull," Staico yelled before he leaped at a younger attacker, coming for him in a blur of speed.

The club came near the tip of Vlad's nose, rammed his chest, and battered his arms until they were sore. He blocked limbs as thick as the club and sliced his opponent's chest at intervals. Bellowing like an enraged bull, the man reached for Vlad's booted foot. He drove his heel hard against his assailant's chest and the man tumbled backward.

Vlad dove and stabbed him in the exposed neck. Afterward, he stared at his fallen foe, who gurgled and wheezed as blood spouted and pooled at his throat. He coughed, flecks of red spittle flying everywhere. The grip on the club loosened. The broad chest no longer rose and fell.

An arrow whizzed by Vlad's ear. He could not think of the dead or consider the import of his first kill. A flurry of arrowheads came at him. He dashed behind a boulder along the road. Behind him, his horse whinnied and snorted before hoof-beats raced away in retreat.

"We'll get the archer, *Domnule*." Tobar and Yoska ran ahead of him. Suddenly, Tobar veered off to the right, defending himself against two swordsmen. Vlad lost sight of Yoska before a guttural cry tore through the evening.

The arrows stopped. He threw aside the wolf-skin, pierced by three fletched shafts. Scant moonbeams shone through a patch of sparse trees. Enough to reveal the archer, crouched at the edge of the grove, with a body prone near his feet.

Vlad plunged into the woodland. The archer misfired in his haste. He nocked another arrow in the bow. Other shafts littered the snow beside him. Vlad roared, whacked the weapon aside, and plunged his sword into the apex of the man's neck and shoulder.

The archer grasped the steel as if he meant to pull it out. Blood seeped between the blunt fingers closed on the blade. Vlad shoved it deeper and twisted in savage fury.

The scent of fresh blood filled his nostrils. Viscous and cloying, it seeped from the man's gaping gash and his wounded hands. Vlad wrenched the sword from his flesh, and he sagged on his side. His stare widened as if in surprise before he breathed his last.

Vlad stood dazed over the body. The act of killing was not what he once expected.

"Brother!"

He spun around at the pitiable sound of Tobar's voice. The Gypsy hovered beside his bloodied twin.

An arrow shaft protruded from the eye of the boy on his back. He groaned and coughed. Tobar patted his sibling's cheek where red flecks dotted the skin.

"*Domnule* killed him. You're safe now." Yet, tears coursed down Tobar's face, like his sibling's blood pooling among the dried leaves.

Vlad went to them and leaned over Yoska. "Don't touch the shaft. We don't know whether it's lodged in bone and flesh."

Somewhere, a distant horn blared.

"Stay with your brother, Tobar. I'll return," Vlad said.

He raced to the road. His uncle and the Gypsies fought on. Everywhere, the sound of steel rang out. There were more bandits. A pair of mounted archers and light-armored men on horseback, though not the Carpathian ponies and Gypsy mounts that had long fled.

A Gypsy staggered backward, clutching at his belly while the intestines spilled out. Vlad hollered a challenge for the killer, who sized him up and urged the horse toward him. The bandit leaned forward in the saddle with his sword held aloft. Vlad waited for him, sliced his unprotected side underneath the arm, and slashed his lower back. The rider gave an agonized howl while his galloping mount hauled him away.

An arrowhead lodged in Staico's thigh made him growl like an angry bear. He hurled his dagger. It caught a mounted archer square in the chest, plunging through his leather cuirass before he slumped and slid off his horse.

The horn blew again. Vlad peered through the dimness in the sound's direction. Multiple hoof-beats rumbled the earth and approached a bend in the road ahead.

More mounted men appeared. They wore full plate and chain mail armor. Narrow slits for the eyes in the helmets. Their archers in the vanguard fired on the marauding riders with deadly precision. The lead knight shot a crossbow and carried a large shield. A black raven painted on a blue background clenched a gold ring in its beak.

This warrior and his men charged into the fray. The swordsmen among them slashed with their weapons and bashed unprotected heads. Soon, a few bandits remained. The knights slaughtered the rest, even a pleading youth who looked no older than Vlad.

When the fight ended, the apparent leader of their rescuers removed his helm and dismounted. A hunting horn hung from a leather cord around his neck. He surveyed the battle's aftermath. Then he ordered his men to round up the horses.

Vlad drew ragged breaths and wiped his stained sword on one of the attacker's cloaks. The knight with the raven shield approached Staico, who tested the shaft embedded in his thigh and cursed. Vlad recalled Yoska. He rushed to the Gypsy's side.

"Over here!" Vlad yelled from the forest. "Help Yoska."

Soon he and three clansmen crouched beside Tobar. Yoska cried out even as his twin spoke softly to him again.

The lead knight joined them in the woods. "The boy lives, though losing his eye is certain. If your Gypsies can bear him up, others of his kind will attend him at Hunyadvár."

Vlad looked at their rescuer, who spoke Hungarian. "Who are you?"

"Vajk Hunyadi, a knight of the court of King Zsigmond." He bowed and quickly straightened. Graying brown hair fell over his dark eyes. "You are a son of Prince Mircea. Your father sent word about you to our liege at Buda Castle. Our king ordered me back to my domain at Hunyadvár to await your arrival and escort you into Hungary."

Something familiar resonated in his gravelly tone, but before Vlad could question it, the Gypsies placed some of their outer furs on the snow-covered ground next to Yoska. Vlad stood aside while they hefted the young slave, who groaned, onto the pelts. Then they wrapped him up from his chest to the thighs. Two pairs of men lifted and bore him away.

Vlad followed and went to Staico, who frowned at a knight tending his leg. "You live, my boy. I did not fail your father. But say I'm old or I should've moved faster, and I'll beat you to death, nephew."

Kneeling beside his uncle, Vlad gave him a blood-spattered glove to bite. Staico examined it before glancing at him.

"It's not my blood. You trained me well."

"Not a cut on you, eh? First-time luck."

"Skills taught to me by the finest sword-master I've ever known."

"One with an arrow stuck in his leg, Vlad."

Staico stuffed the felt glove into his mouth before Vajk's knight tested the edges of the wound where the arrowhead protruded. Staico screeched as blood seeped. He might have walloped the knight, but Vlad flung himself across his uncle's body.

"Let him help you, Staico."

In time, the knight eased the shaft and entire arrowhead from the thigh. He tore the bottom of the wool tunic under his plate and mail and bound Staico's leg.

"That must suffice until we reach Hunyadvár and my lady wife," Vajk said. "We can take those horses your attackers rode, but some of your Gypsies must double up or walk."

"They will wait upon me," Staico said. With aid, he got on his knees in the snow. A grunt escaped the lips that he pressed together. His throat bobbed. He made the sign of the cross, clasped his hands on his chest, closed his eyes, and bowed his head.

Vajk snorted. "There's no time, my lord prince. Your uncle must have the leg tended."

Vlad shook his head and looked down at Staico, whose lips moved in silent prayer. "He would clearly disagree and say there is always time for God."

VLAD TRAVELED THE ENTIRE way beside Yoska and Tobar, riding double. The Gypsy youth's pains as his head slumped on his brother's back made the slow walk the horses took to the castle unbearable. Again, the twins risked possible death, for Vlad's sake. He owed Yoska a debt he could never repay. Except by one means; a grant of freedom.

The clan found half of their horses along the forest tracks, including Staico's mount. As they approached his domain, the castle's lord blew the hunting horn Vlad had heard earlier. The Wallachians and Transilvanians crossed a narrow river bridge and entered the precincts of Hunyadvár, with its gates flung open to receive them. In the torch-lit courtyard, four people waited under heavy fur-lined mantles next to a half-finished tower. Wooden scaffolding rose from its base.

Vajk dismounted with a loud grunt and took off his helm. He joined a pale, broad woman and a small boy. She kissed his cheek, and he smiled before patting the head of the child beside her. Then he whispered to the lady, whose lush mouth gaped before she peered at the Gypsies with their wounded and dying. She picked up the boy and cradled his face against her neck. He whined and turned for a view of everything.

Vlad and Staico came down from their horses at the same time.

"I present Prince Vlad of Wallachia and his uncle, the lord Staico." Vajk introduced them to the others, who bowed. "If you'll permit me, my lord prince, I present my brothers. Also, my lady wife. The boy is our son, János."

The child with a mess of mud-tinged curls perked up at his name.

"Wh-who are those men there?" He pointed to the Gypsies.

An unfortunate lisp afflicted the boy at a tender age. Vlad hoped the impediment would fade in time. He once suffered the same in childhood.

"Those are the fierce Gypsies," he explained. "Very brave men who made sure robbers did not hurt me badly. When they fell on us, your father saved us."

János' brown-eyed stare widened. "Did they want to hurt Father too?"

"They are gone now, don't worry," his parent said.

"Wh-where, Father? Where have they gone?"

"It doesn't matter now, János. We are all safe." Vajk shook his head and patted his wife's stout hand. "My dearest lady, Lord Staico's leg needs tending. A wash, poultice, and bandages. The Gypsies have been wounded. One beyond all hope. There's also a boy... His eye."

"What's wrong with his eye, Father?"

János' interruption made Vlad smile as he recalled his impatient, exuberant youth.

"If Lord Staico will await me in the great hall, I shall attend him," the child's mother said.

"Later, if you please. I must ensure the care of my Gypsies first," Staico insisted.

"As you wish. Direct everyone to our Gypsy tents, my lord husband. The women will look after any wounded. Please let me tell the castle cook we'll need a larger supper and take János to the nursery first."

"I don't want to go!" The child whined, wriggled, and batted a small fist against his mother's high, ample bosom.

Before either of his parents could chide János, Vlad cleared his throat. "That won't do. My family taught me to be kind to ladies. Never raise a hand against them. A man doesn't hurt women. You want to be a man, young János?"

The boy's tantrum ceased. "Yes. I want to be a man. A knight, l-l-l-like my father."

"Then you must be good to your mother. For now, she is your only lady, and a knight would tell his lady he is sorry if he ever hurt her."

János pouted for a moment before looking at his mother. "D-d-did I hurt you?"

"Yes, a little, János." She gave a grave nod.

"S-s-sorry," he mumbled before he burrowed his ruddy face into her neck.

"That will have to suffice for an apology." She smiled at Vlad. "Thank you, my lord prince. I've never been able to make him understand why he mustn't hit."

Once she withdrew into the castle, Vajk directed Vlad, Staico, and the Gypsies to tents beyond Hunyadvár's stables, abutting the eastern walls of the fortress. Women came out of their dwellings and examined the six of the Wallachian clansmen with grave injuries.

"Ah, *dordi*." One female clasped her hands at her chest. She leaned over the disemboweled fighter. She said, "ah, dear," with the emotion reserved for a close relation. Most clans held each other in common kinship.

"Losing even one man pains you." Vlad patted his uncle's shoulder.

"If I may suggest, we should go inside the fortifications. A warm fire and ale await you." Vajk nodded to the Gypsies. "They will do all they can."

The men carrying Yoska ducked inside a tent with him, following directions from another woman. When Tobar would have followed, she barred him. An angry exchange ensued. In the end, he glared at her and sank on the mat before her doorway.

"Come, nephew. Tobar will never leave Yoska." Staico dragged his injured limb as he staggered beside Vlad.

Together, they followed Vajk to the inner courtyard's well. A pageboy awaited them with brushes, buckets, and a bowl of salt. Their host rinsed away the blood from his leather gloves and invited them to do the same. Vlad looked down at the crimson stains marring the felt on his hands and sighed. His mother's handiwork was ruined now.

The castle's master said, "My lord king received word of your impending travel into Hungary at the start of winter, Prince Vlad. I rushed home to Hunyadvár at his command."

Staico rinsed and brushed his plate and chain mail gloves with handfuls of salt in a bucket. The cold water increasingly reddened.

Vajk added, "My lady wife can provide baths and send your clothing to the laundress. I assume you have more in your saddlebags, Lord Staico. Good. Either of my brothers can offer you clean garments, my lord prince. None so fine as you may be used to, of course, but at least they are your size. We'll find your missing mount. Will you bathe before the meal?"

"I thank you, Vajk." Vlad peered at a grimacing Staico. "But, no, we'll eat first."

Afterward, he and his uncle washed the blood from their faces.

"Are bandits common here or across all of Transilvania, even on well-traveled roads?" Staico swiped away droplets from his thick beard.

Silence stretched for the interval of a few breaths.

Vajk scratched his nape and shuffled on his feet. "Er, in winter, anything is possible."

His embarrassment became clear as his cheeks reddened, reminiscent of the water in the buckets. The bold and brutal attack occurred too close to his domain.

"The skirmish is over," Staico said. "That's the most important aspect, Vlad. We won't need to mention it at the Hungarian court, thanks to our valiant host; a fellow countryman."

At last, Vlad understood why Vajk's discourse seemed so familiar.

"I can recognize the Wallachian dialect, even in Hungarian speech," Staico added with a nod to Vajk.

He replied, "I once served among your father's knights, my lord prince, fourteen years ago. At the battle of Nicopolis, he ordered us to save ourselves from the Turkic rout. King Zsigmond remained mired in the rushes alongside the lower Danube, cut off from us. I begged Prince Mircea to let me aid the king's rescue in a fishing boat. When Zsigmond was safe and back at Buda Castle, he demanded my name and service. Your father released me."

After Vajk fell silent, he glanced across the courtyard to where his wife had exited the castle again. She smiled at him and continued toward the Gypsy tents.

"My lady is Transilvanian by birth. The slaves are her inheritance."

"May I check on Yoska after we've supped?" Despite the delicious scents wafting from Hunyadvár's kitchen, Vlad could not forget his loyal Gypsies.

Vajk nodded and waved over an attendant, who took the trio's gloves and outer garments.

Inside the great hall, spacious with trestle tables set along the walls, Vajk bowed beside Vlad. "Allow me, my lord prince, to look in on my son and bid him good night."

Vlad nodded. Once they were alone, Staico took to a bench and sank with a grunt.

"Why do you suppose he continues to speak with us in Hungarian, eh, despite knowing our shared origins, Vlad?"

"It's the language of the court and the king he serves. In Wallachia, our people would have called him 'Voicu' from birth. He might have altered the name to the Hungarian version, to honor his master the king. Vajk is entitled to his preferences."

"Humph, as you say. A knight with such a strategic holding must be important to Zsigmond. Yet, not enough to deserve a noble title too, eh? I wonder why."

"You heard Vajk. He saved the king's life. Hunyadvár must be his reward. A substantial one. Didn't you notice the work on a new tower? The knight must have the means to expand his domain into a great fortress."

Vlad whirled, taking a full view of the dining hall with its tapestries woven with the raven and ring heraldry. Lit beeswax candles set on every table sent the scent of smoke tinged with honey through the otherwise stuffy air. Closed windows kept the cold out.

Staico said, "He should spend monies hiring mercenaries to rid him of bandits."

"Vajk saved us." Vlad ceased his study and frowned at his uncle.

"Yes, at a crucial moment. The bandits never tried to steal our belongings. They only wanted our blood. Strange, eh?"

"Not so. It's easier to rob the dead." Vlad ran his fingers through his hair. "What are you getting at with all these questions?"

"No lookout here could have seen the skirmish, with the trees on the river's eastern bank blocking the view. I wonder how Vajk knew where to find us."

"He expected our arrival. I'm sure my father told Zsigmond about the route we intended; our use of the itinerary Mother gave you. Maybe Vajk was on patrol with his men while we were defending ourselves. Does it matter?"

Staico gave his characteristic shrug. "You don't have the benefit of my age and experiences. Few miraculous things in life are truly happenstance or coincidence."

"Have you considered whether God sent Vajk to us? Do you deny His power to thwart evil? I've never known you to question faith in Him."

"I rely on God, my instincts, and the Gypsies who are loyal to me. I'll never trust the words of strangers outright. You shouldn't either."

Vlad would have reacted, but their host returned and waved to the dais. After they sat, Vajk's brothers joined them. They dined on sweet cheese and bread, followed by a savory soup of sturgeon and vegetables. Roasted venison and boar meat accompanied the meal.

Sore from the saddle and the fight, Vlad concentrated on filling his belly. Staico's suspicions warranted no real concern. Yet, thoughts of them prevailed.

VLAD SAT WITH TOBAR and Yoska each day during the subsequent week as the boy recuperated. It took that length of time for his clansmen to call him Yoska One-Eye. A name Vlad thought cruel, but the Gypsy youth did not appear discomfited. Daily, his caretaker secured a fresh bandage across his face and over his head before tying the ends. He learned from her how to care for his wound and avoid infection.

All but one of the six injured Gypsies recovered. The clan buried their fallen kin and, in their custom, burned his belongings. No wife or children existed to claim them. Staico never complained about his leg. Only fingered it and scowled.

Villagers brought news about the missing ponies and returned the animals for rewards. Vlad paid, maybe more than he should have. He knew how much the Gypsies prized their mounts. He understood the sentiment well after his horse arrived, unharmed, with the baggage and crossbow still tied to the saddle horn.

"We must get on the road if your men are ready," Vajk said at the week's end.

Staico grunted. Vlad frowned at his uncle's rudeness before he nodded and replied, "They are eager to ride. How soon may we leave Hunyadvár?"

"I'm prepared to go tomorrow. If it would please my lord prince."

"That suits me well. And my uncle and the Gypsies."

The next morning, after dawn, Vlad climbed into the saddle again.

He looked over his shoulder. Tobar mounted. Yoska lingered beside a Gypsy girl whose mother healed him. Their heads close together, the young pair shared a laugh before he took to his horse and looked down at her with his good eye. She blushed.

Vlad thought it was a shame that they might never encounter each other again. He did not expect he might bring the Gypsy twins with him through Transilvania in the future.

"You never told me; what did you first feel after you killed those bandits in the forest?" Staico joined him on the adjacent mount. "Battle leaves some men ill. Others remain shocked in the aftermath."

Vlad stared at an idyllic family scene. Vajk kissed his plump wife and four-year-old son. He hailed his brothers, who would oversee work in the castle during his absence. Afterward, the knight drew up his horse to the gatehouse and awaited the Wallachians.

Vlad urged his pony on and Staico joined him, as he said, "At first, I wanted us to live. Then, I wanted to stop the archer who had wounded

Yoska. As men died by my sword, there was nothing, uncle. I felt nothing."

CHAPTER 6

The Ginger Fox's Lair

"The courts of kings are full of people, but empty of friends."-Seneca the Elder (54 BC-39 AD), Roman writer.

IN THE YEAR OF OUR Lord 1410. Buda, Hungary (modern-day Budapest, Hungary)

"You don't find your reaction to your first kill rather odd, Vlad, even days later?"

With a loud sigh, Vlad rolled his eyes heavenward before he turned and glowered at his uncle. "How many times must I answer so?"

"Until I believe you." Staico drank from the skin of ale and handed it to the Gypsy chieftain next to him. "I vomited the first time after I killed a man."

The riders approached a gatehouse with two red-roofed towers. The wind howled and tore at Vlad's pelt like savage wolves. The biting cold blowing eastward from the Danube River irritated him almost as much as the persistent conversation.

"On the road to Hunyadvár, you told me to fight when I must, Staico."

"You'd have me believe you learned the value of that lesson after one battle?"

"The danger we faced showed the truth of your words. For once, I listened and followed your direction. Now, you question my actions."

"No. I wonder about your mood in the aftermath. You've slept well, snoring so loud as to wake the dead. Battle changes a man, much less his first kill. You're just a boy."

"Except I'm not! You refuse to see it." Vlad ground his teeth together and wished he could ram his fist into Staico's face. "My sixteenth birthday arrived the morning after we left Hermannstadt. I haven't felt like a boy for a long time."

In the spring of his seventh year, Mircea the Great had roused him from sleep at dawn and sent him to the practice field. There, Staico waited alongside Vlad's elder brothers. Their uncle put a wooden sword and shield in his grasp and began his instruction.

Then at nine years old came the blunted blade and an iron shield so heavy, at first, he could barely lift it. He learned. As he did two years later with bows and arrows, the shafts thick as his fingers. The strength needed to wield the long-handed ax and mace made his shoulders burn. He never complained. His brother Radu introduced the crossbow, two summers before Vlad's first exile. Also, at twelve, he drew blood for the first time; a spear thrown at a fresh pig carcass. During more than a year spent at Târgoviște, Staico never allowed him a respite from the daily regimen.

How could his family have trained him to wield lethal weapons from such a youthful age and still consider him a child?

As they entered and rode through the town, he studied the houses built of wood and stone, aligned along an old Roman road that followed the river's course. No dormers topped the roofs, unlike the ones found in Transilvania. A sharp spire rose from some unseen structure closer to the unfortified embankment. Gaps between the buildings and scant trees permitted him the sight of the Danube. Snow flurries blustered. He batted at his cold nose.

Midday approached and found some people outdoors, despite the frigid weather. Fishmongers carried baskets of huge salmon and sturgeon. A few denizens hailed Vajk. Likely, the raven shield ensured his recognition.

"Generations of our warriors have preceded you, Vlad," Staico said. "Our ancestor, Basarab, claimed the principality at the tip of a sword. It is our way, eh? Some fighters are reluctant. Others, like Basarab, have no choice. Every life taken should be of some significance, no matter the cause."

Why couldn't he relent?

Exasperated, Vlad ground his teeth together and focused on the extensive swath of the river. Beyond a bend in the waterway and a stone bridge, Buda Castle lay on a wide plateau. He wanted to explore the rooms beneath red and golden spires and take in a full view of the landscape from the windows and balconies. Not carry on an annoying conversation with his uncle. He hoped to end it now and put all the talk of his emotional state aside.

"Our family didn't raise us to be cowards, Staico. When the first man attacked, meaning to murder me, it was my life or his in the balance. I survived. Yoska could have died if the second man, the archer had ruined his eye. The third, he slashed your Gypsy across the belly, spilling the man's guts. The bandits deserved death. Taking their lives meant nothing to me. It was fair recompense for what they did."

"God alone metes out justice, nephew. Don't call what we did by the same name."

"I'm no blasphemer!" He glared at his uncle again. "If anyone attacks me, those whom I care for, or others who depend on me, I will never hesitate."

Staico snorted and leaned forward in the saddle, looking to Vlad's left. "Vajk, do you remember what happened after you cut down your first man?"

"I shit myself!" The knight gave a raucous laugh. His captain rode next to him. The other knights behind them joined in the mirth. Soon he sobered. "Once a battle is over, there are still times my belly knots. Like the lord prince, when faced with an enemy, I do what I must."

He turned his dark-brown stare on Vlad and added, "Despite what other knights or minstrels would have you believe, there is little glory in the sight of a man's light leaving his eyes. When we kill, we recall our mortality. One day, we might be the ones pleading for mercy. Helpless.

Some deaths in battle are expected. Even necessary. All are cruel harbingers of the fate awaiting most warriors. We rarely die old in our beds."

Staico nodded. "That's why I don't concern myself with the manner of the end. It comes for us all. The things we do while we live make a difference for the people whom we love and protect, or honor with the service of our swords. How they recall us matters. I don't want to be thought of as only a butcher of human meat."

Perhaps the reason he acted as a benefactor to the monks at Vodiţa, Vlad reasoned.

Staico hoped to save his immortal soul, assuaging his guilt for the lives taken. He said nothing further and took back the skin of ale. He drained the dregs and belched.

"When I die, I hope I'll be thought a fierce defender of my king," Vajk commented.

The mention of Zsigmond gave Vlad a chance to end an otherwise futile discussion.

He asked, "Will you tell us about him, Vajk?"

"Our king is one of the most formidable, wise, and brilliant men I have ever known. He could have been pope or one of the kingdom's greatest scholars." The knight smiled. "Zsigmond is called 'the ginger fox' by friends and enemies. The first reference is because of his hair, admittedly grayer in recent years than red. He is wily still, much like a fox."

"Beware of men who resort to trickery, Vlad, especially kings," Staico advised.

Vajk's mount snorted and pranced while they crossed the bridge. He brought the animal under swift control.

"Zsigmond's wits simply prevail over those who have none." The knight did not even try to conceal his scowl, although Staico outranked him.

Vlad wondered how the king fostered such devotion. The magnanimity shown in his receipt of a castle aside, Vajk admired Zsigmond.

What inspired loyalty in a vassal? Were acts of bravery and generosity, as the knight knew with his king, enough? Prince Mircea held sway over the Wallachian boyars, although he bargained for peace with their enemies through Arina's marriage.

Six weeks ago, Vlad last saw her, and he left their country. Thirty years beforehand, his mother journeyed between Buda and her husband's lands. She never revisited her birthplace; she said once there was no need in a new life centered on her children.

Would he reunite with her again? Ever return to Wallachia? With his brother Mihail ruling Târgoviște in the south and their father north of the country at Argeş, neither man would welcome his reappearance.

Before the company reached the first royal bulwark, Vlad turned to the mighty Danube a final time. Some vessels, including fishing boats, idled along the docks. A ferryman hurried across the expansive waters. A trio of large ships with men at the oars sluiced upriver in the same direction, striving against the prevailing winds. Had any of their crews journeyed from the southern environs of his homeland?

Vajk seemed to have followed the direction in which Vlad stared.

"The flat plain where the ferryman and those three galleys are going is called Pest, my lord prince. The Mongols ravaged it more than a century ago. North is Óbuda, or old Buda, which the Mongols also destroyed after they crossed the frozen river. Here is new Buda."

Vlad nodded as he took a final look back at the route they had traveled. He did not contemplate the knight's description. Instead, he pledged himself to a new future, which would see him return to the past someday.

I'll make alliances and gain aid, as Zsigmond and my father did. When I'm ready, I'll take Mihail's throne. Wallachia will be mine. When I hold our country, I'll find you, Rina, and free you from the Turks.

His heart thrummed with the vow's solemnity as he urged the pony on.

A FROST-COVERED STREET ascended to Vlad's destination atop the slope of the mound, which Vajk named Várhegy, for 'castle hill' in Hungarian. Behind stout white walls, the castle must offer warmth and hot meals, and the end of an arduous journey. Vlad hoped he might never again venture out in the winter for so long.

After passing through a fortified gateway, they rode in the shadows of square and semicircular towers connected along the ramparts. A town within a town, Várhegy's large estates featured gardens and farms. From the marketplace, where the German tongue dominated conversations, a narrow lane veered to a church with three naves, surrounded by gravestones. Vajk pointed out the Dominican friary of Saint Miklós nearby and north of the square, a chapel dedicated to the Catholic Saint Gheorghe, a venerated slayer of the dragon.

Beyond another gatehouse boundary, they entered a three-sided courtyard. Sunlight on the whitewashed surface of the first edifice revealed rust-colored patterns, which rose five levels to a snow-covered roof with its turreted spire. From the second floor up, there were identical pairs of man-sized stone windows, with columns at their centers. At the base of an adjacent structure, arrow-slits allowed a little light to penetrate. Further east, a stone balcony jutted at the side of another building.

In the central space, men-at-arms encouraged a fight between two ragged, bloodied dogs. Some ladies in sumptuous furs grimaced and huddled in the arched doorway. Knights with the lion rampant heraldry blew hunting horns and raced with canine companions in the direction Vlad came.

"We've reached the great keep, István's Tower." Vajk nodded to him. "This is where we shall part, my lord prince."

Double doors opened. A ruddy, squat, black-bearded man came from the keep. He approached the Wallachians. No taller than Vlad, everything about the stranger's appearance commanded authority. A black mantle of velvet flowed from broad shoulders. He wore no hat or hood. Any flurries alighting on top of his head disappeared among black hair with sparse gray threads, shorn sharp along his furrowed brow and rigid jawline. Wide booted feet splayed out under his mantle.

He stopped beside Vajk, who dismounted and bent on one knee.

"Was there much snow outside Hunyadvár? Our king hoped for your arrival days ago."

At the man's slightly hoarse tone, the knight nodded without looking up. Once the stranger gestured a silent command for Vajk to stand, he did so before turning to Vlad.

"My lord prince of Wallachia, allow me to present Prince Fruzhin of Bulgaria."

"You are most welcome here, Prince Vlad of Wallachia." An unpredictable smile softened the crags of the Bulgarian's stoic visage. He tilted his head.

"Th-thank you, Prince Fruzhin." Vlad swallowed and cursed himself for the return of his childhood stammer. A few onlookers mocked him with chuckles.

Until the Bulgarian's dark stare swept the courtyard. The men-at-arms fell silent. The pair with the dogs on chains dragged the animals apart, leading them away.

"Our king is eager to meet the son of Mircea the Great. Zsigmond of the House of Luxembourg ordered me to welcome you and ensure the protection of your company during your time at court." Prince Fruzhin looked past Vlad to the Gypsies. "Including your deadly protectors. I've heard, although they are slaves, they are also steadfast fighters."

Vlad glanced back at Tobar and Yoska and smiled. "They've earned this reputation. If I may, I present my uncle, Lord Staico."

"Even here," the Bulgarian prince said, as he rounded Vlad's horse, and extended an arm to Staico, "We know of the battles you've fought in the mountain passes and gorges of Wallachia and at Dobrogea and Nicopolis. You are famed for your courage and piety." His laughter, a rich timbre, boomed across the quiet courtyard. "Is that not a contradiction, my lord? You're a killer, as I am, but do you also kneel before God and ask forgiveness?"

"I'm a man of faith and the sword, Prince Fruzhin. Not an angel. The Turks cut off my thumb and index finger at the Battle of Nicopolis, but I can still slaughter them." Staico reached out and grasped his forearm. They grinned and released each other.

Vlad wondered at the ease of their rapport at the first meeting. Before he left home, his mother warned him he would find few friends in Buda Castle.

"The devil's pit, as your father has said. Be careful, Vlad," he recalled her saying.

Since Vajk described King Zsigmond as 'the ginger fox,' perhaps Buda Castle deserved a more apt title as the fox's lair.

"Lord Staico, you and your men may bed down in the castle keep." Their host paused and moved in a circle, as he added with a blustering tone, "Where none shall trouble the Gypsies of your retinue!"

When he halted without another word, Staico shook his head.

"My Gypsies prefer the outdoors, the familiar comforts of their tents, and the proximity of their horses. I like their company and will remain with them." He glanced at Vlad. "We must part here too, for a time."

With a nod, Vlad dismounted and stood at his uncle's side. "May it be brief." He swore, "I'll never forget all you have taught me."

Staico reached out and thumped his shoulder with a heavy fist. Beneath Vlad's wolf-skin and his wool garments, an ache swelled.

"You will remember what the House of Basarab expects of you, nephew. Never bring shame to your princely father or family. Take your saddlebags, and sword, and go."

"Keep the crossbow," Vlad said after he retrieved his belongings.

His uncle took the weapon and clasped it against his chest.

The Bulgarian turned to Vajk. "You and your men are bound for the stables. Show Lord Staico and the Gypsies where they may pitch their tents upwind."

The knight bowed, his stare lingering on Vlad before he turned away. As his men and the Wallachians rode by, Tobar grabbed the reins of Vlad's horse and led the animal.

Vlad stared at their backs until his host cleared his throat.

"You must be hungry. Eager for the warmth of István's Tower. The walls are thick, and a hearth helps keep the cold at bay. Let's go inside."

There beneath the vaulted ceiling, they found men gathered between the arrow-slits at trestle tables arranged around a central hearth. A maid stirred a thick soup for one man-at-arms, who shuffled off with a brimming wooden bowl. Others already gorged on their meals. All lifted their heads and stood. They nodded or bowed before the Bulgarian waved them back to their places. Few eyed Vlad.

"Please, I don't wish to be so formal during the length of my days here," he said to his companion. "Will you call me by my Christian name?"

"I will if you'll do the same for me."

"I could not. You are, er...what I mean to say, is that—"

"I am clearly older than you?" As his counterpart cocked his head, Vlad's cheeks warmed under scrutiny. "How many years would you adjudge me, Wallachian?"

"I don't know."

"Ah, you will not say, for fear of giving offense. How old are you?"

"Sixteen years this past month."

His host scratched his beard and squinted. "It's been eight years since I last saw the age of sixteen."

Vlad gaped. The man guffawed, laugh lines creasing around his mouth.

"So, you will call me by my Christian name too, Vlad, for I'm not that much older than you." He sniffed, and his features fell. "But, I suppose, troubles must have aged me."

Troubles? What could bedevil him when he bore the clear respect of many? He must be important to the king.

"I wondered why you greeted me outside the keep, rather than a steward or some other castle servant, Fruzhin."

"Zsigmond does not tolerate idleness from anyone. There are many of us displaced princes serving as vassals within his court."

Vlad swallowed his natural curiosity, although he wanted to know how Fruzhin came to count himself among such men. Ottoman Turks ruled vast tracts of the Bulgarian countryside. They would claim the entire Balkans, if unchecked.

"I've already eaten here, but let's find you some food and a table so we can talk, Vlad. Except for my grandfather's fickle heart, we could have been relations."

Fruzhin's words stirred Vlad's interest.

"If you don't mind, I'm not hungry. I'd rather hear more about your grandfather."

Fruzhin waved Vlad ahead to the spiral staircase at the back of the room. He climbed but stopped two steps below the landing.

An armored giant stood in his way. Easily the tallest man Vlad ever saw, as wide as Staico.

White-haired, with a great helm tucked under his arm, the warrior's sword dangled at his side. He also hefted the wooden shaft of a morning star, topped by a spiked iron ball. The breastplate of his cuirass bore the heraldic image of a curled-up black dragon. Red flames spurted from the mouth. It lay on its belly, Christ's cross stretched across its back.

"Move off the stairs, runt," the armored man said, his breath redolent with garlic.

A younger version of the gruff brute, yellow bristles sprouting from the face beneath a shaved head, peered over his massive shoulder. "He can't, Father. Fruzhin is behind him."

"He and Fruzhin must retreat so we may come down. I'll be late for the hunt."

"Stibor." Fruzhin sighed. "By the blood of Christ, I swear you're a difficult man and often, for no good reason. Vlad and I would've already reached the top if you gave way."

"Vlad, is it? This is the runt of Prince Mircea's litter you've been awaiting. The one Zsigmond wants for an attendant. He's older than most pageboys. I thought my friend knew the boy's age. That black scruff on his chin might be the beginning of a beard. Or dirt. Either way, did his parents teach him nothing about proper manners before his betters, Fruzhin?"

"I'm sure he understands, as the son of Zsigmond's vassal, he ranks higher than you in any royal court. Please step aside and let him reach the landing."

"Oh, I will." The giant drew back and beckoned Vlad and Fruzhin. "This way, my fine princes." He turned aside to his mirror image, both smirking.

Vlad gulped but mounted the steps. With the saddlebags slung over his shoulder, he stood next to Fruzhin, who put his palms up in the air.

"Neither of us wants any difficulties with you or your namesake, Stibor, but you were in the wrong. Allow me to formally introduce you both."

"We'll have none of your delays, Fruzhin. So, did the runt not see or hear us coming? Are his senses as deficient as his height?" The troublemaker elbowed his son. "Which of these toads shall I squash?"

The younger man's mouth twitched. He tapped his pointed chin. "I think Fruzhin's survived the test of your sword and morning-star enough times, Father. Give the other little one a try."

A tremor ran through Vlad. His gaze dropped to the iron ball's spikes.

In that instant, Stibor leaped at him with the blunt weapon. He barely blocked his assailant's arm, crossing both of his, so the morning star did not land a blow. His bones throbbed anyway, as Stibor wore riveted forearm guards with his plate armor.

"That's not fair!" Fruzhin yelled. "Vlad doesn't have a shield."

Stibor smirked and backed up. He handed his son the morning star and bellowed, "He's got a sword, good reflexes, and strong muscles. Let him prove his worth or die."

Given no other choice, Vlad cast off the wolf pelt, threw down the saddlebags, and drew his blade, as did his opponent. Surely, this contest was about more than who should have taken the stairs first. Bewildered, he shook his head. Wood scraped the floor below before men rushed up the steps and gaped at him. Would they do nothing except watch?

Stibor attacked again, his sword a blinding arc. Vlad whirled away and another slash raked at him, catching his doublet's sleeve. Steel clashed and his arms burned. The older man showed no sign of diminished strength. When he swung, Vlad blocked him repeatedly. He could only defend himself.

"Tired already, runt?"

"I don't want to fight you! I don't know why you're doing this, but—"

Stibor grabbed his wrists in one hand and blunted his weapon with the sword. Vlad gasped as the point of his foe's blade came to rest in the hollow of his throat. He peeked at Fruzhin and others, who stared open-mouthed at him.

Stibor pressed the blade's tip to the skin. Vlad backtracked. Stibor moved with him until he slammed into the masonry.

"You look like Prince Mircea, except for the eyes and hair. Is his whiter than mine now? It's been thirteen years since I last saw him, when you were two years old. I helped remove a usurper from your father's throne. A look of surprise? Did he tell you he did it himself?"

"No, my lord," Vlad whispered. He cleared his throat and repeated himself.

Stibor withdrew the sword. "Zsigmond's demanded the services of Prince Mircea's son. Let's see if the runt has the mettle to become a king's warrior, men."

A crescendo of applause filled the landing. Fruzhin bent and gripped his knees. Vlad wondered what ailed him until he cackled like a madman.

Others traded laughter and stories. "He could've had him good, but the little one defended himself too well. Indeed, he did... I never lasted that long when Stibor tested me. You wouldn't have in your youth. Remember how you looked? A lumbering cow with udders! Stibor knocked you off your feet in one blow!"

Vlad drew deep breaths and cursed between them. "You fought...for their amusement?"

"To test you, runt," Stibor answered. "Bigger and taller men will always look down on you. They'll size you up, judge your youth, and think you won't offer much of a challenge. Use their folly to your advantage. That is my first measure of advice."

"Thank you, my lord. I'll remember it."

"Don't thank me, runt. You're not a member of this court and you have much more to learn about fighting. No one serves our king who doesn't first prove his strength against me. Zsigmond is my sovereign and my friend. I must know he surrounds himself with those who can defend him, even in the privacy of his chambers or the royal tent. The barbarian Turks have sent assassins before."

Vlad drew in a harsh breath and nodded.

"Get out of my way, men!" Stibor sheathed his blade. "Come, son. I'm sure the hunters are already at the edge of the forest."

As the onlookers parted and cleared the route down the steps, Stibor winked at Vlad and left with his lookalike.

Still irritated, Vlad almost turned in a fury as Fruzhin patted his shoulder.

"No harm done, right?"

"No harm?" Vlad repeated. "He hits almost as hard as the morning-star."

Fruzhin covered his mouth but could not suppress another laugh. Vlad scowled at him. Had he and the giant planned this trial together?

"You've survived your first encounter with Stibor of Stiboricz, who governs Transilvania at Zsigmond's behest. A Polish man, he's lived at least threescore years. A great officer of state in the Kingdom of Hungary."

"And everyone must fight him?"

"Only those who match blades with him successfully are worth his interest and approval. He sliced off a boy's thumb once. Sent him back to his lands, crying. If Stibor likes you, your time in this court shall pass with ease. For he alone, not the queen or the palatine who is the highest officer of state, has our king's ear."

Vlad huffed and dragged up the sword and wolf-skin while Fruzhin took up his saddlebags. They moved down the hall, free of spectators, and stopped beside an arrow-slit.

"The morning-star should be that brute's emblem, not a black dragon." Vlad's shoulders aching, he rolled them back.

"You might not want to call him a brute within his hearing," Fruzhin said. "As one of the strongest allies of Zsigmond, Stibor is also a respected member of the Order of the Dragon."

"I've studied the military orders, but never heard of those knights."

"The Order is new, founded one winter season ago."

"Are you a member too?" Vlad scrutinized Fruzhin's black cape for a similar dragon insignia but found none. "Everyone shows you great respect. Is that why?"

"Let's talk about my grandfather. You'd said you wanted to know more."

Vlad sighed. If Fruzhin wished to divulge anything further about the Order of the Dragon, he would do so in time.

Fruzhin said, "When my grandfather came to the throne, he wed a daughter of Basarab."

"Who was my great-great-grandfather," Vlad affirmed.

"Her husband grew tired of her sadness after the births of their four children. A daughter, taken by the plague. Brothers who ruled as emperors in my grandfather's stead, before the Turks, hated by God and His righteous people, killed each sibling. Their mother pined for her homeland, or, as her husband accused, an old lover. Grandfather divorced her and sent her to a nunnery, forcing her to take the vows."

"Why? When he could have let her go home?"

"I've heard the same tales of Basarab you've known since childhood. Does he seem as if he would have permitted the slight against his daughter? My grandfather wanted to punish her for refusing to love him and their children. She went into a convent under a new name, Teofana. Within a year, my grandfather married a former Jewess who birthed another heir. My father. If Teofana's union had lasted and she mothered him instead, you and I would have known each other as kin."

Vlad did not reply. Although he should not think so already, he hoped he and Fruzhin would become friends. Separated from his uncle and the Gypsies, he needed an ally in the castle. Especially with Stibor lurking around.

Outmatched by an old man over three times his age. He lifted his arm with a groan. Fruzhin turned away as if he could have obscured his lingering amusement.

Vlad sneered. "You think it's funny how Lord Stibor torments youths at court?"

"Most don't even try to defend themselves. I did. You remind me of myself." Fruzhin pushed away from the wall behind him. "Let's go downstairs. I'll show you where you can bathe and soak your muscles. You'll bed down here with pageboys, squires, and knights. I once served as you did and still prefer sleeping up in this tower."

They went to the steps again, where Fruzhin paused.

"Never leave the castle or our sovereign's presence without permission. He will want you close at hand. Our king's councilors have dwellings within the town, so they may attend meetings. Hundreds of others live and work in this place. Zsigmond knows them all on sight and those whom he does not know; he seeks to learn more."

"You're saying he cares for the lives of kitchen maids?" Vlad scoffed.

"He calls them by name to his bed if he chooses. Our king has a voracious appetite. For women, food, and the hunt. Even the crowns and thrones of other nations. Serve Zsigmond well, Vlad, and you will succeed. Disappoint him and you'll suffer."

"When will I gain an introduction to him, Fruzhin?"

"This evening. While the court dines."

CHAPTER 7

Blood Pact

"Hope has two beautiful daughters; their names are Anger and Courage. Anger at the way things are, and Courage to see that they do not remain as they are."-Augustine of Hippo (354-430 AD), Roman North African Christian theologian, philosopher, bishop, and Roman Catholic and Eastern Orthodox saint.

IN THE YEAR OF OUR Lord 1410. Buda, Hungary (modern-day Budapest, Hungary)

Once the bells pealed the hour of six in the evening, an army of pageboys in multi-colored velvet livery fanned out along the corridors. They summoned members of the royal council and the nobility of the court to dine with Zsigmond of the House of Luxembourg and his young queen of five years, Borbála of the Styrian House of Celje.

The cacophony of voices and the cloying scents of heavy, perfumed oils guided Vlad from the great keep to the adjacent building. Fruzhin would meet him later, after attending some duty to the king. From István's Tower, the courtyard beyond led to the palatial residence, the royal chapel, and a ceremonial hall.

Courtiers ascended a staircase to a rectangular chamber. The upper great hall where the castle's denizens ate their evening meal seemed the most opulent place. Two stone statues of unicorns stood on either side of the entryway. Marble frames met inlaid oak doors, which gave way to carved pillars beneath coffered wood ceilings. Large stained-glass windows occupied the northern wall. Tapestries and silken royal banners adorned the room. Red brocaded cloth with gold tassels covered each table.

When Fruzhin joined Vlad at last, he said, "Don't become too accustomed to the sights. In the spring, Zsigmond's chief architect arrives from the old Hungarian capital at Visegrád. There will be changes."

Near the double doors, they sat together. In solitude, Vlad could have walked the length of the great hall and measured the number of paces it took. The warmth of the room, stirred by more than the bodies seated close together, stifled him. Perhaps the courtiers preferred heat in their heavily embroidered fashions, almost as ostentatious as their ruler's apparel.

Earlier, after Vlad's bath, Fruzhin took one look at the woolen, velvet, and silk doublets in the saddlebags and shook his head. He explained, the Hungarian courtiers favored longer garments and revealed his under the black mantle; a high-collared, laced-up robe of the same velvet. The emerald-dyed material fell to his booted heels. Cuffs trimmed with sable, which also decorated the neckline, and a wide sash around the waist completed his attire.

Since the pair stood the same height, Fruzhin had told Vlad he would summon a pageboy, to whom he gave instructions for his steward to send clothes.

"I can recommend a Florentine tailor who will fit you with fashionable outfits. He's not far. East of the main marketplace. I'll summon him in the morning. As there are many languages spoken here, the court reflects various influences. When Zsigmond came to the throne, the royal council pleaded with him not to rely on foreigners nor grant them high honors and privileges. The council members never dictated court dress."

The royal attendant had returned with a rust-tinged robe of Italian damask, and the linen undershirt. Fruzhin called the attire a gift, which he had never donned before, but warned Vlad that one guest might recognize the fabric.

So far, that man, if he numbered among those at the tables, did not approach them. No one came near but the pageboys. Occasionally, Vlad felt himself under intent scrutiny. When he looked up from his meal, the sensation ebbed, only to return while he sipped from a cup of mulled wine or spooned the contents of pewter bowls; the succulent, seasoned flesh of spicy fish soup or peppery pork goulash, garnished with parsley sprigs.

"Eat some more." Fruzhin gestured to the half-empty bowl. "Would you have our king take offense and believe the cuisine is not to your liking?"

"There are many people in the great hall. Does he notice each of them, too?"

"Zsigmond sees everyone and everything."

Although seated at some distance from the monarchs, Vlad enjoyed brief glimpses of them in their ermine fur-trimmed robes. Until rows of pageboys brought in the next two courses of the meal with great ceremony, displayed for approval. They served platters of roasted meats, followed by trays piled high with sweet cakes, and candied and jellied fruits. Vlad stopped looking at the royals after Stibor, seated on the king's right, noticed. The Polish lord leaned aside and whispered to Zsigmond, who smiled.

Vlad ate from every bowl and trencher placed before him, although his guts roiled at the end of dinner. The occasion seemed to be the time in which the king permitted his nobles to approach. He beckoned some, but those sharing the dais with him rose of their own accord, came around, and bowed before the sovereign. Brief exchanges followed, often accompanied by Zsigmond's baritone laughter.

"Is it always like this? Crowded with so much food?" Vlad asked.

"Yes, in the evening." Fruzhin relayed, "*Prandium*, the morning meal takes place at the hour of ten. The royal chapel's bell rings at the same time the pageboys come around. The council and most of the royal officers take their breakfast in their townhouses instead."

"At my father's court, minstrels often followed the last meal. Is it so here?"

"That is the queen's discretion. Regardless, Zsigmond won't remain." Fruzhin wiped his mouth with a linen napkin. "Your summons won't be long now. Be ready."

At perhaps some prearranged or hidden signal from the king, Fruzhin cupped Vlad's elbow, and they rose at the same time. Vlad smoothed the fabric of his robe and walked with Fruzhin to the dais.

Dishes rimmed with gold and jeweled chalices covered the tablecloth there. At its center stood a silver pepper mill adorned with two lion figures. Seated behind the mill, the king and queen gazed expectantly at the pair.

"*Sigismundus dei gratia rex Hungariae*," Fruzhin intoned in Latin as he bowed. He added, "King of Dalmatia, Croatia, Rama, Serbia, Halič and Lodomeria, Wallachia, and Bulgaria. Margrave of Brandenburg, arch-chamberlain of the Holy Roman Empire, and heir of Bohemia and Luxembourg. His royal consort, Queen Borbála. May it please Your Royal Majesty, the king, and Your Grace the queen; I have the honor of presenting Prince Vlad, the third son of Prince Mircea of Wallachia."

"I am the humble servant of His Royal Majesty, the king, and the queen." Vlad bowed alongside his companion until the sovereign bade them rise.

Zsigmond chose a fur-trimmed, silk-damask robe, quartered in the same crimson and gold pattern as his wife wore. The egg-sized diamond pendant hanging from his broad necklace outshone all her regalia. Red hair with graying roots sprouted everywhere like wild growth; atop his head, and from his thick russet mustache and neck-length beard. Earlier Fruzhin revealed the king and courtiers celebrated his forty-second birthday last week. The ruddy mouth parted, revealing small, even teeth. A ginger fox, indeed.

"At last, you have come to Us," King Zsigmond said, continuing the Latin discourse before he turned to Stibor. "He has the look of Mircea, as you suggested. We recognize those eyes as his mother Mara's own. Like agate, you can see through their centers."

"And what does His Royal Majesty view there?" The queen's slim fingers clenched a silver and enamel chalice. "A son with his mother or father's temperament?"

Zsigmond smiled but did not regard his wife. "Mircea said this one has his moods. We do not doubt Mara taught her son about duty, the love of family, and chivalry."

"The perfect mother, Your Royal Majesty," the queen replied in a subdued tone that did not match the hard glint in her stare.

Her florid skin and youthful visage reminded Vlad of the woman at Hermannstadt. Even the eyes were almost the same green shade. Except Borbála of Celje possessed no kindly mien. She smirked. Laugh lines marred both sides of her full lips and aged her appearance, although Fruzhin believed her to be only two years older than Vlad. Had five years of marriage already taken a toll?

Her brocaded gown shimmered with gold threads at the ermine-trimmed neckline and sleeves. A jeweled filigree necklace encircled her throat. Yellow hair caught up in a golden caul dotted with pearls and topped by a simple coronet fell beyond her shoulders.

Vlad noticed how the surrounding conversation ceased. Everyone on the dais, including the prelates, counts, and royal council members Fruzhin pointed out earlier, and courtiers seated at the two rows of tables on either side of the room, focused on his presentation. Sweat glided down the middle of his back. A strange, sudden chill jolted him.

"We remember your lady mother with fondness," Zsigmond said, as he stared at Vlad. "Your father, less so."

As the king paused, the court erupted in laughter. A hollow sound, lacking real mirth. Sycophants, no better than the boyars of Wallachia, for all their fine manners and attire. Preening peacocks, like the fat birds served up earlier.

Zsigmond continued, "Mircea was not always a vassal of the Kingdom of Hungary. He feared the papacy and Rome's influence. Thereafter, the Ottoman Turks became his concern and he submitted to Us in an alliance against them. Now We've heard he's married your sister to one of them for the sake of peace on the Transalpine Black Sea border.

When We required a son of his to serve as an assurance of his loyalty, at first, he suggested his last child as a pageboy, aged twelve."

Vlad nodded. His little brother Alex would like Buda Castle too.

"We demanded your service instead once your father described your nature."

Vlad doubted Prince Mircea had made any recommendation of him in that description.

Zsigmond cocked his head. "You're not curious about why We requested you."

"He suffers from a deplorable deficiency of interest, Your Royal Majesty," the queen muttered. "Perhaps, in youthful ignorance, he cannot grasp the solemnity of this honor."

Murmurs swirled around Vlad, but he ignored them. He would be damned if he stood there silently after such an insult.

He raised his chin. "My lady mother taught me the deference owed to a king. If His Royal Majesty wishes to share his reasoning, it would be a pleasure to hear."

Queen Borbála eyed him over her cup's rim for the space of several breaths before setting the vessel down. He admired the gemstone rings on three of the nimble fingers gripping the base of the chalice. But not the wearer. How dare the bitch suggest he possessed no curiosity or lacked discernment!

"We did not require another royal pageboy," Zsigmond added, without as much as a glance at his wife. "The Turkish confrontation demands fighters. Our governor of Transilvania here tells Us you have a good sword arm."

"He does," Stibor avowed, with a nod to Vlad, who bowed in acknowledgment. Soreness still suffused his limbs from the bout with Stibor.

"Is the prince more than his sword?" Borbála asked. "Has he read the classics? Does he speak any of the seven languages my husband His Royal Majesty knows?"

"You need a demonstration of his talent, dearest Borbála, before We consider his future?" The king covered her slender, graceful hand with his larger one.

"I do, Your Royal Majesty." With her forefinger, she tapped the rim of her chalice. "Do you understand the Latin inscription, prince?"

Vlad read aloud, "*Hic est calix novi testamenti in meo sanguine*." Then he provided the Hungarian translation. "This chalice is the New Testament in my blood, saith the Lord."

"And you know the reference?"

"It comes from the Gospel of Saint Luke, chapter twenty-two, verse twenty."

Borbála nodded. "*Parli Italiano*?"

"*Sì*, I can speak Italian," He smiled, recalling the royal tutor at Argeş, a kindly hunchback from Modena in northern Italy. "Although the man my father employed also despaired whether I would ever learn. He realized he kept me most engaged when he reminisced about Mircea the Great's wars."

From somewhere behind him, a chuckle rumbled.

Zsigmond's queen continued to query his comprehension, with German and Greek next, while her husband looked on. Would she question whether he knew his mother's Hungarian tongue, too?

Then Borbála uttered a language he did not know.

He stared at her, mute for the first time. She repeated the same phrase twice, slower the second time, but he could not understand even after hearing it again.

Fruzhin cleared his throat and bowed before her. "If I may, Your Grace?"

"I'll allow it." She sat back in her chair, her nails trailing over the cushioned armrests. Another smirk upturned the corner of her lush mouth.

"The queen asked, in Bohemian," Fruzhin said to Vlad, "if you're aware of the ruler of that country, King Wenceslaus, the half-brother of His Royal Majesty King Zsigmond."

"Ah. I'm aware of him, but obviously, I do not know his language."

"What of Polish?" Borbála snapped. "Stibor is a loyal friend of His Royal Majesty, who can also speak the tongue of his Transilvanian governor! Do you?"

"No," he admitted, with a glance at Stibor. "I am unfamiliar with Polish."

"And no French, I suppose?" When he shook his head, she turned aside to her husband. "Your Royal Majesty, you rely on the warriors here for more than their military prowess. They are your negotiators before a battle begins. Mara of Tolmay has not bothered to teach her son the languages of the nations on Hungary's borders. Even French, while most royal pageboys learn the basics of it by the age of seven."

Zsigmond's forehead creased as if he weighed her words.

Vlad's fingers curled into a fist. His breathing slowed. Why was the queen so determined to embarrass him? He drew back, but Fruzhin's hand closed on his elbow. The Bulgarian stared straight ahead, yet his grasp conveyed a warning. Vlad must control his impulses.

"If he is to be a member of this court," the king pronounced, "then he should learn from the most educated among us. We can think of none more suited than you, Our most beloved queen. You speak all these languages better than anyone else here."

"Your Royal Majesty, you cannot mean it!" She spluttered, trading glances with her husband and Vlad.

His stomach roiled at the idea of Borbála of Celje's company.

Zsigmond held her slender hand. "You will do it because it is what We have decreed."

In his grip, the queen's knuckles whitened. She tried pulling away, a subtle tug between their bodies, which only Vlad and Fruzhin could have seen. Then her lips parted, and she forced a smile.

"It must be as you wish, Your Royal Majesty." After her husband released her, she glanced at Vlad. "Your lessons will begin tomorrow after *prandium*."

"We have concluded, when you are not at Our queen's side, you will undertake an apprenticeship and squire for Stibor," the king added.

Vlad might have gasped without the reminder of Fruzhin's hand at his elbow. He recalled his manners. "I thank His Royal Majesty for the honor, and I pray the lord Stibor may find me worthy and useful at his side."

"Very good. You may leave Us and return to your table."

At the monarch's easy dismissal, Vlad bowed and murmured, "I remain the humble servant of His Royal Majesty, the king, and Your Grace, the queen."

Fruzhin's grip fell away, and the pair of them bowed before backing off. At their table, Vlad sat and stared into another cup of mulled wine.

"Drink it and thank God that the queen's bitter tongue didn't poison her husband's ear."

"Why does she dislike me, Fruzhin?"

"I don't know, but her intent was clear from the start. She meant to discredit you before the court. Never try to leave her presence without consent again."

"Did you see the king's hold on her hand afterward?"

"Don't concern yourself with matters between a husband and wife. Borbála is the mother of Zsigmond's only legitimate child. A daughter less than five months old."

"But his was not...chivalrous behavior. The queen seemed...distressed."

"Then she hid behind the facade of a smile. Think no more of her. Drink."

Vlad did so, and when he set the chalice down, a man in a multi-striped robe approached their table. Slightly taller than Vlad and Fruzhin, his dark eyes twinkled with mirth. His yellowed beard and shoulder-length hair, interspersed with gray, reflected the style the Hungarian male courtiers adopted.

"*Amici*," he greeted them in Italian. "I'll join our king once he leaves the great hall. But I could not let the evening end without an introduction to the son of a fierce comrade-in-arms, Prince Mircea."

Fruzhin smiled and nodded. "I wondered when you would greet Vlad."

"I am Filippo Buondelmonti degli Scolari. Born near Florence. I'm the royal officer responsible for Zsigmond's salt chambers and Temes County, north of Serbia. My friends call me Pipó of Ozora, the latter for my wife's Hungarian estate."

Vlad extended his hand. "My lord Pipó, I'm pleased to know you."

"Ah, I hope I may know you for some time. If training with that savage, Stibor, doesn't kill you too soon!"

As Vlad gaped, Fruzhin and Pipó shared boisterous laughter.

"My old friend makes a joke," Fruzhin reassured Vlad. "You have no real cause for worry. Stibor would earn our king's wrath if you suffered undue harm."

Pipó said, "*Sì*, but will the possibility temper Stibor? Zsigmond will always forgive him."

Once the king and queen rose, the courtiers fell silent and stood. Zsigmond kissed the same fingers he crushed earlier, before leaving his wife. All who sat on his side of the dais followed. He strode between the trestle tables. A taller man than Vlad had first realized. He stopped beside him.

"We leave to discuss matters with Our counselors, as is Our custom in the evening. After the queen finishes with you tomorrow, she will send you to Stibor."

"Thank you, Your Royal Majesty." Vlad bowed and straightened.

The king leaned closer. "Tell Us; is your lady mother still so beautiful?"

From his periphery, Vlad noted how Borbála crossed her slender arms and stood rigid. Understanding dawned. She disliked him because she held Princess Mara in disfavor. What did his mother ever do to such a haughty woman? Borbála left her family's Styrian castle in Celje for Hungary twenty-five years after his mother departed her homeland.

Vlad cleared his throat. "The years have been kind to Princess Mara."

The king withdrew, and his companions followed. The red-faced queen turned away and summoned minstrels.

"*Sì*, the garment looks much better on you than Fruzhin," Pipó said to Vlad before he trailed the sovereign's entourage.

"I told you, Pipó would recall the fabric as a gift he gave me," Fruzhin said.

IN THE DIMNESS OF ISTVÁN'S Tower, where some knights were already snoring, Vlad and Fruzhin stretched out on pallets next to the second-floor wall. Thin moonlight and the cold seeped through a nearby arrow-slit window, although stuffed with cloth. Vlad inquired about the lack of tapestries in the great keep, but Fruzhin said alterations would begin here first, under the king's plan.

"Is what he said about your sister true? She's married a Turk?" Fruzhin asked.

"Not by choice. Arina obeyed our father's dictates," Vlad muttered. "I miss her."

"As I long for my family, especially my mother. One of five elder sisters of the current Serbian ruler. Tall and warlike, as one of the Amazons in Greek myths. At least, she doesn't know we lost our home in Vidin to our treacherous enemies."

Vlad wanted to ask why, but his tongue stayed rooted in his mouth. He sensed Fruzhin's mother no longer lived.

"I hate them! All of them." His companion reared up on his elbow, more than half of his face in shadow, the rest revealed by candlelight. His voice hoarse, he said, "I'll never stop seeking revenge for the deaths and disgraces my father and mother's families suffered because of those wretched Turks."

Vlad rose as well. "If you wish to tell me about your difficulties, I'll listen."

Fruzhin revealed his father died on the orders of the previous Ottoman sultan.

"And my father's eldest son brings shame to the rest of our family," he added. "The persecutors of Christ's cross took my sibling as a small boy. He once bore the same name your younger brother does. He calls himself Iskender now."

Vlad sighed, sorrowing for Fruzhin, who hung his head.

"The Turks seduced Iskender. They seek to do the same throughout the Balkans, offering Christian princes alliances to thwart the papacy. Fools who think Orthodoxy is the sole path to God. It's too late when they realize the truth. Our enemies will never stop until they dominate all Christian lands."

He paused and raised his gaze. "When they could not influence my relations with their accursed religion or persuade us to betray each other, they tore us apart, like vultures and wolves. My mother's brother, Stefan Lazarević, *Despoteses* of the Kingdom of Rascia. The Turks also murdered his father at the Battle of Kosovo. You've heard of it?"

"From my Italian tutor. The conflict occurred over twenty years ago."

"Stefan's mother served as regent in the aftermath. The Patriarch of the Serbian Orthodox Church advised her to submit. At twelve years old, her son became a Turkic vassal. Then, they stirred enmity over the throne between Stefan and his nephew Đurađ Branković, son of my mother's eldest sister. My cousin and uncle still fight over the scraps our wretched enemies have left of their land. Even if he prevails, Stefan has no son."

"He serves the king. You named Zsigmond overlord of Serbia among his titles."

"Uncle Stefan allied with Zsigmond seven years ago, but the Turkish threat never went away. Like your father, my uncle has bargained for the lives of his people. Stefan bent to the will of one among the warring sons of the last Ottoman ruler."

Vlad recalled something his mother spoke about at Târgoviște when she had heralded the imminent arrival of Arina's husband.

"Your uncle sided with Mûsâ Çelebi," he whispered.

"How do you know?" Fruzhin gaped at him.

"Before Arina's unholy union, my mother mentioned your uncle as being one of Mûsâ Çelebi's supporters." Vlad swallowed and stroked a hand over his hair.

"Stefan does what he must for survival." A flush reddened Fruzhin's cheek.

"We all do," Vlad admitted. "Arina is my twin. The coming of the evil Turks and my father's support of them changed her forever. She would not speak to me in our last days together before she married. She did her duty and left us at Mûsâ Çelebi's side."

"I'm sorry, Vlad. That accursed Iskender. He won't talk to me either. I gave up writing letters after he called me an infidel." Fruzhin scrubbed his face with one hand. "He's no longer my brother. He's an enemy of Christendom."

"I could never forsake my sister. I don't blame Arina. Our father ruined her hopes," Vlad murmured. "He thinks he's paid for peace with her life. Some bargains are too costly. I'll never be truly happy until she's safe with our family."

The pair looked at each other. United in grief and loss, and hatred.

"Admit it," Vlad coaxed. "If ever Iskender returned to your side, you'd welcome your sibling with open arms."

"Until now, I imagined no one might understand me as well as he once did. Like a brother," Fruzhin said.

"My brothers have tolerated me. Only Alex ever really liked me. Maybe Radu too," Vlad replied with a rueful laugh.

He felt like crying. He never expected to reveal his misery about Arina's fate to anyone in Hungary. Not in one day. Nor hoped he might find someone reliable outside of Staico.

"I like you well enough, Vlad. You're as brave as Stibor, as amenable as Pipó. We don't share any bond of kinship, but we can be lifelong friends if you wish it. Let's make a vow to remain companions and ensure the destruction of the Turks."

Fruzhin found his eating knife tucked under the pallet.

"They took your sibling, and they took mine. We share a common cause," he said.

He sliced open his palm, and Vlad did the same. They pressed their hands together. A little blood seeped and dribbled on the floor. The rest co-mingled, binding them in vengeance against their mutual enemy.

VLAD FELL INTO A DAILY routine at the Hungarian court. He hated the mornings with Queen Borbála, who delighted in the mistakes he made with his French pronunciation. As he improved, the expression on her otherwise beautiful face soured like spoiled milk. He understood no more of her hostility than he did her resentment of his mother. He suspected Zsigmond's wife had taught him the wrong words or phrases, but in the evening, he found reassurance and any necessary correction with Fruzhin.

In the afternoons, he remained at the mercy of Stibor, a fanatical swordsman. One who extolled the virtues of warfare and battlefield tactics. He often did with the same vigor as he took any of his three Hungarian mistresses behind bales of straw set out on the misty practice field while Vlad on horseback slashed at the hay. At least two nights per week belonged to Staico and the Gypsy twins, who brayed lusty songs the clansmen taught them by firelight until Vlad's head ached and drooped from too much wine.

Staico walked with him to the entrance of István's Tower, where his uncle took away the musty wolf-skin Vlad kept as a reminder of Tobar's kindness. With the vow, "You'll have the pelt the next time you visit us, nephew," his uncle sent him up the spiral staircase to his rest.

Spring neared, and birdsong echoed from the lone tree in the courtyard outside the tower. Foreign knights journeyed to Buda, and some visited the castle, before a tournament Fruzhin revealed would take place on the queen's dower island of Csepel. One of many properties, like Óbuda, apportioned to her in the marriage along with twenty-thousand gold florins per year.

A burly warrior attended the king's evening meal. Seated between Fruzhin and Pipó, who became their constant dinner companion, Vlad gaped at the stranger's heraldic symbols. A muzzled bear and a staff.

"Who is that man whom the king embraces?" Vlad asked.

"*Amico*, that's Richard de Beauchamp, the Earl of Warwick," Pipó answered. "From England. He will take part in the joust, too."

Vlad shook his head. "He's here for a tournament, my lord Pipó?"

"Why so shocked, ah? I've traveled as far west as France for the same reason, no. Those of us who aren't hereditary princes, like you and Fruzhin, must gain horses and wealth. Entering the lists and winning tournaments is one way. I've told you, stop calling me a lord. I'm Pipó to my friends. Besides, you don't make me call you a prince, although you outrank a royal officer of lesser origins like me."

"Vlad shows deference to your obvious age." Fruzhin laughed and veered away when Pipó struck out at him.

"Age! I'm a year younger than Zsigmond, no," Pipó grumbled. "Ah, I'll show you age, Fruzhin, if you're brave enough to face me in the lists."

"I broke two lances against you a summer ago. Have you forgotten?"

Fruzhin chuckled but did not move in time as Pipó reached over and smacked him hard on the back of his head. Fruzhin groaned.

"Do you think Stibor, or the king will ever knight me?" Vlad asked.

Pipó patted his arm. "*Sì*. Show them the potential I see in you with Stibor."

"Prove your mettle and you'll earn the honor," Fruzhin said.

"I will," Vlad vowed.

"I don't doubt you, *amico*," Pipó said, clapping his shoulder.

"You didn't tell him the other reason the earl is here," Fruzhin remarked. "Before her death, Zsigmond's sister Anne of Bohemia became the queen-consort of Richard the second of England. The earl's godfather. Zsigmond had good relations with high-ranking members of the English court thanks to the union."

On the next day, Vlad attended the joust on Csepel Island. Stibor unhorsed a Teutonic knight, who threw his black and silver helm aside and stomped off while a hapless squire fetched the horse, lance, and helmet.

Inside a tent, Stibor ordered Vlad to remove his gauntlets and unbuckle the steel breastplate, and pauldrons covering his shoulders and armpits.

"I'm not fighting for an hour. Find your friends, runt, and leave me be," Stibor whined.

Such a sour mood, despite his win, meant only one thing.

"As you wish, my lord." Vlad's mouth twitched, and he bowed.

Before he left the tent, as he expected, Stibor barked, "Runt, fetch my mistress from the house near the Jewish gate. Not the woman from Bakers' Street. Or the one the palatine thinks he alone beds. A man's lusts turn from blood to women at the end of combat."

Vlad would have gone, but Stibor wrenched his arm.

"I haven't seen you with a woman. Are you a damned virgin and a runt I could still crush?" Stibor yanked his limb harder. "You're not one of those catamites?"

"I'm no virgin, nor do I play a woman's part abed for other men, my lord."

"Then why has no woman spread her legs for you?"

"You assume none have, my lord." Vlad recalled the kitchen maid at Târgoviște. It was none of his master's business that she remained the only one he had ever bedded.

Stibor grinned and finally waved him off. He found the man's preferred mistress and took her to Stibor's tent before he sought Fruzhin. A pageboy directed him to the medical tent. He hastened there and found Pipó cupping his elbow while Fruzhin looked on.

"*Amici*, I jousted and then fought with the sword against some knight whose silver helmet-crest bore a dragon," Pipó said. "No one knows his identity, but he's set to face the English earl next. I want to know who almost tore my limb from the socket."

Vlad and Fruzhin hurried to the list. The king wore a Montauban fur cap with a jeweled pin on its upturned brim. The edge of a sheepskin coat grazed his ankles.

"Zsigmond's always cold, no matter the weather," Fruzhin commented.

Soon, the earl of Warwick rode out on a caparisoned mount. Beside him on foot, his squire hefted his standard. The so-called dragon knight, fitting Pipó's description, appeared at the opposite end of the list. His helmet obscured all facial features, except a red beard.

The riders charged three times; lances raised. When the Englishman twice shattered his weapon against his adversary, many cheered. Except for the king.

The dragon knight raced away from the list, rather than conceding his loss.

"Now we'll never know who Pipó faced," Vlad said. "He'll be disappointed. We must think of a way to cheer him up, Fruzhin. Er, Fruzhin, what distracts you so?"

Although his friend stood close by, he never answered. With an inscrutable expression, Fruzhin stared in the direction the dragon knight rode. Vlad wondered why.

The King's Man

1411-1420

CHAPTER 8

The Convert

"Remember that when you leave this earth, you can take with you nothing that you have received—only what you have given: a full heart, enriched by honest service, love, sacrifice and courage."-Francis of Assisi (1182-1226 AD), Italian friar, deacon, mystic, preacher, and Roman Catholic saint.

IN THE YEAR OF OUR Lord 1411. Buda, Hungary (modern-day Budapest, Hungary), and *Pozsony, Hungary* (modern-day Bratislava, Slovakia)

Vlad dragged on a pair of calf-length leather boots and pinched at bobbles of fibers on the shoulders of his robe. He brushed a hand over the wool fabric, dyed crimson and gold, the pigments his king favored.

"How do I look, Fruzhin?"

"As any fine royal attendant should," his friend replied. "You wear Zsigmond's livery well. You could have let the hair grow a little longer, rather than having it trimmed as soon as you returned to court."

Last year, Vlad traveled to Bosnia at summer's end. He stayed during the king's campaign against an alliance of traitorous Bosnians supporting the Turkish menace until December. Afterward, the Hungarian army departed for home. They reached Buda exactly one week after the feast of the Epiphany.

"The queen's herald came two days ago," Vlad relayed. "She told Zsigmond she won't return from her dower lands until he's confirmed construction is over."

"Then he'll ensure some delay with his master builders and avoid his wife." Fruzhin smiled. "After you arrived from Bosnia, he rode straight to his current mistress' door."

Vlad ground his teeth together and huffed.

"You don't approve of our king's behavior," Fruzhin said. "Didn't you tell me your father has mistresses, although you believe he loves your mother?"

"He also kept his women far from sight," Vlad acknowledged. "He provided for the bastards while shaming his nobly born half-brother, like a hypocrite. There were allotments recorded in the boyar council. My brothers and I should not have searched for the papers, but Radu wanted to know what the nobles did all day. He shouldn't have told our mother about their contents."

"So, you believe as long as your father is discreet, she remains unaffected?"

"I didn't say so! They love each other, but in a complicated manner. Come, hurry."

Together, they left István's Tower nearly an hour after dawn. They emerged into the chaotic start of another day for the king's masons, carpenters, and their apprentices. All were incapable of working without shouting at each other over the racket. Wooden scaffolding remained on the great keep's western facade, although the major work ended two days ago.

The pair walked side by side in a rush. Vlad ducked his bare head and wished for a hat, as well as one of the sheepskin cloaks Fruzhin wore. A chilled mist from the gray-blue Danube River, its banks rimmed with chunks of ice, swept inland. Winter might never abate.

They entered the palatial residence where Vlad rubbed his cold hands together.

"This isn't about my parents." He pitched his voice lower for fear the tone would reverberate within the stone walls. "I've been here eleven months and our king's proven himself a notorious womanizer. I shouldn't judge him, Fruzhin. He doesn't need my approval."

"Glad you recognize that fact."

"Stibor has rutted every day with any bed-warmer he chose, here or on the campaign. At least, his wife is in Poland, unaware of the shame he heaps on her head. Queen Borbála cannot help but know about the king's...activities."

"I never thought she'd have your sympathy or pity, Vlad."

"In this single instance, she's earned it."

"Well, you're welcome to your opinion. Never repeat it to our sovereign."

"I'm no fool. I know my place here."

"Zsigmond's favor is all that should matter," Fruzhin remarked. "The palatine will be late for the meeting, as usual. He reserves his prompt appearances for our king alone. Stibor is typically punctual, and I expect he awaits both the palatine and me. Shall I see you this evening or will you visit your uncle and the Gypsies?"

"I must. I've barely spoken with Staico since my return. He wanted to know if I'd killed anyone in Bosnia, as if Stibor would've let me near the battlefield. But I must hear how my uncle and the twins fared in my months' long absence."

"You think the lord Staico needs a nursemaid?" Fruzhin chuckled. "I've told you already. I ensured his well-being in your absence."

"You're a good friend." Vlad patted his companion's arm. "Sometimes, you're more patient with me than I deserve."

"I was once your age. So very long ago, as you first thought." Both laughed at Fruzhin's reminder of when Vlad believed him much older. "I'll miss your company at dinner, especially without Pipó. He'd sworn, after Zsigmond sent him to the pope, he would spend only a few weeks with his brother Matteo."

"Maybe Pipó has trouble, though I hope not. The roads prevented the king's arrival in time for Epiphany."

"Ah, that reminds me. Today's your birthday. I hope you're able to enjoy some parts of it. I recalled you saying it falls ten days after the feast day."

"You're good to remember, thank you. I doubt anyone else will care." Vlad smiled and smoothed his palms down on the robe. "I must go. Our king–"

"Wait, a little." Fruzhin clutched Vlad's arm before he could have turned away. "I had something made for you in your absence."

Fruzhin pushed up the sleeve of his cloak and drew a ring from his forefinger. He held it up to the light from a stained-glass window over their heads. Fine detailed work in two figures etched on either side of the gold mount. At the center, an ox-blood ruby shone.

"I asked the jeweler to depict the Catholic Saint Erzsébet of Hungary and the infant Christ for your protection, Vlad. Rubies are associated with the sun. It's said they darken when danger is near. They're also considered stones of destiny."

"I hadn't expected...th-thank you, Fruzhin." Vlad sniffled. "You're too kind."

"No stammering now. You can't be that overcome by the trinket. Put it on! Let me see."

Vlad tried the ring on his forefinger first, but the band would not glide past the knuckle joint. Fruzhin laughed at his exasperation while trying every other finger until he pushed it to the base of the smallest one and closed his hand in a fist.

"Good. Now, don't keep our king waiting any longer," Fruzhin said.

The pair bowed before each other and departed in opposite directions. While he walked, Vlad flexed his hand and admired the gift. Before he gripped the balustrade and mounted the stone stairs to Zsigmond's private chamber, he peered down the long corridor at his friend, who turned a corner where two royal guards stood stationed.

Vlad went up the steps, lined with more of the king's sentinels. Two pageboys gave him access to the antechamber. He sighed upon seeing his other counterparts already assembled, although he was not late. The sovereign's chamberlain spoke in low tones with Zsigmond's confessor by the door.

Each year, typically at Epiphany, the king chose forty attendants from among the squires who served the realm. Stibor, Fruzhin, and three others aided in his selection.

Every week, ten of the squires attended the sovereign in the morning and at his mealtimes. A great and lucrative honor, for which they received wages of forty pennies per day or ninety-two Hungarian florins by year's end. Fruzhin assured Vlad the wages were enormous. Mercenary soldiers of the kingdom earned over a third of it in a year's service. The squires also secured new livery at the start of the winter and summer months, and four beeswax candles each quarter.

A bell in the royal chapel pealed at the hour of seven. The signal for the pair of guardsmen stationed within the antechamber to open its doors. As happened the two previous mornings, upon entry into the royal chamber reserved for Zsigmond's sole use, he sat in bed already with the curtains parted.

Everyone bowed before him. "Good morning, Your Royal Majesty."

"With that noise outside? Hardly a good morning," Zsigmond grumbled. "If We hadn't already granted permission for work to begin each day at dawn, We would alter that arrangement now. But the sooner they finish renovations, the better."

Each squire received a daily assignment for the week. One drew back the bed curtains and coverlet, while a counterpart brought a gold cup with water and a basin for Zsigmond, who rinsed his mouth and hands. A gangling youth took the Bible to the sovereign, from which his confessor read before Zsigmond prayed.

Two other squires directed the servants who brought up warm water from the kitchens for the bathtub and laid out the towels and bath tools. Four helped the king wash and select his garments for the day, and brushed his hair, while one squire assisted with footwear.

Vlad shifted on his feet. His turn must come soon. A sigh of relief filled him when the chancellor's aide rushed in and gave him rolls of parchment, none of which bore the great seal of Hungary. If the monarch approved their contents, the chancellor would affix the seal.

Zsigmond sat in a gilded chair while the attendant put on his shoes and laced them up. The king beckoned Vlad, who came to him and set the rolls of parchment down on the adjacent table. At a wave from Zsigmond, he unrolled each document and perused the opening paragraphs to provide a summary.

"If it pleases Your Royal Majesty," Vlad said, "There are letters patent awaiting your review. The proposal of the royal council for a meeting of the king's parliament in two months. Your Royal Majesty's correspondence with the Lithuanian ruler regarding a treaty between his country with Poland and the rebellious Teutonic Knights. The appointment of a new royal officer in Szepes County. Grants of armorial letters for the heraldry of the Garázda and Hideghéti noble families. A charter for the free movement of peasant tenantry."

"Is that all Our chancellor's office composed between yesterday and today?" His Royal Majesty looked around the room, and every attendant, Vlad included, chuckled as required. "The kingdom's business keeps Us occupied but must wait upon mass."

At a knock, one pageboy entered and when the king beckoned, came to him, and whispered in his ear. Zsigmond smiled and waved the small boy off.

"All of you may withdraw. Except for Prince Vlad," he said.

A flurry of feet hurried across the carpet. The king's confessor closed the doors out to the antechamber.

Vlad sucked in his breath. What could Zsigmond want with him in private?

"Our friend Pipó is outside." At the king's assertion, Vlad's heart soared, but he kept his silence while Zsigmond continued. "We required his swift return to court. As you're not a Catholic, you may speak with him while the other squires wait for Us at the chapel doors."

"By your command, Your Royal Majesty."

"Pipó has a special present. We demanded he bring it for you from Florence." The king stood. "We wish you joy on your birthday, Vlad. You need not look so surprised. In his custom, Fruzhin keeps Us informed of all matters. He wrote two months ago, while We were encamped in Bosnia, and mentioned the occasion would come up in the new year. We sent a missive to Pipó, requiring a gift for you."

"Thank you. Your Royal Majesty's consideration means more than I can express."

"You deserve it. Not only did you comport yourself exceedingly well while abroad and here at Buda Castle. You've also met the challenge Borbála assigned, excelling in the languages she's teaching. The lessons must continue but know they do not supersede your duties as a squire of the king's chamber."

"I understand, Your Royal Majesty."

"Very good. We will require only two of your fellows during the meal at *prandium*. Again, the rest of you will come here and eat together in the antechamber, awaiting Our return. Then you shall read these documents aloud, so We may ensure all provisions are as We outlined in Our dictates. Now come, the bell will ring soon."

As if on cue, sonorous peals announced mass. Vlad followed the sovereign into the hall, where Pipó bowed. The pair shared brief pleasantries before Zsigmond led his confessor, chamberlain, guards, and the other squires down the steps.

Out of sight, Vlad and Pipó shared a fierce embrace.

"I thought you meant to stay in Florence forever," Vlad gushed once they drew apart. "At least Fruzhin shall have your company at dinner this evening."

"*Buon compleanno*, Vlad. Seventeen! I remember that age. Did Fruzhin give you his gift already? *Sì*? Good. I've missed you both." Pipó swiped a hand over his mouth. "Riding hard for the capital is thirsty work. Let's find some ale in the great keep and I'll give you Zsigmond's present, as well as my own. He's spoken of it, no?"

Vlad nodded. "In private."

"A rare honor of a personal gift, for a squire of our king's chamber," Pipó said. "He chooses not to, ah, cause ill-feeling among the others by singling you out."

Together, they went to István's Tower. A maid brought two tankards to the table. Vlad asked her for more drinks. Grateful, Pipó downed the first set.

He called his squire, who stood near the doorway with saddlebags. From them, Pipó withdrew the gifts; four ells of gold and silk brocaded cloth weaved with pomegranate motifs, flying birds, and asymmetrical flower compositions. While Vlad gaped at the rich fabric, Pipó gave him the present from the king. An ornamented dagger in a scabbard embellished with jade stones, which also covered the grip.

"I've seen nothing like it." Vlad fingered the blade's slight curvature.

"Ah, that's because it's Turkish."

Vlad pulled his hand away and scowled.

"Trade brings variety in Christian marketplaces," Pipó said over the rim of his drink. "You wouldn't dare disdain Zsigmond, no? He told me to seek that for you."

"Why?"

"To kill Turks. It's fitting if their weapons should take the lives of our enemies, no?"

If he sat alone, Vlad would have flung the dagger outside into the snow and pissed on it. Instead, he grabbed it up and muttered, "That's the only purpose this blade will ever serve."

His duties resumed after *prandium*. When Zsigmond asked how he liked the dagger, he lied to his king for the first time.

LATER IN THE AFTERNOON, Vlad went to training with Stibor. On the practice field, he also found Stibor's namesake son and Fruzhin, alongside a trio of manacled prisoners.

They dressed in tarnished, flopped hats sewn to a point. Their laced-up, knee-length shirts might have been white in the past, but for grime and bloodstains. Red, tattered wide coverings for their legs gathered at the ankles, where the material met shoes dyed black as soot. All wore mustaches, but no beards. A corps of Zsigmond's royal guardsmen, standing shoulder to shoulder, encircled them.

"Turks, runt," Stibor said with a nod toward the captives. His namesake helped him fasten the sides of the cuirass over a padded woolen tunic. "If you're going to fight them and survive, you'll need to learn their battle tactics."

Fruzhin shoved long blades curved slightly from the hilt into the prisoners' hands. They gave him wary stares and traded wide-eyed looks and whispers.

"Vlad, the Ottoman soldiers favor this weapon called the *kilij*," Fruzhin said. "Like the ones we've provided, except they've been dulled. In battle, the Turkish light cavalry is effective. The speed of their mounts allows them to wield a sword with devastating power."

"You would've seen in Bosnia," Stibor added, "how they rain down a cascade of arrows with their mighty bows. If anyone survives the first assault, the Turkish cavalry charges in and slashes with their blades. Not a killing move against heavily armored knights, but remember, the sword is the enemy's secondary weapon."

"You two almost sound as if you admire them," Vlad muttered, his guts roiling with rage against the foes who took his sister from him.

Instant regret filled him. Fruzhin, Stibor, and his son stared at him.

"A healthy regard for an enemy's capabilities will ensure even the most impetuous fighter lives to see another day," Stibor growled. "If you plan on doing the same, learn the difference between respect and admiration for the Turks, runt. I've lost too many friends in battle to favor our natural enemies overmuch."

"My lord. Forgive me," Vlad began, "I meant no offense—"

"We both know what you meant." Fruzhin cut him off. He approached Vlad, placed an arm over his shoulder, and waved a hand at the prisoners. "Their people are savage killers. We must be better than them. Watch Stibor."

Fruzhin left him and returned to the first captive. They spoke words Vlad could not understand, but he assumed they were Turkish. Fruzhin pointed at Stibor, typically an indomitable tower in plate armor. Even without it, as now, a fearsome sight. No wonder the Turk backed away while shaking his head. He threw the sword he had received into the dirt.

Stibor came to them. "Tell him he'll die today. He can choose how. On his knees, his brain splattered across the grass, or on his feet with a blade in hand."

Fruzhin presumably repeated the words. The Turk blanched.

"*Dynatos*, please don't kill me," he pleaded.

Vlad and Fruzhin looked at each other. "He speaks Greek!" They exclaimed.

"What did he say?" Stibor demanded.

"He called you a person of authority and asked you not to murder him," Vlad said.

Fruzhin circled the prisoners. "Janissaries." He scowled and spat into the grass.

"What does that mean?" Vlad asked.

"Like my accursed brother, Iskender. Christian boys, conscripted by force into the Turkish army. After the Battle of Kosovo, their leaders captured males between the ages of seven and eighteen and taught our youth to fight and die for the sultan."

"These are men Zsigmond took as prisoners in Bosnia," Stibor muttered. "Ask them how many Christians they killed there, Fruzhin."

"It doesn't matter. There are other things I must discover."

Fruzhin questioned the captives in Greek, while Stibor frowned and asked Vlad for a translation, which he provided. Fruzhin interrogated them; asked if any heard of his brother, whom all claimed not to know.

The third prisoner did not speak Greek. Fruzhin switched to another unknown tongue before he yelled over his shoulder, "This one's a Serbian!"

"Who cares?" Stibor's son muttered. "They'll all be dead men soon enough."

"Now Fruzhin's telling them if they could face our army in Bosnia," Vlad continued, "they can battle for their lives here. The first man insists he won't fight you, my lord Stibor. You're too big, he says, and there would be no contest. But the one in the middle, he's ready."

Fruzhin finished and relayed the same claim to Stibor, who put on a helmet. He nodded to his would-be opponent, who stood at the same height as Vlad.

"Runt, you've spent the last year seeing our king's mounted knights charging into the fray. No knight always has the advantage of fighting on horseback. I'll show you how to bash a skull at close quarters. Give my foe a shield too, my son. Pay attention, runt. You won't find shields on most battlefields, but in tournaments."

What the captive lacked in size compared with Stibor, he made up for with brute strength. He also outmatched Stibor's agility. He maneuvered the long chain between his shackles, so they did not impede him and weaved and ducked in a circle around the practice field. So far, barely three strikes of Stibor's morning star battered his opponent's shield.

"This one's come to dance with me." Stibor laughed and swept his weapon in a wide arc while his adversary spun away. "It's only a matter of time until he's dead."

"Janissaries never run from a fight." Beside Vlad, Fruzhin whispered in his ear, "Disciplined warriors. The morning star isn't the most effective weapon against a real sword. The janissary doesn't play for time. He's awaiting an opportunity."

Fascinated, Vlad drew closer. The Turk swung, and his blade caught Stibor's arm. Somehow, the tip broke off, perhaps against Stibor's shield, leaving a jagged, sharp edge. The larger man cursed. His enemy smiled, enjoying the unexpected feat. Long enough for Stibor to crush his upper arm. He howled and reeled until Stibor cracked his skull.

The remaining prisoners gaped at the dead man in open shock. Stibor fingered the slit in his sleeve and gave the bloodied morning star to his son.

"What have you learned, runt?" Stibor asked while shooing off his namesake.

"A smaller warrior may have speed, but great skill is required," Vlad answered.

"What else?"

"The morning star doesn't have the range of a sword, my lord."

"True. It's brutal, but a well-balanced weapon with a short shaft. Our determined foes wear chain mail, with plate armor protecting the chest and head. A heavily armored warrior can bludgeon a lone janissary in single combat. Now, Fruzhin will show you what he learned from me years ago."

Fruzhin removed his black cape and handed it to a guardsman. Dressed in the same type of garments Stibor wore, Fruzhin took a shield from Stibor's son and battled the Serbian-born janissary.

The prisoner answered every sweeping stroke, blocking with his shield, while occasionally swinging the blunted sword. When his arms drooped, he gripped the flat blade in both hands and struck Fruzhin's side with the pommel. The last blow he managed before Fruzhin slashed at him repeatedly.

Worn down, the captive soon lost the battered shield and left his flanks exposed. He sagged to his knees in acceptance of defeat. Fruzhin dug into his breastbone, stabbing downward until the sword's cross-guard stopped the piercing steel.

"What did you perceive about that fight, runt?" Stibor asked.

"Swords are more than their blades," Vlad said. "Other parts can be useful for attack or defense, in a skilled combatant's hand."

Fruzhin grunted. "What do you think of our weapons versus the Turks' own?"

Vlad scratched his head. "In hand-to-hand conflict, our swords are superior for thrusting blows and blocking attacks, but we're trained from early with them. Are they better than Turkish weapons? Or do we study how to wield them to an advantage?"

"You'll discover the truth on your own." Fruzhin took a cloth from Stibor's son and wiped the dead man's blood from his weapon. "The last janissary is yours to kill."

Vlad's heart pitched. The fight for survival a year ago outside Hunyadvár, against those who also deserved death, left him almost numb. So why should he feel anything now?

Perhaps the way the last Turk's eyes watered, once he must have accepted that he alone remained. His lips quivered and he stared at Stibor, Fruzhin, and Vlad. Did the prisoner fear the discovery of which one of them he would face?

His concerns were his alone. If Vlad did not meet this test, he would never become a warrior, a leader of men. Stibor would call him a coward. Worse, Fruzhin might think him an oath-breaker, forsaking their blood pact against their devilish opponents made last winter.

When Vlad put on the helmet and took the weapon and shield Stibor's son gave him, the look of fear in his foe's visage receded. Vlad recalled Stibor's advice during their test bout after they first met in István's Tower.

"Bigger and taller men will always look down on you. They'll size you up, judge your youth, and think you won't offer much of a challenge."

Fruzhin shoved the sword the Turkic soldier had once cast aside into his hands again. His throat bobbed, and he accepted the blunted weapon.

Vlad came at him, not with the overwhelming power of Stibor, but with the determination of Fruzhin's earlier attacks. A new dance began between them, where Vlad tried to get his adversary to follow his lead.

The captive never lunged or failed to deflect. His nimbleness with the long chain rivaled the man whom Stibor killed with the morning star.

"Finish him, prince! I haven't eaten for the day," Stibor's son complained.

"Be quiet and let my squire concentrate," his father said. "Or leave now and forfeit the visit to the brothel we planned for tonight."

"Oh, but I...."

Vlad ignored the rest of the exchange. Momentum shifted, and his adversary attacked as if forgetting his weapon possessed no sharp edge. Vlad retreated against a furious battering, which irritated him. He knocked the blade aside and swung the shield, smashing the man's head repeatedly until he toppled backward.

Vlad breathed shakily and let the bloodied shield fall.

"Kill him, runt," Stibor commanded.

A yelp from Fruzhin came at the same time as the prisoner gripped his chain in both hands and swung it at Vlad's lower limbs. Heavy iron links struck his calves and shins, covered only in hose. With a bellow, Vlad drove the tip of the sword downward, but the Turk rolled away. Toward Stibor, who bashed with the morning star. He did not stop until Fruzhin yelled in his ear.

"By the blood of Christ, man, there's nothing left of his face!"

Stibor lowered his arm and swiped at the flecks of blood and crushed bone on his cuirass. "It's always best to be thorough." He staggered a bit before righting himself. "Well, runt...what did you learn this time?"

His bones throbbed so much; Vlad could scarcely breathe or think to answer.

"What was the lesson here?" Stibor insisted.

Aghast, Vlad stared into the open maw of the dead man's features. After the bludgeoning, nothing discernible marked his face as a human.

Stibor rushed at Vlad and seized his arm. "Don't turn from a fight until a corpse lies at your feet."

"WHAT HAPPENED TO YOU, Vlad? Too much time celebrating your birthday?"

His uncle looked up from a spot beside a warm fire, while he tucked a leaf of paper under a muscled thigh. For once, the Gypsy twins were absent from him.

Vlad rested his aching limbs. In a rush of words, he explained the events on the practice field but returned to Zsigmond's gift of a Turkish-style dagger. He handed it over to his uncle for safekeeping, as he had all his other belongings.

"And how does all of this make you feel?" Staico asked.

"I'm glad to be here, learning from Stibor," Vlad murmured as he stared into the flames. "I wonder at fighting prisoners of war who defended themselves with blunted blades. Shouldn't Zsigmond have ransomed them? What could the king mean by giving me one of a Turkic ornamental blade? Does he think I'll kill someone in a pitched battle with it?"

"Your mind darts like a bee from flower to flower," Staico said with a chuckle.

"No words of wisdom, uncle? On our way here, I couldn't get you to stifle the talk about defeating bandits outside Hunyadvár. Now it's bees and flowers!"

"My thoughts wouldn't help, nephew. I'm glad you've raised these quandaries on your own. Consider them. You'll find the right answers in the fullness of time."

Vlad huffed. "You assume so." He looked around. "Where are the twins?"

"Tobar went off with some girl from town. Won't see him until morning. Yoska One-Eye's wrestling his uncles and cousins in the Gypsy camp."

"I wish you wouldn't call him that. One-Eye," Vlad grumbled. He pointed to the paper under Staico's limb. "What were you reading before I joined you?"

His uncle pulled the letter out nimbly with his three fingers. "The monks at Vodița promise more ale if my Gypsies will come and secure the transport."

Satisfied but still weary, Vlad stretched out on his back and studied the myriad stars. Where were his mother and sister on such a night?

"You long for home again, nephew? Where are your thoughts?"

"On Arina and Mother. I wonder about the Dowager and my brothers, except Mihail. Even Father. Mother hasn't written. Do you think he won't allow it?"

"I believe your parents want you focused on a new life," his uncle said as he reclined beside Vlad. "I miss Wallachia but promised never to leave your side."

"My father required that pledge?" Vlad scoffed. "As if he cared for either of us."

"No. I honor the faith your mother, Princess Mara, placed in me."

THE CHANGES VLAD EXPECTED within and outside Buda Castle unfolded at a slow pace. In the spring, the work on the great keep occurred. The king also began a new tower. Fruzhin and Pipó made their farewells to Vlad in the forecourt. Fruzhin rode off to meet a cousin in Bulgaria, where they would plan a new offensive against the Turks. Pipó led a force of twelve thousand to regain Dalmatia from the Venetians.

Midsummer, the court took a northwesterly route to Pozsony, where the king and queen finally reunited. The formal betrothal of Zsigmond and Borbála's two-year-old daughter, Erzsébet occurred, her father pledging one-hundred-thousand florins for the future bride. Vlad thought about the prospective bridegroom Albrecht, the fourteen-year-old Habsburg, dour and sallow.

In late July, four days before the Catholic Saint Jakob's feast, for whom even Hungarians made the pilgrimage to Santiago de Compostela in Spain, a russet-bearded German arrived at court. Fruzhin identified him as Friedrich of the House of Hohenzollern.

The king and courtiers cheered the good tidings Friedrich brought. The death of Zsigmond's rival, who earlier deposed his half-brother

Wenceslaus in Germany and opposed Zsigmond's interests there, meant he would attain that crown finally.

He returned south to the capital on a late summer evening, without the queen, doting on the daughter on his lap. Vlad marveled at a father besotted with his child, auspiciously born, according to Zsigmond, during the Catholic feast day for Saint Francis of Assisi.

However, Erzsébet inherited her mother's moods. After hours of giggling along the journey, she suddenly screeched and wriggled in her parent's arms. Zsigmond let her down to one of her caretakers. The same woman whom Vlad spied from a window in Pozsony's castle, kissing Zsigmond and stroking a bulge at the apex of his hose. A quiet moment in which Vlad read a poetry book, tarnished by the monarch being an unfaithful lout.

Wearied of Zsigmond, his whore, and his insufferable daughter, when the king dismissed him, relief flooded Vlad. He almost ran to Staico's tent, but found him outside under a tree again, hunched over and facing the fire.

"Anyone could sneak up on you, with your back to them, uncle."

Staico yelped and a leaf of paper floated close to the flames. He grabbed the document, but not before Vlad noticed the red wax seal. The lion rampant with which Prince Mircea secured all personal correspondence.

"Vlad, I didn't expect—"

He rounded his uncle and held out his hand. "If it's my mother who's written, I want to read the words myself. I doubt my father would contact you."

"Vlad, you shouldn't worry," Staico began.

"I won't, if you'll show the letter to me."

His uncle handed it over with a sigh. He recognized his mother's handwriting and the significance of her words. Mûsâ Çelebi fought his brothers; winning one major battle last year, a month after his union with Arina, aided by the troops the ruling prince provided him. For the first time, Vlad learned the identity of their captain general. His cousin, Dan Dăneşti, son of the brother many believed Mircea the Great had conspired to murder.

Inexplicably, Arina remained encamped with her husband, rather than in the safety of some walled city. Princess Mara received no more information after the prince lost another conflict with his siblings the previous summer. She confessed her fears to Staico, acknowledging she could never express the same to her husband.

"Why does she write to you?" Vlad demanded. "What can you do in my stead?"

"Nothing," Staico admitted with a shrug. "Except send her calm assurances. You would only increase your mother's concern for Arina."

"Shouldn't we be concerned?"

"My half-brother's commitment of troops to the Turkish cause depends on Arina's well-being. If her letters to your mother ever cease, your father will withdraw his support of Mûsâ Çelebi. Recall the marriage. Your father affirmed the nuptial agreement, not with the great seal of Wallachia, but with his privy seal. He only affixes the signet ring to private communications or significant documents. His daughter means much to him. If the foreign prince wants Wallachian fighters, he must preserve the marriage and your sister's life."

Vlad shook his head. Her fate hung in a precarious balance.

Staico stood and came to him. "Please, concentrate on your responsibilities, nephew."

"You think that despite them, I could ever put Arina from my mind?" Vlad shook his head and turned away. "You won't hide another letter from Mother. I want to read them all. If you truly care for me, you won't conceal their contents ever."

He did not await his uncle's answer.

Four weeks later, Vlad's mother wrote again. Mircea the Great welcomed his nephew Dan Dăneşti to Argeş at summer's end. Dan arrived with news he trusted no herald to deliver. Mûsâ Çelebi's victory took place in mid-February, over six months beforehand. His people proclaimed him the sultan of Rumelia.

"Your sister is well and safe, as promised," Staico said.

Vlad wished he could be as certain of Arina's fate as his uncle could.

When he left Staico, a pageboy found him and gave him the strangest news. The queen returned abruptly and summoned him to Zsigmond's chambers. Did she know Vlad witnessed proof of her husband's illicit affair?

At the door of the king's room, Vlad begged admittance and received it. Zsigmond and Borbála sat by the window overlooking a new garden.

"There he is!" The queen screeched. "Ask him about the letter, Zsigmond."

"Calm yourself, Borbála," the sovereign said. "Let him come to Us now."

Once Vlad reached them, the king handed him an unrolled parchment. Inside, damning correspondence from Prince Mircea to the ruler of Poland, offering him fealty. On the reverse, the personal seal, stamped with the lion-rampant.

Vlad gaped at the royal couple. Even if his parent could explain, his disloyalty jeopardized his son's position in the Hungarian court.

"What do you say about your traitorous father? He would trade one overlord for another, like cattle for coin," Borbála accused. "Does he forget Zsigmond controls your fate? I do not. How shall our king punish you for Mircea's treachery?"

The base of Vlad's throat pulsed so hard. He could barely swallow. Your Grace, my...queen," for it pained him to acknowledge her rank. "I'm not my parent and cannot know his thoughts, nor expect his misdeeds. A just ruler would see the truth."

He forced a measure of calmness into his voice he did not feel, not since hearing the first news of Arina in months. Their father placed her in a precarious state. Vlad could no longer think of the ruling prince of Wallachia, except to blame and revile him. How could he endanger them both? And what of Vlad's plans for their country? Would he lose all hope of ruling there if Zsigmond retaliated and removed Prince Mircea from the throne?

He turned to the king. "I swear from this day forth, Your Royal Majesty, you have my fidelity. I'll do nothing to make you associate me with a worthless parent."

"What proof would you give as a sign of your commitment to Us?" Zsigmond pitched his tone low, like that of a lover. The king did not need to cajole Vlad.

He had spoken the truth with Fruzhin in weeks past; he knew his place in the decadent, brutal world of Zsigmond. Yet, he could not stagnate here. He needed his sovereign's trust and respect. Without either, he would not achieve a knighthood like Stibor, or a command of armies like Pipó. He could never gain royal approval in his quest for Wallachia's crown.

"Your Royal Majesty, I will renounce Eastern Orthodoxy and convert to Catholicism."

"You can cast aside the faith of your birth so easily?" The queen's green, fiery gaze narrowed on him. "Too tractable. A sycophant! You're no better than your profligate father."

"I am!" He met her stare as her golden brows flared. Turning to Zsigmond again, he swallowed the vehemence in his earlier tone. "Your Royal Majesty, I will show you."

CHAPTER 9

The Whims of Kings and Princes

"Pale death knocks with impartial foot at poor men's hovels and kings' palaces."-Horace (65-8 BC), Roman lyric poet.

IN THE YEAR OF OUR Lord 1412. Buda, Hungary (modern-day Budapest, Hungary)

In awe, Vlad became enthralled with the number of monarchs, including kings, princes and their families, nobles, the clergy, and knights who descended on Buda daily. A conclave between the two powerful rivals would occur within weeks. Zsigmond met King Władysław of Poland at the border of their countries in February. They hunted and feasted together for four months before reaching the Hungarian capital.

Seeing their rapport and the amicable relationship between their queens, cousins descended from the House of Celje who both urged peace talks, Vlad sought to learn more about the historic conflicts between the two nations. He also wondered if the hastily arranged meeting did not occur in response to the overture Prince Mircea made to Poland almost a year ago.

Unfortunately, the only person without significant duties during the summit seemed also the least likely member of the court to indulge Vlad's curiosity. After serving Stibor for over two years, he could easily deduce the man's moods. With the right inducement, Vlad's chance to learn would come.

He stood guard beside the brothel room door, through which loud grunts and raspy moans echoed since midday. At least two hours later, if the rumbling of his belly gave proof of time's passage, he could seek answers soon.

A buxom redhead exited another room, her hair tidied beneath a yellow scarf. The law, as enforced by the master bailiff, required her to wear it. Soft skin glowed, flushed, and perfumed with fragrant rosewater beneath a wispy garment. He avoided eye contact with her. To do otherwise would offer an invitation he did not intend. Buda's prostitutes could wait for another occasion. His curiosity about Zsigmond and Władysław would not.

The door beside him creaked. Stibor grunted, ducked his head, and came out. His bulk nearly filled the hallway. He smiled at the woman there but waved her on. She hesitated, peering at Vlad, and waited. He shook his head. She huffed, lifted her chin, and traipsed downstairs presumably to seek her next conquest.

"There's time, runt. We have some hours before dinner. You may stay a little longer. I'm well satisfied and could visit the inn across the street."

"I would not delay you further, even for the pleasures here, my lord."

"You enjoyed yourself?"

"How could I not have, my lord?"

Stibor clapped his back, and he nearly went sprawling. Instead, he grabbed the carved torso of a Venus statuette set along the wooden wall and righted himself.

"Well, if you're certain." Stibor turned aside and sketched a dramatic bow. "Always a pleasure. Another time." Dual peals of feminine laughter ensued. "Come along, runt."

He made for the stairs. Vlad followed, his peripheral gaze catching the pair of women stretched out nude on the curtained bed. He hurried behind Stibor, who jaunted down the steps with the vigor of a younger man. Vlad found the girl chosen earlier for him in the vestibule. A faint smile curved her soft lips. Black curls billowed around her narrow face.

Stibor paused and spoke with the procuress who owned the brothel, while the girl stood by. If they were alone, Vlad might have done something foolish and promised her a future visit. However, he could not waste the rest of the wages saved from last year. He expected more monies, for Zsigmond named him as a squire of the royal chamber again six months ago. Greater needs outweighed those of the flesh.

He stepped outside the establishment in the middle of the narrow Street of Roses or the *Via Rosarum,* and walked toward its southern end. The thatched roof of a crudely built shelter held their horses under the watchful gaze of Stibor's favored mistress' son. Men of every class and dress ducked in and out of the facades of bathhouses interspersed among the brothels. A pair of riders moved in Vlad's direction.

"I don't think you've led us along the right path. Are you certain this is correct?"

The husky feminine tone drew his attention to the diminutive woman sitting sidesaddle. She rode alongside a lightly bearded man with yellow curls sheared at his chin.

"You heard the guard at the eastern gate as well as I did, Călţuna. He told us we would reach the *Platea Iudeorum* if we took this way."

Her companion was not wrong. The Street of the Jews, the main thoroughfare of their quarter, lay on Buda's southern edge. But neither of the travelers wore the distinctive red cloth sewn on the left breast of their cloaks, as required of all Hungarian Jewry. Vlad wondered if they did not know the custom as Jews themselves or did not adhere to that faith, being Christians. Either way, ignorance of the town's laws about Jewish identity or Christian interaction with Jews would not aid them against the master bailiff.

The stranger's voice echoed as he drew closer. "Our host and his eager daughter must already wonder where we are. We should've arrived earlier this morning."

"Let us make haste! I don't like the look of this area." When the lady urged her mount, her wool cowl slid back, revealing golden curls atop her head in the style of an unmarried female. Her jeweled green gaze barely flitted over Vlad before she rode on.

As they retreated from view, a jolt ran through Vlad as he realized he had once seen her somewhere else before. He strove for the memory until it came to him. The lady from the 'city of eyes,' Hermannstadt in Transilvania, whom he met two years ago.

"Are you ready?" Stibor jolted him from reverie.

He released an unsteady breath. "Y-y-yes. I believe so." He looked around but saw no further sign of the woman and her companion. Disappointment filled him. What were they doing in Buda and on the Street of Roses, known to all as a place of prostitution? He had never expected even this briefest of sightings of the lady again. But she was here.

Stibor eyed him. "What's wrong with you, runt?"

"Nothing, I assure you, my lord." Vlad swallowed and nodded.

They rode through the crowded town in the palace's direction. Any opportunity to rediscover the woman receded in the distance. Vlad pushed aside his regret and listened while Stibor sang in a rich timbre. The man's good mood boded well for the conversation Vlad intended to undertake. He could not lose sight of his goal. Besides, how could he expect to ever find the woman from Hermannstadt again in such a large place?

Residency in Buda and Pest swelled temporarily. Every inn and once-vacant townhouse now filled with royal summit attendees. Even Stibor rented out his home to three bishops who bowed before their king in the throne room upon arrival. Vlad lost count of the number of visiting clergymen whom Stibor greeted loudly by name before they exited the Street of Roses.

He laughed and turned in the saddle to Vlad. "These bishops and cardinals with their prattling about God. A man's lusting heart thrums inside their chests. Same as you and me. Or me at least."

Having reached the age of eighteen six months ago, Vlad should take offense. However, contradicting Stibor would not gain him the knowledge he sought.

"How long shall they remain in Buda? When will the conclave end, my lord?"

"Once Zsigmond and Władysław agree about the future."

Vlad bit back a smile at the easy opening Stibor gave him.

"What have they fought about in the past, my lord?"

"Thrones. What else is there of importance to kings?"

"I don't understand, my lord. One monarch rules here, the other in Poland."

"Zsigmond wed the heiress of this country. When she perished alongside his stillborn son, our king still held the crown," Stibor explained. "Władysław was born in Lithuania, and his claim to Poland originally did not differ from that of Zsigmond. It derived from a first marriage. Together, he and his wife sought to rule Hungary after the death of Zsigmond's queen, but they failed. Zsigmond is the grandson of the third King Casimir of Poland. Władysław's current wife, Queen Borbála's cousin, is a granddaughter of the same Casimir."

Vlad's mother once told him much about the Hungarian court, but he never knew how its king gained his crown.

"Why did the previous queen of Hungary die, my lord Stibor, in her childbed?" Vlad wondered whether she suffered much, like his lost sister, Anna.

"A riding accident. Thrown from her horse. The babe came too soon, as a result," Stibor explained before he shook his head. "Talk of dead queens sours my good mood. We should speak of life's enjoyment. Thanks to your suggestion, we both enjoyed a pleasant afternoon. I've killed no one today, nor do I have the urge, satiated as I am. You should be even more joyous than me, for I believe your Bulgarian friend Fruzhin returns this week."

"He does?" Vlad sat straighter in the saddle. "I haven't read a letter from Fruzhin for three months. What happened, my lord? Did he and his cousin win against the Turks?"

"You're more eager to hear of his exploits than you were for the pleasures of that brothel girl." Stibor chuckled. "Zsigmond received a missive from Fruzhin, brought to him after dinner last night. Our king would only say we should expect the Bulgarian this week, and he doesn't travel alone."

Perhaps with his cousin? Would they bring prisoners from Bulgaria? With the enigmatic promise in mind, each subsequent day, Vlad searched a sea of faces. So far, Fruzhin did not number among the arrivals at Buda Castle.

AT THE WEEK'S END, Vlad completed a Polish reading lesson with Borbála and her Polish counterpart. Through the opened window of the Hungarian queen's library, he glimpsed Fruzhin's familiar profile before a larger, red-bearded man eclipsed him on horseback.

Vlad rose and bowed before Borbála, begging her leave to go. She waved him away and turned aside to her kinswoman, dull in all comparisons to Borbála. They were deeply affectionate. They could have been sisters rather than the offspring of two Celje brothers.

Borbála said, "I'm well rid of Prince Vlad, at least until tomorrow, dearest Andlein."

"Cousin, he can hear us! I don't see cause for complaint. The Transalpine prince read the poetic verses well enough. I find his countenance pleasant around the eyes."

Borbála's laughter pealed. "You might not want to let Władysław overhear that."

"You assume my wayward husband has any interest in what I say? He finds me as useless as when I appeared outside Kraków eleven years ago. An illiterate girl, who has only borne him our daughter, Jadwiga, in the last four years. Our child shall inherit the throne—"

The rest of the royal cousins' conversation faded. Vlad rushed outside. He and Fruzhin found each other among the teeming mass of arrivals and well-wishers.

"I didn't think you'd ever come back," Vlad said, while he and his friend embraced. "It's been ten months. Does the return mean you've won?"

"Yes! Lands in the northwest belong to Bulgaria again. At least, a large swath of them!" Fruzhin exclaimed. "Victory couldn't have occurred without my family."

When they drew apart, Vlad noted the large man eyeing them, his beard more russet than full red. Fine lines crinkled the corners of his eyes, as they did the gaze of the radiant beauty beside him. In unison, they dismounted, and Vlad gasped. The pair stood almost as tall as Stibor; surprising for a woman especially. Behind them, an entourage of at least a score remained on horseback. Some women favored Vlad with enchanting smiles.

Fruzhin tugged his arm. "My friend," he said, switching to Greek. "I'm pleased and proud to present you with my mother's Serbian relations. This is her brother, Stefan Lazarević, the *Despoteses* of the Kingdom of Rascia, as old Serbia is called here, and Princess Milena Olivera Lazarević, my uncle's elder sister."

"Not by that much," she insisted in a velvety tone. "How could you, nephew?"

"Forgive me, aunt." Fruzhin bowed. "I implied nothing about your age."

"Nor should you." The Serbian princess curtsied to Vlad. Lustrous hair, like sun-ripened wheat, spilled on either side of her broad shoulders and full breasts.

Vlad stopped staring and made obeisance. "Your title, *Despoteses*. It's an imperial courtesy of the Byzantine court, Fruzhin said. Have you visited Byzantium?"

"Indeed, Prince Vlad," Fruzhin's uncle answered. "The high honor of a reception with the emperor awaited me there, as did the title, second in rank only to that of an emperor. I trust we won't remain as formal with each other while Milena Olivera and I are here."

"I should hope not either, dear brother. With so many ruling houses around us, I refuse to learn everyone's titles."

"I shall simply be Stefan and you, Milena Olivera, to all," he replied. "Remember the deference owed to every other entitled person, sweet sister?"

"As if you would let me forget, Stefan."

Vlad glanced at Fruzhin before he said, "Your nephew has called me by my Christian name at my insistence. Please do the same for me."

Although Milena Olivera smiled, she looked beyond him into the throng, clearly searching. Her brother peeked at her, chuckled, and shook his head.

His appearance drew Vlad's further scrutiny. The silver clasp of Stefan's mantle featured a dragon curled on its belly. The tail wrapped around the neck. Inlaid with small red jewels for eyes, a cross spanned its back. The symbol reminded Vlad of a similar heraldry etched on Stibor's armor. Was Stefan another member of the elusive Order of the Dragon?

"Prince Vlad, if you'll permit, among my retinue is a person who knows you and wishes to speak," Stefan said. "May I call him?"

"Why...yes," Vlad whispered. His temple pulsed. There could be only one Serbian already acquainted with him.

Stefan yelled over his shoulder. Otherwise, his man might not have heard him.

Vlad's eyes watered once a brawny, yellow-haired figure got down off the horse, approached him, and bowed. When Vlad touched his shoulder, he straightened.

"My lord Radič?" Vlad's voice warbled. "Is it truly you?"

Radič Postupović smiled and tilted his head. "It's been too long, but I would know you anywhere. Although you favor the House of Basarab, you have the eyes of your mother, Princess Mara. Same as my darling Anna. If only she had lived to see how well you, her dear sibling, have grown."

The former brothers by marriage shared an overlong hug.

"My God. I never thought to see you again, Radič."

"Nor I, you, after we lost Anna. She smiles down from heaven today."

"And how is your son? He must be big now. Does he look at all like Anna?"

"He must be your height by now." Radič chuckled, as did Vlad, at the impossibility, for his nephew was seven. "It would seem your mother's descendants will be no taller than her. Her grandson trains as a pageboy in Bosnia. He has her eyes too."

"You've never remarried?"

"I lost my heart to the perfect Transalpine beauty at our betrothal. After we finally wed a year later, Anna held my heart in her keeping. It will always be hers."

"I'll admit, I've encouraged Radič to find marital happiness again," Stefan interjected. "He serves as my palatine. I trust him with the administration of the Serbian state and protecting my family. Speaking so, it occurs; Milena Olivera, shouldn't you let Radič escort you to my townhouse while I seek an audience with Zsigmond?"

His sister snorted and continued peering into the masses. Stefan shrugged.

"They're affable." Fruzhin leaned over and whispered in Vlad's ear, "but I'll say, even after our long absences from each other, their forthright manners still shock me."

"Where is she?" Milena Olivera grumbled.

"Sweet sister, she will come." Stefan explained to Vlad, "We hope to see our other older sibling, Jelena, who travels with her new husband to the conclave."

"A husband, whom only you've met, Stefan," Milena Olivera added.

"I approved of his marriage with Jelena to forge strong ties in the Balkans. The Bosnian and Serbian people need each other in defense against the Turks. You're only upset because you couldn't attend the wedding."

"A hasty union invites speculation, brother. If Jelena were not already a mother in her forties, I'd fear the gossip that viper Borbála might spew about our sister's hastiness to marry again."

"Jelena can manage Zsigmond's queen as well as you can."

Already inclined toward Fruzhin's Serbians, Vlad decided he liked Milena Olivera best of all, since she shared his opinion of Borbála.

"Our king waits. There are matters we must discuss," Stefan said. "Sister, if you won't let Radič attend you, shall you remain with your nephew and his friend?"

"Certainly not, if they'll both pardon my insistence." She turned and summoned attendants in the Slavic words Vlad recognized as their native language. When six women came to her side, all curtsied before Stefan with her.

"I'll seek Jelena and find out who won the wager about getting here first," Milena Olivera said once she straightened. "Whatever the outcome of my search, I'll return to the townhouse and come again in time for dinner. Still at the hour of six, dear brother?"

"Your good memory is a blessing, sweet sister."

"Be dutiful in your discussion with Zsigmond."

"Am I not always so? I've done everything he asked, including bringing two thousand loyal vassals to join his Venetian campaign this autumn."

"Kings always want more, Stefan," Milena Olivera murmured as she brushed her lips against his cheek. "You'd do well to remember that fact."

She curtsied to Fruzhin and Vlad before preceding her ladies.

"Won't you take an escort of our guards?" Stefan called out to her.

Her husky laughter mocked him, although Vlad thought she should have heeded the advice. Most males stopped their conversation and eyed the sway of her generous hips below a trim waist. Vlad supposed such a statuesque woman, a ruling prince's sister would always entice eligible suitors and lesser men.

"My sisters. Willful to the core," her brother mused. "How I love them for it."

Vlad parted from Radič, who awaited Milena Olivera with a vow to speak further during the feast. At Fruzhin's side, he followed Stefan to the outskirts of the ceremonial hall below the dining chamber. Inside, Zsigmond greeted the guests. Stefan left them with a curt nod. Vlad wondered why the mood soured once Stefan readied to greet their king.

He would ask Fruzhin for the reason after he pulled him into a nearby alcove. "First, tell me everything about your success in Bulgaria!"

LATER, FRUZHIN EXPLAINED his uncle had arrived in Hungary to renew the terms of vassalage with Zsigmond. Stefan resented the commitment of his Serbian people, reasserting his king's claim on Dalmatia against the Venetians, while Stefan needed every vassal to withstand a future Turkish expansion. For all his uncle's grumbling about their overlord's whims, Fruzhin said Stefan would never reject them.

"He genuinely favors Zsigmond and has pledged himself a liegeman. The two thousand horsemen will go south with us in the autumn to war with the Venetians."

Vlad looked forward to the time in Dalmatia. The prospect of seeing his Florentine friend Pipó again would be worthwhile, even if not on the battlefield. Stibor would not let Vlad fight. He said no squire should, so Vlad would be a spectator from the encampment as on the Bosnian campaign. How could he gain a knighthood as an observer of battle?

He did not underestimate the difference between facing bandits in the forest or janissaries, versus an army formed up to defeat Zsigmond's men. When talk of war filtered through the hallways, he prayed inwardly for two boons. He asked God to let him prove himself a brave and true man devoted to his king, and to give Zsigmond victory.

With the ongoing summit, autumn seemed far away. Vlad still dutifully examined and summarized all courtly correspondence while his sovereign dressed each day. On a gray and dull morning, his task concerned a single letter brought by a herald. He perused the first paragraph in silence, as was customary. Four of Zsigmond's squires held up two mirrors, so he could admire the new robe his queen presented an hour after dawn. The king also bantered with his attendants about who might emerge victorious in the upcoming joust.

Dressed to join her husband at mass, Borbála perched on the edge of the bed, a smile Vlad judged as insincere pasted on her lips. A rare sight in the chamber of her husband. She looked pleased with his appearance and glad to be by his side. Sometimes when no one else observed her, Vlad noted the slight curl of a sneer when she watched their king beneath hooded lids. In other instances, a green fire smoldered in her glare.

Did Zsigmond know she despised him? Did he care? Was that why he cavorted without consideration for her feelings?

Suddenly, Borbála caught Vlad's regard for her when he should have focused on the missive. His gaze flitted to the paper again and found the second paragraph. He gasped, lifted his stare, and met the queen's gaze again.

"What have you there, squire?" She warned, "Don't keep our king waiting."

"Yes, you may read to Us," Zsigmond said, turning from the mirrors.

"If it pleases Your Royal Majesty," Vlad began, "This is not a communication intended for you. Rather, it's for Queen Borbála."

She rose and came to him, snatched it from his hand, and turned away.

Vlad recalled yesterday's presentation of the letter's author. A bull-necked Bosnian magnate called Hrvoje. His coat of arms bore a knight battling a lion, the same as the broken seal on the document. Their king had dismissed the scowling man from the hall in haste. After dinner that night, Hrvoje blundered toward Zsigmond before he withdrew with his counselors. The royal guards barred the Bosnian's way. Behind his back, the governor of Slavonia mocked the stocky man, bellowing like a bull.

While Zsigmond read in silence before cursing, the queen hovered over his shoulder.

"Your Royal Majesty, did you see the date on which he requested aid against our Turkic enemies? The letter's months old, husband. It must've gone astray while we rode in the countryside with King Władysław and my dearest cousin, Andlein."

"You insist on using the same endearment your father does for Queen Anna," Zsigmond said. "Her husband brought her here to aid the peace between our two kingdoms. You and your father have failed to realize she's no longer an ignorant girl. She has roles to fulfill as queen consort. Just like you."

He went to the window and pressed his head against the rain-streaked glass.

"We are the mothers of daughters, Your Royal Majesty, having left the nursery long ago." She came to him. "Why speak of Andlein or my parent, when you're upset with another?"

Although neither her tone nor visage softened, she placed her hand on his upper arm. A semblance of affection.

Vlad did not know how to reconcile the queen's actions and words. Fruzhin and his Serbian relations displayed more genuine affection than the royals of Hungary or Poland did. At least, Zsigmond loved his daughter and accepted that she would rule in his stead.

"All of you may withdraw, except Our queen," he muttered in a flattened tone.

While he followed the other royal attendants, Vlad considered the contents of the queen's letter. Hrvoje appealed to her solely, with the address 'Your Serenity,' rather than her husband. He mentioned some role as godfather of the princess and reminded the queen of his membership in the secretive Order of the Dragon. The second paragraph began in Latin, "*Advertat Serenitas Vestra quomodo ego existo in Societate Dracorum*," or "Your Serenity, recall, I am a member of the Dragon Order."

Again, the mysterious Order reared its head. Vlad pondered Borbála's influence among the members. Though unlikely, for he knew of no women connected with knightly orders, she must be involved somehow.

"No wonder the lord stood so stiff-backed at his presentation," she said as Vlad neared the doorway.

"Christ's blood!" Her husband snapped, "I should care for the traitor's moods now? I've not forgotten how he supported the king of Naples in the quest to take MY crown! Or how he appealed to the same Turks to overthrow the ruler of Bosnia! Must I forgive and rescue Hrvoje from the folly of his own making again?"

"Please, consider this instance, Your Royal Majesty—"

The guards in the antechamber closed the heavy doors on the queen's words.

Vlad clasped his hands behind him, as did the other squires, and mimicked their quiet countenances. But his mind and heart raced.

Stibor, the Bosnian Hrvoje, and by simple reasoning, Fruzhin and his uncle Stefan each belonged to the secretive Order of the Dragon. They enjoyed close companionship with Zsigmond. His troops helped Stefan maintain some control of Serbia. A contingent of Hungarian cavalry and mounted archers also went into Bulgaria with Fruzhin ten months beforehand. Hrvoje relied on them equally against the Turkish menace.

To achieve his aim in Wallachia, Vlad would need his king's support, too. A simple appeal might not grant him Zsigmond's favor. Membership in the Order of the Dragon could. Vlad would have to gain admittance. Through it, he could command a portion of the expanding Hungarian army to take Wallachia, remove his brother Mihail from the throne, and march on Turkic lands to rescue Arina.

To do all that, Vlad must secure a knighthood first. Would such an honor occur during the Venetian campaign in autumn? How could he ensure it without Stibor's permission to fight? How would he prove himself, as his friends advised? The words of ancient Greece's Sophocles guided him. '*Heaven ne'er helps the men who will not act.*'

THE CATHOLIC FEAST of Corpus Christi took place three evenings later. King Zsigmond sat on his throne, placed in the triangular courtyard outside István's Tower. A silk canopy draped on poles sheltered him. Courtiers dressed in their finery stood at the outskirts of the buildings, torchlight setting the facades aglow. Clouds rolled in, heralding more rain.

Twelve squires of their king's chamber carried the Blessed Sacrament in procession from the royal chapel. The rest bore sacred relics on biers, crucifixes, and gilded pictures or sculptures of Hungarian saints. Flowers littered the ground before the noble youths as they proceeded in great reverence to their destination, the Church of the Holy Virgin Margit.

At the forefront of the squires, Vlad kept his gaze on the church door. Except for when he met Fruzhin's open-mouthed visage.

They came together during the night banquet, seated with Fruzhin's Serbian family in the crowded reception hall. Outside the windows, the heavens thundered.

"Why didn't you warn me about your conversion, Vlad?" Fruzhin asked. "I can't say I'm surprised, as some men do become Catholics while serving our king."

"He didn't inspire me. Rather, my father's unfortunate actions did."

Vlad spoke of the intercepted missive from Mircea the Great to the Catholic monarch of Poland, seated with Zsigmond. Their champions would face each other in the joust.

"I pledged myself to Catholicism and put aside the Eastern Orthodox faith. At home, the ruling prince does what he thinks is best for him and I must do the same, aligning myself with our king's interests and proving myself far worthier of his trust than my opportunistic parent. I pray you won't revile me or believe I'm some sycophant. My adherence is real. Do you think the choice is poorly motivated?"

"No. It's a momentous change, and Zsigmond must have accepted it as a true sign of commitment. However, there are other consequences. One day, you may go home and visit your family and people. Will they accept a Catholic prince among them? What about your father? How might he have explained his choice to seek a new alliance with Poland? Didn't he, as a parent, deserve to be heard by our king and you before you converted?"

Stefan and Radič's boisterous laughter prevented further conversation.

"The perfidious bastards! I care not if the warring Ottoman princes kill each other." Stefan set down his wine chalice. Some liquid sloshed over the rim. "Mûsâ Çelebi thought the threat of an Ottoman army at my gates would keep me acquiescent to his demands, for fear his men might overrun Serbia. He never imagined, after sharing his battle plans with me, I'd switch sides and ally with his brother. Soon, he'll learn about the expansion of the Hungarian army and my plans with Zsigmond to eliminate the Turkic threat."

For Vlad, the revelation meant his sister Arina's Turkish husband must rely more on the troops Mircea the Great gave him. Would Stefan's abandonment of Mûsâ Çelebi put Arina's life in greater danger, as her spouse continued fighting his brothers with diminished forces?

"You should not have done it." Beside Stefan, his sister Milena Olivera sat with whitened knuckles, gripping a cup she did not lift. "It was not prudent."

"You accuse me unjustly of having an imprudent mind."

"I never speak without forethought. You've betrayed Mûsâ Çelebi. Your defection from one brother to another caused trouble within our family and among our nobles, who plotted your overthrow last year, rather than risk their futures with a wrathful Turk."

"We discovered the Serbian traitors and finally put down their rebellion in the spring."

"What enmity remains among our countrymen because of your hasty action? You consider Muslims the devil's spawn, but their belief in God is as real as ours. I know what Mûsâ Çelebi's like, better than you ever could. How will our people survive his vengeance?"

"I swear, I'll protect them, sweet sister."

"As you once pledged your troops to Mûsâ Çelebi to stave off our destruction? I daresay, what are our oaths as Christians if we can cast them aside so easily?"

"The Church absolves oaths made under duress." He tugged her hand.

She pulled away. "That doesn't make it right in the eyes of God, Stefan."

He sighed and took up his wine, which he downed before he set the empty chalice aside and reached for his sister's fingers again.

"The noblemen of Serbia, afraid for their futures and families, once asked our father whom he would support. Their words were, 'which realm will you choose—the Ottoman Turks or the Hungarian Catholics?' Our father made his choice and died for it. I've made my decision. I think you've done the same because you are here with me. Not with your daughters and the other children of your former husband."

Milena Olivera did not answer. Nor did she shrug off Stefan's hold.

Vlad pondered Stefan's mention of his sister's children. Why were they of any consequence in a conversation about the damnable Turks?

After Fruzhin parted with his family and Vlad said farewell, the pair hastened to the great keep in drizzling rain. Once indoors, Vlad could no longer contain his curiosity.

"Your uncle holds your aunt in great esteem."

"Yes. Even if he behaves in ways with which she does not always agree."

"Why did she speak of Mûsâ Çelebi in such familiar terms? She said she knew the nature of my sister's husband better than Stefan did. But how could that be?"

"I know little about my aunt's earlier life," Fruzhin admitted. "We've grown closer over the last nine years. For more than a decade before, she lived among the Ottoman Turks, in the palace of their former ruler. As his wife. Mûsâ Çelebi is her stepson by the marriage."

Shocked, Vlad stopped in the shadow of István's Tower. Fruzhin went on a few paces unawares before he looked aside and then over his shoulder.

"Among all the things you've said about your Serbian family, that should have been first." Vlad gaped at him. "You knew my fears for Arina at Mûsâ Çelebi's side."

"I didn't wish to compound them with my limited knowledge. My aunt doesn't speak to me about her time among the Turks," Fruzhin said. "But when I wrote to her and revealed your sister's marriage and your concerns about her future, Milena Olivera insisted on accompanying Stefan here. As we left the dining chamber, she whispered to me, she wants to talk with you in private during the days of the tournament."

CHAPTER 10

The Esther of Her People

"What is better than wisdom? Woman. And what is better than a good woman? Nothing."-Geoffrey Chaucer (circa 1340s-1400 AD), English poet and author.

IN THE YEAR OF OUR Lord 1412. Buda, Hungary (modern-day Budapest, Hungary)

"Have you forgotten how to fasten a breastplate, runt?"

"No, my lord Stibor. I've done so many times in your service."

"Did some whore sap your strength after the night banquet?"

"No, my lord. Yesterday, once Corpus Christi ended, I slept in the great keep."

"Then you should be more than capable of doing your duty now."

However, try as Vlad might, he could not draw the leather straps closer together, so the plates of armor overlapped. Any gaps would see Stibor unprotected in the joust. Even the soft, hollow balsa wood of blunted jousting lances could cause harm. Shattered slivers became projectiles often enough.

"Come on, runt," Stibor urged. "I'm due in the lists in less than an hour."

"I'm nearly finished, my lord." Vlad crouched and swiped at the beads of sweat on his forehead. The damnable day proved too hot. The midmorning sun's rays had already penetrated the linen tent. Why couldn't he be anywhere else?

Half asleep, half awake, his night had passed in dreams and thoughts occupied by his sibling Arina. He could not forget she faced the same fate Fruzhin's aunt once did, alone.

Frustrated, he gave up the effort with Stibor. "My lord, this new aketon meant to protect your chest may be padded too thick to secure the armor over it."

"Or you've grown fat with old age, my friend."

Vlad and Stibor turned as one to the opened tent flap. There stood the darkest-skinned man Vlad had ever seen, his complexion deeper than that of the southern Italian courtiers. Clad entirely in black armor, the same hue as the short curls nestled atop his head, he spoke unaccented Polish.

"Too much rich food consumed at Zsigmond's table?"

Stibor shooed Vlad away and crossed the tent. He enveloped the shorter, younger man in an enormous bear hug.

"I recall you sharing some of those meals right alongside me, Black Knight. Though not so much of late, since your sovereign and mine have quarreled," Stibor said.

"May peace prevail between King Władysław and your Zsigmond, for more than their sake. You and I must ensure the royal summit ends in a peace treaty, so we can always meet as friends."

The two companions of old drew back, regarded each other, and embraced again before Stibor summoned Vlad.

"Here's my new squire, Prince Vlad of Wallachia. Even smaller than you!" He thumped a fist against his friend's shoulder. "Runt, meet Zawisza Czarny, the so-called Black Knight of Poland. A favored champion who's won every tournament in which he's ever competed. Although these days when Zawisza is on horseback, he travels from nation to nation as a diplomat for his ruler Władysław, for whom he negotiated the most recent peace terms between Poland, Lithuania, and the Teutonic Knights."

"But I'm here primarily for this week's tournament."

"It is my honor, my lord Zawisza, to greet you." Vlad bowed.

Once he straightened and lifted his gaze, the Black Knight chuckled and elbowed Stibor. The latter nodded. His friend grabbed Vlad, hauling him up by the collar of his robe.

"You're Prince Mircea's boy?" When Vlad said yes, he gave an even heartier laugh. "You have the look of him. If Stibor chose you for a squire, I can trust your father's fighting spirit endures inside you."

All his life, Vlad had heard of little else but Mircea the Great's victories against Christendom's enemies. Hard to rely on history, given Prince Mircea's subsequent embroilment in Turkish affairs. Zsigmond must have revealed to Stibor the treacherous letter from Wallachia. Even if their king kept the matter private while pursuing peace with Poland, he held Vlad's father in disfavor. Neither he nor his boyars attended the royal summit. Bitterness ruled Vlad, who refused to think or speak of his parent.

Zawisza let him go. Still, he studied the man's swarthy complexion. The deep lines carved crags as if etched in stone. Obsidian eyes bulged beneath a heavy brow ridge.

"You'd like to ask me a question," Zawisza observed.

"Forgive me, please." Vlad's stare fell away. "I wouldn't want to offend."

"An intriguing start to your inquiry," Zawisza replied. "Ask what you will. I'm not in the habit of pummeling squires, even for staring with outright impudence."

"I know what he wants to hear." Stibor winked and clasped Zawisza's shoulder.

"Well, I wondered...." Vlad swallowed. "Do you have Moorish blood, my lord? Again, I mean no offense to suggest a Christian knight resembles any heathen Moor, but your countenance favors the descriptions I've read about them."

Stibor and Zawisza looked at each other and guffawed.

"I told you in my last letter, he would ask upon first sight of you," Stibor said. "He thinks you're another Saint Maurice come to life. The runt enjoys reading almost as much as swordplay. Too much imagination."

"There is no such thing. He has the makings of a virtuous knight, who must be fierce in battle, but also well-educated." Zawisza admitted, "You were right about him. I owe you one gold florin, my friend."

He addressed Vlad next. "It's not the first time anyone has questioned me so. I don't take offense easily. My parents lived in Poland, where my father descends from a local noble family at least two generations old. If any had a Moorish heritage, I would not know."

"But how did you gain the sobriquet of the Black Knight?"

"Zawisza's indulged your curiosity long enough, runt. Fetch my old aketon from my son's tent," Stibor ordered. "He isn't jousting today, so I won't need his loaner after all."

"I haven't seen your namesake in years, but I imagine he looks like you."

Vlad left while the gruff exchange continued at the tent's opening.

"He's inherited my height, strength, and love of whores!" The pair laughed. "Did you bring your sons?"

"All four. They wanted to meet the giant Stibor. Who do you face in the lists?"

"That cow-faced Habsburg idiot called the Iron Duke is first. Ernest brought the betrothed of Zsigmond's daughter with him. Albrecht. Another sallow-looking wretch, like soured milk, with drooping lips and a long nose."

The tent of Stibor's namesake lay pitched halfway across the camp. To reach it, Vlad tramped through muddied earth among knights, their squires, and pageboys, all of whom spoke in a variety of tongues. Unlike those others, he could not understand the envoys of the Mongols' Golden Horde. They pestered King Władysław's majordomo outside the Polish royal tent until he scowled and waved them off. What did the Mongol khan want?

Vlad also spotted Fruzhin's family gathered around Vlad's former brother by marriage, Radič in silver and gold plate armor. Stefan stood between his siblings Milena Olivera, and the newly arrived Jelena. As Vlad bypassed them, he shared a nod with Stefan. Milena Olivera gave him a lingering look before her equally lovely sister drew her aside.

Despite the urgent errand, Vlad's mind loitered on Fruzhin's youngest aunt. When would he talk to Milena Olivera? If she knew the sort of man their father forced on Vlad's sister, might the Serbian princess also tell him anything about Arina's likely circumstances? Could he reach his sibling through Milena Olivera's good graces?

Even after several years, the woman must have some connection to her former life. Would she be willing to revisit the past for him?

KINGS ZSIGMOND AND Władysław intended the tournament to last all week. When the final victor emerged, a knight who supported either ruler would receive the title of tournament champion and a white horse bedecked in a golden bridle. Stibor fought in the lists before midday and dueled each afternoon. He emerged victorious, even against knights half his age. Two of his slated competitors, rather than complete any of the three courses required by jousting rules, withdrew.

Once Vlad finished his duties to the Hungarian king in the morning, he attended Stibor, who held him responsible for the maintenance of the sword, shield, and lances. After the jousts, Vlad visited the armorer, who checked for any defects in the weaponry.

Most late afternoons, when spectators abandoned the tournament grounds, found Vlad in Stibor's tent polishing plate armor until his thin, ruddy face with its heavy black brows and large, aquiline nose reflected in the steel. Often, he thought himself a miserable sight. How could he be truly happy while concerns for Arina haunted him?

This evening he stared at his visage for so long, he did not hear the royal pageboy who pecked at his sleeve to deliver a summons to the impending feast. Startled, he drew the sword on the frightened youngster, who fled before Vlad could think to apologize.

He arrived late to the dining hall, beeswax candles scenting the air. He drew quizzical glances from Fruzhin and Stefan, but not the person whom he sought.

Milena Olivera remained absent. She preferred eating with her sister's new family and retainers since their late arrival. Had she forgotten about her request to speak with him? Disappointed, he sank beside Fruzhin, who was talking with Stefan and Radič.

"Tomorrow is the last day of the contests," Radič commented, "where all the winners at the end of each day face off in the tourney. Whom do any of you favor as the final victor and his king's champion?"

"I've bet five hundred florins on Stibor," Stefan said. "None can best him."

"An unfortunate wager, uncle," Fruzhin replied. "Many believe the Black Knight Zawisza will be champion, as in the past."

"Zawisza?" Stefan snorted. "He hasn't competed in the last three years at least. One year, he left the Teutonic Knights, who called him a brother. He fought against them on Poland's behalf in the next, and last year, spent weeks negotiating terms between his country and the same knights."

"You've been seated with Zsigmond under his pavilion, where the courtiers extol Stibor's skills. In the spectator stands, a much younger Zawisza rules hearts and minds."

"So, you've bet against a friend, nephew? I thought you liked Stibor."

"I tolerate the man because...well, for reasons you already know. I've laid no wager, uncle. You saw what the Bulgarian campaign cost me, and no, again, I'll take no loan or gift of monies from you. I have what I need. I don't want any excess, simply to guess at the tournament champion. But mark me, Zawisza will win."

"Humph. What do you think, Radič?"

"That I stood no chance against either man in the competition, as proved by my being unhorsed yesterday. It was wise to lay a wager on Stibor with the Polish knights who accompanied King Władysław and on Zawisza, among Zsigmond's retinue."

Fruzhin and his uncle laughed at Radič's strategy of a second bet hedged against his first. However, Vlad stared into his chalice, still filled with wine. Even in the candlelit room filled with people, seated among those he admired, he never felt more desolate. How could he join their talk of sport with his sister trapped by Christendom's enemy?

Fruzhin's tug on his arm drew him from reverie. He looked up to find three expectant gazes on him.

"My uncle asked whom do you favor to win?"

"Stibor, of course," he murmured. However, like his best friend, he made no wager.

The competition, unlike anything he witnessed two years ago at the last royal tournament on Csepel Island, featured fifteen combatants each on the Hungarian and Polish side. The knights mounted up in opposing positions across the grassy field, grown lush after recent rainfall. A herald emphasized the last two rules.

Although a tourney, there would be no payment of ransoms or surrender of horses to those who bore them to the ground. The fighting would cease when the last knight remained atop his horse.

Standing with other Hungarian squires at the edge of a muddied area, Vlad's heart fluttered like the birds in Zsigmond's mews whenever Stibor charged alongside the other knights. First with the blunted lances, which cleared half the combatants among the Poles, and again, with upraised swords. Clumps of grass and curses flew.

The rest of King Władysław's warriors fought on and took down ten of Zsigmond's knights. Afterward, each man scrambled across slogged earth away from thunderous hooves before the next charge. Soon five Hungarians remained to face eight opponents.

Vlad lost sight of Stibor, surrounded by three Teutonic Knights. They wanted his chance at winning ruined. Even with the unfair odds of three against one, Stibor held out. He hammered one adversary's head with his pommel so hard; the man cried out.

Jousting saddles were fashioned higher at the rump to keep riders secure. He must have injured his back. He slid down from the mount and lost his great helm. Two squires, who surely had heard the rules as Vlad did, skidded across the field. Their white tunics bore the black cross emblazoned on all the attire of the Teutonic Order. They dragged the fallen man away together by his feet. Not before a hoof kicked him square in the jaw.

Stibor's remaining attackers would not give up, slashing and hammering him with powerful blows. Around them, the tourney devolved into frenzied fighting. Vlad turned to his king's pavilion, built of wood with a painted leather canopy for shelter. Zsigmond leaned forward in his chair and gripped the cushioned armrest.

Stefan rose out of his seat, screaming curses at the top of his lungs, which made several ladies blush. Except for Borbála, who also stood, gripping the post next to the stairs. Her gaze rapt, she smiled.

Collective groans filled the royal pavilion, and Vlad peered at Stibor again, who slipped from his horse. By the rules of the joust, he would yield, and the Teutonic Knights must accept his surrender. However, both men dismounted with swords held aloft.

Stefan swung to his king. "Tell them to stop! This isn't allowed."

The knights advanced on Stibor. Zsigmond and his royal counterpart stood at the same time under opposing pavilions and demanded an end to the fighting. Most combatants rode their horses from the grassy area or limped away.

Across the field, Stibor's opponents ignored the dual commands and swung at him. He blocked them with his blade and shield.

"Whoresons! I'll teach you to attack a lone knight on his back." At the furthest edge of the tourney from Stibor, near Vlad, his friend Zawisza lowered his visor and charged.

One villain stabbed downward. Stibor rolled away. The other man found the undersides of Stibor's padded thighs and dug his sword into one leg, then the other. He twisted the blade both times.

Stibor's howl of fury sent a chill up Vlad's spine. The rules allowed only mounted participants on the field for everyone's safety. Yet, resolve settled in his heart.

He pelted across the ground in Zawisza's wake. Zawisza leaped down from his horse and engaged the closest combatant, a fellow member of the Polish side. The remaining warrior thrust at Stibor's helmet, trying to pierce the visor.

Boot heels slipping and squelching, Vlad barreled into the Teutonic knight. Although he met full resistance from plate armor, his action caused surprise. Long enough for him to find an abandoned sword. He readied to defend himself and Stibor, whose battered shield he wrested away.

"A little squire dares interfere," the knight muttered. "Stibor's king betrayed us in our war with Poland, but my Order will have vengeance. Your death will do for now."

Vlad safeguarded himself and Stibor while their assailant bore down on him, striking hard against the shield he raised. There was no time to consider the stupidity of running in garments with light padding underneath into a contest against a fully armored man.

Swift slashes to his upper arm and hip ripped through his clothes. Flesh stung and warned him of bleeding. He shook off the dizzying sensation. He must survive long enough and perhaps a chance would come to wound his foe. It never did.

He faltered and slid in the slick gore of Stibor's blood seeping into the grass. Although he regained his footing, the enemy knight laughed and raised the blade.

"I promised no mercy for you, stupid squire—"

"He doesn't need it, not when I'll kill you before you can slaughter him!" Zawisza slashed at the man's side and gained his full attention.

Vlad backed away and almost tumbled over Stibor before sucking in a harsh breath and sagging next to him on the damp ground. Its loamy odor invaded his nostrils.

"Runt. That was the most foolish and... courageous thing...I've ever seen you do." Stibor yanked off his helmet and revealed his bruised nose and temples. His hands still covered in gauntlets, he reached for Vlad's cheek. "By God. If the so-called Mircea the Great could see you now, he would know his prowess in battle alone has not earned him the epithet. It's also well-deserved for the fine warrior son he has raised."

"Let me help you, my lord," Vlad wheezed. His chest burned worse than the cuts to his limb and side.

"You can't do it alone, boy!" Stibor's son, nimble for such a large man, skittered beside them. "No matter how many Teutonic Knights you thought you could face by yourself. Come, Father, we'll take you to the surgeon. Our king summoned him."

Though Vlad grunted beneath the weight, he aided Stibor's removal.

"Get him into my tent, now!" Zsigmond commanded.

HOURS LATER, ON HIS back with wounds sewn closed, Vlad tried to rise in the medical tent. Fruzhin and his uncle arrived and forestalled his vain effort. An odd, purple bruise discolored the lower left side of Stefan's face.

"Pipó won't believe this story if I tell it after we arrive in Italy," Fruzhin exclaimed. "So, you must share the full details, Vlad. Everyone's talking about you."

"How foolish I was?" He groaned.

"Not your folly alone," Stefan said. "Your valor too. The Teutonic Knights violated the rules and paid with their lives. Rest. I've sent a servant to fetch Radič and your uncle."

"Staico? What happened? Why's he with Radič?"

"Your uncle heard about your injuries while the surgeon tended to Stibor," Fruzhin replied. "Staico came to the tourney grounds, a sword and loaded crossbow in hand. He bayed for the blood of that treacherous Teutonic knight. I could barely restrain Staico; much less get him to see the devil already lay dead at Zawisza's feet."

"Remind me never to stand in your uncle's way." Stefan chuckled. "I met him outside the medical tent and tried to hold him back, as Fruzhin did on the field. Told him you would be well. In need of a few stitches." Stefan fingered his battered cheek. "Hurts. Staico hits harder than Stibor's morning star. Prince Mircea's hot blood runs in his son and half-brother. Radič took your uncle away after I swore to send word again."

"I'm sorry. He's protective of me."

Stefan gripped Fruzhin's shoulder. "I understand."

"But what of Stibor?" Vlad asked. "Has our king's surgeon finished with him?"

"He's sorry the Black Knight, unaided, killed his attackers." Fruzhin shrugged.

"It's a little more serious than my nephew suggests." Stefan removed his hand only to smack Fruzhin hard in the back of his head. "The blade dug into flesh and bone. Stibor bled so much; he looked paler than any of those Habsburg wretches do. But he'll live, much to Fruzhin's chagrin."

"For shame, uncle! I've never wished for Stibor's death." Fruzhin massaged his nape. "After this brush with it, I pray God will temper his lusts for blood and women."

"Before your uncle comes, Vlad, another person wants to see you." Stefan called out. "Milena Olivera, come here!"

Yellow silk shimmered in torchlight at the open tent flap before she entered.

"I was right there, dear brother. You didn't need to shout." She joined them; her gaze locked on Vlad. "Will you speak with me alone, prince?"

He swallowed. Why did she choose this time to seek him?

"Sister," Stefan warned. "What will the gossips say about you and the prince in a tent?"

"Little, if you'll wait outside with Fruzhin."

Uncle and nephew bowed before they withdrew.

Milena Olivera hovered next to Vlad. "I saw you on the tourney grounds. How you rescued Stibor. You're much foolhardier than my nephew thinks."

"I'm sure Fruzhin's since revised his opinion of me downward."

"Impulsive people often die by their folly. Or, if they live long enough, they show the world something unexpected. When my father died, the Turks proposed terms for our surrender to my mother. I suggested a final proof of our commitment. My union with Bāyazīd Hân."

"Who?"

"The last imperial Ottoman ruler. His name was Bāyazīd. The title Hân follows the personal names of all Turkic sultans. His people called him *Yildirim*, or 'thunderbolt' in their language. Like you, on the field here, I once thought I must do something bold; by contracting a marriage with him, if those whom I loved would survive."

"Did your marital union help them?"

"In a certain way. Stefan escorted me to the Ottoman encampment. Bāyazīd accepted me and I married the man who had decreed my father's beheading."

Vlad gaped at her. Silence swelled between them.

"I knew he gave the order without being told," she resumed. "He never apologized or begged my forgiveness. After the wedding ceremony, once Stefan and Bāyazīd's chief minister signed the nuptial agreement, my new husband promised he would not intrude on my life or touch me unless I wished it. His chamberlain threatened otherwise; warned Stefan, and our people would suffer if I withheld myself."

She sank beside Vlad on the ground and drew up her knees like a young girl, covering the silk dress with her mantle.

"A year later, Bāyazīd feted my brother and invited me to dine with them. After Stefan left the palace in Būrsâ, I remained in Bāyazīd's chamber. I let him do to me, as husbands will. I hated him but never resisted. He grew to love me. As much as a man with other wives and many concubines can. He called me Despina Hatun; the former for my status as a sister of the *Despoteses*, the latter being the courtesy title all Ottoman women bear."

She picked at the mantle's golden tassels on its fringe with a wistful gaze.

"I didn't comprehend his heart until our three daughters arrived. A son followed, but he lived less than a fortnight. When I woke beside his cradle, the blanket lay over his face, which had turned blue in death. Bāyazīd said he must have tugged it in the night, and his breathing stopped. I knew one of the other wives ordered our child's life snuffed out. Bāyazīd comforted me and I did the same for him because by then, I loved him dearly."

"You fell in love with the man who killed your father?" Incredulous, Vlad looked away. Could Arina succumb to such emotion? For love, would she refuse his help in the end?

"You wonder how it's possible. How could hearts bridge the divide between a cherished daughter and her father's murderer? One a Christian and the other, the Turkic conqueror of her people. Like the

Jewess Esther, such are the lives of peace-weavers. The women who wed their nation's enemies after men's wars have ravaged the land."

He swallowed and turned his head on the pillow again. Their gazes met. Like her, his sibling entered a union for the benefit of the Turkish and Wallachian peoples. Arina despaired of it at first. What might have occurred between her and her husband since?

"You don't hide thoughts or emotions as well as you might like, prince. You ponder whether your sister, also a peace-weaver, could achieve the same happiness I did."

"Mûsâ Çelebi's her enemy!" Vlad insisted.

"Is he?" Milena Olivera cocked her head. "How do you know?"

"Because he's a Turk!" Try as he might, he sounded like a petulant child.

"Mûsâ Çelebi may sire children with your sibling. Bāyazīd bound my heart with our lovely, black-haired brood. Your sister has even less reason than me to despise the prince she wed. Tell me about her."

Awash in memories, he described Arina's features and personality.

"Her husband could have no appreciation of such qualities," he concluded.

"Mûsâ Çelebi grew up surrounded by beauty in the harem. That's where a Turkish family lives; mothers, daughters, and sisters before they wed, and young males until their ages merit households of their own. As a little boy, Mûsâ Çelebi liked to laugh and sit in Bāyazīd's lap while his father told stories of the dynasty's progenitors; Süleyman Shah, his son Ertuğrul Bey, and his grandson, Osman Bey. The conquerors of Anatolia."

"I saw Mûsâ Çelebi in the days before he married my sister. He did not have a kind look about him. Is he trying to emulate his warrior ancestors?"

"Losses made him bitter. His laughter and smiles died the same day Mûsâ Çelebi's mother did. I helped raise him afterward. When he came to manhood and received the first slave girls of his harem, he favored a red-haired Albanian. He will enjoy your sister."

Vlad pounded the thin mattress on which he rested with his fists.

"Don't agitate him, Milena Olivera," Stefan said over his shoulder outside the tent.

"It's impolite to listen to other people's conversations," she snapped before she sighed and wiped her brow. "What if you discovered she is happy in Anatolia?"

"She cannot be content at the side of an evil Turk."

"He's neither evil nor good. In life, there is more than light and dark, love and hate. An arranged marriage does not always result in unhappiness, nor is any union born of passion certain to weather time. Do you want your sister to know joy again?"

"Of course! From childhood, her sadness pained me more than my own." He rolled and regretted it in the next breath. A searing pain coursed along the stitches in his hip. "How can I find out where she is? Where does the sultan live?"

"Like my Bāyazīd before him, Mûsâ Çelebi would live at Būrsâ Palace."

Relief flooded Vlad. Milena Olivera proved more helpful than he had hoped.

"Are your daughters in the palace, too? Could they reach Arina?"

Milena Olivera lowered her gaze. He admired her thick tresses spilling over bountiful breasts. No wonder the old Ottoman sultan adored this glorious goddess.

Then he realized how her shoulders quivered. Had he asked too much? Was the talk about her daughters painful? She must have left them with their father's family.

"Forgive me, please," Vlad pleaded. "Your children remain in Turkic lands?"

She shook her head. "I lost my husband at the Battle of Ankara ten years ago. The vicious Mongol Temur Leng took my Bāyazīd captive. Me too. He came for our daughters next. We survived, but my beloved, their father, did not. Temur Leng's dead too, the savage! Before God struck him down, he had married my three children off to a Turk loyal to him, a Persian, and a general of his army. My daughters are not at Būrsâ Palace."

He cursed under his breath and then apologized in haste.

"I'm older than you, remember? I've heard worse. Perhaps said it." Milena Olivera raised her face and wiped her tear-stained cheeks.

"Could you write Mûsâ Çelebi on my behalf? He must understand my worry."

"Your sister is a foreigner. She will have little privacy. No loyalty from palace servants. No letter shall enter her chamber without scrutiny. The former Despina Hatun, if she remained in Ottoman lands, could send such a missive, and expect it might be well-received. But a Serbian princess, whose brother ransomed her from Temur Leng nine years ago? Mûsâ Çelebi would disregard her words. His people blamed me for the Ankara disaster. Said I bewitched his father Bāyazīd and drove him to drink."

Vlad shook his head. Did no hope remain?

"Still, I shall contact each of my daughters. They may have ties to our former servants."

"Thank you, Milena Olivera. May I beg another boon? Whatever you discover; good or bad, promise you will not hide it from me."

Later, he saw his uncle, but omitted the earlier conversation with the Serbian princess. Staico would only chide his inquiry. He also begged Fruzhin to ask Zsigmond if he could see Stibor on the morrow.

The summons to their king's tent came the next evening. Vlad's uncle returned and helped him wash and dress. The injuries caused lingering aches. With Staico at his back, he entered the royal tent. Inside, he found Zsigmond beside Stibor, resting on a pallet. Stefan, Fruzhin, and Zawisza also stood there.

"Come to Us," Zsigmond intoned, his Bible in hand. "Your uncle may join the others."

Vlad peeked at Stefan. Did he reveal how he came by the dark bruise on his face to their king? Wary of the royal wrath, Vlad approached and bowed with a grunt.

"Kneel," his sovereign commanded, "And swear fealty to your God and king."

An oath of loyalty, as those on the verge of knighthood swore. Could it be...?

His king peered down at him. "Speak the words," Zsigmond said.

Although bewildered, Vlad cleared his throat and placed his hand on Zsigmond's Bible. "I promise to serve God, and my king in valor and faith." He peered up at his uncle, who smiled and nodded. "To defend the Cross of Christ against the perfidious enemy Turks and all ungodly pagans and serve the holy religion of Christian faith until death claims me."

Fruzhin poured a small measure of oil from a gilded cup over Vlad's head. Their king gave the Bible to Fruzhin, drew a sword, and tapped Vlad's shoulders.

"Arise, good and faithful prince, an anointed knight of the Kingdom of Hungary. Go forth and be brave and bold as when you served Us while saving the life of Our dear friend. Such an achievement deserves no less than a knighthood."

His heart full to bursting at the honor, Vlad rose on shaky legs. His uncle and Fruzhin hugged him and kissed his cheeks. Stefan and Zawisza congratulated him.

Stibor yanked him down. The pair embraced for the first time. Several agonized breaths issued from both men before they drew apart.

"An anointed knight," Stibor repeated. "God bless you." His gray eyes shone like steel.

Of all those gathered around him, even his uncle, Fruzhin, and their king, that final approval from Stibor meant the most to Vlad.

CHAPTER 11

Wreathed in Flame

"In each fire there is a spirit; Each one is wrapped in what is burning him."-Dante (circa 1265-1321 AD), Italian poet, writer, and philosopher.

IN THE YEAR OF OUR Lord 1412. Buda, Hungary (modern-day Budapest, Hungary)

Autumnal breezes swept through the palatial courtyard. Dry leaves showered Vlad's cloak while he sat under the lone tree after dawn. Hours of fitful sleep earlier drove him from the great keep of István's Tower, where he spread the cloak on the dew-covered grass.

A few men-at-arms shuffled around, but none acknowledged him. One stray dog edged closer and sniffled his hand. Vlad smiled and beckoned it closer for a petting. The wary animal fled. Vlad closed his eyes and leaned back against the bark, digging at his scalp. After today, there would be few comforts except a warm fire at night.

Once morning mass concluded, he would depart with Zsigmond's army for Friuli, one of many ecclesiastical states encompassing the Holy Roman Empire. The Doge Michele Steno of Venice wanted the area under his control. As the newly elected king of Germany, Zsigmond would vigorously defend Friuli at the behest of his half-blood brother

King Wenceslaus. The deposed German king and former head of the empire.

No blood bond strengthened the relations between the siblings. Nor could Wenceslaus hold the hope of regaining the lands lost to him twelve years past. If Vlad guessed right, since Zsigmond would inherit his brother's power, he would try to prove himself the better man to the pope, the only person who could appoint him as Holy Roman Emperor.

Vlad could only guess at his king's other ambitions but might never have expected how much they cost Hungary. At the end of the conclave with Poland, Zsigmond formally admitted Vlad to his company of household knights, but not before the chancellor's aide made an error and brought Vlad royal correspondence outside their king's bedchamber.

He shouldn't have looked at any of it; for on the previous night, Stibor made the purpose of Zsigmond's summons the next morning clear. A new squire would take over Vlad's previous duties.

However, one word at the top of the first parchment drew his attention. The reference to a loan. As part of the peace treaty Stibor and Zawisza negotiated on behalf of their masters, Zsigmond pledged sixteen Hungarian settlements and castles to Poland's king in exchange for the grant of monies to fund the war in Friuli. More letters detailed currency devaluation, church taxation, and an increase in the duties collected from foreign merchants.

Then, there were requests to settle outstanding royal debts; the costs of the royal retinue's travels during the Bosnian campaign, and the mercenaries he employed there. Another petition asked for repayment of two thousand florins a widow gave their king while on his way to the Battle of Nicopolis, which occurred sixteen years ago.

Since the discovery of such monetary burdens, Vlad reassessed everything he knew about his sovereign, including his dual nature. A womanizer and a devoted father. A warmonger who prayed each day at Catholic mass for peace throughout the world. A spendthrift with clear financial difficulties, who enjoyed the loyalty and support of the people he unduly taxed.

The riddle of Zsigmond bedeviled Vlad, but he knew one thing: his king's every action required further scrutiny. Whatever the motives, the outcomes did not always suit the needs of the nation or those who favored Zsigmond.

"Some concern made you restless in the night?" Fruzhin yawned and wrapped his velvety black mantle around him while he rose beside Vlad. "You tossed and turned as if bad dreams afflicted you."

"I hope I didn't keep you awake too long," Vlad replied.

"In time I drifted, although you were not asleep by then. What ails you?"

Vlad dared not admit the truth, knowing Fruzhin's devotion to their king.

"Do you think your aunt Milena Olivera will hear from any of her daughters while we are in Italy?" Vlad asked instead. "It's been three months since she wrote them."

"You know everything takes time. Word will come to her, and she'll send a herald at once." Fruzhin clapped his shoulder. "Try not to die in battle before then."

"I won't." Vlad laughed. "Not when you've extolled the delights of Italy's courtesans."

"I vow they are the most beautiful, sensuous women in the world! You'll enjoy them."

More activity stirred in the courtyard. A Styrian squire of their king's chamber, whom Vlad had long disliked, stumbled out of the great keep. The fool hopped on one leg while shoving his foot into a shoe without unlacing it. When he fell, in his hasty carelessness, the men-at-arms, Vlad and Fruzhin, laughed at him. He got to his feet and scampered away. Vlad stared in the direction he'd gone long after his disappearance.

"Don't be jealous. You've earned a knighthood and a permanent place at Zsigmond's side if you choose," Fruzhin said.

"Jealous?" Vlad snorted. "Of that preening pig? I am a knight. He is not. Besides, he always made faces at me behind our king while I read for him."

"What? You should've told Zsigmond. He doesn't tolerate childish insolence."

"It no longer matters." Vlad got to his feet, took up his cloak, and with a grin, tugged Fruzhin along and teased him. "Come on, old man. Are your saddlebags packed?"

"I finished the task before coming out here. Let's eat. I'm starving. We won't have our familiar fare while on the road to Friuli."

"Maybe that's a good thing?" Vlad buffeted his friend's shoulder. Together, they returned to István's Tower.

After a meal, Vlad sought his uncle and the Gypsy twins. Tobar and Yoska washed him in a wooden tub behind the royal stables. Staico waited inside the tent, pitched north of the dunghills. He, along with Fruzhin and Stibor each paid the armorer some money for the plate and chain mail Vlad would wear.

Tobar and Yoska helped him into the armor. When they finished, Staico handed him silver spurs and a helm, both presents from his king.

His hands covered in gauntlets; Vlad patted his uncle's arm. "I'll come back."

"By God's grace." Staico touched the center of the breastplate. "Your heart is true. Be brave and merciful. A good knight vanquishes his foes and protects the innocent."

He turned aside and drew out the folded wolf-skin Vlad wore into Hungary. Wrapped inside the pelt was another royal gift. His new sword was set in a belted, red leather scabbard. The ruby centerpiece of the pommel matched Fruzhin's gift, almost two years past, of the ring worn on Vlad's smallest finger.

"You'll need more than a weapon," Staico said. "The northern Italian mountains may be cold. The wolf's fur will help."

With a smile at Tobar, Vlad took the pelt and sword under his arm before he hesitated.

"What is it, nephew? Are you nervous?"

"No. I don't know how long this campaign will last," Vlad confessed. "Why don't you come with me? You love a good bout, and you and your Gypsies haven't enjoyed one since we arrived in Hungary over two years ago."

"I don't think the choice is yours, whether we can fight in Italy." His uncle gave him a sheepish grin. "Though I do like your reminder. Maybe while you're gone...."

"You won't stir troubles with any Teutonic Knights! Their feud with our king is over." Vlad gave Staico back the animal skin, the sword, the helm, and the spurs. "Wait here."

"But where are you going, nephew?"

"To Zsigmond. I'm part of his household and I've never asked him for anything. I will beg his permission for you and the Gypsies to join us."

"What if his answer is no?"

"We part here as previously intended. My mind won't be at ease while I'm away, left pondering whether the bold request might have gained his approval. I must hurry and catch him before he reaches the chapel."

Vlad moved well in the armor, lighter than he expected, and a credit to great workmanship. Ladies in the courtyard cast him admiring glances while he begged their pardon and weaved a path through clusters of them, gathered to send off their king and his knights. He found Zsigmond near the bottom of the stairs to his chamber. His queen and squires stood beside him.

"Why do you frown so, Borbála? Is this not what you've wished," her husband asked, "for more authority? There is none higher than serving as Our regent."

"But you knew I planned to accompany you on the journey as far south as my dower lands, there to remain until next spring," the queen complained.

"You may do so! Our pronouncement does not interfere with your intent."

The bell had not pealed for mass. Vlad halted in his king's path, away from the steps.

Zsigmond spotted him. "How well you look! Doesn't the armor suit him, Borbála?"

"As you say, Your Royal Majesty." She directed her scowl at Vlad as if he had affected her plans. She should be ecstatic at her appointment as regent, signifying her husband's trust. Praise be, last week she announced Vlad's tutelage would end, given his knighthood.

"Your Royal Majesty, may I beg your favor?" he asked.

"Can't you see he's dressed for mass?" The queen snapped, "Stand aside! You'll have time to make your plea on the way to Friuli."

Accustomed to her rudeness, Vlad would not let it dissuade him.

"Please, Your Royal Majesty. My request cannot wait."

"Borbála, you may go on and We shall join you shortly," their king said.

She huffed and left them, her heels striking the marble floor in angry strides.

"The Lord truly planned to test Us when We wed such a harpy." Zsigmond shook his head and urged Vlad up. "Speak in haste."

After Vlad relayed his request, his sovereign peered down his nose with a frown, mirroring that of his wife.

"We've assembled forty thousand men, with innumerable camp followers certain to join us. You truly believed Our permission was necessary for your uncle and his Gypsies to do the same?"

"I dared not take liberties that my king never granted, Your Royal Majesty," Vlad said.

"You do well to offer the deference owed to a monarch." A smile softened Zsigmond's leathery visage. "You could teach your fickle father about a vassal's courtesy."

Although the mention of his parent made Vlad's heart jolt, his king put a hand on his shoulder and he soon relaxed.

"Walk with Us. You understand you're entirely responsible for the behavior of those you've chosen to accompany you?"

"I do, Your Royal Majesty."

"Good. Have them prepared, for We'll leave immediately. Then attend Catholic mass in the royal chapel where We expect to see you among the congregants."

"As my king commands. Thank you, Your Royal Majesty."

Vlad bowed again and rushed off to his uncle. Afterward, he returned for the rite of mass. At the chapel door, he hesitated, spying Fruzhin ensconced with his aunt and uncle. Stefan folded and crushed a missive in both hands. Milena Olivera touched his arm, pried his fingers open, and smoothed out the paper. Fruzhin whispered in his uncle's ear, but Stefan shook his head and turned away.

A quarrel began, which Vlad could not overhear. He perceived the meaning behind raised voices, wild gesticulations, and the crinkled brow of his closest friend. Although curious, he darted inside his king's chapel.

WHEN THE CATHOLIC MASS concluded and Zsigmond withdrew to his chamber to don attire fit for travel, Vlad sought Fruzhin. A pageboy directed him to the royal garden, where he overheard the feuding family in a grove.

"I owe him nothing!" Stefan shouted. "He's my nephew also, Fruzhin, but he's worse than his father who conspired against me and lost his head for attacking the Turks."

"You cannot ignore this plea, uncle!" Fruzhin clapped his hands atop his head. "Your sisters; my cousin's mother and my other aunts are right. You don't have an heir—"

"I would if you agreed to my wish."

"But I don't want to rule Serbia once you're gone! I love you; I love all my mother's Serbian family, but I will have the lordship of Bulgaria or nothing. Please see reason. After years of strife, my cousin offers reconciliation. He's proven himself a great warrior against the Ottomans, and even you. You can trust him to defend Serbia. Go to him."

"Do you think Zsigmond will allow me to return home after I've already pledged myself his vassal again and vowed to be at his side in warfare?"

"Dearest brother, you know Radič can command your men ably in Friuli while you and I meet our nephew in Belgrade." Milena Olivera stood behind her sibling and massaged his nape. "Our retinue has been already prepared. We'll leave Hungary this afternoon as planned once our king's army withdraws. Please, Stefan, put aside your pride and old enmities. Let there be a new dawn of peace between you and Đurađ Branković."

Vlad turned away, having intruded long enough.

"Who goes there?" Fruzhin's hoarse voice chased him.

He stopped and turned around, stepping into full view from behind the wide tree trunk. With his head bowed, he shuffled on his feet.

"Ah, Vlad! I'm so happy we'll see each other before you leave." Milena Olivera came around her brother and reached for Vlad's hands.

"Forgive me. I didn't mean to interrupt," he murmured.

"Nonsense. You are welcome among us as always, for you've become dear to me, like my brother and nephew here." She tugged him to join them.

They all commented on how well the armor suited him. He could have said the same for Stefan and Fruzhin, but their similar glares at each other warned of lingering resentments needing swift resolution.

Stefan gave over first. He drew Fruzhin close to his chest.

"Forgive me, nephew. I've never doubted your affections or your desire to rule Bulgaria in your father's stead. I have no right to expect you would abandon the aim."

"Your trust and faith in me are great treasures, uncle." Fruzhin pulled back and fingered Stefan's bearded cheek. "I can't set aside my ambition to be a Bulgarian emperor, even to fulfill your wish. Name Đurađ your official heir. If you are to meet with him as he proposes, then you must speak to Zsigmond now."

"Let's go together. We'll find Radič on the way."

"Before you leave...." Milena Olivera gripped Stefan's burly arm and tugged him away. While she whispered in his ear, Vlad and Fruzhin turned their backs and stood aside.

"You overheard enough, so I won't need to explain," Fruzhin said.

Vlad nodded, still ashamed.

"Then you've saved me the trouble." Fruzhin patted his forearm. "I must offer gratitude. Since my aunt revisited her past with you, she's told me more about my Turkic cousins. You've opened a window to her heart, long closed off to me because she feared I wouldn't understand how much she misses her children. I do. I feel the same way about my brother Iskender. Love never dies, Vlad. I thank you for the reminder."

"I've done nothing you couldn't have achieved on your own."

"No, our accord is due to you. You're my greatest friend and a brother in arms. I shall always be yours, even when our king's wars are done."

Afterward, the pair embraced.

"Grant me one boon before we set off on the campaign, Vlad."

"Anything, Fruzhin. You know that already."

"When we reunite with our Pipó in Italy, don't mention your religious conversion."

"Why? He's my friend too and a fellow Catholic."

"I think you know why it is best if fewer people can attest to your conversion."

Stefan and Milena Olivera rejoined them before Vlad could reply. Fruzhin and his uncle went away, while his aunt drew Vlad beneath a tree with cascading autumn leaves.

"I wanted to see you earlier, but Fruzhin said you'd gone to your uncle," she told him.

"Yes, for the armor." Full morning light glinted off the plate covering his chest.

"I've fulfilled my promise." She leaned against the tree. "A letter came late last night after we dined from my youngest daughter Oruz Hatun."

He drew apart from her with a loud gasp. "Word of my sister Arina?"

"It would do no good to show it to you. It's in Turkish. The Transalpine princess lives, but she is not altogether well. She miscarried Mûsâ Çelebi's son in the middle of her first pregnancy this past summer, while Zsigmond's conclave with the Polish king took place."

Vlad's heart seemed to sink into the hollow pit of his stomach. *Dear Rina, I grieve with you and long to comfort you. Will the sweet sound of your voice remain a distant memory?*

"She will recover eventually," Milena Olivera continued. "The loss likely resulted when one of her husband's brothers attacked Būrsâ Palace and almost breached its grounds. Ottoman medicine and midwives are among the best in the world. They can ease the body. Grief is beyond their capabilities. A woman carrying a child cannot bear great shock."

Vlad turned away, reminded of his eldest sister, Anna. The shared heartbreak of his family and her widower Radič at her loss.

"I'm aware of your fear, but don't worry overmuch. If she is otherwise healthy, the princess can try again in a few months." Milena Olivera's rosewater scent drew closer.

"That concern lies at the heart of my worries." He raked a hand through his hair. "My sister is a means to an end for Mûsâ Çelebi. No more, no matter how you try to convince me love can grow between them. If Arina gives him a son, the birth will ensure more Wallachian men fight and die for the prince in battles with his brothers. He will have that child, even if my sister's lifeblood must soak the birthing bed."

"It won't!"

"You didn't know her or Anna. Both frail and small in our childhood, they stayed so."

"Yet, your eldest sister survived to give Radič his son."

"But not the daughter he and Anna wanted. I fear Arina may suffer the same fate."

Milena Olivera shook her head and appeared at a loss to reassure him with more words. She enfolded him in her arms. After a few agonized breaths, he let her hold him.

Within an hour, she and Stefan bid him and Fruzhin goodbye. Her tears trickled. She hugged them with a mother's fervor and kissed their foreheads.

Before he mounted the horse he had recently bought, he looked down the long length of the column. His king and Borbála led them. Staico and the Gypsies brought up the rearguard. Then came the supply wagons. Broad smiles lit Tobar's and Yoska's faces.

IN THE YEAR OF OUR Lord 1412-1413. Friuli, northern Italy (modern-day Friuli Venezia Giulia, Italy)

A month later in October, Zsigmond's army reached Friuli. After a brief exchange with Vlad and Fruzhin, Pipó withdrew into his tent at their king's side to discuss the latest Venetian rout of the Hungarian forces.

Little improved the army's plight, even with the additional fighters. A planned siege of the city of Vicenza, southwest of Friuli, failed within weeks of their arrival.

Stibor, never as agile in the wake of the summer tournament, suffered again. Blows from a mace dented his great helm. Before winter descended in full, their king sent him home to recuperate. With no end to the campaign in sight, the combatants agreed to a five-year term of peace beginning in mid-April 1413.

Friuli remained far from the reach of Venice's doge. After having discovered his king's ambitions, Vlad knew no great man abandoned long-held desires.

IN THE YEAR OF OUR Lord 1413. Buda, Hungary (modern-day Budapest, Hungary)

Vlad returned to Hungary a month later, taking up duties with Stibor's knights, who upgraded the defenses of fifteen among the thirty strongholds he owned. While on the road, the pair discussed Stibor's plans to sponsor an Augustinian chapter house. Despite the comfort offered at each of his castles, at night, he bivouacked under the stars.

"You've changed, my lord," Vlad observed, while he sat before a fire and shared Stibor's wineskin. "You rush hither and thither to your domains as if fearful you won't accomplish your goals. The whores must regret your long absence. This chapter house is a surprise too. If you'll forgive, you've never struck me as a devout man."

Stibor's laughter boomed, stirring some animal in the brush and one of his knights, all of whom snored. The man opened an eye before he rolled away from the fire's glare.

"Perhaps I'm making up for the lapses of youth, runt," Stibor replied. "I feel my age upon me. I've not been the same since last year's summer tournament." He tugged a blanket around his bowed shoulders. "I think I'm dying."

Vlad chuckled but turned away from the truth in the darkening hollows underneath Stibor's eyes. The persistent headache complaints while he hunched in the saddle daily.

"I don't mean to argue, but you're wrong, my lord," Vlad said. One who embraced each day with passion and vigor as his master did would not find an end too soon.

"I've lived a good life," Stibor said. "Sired children. Seen my heir come to manhood and married. Witnessed your attainment of knighthood. What will you do with it?"

"Rise in the ranks of Zsigmond's household, I hope." Vlad drank deeply of the wine and passed the skin before he belched. "Get a command or become castellan of one of the royal fortresses. Maybe even gain as much authority and lands as you have."

"You could. However, I doubt any of it would satisfy you. What do you really want from life? You may confess, for I'll carry your revelation to the grave soon."

Vlad considered what he should say to such a man. He respected this devoted partisan of the Hungarian king, whom Vlad viewed with greater caution these days.

"To know my family is safe," he said, "wherever they may be."

"All of your family?" Stibor arched a shaggy eyebrow. "Three years ago, before your arrival, Zsigmond said your father deemed you the most stubborn of his offspring. 'Unlikely to follow directions as a royal retainer,' he once advised. Our king gleaned from the lack of praise that some strength of spirit must lie within you. He believed adversity would never strike you down in the viper's nest of his court. He admires your perseverance and dedication."

Vlad hesitated, uncertain how to respond, given the late revelation of Prince Mircea's opinion about him. The words shouldn't matter, since Zsigmond disregarded them.

"You've served me dutifully as a squire," Stibor added, "because you hoped to gain knighthood. Why?"

"To gain the support of others and sit on the throne of Wallachia in the place of my eldest brother Mihail," Vlad confessed. "To rule at the side of our father or independently after our father dies."

His master smiled and nodded. "What wouldn't you do to achieve such a goal?"

Stibor's two brothers had joined them for the first half of their journey. The closeness of the trio often made Vlad reflect on why he and Mihail lived at odds.

"You're asking if I could usurp a sibling," he said. "If I held Wallachia; our family, my sister Arina, whom our father traded, would be safe. I can do anything for her."

"If you want to reign, don't hide behind lofty ideals. Don't fear the power you seek. Claim it. Only the strong survive and need not apologize for their strength."

Stibor drained the last of the ale and swiped at his mouth. After a roaring yawn, he stretched out on the fir branches with which his knights covered the cool ground. Early autumn winds descended.

Vlad lay down on his wolf pelt and exhaled. His breath floated in a white wisp.

"And, runt, I meant what I said. I'll take what you've shared with me to the grave."

"Thank you, my lord. Though you won't die."

"Don't blaspheme! Everyone and everything will die. What does not is pure evil, of the devil's making, not God's creation. You know what I mean. I will not say the names."

It would be best not to. The *moroi* and *strigoi* haunted Vlad's homeland, the undead blood-drinkers and shapeshifters who robbed parents of their children in nightmares.

Stibor continued, "Heed my advice. Never tell Zsigmond of your heart's desire. He is our liege and my friend. He can also thwart you if his intent differs from yours."

"Why would it, my lord?" Vlad's heart thrummed. Without his king's influence in Wallachia, he wouldn't succeed.

"At a whim, any monarch can elevate or cast down a man." Stibor wriggled and rolled away on his side. "Don't rely on Zsigmond only. I didn't. Secure a path to the throne."

On winter nights, as Vlad dreamed, a faint voice echoed in his mind. *Find me, free me.*

IN THE YEAR OF OUR Lord 1414. Buda, Hungary (modern-day Budapest, Hungary)

Stibor died in mid-February of the next year. Knights among his retinue, much older than Vlad, sank onto snow-covered castle grounds and wept like children. Although twenty years old, he felt no shame in joining them. He mourned the master who taught him about the joys of life and warfare's brutal nature. Their king sent a decree for Stibor's body to rest in the royal sepulcher. Vlad became part of the honor guard who escorted the coffin.

After the funeral, he rode with Zsigmond's retinue to Buda Castle at the side of Fruzhin and his uncle Stefan. The latter relayed occurrences in the intervening months since their parting, including the Epiphany announcement of Đurađ Branković, as Stefan's official heir. Fruzhin remained quiet. Despite his friend's fixation on ruling Bulgaria, Vlad wondered whether the lordship of Serbia might not have satisfied Fruzhin. Did he regret his choice or resent his cousin Đurađ's appointment, after all?

"You've earned the admiration of Milena Olivera," Stefan said to Vlad. "The bond between siblings is resolute. Mine explained her role in your quest to find your sister."

"Some call it a waste of time," Vlad murmured. "Say it is only a fool's wish."

"Not me. I offered Milena Olivera's hand in union with a Turkish sultan, but I never gave up on her return. Never! Even after the Mongols found her and her children. Love and hope are never folly. Don't let present circumstances dictate or deny your plans."

Once Stefan rode ahead, Vlad questioned Fruzhin's unusual silence.

"Vlad, I should mourn Stibor, but other thoughts occupy me. Iskender now serves as the governor of İzmir, what Christians called Smyrna on the northern Aegean coast. He's devoted himself entirely to the enemy. The sibling I knew has gone forever."

Words of comfort eluded Vlad, for he feared the same would happen with Arina.

"Before Stibor's burial occurred," Fruzhin added, "I also received news from my Bulgarian cousin. We've lost all the territory he and I regained two years ago."

"I'm truly sorry. When will you campaign against the Turks once more?"

"Uncle Stefan and Đurađ have promised to commit Serbian forces. My heart wavers. Iskender would be among my foes. His ships can reach the Bulgarian coast in less than a day. The Ottomans always destroy Christian ruling families from within. No wonder the new sultan named Iskender as governor so soon after Mûsâ Çelebi's death."

Vlad pulled sharply on the reins. His mount gave a furious snort. He calmed it.

"What did you say? My sister's husband, Mûsâ Çelebi, is dead?"

"Yes. Vlad, I thought you knew! I assumed Zsigmond made mention to Stibor."

"If our king did, Stibor never told me. Where's Arina now?"

"I don't know, but once her husband's fate came to light, I wrote to my aunt Milena Olivera on your behalf, seeking information I knew you would want."

"Thank you. I wish you'd sent word to me directly. How long ago did this happen?"

"Six weeks after we came back from Friuli, when you and Stibor left the capital. Mûsâ Çelebi died at the start of July last year, near Sofia within Turkic-controlled Bulgaria. Strangled by the men of his brother, who reigns as sultan. *Sic semper tyrannis.*"

"Yes, 'thus always to tyrants,' indeed," Vlad said, as he looked away and wondered about his sister's life, which drastically altered seven months ago with the loss of a husband.

Fruzhin regained his attention with a hand on his shoulder. "Stefan didn't say. He's perhaps ashamed to admit it, but he and Radič led Serbian troops to support the victor's army. The Turks are too strong, and my uncle couldn't withstand their threats. He did what was necessary for those whom he loves and protects."

"As we all must," Vlad echoed, but his thoughts dwelled on his sister. *Rina, how can I help you in this dire circumstance if you will not reach out?*

Upon arriving in the triangular courtyard beneath the great keep, dusk fell over Buda. Their king and courtiers received the welcome of squires and pageboys, one of whom sought Fruzhin's immediate attention.

Vlad parted from him, eager for the familiar visage of his uncle with whom he shared the fate of Arina's husband. He got no further than the mention of Mûsâ Çelebi's death before Fruzhin raced beyond the stables toward them, shouting Vlad's name.

Staico pushed aside the tent flaps so he and Vlad might emerge. Nearby, the Gypsies observed the scene, Tobar and Yoska standing among their seated relations.

"I'm here," Vlad called. "What is it? Does Zsigmond summon me?"

"No, you have a letter!" Fruzhin stopped and gripped his knees as he gulped air. "From Milena Olivera. A herald brought it earlier this morning; told the pageboy it contained urgent news for Prince Vlad of Wallachia about his sister, Princess Arina."

An instant ache pulsed in the middle of Vlad's forehead. His hands shook.

"When I last saw Fruzhin's aunt," he said, turning aside to his uncle, "I asked for her help. She is the widow of Sultan Bāyazīd, who fathered Arina's former husband."

Staico's throat bobbed. "You must learn how she fares in widowhood."

Vlad reached for the rolled parchment, but his icy fingers fell away the moment they touched the material. "I can't. My heart is too full."

"Your uncle should read then," Fruzhin said with a nod while he patted Vlad's arm.

Staico broke the seal. His lips quivered before he spoke.

"Greetings, Prince Vlad, in the name of our Lord and Savior, Jesus Christ. I, Princess Milena Olivera, write to you from Belgrade with news of great concern to you. All Christendom must know the Turkish civil war is over. Prince Mûsâ Çelebi fell to the forces of his brother. My daughter Oruz Hatun went with her husband, and my grandson and granddaughter to pledge loyalty to the new sultan. After an apt interval, Oruz asked about the harem of Mûsâ Çelebi, his Christian wife. Whether she had moved to the old palace.

"The sultan brought forth a lady whom he held for ransom from her father. Oruz asked to speak in private with her but discovered a Byzantine noblewoman. The bastard daughter of Carlo Tocco, the ruler of the Greek isle, Cephalonia. Married and widowed the previous summer by Mûsâ Çelebi. Confused, my Oruz next asked her victorious brother for the first wife of the deceased prince and described her as you did for me. With great sadness, I must confirm the worst. Your sister Princess Arina of Wallachia died...."

Staico trailed off. The missive slipped to the ground. He clutched his chest.

His lips gaping, Fruzhin bent, picked up the letter, and continued reading.

"Arina of Wallachia died in childbed on the last day of December, five months after her husband's murder. One of the sultan's wives took my Oruz to the mausoleum where, presumably, the infant lies entombed beside your sister. With sorrow and sympathy, I remain your friend, Milena Olivera."

A strange sound, the rushing of river water, pulsed and overwhelmed Vlad's senses. He collapsed in despair, powerless as if tossed about by waves. His awareness dulling, he tried to hold on to a semblance of a rapidly altered reality.

How could Arina be dead? How had he not felt her passing? Was the bond between them closed forever? He couldn't comprehend it.

His eyes and throat burned like hellfire. He would gladly sink into the devil's pit if only it ended the gnawing chasm of pain that swelled inside him.

Tobar and Yoska, having rushed to them, bore up a sobbing Staico. Fruzhin kneeled, framing Vlad's face between deathly cold hands. His lips moved, but Vlad couldn't hear him because someone was screaming.

Everything in his awareness faded except that awful sound. The guttural howls, those of a wounded animal, echoing into the deep recesses of the night. Only when his throat tightened, did he realize the noises came from him.

So much time spent on heartbreak and worry. Then the faintest hope sparked, rekindled by Milena Olivera's efforts to help him find Arina. All ended now.

Vlad's plans lay dashed in the dust. Nothing but ruin and death remained.

CHAPTER 12

The Fiery Cross of Death

"There is no worse death than the end of hope."-Pelagius (circa 354/360-420 AD), British Christian monk and theologian.

IN THE YEAR OF OUR Lord 1414-1415. Aachen and *Konstanz, Germany*

Light intruded, and its glare stirred a deep ache, radiating from the center of Vlad's forehead. He squeezed his eyelids shut, raised a hand, and rubbed his brow. He rolled away on something soft, but the brilliance would not fade. Nor did the voices.

"Pipó told me he hasn't stirred. He can't sleep forever, Lord Staico."

"I know, Prince Fruzhin, I know. But he returned to the tent late last night...."

At least, they were the sounds of the living. The dead did not shout.

In the rare dream Vlad could recall, after a night spent carousing, a plaintive voice had haunted his imagination. *Find me, free me.*

From Arina. He was desperate to believe it, but that could not be. She lay cold in her grave. Maybe his wine-addled mind concocted a vision, where she still lived and spoke through the old bond. He opened his eyes and forced himself to see his reality.

Why was he here, in a tent? Why wasn't he on the second floor of István's Tower? Then he remembered the court had left Buda at the start of autumn. A journey by ship and then overland. They were in Germany, encamped outside Aachen.

The voices from outside intruded again and grew louder.

"You're his uncle, but it's time he did his duty as a knight of our king's household!"

"I beg you, my prince, to lower your voice if you care for my nephew to remain so. Would you jeopardize his status?"

"He does so on his own. Does he still think he's the only person who's ever known grief and loss? I've been patient with him for nine months, sobered him up every morning, and hidden his nightly transgressions from Zsigmond. However, our king won't care for any delay, not when he's given the order to strike camp and ride for Aachen by this afternoon. Get Vlad into his armor and ready for the day. We'll leave soon."

"I understand, Prince Fruzhin."

"Now, will you allow me inside your tent?"

"Yes. I can deny you nothing. You're Vlad's greatest friend."

"Let's see if I can persuade him to acknowledge that."

Vlad held his breath and shuttered his gaze again. A growing awareness warned of Fruzhin's approach. An acrid scent from the recent use of linseed oil for armor polish invaded Vlad's nostrils. It vied with the rank odor of his mouth.

"You're awake," Fruzhin said. "The snores and breaking of wind ceased after I began talking to your uncle. He's worried about you. We all are, your Gypsies included. They blocked my path into Staico's tent until he told them to stand aside."

Vlad refused to speak.

"The time for hiding from the future is over. Our king must reach Aachen. You know prolonged illness already delayed him, but his coronation as the German ruler occurs in three days. Rouse yourself, throw off the wolf-skin, and wash away last night's drunken folly. If Zsigmond learns how you've behaved, and Pipó's and my part in keeping the truth from him for months, he'll dismiss us all."

A truth Vlad already perceived. He wasn't sure he cared.

"Get up! I won't let you ruin your life or others." Fruzhin seized his forearm, nearly pulling the limb from his socket, and tugged him onto his back. “Get to your feet! Are you a knight of our king’s household?” Fruzhin reached for the other arm.

“Leave me be.” Vlad warded him off with his hand. A feeble attempt, made in the full light of another unwelcome autumn dawn. He cursed while Fruzhin yanked and hauled him into a sitting position. Groggy, he protested again, “I said, leave off, man.”

“I should, for your foul stench would make a weaker person vomit. You stink of more than drink. Did you piss your hose also? Now I understand why your uncle and the Gypsies slept on cloaks outside the tent. The scent of well-used women lingers on your body. You’re lucky there aren’t camp followers with signs of the burning sickness or other corruption. You’ve imbibed enough strong drink and rutted each night. That is not a life.”

“What would you know about life?” Vlad swiped at the clumps of hair falling over his face. His tongue seemed swollen twice its usual size.

“I’ve enjoyed whore-mongering and drunken revelries.” Fruzhin’s hands fell to his sides as he peered down at him. “But never when my king needed me.”

“He doesn’t need me,” Vlad growled. Acerbic fury swelled in his heart. “Besides, I’m talking about life. You’re here to witness Zsigmond donning another of Europe’s crowns when you should be in Bulgaria, fighting for your lost lands. You let the Turks take them and all you do is wait on the whims of another. Why won’t you ask him or your uncle Stefan for the money and men you need? Pipó and I would fight for you. Why are you here?”

“We’ve remained by your side, ensuring our sovereign never discovers your inebriated state. He must wonder why you’ve developed an odd taste for breaking your nightly fast with eels in a vinegar brine. It’s the only way you can recover.”

“Well, I don’t need you or any foul cure!” Steeped in resentment and bitterness, virulent as wine, Vlad rolled on his side and tried to rise. However, his legs wouldn’t cooperate and collapsed under him. The throbbing between his eyebrows increased, made worse by Fruzhin’s unrepentant laughter.

"You'd fight for me? You can barely stand." Fruzhin held out a hand. "Come—"

"Get away from me!" Vlad slapped aside the short, blunt fingers. "You make laughing sport of a man who suffers, when I've called you my best friend."

"I will be so until the end of time. Have you neglected our blood oath?"

"You have, and I don't want to be friends with a coward who won't fight the Turks!"

Fruzhin lunged, grappled with the collar of Vlad's shirt, and rammed a fist into his face. Then twice more, with each blow harder than the first. Blood spurted, and Vlad flopped on his back, dazed.

He gaped up at the tent's ceiling. Staico came into view beside Fruzhin.

"Our companionship is the sole reason I won't smash your face to a pulp." Fruzhin staggered off a few paces and rubbed his red knuckles. "It also ensures I'll never abandon you to your stupidity. Your sister's been dead for over ten months, but you're here. After all you've endured, you breathe. Now, live again."

Staico bent and offered to help Vlad, but he scowled and stood of his own accord. His vision swam for the space of some malodorous breaths before he glared at Fruzhin.

"You are right. Arina is gone. She has left me behind. What purpose do I serve now in her absence, when I can no longer free her from the Turks?"

"I understand your pain." Fruzhin came to him and palmed the cheek he hammered earlier. Vlad reeled away.

"No, you can't know, not truly. Your brother Iskender is alive, though he may be lost to you. I promised to safeguard Arina. I have failed—"

"But you didn't, Vlad." Wetness brimmed in Staico's eyes. "You never gave up hope."

"What do I have now in a future without hope or choices or Arina?"

"Vengeance!" Fruzhin framed Vlad's face in both hands and pressed their foreheads together. "If you think there's nothing left for you, live to avenge her loss."

"The birthing stole Arina. The husband who got her with child is also dead."

"The Ottoman sultan and his armies are resolved to destroy Christendom. Despite your sister's sacrifice in marriage, the threat of Turkish expansion increases. She died in their lackluster care. Help Zsigmond thwart our enemy. Remember our blood pact."

Fruzhin released him and turned to Staico. "Take him down to the river nearby, my lord, and let him wash. His nose is likely broken, so tend to him. Do it quickly while the Gypsy boys pack your belongings."

"What about my father?" Vlad asked, as blood dribbled over his lips.

Staico shook his head. "Although we are not there to see, you must know he suffers in Wallachia over the loss of a third child of his."

"Not enough. Who but he should deserve the pain? Not one word from Mother since you wrote about Arina's death. Maybe Mother knew beforehand and hid the news. My sister would be among the living, but our father bartered her like cattle."

"You're wrong, Vlad. He made a calculated choice and found himself worse off for it. He's always loved her. He didn't intend her death."

"But he foresaw the possibility of it. He is at fault."

"Even if so, your anger toward him in this single instance isn't justified. I'll never agree with any plot you devise, but I won't stop you, either."

"Do as you like. There is one way to hurt him now. You know it."

Staico gaped at him. "You'd make a bid for the throne? Divide the boyar council? Even if you could achieve this miracle, lacking men and money for bribes, your father would not let it stand. He would march upon you. He'll never let you usurp what he sees as Mihail's birthright. Do you understand you'd be fighting your father and Mihail?"

Vlad wondered; could he kill for a crown? Stibor asked him the same a year ago, but regarding Mihail alone. Not their parent. In Vlad's tortured thoughts where rage festered since childhood, he knew the answer he gave Stibor remained unchanged. Even if Prince Mircea's blood might stain his hands. Their personal history and that of the House of Basarab warned any such clash would be brutal.

He gripped Fruzhin. "If I must oppose them, will you stand with me against my foes?"

"Do your duty to our king and I will fight for you. My sword is yours, to strike down any whom you call an enemy. I pledge myself as a companion in times of war and peace."

Staico turned away from them. "I want no part of this foolery." He marched outside, shaded his gaze with his good hand, and gave blustery orders to Tobar and Yoska.

HURT AND ANGER BOILED beneath Vlad's skin, but he trudged to the embankment. There, he stripped off his musty garments and told Staico to burn them. He dunked his whole body into the frigid river with a great splash. Icy nettles of pain pricked his skin. He swallowed any outcry and scrubbed with a bathing rag from his face, including his battered nose, down to his feet. He willed the water to cleanse away sorrow and regret.

Arina's sad end meant his life must begin anew. He vowed his sword would be the instrument with which he destroyed every Turk, and one day, his brother and father.

His heart hammered as though brimming with vigor for the first time in a long time. Savage fury burned inside him so hot, the river's chill subsided. He emerged, and Staico bundled him in a drying blanket. Once he removed it, frosty air surged and cooled the fire roiling inside him. He dressed before his uncle examined and tended his broken nose, then fetched his armor and helped him into it.

"Prince Fruzhin sent a bowl of the eels pickled in vinegar," Staico said, his mouth twisted in a grimace. "Will you have them here?"

Vlad desired no quick remedy to cast off the night's disgrace. The pounding of his head must cease, eventually. He embraced his pain and the cold swirling around him, willing the latter to seep beneath the armor, through flesh and bone. His hurts would serve as a reminder of the terrible difficulties he had survived.

"I need nothing, uncle." He pulled on the gauntlets and girded his sword.

With dexterity, Staico affixed the last steel pauldron at his shoulder. "You should eat it before we get on the road. If sweet Arina could see you now, a knight in armor—"

"No. You will not speak her name again, nor will I."

"But Vlad...." Staico trailed off once their gazes met.

"No, uncle. No more talk of her or the past. If vengeance and bitter memories are all I have left, they must sustain me. Come, I won't keep my king waiting."

Outside the royal tent, Fruzhin spoke with Pipó, and the palatine, and the governor of Slavonia. The latter mimicked a bull's horns with his fingers and bellowed.

An idling Hermann of Celje, Borbála's father, laughed. Fruzhin joined Vlad, who acknowledged Pipó's quirked eyebrows with a nod, before the queen's parent demanded Pipó's attention.

"What has happened?" Vlad asked Fruzhin.

"The Turkish invasion of Bosnia began a few weeks ago. Pipó's not coming with us. He'll ride for Buda to bring word and summon council members. Our queen received a message before we left Bonn. A Bosnian noble, whom Zsigmond has often quarreled with; he has betrayed his people and aided our enemy."

"I suppose he is the stubborn Hrvoje, the same magnate whom our king dismissed at the start of the summer summit with King Władysław of Poland."

"Your memory remains indefatigable. Praise God. Zsigmond took back Hrvoje's Hungarian lands for repeated treachery with the Turks. This is the Bosnian's revenge."

"Are we marching in his country?" Vlad clutched the pommel of his sword.

"No. Nothing can interrupt the coronation plans."

Vlad burned for a fight with the Turks, but he huffed and nodded.

"Zsigmond won't permit the fall of the Balkans." Fruzhin patted his shoulder.

THEIR KING, HIS QUEEN, and their companions came to Aachen by midafternoon, as planned. Zsigmond prayed with Borbála in the cathedral while Vlad and the other household knights stood guard outside. Three days later, their sovereign donned the gold and cloisonné enamel crown of Germany, studded with pearls and glittering stones.

Vlad and Fruzhin stood a few paces behind Stibor's son, and Earl Richard de Beauchamp of Warwick, and the red-bearded Friedrich of the House of Hohenzollern, whom Vlad recalled brought welcome news about the German crown to Zsigmond.

"But why would our king attend the council so soon when he knows the danger Bosnia faces?" Vlad tried hard to subdue the annoyance in his tone, realizing he must have failed once the earl peeked over his shoulder with raised, bushy eyebrows.

"The ecclesiastical Council of Konstanz meets to discuss the Great Schism. Three named popes, each claiming to be the lawful vicar of Christ and excommunicating each other," Fruzhin replied. "A meeting as important to a Catholic like Zsigmond as is any Balkan invasion. All rival papal claimants must be heard, and their disputes resolved before the rightful pope can declare a crusade against the Turks."

"The Bosnian people can't wait upon such a determination," Vlad muttered. "I wish Stibor were here. He would share my view and advise our king."

He groaned when Stibor's namesake son turned and gave them a baleful glare. Afterward, they were silent until the end of the ceremony. Zsigmond and Borbála went from the cathedral grounds to where they would receive homage to the city hall.

With a nod to Stibor's heir, far ahead of them, Vlad asked, "Is the rumor true?"

"That he's turned into everything his father was not? A defiler of women and a callous murderer." Fruzhin cursed under his breath, but a lady walking nearby giggled and flashed him a wicked smile. "Our sovereign, in deference to his friend's memory, has cautioned the son against further crimes. There will be no additional warning. It's good you've taken note. He's a cautionary example. In his grief over Stibor, the son lashes out at his people."

Determined to be a better person and a worthier ruling prince of Wallachia than the current leaders, Vlad said nothing. At length, he and Fruzhin approached their king.

Zsigmond held out his hand, which each man kneeled and kissed. He said, "My young princes have reconciled. I knew whatever trouble arose between you, it could not last."

Vlad looked askance at his closest friend, who shrugged. Of course, he'd already divulged even the minor trouble. A new worry bloomed. Since Fruzhin kept no secrets from their king, did Vlad miscalculate by revealing his plans for Wallachia to his friend?

"Peace reigns once more, Your Royal Majesty," Fruzhin said, "among your courtiers and over the German lands, which you may call your own at last."

"God be praised, though We will not enjoy this triumph for long. The church council reconvenes at the start of the year. Our departure south shall occur in four days. I expect we will winter in Konstanz."

The pair bowed and left their sovereign. Perhaps at Konstanz, Zsigmond would realize the importance of sending his army into Bosnia soon. If their king did not, Vlad feared the fates of beleaguered Albania, Bulgaria, and Serbia would befall Bosnia. More than his concern for the Balkan states, he also craved a bloody encounter with the Turks. They must pay for his bitter loss. Vengeance would be his.

IN THE YEAR OF OUR Lord 1414-1415. Konstanz, Germany

After crossing into France for a tournament in December, King Zsigmond with his queen entered Germany again by boat on a frigid night. Vlad and other courtiers followed on other smaller vessels sailed across Bodensee Lake toward their destination at Konstanz's town hall.

From astern on another boat, Vlad made out the white basilica of the Konstanzer Münster.

The king's company arrived well after the sentries must have already called the midnight hour. Scant moonlight could not rival the light cast by innumerable torches carried with great ceremony as Zsigmond and Borbála led the way. To onlookers, who shivered and breathed out white wisps, Vlad imagined the illumination might have looked like a fast-moving fire approaching the town. The royal couple planned to celebrate a pre-dawn Nativity mass on Christmas Eve.

Bone-weary after a day-long journey through inclement weather and the night-time crossing in the boat, Vlad longed for sleep. But the expected length of the service meant sleep would not come soon. Once the council meetings resumed, he would seek solitude and solace along the shores of Lake Konstanz, home to reeds and moorland fed by the Rhine River.

Absent the oblivion the bottom of a wineskin offered, nightmares plagued him. In them, Mircea the Great fell with a sword protruding from his back. But who had delivered the death blow?

Pushing aside such errant thoughts, Vlad asked Fruzhin, "Have you mentioned my plans for Wallachia to Zsigmond?"

"Why would I?" His best friend leaned forward in the saddle. "Besides, your intent doesn't conflict with his wishes."

"He'll aid me?" Vlad recalled Stibor's advice not to rely solely on their king.

"He hopes you'll prosper and earn the trust of other men and inspire them. Prove yourself worthy of command. You'll be but twenty-one years old in less than two weeks."

"What bearing does my age have?" Vlad snapped. "Can I count on Zsigmond?"

"I believe so." Fruzhin cocked his head and nodded. "When the right time comes."

Vlad heard the inherent counsel of his friend. Their leader did not think he was ready to rule. Knighthood and a place in the royal household were not enough proof of his merits.

"You're only eight years older than me," he said. "How did you gain entry into the Order of the Dragon before I arrived in Buda?"

"Who says I've been inducted?" Fruzhin offered him a tight-lipped smile.

"You and Zsigmond. Your constancy and his reliance betray some connection."

"Our king is close with many of his courtiers."

The earl of Warwick's trumpeters and fifers proclaimed their arrival, stymieing further discussion.

"Yours and your uncle Stefan's relations with Zsigmond differ from other men," Vlad resumed in the aftermath. "Much like Stibor with the dragon on his armor. He must have been a member of the Order. The Bosnian Hrvoje invoked his membership in a letter to the queen. Is Pipó one of your brethren? Shall I ask when we see him again?"

"The Order is not your concern, Vlad," Fruzhin replied as they slowed the horses. "You have more to learn about fighting and command. Concentrate."

Hardly appeased, Vlad caught sight of another awaiting them.

Since Stibor's death, which Vlad informed the Black Knight Zawisza in a message to the Polish court, the pair began an exchange of letters. They did more than inform each other about occurrences within their separate kingdoms and commiserate over their mutual loss of a friend. Whenever he sobered enough, Vlad imparted his hatred for the Turks. He even composed one missive about his heartbreak before he drank himself into a stupor. He never sent that letter. Zawisza might have already known his worries from Stibor.

"Have you not slept?" Zawisza searched his face. "Your eyes are reddened. Your countenance betrays the turmoil of an older man. Will you take some wine with me?"

"He will not," Fruzhin interjected. "All we need now is several hours of rest after our sovereign attends mass."

Though embittered by an answer made on his behalf, like some child, Vlad accepted it. Shame filled him at the memory of his drunkenness. He would not consider the source of the loss or admit the pain of it still knifed him each day.

"I arrived one day ago, same as Zsigmond's herald," the Black Knight said, drawing him from past miseries to present circumstances. "Not at the behest of my good King Władysław. Resolution of the Hussite matter concerns me."

Before the Hungarians went to Aachen, Zsigmond boasted of a personal guarantee of *salvus conductus* to Jan Hus, a Bohemian theologian whom some Catholics called heretical. The church council of Konstanz would decide his fate.

"Why does Jan Hus worry you more than the new vicar of Christ?" Vlad asked.

"Poor choices can lead to war," Zawisza replied. "Conflict with Jan Hus' adherents in Bohemia will spill over the borders and become Europe's trouble. Like the Turks."

THE BOHEMIAN THEOLOGIAN arrived a year to the day of the coronation in Aachen. Nothing threatening in the thick-bearded and plainly dressed appearance of the man, but Vlad soon knew why the Church feared Hus so. He caused resentment of the Catholic hierarchy among his followers and the Germans to whom he preached daily, against repeated remonstrance from the council.

The papacy required complete obedience and submission to the pope, who served as the head of Christ's church with the cardinals as its body. Within the month, they took Hus captive, although Zsigmond threatened the dismissal of the council. No king's oath of safe passage to and from Konstanz would sway them.

Too many common people questioned long-held doctrines, or so Pipó said once he rejoined them in February of the following year. The Catholic prelates rallied and warned Zsigmond against interfering in a church matter. For all the guarantees a writ of safe conduct offered, Vlad thought his king had abandoned Hus.

In the first week of June, during which Catholics celebrated the feast of Saint Boniface, screams and the screeches of birds vied over Konstanz.

Vlad fled a lakeside tavern in the wake of his companions and their king's warriors, who had gathered to share their first meal of the day. Their shouts mingled with the city's cries. Priests left their celebrations of mass. One shouted the verses of Psalm 51 to the heavens. An eclipse occurred.

People rushed back indoors, even some of Zsigmond's most stalwart fighters. Pipó and Fruzhin made the sign of the cross.

Vlad stared without saying a word. The sky darkened, obliterating all light. The waters of the lake blackened, the surface becoming a sheen of hammered steel. The stars were visible. Several birds fell, littering the ground in a morass of feathers. Women shrieked and shielded their crying children. The total eclipse lasted an interminable time.

Zawisza asked no one in particular, "Is this the world's end?"

Vlad did not share the fearful sentiment. He recalled what his grandmother told him at Argeş about the celestial dragon. "*A herald of great change for you,*" which he must not fear, she had said.

Long after the sun returned, he shaded his eyes and stayed outdoors.

Within weeks, a trio of bishops oversaw the summer trial of Jan Hus. The accused reiterated his beliefs that only God could judge him.

The churchmen thought otherwise. Vlad stood with Fruzhin, Pipó, and Zawisza on a humid, pitiless July day while the council condemned Hus as a heretic, stripped him of priestly vestments, and sentenced him to a fiery death.

"*Amici*, we will regret this sight, no?" Pipó said.

"It hardly matters. We'll be at war in Bohemia soon," Fruzhin said.

Vlad disagreed with his best friend but did not say so while he regarded Jan Hus. At a stake piled high with wood and straw, the man burned alive, fingers clutching a metal crucifix, perhaps hidden in his sleeve. The cross fired sparks, catching the clothing of a prelate who stood too close. While a few doused his clothing, most observers fled.

A deafening roar made Vlad cover his ears. He imagined the sound must be the same as the damned uttered, burning in hellfire for eternity. Out of the pyre, a dark specter rose above the stake. The form stretched overhead and hovered in the sky like a cloak of ravens' wings. The phantom thing cast no shadow.

Vlad's heart pitched in terror. It must be a harbinger of evil. His friends went on speaking and pointing at the charred corpse as though nothing afflicted them. Was it possible he was the only one who saw the dreadful omen?

IN THE MIDDLE OF THE next month, their king announced Pipó would accompany him there when he left the Freiburg Court, where he had lived separately from his queen, for a new journey beginning with Spain's Kingdom of Aragon. Ten days earlier, Borbála had left them for Hungary. That's when the troubles began.

Some quarrel arose at dinner between Zsigmond and a German noble, who insulted the honor of the queen, publicly naming Friedrich of the House of Hohenzollern as her lover. Zsigmond warranted the claim as a personal affront to his marriage. Richard de Beauchamp, the earl of Warwick, rose first to become the champion of the royal couple.

He and the German broke two lances against each other the next dawn. On the third joust, the tip of Warwick's weapon shattered and pierced the German's chest. As he lay dying, his opponent's herald presented Zsigmond with the emblem of the earl, a bear on a ragged staff.

"Our king is satisfied, and the scandal is put to rest," Fruzhin told Vlad afterward. "Still, I'm unsure what to make of the accusation, given the absence of Queen Borbála, already headed along the Rhine for Hungary. Friedrich lives in Berlin. Zsigmond has long relied on him, and he's guaranteed the loans our king borrowed before his European travels. Why do you suppose Warwick defended the royal honor?"

"Maybe the queen and earl are lovers, too," Vlad replied, while Fruzhin gaped at him.

"Don't say so again. No man likes to be assumed a cuckold, least of all, a king."

IN THE YEAR OF OUR Lord 1415. Doboj, Bosnia (modern-day Doboj, Bosnia and Herzegovina)

Six weeks later, Vlad stood atop the tallest tower of Bosnia's Doboj Fortress. Summer stars streaked through the sky in a display Catholics called the tears of martyred Saint Laurentius. In Wallachia, court astrologers named those celestial bodies, the Perseids.

By Zsigmond's order, Vlad with Staico and the Gypsies, and Fruzhin at the head of his mercenaries followed a Hungarian army south. The governor of Slavonia, although in tripartite command of their forces, ensured everyone knew he alone would order the initial attack. Vlad thought him boastful and immature, bellowing like a bull as he ridiculed Hrvoje, the stout Bosnian magnate they would face. A man who reviled Zsigmond so much, he bowed before the Turkic enemies of Christendom.

Doboj's defenses, built five floors high, allowed a magnificent view of the surrounding valley and the confluence of two rivers. The lands of Croatia, in Hungarian control, and Styria, the queen's home, lay along the northern border. To the west, beleaguered Serbia.

In the night, small fires smoldered, and smoke billowed. Vlad came to the fortress one week ago. Their captain general dispatched soldiers to nearby settlements with orders to clear out. Flames devoured houses. Soldiers killed dogs, polluting wells with the carcasses. Villagers huddled in the stronghold's courtyard. The cries of children and fervent prayers from their parents vied with animals, a daily cacophony from which Vlad sought to escape.

A warm gust of wind buffeted him. He looked around as Fruzhin appeared with a grim expression. Vlad returned his attention to the starlit southern lands.

"No word from your aunt Jelena," he surmised, "about whether her husband will join us in defense of his country or ally with the traitor Hrvoje who sides with Turks."

"Sometimes no answer is an answer, Vlad." Fruzhin gripped the thick edge of the rough-hewn stone walls. "From this vantage, we'll see the arriving Turks for leagues."

"The governor of Slavonia will have this view while we're on the field."

"As we both wish. Doboj is the heart of Bosnia, Vlad. A gateway to Christendom. We must stop the Turks here or our religion dies with us."

Encamped on the plain below the defensive walls, the Hungarians blended with German, Bohemian, Lithuanian, and Polish troops, including Zawisza. He diced with his countrymen until midafternoon of the following day before strolling between Vlad and Fruzhin at the camp's southern edge. The scent of boiling meats and soups wafted from wood fires. Birdsong echoed on the waterway.

"Have scouts reported in since last night?" Zawisza plucked a blade of grass while Fruzhin shook his head. "That's not so good. We don't know how many we'll truly face."

"Our spies suggested even odds with the Turks at fifteen thousand strong," Fruzhin murmured. "We don't have the number of Bosnian traitors who'll join Hrvoje."

A flurry of shouts echoed from the southern bastion, arranged with six cannons. From the tree line in the distance, the Turkish army emerged alongside two others. Christians, by their banners. The bells of Doboj's fortress pealed in sonorous repetition.

"Jelena's husband chose. I see his heraldry." Fruzhin scrubbed at his clean-shaven face, which turned pallid. "I'd hate for my aunt to be widowed again, but God alone will decide."

THE NEXT DAWN CHASED away traces of the lilac sky on the horizon and found Vlad in the saddle. He sat at the center of three square-shaped units formed up along the slopes in opposition to the enemy. An unholy alliance of Turkmen and several thousand Bosnian knights. Their light cavalry and men-at-arms outnumbered the Hungarians.

Smoke gray mist from the burning land snaked its way along the river valley, obscuring Vlad's lower limbs halfway up the greaves. The acrid scent suffused his nostrils. In the third of seven rows of heavy cavalry, mostly Hungarian and German knights surrounded him. He patted his skittish mount as it snorted and shattered the unearthly quiet. Did the stallion feel his restlessness?

A glimpse of Fruzhin or Zawisza, commanding the other bands below the foothills, might have soothed him. Instead, he glanced at the pair of unknown knights on either side of him. Neither wore his helm. One kissed the wooden German-style crucifix slung around his neck on a leather cord. The next man prayed in Polish. Strangers united to defend a country not their own. Their sun-bronzed faces mirrored more solemn visages.

The governor of Slavonia, who called up the levies at Zsigmond's behest, brought militia. Peasant archers, crossbowmen, and spearmen swelled the Hungarian ranks.

The fog obscured their adversaries' camp except for pennants snapping in the stiff breeze. Vlad recalled Stibor's training. The Turks would depend first on their archers' assaults. He looked for Staico and the Gypsies, relegated to Hungarian light cavalry. God shield them, he thought. In such uneven odds, Zsigmond's army needed every fighter.

He lifted his sword in hand. Did he imagine the center of his ruby ring looked darker? When Fruzhin gave him the gift, he said it would dim, warning of times of peril. Perhaps the scant morning light played a trick on his eyes.

Enemy drums pounded, horns rumbled, and river fowl and insects took flight from the marshes. The Turkic standards drew up in vivid shades emblazoned with slanted, black lettering. Ox-blood flags bearing the silver crescent moon dominated the skyline.

The cannons atop Doboj's fortress belched the first red flames. Stone balls arced in the air and the initial volley sliced through the first three or four Turkic infantry ranks, crumbling their front line. The survivors answered with arrows blotting out an ascendant sun. Vlad watched their trajectory in the sky briefly. Black iron shafts littered the foreground, well away from the Hungarian vanguard, who cheered.

When the order came to charge, Zsigmond's lions, as the household knights called themselves, roared their battle readiness. "For Christ's glory and the king's honor!"

In another ear-splitting boom, a barrage of cannonballs ravaged the Turkish lines. Clumps of grass and dirt exploded into the air, filled with the cries of dying men.

Vlad pulled on his helm and gauntlets, drew his sword, and spurred his horse across the valley floor. Waves of memory of his sister cascaded for the first time in nearly a year. Not their joyous days, but the final week before their bitter farewell. The foes he thundered toward had taken her away. Their lives would be small recompense.

He aimed his sword at the enemy. "You will all die, worse than she did."

The power of a cavalry charge, unlike any other heady feeling, roused Vlad's angry bellow. Clustered knights fanned out and stabbed from overhead with rabid savagery.

Vlad plunged into their midst. He found the first Turk in the fray. Blind hate propelled his sword arm. He aimed at a thin gap between the mail ringing the sides of the helmet and the armored shoulder. Steel scraped the iron before the blade stabbed deep. Blood spurted from the man's neck and sprayed Vlad's gauntlets. His horse opened its mouth and snapped at the Turk's wide-flung hand before sidestepping.

Another man came at him to die like the first, although he fought on his knees until the mount kicked him in his chest. Vlad panted but did not stop slashing. Soon gore covered him and the warhorse, mangled corpses with crushed skulls in the dirt.

No matter how many he slaughtered, more Turks filled the void. The sunlight glared. Perspiration stung his eyes. Hair became an irritant, a clingy, sopping mess at his neck. Still, he drove his mount forward into the wild feast of bloodshed. Like a wild beast tasting blood, he could not get his fill. The carnage whetted his appetite for revenge.

A spear caught his horse in the chest. It reared, and Vlad tumbled from the saddle. An iron-shod hoof struck his helmet, and he rolled across the bloodied muck. He rose quickly but slid in the slick rope of some knight's entrails. He dived for the blade lost at the side of his fallen mount. He stabbed an attacking Turk before crouching beside the dying warhorse. Blood trickled from its nostrils. Anguished pangs filled Vlad's throat.

He swallowed bile. Ragged breaths burned his chest. The helmet stifled. A glance showed how the enemy flanked the Hungarian army. A wolf set to devour them.

He looked up at the sky and recoiled. The unearthly specter he witnessed in the burning of Jan Hus now hung over the battleground. His gaze flitted across the site, but no one else gaped at the spectacle. He clapped his hands to his head. Was he going crazy?

"Vlad!"

He shook his head, mind muddled, for the wind carried his name. Arrows whistled by. He dove over the dead horse before a flurry of black arrowheads pierced the carcass.

"Vlad! Where are you? Vlad! Answer me if you still live."

No mistaking the sound this time. Pounding hooves neared. He gripped the sword, poised to spring out. No awaiting death on this bloodied field.

"Come on, Vlad! Too many of us have fallen. The Turks have brought up artillery."

He barely recognized Fruzhin atop a mount with no saddle, armor steeped in crimson remnants of butchery. His friend held out a hand.

Vlad surged to his feet and stumbled across the broken bodies. He grabbed Fruzhin's forearm and leaped onto the horse. They fled to the fortress with others. From the eastern bank, Turkish cannons traded fire with the towers' defenses. A loud boom rocked the southern bastion. The masonry shuddered. Pulverized stone sprayed. Both men ducked low over the back of the horse.

"The tower will crumble!" Fruzhin yelled. "The battle is lost. We can't stay, Vlad."

"You'd have us flee like cowards." He cursed the Turkish artillery's arrival.

"There's no shame in retreat. We live to fight another day against the barbarians."

Although frightened, Vlad sought the phantom that haunted the battlefield. He shuddered at the sight of it lingering above the slaughter. What did it mean, and why was he the only one who could envision it?

Riding double with Fruzhin still, well north of the road to the fortress alongside other survivors, he found a bloodied Staico and his Gypsies, including the twins. They saw two of their uncles and five cousins killed. Rapid word spread of the Turkish capture of Doboj, the slaughter of all Christian defenders, and the enslavement of those inside the fort.

"Our fellow travelers say the Turks brought the governor of Slavonia to the enemy Bosnians. They sewed him inside an ox's hide and set it alight," Fruzhin muttered.

Vlad seethed at their defeat. Where was Zawisza? Had their foes tortured and killed him too? Would the rest of Bosnia endure the fate of Doboj? When would he have another chance at vengeance against the enemy of all Christians? How much of their blood would suffice for the chasm in his heart?

Even in dreams, he found no rest. The voice he imagined must be Arina always disturbed him. *Find me, free me.*

CHAPTER 13

Forbidden

"Nothing is sweeter than love, nothing higher, nothing stronger, nothing larger, nothing more joyful, nothing fuller, and nothing better in heaven or on earth."-Thomas à Kempis (1380-1471 AD), German-Dutch Christian canon.

IN THE YEAR OF OUR Lord 1418. Buda, Hungary (modern-day Budapest, Hungary)

The Council of Konstanz wore on until its conclusion in the spring of 1418, and satisfied with the choice of a new pope, Zsigmond sent half of his courtiers and retainers ahead of him. They rode in the middle of a wide column snaking across a Hungarian forest tract, expecting to see their destination over the next rise.

Although pleased to leave Konstanz after the long sojourn of a year and a half, Vlad reflected on their monarch's choices with continued concern. Rather than seek the blessing of the new vicar of Christ for an immediate reprisal after the Bosnian loss, Zsigmond harried his people for the ransom of sixty-five thousand gold florins the Turks demanded. At least, the money ensured Zawisza's return.

The Bosnian nobleman Hrvoje, who gave Doboj Fortress to his Turkish allies, died within a year of the battle. A fitting end for the traitor. From that time, their king led Hungarian courtiers through the western countries, even crossing at Calais for the London palace of England's King Henry the Fifth. He boasted about the French defeat at Agincourt last autumn rather than listening to whatever Zsigmond said in his ear.

"Why does Zsigmond stay behind in Konstanz when we must prepare for war?" Vlad shook his head, bewildered by his king, and irritable from lack of a proper night's sleep. "There should be a new crusade. It's been three years since the people of Bosnia faced the Turkish menace. We've idled in Germany for seventeen months and visited the cities of Spain, France, and England—"

"Lower your voice," Fruzhin ordered. He held command of the returning knights.

"I will not! Besides, others agree with me." For affirmation, Vlad looked to his left and right. Some warriors nodded or grunted. Only two men in the same row sat stone-faced in the saddle and denied him their regard.

He added, "Pipó led an army into Bosnia again, more than a year after Doboj fell, but nothing changed. Why is Zsigmond still hesitating?"

Fruzhin sighed. "Impetuousness won't win us any wars. You've forgotten there's a reason our king is 'the ginger fox.' He learned from the failure at Doboj. There is no coalition of nations in the east large enough to stop the Turks. He went to Spain, France, and England to seek help from their rulers. We need an alliance of western and eastern powers to defeat the Ottomans. Why else would Zsigmond befriend warring France and England, or seek help from Spain, preoccupied with the obliteration of Moorish Granada?"

Vlad recalled the last two years of travels. If his king still deemed Christian control of the Balkans important, his dalliances with other countries gave no urgency to the crisis.

Vlad eyed Fruzhin. "Well? Will the western countries help us?"

"Time will tell, my friend."

"Meaning, you don't know." Vlad scoffed and turned aside.

"Your zeal for Turkish blood will not ensure aid comes any faster." Fruzhin maneuvered his horse closer and pitched his voice low. "Until our arrival, I'm your captain general. Use that surly tone with me again, and I'll do more than break your nose."

Fruzhin spurred his steed, and Vlad stared hard at his back before the hills around Buda came into view. Soon, Vlad caught up with Fruzhin again. They rode side by side in silence. His lips pressed tightly together, Vlad huffed and looked away until he could not bear the tension.

"Forgive me, friend," he said, turning to Fruzhin. "I let impatience influence my hasty tongue and ignored your role as the captain general. It will never happen again."

"See that it does not." Fruzhin gave him a curt nod. "I value our bond, but my duties to our king supersede all else." Fruzhin nudged the horse closer again. "I'm to escort the queen to her dower lands a month from today. While I'm gone, contemplate what I will say next. You're a man full-grown, yet the rebellious child within still governs you. The world has many unpleasant surprises. Learn to control yourself and master your destiny."

Although the import of the harsh words soured in his stomach, Vlad nodded. He hoped to live by Fruzhin's guidance, but his guts still roiled with fury against the Turks.

Inside the crowded courtyard of the great keep of István's Tower, a saddle-sore Vlad clambered down and patted his horse's rump. Courtiers thronged the area. They embraced men absent for some years, introduced children born since their fathers' departures, and mourned fallen kin who would never return from Bosnia.

No one welcomed him, but Vlad's mood lifted at the reunions. He thought of Buda Castle as home too, at least for a time. Afterward, he spoke to his uncle and the Gypsies. Of the band of thirty-two who left Wallachia eight years ago, they'd lost a third of their number. The rest raised families with women they found in Hungary. Even Tobar hoped to marry a girl who had captured his heart four years ago. Knowing the Gypsies' desire to embrace others, Vlad dismissed them and his uncle.

He alone awaited Fruzhin. The Bulgarian addressed a gray-haired knight who rested his hand on the curls, mud-colored at the roots until turning auburn, of a wiry boy. Once Fruzhin shook his head, the knight's face became crestfallen. He nodded and patted the youth before they bowed and departed.

When Fruzhin rejoined him, Vlad asked about the identities of the pair.

"I'm not entirely surprised you don't recognize them. It's been eight years since Vajk Hunyadi escorted you from Transilvania into Hungary." As Vlad's recognition dawned in full, Fruzhin asked, "Do you recall meeting his son János at Hunyadvár?"

"Yes. A boy of four with an unfortunate lisp I hoped he might outgrow."

"He's twelve and still has it. He serves as a pageboy in Transilvania, under Stibor's successor to the governorship. Vajk wants a place for him here. He hoped Zsigmond had arrived with us. When I said our king would not return right away, the father asked if I'd take his boy on in an apprenticeship as my squire. I won't. Vajk is ambitious for his son. I hold no lands or honors with which to gift János and better his prospects—"

While Fruzhin spoke, Vlad's name rose above the din in the courtyard from somewhere behind him. He and Fruzhin turned as one.

A tremor ran down the length of Vlad's body. His mother stood in the great keep's doorway, dressed in black. Time remained kind, despite deep lines etched at the corners of her eyes and around her mouth. Spring breezes lifted the trailing edge of her veil.

One man lingered near her, his slender face with shaggy hair falling on either side reminiscent of a wolf. Something familiar in his features tugged at Vlad's memory.

"Who are they?" Fruzhin grasped his forearm.

"I don't know the man, but I've seen him at home. The woman is my mother."

"Princess Mara. Why do you believe she has come after all this time?"

"I can think of a single reason." Vlad forced his limbs into action.

His mother cried out behind the hand over her lips before she rushed at him. They did not embrace. She reached for his bearded cheek and ran her fingers over the bristles until he caught her hand. He searched crystalline agate eyes like his.

"Oh, my Vlad," she whispered. "You've grown so much, but I would know you anywhere. If only your father could have...." She trailed off and hiccupped a sob.

As she quivered, his arms came around her and he bore her up. Her tears seeped beneath the armor worn at his neck.

"You're here because he is dead," Vlad murmured, his cheek against hers.

THEY FOUND A TABLE and sat in the hall of István's Tower, where their king's knights ate. Fruzhin brought three bowls of goulash and offered his condolences before leaving.

"Who are you?" Vlad eyed the stranger. "Certainly, no halberdier by your look."

"This is Vlậcsan of the Florea clan. A boyar who serves Mihail," his mother said.

Vlậcsan tilted his head before he spooned pork fat from the rich broth.

Vlad ignored the food. Rancorous thoughts turned to his brother, the sole ruler. When he moved against him, at least their father's blood would not taint Vlad's hands.

"Have you nothing else to say or ask?" His mother tugged his arm. "Don't you want to know when or how your father met his demise?"

In his vengeful heart, Prince Mircea perished long ago. Her watery gaze kept him from saying so. When he would not speak, she revealed her husband's last act. A treaty with the new Turkish sultan before dying in his sleep near January's end.

Afterward, Mara buried him in his favored foundation of Cozia Monastery, in the Olt River Valley. His pledge of three thousand gold pieces per year should have bought the Ottomans off. However, Mihail faced a new demand for both of his sons as hostages.

"My poor first boy," their mother whimpered. "Such a choice, if I can call it that."

"If Mihail sends his children, he's a coward."

"Don't reproach him for struggling with a decision," their mother chided. "There are no absolutes in any of our lives. Not where the Turks are concerned. We never know what we will sacrifice in a crisis until the moment is upon us."

She was wrong. If faced with such a barbaric order from the Ottomans, Vlad would never submit. God help his brother's children, cursed with a craven fool for a parent.

"Your husband gave up my sister for peace. He gained what? A few years of respite?"

She gaped while he glanced at Vlậcsan again, who soaked bread in the goulash.

"You're still angry with your father about Arina, and with me," his mother said.

He could not deny it. He'd spent more time mired in anger than any other emotion.

"You never sent word when she died," he said. "You came only after your husband breathed his last. Did you think his passing would mean more than her ending?"

"He was a father to you both."

"He barely remembered," Vlad muttered. "He sent her to her death."

"You can't blame him for it!" His mother protested. "How could he have known? I won't let you dishonor his memory by accusing him of abandoning our daughter."

"I'm a man of twenty-four years. You'll never dictate to me. Do you deny your husband wrote to the king of Poland, offering fealty, and forsaking his role as Zsigmond's vassal?"

She blinked rapidly and looked away, fingers on her trembling lips.

He touched her chin and compelled her to look at him. "What did you think would happen to me afterward? A youth at the mercy of a king."

"I feared for you!" Her abruptness drew the gaze of the knights nearby. At a harsh glare from Vlad, they looked away. She sighed. "But Mircea said it all came to naught. Władysław of Poland ignored the overture."

She acted as if the outcome alone should matter to him. If he came to Hungary as a hostage instead of an attendant, Zsigmond could have claimed his life in payment for his parent's treachery.

"Your husband told you to ignore me, too? You wrote to Staico, never me."

"I charged him with your safety while fearing your imprudence for good reason. You'll always be my beloved, impulsive son. I didn't want you distracted in your service."

"Absent news, my fears grew. You knew of my sister's death before Staico wrote?"

"No. Arina always sent missives twice a year, after January and around Michaelmas in September. Then nothing from her that year until your uncle's letter came. But a mother's heart perceives when her child is in peril."

"You remembered how close we were as children but gave no consideration to how I might have grieved her loss."

"I ached for you, myself, and Mircea." She lifted her chin with a dull look in her eyes. "We all lost Arina." She faced him again. "There's more misery in you than her death or my long absence could've inflicted. My Vlad! What have Zsigmond and his wars done to you?"

What else but give him purpose? Would she think him a monster if he admitted he liked the killing? The splash of a Turk's blood, a warm balm for his savage soul.

She said, "I've waited here for three months since the funeral. An eternity, no less lonely than when I let my dear boy ride off eight years ago. A cold warrior sits in his place. One who has surely seen death. Dealt it to others. Is there anything left of the son I knew?"

He stood and pushed back the stool. Her breath hitched and a small, wounded cry came from her throat.

"Finish your food while I fetch Staico," he said. "He'll want to know you're here."

He would always be her son. If only she remembered how to show a mother's love.

He sent Staico to her but lingered inside his uncle's tent. Forlornly, he wept. Whether for his dead father, his mother, himself, or the lost years between them, he could not tell.

He dried his face sometime later. The pathways of the past could not change. However, he and his mother might track a new course toward forgiveness. The sentiment, buried beneath his resentment, must be uncovered again.

Fruzhin was right. The child inside him still lived, though wounded. Something remained of a boy longing for his mother's comfort.

THE NEXT MONTH, WHILE the courtiers gathered for the queen's departure, Vlad embraced Fruzhin and looked on over his friend's shoulder. His mother made her obeisance before Zsigmond's wife. Borbála's face was mottled before she left. Vlad joined his parent.

"Why does she dislike you?" He leaned close to her ear.

"She doesn't have any peculiar feelings for me." His mother watched the household knights lead the queen away at Fruzhin's order. "Her husband enjoys beautiful women. She tolerates what all wives do. As I did. Unlike her, I remain above suspicion."

"Are you accusing her of being no better than Zsigmond? How would you know?"

"Recall, I left family and friends behind among the courtiers here. Our king and queen are two sides of the same coin. *Infidus namque maritus infidam facit uxorem.*"

"The unfaithful husband made the wife unfaithful," he translated from Latin.

"Come with me to the herb garden before you assume your patrol on the walls." His mother tucked her hand in the crook of his elbow. "Let us talk about the royals."

"Did Zsigmond once desire you and try to take liberties?"

She smacked his forearm as they ambled outside. "We met at the Bavarian imperial castle, the Kaiserburg Nürnberg, in the same year my father considered Mircea's request for my hand. I was then fifteen years old. Zsigmond was two years younger. A lusty, bold youth, he came to Hungary when he was eleven for his education and to meet his first wife. I entered your father's bed, my maidenhood intact despite Zsigmond's...rigorous attempts to claim it. He received the crown of Hungary six years later."

"He's never forgotten you."

"It's likely he's bedded every female he's ever wanted, except for me."

Despite the initial strain, over the subsequent autumn and winter months, mother and son rebuilt their bond. She surprised him with the news that his grandmother thrived, unaltered by grief for her dead and buried child.

Mara also spent hours in prayer or with Staico and the Gypsies. Knowing his uncle's heart, Vlad often turned on the wall and watched them strolling through the grounds north of the stables. Staico seemed at peace beside Mara and her, with him. She balled up the snow in her hands and playfully lobbed it at his face. Only the affection of old friends.

IN THE YEAR OF OUR Lord 1419. Buda, Hungary (modern-day Budapest, Hungary)

Hungary's king and his queen, under Fruzhin's protection, returned to Buda within days of each other as the winter ended. For once, Vlad and Zsigmond's wife shared similar concerns, as their king paid particular attention to Mara on every occasion they met.

"Even in your widowhood, you look exceedingly lovely, my dear princess," he murmured over her hand before his expected departure from the dining hall.

"Your Royal Majesty remains too kind," Mara replied in a cool tone.

Vlad winced as her nails dug into his forearm below the tablecloth. He turned from the view of a scowling Borbála on the dais. He rose with Mara. After more pleasantries, their king released her and left.

Fruzhin did not attend the meal. During the week, he mourned the death of his brother Iskender, killed at the end of last year by Turks loyal to Mûsâ Çelebi's memory.

"You should comfort your friend. Fruzhin is good to you." Vlad's mother sat with him again. "Besides, it's time I summoned the royal halberdiers to escort me home."

"The boyar Vlậcsan has never joined us at mealtimes."

"He has a townhouse nearby. He did not think he would be welcome at your side."

"Something about him disturbs me. The feral look of him, draped in that gray pelt."

"He's called Vlậcsan the Wolf rightly." She smiled and patted his fingers.

"I first saw him with Grandmother years ago. Why did you bring him here?"

"Vlậcsan is her brother's son. A cousin to your late father. It's not your fault you don't know all your relations. The Dowager trusts her nephew and I trust her."

While Vlad contemplated the revelation, his mother raised his hand and kissed it.

They parted at the start of spring with a mutual vow to write to each other at least quarterly. He gazed at her, memorizing the contours of her face. As if they might never see each other again. She and Vlậcsan rode away between two rows of armored halberdiers.

Later, Vlad patrolled the wall in the shadow of a half-finished tower begun seven years ago. Zsigmond's wars and poor money habits left him unable to finish the work. After dinner, where his king and Queen Borbála appeared resplendent in purple and crimson garments shot through with gold thread, Vlad took up the night duty.

Movement between the base of the wall and the tower drew his scrutiny. Hand in hand, a pair raced to the structure. An armored knight, his head covered by a helmet, its crest shaped like a dragon. His companion wore a hooded mantle. Cool air brushed aside its trailing edge, revealing shimmery dark material.

A woman's velvety laughter pealed before the couple withdrew inside the half-finished construction. After some time, Vlad assumed the lovers had made their escape through some other path. They re-emerged below his station. The full moon revealed them as they embraced and kissed, the lower half of the knight's face concealed but for a russet-hued beard. He fled afterward.

Vlad recalled a mysterious dragon knight from years ago who vanquished Pipó but lost in the joust against the English earl of Warwick. Was the same warrior also the woman's paramour? She turned from watching his departure. Cold fingers of air currents ripped at her mantle's lower half, exposing quartered skirts dyed purple and red. She raised her head, although the hood never slipped. A clear glance shot at the rampart where Vlad stood before she left.

He clenched the masonry. Did he truly glimpse proof of the queen's infidelity?

THE END OF SUMMER BROUGHT momentous news to the Hungarian court. Their king's half-brother Wenceslaus died after his heart gave out.

As he dined in the aftermath, Zsigmond raised a wine chalice. "To Wenceslaus."

"To Wenceslaus," his courtiers repeated as they drank with their king.

"A greater drunkard never lived!" He drained his vessel and waved for more wine.

He made a pretense of solemn grief in public until the Turks attacked southern Hungary. At the head of Zsigmond's Bulgarian mercenaries, Fruzhin fought the enemy for two months. In a letter for Vlad, his best friend celebrated minor border victories.

Vlad did not reply with how Bohemian Hussites celebrated the death of Wenceslaus and rejected his heir Zsigmond, who failed to protect their martyred theologian, Jan Hus. In defiance of Catholic rules, where only clergy received the communion chalice, the radicalized reformists' congregations also drank the wine.

A staunch Catholic, equally affronted by the Hussite practices and their rebellion against his future rule, Zsigmond promised war bands would fall upon Bohemia. He called up the levies once Fruzhin returned to Buda.

"*Amici*, will we fight the Ottomans or Bohemians?" Pipó asked while he, Vlad, and Fruzhin sat under the lone tree in the castle courtyard. Dried leaves fell around them as Pipó removed a shoe and rubbed his big toe.

"We can't wage two wars and win. This country is supposed to be the bulwark of Christianity," Vlad answered. "We've lost too many in Bosnia. When our king should've replenished our ranks, he let the papal issue at Konstanz hold sway. I don't care how you scowl at me, Fruzhin. It's true."

"Whatever course Zsigmond chooses, we have a duty to him," his best friend said.

Later, to the trio's collective disgust, their sovereign chose peace with the Turks.

"A five-year truce." Fruzhin kicked the pile of rotting leaves clumped beneath the courtyard's tree. "The Ottoman envoy will arrive at Várad in Transilvania."

"Truly, *amico*?" Pipó flung aside the last of the walnut roll pilfered during *prandium* that morning. A stray dog snatched the half-eaten pastry and scampered.

Vlad huffed and frowned at his friends before he turned on his heels. Fury surged inside him. Damnable Turks! By the blood of Christ, how could they evade his sword again? Must his vengeance wait on Zsigmond's whims alone?

"Where are you going, Vlad?" Fruzhin called out. "What about your duty on the wall at noon?"

He would not neglect it. Except for a curt nod to the gatekeeper's men, he acknowledged no one. He ambled without purpose; head bowed.

On the quayside, sailors shouted to each other on ships sailing up the Danube River in the recesses of his mind. Thoughts muddled, he only stopped when a child's leather ball rolled into his path. He retrieved it and looked around for the owner. Three little boys blanched and ran away.

"It is no wonder they fled, for you are a fearsome warrior, my prince."

The children's ball fell from his grasp and rolled away, forgotten, as the woman from the streets of Hermannstadt, the city with eyes, reappeared before him. Nine years after the first encounter and seven years since he last glimpsed her riding in search of Buda's Jewish neighborhood.

"You've not changed," he gushed. A lie, for she seemed even lovelier than memory.

"The prince recalls me? An honor." She laughed, a tinkling melody. "Your face is beardless as when we met in Hermannstadt. The armor is new."

"Please tell me your name at once! I must know it."

"As I remember, you once concluded I was not worthy of your interest."

Mortified, he recalled his pompous introduction and abrupt leave-taking of her.

"My name is Călțuna," she offered amid his silence.

He sighed. Somehow, he had heard it before but did not recall exactly when; in Hermannstadt or on the Street of Roses. Now, he would never forget the name.

"I'm pleased to see you again. Call me Vlad. My friends do. Not that I suggest we are already friends. I mean to say, I don't assume you would choose...." He trailed off as her amused expression made him conscious of babbling. "Er, you're far from home."

"I've come here with my father and youngest brother for marital negotiations."

He swallowed. His chest tightened. Heaviness suffused it. He looked at his feet and berated himself for his eager openness with her. She belonged to someone else.

"I wish you great joy." He cleared his throat. "And hope you'll be content."

"To see my last sibling married and settled here, so far from us? Even if he is marrying a rich merchant's daughter, no, I do not think that will make me happy."

He perked up. The edges of her full lips twitched.

"You did that on purpose!" He ground his teeth before saying, "You knew I—"

"Knew what?" Her mirth cooled in an instant. Those emerald eyes pierced him.

"Nothing," he muttered before raking a damp hand over his head. "Your father lets you walk without an escort?"

"He and my brother remain nearby at the place we have rented while in town." She pointed to the back garden of a house at the end of the row. "I vowed not to venture beyond where they can see me from a window."

The sun's rays filtered through thin clouds, reminding him of noon's approach.

"Forgive me, but I can't stay any longer. A knight of a king's household has duties." Although her smile mocked him, he rushed on. "I'd like to see and speak with you again. Can you come to this same spot when the city's bells peal at ten tomorrow morning?"

"If my father allows it," Călțuna answered.

"I shall wait for you," he promised. "Until then, I bid you a good day."

"Good day, knight of the realm." Despite her somewhat teasing tone, she curtsied.

He hurried away, his thoughts on her. One glimpse made him forget his king's treaty and the perfidious Turks. Her bright visage soothed him, although his heart fluttered.

As he approached the castle's southern gate, he chided himself. He hadn't thought of the woman in years yet behaved like a fool the moment she reappeared. She probably would not meet him the next day, thinking no better of him than before.

EXCEPT, SHE WAITED at the appointed time in the same spot, and every day afterward for three weeks. After he mentioned the second sighting of her two years after they met in Hermannstadt, she could not recall having seen him.

"Are you certain you saw me seven years ago, my prince?"

They traipsed through the marketplace, the grounds covered in winter's first snow.

"I could never forget you, dear lady. Our gazes met before you rode on with your companion, presumably a sibling."

"He and I visited Buda with Father's permission seven years ago. To learn more about the woman who's claimed my brother's heart. Where did you encounter me?"

"Er, on a narrow street. Ah, let's have some food!" He hoped she would not pursue more details. Otherwise, she would learn his observation of her occurred on the notorious Street of Roses with its houses of prostitution.

He found the German baker of pretzels and bought one for Călţuna. They enjoyed tankards of brew too, as he had neglected the *prandium* meal to join her briefly.

"You were born in Transilvania?" He drank in the sight of her, headier than ale.

"No, I am Wallachian by birth like you. I grew up in Hermannstadt, where my father fled and raised me on his own. My mother passed away during the birthing. All my brothers are younger. Another woman, who has also since died, gave birth to them. They have been protective of me since girlhood, like our father."

"It's a wonder he's allowed you to be here with me each day."

With her drinking vessel, she indicated two young men who eyed them while eating sausages at the opposite stall. "Father's servants ensure my safety."

"And my proper behavior?" When she chuckled, he joined her. "I could listen to your voice and laughter every hour of every day, Călţuna."

"But you must attend to your duties. May I walk with you to the castle gate?"

"The only thing I'd like more would be for you to stay by my side forever."

Her cheeks flushed as he took their tankards, returned them to the brewer, and left the market. He darted a look over his shoulder. Her guardians followed.

"There's another reason Father left Wallachia," Călţuna said. "He hated your late father's high taxes and favored the rate the lord Stibor administered in Transilvania."

"I knew Stibor well," Vlad replied. "He trained me for warfare."

"Was he a bold fighter, as many say?"

"The bravest I've ever known. I miss his courage and wisdom." He glanced at her. "Your youngest sibling must be well in his youth, but he weds before you do. How many years separated your births? How old are you?"

"Such poor manners! Never ask a lady her age." She smacked his forearm and giggled. "I'm no decrepit maid. My little brother is sixteen and I am twelve years older."

And three years older than Vlad. He commented, "But you have no husband."

"By choice. I don't want to leave Father unattended. He's surrendered all thoughts of marrying me off. I'll take care of him. My future as a spinster may befit me."

"Never! You're too beautiful for that, Călţuna." As she blushed like a young girl, he asked, "What if you found a husband who could also ensure your father's well-being?"

"Do such miracles exist? An unselfish man with vast riches?" They shared another laugh. "I've always wished for a sister, in part, so we could share the duty of our father."

"Sisters are a blessing. I loved both of mine. They died years apart in childbirth. I remember their joy in our youth with fondness."

He realized, for the first time, it did not hurt to speak of Anna and Arina. Their names no longer evoked bittersweet memories alone. Love abided.

He looked toward the woman, smiling at him. Had she helped ease his sorrow?

“Most brothers find sisters are an unbearable nuisance,” she said. “Mine did, because I am the eldest of our father’s brood.”

“Perhaps they were a little jealous, for he must view you as his precious pearl.”

Her ensuing silence told Vlad he guessed correctly. Too soon, they reached the base of Castle Hill. She halted, and he turned to her.

“May I see you tomorrow as well, Călţuna? I’ll attend Catholic mass as usual with my king in the morning, but afterward?”

He shared so much about his life with her in three weeks, including his conversion. A fact he never admitted to his mother. Although not Catholic, Călţuna did not judge him.

“As you wish.” She curtsied. “Until tomorrow, Vlad.”

His name on her lips summoned a deep sigh of contentment. With the usual regret, he left her. Near the palace’s southern gate, he stopped, turned, and made out her diminutive figure covered in a blue mantle. Snow flurries swirled around her, but she appeared not to waver in the cold.

It did not affect him, either. Warmth suffused his heart. Later, he also enjoyed his first good night of sleep in several years. No phantom words disrupted his rest.

AFTER THE RITE OF mass occurred the next day, they strolled on the dock under dull midday sunshine. Their last meeting. Călţuna’s family would leave for Hermannstadt the next morning.

Certainty lightened Vlad’s footsteps. Love bloomed inside him. What did she feel?

“You’re brooding.” She pecked his sleeve with a gloved hand. “Will you miss me?”

“You’ll never leave my thoughts or my heart.” He paused near the house her father rented. “You took no escorts today. Does that mean you trust me?”

"No! I hardly know you." When he frowned, she giggled and rested her fingers on his forearm. "But I wish it. There's one thing I want to know now. The taste of your lips."

She edged closer and pressed her soft mouth to his. Surprised at her boldness, he barely responded before she drew back.

"I've displeased you," she whispered. "Do you fear I give kisses too easily?"

"No, dear Călţuna." He stroked her cool cheek. "I could never think poorly of you."

"My father advised caution. He feared a prince would only dally with me. I knew if I waited for your kiss, it would seem an eternity. We no longer have the time."

He tugged her into his arms and kissed her as he'd longed to do for days. Their breaths melded, and he swallowed the moan in her throat. His metal codpiece spared her the obvious sign of his lust, although he wasn't sure she didn't desire him equally. Her thumb stroked the edge of his mouth. She shivered in his grasp.

"Write to me," he pleaded when they drew apart. "We're going to Bohemia, but I can ask another knight to bring your letters wherever I may be. I'll reply when I can."

She tiptoed, pressed her forehead to his chin, and nodded.

That night, he searched the grounds until he found the household knight whom he had referenced earlier with Călţuna. Vajk Hunyadi bowed with a barely stifled grunt.

"Prince Vlad. Your remembrance honors me," he said.

"As you once honored me, risking your life against forest bandits," Vlad replied.

"Ages ago. How may I aid you now?"

"You'll be among the knights defending Buda during the Bohemian campaign."

"I'm old. I've languished at Hunyadvár too long." Something flickered in Vajk's rheumy brown eyes. The knight shifted on bowed legs and hung his head. "Not as fit for battle as you and others, I suppose."

"But you can still ride a horse well. I ask for a boon," Vlad said. "If any letters should come for me in my absence, I trust you can deliver them in Bohemia."

"I'll need to ask the captain general, but if he consents, I can travel to you."

"As thanks, I'll secure your son's post as a royal attendant. Fruzhin told me about your wish. János won't be our king's priority, but I'll never give up. You have my vow."

The older man's gaze flickered. "You honor me again, prince."

Vlad patted Vajk's shoulder.

Later, while bedding down in István's Tower, Vlad told Fruzhin about Călțuna, confessing his love and the plan for maintaining a connection with her.

"I'm glad your heart heals from loss and grief," Fruzhin replied. "I'd never forbid your feelings, but don't let them distract you from duties to Zsigmond."

Once their king accepted the offer of the crown of Bohemia, Zawisza arrived at the court. Vlad took duty in the throne room where Zsigmond and the Black Knight spoke. Whatever the latter said, their sovereign laughed and dismissed him.

Afterward, the chamber's double doors closed. Zsigmond's smile devolved into a scowl. He pounded his fists on the throne's velvet-covered armrests.

"Ha! He would divorce his lawful wife to seek the bed of my brother's widow. Preposterous! My Žofie in Zawisza's arms instead of mine? Never," he muttered.

More foreign knights joined the Hussite campaign. Vlad joined the ranks of Zawisza's four vice-captains in Bohemia. His friends and uncle congratulated him.

NEARING THE END OF the year, the Hungarian army departed under the cover of light December snow. Vlad came out of István's Tower and found Borbála locked in a passionate embrace with Zsigmond. Neither cared how others smirked. Once their king released her and clambered atop his horse, she pressed her lips to his gauntleted hand and drew back.

Vlad ensured the readiness of Zawisza's men, shared a nod with his uncle and the Gypsy twins at the end of the column, and then approached his mount. Borbála watched him. He offered her a deferential nod, although the viper deserved none.

"I trust you'll defend my husband and keep him focused on the war effort." She drew closer. "I know you saw me that night in the spring after your mother went home," she whispered. "It would do no good to revisit a distant past. Especially with our king. You should be careful on the road. Dangers abound. Even more so for a foreign prince."

He got on the horse and spurred it away from her clear warning.

CHAPTER 14

Leviathan

"Truth is the daughter of time."-Aulus Gellius (circa 125-circa 180 AD), Roman author and grammarian.

IN THE YEAR OF OUR Lord 1420. Mìlník, Bohemia (Mělník, modern-day Czech Republic)

Along the northern journey, Vlad kept vigil for a red-bearded knight in a dragon-crest helm. Pipó and Zawisza could not think of whom he meant. Each man asked why the discovery mattered to Vlad. He explained his interest as idle curiosity. Fruzhin stared at him and shrugged when questioned.

So far, he had kept himself safe from the threat Borbála posed. He chose no other mounts except the Carpathian ponies bred from the original stock the Gypsies brought into Hungary. He declined every royal squire's offer to saddle his horse and inspected all the riding equipment himself. Vulnerabilities remained where he squatted in the bush and relieved his bowels.

On rare occasions when he chanced to see and speak with his uncle, Staico frowned and questioned the wariness reflected in his gaze and furrowed brow. He didn't reveal his concerns, remembering how his uncle once barged into a muddy tourney field with a sword and crossbow, seeking revenge on Vlad's Teutonic attackers. Borbála or her lover would be foes that are far more dangerous.

Vlad reasoned that the queen's paramour must be part of the campaign. Why else would she have warned against betraying her conduct to her husband? Not that Vlad intended to do so. During his mother's stay in Hungary, she opined Zsigmond and Borbála vied with each other in a cruel game only they understood. Mara must be wrong. Vlad could not believe a husband would tolerate his wife's open infidelity.

Encamped at Mìlník, the dower town of Bohemian queens for centuries, according to Zsigmond, Vlad brought Wenceslaus' widow to his king. Borbála was perhaps less haughty than Žofie of Bavaria in Vlad's opinion. On duty with other knights outside the royal tent, they overheard her ardent shrieks and moans. Although he frowned, his companions jeered and silently mocked the Bohemian queen's exhortations.

Some days later, she screeched, though not in the throes of passion. Vlad gaped at her. Red-faced, she parted the tent flaps and rushed out. Zsigmond followed, his open robe revealing an unlaced shirt. He dragged up the hose below his waist.

"Come back here, Žofie!" He roared. "I am your king, and you'll obey!"

"No, I will not, Zsigmond." She turned and faced him. "I've kept my word and withdrawn support of the Hussites, but you haven't held onto your oath. I'm done with your false promises! Wenceslaus is dead, as God willed it. Still, you hesitate."

"What do you want from me, woman?"

"Keep the vow you made. If you truly want me, get rid of your wife!"

She did not await their king's reply. For the best, Vlad thought, since Zsigmond gave none. She huffed and called her attendants. The Bohemians left in a flurry of dust.

VLAD KEPT TO HIS DUTIES while a foul temperament consumed Zsigmond for two weeks. No more references to his royal personage in formal address, as he muttered to himself. His forked beard grew overlong, the tips touching his chest. He guzzled wine with the same wanton abandon he once accused his cuckold of a half-brother.

Though despairing of Zsigmond's behavior, Vlad never commented on it, even with friends, having once sought a remedy for his battered soul by the same means. He would not judge now.

Their king deigned to consider the war operation again. He summoned Vlad, along with other vice-captains and their immediate subordinates to the royal tent at noon during the next week.

Vlad looked on in silence. He trusted leaders of the Hungarian war bands, among them his friends Zawisza, Fruzhin, and Pipó, the latter named as their captain general, to ease Zsigmond's mood.

"Your Royal Majesty, we cannot, ah, ignore the reports of our spies." Pipó stroked a graying beard. "The Hussites are building wagons reinforced with heavy—"

"Pipó! You think their wagon trains are a concern for me?" With his forefinger, their king stabbed a calfskin map stretched across the makeshift wooden table. "They're encamped here, twenty-five leagues away! It's less than two days' ride. I care not how they move their equipment and supplies when they could attack at any moment."

"If you'll forgive, Your Royal Majesty, they won't assail us. *Sì*, they're too busy with the wagons. The Hussite's foremost leader, Jan Žižka, began life as a squire, admitted to King Wenceslaus' royal guards before he was appointed chamberlain in Queen Žofie's retinue." Pipó rushed on as Zsigmond frowned at her mention. "Despite her later dismissal, Žižka came away from royal service well-steeped in its traditions and your half-brother's battle tactics. What if he hides something else inside the wagons, no?"

Their king snarled, "The scouts must tell us! Have wars been won with unreliable information? If our spies can't learn the truth, eliminate them! Find better spies!"

No one else spoke in the wake of the callous command, but Vlad looked at Fruzhin, who barely shook his head in warning.

"You heard me, Pipó!" Their king's brow furrowed, and his face reddened, fiercely bestial like a lion, the heraldic symbol of his House of Luxembourg. "Now leave my tent and get me what I need. Go from me, all of you! Vlad, you still have the duty of my protection. Tell one of your men on guard to find my chief barber while you bring the palatine to me now! Have him come with any new royal correspondence."

The courtiers bowed and left Zsigmond, Vlad last among them. He gave their monarch's instruction to a knight near the tent flap before seeking the palatine.

After he delivered their king's order, Miklós' beady brown gaze darted to the opened box of rolled and sealed letters on the parchment. "I would've brought them to His Royal Majesty myself without—"

"Shall I carry them for you?" Vlad cut him off, despising his unctuousness.

In the royal tent, the palatine shuffled on his feet and Vlad awaited Zsigmond's dismissal, which did not come. The chief barber arrived, and their king took to a stool, demanding the hair of his head and beard shorn to a decent length.

"Miklós, what letters do you have for me today?" Zsigmond asked while the barber draped him in a woolen towel. "Has anything come bearing Wenceslaus' seal?"

"Er, no, Your Royal Majesty." The palatine made another furtive glance at the missives rather than face Zsigmond's glower. "Not today, Your Royal Majesty, but I am vigilant."

"Damn Žofie for a stubborn bitch!" Their king slapped his muscled thigh, clad in crimson hose. "Vlad, you are lucky. No desires for one woman have encumbered you."

He could never describe Călţuna or his love for her as a burden. He would not reveal her to Zsigmond, who might disdain genuine interest in a boyar's likely bastard.

Vlad chided himself for letting her leave Buda without introducing himself to Călţuna's father and determining her lineage. He never asked his love if the woman who bore her had also married her father. A Wallachian prince in Hungarian royal society should care about his would-be wife's heritage. He had not inquired, because only his happiness with Călțuna mattered to him. A fierce protectiveness of her swelled inside him.

"Did you hear what I said, Vlad?" Zsigmond snapped. "Where is your mind?"

Pleasantly engrossed, Vlad blinked then, brought back to awareness. "Forgive me, Your Royal Majesty. I humbly ask for your lenience."

"So, you admit you were ignoring me? At least, you're no liar, but how dare you disregard your king! Don't do it again. I've commanded you to read the royal letters."

As Vlad approached the table, Miklós murmured, "Er, I could call a royal squire...."

"Did I ask for one?" Their king turned his glare on the palatine. "Vlad can undertake the task, having done so years ago. Christ's bones!" Despite his obvious exasperation, Zsigmond closed his eyes and allowed his barber's attention to resume.

Vlad broke the seals on his king's correspondence and scrutinized their contents. The queen served as regent and consulted her husband, a month after his departure, in resolving disputes, confirmation of ownership rights, and issuing charters. Vlad perused several letters from her requiring Zsigmond's opinion.

Another document detailed a quarrel between Borbála and an archbishop whom her husband relied on; she would not do the same regarding her dower property and begged Zsigmond to support her. Vlad bit back a sigh at the usual requests for settlement of the royal debt, which preceded another letter bearing a plain wax seal without insignia.

As Vlad scanned it, he recognized the immediate significance. Absent a signature and date, the delicate, cursive writing damned the queen. His gaze fled to their king, who met his regard at the same time.

"You've paled," Zsigmond said. "Is there some new difficulty mentioned in that missive? Read it to me first."

Vlad swallowed and glanced at the words again, as though wishing to blot them from sight. He cleared his throat and began, "To His Most Serene Majesty, King Zsigmond—"

"Dispense with the salutation and preliminaries. I need to know if there's trouble." His sovereign shifted on the stool and waved to his barber, still trimming the beard.

Skipping the first paragraph, Vlad read, "I write to you with word of Friedrich of the House of Hohenzollern—"

"Oh, why would I wish to be bothered about him?" Zsigmond complained and turned his head. His barber's yelp seemed to go unnoticed, as did the lopsided cut of the beard with a blade. Their king continued, "He's at home in Berlin, isn't he, Miklós?"

"Er, yes, Your Royal Majesty," the palatine replied.

"He donned that silver dragon-crest helm without my consent. Borbála let him. As if I would've allowed him membership in the Order after he questioned my fight against the Hussites and refused to commit his men-at-arms." Zsigmond's thick brows flared before he added, "I suppose I must hear about Friedrich. He settled a large sum of the royal debt after I traveled to France. As any loyal courtier should! Vlad, tell me what's been said of him." He turned to his barber. "Take better care with the blade."

The hapless servant accepted the blame with a nod.

Vlad cleared his throat and resumed reading. "I am unknown to you, Your Royal Majesty, and wish to remain so. I must preserve the sanctity of my life, but as a loyal subject of your court at Buda Castle, I cannot conceal the horrid truth. Friedrich, whom you've long relied upon, had carnal knowledge of your queen, Borbála of Celje, for years, and got her with a child last spring. A bastard she rid herself of soon after...."

Trailing off at the sight of his patron's baleful stare, Vlad held his breath as Zsigmond shoved aside his barber and came and snatched the letter. His hot gaze flitted over the damnable words before he glared at Vlad, the palatine, and the servant.

Who could have written the words? Vlad wondered whether a disgruntled maid in the queen's retinue did so. Maybe even the former governess of her child, whom Zsigmond took as a lover at Pozsony some summers ago, before discarding her.

"You will each swear an oath to Us now." Their sovereign drew himself up to his full height and crushed the paper in his hand. "What you have heard will not leave this tent."

In order of courtly rank, from the palatine to the chief barber, each man got on his knees and made a solemn vow. As he did so, Vlad's mind warred with his conscience. After confirmation that Friedrich of the House of Hohenzollern once wore the dragon-headed helmet and rutted with the queen, he could not conceal having witnessed them last spring. Flanked by the other two men, he asked Zsigmond's permission to speak.

"Your Royal Majesty, I have direct knowledge of events pertaining to the accusation," he admitted.

His king's frosty glare fell on him. "You dare tell Us this only now?"

"I saw an incident suggesting Friedrich and... the queen's involvement, but your remark about his heraldry gave the final proof. He is the same knight who rode against the earl of Warwick after defeating Pipó in a joust on Csepel Island. I recall Your Royal Majesty's vexation at the knight as he left the lists."

Zsigmond hovered closer. "Say what you saw of Friedrich and Borbála."

Vlad swallowed and spoke in full of the night in which he recognized the queen by her dress, the quartered skirts in deep crimson and purple. With each word, her husband and king reddened with rage and his fists shook.

In the end, Vlad bowed his head. The truth was disclosed at last. Would Zsigmond punish him for its revelation now after having hidden it for eight months? His king's hand alighted on his head and fisted in his hair.

"I've lived with her betrayals long enough that they don't offend. Only her lack of discretion matters," Zsigmond muttered over his head. "She will pay for her carelessness."

The truth of his mother's opinion reverberated in Vlad's mind. For his king knew about his wife's extramarital partners the same way she knew about his lovers. He only demanded she spare him any disgrace, including a bastard's taint.

"You will never mention the incident again, except for the trial records, Vlad."

Heart thudding, Vlad understood the disclosure heralded disgrace alone for his sovereign. The perfidious game Zsigmond and Borbála played required her secrecy, so no man might deem her husband a cuckold. Now, three others knew his shame.

As though poised on a precipice, Vlad realized there could be no turning back. In the legal proceedings to follow, his king required his testimony against a woman who never liked him from the start. Surely, after the trial, she would mark him as an eternal enemy.

The palatine Miklós gasped once Zsigmond withdrew his hand and looked down at him before he rushed to say, "Your Royal Majesty, er, please let me—"

"For fifteen years, you've been married to that bitch's sister. You once counseled Our wedding with Borbála. Now, you shall begin Our efforts to undo the union. Write to the treasurer of Our royal council and cut off all her monies. She's not to have another florin of income from her dower lands! I will not see or speak with her, or any of her officials. We will convene a tribunal at Várad in Transilvania against the whore. She conceived a bastard and hid it. She shall know nothing but Our wrath for this affront!"

Zsigmond went to a chest from which he withdrew sheaves of paper, bottles of ink, and goose-feathered quills. He littered the map on the makeshift table with them. A vessel overturned, but its cork stopper prevented the contents from spilling.

"You shall write Our decree to the royal council, Miklós. When the marriage of Our daughter Erzsébet occurs with that pale-faced Habsburg prince, Albrecht, We'll name that boy Our official heir—"

"Er, Your Royal Majesty, the council must discuss the matter!" The palatine scuttled across the tent on his hands and knees, only stopping when Zsigmond hauled him up.

"How dare you speak when We have given no permission?" He shoved Miklós aside, fetched his stool, and slammed it beside the table. "Set the quill to paper now."

The palatine scrambled to do so before Zsigmond shouted at his barber, "Get up and find another stool! Finish your task. We'll leave for Várad tomorrow morning with Our guards and half the court retinue."

BEFORE MIDNIGHT, WHEN Vlad would have surrendered his king's protection to one of Fruzhin's vice-captains, a scout arrived at the camp. Pipó and Fruzhin brought him to the royal tent, while Vlad woke Zsigmond. Cursing under his breath, their sovereign rose and allowed the spy inside the royal tent with his officers.

There, the scout informed them of a skirmish one week ago where a Bohemian nobleman loyal to Zsigmond confronted the Hussites. At a place they attacked called Nekmíř, near their encampment, Jan Žižka faced two thousand soldiers with less than a quarter of their number and escaped. The Catholic forces endured heavy losses.

Fruzhin bowed and begged Zsigmond's leave to speak first. "If you'll allow, Your Royal Majesty, the numbers seem unlikely to have resulted in defeat for the Catholics."

Vlad nodded with Pipó and added, "It's only possible if there's some new weapon or tactic against mounted soldiers, which His Royal Majesty's loyalists never encountered."

Fruzhin turned from their king to the spy again. "How did Žižka escape?"

"With support from men in war wagons," the scout said. "Seven of them lashed wheel to wheel like a moving fortress. Less than a third of the height of a siege tower, they have arrow slits between extra planking, secured by ropes. A wagon nearly turned over and some inside spilled out. I counted men with flails and spears, and crossbowmen and hand gunners, who held their weapons against their bodies and lit gunpowder with a free hand. Behind the wagons, Žižka placed Hussite artillery, unlike cannons."

"How so?" Pipó demanded. "Leave nothing untold."

The scout bowed. "The barrel is shorter, but it moves on two wheels. It doesn't fire large stone balls. Instead, the shot the men loaded was smaller. At close range, it tore through the ranks of armored cavalry. The Hussites won with artillery and war wagons."

No one, including their king, said a word. Vlad ground his teeth together. A makeshift band of religious rebels led by a former Bohemian king's trusted guardsman seemed as formidable as any Turks Zsigmond ever encountered. Would they prevail?

ARRIVING FROM BOHEMIA before sunset, Vlad received Zawisza's command to guard their king's chamber. The next dawn, before seeking his rest, Vlad sent a letter to Călţuna. Despite parting from her only two months before, he longed for the sight of her again. A salve that also set his soul afire. She alone helped mend his wounded heart.

As the last royal council members made their way into the Episcopal city of Várad, she arrived. While Vlad kept watch outside Zsigmond's meetings about the upcoming trial, a pageboy brought her short letter to Vlad. Rapture filled him and deep longing. Throughout the day, his obligation kept him from her side at an inn.

Raised voices filtered beyond his king's chamber into the passageway as some counseled Zsigmond against rash actions. Twice, the door slammed back on its hinges, and he shouted for the removal of some frightened courtier. Vlad did not know who among them would give testimonials against the queen, for the palatine summoned them in private soon after they came to Várad.

After Vlad surrendered his post to another of Zawisza's vice-captains, he hastened to the inn an hour before midnight. The innkeeper scowled but let him in after he flashed a gold florin. He took the stairs two at a time, arriving at the first door on the second floor. Călţuna peered out into the dimness and ushered him inside.

They rushed at each other in a flurry of kisses and tangled limbs. He wanted to nip her slender throat and the small breasts pressed to him, no bigger than apples with their stiff nipples jutting. Her hold on his nape tightened, keeping their mouths melded together while her fingers roved his breastplate, seeking to unfasten the sides of it one-handed. Damn. He should have called a pageboy and removed the armor at court.

He tore away from her. "My sweet, you'll bruise your fingertips on the metal."

"I don't care!" She tugged off his helmet and pulled him into the center of the chamber, where for the first time, in the low candlelight Vlad noticed two forms huddled beneath a blanket, another woman with a little girl, both deep in slumber.

Vlad grasped Călţuna's slender arms when she would have drawn him closer again. "Stop," he pleaded. "Our reunion can't happen in the room you are sharing. We don't know who this woman may be. She may talk."

"There's a stable behind the inn. Let's go there," she whispered.

He smothered giddy laughter behind the gauntlet on his hand and removed his mantle. Wrapping her inside it, they crept down the stairs and lifted the bar on the inn's door. The wood creaked, and the innkeeper peered out with a candle precariously close to his nose. As he scowled into the darkness, they rushed out into cold and snow flurries.

Merry as children, they ran to the horse barn, hand in hand. Inside, the animals greeted them with neighs while Vlad picked his way through piles of straw and grimaced at the pungent scent of the offal. They found a stall.

The whites of a groom's eyes met Vlad's own.

"One florin, if you sleep outside and don't betray us to anyone," he vowed.

Afterward, Călţuna giggled and pulled him down on dry hay. They kissed at their leisure until he lifted his head.

"How did you leave Hermannstadt?"

"My youngest brother helped. He found a band of pilgrims coming here in honor of the sainted Hungarian king László." She ran her fingertips over the short bristles on his face. "We knew Father would be angry, but I swore I loved you too much to stay away."

Despite hearing the truth on her lips, he rose above her. "Do you really love me?"

"Yes," she answered in the darkness. "Do you doubt me?"

"Well, it's the first time you've said it. You didn't write back after I sent word of my arrival at Mělník in Bohemia."

"My father found your first letter and burned it. He swore no good could come of my feelings for you. I dared not write back, but when I heard you were in Transilvania again, nothing could keep me from your side. I love you, Vlad."

He enfolded her in his arms and kissed her everywhere he wished. She never protested, even when his mouth closed on a taut nipple and tugged at it through the linen. She moaned and caught his nape again. He rose and nibbled at her neck.

"I love you with all my heart, Călțuna, with everything inside of me. Now and always, I am yours. I want you to be mine."

"I am yours also, forever," she whispered against his hair.

"Then say you'll marry me," he pleaded.

"Ask me later." She pushed him back at the shoulders with surprising strength for so small a woman. Or perhaps, lost in desire, he let her.

She removed her garment and helped him with the armor. When they were naked and his fingers splayed across her maiden-flat belly, he imagined a child nestled there.

"Why do you hesitate?" She panted. "I've seen the kitchen servants with my brothers when Father wasn't at home. I'm unafraid and wish you would claim me."

"I know, Călțuna," He rose above her. "I fear hurting you. There will be joy too."

She clutched his shoulder and sought his lips. "You could never hurt me."

He assured her he would not.

MORNING CAME TOO SOON, and a pair of voices outside the stable woke Vlad.

"Are you lying, boy? I didn't father you, but I'll beat you all the same if you lie. You're sure no knight and a woman came out here yesterday?"

"No, I never saw them."

As the man went away, mutters echoing behind him, Călţuna stirred and brushed Vlad's arm. He looked down at her and stroked the contour of her cheek.

"Did we get the poor groom into trouble, my Vlad?"

"He handled it." He kissed her forehead. "I'll have an extra florin for him as thanks. You must go back inside before I return to Zsigmond."

Yet, he would not let her up, kissing and caressing her. When she responded with her soft sighs and moans, Vlad's restraint broke. Only later, when he noticed the darkening bruise on her throat, did he regret his lack of gentle care.

She pulled on her sleeping tunic and brushed at the straw sticking out of her hair. He dressed in all but armor while she went to the stable door and summoned the groom. "Help this knight with the rest, and he'll have two florins for you."

Vlad scowled at the back of her head for her free hand with his money, but upon sight of her broad smile, he laughed at her audacity. His future wife should be so bold.

The groom left them afterward, richer with three gold coins that Vlad doubted the boy's stepfather would ever discover.

"I could not love you more if you were my king or less, if you lived as a pauper's son." Călţuna ran her fingers up his breastplate to the base of his throat, pulsing beneath her light touch. "There's something I must share, a long-held secret, which my father confessed to warn me away from you. I should have told you the moment we reunited."

Thrilled by her declaration, he silenced her with a kiss. "It can wait. I must leave. We have time," he murmured against her lips. "I'm not letting you go home without writing to your father. He must know of my devotion. I'd give you the world if I could, but you must be content with the heart I offer and the promise of marriage. All of it must wait on Zsigmond. Go."

Călţuna sighed and nodded. "My heart is always with you, wherever you may be."

They parted after another lingering embrace.

TO HIS DISMAY, VLAD could not escape for even an hour during the week to see Călţuna again or hear her revelation. Two of Zawisza's vice-captains showed signs of the burning sickness from prostitutes they frequented. Vlad performed the extra guard duty.

He witnessed the queen's afternoon arrival at the end of the week. She rode with a young man who favored her other companion, her parent Hermann, Count of Celje. The men could only be father and son. Borbála, all dressed in the somber black of mourning, shouted her demand for a meeting with her husband. Even worse, she brought their daughter Erzsébet, a girl of ten years, seated with a downcast expression on her pony.

Vlad stepped away from the door once Zsigmond emerged. He gripped the stone balustrade, staring down at his wife in the inner courtyard. Neither spoke.

"Your Royal Majesty, gracious and good," Hermann said as he dismounted and bowed. "My son Friderik and I have come seeking your benevolence for our dear Borbála's sake."

"No! You've arrived, thinking to prevent Us from exposing that whore's betrayal."

"If His Royal Majesty would give a kind ear to her pleas, our queenly daughter would beg forgiveness for any manner in which she may have wronged you."

"The slut's opened her legs too many times for Us to believe her contrite now."

A collective gasp rippled through the onlookers in the courtyard, obliterating the secrecy on which their king once insisted. Stationed behind him, Vlad groaned at the spectacle. He had kept his vow made in Zsigmond's tent and told none of his friends the details leading up to the queen's trial. Borbála deserved no sympathy, but shaming before the courtiers and men-at-arms tainted her husband too. Zsigmond would have done better to speak in private, far from prying eyes and loose tongues.

"If His Royal Majesty spurns the true penitence of our dear Borbála," Hermann bowed and approached, "will he not consider the words of a mere servant whose son helped save your most precious life at the Battle of Nicopolis over twenty years ago? Will His Royal Majesty give no ear to the man who thwarted rebellious Hungarian nobles when they imprisoned him for six months in the aftermath?"

At last, Vlad understood why Borbála had arrived with her father and brother. Zsigmond owed each man some personal debt. He might not be the ruler of Hungary without them. It seemed their king remembered well, for eventually, he spoke with both men in private. Later, a herald called for Borbála.

She murmured to her child, who waited on horseback. The queen's head held high. She got down off her horse without aid and mounted the steps. At the top of them, her gaze found Vlad. Cold fury in her narrowed stare and furrowed brow made him shudder.

She joined her husband, father, and brother. A summons came for three other high-ranked courtiers who came and went before dusk.

Afterward, Zsigmond and Borbála approached the balustrade side by side, and both waved Erzsébet up the steps. The assembly grew in their absence, once word spread of their king's accusation. He proclaimed there would be no trial. Exclamations of surprise followed. He would return to Buda Castle in two days and share the news of Bohemian war wagons and artillery while Borbála journeyed on to her southern Hungarian estate at Kelmek. Then he withdrew to his chambers alone.

Vlad followed, but not before catching sight of the queen with her father. Over his shoulder, she shot Vlad a dark stare filled with the promise of enmity. Even though a letter from someone else at court had damned her, she would still blame him. If she spoke with the palatine, she would learn how Vlad's confession bolstered the revelation of her secret.

Having roused a leviathan, when and how would she strike at him?

PREPARATIONS FOR THE short sojourn at Buda Castle kept Vlad busy. He managed only a short letter for Călţuna. The next morning, a cheerful pageboy delivered it at Vlad's behest and awaited her answer. Although sorrowful, she thought it best if they parted then rather than waiting for his leave-taking. In his reply, he begged her to stay and promised to see her that night. However, when he came to the inn again, Călţuna was not there.

The innkeeper, his wife, or his stepson saw her after the morning when she broke her fast. No threats or attempts to cajole altered their insistence on not knowing where she went afterward. Vlad did not believe she fled with no word of farewell.

"You've worn a frown all day, *amico*, no?" Pipó joined him outside Zsigmond's chamber. "Everyone saw and knew something bothered you, especially those who love you well. Fruzhin's with the palatine completing plans for our return to Bohemia a week after we reach Buda Castle. Will you unburden yourself to me, even if I'm not Fruzhin?"

Vlad took Pipó's arm and drew him away from the other guards into the shadows at the end of the passage. There, Vlad confessed all about Călţuna and his wish to wed.

"How do you know she wants the same, ah?" Pipó patted his shoulder. "You've loved this woman for what, three or four months, no? *Sì*, you don't truly know her."

"Not so!" He looked around and tried to lower his voice, for they drew scrutiny. "I feel as if I've known Călţuna all my life. I love her and want her for my wife. Why shouldn't I have a chance at the love my parents enjoyed? I don't know what's happened to Călţuna. Maybe she visited her father, to show I did her no harm—"

"No harm?" Pipó waggled his eyebrows. "Didn't you, ah, claim her maidenhead?"

"Yes! You knew I meant otherwise."

"*Sì*, I did!" Pipó laughed before he clasped Vlad's forearm. "I remember the throes of first love. Only ensure the woman you want is worthy of a prince's heart, ah?"

"She is," Vlad replied. "I will ask for her at every city gate. I'd cover all the exits faster with a friend's help if he took half of them while I visited the others."

"*Sì*, help you shall have, *amico*," Pipó swore. "*Prego*."

EVEN WITH PIPÓ'S AID, Vlad came no closer to learning the truth of Călţuna's whereabouts. His heart heavy, he rejoined the courtiers, preparing to depart with their king. Where was his lady love?

A squire interrupted his thoughts and brought Zsigmond's summons. Upon entering the royal chamber, he found his sovereign and Queen Borbála seated side by side. At their feet, a pageboy kneeled as did a blue hooded figure, both backing him.

"Come to us, Vlad." His king beckoned him with a wave.

As he stood between the kneeling pair, Călţuna threw off the hood and clutched his ankles. Stunned into silence, he could not muster a word.

Borbála leaned forward. "Boy, as a servant of His Royal Majesty's court, I charge you to answer truthfully. Did you carry an exchange of letters between this knight and this woman two days ago?"

The little attendant lifted his bowed head, revealing the wetness under his eyes. "Yes." Once she glared at him, he added, "Yes...my...queen." His small voice warbled.

"You may leave Us, child," Zsigmond said.

With a sorrowful look at Vlad, the pageboy scrambled to his feet and fled.

Their sovereign asked, "Vlad, is it true what Our queen has told Us? You've pledged your heart to this woman, already bedded her, and offered her marriage?"

"It is all true, Your Royal Majesty." He glanced down at Călţuna and stroked her hair. "I love her and wish to be her husband." He regarded Zsigmond and Borbála again. How dare they sit in judgment when neither respected the sanctity of marriage!

Vlad balked when Borbála laughed and nudged Călţuna's knee with the tip of her black, velvet-covered foot. "Tell him why he can't have you for a wife."

A dull ache throbbed in the center of his forehead. What did the queen mean?

"I've wanted to say it..." Călţuna's voice croaked. She collapsed in despair, sobbing.

"You've sullied yourself with oaths you cannot fulfill, prince." Borbála stood, her hands clasped together, a serene image hiding behind a monstrosity. "The bride you want is not nobly born. She is her father's bastard, born from his adulterous love for a Jewish maidservant, another man's wife. Whom he could never wed over his parents' objections. She died in childbirth, leaving this one's father to raise her alone."

With his suspicions affirmed, Vlad raised Călţuna's tear-stained face. "I don't care."

She hiccupped and held his gaze. All else receded in a world where only their love for each other existed. Nothing beyond that truly mattered.

"We care!" Zsigmond's bluster shattered their intimacy. "Aim higher in your ambitions as a king's knight. You are the third-born son of a vassal state, yes, but a Transalpine prince. Your marital arrangements must benefit Us." He stood even as Vlad shook his head. "This baseborn woman is not fit to wed. Find another."

The royal couple left them. Călţuna cried loudly, and Vlad stared without seeing. His desire for her was the equal of his hopes for his late sister or the Wallachian throne. Denied by the sole power on earth who could thwart him, alongside a vengeful queen. He recalled her regard two days ago, the promise of retribution in her hard, glittering stare.

He wavered on unsteady legs. After several gulps of air, he reached down and aided Călţuna. They embraced. Her sobs tore at the depths of his heart, almost unmanned him.

"When the queen's men came to the market and brought me before her, I feared the worst. But with you, I'm never afraid." The words, though muffled against his armor, reached him. "I can't leave you, my Vlad. I'll be your mistress. I'll be anything you wish."

"No, dearest Călţuna." He nuzzled her brow. "I can't let that viper Borbála with her forked tongue condemn you. The courtiers would name any children of ours, bastards."

"When I lay with you, I knew there could be a child. You'll protect us, I know it."

He recalled when members of his family shunned Staico and shuddered at the thought of his sons and daughters with Călţuna, burdened by ugly whispers.

Another truth existed, which he could never admit to her. He needed Zsigmond's support if he might ever rule his homeland. He could not defy his king.

"I love you too much to condemn you to a life of recriminations." He hoped she would accept those words instead. At least they were true. He grabbed her hand and headed for the door, although she wept. "Pilgrims are leaving Várad each day. I'll see you safely on the road with them before my departure to Hungary. Hurry!"

"No, Vlad," she cried. "Please take me with you. Don't send me away."

She thrashed, but he forced her bodily through the door, toward the stairs. She screeched his name, alerting the courtiers gathered to ride for Buda.

He rounded on her. "You must go! Can't you see this is how it must be now?"

"No!" Flecks of her spittle spattered his face. "All I see is your weakness. You love me, but your king holds more influence over you than me. You send me away because of him."

When she struggled resolutely again, he released her. Momentum carried her forward. She fell, shouting for help. He rushed down the steps, horrified. As he reached for her, she shrieked and warded him off. Blood trickled from a small cut at her hairline.

"Călţuna," he whispered, kneeling beside her.

"Don't come any closer. Please." She sobbed anew and swiped at her runny nose. Like a newborn foal, she struggled to her feet. Courtiers pointed and laughed.

Vlad snarled and stood. He drew his sword and brandished it at them. Most reared back. Once he turned again, he offered his hand to Călţuna.

She flinched. "Liar! Monster! You vowed you'd never hurt me."

Călţuna fled. He let her go.

A Warrior for God

1420-1427

CHAPTER 15

The Sword and Shield of the Realm

"Remember this. When people choose to withdraw far from a fire, the fire continues to give warmth, but they grow cold. When people choose to withdraw far from light, the light continues to be bright in itself, but they are in darkness. This is also the case when people withdraw from God."-Augustine of Hippo (354-430 AD), Roman North African Christian theologian, philosopher, bishop, and saint.

IN THE YEAR OF OUR Lord 1420. Sudoměř, Bohemia (Sudoměř, modern-day Czech Republic)

Dusk fell over Vlad while the Hungarian army with its Bohemian supporters and their camp followers traveled northwest, nearing the town of Sudoměř. The scouts kept watch beneath the trees, alert for any Hussite ambush. The enemy's strongest captain, Jan Žižka, proved a daring foe and hard to kill. Five or six abreast cavalry units and infantrymen delved deeper into the encroaching darkness.

Vlad kept silent for most of the journey from Buda. What was there to say?

"I still don't understand why you never warned me of your discovery about Borbála." Fruzhin glanced at him before staring straight ahead. "The palatine said you would have given testimony if a trial had occurred. Why did I hear so from him, not you?"

"You never revealed Friedrich's identity as the dragon knight." Vlad did not turn in the saddle. "I asked you about him twice. During our entry into Bohemia, two months ago, and on Csepel Island after he rode away from the lists, victorious over Pipó but defeated by the earl of Warwick. I remember you stared in his wake."

"I didn't know it was the same man all those years ago."

"You suspected. Did you think he and the queen were lovers then?"

"I knew not and did not care. What she does, and what her husband does with others is not our concern. Is this why you've been so quiet on the way here? Are you angry with me because I did not confirm Friedrich's identity? Does parting from the woman at Várad silence your tongue instead? The palatine told me about that as well."

"He expected the letter about the queen. Maybe he even knows who wrote the missive. All of you courtiers like keeping so many secrets. Allow me mine."

"The palatine's no better than an old woman. I warned him about the gossip-mongering, expecting you would explain what happened to your lady in full. But you haven't, as is your right."

"I will not do so now either." Vlad would not speak of his frustrations, even with his greatest friend. His time with Călţuna, all too briefly, was over. Now the battle lay ahead.

None of his fellow warriors seemed to fear the Hussites and their war wagons. With so many knights and cavalry units, they boasted about trampling Žižka's rabble, which included women, underfoot. Vlad shook his head at their bravado.

"Please, friend." Fruzhin disrupted his thoughts. "I can't help if you won't talk. I saw you cared deeply, but I still don't know what happened with you and your woman—"

"She is not mine," Vlad muttered. "Nor can she ever be. Let me mourn in peace."

He emerged with the army on the wide river plain outside the village of Sudoměř, where they bivouacked for the night. Scouts found fishponds bordered by marshland and a northbound river well stocked with carp, so their forces ate well.

Although surrounded by allies, Vlad hardly spoke. He thought of Staico, left behind. Despite his uncle having joined him in the initial campaign, this time Vlad ordered him and the Gypsies to remain in Buda. Although disgruntled, Staico had agreed.

Vlad struggled with the conclusions he drew after returning to Hungary. He questioned the morality of the coming conflict. Zsigmond persecuted Hussite Christians because they rejected his kingship, not for their practice of the Holy Eucharist.

Disillusioned with the Catholic faith, once embraced on an impulse, Vlad could not speak about his qualms. Not with the absent uncle still unaware of his conversion or his comrades devoted to their king's cause, who would kill as Zsigmond willed.

As he brooded, an emerald-green dragonfly landed on his bare hand. The campfire's light revealed patterned spots in varied golden hues. The insect flew away quickly, but its colors summoned thoughts of Călţuna.

Vlad wondered how she would view his misgivings. His hands itched to hold his lover against him. She tortured every fervent dream and waking hour. Somehow, he must master control of his thoughts about her. They could never be together again, not in the way he wished.

HE FELL ASLEEP ON THE open ground next to the fire, weighed by concerns. His fellow vice-captain woke him for the night duty; protection of their monarch.

He rubbed his eyes and looked over at Pipó, Fruzhin, and Zawisza, all of whom snored. God protect them.

For love and loyalty to his brothers in arms alone, not his king, he would fight the Hussites with the same determination as he showed their Turkish foes.

Rousing those who would protect the royal tent with him, he ensured they set up a perimeter at similar distances between them. Staring hard at any fellow guardsman who yawned or complained about the chill, he took his place at the entrance. Zsigmond's loud snores rumbled like a wild boar before subsiding to a rattling racket.

Then a sonorous, rich song reached Vlad at the center of the camp. Scouts mentioned a castle and rocky low hillsides surmounting the village of Sudoměř, not religious houses. There must be one in the woodlands, where Catholic nuns lived. They sang:

"*Ave Regina coelorum.*

Ave Domina Angelorum,
Salve radix, salve porta,
Ex qua mundo lux est orta."
"Gaude Virgo gloriosa,
Super omnes speciosa,
Vale, o valde decora,
Et pro nobis Christum exora."

"What is it?" The nearest man asked in a thick Serbian accent. "What do they say?"

Since his companion was clearly not a Catholic, Vlad replied, "It is a chant devoted to the Virgin Mary, recited during Lent, which ends tonight. I've never heard it sung."

As the nuns repeated the verses, he translated for those who did not know Latin.

"Hail, Queen of Heaven.
Hail, Lady of Angels
Hail, root; hail, gate
From whom unto the world a light has arisen."
"Rejoice, glorious Virgin,
Lovely beyond all others,
Farewell, most beautiful maiden.
And ever pray for us to Christ."

The last line became a litany in his mind as he considered the coming struggle. *And ever pray for us to Christ.*

RAGGED RED FLAGS BEARING the symbol of a chalice billowed before Vlad's eyes. The Hussite units arrived and met the Hungarian army well after the next dawn. Their king and his closest companions erupted in jeers, mimicked by others. Not just at the laughable sight of women carrying flails and spears in the enemy company.

Vlad studied the lone man on horseback who led them. He wore a black patch of cloth over one eye. Bohemian loyalists affirmed his identity as Jan Žižka. No one fathomed why he defended the area of dammed small lakes turned into bucolic fishponds.

"A blind and vain fool guides them into battle, to their ends!" Zsigmond brayed from beside his tent. "When the fighting is done, do what you will with their women, stupid enough to think they can withstand armored warriors." Lusty approval interrupted their king's speech before he went on. "They'll all be carrion for crows!"

Although his men cheered, Vlad, who stood beside trusted companions, said, "We shouldn't underestimate the Hussites. This is their land. They'll fight and die for it."

"A paltry force, but even the wind may strip the face of a mountain bare. Look, there's some cavalry with them at last." Fruzhin nodded. "Vlad is right. If their women will fight us, it is but a sign of how much the cause means to them. Prepare yourselves."

Zsigmond's lions assembled and advanced on the enemy. War pennants fluttered in the morning breeze. Dragonflies rose in clusters from the marsh up ahead. The humidity rose early in the spring morning.

In the vanguard, Vlad maneuvered his warhorse at Zawisza's side, the animal strangely skittish. He patted the stallion, nickering at unexpected dips in the sodden earth. The mounted knights of the Hungarian and Bohemian units rode with him behind infantry archers, clad mainly in little plate armor over mail shirts. Bands of sunlight rippled across rows of steel.

"We draw near the wetlands, *amici*," the captain general Pipó warned as he led his war band.

The muck, thicker in some low-lying areas, mired their mounts' legs and meant a heavy slog through grass patches, moss tufts, and tangled marsh plants. Vlad noted where horses floundered, no matter how their riders urged them. He guided his mount with care. The animal snorted as the drone and hum of insects buzzed around its head.

The Hussite bowmen lined up along tangled reed beds behind those hefting spears, who threw their weapons just before arrows whistled in the air. Some found their marks among Pipó's soldiers, first in the foray. Men and horses panicked.

"Dismount! Dismount!" Fruzhin yelled. "The ground's too wet and unstable."

Vlad drew his sword and left his horse behind. He trudged, sinking into the cold sludge up to his thighs covered in plate armor. Viscous liquid seeped everywhere. The Hungarian spearmen and bowmen aimed at Hussite targets and found them.

Intent on reaching the enemy's front line, Vlad led the men behind Zawisza. Their foes lobbed more than arrows and spears; even rocks and wet branches as projectiles. One dizzying throw dinged Vlad's helm and made him blink rapidly and stumble a little. He dragged his limbs through the fetid marshland vegetation.

A thicket of Hussite skirmishers swung long-handled flails attached by chains to spiked heads. Vlad brandished his sword against a man whose weapon slammed his arm, denting the armor and sending a spiraling rush of pain through the limb. Brutish as the morning star Stibor once carried.

Vlad stabbed his assailant below the belly, where a breastplate provided no covering, and shoved him to the ground, piercing one eye socket and twisting his blade. His spur cut into the dead man's cheek as he slogged on.

Another attacker came. A beardless youth by his look, he wielded a spear with an old warrior's ferocity. With lightning speed, he aimed for the slit in the helm and any gaps between the plate armor. Vlad reeled back on the defensive.

When his foe's nimbleness ebbed, Vlad bashed his face with the sword's guard and sliced the belly. The youth slumped to his knees, spear sinking in the muck. Vlad took his head with one blow. A Hussite clad in dented, rusted mail, a relic of bygone battles, waded through the swamp toward him.

Hemmed in by the surge of men at his back, all earlier doubts receded. Were the Hussites not his king's enemies, Vlad could have admired their battle courage. He fought them, driven by the will to survive alone. His shoulders tightened and burned beneath his pauldrons. At last, he stood in the vanguard at the side of a panting Zawisza.

Žižka unleashed the men and artillery of the war wagons, twelve of them by Vlad's earlier count, arranged in an arc. A volley of arrows preceded fire from the hand-gunners in the Hussites' wheeled defenses.

Behind the hand-gunners, great crossbows manned by two or three Hussite fighters and other artillery tore into the Hungarian vanguard. White smoke billowed from the guns, stinging Vlad's eyes. Screams warned the shots found targets; piercing thigh armor made thinner for agility. The wounded clutched their injuries and cried out for help. Even Zawisza yelped.

A dead man crumpled at Vlad's feet on the grasses with an upturned, bloodied face; both eye sockets ravaged. Vlad bent and cradled the head of the Serbian who asked about the singing nuns on the preceding night.

Although Zawisza urged them on, all around Vlad, the vanguard faltered under the intensity of the enemy's attacks. Warriors who had mocked their adversaries earlier now fled. Knights retreated, not just from Zawisza's command.

"*Bastardo*!" Pipó's yell reverberated above the din as he struggled for the arm of one of his vice-captains, who pulled away and stumbled backward into the marsh.

Vlad backtracked with them, protecting Zawisza's right flank as blood seeped from under the armor and ran down the side of his leg, disappearing into the sludge oozing at their feet. Each time Zawisza lifted the injured limb, a grimace and grunt escaped him.

"Lean on me, if you can," Vlad urged.

"I won't let these heretical mongrels and bitches see me limp away," Zawisza muttered. "This isn't over! I will have their blood!"

A chill swept up Vlad's spine, colder than the sludge in the marsh. He did not need to turn back and look for the phantom vision in the sky, but he found it all the same.

He swallowed and trudged on beside Zawisza. "Come. We are not defeated." His head and heart, still pounding after a glimpse of the awful sight, warned him otherwise.

AFTER TWO LULLS IN the battle before midday and in the afternoon, during which the Hussites retrieved their dead and looted corpses for armor, Vlad fought on after more than half a day since the first skirmish. An orange sunset blazed across the sky, yet still no sign of victory appeared. The murky specter loomed above.

Vlad answered a flail swung at his helm with blistering slashes of the sword. His opponent arced out of reach each time only to assail him again. After a feint, his blade at last pierced the breastbone of his diminutive attacker, who cried out.

"My poor children! Their mother has failed them."

For the first time, Vlad studied the slender hands gripping the edges of his weapon. Viscous blood bubbled between the fingers and trickled down the palms to sleeves laced tightly at the wrists. He wrenched the sword away. His victim collapsed.

The rounded helmet with a wide brim rolled away, revealing sodden yellow curls clinging to the temples of a woman. A short, ragged scar bisected her left eyebrow.

He kneeled at her side and looked into eyes lit by the last embers of a dying sun, their tint a similar shade to his. With each of her ragged breaths, her stare darkened like the mosses near the marshland. She grunted and gasped, palming a gaping chest wound.

"I'm sorry," he whispered, without knowing exactly why he apologized.

She did not deserve it. Her sex certainly did not matter once she fought him. He had battled for his king. Her for her country and faith. Neither sought the encounter of their own accord.

She coughed and spluttered, spraying his face with flecks of bloodied spittle. One final wheeze before the light left her gaze. Her stained and bleeding hand slid into the grass. She lay utterly still until a cool evening wind rippled through the river valley and swiped at the hair nestled against her neck. The sun's last embers died, and night fell.

Vlad signaled his men when, with the sudden onset of fog and darkness, cow's war wagons retreated in haste. The last Hussite defenders gave their lives. Vlad plunged into the night and pursued the rest. He and his companions captured wounded stragglers, numbering thirty in total. Zsigmond wanted them to be questioned about where their leader would strike next. He appointed Fruzhin to the task.

Grim-faced, his best friend shared a look with Vlad before nodding. After the dismissal, he left the royal tent in Fruzhin's wake and stumbled through the encampment, seeking those who remained under his vice-captaincy. Some suffered grievous wounds, but over half of them survived. He prayed beside the fallen bodies. There would be more retrieved in the morning when he searched the wetlands.

A little before midnight, he sat with Pipó and Zawisza beside a fire. Fatigued, his armor weighed him down. Pageboys brought bowls of goulash, but Vlad lifted the wooden spoon three times before he plopped it into the food and set the vessel aside.

The day proved long, but the night grew longer still. Shrieks rose from the tent where Fruzhin summoned each of their prisoners.

Vlad scratched at his aching forehead before pinching the bridge of his nose. His eyes burned; body bereft of sleep. His soul was ensnared by the recollection of the woman he killed. Her golden hair and green eyes also summoned memories of Călțuna.

She would surely shrink from him now, as she did the last day they saw each other, with the stink of battle and the marsh on him. If she were here, could she forgive him for the Christian blood spilled by his sword, and love him still? Would God?

THE NEXT MORNING, VLAD supervised the retrieval of the Hungarian dead. Cartloads piled high with waterlogged bodies left the soppy earth, pulled by teams of oxen taken from the villagers of Sudoměř, who protested at the loss of their animals. Although Pipó urged mercy, their king still considered whether to raze the area for suspected support of the embattled Hussites.

A squire came to the murky marshland with Zsigmond's summons for Vlad. Mired in gore for over two days, he shook his head and returned to camp. After he entered the royal tent by consent, he found Zsigmond, seated alone at the makeshift table covered with silk cloth instead of the map of Bohemia.

"You're quite a sight. And you smell." The king coughed behind his fisted hand.

Vlad kneeled and bowed. "Forgive my appearance and odor, Your Royal Majesty."

"But you do a necessary service for Our fallen martyrs, ensuring them a proper Christian burial. The Hussites sent an envoy. They want their dead. We will allow the retrieval after Our warriors are recovered from the swampland."

"I'm unsure when the men shall complete the grim duty, Your Royal Majesty."

"That is a determination another will make." Zsigmond shifted in his seat, the wood creaking beneath his bulk. "Zawisza spoke of your courage. You saved his life."

"He's a brave captain, devoted to your cause, as I am, my king."

"He's become a companion of yours, like Pipó and Fruzhin. All three expressed some concern that, although you fought tirelessly, some worry vexed you."

"Not so, my great king!" Vlad swore. The lie came easily. Expressing any of his doubts about the campaign would ruin his quest for Zsigmond's trust. "I don't mean to contradict you, except in this matter. The fight occupied me." That, at least, veered closer to the truth.

"No thoughts since then of the woman with whom you parted from at Várad?"

This time, Vlad could not deny the truth, even if he wished. He bowed his head and began, "Your Royal Majesty, I—"

"Let Us speak before you perjure yourself. Let Us be magnanimous given your recent break with the woman, which Our bitch of a queen wrought, to harm you."

Zsigmond rose. His feet covered in velvet shoes came into view under the robe.

"You are a sword and shield of the realm and would never defy Us or leave the army without permission. The consequences of desertion are clear for you and your family's holdings, which We would seize. The Hussites have begged for a truce. We can be generous and allow it. Our focus turns to the siege of Prague, to be wrested from the Hussites before Our coronation can occur there in summer."

Vlad reasoned the enemy would not give up the capital without bitter fighting. Did Zsigmond imagine he could claim full authority over a country in revolt?

"We ride northeast in three weeks to Prague," his monarch continued. "We grant you the same term in which to find the one who holds your heart. If you marry a boyar's bastard, We will be displeased. However, many men have mistresses whom they love more than wives. Find your woman and follow Our army's trail north."

With bated breath, Vlad looked up. Zsigmond covered his nose and mouth with a perfumed kerchief, doused in rosewater and cassia. Nothing could hide the mirthful crinkles around his eyes, or the kindly mien reflected within them.

"Well, why do you linger? Awaiting permission to leave Us? You may go."

With a brimming heart, Vlad exhaled, rose, and fled the tent. Shock slowed and overcame him at the sight of Fruzhin, one hand holding the reins of a saddled horse.

"Fresh water from the river north of here. There's a change of clothing." He hefted a skin brimming with liquid and a stuffed bag. "I would assume you'll wash before greeting your lady. You truly reek, my friend."

"Why...why does our king allow this? He's not sentimental."

"A warrior's head and heart must be clear of purpose in battle. A near-impossible task when a woman's love beckons. Go find her and come back to us."

Despite the grime besmirching them, the pair embraced. Vlad mounted and took the bag and skin. He offered a lingering look at Fruzhin, who slapped the horse's rump.

VLAD HASTENED SOUTH along snow-covered pathways through the hilly forests, determined he would reach Hermannstadt, well over two hundred leagues away. If the weather and the horse cooperated, he might enter the city by the time Zsigmond broke camp and got on the road to Prague.

After he discovered Călțuna, how would he convince her to accompany him? Bitter memories of their parting and the revulsion in her watery gaze still wounded him. If he could persuade her, he vowed never to hurt her again. His high-minded ideals about marriage no longer mattered. Only a life at her side did. If children came, he would protect them from the stigma of bastardy as best he could.

A frosty wind carried the snorts of horses and their hoof beats. He glanced behind him but saw no one. Riders in pursuit drew nearer, though. Snow cascaded through the tree line and down the knoll on his right side, spraying him in a pristine white shower. He slowed his mount before drawing the sword.

"*Domnule*!"

At the gruff voices, he peered through the dense firs, his heart pounding in a steady, furious tattoo. In their animal skins blanketed with as much snow as on the treetops, the Gypsy twins guided their mounts to him.

Vlad gaped at Tobar and Yoska in disbelief before he demanded, "What in God's name are you doing here? You're supposed to be at Buda Castle."

The twins looked at each other, then at him, and said, "We followed."

"You've secretly tracked the entire Hungarian army into this country for weeks?" The scouts never realized this? Perhaps Zsigmond deserved better spies.

Vlad shook his head. "Do you realize you're both still slaves? You've disobeyed my order to remain with the clan and my uncle in Hungary. The penalty is a whipping."

"Yes, *Domnule*," they replied in unison, though coupled with unrepentant stares.

In the lonely wilderness, he could not order any punishment, even if he wished it. Yet, they must recognize the consequences of defiance and avoid repeat incidents.

"Did my uncle tell you to do this?" He asked. "Does he know where you are?"

"Yes, *Domnule*." Tobar alone replied. "He worries."

An insufferable Staico deserved a thrashing too, for...what? Vlad cursed. Fears for his well-being? During their king's initial foray into Bohemia, Borbála's threat and the resulting concern remained a secret from everyone around Vlad. His uncle understood his moods well enough to perceive some problem existed.

"Tobar," Vlad explained, "Staico did not know, but at the end of the year I found myself at odds with the queen and her lover."

"He could have friends, *Domnule*, who want you to be dead," Tobar murmured.

Yoska nodded. "She could have more lovers, *Domnule*, who want the same."

Truths he could not deny. He scanned the woodland and track behind him, thinking how his solo departure from the camp might have exposed him to danger, but for the Gypsies' timely arrival. He gave no thought to the possibility of an ambush while rushing headlong to Hermannstadt. Borbála wounded him by exposing Călțuna to Zsigmond's censure, but Vlad would be a fool to think the queen's ire cooled.

"It was wrong of you to ignore my command," he admonished the Gypsies.

As expected, neither man's expression altered. They would never know shame if they also believed in the rightness of their actions.

He added, "But I would not rely on any others as much as you two for this journey. I'm going to Hermannstadt to find the woman I love. Ride with me."

IN THE YEAR OF OUR Lord 1420. Hermannstadt and *Hunyadvár, Transilvania,* (modern-day Sibiu and Hunedoara, Romania)

Vlad arrived a full two weeks after leaving Bohemia, as the day's trading closed. Some foreign merchants would get on the road rather than remain behind the town walls until the morning. Shrouded in a hooded mantle pulled low over his eyes and covering plain garments Fruzhin packed for him, he rode without a saddle ahead of Tobar and Yoska, searching for Călţuna. He found her sooner than expected.

She strolled ahead of him at the edge of the marketplace along a slight incline leading to her home. He would recognize her anywhere by the glorious yellow curls, the proud tilt of her head, and the slight sway of her hips beneath her favored cerulean blue mantle. Although his plan required a hasty retreat from Hermannstadt, he would never succeed by frightening her. Leaving the Gypsy twins near the western gate where they entered, he walked the horse behind her.

Her voice drifted to him as she sang a melancholy tune never heard before. With slow, plodding steps barely avoiding the offal in the cobblestone street, she moved on. Her song grieved him. From the moment of their first reunion, she always brought such joy and laughter into his life. Had their parting of nearly two months saddened her so much? He could not bear it.

As he closed in on her, she stepped aside, turned, and looked up. Her stare widened. She almost dropped the small wicker basket tucked against her hip.

He stopped his mount and leaned down. "Dear lady, will you speak with me?"

She scanned the empty row between houses. "Why did you come, Vlad?"

"Why else would I be here, except for you?" He ached to hold her close, but tempered the impulse, as a dismount would delay his escape. "I love you, Călţuna."

"Leave while the gates are still open." She backed away until the brick facade of a townhouse stopped her. Her gaze flooded. She glared at him through bitter tears. "You can have nothing to say to me after what happened in Várad. Don't speak of love when you let your king dictate the course of it between us."

"Zsigmond gave his permission for my journey. I'm never abandoning you again. It was the worst mistake of my life. I won't ever repeat it."

"Don't make promises you can't keep!" She pressed against the wall.

He edged the horse closer. "I'm not going away without you."

She peered up at him, trembling. The contents of her basket, the fruits and vegetables rattled. "You can't! My father...I won't make him fear for my safety again. Don't do it. I'll scream if you come any closer, Vlad."

He never doubted she would. However, his determination to win her love in full again made him reckless. He reached down and grappled with her waist. An ear-splitting shriek issued from her as she lost hold of her purchases, now scattered to the ground. Although she squirmed and pummeled him, he pulled her up bodily and onto the horse. Nearly his same height, she could never match him for strength. She delivered quite a wallop to his unprotected thighs with her hands clasped tight together.

"Release me now!" She screeched. "Let me go!"

He resisted the urge to slap the curves of her rump. Instead, he wheeled the horse around while a man's ruddy face appeared at the townhouse window. As his shouts rose, Vlad raced away with Călţuna. Her cries drew attention he did not need.

She also did not make it easy for him to hold her across the animal's back. On her belly, she could slip off and break her damnably lovely neck.

Once outside the town, he would maneuver her into a sitting position and hold her wrists in one hand. If he managed their flight. Although the market area thinned out, tradespeople awaited their turn at the eastern gate. Tobar and Yoska rode hard for him.

"It's no good that way, *Domnule*," the latter warned him. "Too many animals."

He scanned two gates with five towers between them to the east. Three entryways, much more fortified in the south. All reasons he had selected the sole narrow western exit from town while devising an escape plan.

"I see it, Yoska," he muttered. "Still, I think we must try."

Denizens yelled at them and foolishly tried to block their path with outstretched arms. The Carpathian ponies snapped with large teeth like a warhorse in battle.

Vlad kicked his mount again and bore down on the merchants, cursing at them. The Gypsy twins stole two torches already lit, although the sun barely began its descent. While he thundered at the cattle trader in his path, the Gypsies scattered the herd.

Pandemonium followed, and guards along the ramparts and in the towers rushed to the walls. Two aimed and fired crossbows, but not before Vlad withdrew into the shadow of the gatehouse. His Gypsies fought men on all sides with their long knives, while he circled his pony before he rode for those desperate to close the gate. The cowards scrambled from the path rather than die under the horse's shod hooves.

With heart-racing speed, Vlad made his escape, the twins at his back. Călțuna cursed him but held his leg tight as they fled west in the glare of the dying sunlight.

RESTING THE HORSES for two nights, they approached the next destination Vlad intended on the third morning. Sunlight burnished the roof and towers of Hunyadvár, larger than in his recollection. The old knight Vajk must have completed work on the fortress since Vlad last saw him, at least four months beforehand.

"Is that where you're taking me? Hunyadi's stronghold." Călțuna shifted in front of him, holding on to the mane with bound hands.

She attempted an escape the evening before and, despite his regrets, afterward, he tied her with rope from Tobar.

"We won't stay," Vlad said. "I'll rejoin the army headed for the Bohemian capital."

She asked, "How far is it from here?"

He would not allow the calm tone to lull him into revealing information she might use to find her way home. His fight for her heart would be harrowing. She remained tense and turned and glowered at him whenever his hands covered her smaller ones.

"It's far enough, Călţuna, which is why we cannot linger."

He urged his mount across a wooden bridge and approached the gatehouse. He identified himself and sought the lord's permission for entry. The guards made him wait an insurmountable time before the woman he recalled as Vajk's wife approached with their auburn-haired son János. Both wore black garments and the lady fingered rosary beads in her grasp. Agape, they stared in silence.

Vlad tossed his reins at Yoska and silently signaled Tobar to watch over Călţuna before she bolted with the horse. He dismounted and preceded with upraised palms.

"My lady of Hunyadvár, it is an honor to greet you and the son of Vajk Hunyadi again. I am Prince Vlad of Wallachia, a knight in the service of King Zsigmond."

"I know," the woman said as she made obeisance and gestured for János to do the same. "Even if my late husband never spoke of you, I would remember."

"Late husband?" He repeated. "Vajk's dead? I met him at the end of last year."

"He came home with young János on the last day of December, visibly drained by the journey. We dined. My husband spoke of you and the vow you made. Afterward, he went to bed and never woke. The Transilvanian governor won't take my János back into his service. He sent him home, saying the prior agreement was only a kindness to Vajk."

She sniffled, as did her child. He brushed away the curls tumbling over his forehead. The same hue as the eyes his father once possessed stared unblinking at Vlad.

"How has your family fared?" he asked. "In the absence of your husband?"

"My children and I have the support of Vajk's brother, responsible for our family's affairs." She sighed and clasped her hands in front of her. "How may we aid you?"

"I don't wish to burden you. We seek a small portion of food that would supplement our daily hunting and the service of a messenger—"

"I need your help, my lady!" Călţuna shouted. "The prince took me from my father in Hermannstadt against my will. Please don't let him steal me away from Transilvania."

Vajk's widow gasped. Vlad cursed under his breath. A harsher and, admittedly, wiser man would have gagged Călţuna and left her under guard some distance away. As much as he never wanted to hurt her again, he desired her closeness.

"She speaks the truth," he confessed. "I absconded with her because we love each other but cannot wed without our king's consent. I would make amends to her."

"By the commission of further sins, Prince Vlad?" The widow shook her head. "That doesn't seem wise. Besides, princes and nobles rarely marry for love. Why should you deserve the chance?" She edged closer. "Will you let me speak with your captive?"

"You may." He drew back and she passed beneath the portcullis, coming to Călţuna. After a wary glance at the rope, she frowned at Vlad briefly.

She asked Călţuna, "Do your wrists hurt, lady? Are you injured in any way?"

"I'm not bound tightly. The only injury is to my pride at being so easily abducted."

"My brother by marriage has command of the castle and its men-at-arms, but they would obey if I ordered them to rescue you from this man's clutches. Still, he is a prince, and I recall the fierce fighting reputation and loyalty of his Gypsies. You understand my dilemma?" The lady wrung her hands. "I'm a Catholic Christian and can't condone his theft of you. But it would've been better if none of you came here."

"Lady, I don't wish to cause you difficulty or stir a fight," Vlad said. "Grant me your favor and carry out my requests, so we may take our troubles away."

Vajk's widow ignored him. "Did he speak the truth? Do you two love each other?"

Călţuna's long sigh and sudden watery gaze betrayed her inner turmoil. Vlad longed to offer some comfort, but feared she might recoil.

"I love him to the depths of my soul," she whispered, "but we have no future."

Vlad kneeled on one knee. "I cannot give you up, Călţuna. Please understand." He said to Vajk's widow, "Help me allay her father's worries with the aid of your herald."

She stared at him, wide-eyed. "He shall surely appeal to King Zsigmond."

He nodded. "By then, I hope I will have convinced my beloved to stay at my side."

"Tell me why I shouldn't order the castle's defenders to drive you and your troubles away this instant."

"My purpose in coming here is twofold. Not only must I have your help, but also, I can offer recompense. I will fulfill a final promise made to Vajk Hunyadi to secure a royal post for young János. When I leave here, I would take the boy with me."

"Mother, p-p-please let me go!" The youth rushed to her. "It's all I ever wanted."

"Hush! You don't know what you're saying. You're only fourteen years old."

"But Father told me of Prince Vlad's promise. I want to go with him!"

"He has abducted this woman? Didn't you overhear?"

Her son approached Călţuna. "D-do you trust the prince?"

"What? Well, of course, I do. I know him. He would never see me imperiled and not...." As she trailed off and bowed her head, tears trickled down her cheeks.

Vlad rose and went to her. He brushed a thumb against her soft skin, wiping her sadness away. "Thank you for having some faith in me still, dearest. It is not misplaced."

He looked at János' mother. "Nor is your son's confidence, since I'm a good Catholic like you." He dismissed her gasp of shock. "Do as I've asked, and I shall fulfill the vow given to the boy's father before he died. János will serve our king as I have."

BEFORE MIDDAY, FOUR horses laden with foodstuff and water skins waited outside Hunyadvár in the care of the Gypsy twins. Vlad stood beside his mount and Călţuna.

János hugged each of his younger siblings, smoothing tears from the rounded cheeks of a favored little sister before he shared a fervent embrace with his mother. She kissed his curls and blessed him. Afterward, she directed a herald who led a horse to Vlad. He gave him a folded letter.

"When you see my father, tell him I love him and say I am also unharmed," Călţuna said before the messenger nodded, mounted, and rode eastward.

Vlad got on the horse. She scooted away from him, same as the previous day, but did not move again once his arms came around her and he took the reins from Tobar. He stared at the back of her head. God willing, she would forgive his recklessness one day. Even if it took forever, he would heal the rift between them.

"Whenever the authorities arrive from Hermannstadt," János' parent said, "I'll admit I have seen you and the lady Călţuna, but because you're a prince, I let you pass."

He nodded. "I would expect nothing less from you as a fellow Catholic."

"I pray you will seek God's forgiveness for the errors you've made, but most of all, I wish you, my son and your lady and companions would reach King Zsigmond in safety."

"I will protect them, including János, with my life. You have my oath. Not only as a prince and a knight of our king's household but as a defender of Christ's faith."

She sniffled. With another nod to her, he led his company away, bound for the Hungarian army riding far ahead of them in Bohemia.

CHAPTER 16

Nature's Fire

"We are ever striving after what is forbidden, and coveting what is denied us."-Ovid (43 BC-17/18 AD), Roman poet.

IN THE YEAR OF OUR Lord 1420. Hradčany and *Vyšehrad, Bohemia* (Hradčany and Vyšehrad, modern-day Czech Republic)

Could a man call himself ruler of any land if he exercised limited power within its borders? Vlad considered the question while standing beside the king's door an hour after dawn. Would the Wallachian people reject Vlad as a candidate for the ruling prince, just as the Hussites rebuffed his king's claim to their land?

Five weeks after the battle of Sudoměř, the sovereign met other Bohemian loyalists who besieged the castle they now occupied in Hradčany. Zsigmond's chief aim, the elimination of the Hussites and their leader Jan Žižka remained elusive.

As did Vlad's quest for peace with Călţuna. Lodged at a nearby inn with Tobar and Yoska taking turns guarding her room and its sole window, her anger remained unabated, although an additional four months had elapsed since the army took Hradčany. He prayed daily for a change as the autumn breezes stirred.

Each time he visited Călţuna, she kept the door barred on the inside. The twins confirmed she left the room for food or womanly needs only.

János gave Vlad a three-week-old letter a pageboy brought to the chamber at midday during his duty. A jolt like lightning thrummed his body at his mother's announcement of Mihail's death. Thinking only of what his elder brother's demise would mean for the future of their homeland, he thanked János and sent him away.

The rest of the missive left him breathless and made him knock on the adjacent door. Fruzhin answered, peering out from the gap in the entryway.

"What is it, Vlad? Our king isn't finished with the war council."

"I have received urgent news. My brother Mihail is dead—"

Fruzhin stepped out into the passage, not pulling in the aperture behind him fully. "Great God." He muttered. "When will you control your impulses? How many times must I lecture you about them?"

"But this isn't just about my brother—"

"Fruzhin!" Zsigmond thundered from inside. "You dared leave without consent?"

"Don't interrupt us again, Vlad, if you value your life as Zsigmond's man. That's an order." Fruzhin glared at him before he entered the king's chamber again. "Forgive me, Your Royal Majesty. I beg your great favor...."

With a grunt of irritation, Vlad crushed the missive in his hand.

Hours later, when sunset sent golden-orange light blaring through the castle's windows and arrow slits, the door opened once more. The Bohemian captains came first, quarreling among themselves. Zawisza exited next, eyeing Vlad.

"You shouldn't have interrupted a war council," he said. "You know this as my vice-captain. Unless the news heralded a disaster for this campaign, you should've waited."

"I understand."

Then Zawisza embraced him. "Fruzhin spoke of your brother's death. I'm sorry."

"I hated Mihail," Vlad conceded. "My concern lies with my mother, who's lost four of her seven children. I regret the inability to comfort her. The duty of others now."

Fruzhin joined them. "The king will see you, Vlad. He's in a poor mood with news of the Hussite siege of Vyšehrad, so soon after our losses in Prague and at the battle of Vitkov Hill two months ago. Say what you will and leave him to his thoughts."

Vlad nodded and reached for the door handle before Fruzhin touched his arm.

"I know it's hard to accept the loss of a sibling with whom you've long quarreled. There's no chance for peaceful accord in the future. I cannot replace your relations, but we are blood brothers. You are not alone. Don't forget." He patted Vlad's cheek before taking his leave with Zawisza.

Inside the king's chamber, dimly lit by candles with the shutters closed, Zsigmond stood. His arms folded over his broad chest; a stony visage remained unwavering while Vlad kneeled before him.

"You interrupted Our war council," his sovereign said. "For what purpose?"

"My mother has written, Your Royal Majesty." Vlad regretted how he crumpled the letter, as the king might desire to read it. "My eldest brother, Prince Mihail of Wallachia, is dead. Our cousin Dan Dăneşti attacked him with the support of Turkish mercenaries near the end of August almost four weeks ago."

"Yes, We are aware of this," Zsigmond replied before turning to the fireplace. "To support Mihail, we dispatched some men from here under Pipó and those defending Buda Castle in the governor of Transilvania's war band. They have failed Us."

Staring hard at his king's back, Vlad fought for composure. So, Pipó went away into Wallachia last month, because Zsigmond knew about the perils the principality faced. Neither of them warned Vlad. The king must have told Pipó not to do it. Why?

"Your Royal Majesty, under a usurper loyal to the Turks, my country will fall."

"It will not. Prince Dan sent a letter some days ago. He assured Us, he but used the enemy to rid him of Mihail and has already broken faith with those wicked barbarians."

"Then you will aid Dan?" Incredulous, Vlad shook his head.

Zsigmond looked over his shoulder. "Whom else would you have Us support?"

Vlad swallowed, recalling Stibor's words. *"Never tell Zsigmond of your heart's desire."*

"Your Royal Majesty, there is my elder brother Radu," he suggested instead.

"The one your people call the epithet 'Praznaglava' or were you unaware?"

The term 'empty-headed' would be inadequate, for as Vlad remembered, his second brother Radu focused on three aspects of life with great vigor: filling his belly, rutting with whores, and warfare. He would defend their people. Would their cousin Dan do the same?

"Your Royal Majesty, Radu is a fighter," Vlad began.

"Battle-tested like Dan during the Turkish civil war? He helped your late sister's husband in his conquest. Would that Dan had stayed and ensured the princess' survival."

Although bristling at the casual mention of Arina's tragic end, Vlad swallowed his bitterness. "Your Royal Majesty, Wallachia's future means everything to me. If Dan associates with the Turks, he's not trustworthy. You can't rely on him to hold the southern border. Don't let him keep the throne."

A short, rueful laugh preceded the king's turn to him in full. "How old are you? Several years more than a score by Our reckoning. An age where you should have outgrown naivete. Your cousin Dan is pragmatic. There is a time for enmity and a time for practicality. Our forces are committed to the Hussite cause. We will not intervene."

Zsigmond faced the fire once more, rubbing his leathery hands together, palms crackling like the glowing red embers at his feet. "At least you did not disappoint Us by recommending yourself as Dan's replacement. You still must learn about the arts of warfare and diplomacy. Rid Us of the Hussites and you will achieve the first task. Watch your cousin's rule unfold and you'll discover something about the second."

Hot, caustic fury blazed and churned inside Vlad's belly. How dare Zsigmond, to whom he offered loyalty and the strength of his sword arm in every battle, dismiss him so easily in favor of a usurper? How could the king ignore the threat Dan and the Turks posed? Every breath Vlad drew fed the furor.

Incensed, he roared, "You don't care for my country, only your wars! You want me here murdering the Hussites, fellow Christians. We should destroy the Turks before they take the entire Balkans and seize my homeland."

If Fruzhin saw him now, his best friend would be appalled. Vlad did not care for the good opinion of anyone else, not when the king to whom he devoted ten years, almost half of his life, could treat him and his homeland with such disdain.

Zsigmond shrugged and avoided his regard. "You're good at killing people. Why would We release you from Our service? Besides, Hungary concluded treaty terms with the Ottomans at Várad last year. We see no reason to violate the agreement. Dan must hold the Transalpine land. It is his birthplace, too."

"The Council of Konstanz ended three months after my father died. You concealed that truth as well and kept me by your side, Your Royal Majesty," Vlad spat. "Fighting while you cared nothing for the losses and changes Wallachia endured."

The king gave him a withering glance. "Of course. We hid your father's death. It hardly mattered to you. Remember, you abandoned him as you did the Eastern Orthodox religion, as proof of your loyalty to Us. A choice made of your own volition. Shall We question that oath now? Even if you cared when Mircea died, a grieving warrior would've done Us no good. Your pursuit of the Transilvanian woman proves We cannot allow you too many distractions. Desire is nature's fire."

Zsigmond approached him again, with a visage set in stone, and thumped his pauldron covering the shoulder. "Understand Us well. Your family. Your country and its people. None of them matter to Us. Not in this war with the Hussites. We will claim Bohemia in its entirety and drive out the Hussite menace! We need Bohemia's warriors to help Us defeat the Turks. If you ever want to go home again by Our permit, you'll pledge yourself to this fight. Now, get out. Don't come again until We summon you."

Vlad gritted his teeth and bowed his head. “By your order, Your Royal Majesty.”

Zsigmond said as he turned away, “Before returning to your post, summon the palatine to Us. We must answer the Bohemian castellan of Vyšehrad before he capitulates Our fortress there.”

While he went away, the rancor filled Vlad. He asked God’s forgiveness of Zsigmond for keeping vital secrets from him. He would never forgive the king and swore no man would rule his fate. Not even a king and overlord would dictate Wallachia’s destiny.

NOT LONG AFTER TWILIGHT, Vlad plodded to the inn where Călţuna lodged. He carried a sealed missive a pageboy brought, delivered an hour beforehand. The message came from Hermannstadt. Călţuna received her first letter in five months. The creased and spotted surface of the paper suggested some length of time had passed since its author inked the words inside.

He nodded to Yoska stationed at Călţuna’s door. The Gypsy stared back at him with his good eye, for which the entire clan called him ‘Yoska One-Eye.’ Still deeming the term derogatory, Vlad refused its usage.

He asked the twins, “Has she come out since morning? Did she eat anything today?”

“No, *Domnule*. I heard her crying through the door at noon,” Yoska replied in his usual gruff tone. “Nothing since then.”

Vlad sighed, glad he thought to bring two sacks of fresh rye bread, an odorous but tasty piece of cheese, and small cakes filled with ground poppy seed from the fortress’ kitchen. He gave half of the food to Yoska.

“I saw your brother outside, below Călţuna’s window. Share the meal with him.”

“Yes, *Domnule*.”

After Yoska left, Vlad knocked. No answer came or noise from within the room, as he expected. He rapped his knuckles against the stout, faded wood. An elderly couple in simple dress came up the steps and bypassed him. He waited until they disappeared and tried pushing the door. Resistance warned him Călțuna had once again barred the door. He bent and ran his forefinger along the space between wood and floor before slipping the letter inside. He sat on the ground and waited. So long, he fell asleep.

A soft creak woke him. He looked up and found Călțuna framed in the entryway. Yellow hair hung in hanks around her shoulders, which shook as she covered her mouth while crying. He stood and tugged her into his arms. For the first time in months, she did not resist. He scooped her up and carried her into the small room, kicking the door shut behind him.

Setting her on the fusty mattress with the food sack beside her, Vlad crouched at her feet. She gripped the crumpled paper in her slim hand.

"Father's not angry with me." She sniffled. "He doesn't blame me at all, just you."

As he should, Vlad thought. He maintained his silence, letting her speak again when she wanted. The least he could do.

"He hasn't written to King Zsigmond, reasoning an appeal against a king's knight will do no good. He vows not to denounce you if you'll just let me go home. Will you?"

"You know I cannot." He bowed his head.

"You mean, will not."

As he raised his gaze, her tear-stricken, jeweled eyes and furrowed brow filled him with regret. He despised making her so unhappy.

"Călțuna, I am as incapable of releasing you as I am of taking my own life. If I gave you up, it would be akin to death for me."

She put the letter beside the sack. "You let me leave Várad where I declared myself happy to be your mistress. The king and queen drove us apart. You accepted the decree."

He could not deny the accusation. "I will regret that until my death. Even if it takes the rest of my days, I'll atone. Prove Zsigmond doesn't mean more than your love."

She wiped beneath her eyes. "I don't know how to believe you."

"Will you at least allow me to convince you?" His knees hit the floor. "Permit me to love you and open your heart to me once more?"

She reached for him and clutched his face between her slim fingers. "You ignorant fool. How could you ever think I've closed my heart to you? It belongs to your keeping. Don't you see? I've been as angry with myself as with you for wanting nothing more than to stay by your side, even after you let the king and queen shame me. For desiring you more than my father's goodwill and approval. I love you, Vlad."

He pressed her palm to his bearded cheek and murmured, "Then you will stay with me forever? You won't return to your father in Hermannstadt?"

"God damn me for a disgraceful daughter, but no one can make me leave your side. Say you'll never let me go again," she whispered before pressing her lips to his.

He tugged her down atop him, his fingers delving into her hair, raking her scalp. She cried out when he bit her lower lip before soothing her with sensuous kisses. Every pent-up desire and fear between them found release as they moaned into each other's mouths and ripped and tugged at the clothes separating their bodies. He winced once her nails raked across his back and arms, certain she drew blood in her passion.

Later, spent and with perspiration stinging the cuts on his skin, he drew circles in the small of her back. Ragged breaths seemed torn from her chest. He kissed her.

"If you abandon me once more, I will never return to you, Vlad."

At the heated vow, muffled atop his chest, he stilled his hand. He lay awake, staring at the ceiling long after her even breaths subsided into sleep.

DESPITE A RESTLESS night, wherein Vlad gripped Călţuna tightly in fear of their parting, he left her before dawn with a kiss at the inn's entrance. Tobar and Yoska stood on either of her. Vlad mounted the horse János brought, and together, they joined the Hungarian warriors bound south for Vyšehrad.

As they rode, Vlad considered János and regretted the inability to take the beardless youth on as his squire. For the boy hunted and rode well and completed every task with speed. His mother and former master taught him enough basic manners.

A chance for his betterment might come. Pipó lost a squire in the summer battle of Vitkov Hill, one on the cusp of manhood who was trampled and drowned in the nearby river as Zsigmond's forces retreated. Vlad would talk to Pipó after the siege of Vyšehrad.

"You will not fight, János," Vlad said. "If I should fall, flee to Călţuna."

"Yes...my lord prince," the boy replied.

"I'm not your prince. I'm not your lord, either," Vlad admonished him.

"But why can't I stay with you? I'd s-s-serve you well," János whined and sulked.

"We're no help to each other!" As Vlad answered, the boy's face fell, and he looked away, so Vlad explained. "I promised your father you would have a place in the royal household. You won't get far in life serving a landless knight like me."

The pair lapsed into a tense silence, but when János opened and closed his mouth without speaking, Vlad urged him on. "Say what you will, as long as you don't complain about impossible paths for your future."

"I only wanted to say...I like your horse. Is it a good companion in a fight?"

How could the boy still be ignorant of the difference between the mounts used for travel and in a conflict? He must have had a feckless benefactor.

Vlad said, "Although fierce, this Carpathian pony is not trained for combat. Squires of the king's chambers lead each knight's battle-hardened warhorse."

"D-do you have any favored mount?" János asked.

"Warhorses die in battle. I've learned to form no attachment in the purchase of one." Love and loss of the people in Vlad's life had already caused him enough pain. "Didn't you see your former master go off to fight?"

János shook his head. "He made me...stay...in the pitched tent."

"By my will, you'll find a worthier patron who will show you real battle and teach you about survival. From where in Wallachia did your ancestors hail?"

"They came from...Keve."

An island formed by the branching of the Danube River on the border that southern Wallachia shared with Serbia, territory stolen by the Ottoman Turks. Even Vlad knew from his childhood about the incessant attacks Keve endured.

"It's part of Temes County." He nodded, recalling Pipó held the lands there from Zsigmond. Indeed, Pipó seemed the best choice for János' prospects. "And the family moved to Hunyadvár when your father entered Zsigmond's service?"

As János nodded, Vlad mulled over the boy's father. But for the letters patent with which the sovereign granted Vajk the lands and castle, János would not be at Vlad's side now. The boy's father owed the king much for setting the son on a path.

"Your relations likely left Keve for their survival, dreaming of better, safer prospects in Transilvania. Your father and your family can't decide your fate. What do you want, János?"

"T-t-t...." The stuttering youth's body sagged in the saddle. Curls fell over his eyes, shielding them from view.

Vlad's fellow vice-captains beside them chuckled. His glare silenced them.

"Look at me, boy," he ordered.

When János did so with watering brown eyes, Vlad shook his head. "I've told you about my childhood stammer. Have you ever heard me speak so in manhood?"

Only a childish whimper followed.

"There is no shame in the impediment. It's not an affliction of God or the devil, because you can control it eventually if you try hard. My mother helped me surmount the challenge, as I will do for you. Your stammer comes only when in an excitable mood. Thoughts of your destiny rouse you, do they not? Is it because you want to be a king's knight like your father and gain command over an army?"

János gave a slow nod and swiped at his dampened cheeks.

"Then you'll be able to tell me so one day without a stutter. After you do as I say. Before you talk, breathe deeply. Master your exuberance and think of what you must convey. Repeat the statement in your head before uttering it. Then speak a few words at a time before breathing once more. Try now. What do you want from life?"

His eyes squeezed shut. János' chest rose and fell in the space of several breaths. "I... I want...to be...I want to...be the king's knight."

"Say it once again," Vlad ordered.

"I want to be...the king's knight," the boy said, without forcing every word.

Vlad nodded. "Learn to control the way you speak, as you would similarly train with a wooden sword each day. When we are encamped outside Vyšehrad, you repeat that phrase one hundred times out loud until you can do so without hesitation."

"One...hundred?" János whispered. "So many?"

"Take a practice weapon and stab it into the campground each time you repeat your goal. When there are one hundred holes in the earth, the task is complete."

"I will...do it," János promised.

"You'll succeed by your father's strength and a family's determination."

THE KING'S ARMY REACHED Vyšehrad early that same morning. They found not only Hussite forces encircling the fortress. The banner of Jan Žižka bore a chalice and billowed atop the ramparts. Zsigmond cursed and slapped his thigh. A herald with the white flag of truce led the former officer in charge of the castle.

He pleaded for mercy from their sovereign, claiming no other choice except surrender remained once he did not hear from Zsigmond.

"We sent our herald one morning ago!" The king thundered. "We ordered you not to give over this fortress, for we would break the siege. How dare you capitulate?"

"But Your Royal Majesty's messenger never arrived. I only saw the letter he carried when Žižka brought it to me. The Hussites intercepted your man. That's not all. Žižka surrounded Vyšehrad with more men and artillery than the day before. Fifteen hundred fighters defected from the town of Hory Kutné and aided his seizure."

"How many more of you will fail me?" Red-faced and apoplectic, Zsigmond struggled for control of his snorting, rearing mount. "How much more incompetence must I bear? Go from my sight!" He yelled for Pipó. "We do not accept this surrender of Vyšehrad. Take it back as Our captain general! Summon all the Bohemian loyalist leaders and their vice-captains to meet with their counterparts in Our army."

As Vlad feared, neither the king's rage nor the plans Pipó pursued made an impact. Countermanding him and the former castellan of the castle, Zsigmond ordered an attack on what proved the strongest defensive point.

The Bohemian loyalists, perhaps eager to regain their sovereign's trust fought harder and longer than the Hungarians. By the end of the day, the leaders left to them estimated their losses because of death and capture at over one thousand men and at least a third of their warhorses. Despairing, the king ordered the remnants of his forces back to Hradčany and there, descended into a frosty silence from which none could stir him.

Vlad felt rather than saw the dark specter at first. He grew convinced that the sighting of it cursed his fellow warriors. Maybe at Jan Hus' death, the bowels of Hell spat up a phantom menace to doom those who helped make a martyr of the theologian.

During the fight, Vlad suffered a dislocated shoulder caused by a peasant's flail. After treatment in the medical tent, he sought the balm of Călţuna's company.

"It's not right," he admitted, lying back in her arms while she crooned against his hair. "They're former Christians and can return to the Church. Each time there is a battle, I recall this before slaughtering them as the king commands. Until the Hussite wars, I never gave thought to killing where Zsigmond willed. I told myself, the lives of his enemies could not mean more than mine. Am I only my sword?"

"You are my Vlad." She nuzzled him. "My heart's home, my lover, my prince."

He shook his head against her slight shoulder. The monarch's martial ambitions took Vlad further away from Wallachia and its fight against the Turkish menace.

"Dear God, don't let my faith fail and my country fall," he whispered.

IN THE YEAR OF OUR Lord 1421. Pozsony, Hungary (modern-day Bratislava, Slovakia)

Vlad left Bohemia with King Zsigmond, who, frustrated with his continued failures in battle, must conclude negotiations of his daughter's union with Albrecht the Habsburg. The traveling court followed.

To some chagrin, so did Žofie of Bavaria. Whether her rival, Zsigmond's queen concerned her, Vlad could not know. Borbála busied herself, determining the profits lost from her dower lands, newly returned to her. Vlad brought Călţuna with him, bundled in a cart at the rear of the column with the Gypsy twins as her stalwart protectors. Autumnal leaves turned to gold, like her hair.

They arrived near dusk in Pozsony, northwestern Hungary, and rode past wooden ramparts. From the cathedral, a steep torch-lit ascent overlooking the banks of the Danube River led them through the stout eastern gate. Lodged within the castle overnight, as Zsigmond would greet negotiators in the morning before adjourning to his preferred residence below the castle's walls, the courtiers dined and retired late.

Rather than joining Călţuna and the others at a central inn, Vlad guarded the king's room. With Pozsony's fortress so close to the Bohemian border and shielded only by a wooden palisade, the court's mood on the eve of the nuptials remained cautious.

The door of the royal chamber creaked. The last of the king's favored counselors, Pipó stepped into the hallway and wished him well before pulling the handle in.

With deep lines etched into his brow, Pipó scrubbed a hand over his puffy face, rubbed at reddened eyes, and yawned. Still, Vlad pushed back from the opposing wall.

"I didn't forget about your request, *amico*," Pipó mumbled.

Vlad rubbed the back of his neck. "You spoke of János? What did Zsigmond say?"

"*Sì*. He'll let me take the boy into my service."

Recalling those soldiers also stationed outside the king's room, Vlad refrained from hugging their captain general. He exhaled a breathy sigh.

"I promise János will serve you well. He can ride and hunt and defend. Each day, he practices with his sword. He's grown confident in his reading and arithmetic—"

"No need to praise his virtues again, Vlad. I accepted him upon your recommendation and sought His Royal Majesty's approval. Why does the boy's fate matter?"

Vlad shrugged. "I suppose János reminds me of myself at the same age. Newly arrived among the courtiers, desiring to prove his mettle and earn his king's favor."

"But not so much of the latter for you now, no? You've been battle-tested countless times, but your view of our monarch has changed." When Vlad would have interjected, Pipó said, "I'm twenty-five years older than you, but these eyes still see as well as yours."

He grasped Vlad's arm and tugged him to the end of the passage with a curt nod of dismissal for a guardsman who bowed and moved to a counterpart a short span away.

"You're disenchanted with Zsigmond's view of Transalpine politics," Pipó continued. "He has said you quarreled with him before last winter about your country's destiny. You didn't like His Royal Majesty's refusal to interfere there."

"Dan Dăneşti's always been an ambitious cousin. He's a traitor to the faith my father placed in him. After my brother Mihail's rule ended on the battlefield, our sibling Radu should have claimed the throne. He could've if the king...if our king wanted it."

"The *Signoria*, the leadership of Florence, is, ah, not so different from how you've described the nobles of your homeland. The power of ruling families is all that matters. They did not want your brother Radu, or they would have supported him, no?"

A truth Vlad already conceded. He hoped such circumstances did not herald his future. What would happen when he sought power? Would the boyars deny him as well? What about King Zsigmond?

Pipó scrutinized his features beneath the torches fixed along the wall. What did his friend seek? Truths Vlad could never reveal. Despite their decade-long friendship, he would keep his goal for Wallachia a secret from even such a companion.

"You're right about Radu. God shall decide his fate. It's not my concern." He drew back and saluted. "I bid you a good night's rest."

With a slow smile, Pipó's hold slid away. "*Buona notte, amico. Grazie.*"

THE NEGOTIATIONS OF the princess' marriage arrangements concluded at the end of the week, one day before the feast of Michaelmas. Albrecht, recognized by the courtiers as Zsigmond's heir, conceded his support of the rights of Queen Borbála to all her dower lands if the king predeceased her. A raucous celebration occurred one evening later.

Over ten years separated Erzsébet and Albrecht's ages, so perhaps Zsigmond's heir found little interest in his youthful bride. He did exchange sharp glances with her mother where Borbála sneered before she turned away. Was the princess fated to endure the same poor semblance of a marital union as the queen?

"With the loveliness of your mistress, it's a wonder the royal ladies at the dais draw your attention so frequently," Fruzhin whispered in Vlad's ear.

He reached for Călţuna's hand beneath the embroidered tablecloth. She giggled at something János said from his place next to her before she gave a winsome smile to Vlad. He grasped her fingertips and brought them to his lips.

She leaned closer. "What was that for, my love?"

"You're the most beautiful woman in this room. I won't neglect you," he said.

She laughed and kissed his cheek. "As if I would ever let you."

From a table closer to the dais, Pipó rose and signaled János, whose smile faded. A flush crept across his wan cheeks. He stood with his chin dipped down to the collar of his quartered blue and black robe.

Vlad cleared his throat. "Remember who you are, young János, son of Vajk Hunyadi, a knight of the king and lord of Hunyadvár. Straighten your back and breathe deeply."

János nodded and forced a smile, which turned genuine once Călţuna patted his forearm and urged him on. Each day, with routine diligence, he fought his stammer. He joined Pipó, who formally introduced him to Zsigmond.

A hush fell over the room while everyone eyed the newest attendant. János spoke slowly and deliberately, without embarrassing himself. The king asked after his mother, Vlad supposed, in a polite gesture. His heart soared with pride when Zsigmond charged the youth to be a dutiful squire in the service of Pipó before dismissing them both.

"Did you once face our sovereign before many others, my Vlad?" Călţuna asked.

"I did." He glanced at Fruzhin. "And I have my Bulgarian friend here to thank for aiding me." After they raised their wine goblets in salute to each other, he turned to Călţuna again. "The queen did not look at me with much favor, then."

"Nor me, now," she replied.

The few spiteful glances Borbála sent down the row of trestle tables never perturbed Vlad. He assumed she reserved her scowls for him after the revelation of her infidelity. What grudge could she bear his mistress?

Vlad tugged Călţuna close, and she rested her head on his shoulder. He whispered, "Never fear. I'll keep you safe from her. No one can harm you while I draw breath."

The musicians played a lively tune on fiddles, snare drums, and pipes. Zsigmond drew his daughter to the stone floor between the tables. They danced, eliciting her first smiles of the evening. Courtiers joined them and Călţuna requested Vlad do the same.

"My sweet, your toes would not survive." He begged off and looked for János standing behind Pipó against the wall, as he smoothed the folds of the robe while the other hand ran over his hair. "It appears our young friend wants to try. Shall I fetch him?"

"No, my love." Călţuna rose nimbly. "I'll charm him so he cannot refuse."

She dashed to János' side. Although he blushed up to the dark roots of his auburn hair, he bowed and offered his arm. While they danced, Vlad admired their bright smiles.

"The lady's brought great joy to your life," Fruzhin said over the rim of his chalice.

Vlad nodded. "Only one thing would make me happier; to call her my bride."

"Find your contentment where you can, my friend. We'll be at war soon enough."

"What?" Vlad dragged his gaze away from the alluring sight of Călţuna. "When?"

Fruzhin sipped the wine before he said, "Our king has not forgotten the fifteen hundred men who abandoned the town of Hory Kutné and aided the Hussites' successful siege of Vyšehrad. You and the others of Zsigmond's lions will roar again before year's end at Hory Kutné."

Vlad's stomach tautened at the thought of killing more Christians.

Two days later, another letter arrived for Călţuna from her father, as did a personal missive for János, both sent one month ago by his mother.

After several recriminations reserved for Vlad, Călţuna's father blessed her and pleaded with her to seek absolution in a convent. While she sobbed, she clung to Vlad. He consoled her and held on just as tightly. No way for him to ease her guilt or honor her as his wife and no means by which he could give her up. He despaired at the difficulties his love and desire caused her.

CHAPTER 17

The Child

"Whoever cannot seek the unforeseen sees nothing for the known way is an impasse."-Heraclitus (535-c. 475 BC), Greek philosopher.

IN THE YEAR OF OUR Lord 1421. Hory Kutné, Bohemia (modern-day Kutná Hora, Czech Republic)

Fifty-thousand Hungarian and German knights and light cavalry, attended by loyalists, descended on Hory Kutné in eastern Bohemia. They encircled the town under Hussite control. After several hours, Zsigmond ordered no siege, and Vlad wondered why. He searched the skies, fearing and expecting the phantom vision that stalked Hungarian battlefields. It never appeared. His heart buoyed. Would there be a different outcome?

He sat atop a warhorse with the rest of Zawisza's mounted company beneath bleak winter skies. Ghost-gray steam writhed and crawled over the crags and trees, encroaching on the town. As the morning wore on, silver icicles of rainfall splattered armor. The animals grew restless, shifting in hoof-deep puddles. Except for their snorts, an eerie stillness settled over the land. As if the denizens of Hory Kutné simply awaited their fate.

The fortified war wagons positioned on three sides of the town showed otherwise. Whenever Zsigmond sent out light skirmishers, the frightened horses kept a distance from crossbows, volleys, the flash of gunpowder, and the boom of short guns the Hussites called *haufnitzes* alongside their bombard cannons. Black smoke billowed.

Jan Žižka's tactics might have earned Vlad's admiration if he and the rest of Zawisza's war band were not on the receiving end of Hussite artillery fire. Žižka rightly perceived his rabble, heavily reliant on their peasant flails and pikes, could never withstand Zsigmond's heavy horsemen in full charges. The key to Hussite survival lay in forcing the king's knights to dismount, as Žižka did in the marshland outside Sudoměř, nineteen months past.

Vlad sighed at the recognition of how long he had been killing his fellow Christians. When would he have another chance at fighting his true foes, the Turks? The bloodied battlefield in Bosnia seemed a distant memory of six years ago.

Zsigmond would not allow the wet ground outside Hory Kutné to give their Hussite enemy any advantage. Why did the king delay his siege of the town? Did he fear the destruction of its minting operation, one of the largest in the country? Vlad surmised, no matter the outcome of this day, silver would still flow from the nearby mines. Whether to Zsigmond's coffers or those of his adversary, God alone would determine.

The Hungarian light cavalry sallied forth again throughout the afternoon at regular intervals, remaining just out of the range of Žižka's guns. During this, Pipó summoned all the captains to the camp twice. As evening approached, Vlad turned in the saddle and saluted Zawisza, who brought all four of his vice-captains together.

"We won't stay here into the night. I have our king's edict," he said. "When the sun sets and darkness encroaches, lead your men to the rear gate of the town alongside Fruzhin's war bands. Stay beyond the reach of any Hussites with a view of the ramparts."

Beneath the raised visors of their helms or from the slits between them, each of Vlad's fellow vice-captains stared in silence. His horse snorted and he patted the animal, its forelegs and his boots covered in splashed muck.

He cleared his throat. "As you command, Zawisza. But why do we move to what is surely the strongest Hussite defensive position, a stout walled area where there is no tree line to which we may withdraw if necessary?"

Zawisza chuckled and clapped Vlad's shoulder. "Because there will be no retreat. No Hussite defenders line the wall there; at least not those who truly support their cause. Hory Kutné will fall today because there are enough loyalists inside who'll aid us."

Vlad hated the suggestion of subterfuge. Zawisza implied an easy victory for Zsigmond, thanks to traitors. Honor no longer mattered to the king.

If the other vice-captains shared Vlad's misgivings, none showed them. They saluted Zawisza and gathered their warriors. Once the last orange rays of the sun died beneath the horizon, they rode out. Vlad led his company and met Fruzhin's favored vice-captain at the wall's outskirts. They nodded to each other before eyeing the figures on the ramparts, where Žižka's banners bearing the gold chalice hung limp, drenched by the incessant rain.

The two war bands under Fruzhin and Zawisza hung back until one of those Hussite symbols on a flagpole toppled. Some unseen hand threw the metal and red cloth into watery mud. Disciplined, the Hungarians stayed quiet while the gates creaked and slowly unfurled until the doors hung back on their hinges.

At the signal of their captains, Vlad, along with other vice-captains ordered their men to unsheathe their swords or draw bows.

A lone, grizzled fighter emerged from the town. Mud caked the hem of his ragged tabard, emblazoned with Žižka's chalice symbol on the front of the long garment. He drew near them with arms and palms spread wide. He bowed and straightened before turning in a slow circle and facing them again with no visible weapon.

"I'm a nobleman devoted to the cause and claim of our good Catholic king, Zsigmond of the House of Luxembourg," he said, "to whom Hory Kutné may belong if God wills it."

As Fruzhin urged his mount on, a cold unease filled Vlad with the next lungful of breath. Fruzhin drew abreast of the man and reined in the horse. He nodded to the Bohemian traitor before swinging the sword in a wide arc.

The blade sliced through the stranger's throat. He clutched the wound, eyes bulging. A torrent of blood that not even the steady rain could wash away spilled over his hands. Then he collapsed on the sodden earth. At a wordless command from Fruzhin, the mounted archers of his war band fired at those on the walls, while Zawisza ordered the other knights inside.

"Kill those traitors where they stand!"

Despite his shock and dismay, Vlad led riders through the gate. His companions fell on the betrayers of Hory Kutné.

"But we've surrendered to you!" A Hussite ran at him, sword drawn. "We didn't want a fight. You butcher!"

Vlad plunged the sword into his exposed neck and kicked him in the chest. Flung backward, he perished, as did all his companions, hacked to death with stunned looks of surprise immortalized on their faces.

In the aftermath, when Fruzhin reached him, Vlad grabbed the throat latch of his best friend's horse. The pair of men stared at each other in tense silence, ragged breaths issued in white, smoky wisps.

"Would you have trusted those who betrayed this town to us?" Fruzhin asked.

"Of course not." Vlad gave a curt nod. "Did Zsigmond command their deaths?"

"Do I ever do anything that is not the will of our king? I am loyal and never question Zsigmond. Not once."

Implicit in the reply, the opposite opinion about Vlad. A belief he could not deny even if he wished. He believed some of the king's orders were wrong. His former enemies who capitulated in secret pacts did not merit trust, but their deaths were unnecessary.

Vlad's hold on Fruzhin's mount fell away. "What happens now?"

Zawisza joined them. "We move through the town. Cut down all those who stand in our sovereign's way. We take this place as Zsigmond willed."

Vlad wondered, was it God's purpose as well?

BLACK MIDNIGHT SKIES unleashed a deluge. As if the very heavens wept for the dead of Hory Kutné. Corpses littered the cobblestone streets. Dogs roamed in packs. When they gorged, the Hungarian bowmen scattered or shot them on the spot. Torches revealed rivulets of red sluicing along the pathways between former homes and burned-out shops. Fighting continued outside the town, but once the Hungarian army controlled every city gate, their king sent word for Fruzhin and Zawisza's men to hold Hory Kutné.

Whether Zsigmond also ordered the massacre of the Hussites inside the walls; men and women, old and young, Vlad did not ask and expected he might never know. Blood lust consumed the two war bands. So many died, Vlad lost count of the souls his sword claimed. He could not say with certainty all the dead were Hussites, either.

Afterward, he lingered in the pouring rain outside the central square, removed his helmet, and let the water wash over him. Once it abated, he stood chilled to the bone.

Then he went through the town's rear gate again and sought the reassuring warmth of Călţuna at the king's encampment. Tobar and Yoska stood guard outside the tent Vlad had pitched earlier. Inside, Călţuna sat with her head bowed in both hands until he called her name. She rushed at him and clung to his waist. Although wet and blood-splattered, he held her close and kissed her forehead. She leaned against him and sighed.

"Oh, my Vlad," she whispered against his shoulder after a few breaths. "I heard terrible screams and the wails of women. I feared the worse for you."

"My scars will heal, my Călţuna, but if you were in danger, the pain would be unbearable. The battle rages on outside the gates. Even knowing my Gypsies would die for you if the Camp became overrun, I must ensure your well-being or worry will distract me. Can you bear the sight of me tonight? Please come with me into the town."

She drew back in the circle of his arms and smoothed a fingertip over the mustache he'd let grow overlong until it drooped on either side of his mouth. "I wish to be wherever you are. I will love you always."

"I must warn you." He gripped her small hands. "There is carnage everywhere. When armies fight...their beastly natures consume them."

She reached for the blue cords of her mantle, tightened them, and pulled up the hood. "I'm ready."

Outside the tent, Vlad gave the twins instructions to guard his possessions. From among them, he took his wolf pelt and hunting blade. Hand in hand with Călţuna, he went to his horse and entered the town again.

The victors reveled in grisly trophies; the heads, limbs, and private parts of the Hussites heaped into piles. Some men caroused with beakers of wine and harassed survivors in their homes, breaking down doors and intruding on privacy. Zawisza and Fruzhin took over the largest inn in the central square ostensibly for the king and his war council, while the vice-captains seized all nearby dwellings for themselves and their superiors.

Vlad claimed the remaining chamber in a charred house. He and Călţuna bedded down on a stained mattress, which he covered in his wolf fur. They held each other in the darkness. His hands rubbed her back until a light snore emanated. Sleep evaded him.

Across the distance, cannons fired as the siege continued. Žižka's war wagons must remain trapped between the town that he no longer controlled and the king's front lines.

Exhaustion suffused each of Vlad's limbs. His eyes throbbed. The savagery of the past evening replayed in his mind. Zsigmond's focus on the Hussite problem made a mockery of Vlad's oath to fight the perfidious Turks.

What was he doing, year after year, killing Christians? Instead of preparing for the feast of Christmas in four days, his last hours were mired in the slaughter of those who also believed in Jesus. He must fulfill his vow of revenge against the faith's true enemies.

Shrieks drove him from Călțuna's side to the sole window. He wiped the pane for a view, smearing black grime on his palm. He looked down into the central square, where several makeshift fires flared.

Soldiers encircled a trio of women, Hussites, by their dress embroidered with the golden chalice on what remained of shredded bodices or skirts. The women screamed and hugged each other close as the men pawed at them and dragged them by the tattered cloth. Moonlight revealed pale breasts and calves covered in finger or handprints in the dark smear of gunpowder residue.

Vlad's jaw tightened as he surveyed the grim scene. Where were Fruzhin and Zawisza? The king ordered them to control Hory Kutné, and not allow discipline to fall away.

Three fighters grew tired of their sick game and wrenched the smallest woman between them by her unkempt, inky curls. Others laughed and looked on while they shoved her on her back. A man raped her. His cohorts held her down and stifled her cries.

"Vlad? What's happened? Who's making those sounds?" Călțuna asked behind him.

Before he could turn and answer her, Fruzhin appeared south of the square, hauling a thin, red-haired woman. She stood taller than he did. Her tiny fists tied together with a rope he lugged. The men cheered Fruzhin on. A knight slapped the woman on her rump. Fruzhin drew his sword and brandished it frantically, stumbling while dragging her.

"Vlad?" Călțuna's plaintive voice interrupted his trance. What would he do if someone treated her the same way? He could never abide it.

His gorge rose in his throat. He drew the hunting knife tucked into its sheath. Long as his forearm and crafted with a thick blade fitted to a walnut hilt, the Gypsy twins crafted and gave it to Vlad before they left Pozsony with him. He handed the weapon to Călțuna and squeezed her fingers around the leather.

"Stay abed. Don't look out of the window. If any man except me comes here—"

"He will not leave this room alive," she swore. "I've skinned my father's deer and rabbits with Gypsy blades. I can defend myself with one, too."

He pressed a kiss to her lips and hurried outside, intercepting Fruzhin at the base of the inn's stairs. Up close, Vlad took in his friend's beardless, grubby cheek coated in someone's dried blood; red-eyed and dazed, as if he had never slept the night before.

The woman with him, taller and thinner than Vlad first assumed, struggled against, cursed, and kicked her captor. He wrenched her arms hard. Her slim wrists bore reddened marks. The same shade streaked across the whites of her eyes. She looked at Vlad as if assessing whether he posed the same threat as Fruzhin did. Her efforts renewed.

"What are you doing with her?" Vlad gripped the rickety wood railing.

Fruzhin blinked rapidly before peering at him. "Come...to take...my woman? Don't you have your lady?" He weaved before slurring, "Go back to...her."

"This one is clearly unwilling to have you. Besides, you're drunk."

"I. Will. Take. Her." Fruzhin leaned against the banister.

His captive gave a hard twist, but he barely budged.

She yelled, "Let me go! Wretched mongrel, you're worse than a dog in heat."

He yanked her hard against him once more and after some careless fumbling, grasped her chin. "I'll put that mouth to good use once I get you upstairs."

Vlad gripped Fruzhin's arm. "There must be whores who won't care whether the coin they earn tonight comes from Bohemians, Hungarians, or Bulgarians. Leave her be. This isn't you, my friend. I've seen you after countless battles and sieges with camp followers in your arms, willing to slake your lust. You're not one of those animals outside, defiling defenseless Hussite women. You're no monster—"

"No." Fruzhin pulled away from Vlad and pushed himself upright. "I'm...a killer. Have been...since the age of ten." He shook his head. "I stabbed my first Turk then. After he and those barbarians invaded my father's land and tried to rape my mother."

"What you would do with this woman...it's the same! You have no right."

Fruzhin gaped at him and then laughed in his face. "You stole...ha; you stole a woman from her homeland and think...to tell me who I can take?" He looked aside at the woman again. "This one's...a whore, paid for with good coin already. Not some nobleman's daughter. And you...you're a killer, just like me, Vlad. Look at the blood on you! Even the rain couldn't wash it all...." He mounted the first step and hauled the struggling female up alongside him. "Don't you...don't you dare judge me!"

Vlad reached for him, but Fruzhin whipped the sword in his face.

"Damn you for a drunken fool!" Vlad slammed his palm against the wood. "We are blood brothers, Fruzhin. We never draw real weapons on each other."

"Go...go back to your woman, Vlad. Don't interfere." Fruzhin continued his ascent, a struggle at every step.

Stunned into defeat, Vlad eyed him while he retreated with his ill-gotten prize.

VLAD RETURNED TO THE room where Călțuna waited until Zawisza sought him out.

"Pipó calls for our war bands. The Hussites are trying to break free through our lines with their wagons. Our king demands we stop them. We will not fail him!"

The pair emerged under a dark blue-purple night sky. Other fighters held the reins of their horses. Vlad got on his mount and dragged on his gauntlets. Snow flurries began and frigid air seeped beneath his armor. He looked up once at the window of the room where Călțuna slept behind a barred door. God protect her, he prayed.

"Where's Fruzhin?" Zawisza scanned the faces of riders already mounted across the central square. "Who has seen him?"

"I did. Earlier," Vlad muttered, still embittered at the memory. "Inside the inn."

"He wasn't there when I searched from room to room," Zawisza replied. "He'd better find himself at the head of his war band soon. Ride now, men! Not one of these heretics or their war wagons is escaping Hory Kutné tonight."

In time, Vlad found Fruzhin, already attacking the rear guard of the Hussites with some of his men in the rising disarray. His mounted archers fired while knights and light cavalry harassed the Hussite artillerymen and those concealed in the war wagons.

Vlad urged on his company. "Don't let them break free!"

Around him, madness ensued. A bombard cannon somewhere in the center of the Hussites exploded. Pieces of flesh mingled with dirt and snow spewed into the air. Thick, choking black smoke made Vlad reel in the saddle. He coughed and spluttered.

The vapors parted in front of him, revealing the explosion that devastated some and scattered the rest of the king's warriors. The Hussite war wagons moved for the gap created in the front line.

"Damn them, no!" Zawisza shouted. He waved his arms furiously and yelled for the standard-bearer with the war band's flag. "Signal our cohorts to re-form the line now!"

Yet, the Hussites kept advancing and their artillery fire never ceased, driving back Zsigmond's horsemen in the rear and vanguard.

"Get after them!" Zawisza ordered, rallying their fighters.

More smoke billowed and the snowfall thickened, blanketing the muddied battlefield outside the town walls. Warriors and their horses screamed as the Hussite artillery tore through them. Two other bombard cannons detonated.

Vlad's mount went down on its forelegs, throwing him over its head. He landed on his back, dazed and blinking. An awful ringing reverberated in his ears. Fingering the lobe, blood came away on the tip of the mail glove. He forced himself to concentrate and peered through the blackened mist and swirling snow.

The world no longer made sense. The barrels of Hussite cannons discharged volley after volley of heated stones, but he could not hear them. One of his men rolled beside him, blood streaming from his gaping lips. The eye sockets emptied like crimson chasms. He mouthed something Vlad never made out before oblivion came to the man. Debris littered the ground, including the remnants of humans and their horses.

Vlad blinked and stared in the deafening silence as Zsigmond's enemies made a determined escape.

"I SHOULD dismiss you all from your posts!" Zsigmond railed inside the royal tent against the vice-captains, their superiors, and his captain general. "Žižka made a fool of me again. You let his forces get free, Pipó! And you, Fruzhin and Zawisza, I know about the collapse of order in the town. Your war bands caroused with women and drank rather than holding Hory Kutné. Fools! What were you thinking? Or did nothing but rutting occupy your mind? Don't answer! I don't care. Go from me. Useless wretches."

Vlad bowed his head and exited alongside the others. None of them spoke before they dispersed beneath a dove-gray dawn. The cool air stank with the residual pungency of cannon fire and the rot of death. Zawisza ordered his war band back to the town.

"What about the dead there?" Vlad asked. "Do we leave corpses in the streets?"

"If you care for those heretics, organize their burial," Zawisza snapped. "Zsigmond hasn't rescinded his permission for my hunt, and I'll take advantage before he changes his mind. Our fighters won't be digging the graves. Take some of your company and get the town's residents out of their homes. Make them bury their neighbors."

"By your order." Vlad saluted Zawisza, selected a few soldiers who would reinforce his command, and requisitioned the carts and tools for grave ditches. Late in the evening, he returned to Călțuna and brought her to the inn for food. He found most of the vice-captains and other officers there, among them Fruzhin with his victim from the previous night held in a tight grip on his lap.

Vlad kept Călţuna away from the rest of the room's occupants, close to the door, at a table with scant company. He urged her to eat before the stringy, watery stew grew cold. He wanted to leave. Fruzhin's behavior with the woman still disgusted him.

She wore the same thin garment, torn now. Livid bruises around her elongated neck and wrists coupled with soot and grime made her an awful sight. Even more pitiable, she seemed subdued, her spirit broken. Tears ran down her cheek as Fruzhin pawed her small teats peeking through the cloth. If she debased herself willingly as a whore, why did she weep so? Was Fruzhin so cruel to her?

Vlad's guts roiled at the thought. Was his best friend of eleven years only a butcher and an animal? What about a knight's duty to defend the weak? Mere words.

"You haven't eaten or said a word, my love." Călţuna placed her hand on his.

He pushed his untouched, greasy bowl at her, but she shook her head.

"One awful serving was enough. What is it? What perturbs you, my Vlad?"

"Let's go. I'm not hungry." He rose and grasped her fingers.

She protested briefly. "But you have eaten nothing today."

He tugged her away, while behind her, Fruzhin's woman's wet gaze fixed on him.

In the chamber, while Călţuna helped him remove steel plates, he stilled her hands. A thicket of emotions ensnared him. For her, he would find a path through them.

"The first time I donned this armor, my uncle Staico reminded me of a good knight's duty. Protect the innocent. Vanquish the enemy. They are fine ideals, but far from the truth. A good knight is also a well-trained killer. His only goal is survival. There was no honorable war here against the Hussites. I want to be more than a butcher of flesh. Let us find comfort with each other in this cruel world and see our children grow. Give me a child, Călţuna, so my wretched life may have a new purpose."

He made love to her with such tenderness that night. Tears spilled. He kissed hers away and held her close until she slumbered beside him, sated. Sleep did not claim him. His soul, wearied and conflicted, could no longer bear the killing of his fellow Christians. For the first time in half a life spent wielding his sword, the deaths of others whom he fought and killed at Zsigmond's command mattered.

Although bone-weary, Vlad rose the next dawn and oversaw the burials of the last corpses. Least among them was a child wrapped in his burial shroud; the sole body Vlad placed into the grave. He covered it on his own. He dismissed the townspeople and staggered back to Călțuna. Except, no one occupied the chamber they shared.

Momentary panic seized him. Where was she? His thoughts whirled. She promised never to leave him. He could not lose her. He would not lose her again!

He raced to the inn. Perhaps she sought food. However, she was not there. No one inside recalled seeing his mistress for the day. He emerged from the din, his mind racing again. He scoured the central square, finding dogs that nosed for scraps.

Head in his hands, he sank beside a decrepit fountain. One of the king's squires found him. Summoned to Zsigmond after midday, he learned the entire army would disperse to their respective winter quarters the next morning and leave the town to the loyalists. The king dismissed the captains and vice-captains.

Zawisza never attended the meeting, which a perturbed Zsigmond seemed not to care about, while no one else remarked on the absence. Pipó hastened away before Vlad could ask after their Polish friend's whereabouts.

Fruzhin caught his arm at a distance from the royal tent. "Have you seen Margit?"

"Who?"

"The...whore I've been with since...." Fruzhin trailed off, his visage reddened, his head and shoulders bowed before releasing Vlad.

He frowned at Fruzhin. "No, I have not seen her, and if I did, I wouldn't tell you."

Vlad tromped away through the mud, resuming his search for Călțuna. He found her in the inn this time, but not alone. She sat on a bench with the woman whom Fruzhin wanted. Pipó and János were nearby, but he acknowledged their greetings with the slightest of nods.

"Where have you been?" Vlad grasped Călţuna's hand. "Fruzhin's looking for her."

"So, he can force her to his bed again?" Călţuna stood. "You must save Margit from his attention. She doesn't want them. No girl of fourteen years should suffer them."

"What?" Vlad released her and scrutinized the female on the bench. Where he once thought her tall for a woman, he recognized the lanky length of someone younger in her form and the small roundness of her breasts, the flush of youth in her tear-streaked face.

"But Fruzhin said she is a whore." He touched and raised Călţuna's chin.

"Not by choice," she whispered. "Margit's father owed a debt to the girl's aunt, who demanded her services and sold her to a whoremaster. She was a virgin."

The cold wind blew in before Fruzhin entered. His turbulent gaze met Vlad's own before alighting on the girl. He came over and hauled her up by the arm.

"I've been looking everywhere! I told you, it's not safe. Did someone else touch you?"

She cried and slapped his chest repeatedly until he restrained her.

"You should let her go, Prince Fruzhin," Călţuna said. "You shame yourself."

He glared at her before sneering at Vlad. "I've told you not to interfere." Fruzhin herded the girl ahead of him up the stairs.

Vlad summoned Tobar for Călţuna's protection and searched for Zawisza with Yoska. No one saw the Polish officer in the past two mornings after he left for the western woodlands with a small hunting party. Despite Yoska's unblemished reputation as a tracker of men and beasts, no sign of Zawisza occurred.

On his return to the central square, Vlad spied Fruzhin leading the girl Margit through the streets and followed them at a discreet distance. Several rows of houses later, Fruzhin gave over the girl to a red-haired man in a Jewish skullcap, who sobbed and embraced her.

From under his black cloak, Fruzhin drew a leather sack the size of his fist and rendered it to the girl. After wiping her running nose, she snatched the offering before spitting in his face. The duo entered the residence behind them and closed the door.

Fruzhin scrubbed a hand over his mouth and went to the town's rear gate.

Vlad sent Yoska to his twin brother Tobar and Călţuna, before seeking Zsigmond. The king received him after some delay, despite the absence of anyone else in the tent.

"Your Royal Majesty, the captain Zawisza is still not here."

"What do you mean? We permitted him two days of hunting only in the west woods. He should have returned last night. Send out riders and find him. We must leave today for the Christmas festival tomorrow."

One of the king's guards begged entry and whispered to Zsigmond, who scowled. "Tell Pipó to bring him to Us. Vlad, remain here with your sword ready."

A Hussite envoy entered with a white flag of truce tied to a pole. Without a preamble and no permission from the king, he proclaimed, "We have your Black Knight, Zawisza Czarny. He and his hunting party are our hostages. Jan Žižka wishes to negotiate for temporary peace. If you refuse, he will order the deaths of your men in a week. Žižka is a warrior for God and a man of his word. We don't waste food and water on prisoners."

Outside the tent, Vlad found what he expected in an otherwise ordinary skyscape. The black phantom. Would Hell's nightmarish apparition forever haunt the Hungarian army?

His hands fisted at his sides. They must rescue Zawisza before Žižka killed him.

IN THE YEAR OF OUR Lord 1422. Vienna, Austria, Holy Roman Empire (modern-day Vienna, Austria)

The city of Vienna, the capital of the Holy Roman Empire, thronged with guests before Princess Erzsébet's April nuptials. Vlad's mother declined King Zsigmond's invitation. Although sorrowful, for the occasion would have permitted a meeting between Princess Mara and Călţuna, Vlad focused on securing a dressmaker's services for the latter.

One week before the ceremony, she twirled in an albescent and forest-green garment with silvery swirls and stars shot through the skirt. The pale folds of the cloth reminded him of the florid skin underneath. How much he desired the touch, taste, and feel of it.

"Not even the bride could be as beautiful as you, love," he acknowledged.

"You must never let her, or the queen hear you say so. Every woman wants to be the envy of other females at her wedding. Such fine garb." She peeked at the dressmaker's assistant before whispering, "At seventy florins, my Vlad, it's an extravagance."

"The sight of you in it is worth the cost," he replied, paying for Călţuna's gift.

He took her hand. They rode through a crowd toward Hofburg Castle, a branch of the Danube behind them. Tobar and Yoska followed closely.

"Do you believe your former superior shall arrive before the wedding?"

"Zawisza's letter after my last birthday did not speak of his intent in spring. I asked no such question in my reply. I'd be glad to see him, know he is well, and his brief captivity with the Hussites last Christmas has not altered him."

They entered the square-shaped precincts of the Habsburg royal residence by a moated drawbridge. Four turrets rose above their heads. Each spring day, the courtyard thronged with guests. Vlad glimpsed Zsigmond's widowed sister-in-law Žofie of Bavaria with the two brothers she expected would attend the ceremony at Stephansdom Cathedral. Then he noted Fruzhin standing in a circle of his Serbian family.

Despite the long-term tension simmering between them, Vlad could not restrain a smile at Fruzhin's happiness. He was never happier than when he embraced his maternal uncle and aunt. Vlad searched their entourage for any sign of Radič, his former brother by marriage. Did Stefan's trusted palatine remain in Belgrade?

"Who is that beautiful and very tall woman with Prince Fruzhin?" Călţuna asked.

"She is the Serbian princess Milena Olivera Lazarević, sister of the *Despoteses* of the Kingdom of Rascia, Stefan Lazarević. He is Fruzhin's maternal uncle," Vlad explained.

He withheld how Fruzhin's aunt helped him uncover the fate of his lost sister. No use in ruminating about reunions that would never happen.

"You must greet the Serbians now," Călţuna said.

He shook his head. "No, love, I wouldn't want to intrude."

"But how could you? Fruzhin is your friend, no matter the horrid events at Hory Kutné." She reached for his fingers. "Forgive him. Please. The distance between you has lingered for almost four months and frayed your bond. It's time for unity. Go to him."

A long sigh escaped him. He dismounted and looked up at her again.

"Go on," she urged, taking his horse's reins.

He trudged and weaved among the crowd before reaching the Serbians. Fruzhin turned from the conversation he held with another man, and Vlad bowed.

"Oh, none of that!" Milena Olivera tugged him, and he straightened before she dwarfed and enveloped him in her effusive embrace. "It's been too long since we last stood together at Buda Castle. Now, look at you, with a broad mustache that meets your beard. How fine you appear! Does he not seem well and happy, dear brother?"

"I can't tell since you won't release him and let me have a look," Stefan murmured.

Milena Olivera's husky laugh followed before she let go. Despite her praise, tiny lines formed and furrowed her brow. Before Vlad could consider the sudden change in her mien, her brother reached for him and offered the kiss of peace.

"You've survived our king's Hussite wars. God bless you," Stefan said once they drew apart. "Let me offer my condolences. In Belgrade, we heard of your brother Mihail."

He waved to the man standing beside Fruzhin. "Greet my nephew, Đurađ Branković, the heir of Serbia. Well, if Zsigmond consents to my choice. Đurađ, this is the friend Fruzhin has always spoken so highly of in his letters, Prince Vlad of Wallachia."

Whatever Vlad might have expected of Fruzhin's cousin, he never expected the lined visage and graying brown hair of a man who could be Stefan's brother, rather than a sister's child. Đurađ bowed, and Vlad did the same before asking after Radič.

"He and his son are well, and regret their absence," Stefan said.

"Then Anna's son, my nephew, is home from Bosnia?"

"Yes. He attained his knighthood before spring arrived. He is touring the silver mines with his father before they visit the pair of monastic orders Radič founded."

Vlad smiled, thinking his sibling would be proud of her son and widowed husband.

"Come, Milena Olivera. Đurađ." Stefan clapped his heir's thin shoulder. "We still have the travel dust on us but must greet our king."

As Vlad parted with them and they entered Hofburg Castle, he leaned toward Fruzhin. "When you first told me about Đurađ, I imagined him being your age."

"Careful now, for a short span separates the ages of my uncle and cousin." Fruzhin continued, "You thought me much older when we first met."

They shared a grin, the first in long months. How easily they lapsed into their usual camaraderie. As if they could truly put the awful brutality of their lives behind them.

"I've missed talking with you like this." Fruzhin's throat bobbed. "We stopped after Hory Kutné. Mainly because I behaved...as I did. The memory shames and haunts me."

"It should. You have aunts and female cousins. And you're a king's knight, not an animal. As you always demand the best of me, I expect the same of you." Once Fruzhin colored, blinked rapidly, and looked away, Vlad softened his tone. "None of us can change the past. We may only amend our lives for the future. It is all that matters."

ZSIGMOND'S DAUGHTER united with his heir, Albrecht. The nuptial festivities spilled beyond the expansive banquet hall. Vlad sat on crisp spring grass covered in large, white linen squares with Călțuna, and Fruzhin and his family. Vlad's lover and Milena Olivera fell into an easy rapport in Greek, a language he never knew Călțuna spoke. Both women were so amiable, he never doubted differences in their heritage would fade upon their introduction. Milena Olivera frowned at the Gypsy twins standing guard.

Stefan and Đurađ focused on matters in Serbia, whose fortresses of Belgrade and Galambóc the king wished to have in exchange for accepting Stefan's choice of an heir.

"My cousin must be strong once he shoulders our uncle's burden," Fruzhin said, while he and Vlad reclined apart from the other men. "The greedy Turkic sultan wants more Serbian land. Đurađ worries about the legacy of his four sons and daughters."

"Dear Fruzhin and Vlad, may I interrupt?" Milena Olivera asked. "I think we can both trust your best friend will entertain your lady, Vlad, if we speak in private."

He patted Fruzhin's shoulder. "I rely on him for many things."

Vlad rose and offered Milena Olivera his forearm before smiling at Călțuna. She beamed up at him and slid a platter of apples, dried quinces, and cheese over to Fruzhin. Vlad waved off Tobar and Yoska before they could follow him.

"Now I know the source of your radiant joy." Milena Olivera leaned on his limb. "Thus, I hesitated before inviting you to revive a long-buried past. But you once made me promise never to hide anything I discovered about your sister, Princess Arina."

He halted with her beside a white willow. "What are you saying?"

"I think her child survived the birthing, Vlad, and may thrive even to this very day."

The shock reverberated through him.

Milena Olivera spoke. Two months ago, her youngest daughter Oruz Hatun took her children on a winter pilgrimage to Iznik, which Christians formerly knew as Nicea. Now in the Turkish province of Būrsâ, there Oruz met the family of Bedreddin, who once served Mûsâ Çelebi's interests up to the latter's death. Later Bedreddin also died, executed at the command of the former sultan, Oruz's now-deceased half-brother.

Vlad recalled how Bedreddin had shadowed Arina's husband before their wedding.

"In Iznik, Bedreddin's son Ismail held the hand of a girl younger than my two grandchildren from Oruz," Milena Olivera continued. "A child with light green eyes and dark red hair, whom Ismail called his sister, which puzzled my Oruz. God blessed Bedreddin with four sons. No mention of so young a daughter, whom her brother called the moon of his father's soul. He also said the girl was ten years old, adopted as a baby after her parents died in the year of her birth. He gave no clues as to their identities."

Robbed of his speech, Vlad's fingers scrabbled at the rough tree bark.

Milena Olivera touched his shoulder. "My daughter could not pry about the adoption. The girl's description and her age fit the circumstances of your late sister. What if her child lived? You must see the possibility, as my Oruz did. The child is her niece as much as yours, a granddaughter of my Bāyazīd Hân. It's why Oruz wrote to me in such haste afterward. Do you see why I come to you now with this news?"

He did. By God, a daughter of Arina. Alive after so long. A child of two disparate experiences, the blood of his people and his enemies coursing through her. No matter how he tried to relinquish the past, it seemed fate would not let him.

Now that he knew about the girl, there could be no question of what he must do next. He must find her. But, how? He sank to his knees below the white willow and prayed for her endurance, but also that God in His infinite wisdom would forge the path between them to discover each other.

CHAPTER 18

Hour of the Wolf

"Where there are sheep, the wolves are never very far away."-Plautus (circa 254-184 BC), Roman playwright.

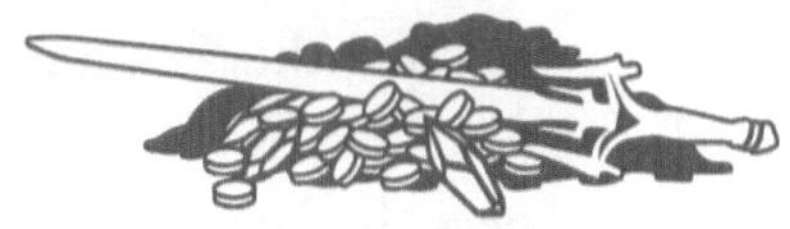

IN THE YEAR OF OUR Lord 1422. Pozsony and *Buda, Hungary* (modern-day Bratislava, Slovakia and Budapest, Hungary)

One week after the Hungarian princess Erzsébet's wedding, Vlad composed a letter intended for his mother the moment he arrived at Pozsony's castle. The royals along with the widowed Bohemian queen Žofie of Bavaria would stay a few days before the newlyweds toured the Hungarian kingdom. At midnight, Zsigmond did not choose Vlad to guard the royal chamber within the king's private residence.

By the light of a beeswax candle set on the ledge above his head, Vlad braced his back along the wall of the castle's dining hall, drew up his knees, and scribbled words that sent his mind racing ever since he first heard them from Milena Olivera in Vienna.

Fruzhin rolled and rubbed the back of his fingers over his eyes. "You're still at it?"

"I've abandoned my first mad ramblings and started afresh four times. Sentries on the wall called the midnight watch hours ago," Vlad replied. "One of my Gypsies will ride to Wallachia with the missive. The twins have never separated before."

Fruzhin asked, "Then you believe all my aunt and Turkic cousin have relayed."

Vlad sighed and set the quill with its blackened tip atop the bottle of ink. "It's hard to know what to think. I remember the man Bedreddin."

"I know the name, too. Not just from my aunt's mention of him to you. Iskender, who turned his back on our Bulgarian homeland and family; his sultan sent him to capture one of Bedreddin's most faithful adherents. A mission that ended in the death of my sibling."

The pair looked at each other. Vlad wondered whether they were always fated to not only come together as blood brothers, but to share strained ties with the Turks.

"Did my sister Arina form an acquaintance with this Bedreddin? Had her husband arranged for Bedreddin to raise their child in case of trouble? How did either of them know they could trust him? Will I ever resolve these musings? The child, if she is Arina's own and truly lives, is thousands of leagues away. I'll never find her."

"Yet, you'll try." Fruzhin scrubbed his palm over his face. "Vlad, our king won't permit you to leave the court."

"Did I say I wanted to abandon Zsigmond?"

"You don't have to!" Fruzhin fell silent as the knight next to him groaned and glared at them before muttering curses and pulling a wool blanket over his head.

Fruzhin pointed to the steps at the end of the passageway. "Let's go outside."

Vlad held up the long length of the paper and exhaled warm breath over the last lines he wrote, willing the ink to dry. Then he tucked the letter, quill, and ink bottle under the edge of his coverlet. With Fruzhin, he rose and crept through the long lines of prone bodies stretched out in the keep. Snores and farts emanated from those warriors who'd found their rest. Vlad wondered whether he could do the same soon. If only the restless thoughts centered on Arina's daughter would abate.

He emerged outside with Fruzhin. Yawning guards patrolled the grounds. Vlad sat on a grassy knoll near the gatehouse and pulled Fruzhin down next to him.

"I know my duty and will never abandon the king," he began before Fruzhin placed a hand on his arm. "Even for my sister's child."

"You think Zsigmond does not see what I do, what Pipó and Zawisza have noted?" A soldier walked by and tilted his head toward them before moving on. Fruzhin pitched his voice lower. "Defiance and resentment of our monarch resonate in your tone."

"My tone? By Christ and all His saints, I've shed blood for the king infinite times."

"Humph. You don't even hear yourself. You call him 'the king' now, whereas once you acclaimed him as 'my king.' Something changed inside you at Hory Kutné, or maybe before in Hradčany, when you argued with Zsigmond over your homeland's future, a year past."

Vlad drew apart from his friend. "Did Pipó write to you about that?"

Fruzhin rolled his eyes.

"Zsigmond then. He is still displeased with me." As Vlad was with the king, he acknowledged inwardly. Fruzhin was right.

"Let me assure you; I understand why your cousin Dan Dăneşti's rule over the Transalpine land concerns you. Because we are blood brothers, I have kept your ambitions a secret. I will never betray your trust, even for our liege, if you do not deceive him. No one can hold your country without our king's support. You never shirk your duty. You give your blood in battle. Nothing less, but nothing more of yourself. There's a reason another knight guards our king at the hour of the wolf."

"He no longer trusts me because I dared question him? I am a prince."

"You're a knight sworn to serve! The homeland your cousin rules is a vassal state of Hungary. You have no right to demand anything from Zsigmond. When you show him obedience, he will rely on you again."

Vlad's guts roiled and tightened. He huffed, pressed his lips together, and looked away. Unbidden, one of his favorite truisms from the Greek philosopher Aristotle filled his thoughts. *'I count him braver who overcomes his desires than him who conquers his enemies, for the hardest victory is over self.'*

"Don't let pride rob you of the support you'll need in the future." Fruzhin's grip on his arm increased and tore him from his reverie. "Listen to me and humble yourself! Accept our king's dictates and do what you must. Regain his favor. In this battle, you must submit."

A fact Vlad accepted, even as the ever-persistent refrain of his long-dead master's recommendation came to mind. *"Don't rely on Zsigmond."*

He would allow no one mastery of his destiny, even a king. Indeed, he would control himself and secure his future.

Thunder rumbled overhead, shattering the relative quietude. A stiff riverine breeze howled and gusted from the Danube below, buffeting him, accompanied by an earthy redolence. Moisture saturated the air, whipping hair across his face.

He looked at Fruzhin. "I've been fortunate to know real father figures besides the man who sired me. Staico put a wooden sword in my childish grasp, and Stibor taught me to wield a real weapon with a deadly purpose. In the absence of either man, I would not be the knight you see today. King Zsigmond could never mean as much as my uncle and Stibor, but I pledged myself and placed the same faith in him. I trusted him."

"And you feel he broke that trust when he neglected your country's fate?" Fruzhin stroked the length of his graying black beard. "In the smallest part of my heart and soul dwells a deep longing for my Bulgarian homeland. Zsigmond would give me the men and money to reclaim it. Even if I take the throne left by my beloved father, I'll never have peace there, the comforts of a wife and children to whom I may bequeath an imperial legacy free from Turkish threats.

"There is contentment for me at Zsigmond's side. You can have the same. I'm not asking you to put aside ambitions forever. Your fulfillment will come. For now, our king calls you to his service. I remind you of a knight's perpetual oath. To serve."

The first words of the vow Vlad once undertook in the royal tent more than a decade ago rushed to his mind. *"I promise to serve God, and my king in valor and faith."*

He heaved a long sigh. "How may I serve our king? Prove my loyalty again?"

"I expect King Władysław of Poland will fulfill his commitment to Zsigmond, allowing Zawisza's service soon. He's sworn you saved his life at the battle of Sudoměř against the Hussites and will surely reappoint you as an officer."

Although Vlad balked at killing Christians, he said, "It's a pity you cannot do it."

"I'm glad you recognize why I must not show favoritism by selecting you."

"Nor would I impose on you. Then our king will not oppose Zawisza?"

"Don't give Zsigmond reason to do so. Let's go indoors. There's rain on the wind."

Vlad sensed something more, though he could not ascribe a name to the feeling. The gatehouse's iron bolts groaned as the entryway opened. Vlad and Fruzhin stood while guards with lances and crossbows at the ready surrounded a lone rider entering the innermost precinct of the castle. Shrouded in a hooded cloak topped by a gray wolf's skin draped around the shoulders, he slowed his horse, lifted his hands with palms spread wide, and spoke to the gatekeeper there.

"Who is this person to come among us at such a time?" Vlad mused. "Our sentries surround him as if he poses some danger, yet they permitted him inside."

"He must have an urgent need to arrive at this hour," Fruzhin said. He crossed the ground while Vlad remained under the tree. "Who is this?"

Vlad could not overhear the subsequent exchange. Once Fruzhin turned and stared at him for a moment, suspicion ran through him before his best friend shouted, "A boyar from your country! He's here for you. He calls himself Vlậcsan the Wolf."

His grandmother's nephew. Heart thudding with concern for the Dowager and his mother, Vlad lurched toward the nobleman. "Why are you so far from home? Has something happened to my family?"

Fat droplets preceded a deluge of heavy, almost stinging rain, pouring as if from buckets in the heavens. The guards yelped and scattered for the shelter of the gatehouse, but Vlad and Fruzhin stood beneath a sky that turned purple where lightning forked.

Atop the Carpathian pony, Vlậcsan reached for his hood and pulled it back. A drab pelt of unkempt dark russet hair below his shoulders framed his lean face, thin mustache, and elongated beard. He bowed in the saddle.

"Prince Vlad." He spoke the tongue of their Wallachian homeland in a low, raspy voice. "I've traveled to Vienna, Buda, and north again to find you here. We must speak."

AFTER FRUZHIN WENT inside the keep, Vlad and Vlậcsan stood together and dried themselves before the kitchen's central hearth. The cook and kitchen maids left the morning meal they barely started atop tables. Embers in the fire pit crackled, intruding on the otherwise silent interlude the pair shared.

In the low light, Vlad studied his late-night visitor, whose hose-encased legs ended in short leather boots. Despite the urgency Vlậcsan stated, he splayed long fingers tipped with ragged nails toward the small flame and stared in silence. Accustomed to perceiving the disposition and motives of most people at the first meeting, Vlad sensed the enigma of Vlậcsan the Wolf would endure.

"Why did you insist we talk at such an hour?" Vlad demanded. "Are my mother or grandmother in poor health?"

"No, neither are. In their joint instructions, both bade me wish you well and warned you to concentrate on your duties to the king, even after we spoke."

"Then it is a matter of some great concern to Mother and Grandmother?"

"I would not be here otherwise, Prince Vlad. The current situation in our birthplace is such that both princesses sent me here. I suppose you wonder why they rely on me."

"I have some idea. Mother once told me we are relations."

"My father, Florea, said the same a year before he died, which the Dowager Princess Ana-Călina affirmed when we met. Father told me to seek her. I did at the same time you returned to Argeş for your sister Princess Arina's wedding. God rest her soul."

"God rest her soul," Vlad repeated, crossing himself. "So, when I saw you in the chapel there, that was my grandmother's first encounter with you. She must have known about you, but I don't recall her ever speaking of a brother and his son in my childhood."

Vlậcsan removed the light gray wolf pelt and draped it over his forearm. He pointed to the emblem stitched at the right breast of his cloak. A blossom with its crown of petals formed by white threads, surrounded by yellow four-pointed stars.

"*Floare*," he said. Flower in their native tongue. "This is the coat of arms the House of Florea in Transilvania, adopted once my ancestors rose from obscurity. Afterward, the Wallachian ruling prince chose your grandmother from among us as his second wife. He built the Tismana Monastery on land belonging to the Floreas. The future Dowager and her brother ensured its prosperity as a powerful monastic fortress.

"Fickle fate turned against my father. Or, I should say, your father did." He faced Vlad fully. Even in the scant illumination, something strange and almost otherworldly flickered at the centers of Vlậcsan's amber-flecked eyes. "He invited mine to join the noble council of boyars and consider an alliance with the Catholic King Zsigmond."

"Your father refused," Vlad surmised.

"We of the Eastern Orthodox faith learned to never trust the Latin West after the sack of Constantinople, the Queen of Cities. As my father's punishment, Prince Mircea gave the mountain settlements my father long held to the monks of Tismana. Now, Wallachian cousins are at war with each other again, this time for the throne."

"You mean my brother Radu and our cousin Dan Dăneşti. When I last saw Mother, she told me our eldest sibling, Mihail, fought a losing battle against the Ottoman Turks. In her letter afterward, I learned he sent his two sons as hostages to our enemies."

"Then the most powerful of Wallachian boyars abandoned Prince Mihail and defected to the side of Dan Dăneşti, who sensed your brother's weakness, and sought and received Turkish support for an alternative claim."

"He had no right!"

"His father was the predecessor and brother of Prince Mircea. He is from the House of Basarab. You cannot deny it, even if feelings of loyalty to Prince Radu may inspire you."

Their relations as siblings did not compel Vlad's sentiments. As Stibor also once said, only the strong endured. If Radu succumbed to their cousin, many would doubt whether any of Mircea the Great's remaining sons deserved allegiance. Including Vlad.

"Upon Prince Mihail's death," Vlậcsan said, "Dan Dăneşti claimed the principality and ruled from Argeş, while south at Târgovişte, Radu held dominion. He marched on his rival at the end of spring last year and won but could not keep his rival at bay for over six months. Your lady mother and grandmother beg you to intercede. Convince King Zsigmond to support Radu and our boyars will do the same."

Vlad slapped his forehead. "I've already tried. Zsigmond would not listen. He said he could spare none of his forces needed to fight the Hussite wars."

Vlậcsan turned from him to the fire again. Wind gusts rattled the window shutters.

"Only a strong and cunning prince can unite Wallachia and ensure our people survive," the boyar said. "Such a man would be a worthy successor of your bold father."

"Do you think this prince shall ever exist again within the House of Basarab?"

Vlậcsan peered at him. "I believe he already does."

They held each other's gazes for an interminable time until Vlad looked away. Why did this nobleman unsettle him so? Vlậcsan possessed the complex nature of a wolf, too.

"Dan Dăneşti is wily, but he is not the man to lead the country," Vlad muttered. "To overcome Mihail, our cousin bowed before the will of the Ottomans."

"He kept them from our lands while gathering supporters to withstand them in the future. An appeasement policy. He knows when he should fight and when he should not."

Vlad shook his head. "You admire him. Is my grandmother aware?"

"The Dowager appreciates strength," Vlậcsan replied. "She raised a strong son and hoped he did the same with his heirs. She would never abandon your brother."

"But you could," Vlad surmised. "I think you might justify any choice, with reason."

After they regarded each other again for the space of several breaths, Vlậcsan turned aside this time. "Have you ever seen a wolf pack on the hunt, Prince Vlad? They are a family, united by a single aim. I am loyal and will never betray your grandmother.

"However, I understand the political realities she will not consider. True power has its costs," he rasped. "Chief among them is patience. The pack bides time to ensure success. Your cousin perceives this truth. Your sibling does not."

"Patience is a luxury many cannot afford, while the Turk wolves invade our borders, stealing land for their expansion and our people for their slave markets."

"Some losses are expected, even vital, in the quest for survival."

"How dare you say so?" Vlad glared at the boyar. "Did you tell the Dowager and my mother the same after Arina died?"

Vlậcsan peered at him. "I, too, understand loss, Prince Vlad."

"Do you suffer like my mother? Her eldest son perished because of our cousin's treachery with the Turks, to whom Mihail lost his children. Both her daughters died in childbed, leaving children, including a granddaughter whom my mother will never know."

"Princess Arina's child lived?" Vlậcsan gaped. "Are you certain?"

"What do you know about it?" Vlad demanded, his voice booming against the rafters. He grabbed the leather strings of the boyar's cloak. "What haven't you told me?"

Vlậcsan looked down at his hand, but Vlad did not loosen his hold.

"Why would you have an interest in Arina or her babe? Speak now. No half-truths."

"As I've said before, Prince Vlad, I'm also devoted to family, no matter the extent of the relation. Please, release me, and let us continue to speak as kin."

When Vlad did so, Vlậcsan rubbed the back of his neck.

"My interest, as you term it, began when Prince Mircea proposed the marriage of his daughter to Prince Mûsâ Çelebi. Your father believed him the easiest to control among his warring brothers. The Dowager feared only for her remaining granddaughter's future. She wrote to my father in secret, seeking comfortable lives for you and your sister in Moldavia. My parent, who suffered a long-standing illness, charged me with the duty."

Vlad recalled one of the last conversations with his grandmother, in which she upbraided him for the theft of her jewels while assuring him she had made all the preparations for him and his sister. Through her nephew, he realized.

"In the weeks before the young princess wed Mûsâ Çelebi, the Dowager summoned me to Wallachia at the behest of her son. He wanted my aid for his daughter."

Surprised his parent cared so much, Vlad asked, "Why did he seek your help?"

"Before the wedding, I had formed an acquaintance with one among the retinue of Prince Mûsâ Çelebi; his closest companion."

"Bedreddin." Vlad whispered the dead Turk's name as if saying it louder might summon a ghost. Perhaps it did.

Shades of the past stirred to life. Joyful memories of Arina, and him riding side by side with her in the Wallachian countryside and foothills. Crystalline peals of laughter cascaded through his thoughts, shattered by her awful tears and the utter stillness with which she stood beside a new husband in white winter furs.

"You know of Bedreddin?" Vlậcsan's voice called him back to the present.

He nodded. "I once asked my brother Radu why the man shadowed Mûsâ Çelebi."

"Bedreddin first counseled the union with your sister. His mother was also Christian, and he knew the difficult changes Mûsâ Çelebi's new Christian bride would have faced. His teachings about tolerance suggested Bedreddin believed our two religions shared the same path toward God's salvation. He hoped the marriage, like that of his parents, could show the world his faith and ours might co-exist."

"Then this Bedreddin was a fool. We are nothing like the worshipers of Allah."

"Are we not?" When Vlad did not answer, Vlâcsan continued, "I secured a vow from Bedreddin. He would help Princess Arina adjust to the Ottoman way of life and teach her husband to make his bride happy. To honor the faith the Dowager placed in me, I required one other boon of the Turk. He must secure the survival of your sister and any children she might bear her husband if ever he lost his bid for control of the empire."

"Bedreddin owed you no such kindness. You have not said how you induced him."

"No, I did not."

Vlad shook his head, knowing he could never compel the revelation.

Vlâcsan added, "When your grandmother told me of the princess' death alongside her baby, I wrote to Bedreddin. By then, the new sultan sought the deaths of Mûsâ Çelebi's adherents; Bedreddin, chief among them. How did you learn about the child?"

Vlad imparted all Milena Olivera told him. Vlâcsan sighed.

"Then the Turk kept his word as best he could. He not only saved your sister's babe, but he gained a measure of peace for her at her husband's side."

"How can you know that?"

"In letters to Princess Mara, which the Dowager relayed, your sister spoke of the contentment she found at Būrsâ Palace. Her husband created a little garden with a chapel at its center and secured the daily services of a Christian priest. Her maidservants were Wallachian slaves. Bedreddin's influence."

Vlad scrubbed a hand over his face. "Was Arina happy with her prince?"

Vlâcsan glanced at him. "She found small joys for a time." His stare flitted to the ground before he opened his mouth again yet said nothing more.

A measure of Vlad's concerns about his lost sister lifted with the boyar's assurances. The chief worries of the past could subside. At least

Vlad knew Arina had led no miserable life with her husband, bereft of family and forlorn. That knowledge alone must suffice.

"I want you to do three things, Vlậcsan the Wolf. My grandmother would approve."

"You have but to ask, Prince Vlad."

He squatted in front of the hearth. Dying embers warmed his hands. Dawn would banish the hour of the wolf soon.

"Take the letter I shall finish to my mother. She and my grandmother should read it together, so they may know the prospect of Arina's daughter. Then, discover the whereabouts of Bedreddin's family; do they live in former Christian Nicea or elsewhere with my sister's child? You will not delay in sending me word, no matter how small of her existence. It is most precious to me, like her mother's life."

"And the third matter?" Vlậcsan asked.

Vlad rose again and gazed at the boyar. "You will keep me apprised of the struggles between my brother and our cousin. I must know the moment either of the thrones at Argeş or Târgovişte becomes vacant. I won't leave our country's fate to Radu, Dan Dăneşti, or even King Zsigmond."

"MY VLAD." CĂLŢUNA BEAMED up at him one week after Vlậcsan left his side. She rocked on her heels and clutched his hands. "I think I may carry your child."

They stood beside the mighty Danube. He cocked his head. Uncertain that he heard right, he asked, "Did you truly say you're pregnant?"

"I actually said, I believe I might be—"

He did not allow her to finish as he swooped her up in his arms and twirled around with her. He glimpsed the stares of passersby, but their expressions hardly mattered with Călţuna in his arms and their child in her belly.

"Oh! My Vlad, stop the spinning. You'll make me dizzy. Oh, no, I already am!"

When he put her down, she lurched from his side, ran to the wooden railing, and heaved the breakfast of bread and beer they had downed only moments before.

As she straightened, he came to her and nestled his chin atop her hair. "Forgive me, please, but you've made me so happy. I'm surprised it's happened now. We've shared a bed for almost two years."

She leaned back against him. "By the time you took me from Hermannstadt into Bohemia, riven by warfare, I became circumspect. If I conceived our baby then, what would we do if God took you from us in battle? After we came together again at the inn, I asked the wife of the innkeeper for herbs certain to prevent conception. But when you told me of your desire for a child in Hory Kutné, I ceased using the concoction."

"If I ever fall in battle, my uncle and the Gypsies will protect you. Don't fear."

"Impossible. You'll be at war in Bohemia again soon enough, leaving me behind."

He tugged her closer. "I'll find us a house in Buda. You'll stay there for your safety. Staico shall be at hand. I trust him with your life and will write to him about the child."

"No! Please. I only suspect the possibility. Let's wait until we may be certain."

"As you wish, Călțuna." He rubbed her shoulders, kissed her head, and sighed. A child sired of their love would make all past struggles between them worthwhile.

Nothing could alter his happiness. Days later, he accepted increased guard duty along the castle's perimeter, ignoring Zsigmond's snub. He thought of the Buda townhouse he wanted, anticipating the comfort of Călțuna and his uncle.

Queen Žofie of Bavaria kept up an appearance each morning at their king's chamber where Vlad overheard her insisting on the rights lost to Borbála in Bohemia. Somehow, Zsigmond's viper of a wife had slithered back into his bed and heart, leaving his former lover bitter. One morning, Žofie left Zsigmond's room incensed and never came again after he ordered her not to leave Pozsony for Bohemia. She still supported the Hussites.

While Zsigmond ordered the court's departure to Várad in Transilvania and planned a midsummer summit with his councilors in Germany, Vlad left Călţuna in Fruzhin's care, seeking a house for her and his uncle. The men located a suitable Buda property. After initial negotiations for its purchase proved fruitful, Vlad discussed part of his plans with Staico as they walked up Castle Hill from the town center.

"The Gypsy women and their daughters can aid my mistress in making our home comfortable, while their men secure the surroundings. They can hunt with you each week, as is customary. You'll entertain Călţuna and have the comfort of a real bed, uncle."

Staico frowned. "That's it. You think I'm growing old, eh?"

"You've been at my side in Hungary for twelve years." Vlad patted the thick muscle of his uncle's burly shoulder and eyed him. "Most of them spent sleeping on the ground in a tent. If that is preferable to your own room, Călţuna may have the house to herself."

The glower deepened. "You're trying to guilt me into becoming her nursemaid."

"You'll be her protector, Staico. She's long left childhood behind," Vlad corrected. "I'm not appealing to any sense of duty on your part. She's not your woman."

"No. She's yours and since your return here, I've seen how merely speaking of her fills your heart with a hopefulness lost for many years. I have some curiosity, eh, a wish to learn more about the mistress who's improved your foul moods."

"So, you'll join her?" Vlad hauled his uncle aside. A lone golden-haired rider dressed in drab tones bore down on them before he approached the castle gatehouse.

Even with the dust the horse kicked up, Vlad recognized the queen's sibling, strangely, without the usual retinue of guards who might accompany the heir to the House of Celje. He left Castle Hill faster than his hasty arrival.

"Who's he to draw such interest, eh?" Staico asked at Vlad's shoulder.

"Friderik of Celje, Borbála's brother, who came alone. That does not bode well."

"Nothing surrounding Zsigmond's queen ever does," Staico muttered. "I've heard rumors about her aborted trial for fornication in Transilvania two years past. There's been talk of your involvement somehow, as a witness of the transgression, eh? Have you asked me to remain so far from you because of her?"

"I did not want you to worry." Vlad sighed. When his uncle snorted, he added, "Like an old nursemaid."

Staico's iron fist rammed into his shoulder. He stumbled before righting himself. His scowl countered his uncle's wide grin. The pair of them shared a gruff laugh.

Vlad reminded him, "You still haven't said if you'll share the house with Călțuna."

His uncle's delayed huff preceded a nod. "I will write when you may claim it and shall settle comfortably at your mistress' side. I hope you'll join us soon afterward."

"As do I. Remember, the choice to live there is yours, as it always will be, uncle."

"You're out of danger, eh, Vlad? I need not worry when you go to Várad tomorrow with your king's court?"

He shook his head. "Queen Borbála has the nature of a snake. I remain watchful for any sign of treachery. She'll never forget my role in her near downfall."

IN THE YEAR OF OUR Lord 1422. Várad, Transilvania (modern-day Oradea, Romania)

Within days of Friderik of Celje's arrival at his sister's side, gossip followed him from Styria. News about his dead wife. Her nephew came to Várad and insisted Zsigmond let him duel Friderik. The chambermaid who found the body marked blotches around the woman's neck and the reddened pupils of her sightless eyes.

Several servants claimed a loud quarrel between the couple echoed into the night, just before Friderik's solo journey into Hungary early the next day. His wife once purportedly cursed the name Veronika Deseniška, calling her Friderik's whore.

Vlad stood in Zsigmond's circle of thirty guards at the end of the morning mass in Várad's cathedral. Again, he commanded those who protected their king as a new day dawned. Zsigmond calmed the woman's nephew and directed him to the confessional, lest the young man rushed at Friderik with a sword in hand.

Outside the open doors, courtiers milled awaiting their king. In an hour, everyone would join the huntsmen, kennel masters, and dogs assembled for a hunt his queen proposed two evenings ago.

Zsigmond tugged at his graying russet beard and muttered to himself before he glanced at Vlad. "You know what We require. Do it quickly. Let none interfere."

"I understand, Your Royal Majesty." Vlad gave a stiff nod and dismissed the warning blaring in his head. He could not refuse any order from Zsigmond, even if the action would once again rouse the queen's choler.

He took ten of their king's protectors with him. In silence, they pushed their way through the crowd at the cathedral's entrance where Friderik talked with his sister, she garbed in all black as became her custom after her husband's accusation of adultery.

"My lord Friderik of Celje, you are accused by members of your household in Styria of murder; the death of your lady wife." Vlad ignored the flash of fury in Borbála's green gaze. As cries of alarm and a cacophony of voices rose, he shouted them down. "By the command of His Royal Majesty, King Zsigmond, you must surrender. The king awaits."

"How dare you!" The queen stepped in front of her red-faced brother. "You will not touch my brother, Prince Vlad."

He drew a step closer. "I have our king's order."

"He will rescind it!" Borbála stamped her velvet-covered foot. "I won't allow this. Where are Friderik's accusers? Are they here with this foul accusation?" She called for her guards. "Don't allow Prince Vlad to claim my brother before I speak to Zsigmond."

Her protectors did not move. Vlad met the gaze of her captain, who nodded and drew back a pace, as did the rest of her retinue.

Vlad turned to the men in his command. "You all heard King Zsigmond when he said, 'let none interfere.' Take the lord Friderik before him now."

The queen raised her hands, nails aimed at his face. He clutched her wrists and glared at her, while the soldiers secured her brother, who did not struggle.

"Unhand me and my brother!" Borbála screeched and spat in Vlad's face.

The spittle dribbled down his cheek and spattered on the armor. How tempting to squeeze her flesh hard right down to the bone until she cried out. She deserved the pain and much worse as she heaped curses on his head and tried in vain to kick him.

Friderik gave her a downcast stare, watery like her own, before he bowed his head and permitted the escort to lead him to their waiting king.

Only then did Vlad release the queen. Her palm flew to her mouth and smothered a cry inside her throat. She gazed in the direction her sibling went before she looked at Vlad and blinked back those tears.

"You will regret this," she muttered, pushing past her guardsmen who followed.

Vlad raked his cheek with the gauntlet on his hand before rejoining Zsigmond.

THE FATHER OF QUEEN Borbála and Friderik, Count Hermann, arrived at Várad within the week while Zsigmond's councilors heard evidence in Buda. He would not allow Hermann to see his son there. Their king expressed more irritation at the canceled summer hunt and ordered it postponed.

Afterward, whenever Vlad undertook the daily protection of Zsigmond, vicious arguments echoed beyond the royal chamber until Borbála or her parent left. Upon exiting, both reserved their fiery scowls for Vlad.

Their moods aside, bliss pervaded his existence. He secured his house. Although Călţuna left for Buda, he found happiness in two letters sent from her and Staico. After their initial meeting, the pair of them behaved like a father and daughter.

Zsigmond planned his departure from Várad for Nürnberg at last. Călţuna returned, radiant with the pregnancy a local midwife confirmed. She brought Staico. Their easy companionship gave Vlad's heart joy, for he knew how much she missed her parent in Hermannstadt, and her presence summoned his uncle's protective nature. Staico's gray eyes brimmed with unspent tears once she and Vlad revealed their news.

On the morning of the resumed hunt, Vlad received his king's permission for the Gypsies to join, extolling their skills as trackers. Staico and Călţuna met Vlad in the courtyard. He smiled down at her as she leaned on his uncle's arm and gaped at a spirited black horse as two grooms struggled to control. Hooves pawed the ground.

"Whose eager mount is that?" Călţuna asked, framed by dawn's hues.

"It belongs to the queen," Fruzhin said as he reined in his mare beside Vlad's Carpathian pony. "A gift brought by her father. I've never seen it outside the stables."

Vlad admired the long, arched neck, thick mane, swishing tail, and feathering on the animal's lower legs. "A breed better suited to warfare than the hunt, my friend."

"Perhaps, but Borbála intends to ride it this morning. Ah, she comes now."

The queen emerged from the palace; the blackness of her garments akin to her horse's coat. She barely spared a glance at her husband, already in the saddle, and engrossed with his chief huntsman. Her chin lifted as she found Vlad.

He returned her regard. "I thought she would plot her brother's freedom instead."

"She will never forget your role in his imprisonment." Fruzhin sighed.

"The queen has an enduring memory, but so do I." Vlad patted his pony's short neck, thankful for the mount's placid disposition compared to the choice Borbála made for the hunt. "She robbed me of marital joy with the woman I love more than life."

"My Vlad, think no more of her." Călțuna gazed up at him and reached for his hand.

He enclosed her fingers in his hold. "She can never part us again, my dearest."

As Borbála approached, the black horse snorted and shied away from the hapless grooms. She shouted vituperation and threatened them with a riding whip.

"Subdue him, you inept fools! I'll show you how it's done."

Borbála reached for the throatlatch, but her yelp followed as the gelding's large teeth snapped closed near her gloved hand. With a head toss, the animal kicked and backed away from her. Face purple, she wielded the leather wildly.

Vlad stared into the whites of her eyes just before the horse bucked and broke free, aiming straight for him. He barely shouted a warning for Călțuna and Staico, who tugged her away. But not in time. The runaway barreled into them and bolted across the courtyard, stirring shouts and cries as everyone else in its path scattered.

Leaping from the back of his pony, Vlad dashed to the side of his lover and uncle.

She gasped and groaned as he cradled her by the shoulders against his chest. Fruzhin appeared next to Staico, who gripped his arm and shuddered, with his leg bent at the knee at an odd angle under him.

"Călțuna? Sweet Călțuna, are you in pain?" Vlad breathed.

She blinked and looked up at him. "My back hurts where I fell, but..." Then she parted her mantle, palmed her lower belly, and lifted her hand. Crimson blotches dotted her fingertips. A stain seeped into her skirt. She gaped as it spread. "My Vlad...."

Fruzhin tugged his arm. "We must have help now."

Vlad lifted his head. In a daze, he found Borbála watching him. With lips pressed tightly together, her eyes became slits. She coiled the length of the whip around her palm slowly before she led her guards away, ignoring the blustery calls of her husband.

Aid came to Călţuna and Staico, whose fractured knee and broken arm received the tender care of Gypsy women, but the nearest midwife could not save Vlad's child. He howled as its life's blood soaked the bedding. Weepy with exhaustion, Călţuna collapsed and slept, waking only to sob while Vlad held and kissed her hand.

He sent Fruzhin away with one task and received him later at the healer's home. As they delved into the dark, moonless night, Vlad's Gypsies nodded to him while they patrolled the house's perimeter. The midwife seethed and huffed for four days, wanting them gone. Vlad refused until Călţuna and Staico were well enough for travel. When they returned to Buda, Vlad would be in the Germanic province of Bavaria at Nürnberg.

He asked Fruzhin, "Did Zsigmond's bitch know about Călţuna's pregnancy?"

His best friend shook his head. "Nothing is certain. The midwife your lady first visited has since disappeared. Her husband swears she would have never left him and their children in Várad. When I asked if anything odd occurred beforehand, he confessed she had lately received a large sum of coin she claimed came from one rich patron."

"And what about the horse?"

"Borbála ordered it locked away upon arrival a month ago. I questioned the pair of groomsmen. They said the animal acted that morning the same as whenever Borbála visited. In the stall, it always shied away from her and kicked until she left. They also could not understand why she chose the mount."

"I do." Vlad cursed under his breath. "She meant to harm me by killing Staico or Călţuna with a runaway horse. Even my babe. Borbála promised vengeance. She's had it."

"I'm sorrier than I can say about your grief, but you make a serious accusation. How did the queen know about your child? How could she be sure your lady and Lord Staico would see you off to the hunt? It was a tragic accident. No more."

Vlad gave a rueful chuckle, his heart brimming with fiery anger. "You can think so if you like, but I feel the truth burning inside me as much as the pain of loss. I forced Borbála's brother to submit. She sought to steal the lives of those dearest to me."

"Even if that's true, how can you prevent her machinations again?"

"I must. That is all. I will NOT lose another person I love." Even Vlad knew he did not have a way to thwart such a vicious enemy as Zsigmond's queen.

CHAPTER 19

A Son of New Rome

"There is no greater sorrow than to be mindful of the happy time, in misery."-Dante (circa 1265-1321 AD), Italian poet, writer, and philosopher.

IN THE YEAR OF OUR Lord 1424. Buda, Hungary (modern-day Budapest, Hungary)

Hours after dawn, Vlad left the newly enlarged quadrangle outside István's Tower, grateful for an escape from the cacophony of craftsmen, stone builders, and architects with the tools of their trade. Dust coated everything, even the new balconets beneath the windows. The acrid scent of lime-wash filled the air.

At last, the changes at Buda Castle, which Fruzhin foreshadowed fourteen years ago upon Vlad's arrival, neared completion. In his view, the end could not come soon enough. A long and hot summer night standing outside Zsigmond's chamber and ensuring the occupant's safety made Vlad desire only the harmony of his home.

He yawned, walking a familiar path down from Castle Hill to his townhouse. A century-old structure, it occupied two merged plots with the front opening onto Saint Gheorghe's Street. In the central courtyard, the Gypsies routinely monitored all passersby and questioned all visitors.

Vlad's immediate neighbors were the palatine and his brother, but he avoided them in the street as he did at court.

Vaulted storerooms occupied the ground floor of his home, where the clansmen and their families bedded down at night. Reaching the house, he found a few young mothers with their children playing between wine barrels. The wife of Tobar huddled beside her husband. Above the racket the children made, the echo of crying came from the upper floor. So much for peace.

"*Domnule*." Tobar approached him. "Your mistress has been sad all morning. She would not eat the meal my *romni* prepared and forced her from the kitchen."

"What ails Călţuna?" Vlad asked Tobar's wife, named Dika.

She replied, "The lady is sick, *Domnule*. She will not say more."

Vlad took the stairs two at a time from the storeroom and entered a heated area that he, his uncle, and Călţuna used for bathing with warmed water. He rushed into a long passageway to the bedrooms with their southern view.

Staico paced outside Călţuna's chamber, rubbing the joints of his mutilated hand. He knew no more about the cause of her poor state than the Gypsies. Her loud sobs resounded outside the closed door, which Vlad pounded in haste.

"My love, I'm here. Why have you locked yourself in? Please say what's wrong."

She bounded to his side; the door slamming back on its hinges behind her. She buried herself in his embrace.

"Dearest Călţuna, why must you weep so?" He hugged her tightly.

"I'm pregnant again and don't know what to do. What if this babe dies as well?"

Vlad lifted his head and stared at his uncle, who pressed his gaping lips together, bowed, and withdrew in the direction Vlad came. He waited until Staico's booted footfalls receded before taking Călţuna into her oriel-windowed chamber. He sat with her on the bed, still holding her.

"You mustn't fear," he counseled. "You and our child are not in any danger."

The knot in his stomach warred with the reassurance he gave her. Two years after the first disaster they suffered, he did not know how to keep his lover and their babe safe from the queen.

More than a decade on, the petty enmity with which she viewed Vlad, stemming from her adulterous husband's attention to Vlad's mother, grew more perilous. Vlad never doubted Borbála cost him the life of his first baby and might try again to rob him of renewed happiness at the prospect of a second child, especially since her brother Friderik still languished in Zsigmond's Buda Castle dungeon.

"We can never know the future, my Vlad," his mistress said. "This new pregnancy is proof. Just when I despaired about us ever creating another life, it has happened."

"Why did you worry so?"

"Well, this is my thirty-third summer. I thought perhaps my only chance at having children came and went two years ago after our baby died."

He kissed her hair and lifted her chin so she could look at him. He thumbed the faint crinkles at the outer corners of her eyes. She would always be beautiful to him.

"Now you know differently, my Călţuna. When did you first suspect you carried another child?"

"I haven't bled for three months, once you started the Catholic Lenten season. How have you never noticed?"

"Duties kept me from your bed at times, love." His hands encompassed the expanse of her waist. "I wondered if you were eating more of the rich foods Dika prepares in our kitchen and getting a little fatter."

She frowned and clouted his chin with her small fist. He pretended the blow hurt him and reeled away. She giggled and nuzzled his nose.

"Trust in God," he said. "We shall hold our baby, dearest Călţuna."

He would also take precautions. At court the next day, he found Fruzhin, ushered him to the spot where the lonely tree once flourished outside István's Tower, and told him the news. His best friend whistled and leaned against the thigh-length stump.

"God bless you both. But the old worries bedevil you if the lines on your forehead betray the truth. A man of thirty years should not have these cares."

"I wouldn't if Zsigmond's queen possessed Călţuna's nature. What shall I do?"

"You still believe Borbála is guilty of some crime against you. Even if she is, do you think she would be so stupid as to try again? She is no fool, I assure you. Examine her purported actions in full. *Cui bono*?"

"Who benefits?" Vlad repeated a translation of the Latin phrase. "Hurting me by Călţuna's pain or death, coupled with the loss of another child would give the queen joy."

As he said so, he turned away from Fruzhin. A secondary thought intruded. Not only might Borbála have rejoiced at his ruin. Zsigmond also resented Vlad's mistress as a distraction. Enough to harm her once the king learned of their child?

Vlad dared not utter the errant musing. "I won't give anyone a chance to hurt me or Călţuna. No one will gain from such a crime." His fists closed.

"Then, if you wish to keep your lady safe, you already know what you must do."

Vlad turned to Fruzhin again. The pair stared at each other until Vlad gaped and shook his head. "No!"

"Ah. The road lies ahead of you always, but you will not tread it."

"Alone? Without Călţuna? She and our child are my life. If I can't have them at my side, what is there for me in this world? I won't send her away."

"Vlad...."

"No, Fruzhin! I've heard you. We will not speak further on the matter."

"As you wish. Let's talk about something else. Before you sought me out today, I intended to find you. Recall our king will host a summit one week from now. He requires your service, Vlad. A matter of the greatest importance."

"I am his man. Though the level of secrecy involved in this meeting puzzles me. Who can we expect this time? Another king like Zsigmond's

Danish cousin Eric, who delighted the queen and her ladies before leaving us in the spring? Some Roman cardinal? No, surely a potentate of great importance. The new Turkic sultan?" He ended with a chuckle at such a preposterous idea.

"The younger emperor of Constantinople. He's directed the empire's fortunes since his father and co-ruler suffered apoplexy almost two years before. The eighth Iōannēs Palaeologus follows in the wake of his namesake grandfather, who also once sought a Hungarian king's aid against Turks, but lost Gallipoli and Adrianople." Fruzhin added, "King Eric plans to rejoin our sovereign in a week as well."

Vlad swallowed any further glib remarks, his interest engaged. Their enemy last attacked Constantinople exactly two summers ago. Was Iōannēs Palaeologus' arrival the precursor of taking the fight to Christendom's eternal foe? Would the emperor also offer Vlad a long-overdue opportunity for vengeance?

"Will Zsigmond's help be forthcoming?" Vlad fingered the sword hilt at his hip.

"Depends on the emperor's persuasiveness. You know our king wants an end to the Hussite conflict. While support endures among his Bohemian loyalists, they've made few gains and suffered further losses."

"What about the fighting we heard would occur south of Hory Kutné?"

"Our scouts were...badly misinformed," Fruzhin muttered. "A rival faction fell there before Jan Žižka a week ago. The loyalists were not involved after all."

"Zsigmond refuses to believe the Hussite matter is best resolved between the Bohemian people of the Catholic and reformist faiths. No matter which side wins in the end, we've already lost too many men."

"The belligerence keeps our sovereign from his rightful throne in Bohemia. You can't expect he will abandon that cause. Would you in your quest to rule? Perhaps the young emperor or King Eric may intervene and find Zsigmond a compromise with the Hussites."

"Why does Iōannēs Palaeologus visit in such secrecy?"

"He left Constantinople in November and since then, has traveled throughout the land, summoning Eastern Orthodox and Catholic territories to his cause. But he is cautious. Assassins abound, as our king is aware. Remember the black pepper incident?"

After a long period, no one, not even the Venetian doctor who saved Zsigmond's life knew whether his enemies or some resentful queen; his wife, or his Bohemian former lover Žofie of Bavaria, ordered the treacherous deed.

"What is my king's command?" Vlad asked.

"Meet the Byzantines and escort them safely here. You'll leave at dawn."

"Do I have royal authority to select men who will accompany me?"

"No. You alone must do this. The Byzantines have their guards. Ours will invite more speculation than either ruler desires."

A solo enterprise? Vlad shook his head. Did their king not even trust the rest of his household knights? Was there the chance of treachery everywhere Zsigmond looked?

"I applaud you, Vlad. You've revived our king's faith in you."

"Not just his belief in my biddable, conciliatory nature?" Vlad chuckled. "He doesn't expect I'll trouble him further about Dan Dăneşti's usurpation in Wallachia, does he?"

"It matters not as long as Zsigmond relies on you." Fruzhin clapped his shoulder. "Come to the royal stables and hear more of his instructions while you select a horse."

"I would prefer a pony from my homeland. The Gypsies will see to it." While they walked, Vlad inquired, "Has Zsigmond received further news from Pipó? Are he and young János still repairing the riverine fortresses along the Danube? Has Pipó mentioned anything else since he wrote to me in the spring about János acquitting himself well on the practice field?"

"You dote on that youth as I did with you fourteen years ago." Fruzhin elbowed him. "János will remain with Pipó after they leave the southern Transalpine region in a few days and cross the Iron Gates gorge into Serbia. Pipó's forces shall aid my uncle Stefan against a Turkish incursion."

"God shield our fighters," Vlad murmured. Worrying would change nothing. He could not protect young János from any challenges ahead of him or the brutal nature of battle. Vlad hoped the boy's forays into war would never herald some disastrous end.

VLAD GUIDED HIS HORSE and delved into the humid, murky forest, laden with pine resin odor and damp, loamy soil. Not even the tiniest sliver of light perforated the canopy. He could not shake the feeling someone or something watched him. He hoped only the emperor's retinue expected him.

The usual grunts of wild boars and their piglets, and the cries of songbirds and woodpeckers did not concern him. He slowed the pony in a clearing and craned his neck, peering into the gray mist swirling through the greenery. He saw nothing but secured the old crossbow he brought into Hungary across his lap.

Fruzhin told him the Byzantines would wait at the northwestern edge of the woods, along the lake shore they circumnavigated after leaving the Polish capital. When he took them south to Buda, King Zsigmond and a few courtiers would welcome them on the city's outskirts.

Something trampled the brush behind him. He wheeled his mount sharply. He shouldered the crossbow, bolt at the ready. But no man or beast came from the brush.

"Vlad, calm yourself," he muttered as sweat trickled down his back under the cloak. "Would you have Zsigmond's guests think you're afraid of your own shadow?"

"If only shadows were the sole thing brave men must fear."

He turned quickly again, seeking the source of the disembodied voice speaking in heavily accented Latin. A thin shaft of light permitted a glimpse of the stoop-shouldered man on horseback. He peered at Vlad, his long visage upturned beneath a broad-brimmed hat, akin to those worn by Roman cardinals. His narrow olive-brown features ended in a pointed beard. Lustrous curls gathered at his shoulders.

As Vlad eyed him in return, something other than youthful brashness made the stranger push those shoulders back. How had he approached with such stealth?

"I am *Dominus* Loukas Notaras, a member of the Byzantine imperial court and the official translator along this journey. Who are you?"

Vlad settled the weapon in his lap again. "I am Vlad of Wallachia, a knight of King Zsigmond's court, charged with providing your master safe conduct to Buda."

"Not a *Princeps* Vlad?" The Byzantine nobleman sniggered. "Are you no son of Mircea the Great, then? Or did you give up your princely title upon entering the king's household?"

"A knight lives to serve," Vlad pronounced through gritted teeth.

"What's that? I can't hear you when you mumble—"

"We waste time here, Loukas. It's hot and uncomfortable in this thicket."

A querulous tone preceded out of the mist before other riders in a single procession emerged into the clearing. Vlad marked the imperial insignia, the double-headed eagle, painted on pennons near the tips of spears thrust heavenward.

One man wore a smaller version of the same heraldry, barely noticeable, but for Vlad's keen observance, at the shoulder of his voluminous red cloak. Dark-haired with a prominent nose and smoother skin than any man two years older than Vlad should possess, something in Emperor Iōannēs Palaeologus' dark stare warned of fraudulence. His entire mien seemed at odds with whatever Vlad expected of a Byzantine ruler.

He could not shake the sentiment and knew in an instant he could not join the fight against the Turks under such leadership, no matter if King Zsigmond followed.

"You've silenced our escort, Loukas. I fear he's offended and will not take us to Buda as planned. Imagine poor me, a son of new Rome, left to fend for myself with only my guards and you in this forbidding forest," the emperor drawled in Greek. He appeared more bored than worried about abandonment.

"As my *basileús* and *autokrator* already knows, we would give our lives for you," Loukas replied, bowing in the saddle before he regarded Vlad. "*Princeps*," he switched back to Latin, "you will understand the Greek language comes easily to us."

"Converse freely, *Dominus*, unless there's some private matter between you, in your capacity as a translator, and your *basileús* and *autokrator*," Vlad replied. "If the need arises, I can always ride at a discreet distance from you."

His easy use of Greek made both men sit straighter in the saddle. Oddly, the ruler Iōannēs looked with quirked eyebrows at Loukas, whose thin-lipped smile widened before he nodded to the man whom he called his emperor and autocrat.

"You should lead on then, Vlad of Wallachia, knight of the king," Loukas said.

"Yes, you should," the emperor added as if remembering his status and authority.

Vlad brought them through the forest with the same speed as when he entered it. All the while unable to fathom his misgivings about Iōannēs Palaeologus coupled with growing concerns about Loukas, whose arrogance bothered Vlad. The foreign lord must think of himself as an equal or better than a prince by association with an emperor.

While Vlad scanned their environs for any signs of a potential ambush, the Byzantine twosome made a mockery of his caution by speaking loudly and overmuch. Whenever Vlad attended their words, a strange suspicion grew as the supposed ruler expressed himself with unusual deference to his subordinate.

After they emerged from the woods into the summer sun's glare and traveled downhill, the full morning light revealed the pair in full. From his periphery, Vlad studied Iōannēs and Loukas, riding side by side between double rows of guards next to him. Loukas, of a larger build and well-proportioned compared to his companion, held himself with a dignified air despite his ill-mannered greeting in the forest. Did Vlad imagine Loukas might be his age, while the emperor, with his pointed beard, appeared younger than expected?

Vlad uncovered the enigma of the duo's incongruence just before sighting King Zsigmond with a cadre of guards at the next crest. The walls and towers of Buda Castle rose in the distance.

In more than a decade at his sovereign's side, Vlad heard him express little knowledge of the young emperor. Certain Zsigmond had never met the man before, Vlad would not permit any embarrassment, no matter the reasons the Byzantines thought it necessary to employ deceit.

He dismounted and kneeled before his king, who greeted him warmly and with thanks, before requiring him to make the introductions.

"*Sigismundus dei gratia Romanorum rex Semper Augustus*," he began in Latin, acknowledging the Germanic title of 'king of the Romans' before adding the other ponderous appellations, "King of Hungary, Dalmatia, Croatia...."

Once finished, he moved and stood before "Loukas," who peered down at him from the saddle. With a wave of his hand to the man, Vlad indicated, "My king, I present His Royal Majesty, emperor and autocrat of Constantinople, the eighth Iōannēs Palaeologus."

In the revelation's face, the Byzantine ruler gave a hearty laugh and abandoned the feigned identity of Loukas Notaras, removing his crimson hat.

He nodded to Vlad. "Well, the correct title is 'emperor and autocrat of the Romans,' but how could I expect you to know that?" Then he looked at his host. "King Zsigmond, I thank you for the fine services of this knight. Not only did he bring us with alacrity through the forest," the emperor said with a wink at Vlad, "but his sharp-eyed sensibilities and wit would be helpful on this journey. May I steal him from you? I could use a man of his skill."

Vlad swallowed in a suddenly dry throat, certain the redness suffusing his sovereign's cheeks could not have come from sunburn so soon.

"Let us speak further on this," Zsigmond said, "and many more important matters at my palace where we may be assured of your continued safety, Emperor Iōannēs."

The royal pair rode ahead. Vlad followed in the mix of Hungarian knights and the Byzantines. To his distaste, he found himself beside the real Loukas when the nobleman slowed his horse and stroked the pointed beard.

"How did you know I was not the emperor when he imitated me so well?"

So Loukas admitted to having a boorish nature? Vlad tamped his lips together and kept that question behind his teeth.

"For one, your natures are different. And if you want the charade to continue to protect the emperor, don't defer to him so openly."

Before Loukas could ask more, Vlad spurred his horse, eager to part from the younger man who played at being a ruler of the Byzantines.

Nine days later, a total eclipse occurred, visible all over Hungary. While the frightened, superstitious populace shrieked, Vlad wondered what changes the celestial dragon's appearance would herald.

DURING EIGHT WEEKS at Buda Castle, the emperor recommended not only renewed fighting against the Turks. Iōannēs also urged the union of the Latin West and Eastern Orthodox churches, a proposition Vlad did not expect would be popular among the latter. The general populace's recollections of tales from their ancestors about the Crusaders' sack of Constantinople were longer than the memories of Ottoman degradation.

The kingdom's concerns receded when Vlad held Călţuna at night. She slept naked in the warm room and though her flesh tempted him, they both adhered to the strict admonition of a Gypsy midwife and shared only chaste kisses and hugs. As his dainty mistress' waist thickened and her belly expanded, Vlad delighted in the first subtle and then firmer movements of their baby.

At his insistence, Călţuna also kept indoors and well away from opened windows. No one outside the home could know of her pregnancy, lest the queen discovered it. Although Călţuna chafed at the restriction, she allowed Staico's visits to the marketplace with Tobar's wife.

While Vlad kissed and palmed her bared belly, his lover huffed. "May I not even have a visitor in this townhouse? Tobar told me a man claiming to be my youngest brother arrived here and your Gypsies sent him away before I could identify him."

"Tobar warned me." He sighed. "He keeps outsiders away for your protection."

"But what if there is some difficulty? Why else would my sibling seek me out? He's never done so since his marriage and move to Buda until now."

"If he comes again, Tobar will question him. There must be something only you and your brother would know."

"Well, there was the time we took that horse out of the stables, and it nearly killed me in Dumbrava Forest."

He pressed his mouth to hers. "The happiest day of my life. We met back then."

"Are you certain it shall always be the best day?" As she stroked her belly, some limb of their child twisted beneath the florid skin.

He stared in fascination. "Only two other events could supersede it. Our wedding or the birth of our babe."

"Our son," she insisted. "It's a boy. No girl would be so unruly while I try to rest."

"Even one with an audacious mother like you?"

Her husky laugh followed. He kissed her a final time before letting go. Once he went through the door, he dared not look back at the temptation she offered.

She called to him, "My Vlad, may János dine with us while he's in the capital?"

He grinned, but never slowed his strides. Staico awaited him with the armor, as did Tobar and Yoska, who would escort him to Castle Hill. "The Hunyadi attendant has his duties as a squire, Călțuna!"

Yet, he already intended to persuade Pipó and the youth to join them here. Vlad missed them during their nearly three years of absence. A tour of his townhouse and a fine meal would offer a better opportunity to converse with the pair than in recent weeks.

János and Pipó had arrived one day after the feast of Corpus Christi at the side of a victorious Stefan from Serbia. He hailed Vlad with the same warmth as he showed his nephew Fruzhin, before presenting their king with the spoils from a Turkic skirmish. Soon, silken textiles and the enemy's war drums covered in fine leather littered the dais.

Once Vlad reunited with him, János barely spoke. He seemed oddly timid and taciturn. Perhaps the Ottoman campaign unsettled him. With little evidence of the eighteen-year-old's stammer, Vlad could not understand the youth's mood, but also planned to coax him out of his reticence.

A chance came upon Vlad's arrival at the royal court where he dismissed his Gypsies. Dawn approached and people thronged Buda Castle. Vlad spied János immediately, his dark auburn curls rustled by the morning wind. Their gazes met as gangling legs took János to the great keep.

Since that was not Vlad's destination, he raised his arm and called out, "János, wait! We must—" but the youth darted inside István's Tower.

Vlad mused, "Surely, he heard, so why would he hasten away as if avoiding me?" He detoured to the great keep. No sign of János materialized inside. The youth might have gone up the stairs on an urgent errand for Pipó.

"I'll find him another time." Vlad could not search now, as guard duty awaited.

He turned and slammed his shoulder into the ragged form of Vlậcsan the Wolf.

They exchanged greetings, while Vlad wondered whether Wallachian or personal interests brought the boyar into Hungary again. Despite the passing of two years, he'd uncovered nothing about the Turk Bedreddin's family in old Nicea or elsewhere.

Vlậcsan said, "Officially, I arrived on behalf of Prince Dan Dăneşti. He demanded I hear the emperor's proposal to reunite the Western and Eastern churches and give a report."

Vlad balked and drew back. "I never noticed you among the conference attendees. You didn't seek me out because my treacherous cousin sent you. Does Grandmother know?"

"She understands when the ruling prince of Wallachia makes a demand of any boyar, he must obey. She recalls how your father dealt with mine."

The kin glared at each other until Vlad muttered, "Well, you've done your duty. Why haven't you gone home?"

"I will today, but I waited for news that arrived yesterday. Of consequence to you."

The breath hitched in Vlad's throat. "About Arina's child?" He dared to hold hope.

After Vlậcsan nodded, Vlad drew him to the kitchen of the great keep, where one look sent the cook and maids scurrying, leaving freshly baked bread on tables and a thick, bubbling pottage unattended on the hearth.

"Speak," Vlad commanded.

"After Princess Arina died in Turkish Adrianople," Vlậcsan said, "one of her Wallachian servants smuggled out her nameless baby daughter and placed her in the home of Bedreddin, where she grew up. The girl is certainly your sister's child."

Support of Milena Olivera's supposition stunned Vlad into silence. He turned away; his palm flattened against the cold wall. With deep breaths, he slowed his rapid heartbeats.

"Since affirming that fact, I sought more information," Vlậcsan continued. "But my...youthful contact was less than circumspect and stirred suspicion by making inquiries about the distant past. Bedreddin's family fled to parts unknown."

"That cannot be," Vlad insisted, roused from his torpor. "As a descendant of the House of Basarab, my family's last connection with Arina, her daughter must be found!"

"She is also a member of the Ottoman dynasty, whom the enemies of her uncle the former sultan raised in secret. Her adoptive family safeguards their lives by hiding her."

Swiping a hand across his brow, Vlad sighed. "What is her name?" He should have asked Milena Olivera when he last saw her. Pity she did not travel to Buda with her brother Stefan.

"My spy doesn't know. She could be anywhere in Turkic lands or beyond. The Ottoman domain is vast and growing steadily, encompassing former Christian lands."

Vlad cursed under his breath. Until a century ago, the damnable Turkish people were a ragged band of nomads who lived in tents. Since that time, they gained an empire. Large enough to ensure a little girl's secret identity could stay hidden for a long time.

Still, he instructed Vlậcsan, "You will not give up the quest."

The Wolf grinned like his totem and rasped, "The hunt is never over just because the quarry has gone to ground."

"Indeed. I must leave you and greet Zsigmond. Go with God."

Before Vlậcsan departed, he touched Vlad's shoulder. "Beware the Hungarian king's taciturn nature. A few weeks ago, emissaries from Zsigmond's court met your brother Radu to support his claim to the Wallachian throne in secret. Radu also seeks Turkish help."

"Did you warn your master Dan Dăneşti?" Vlad asked. His sibling must be desperate if he threw his lot behind Zsigmond and their Turkish foes.

"I serve your grandmother, not Dan Dăneşti's interests."

Vlad made no reply. He suspected Vlậcsan the Wolf weighed costs and benefits to himself in every move he made, no matter his claim of loyalty.

The man's pallor changed. He coughed behind his hand.

"What is it?" Vlad asked. "You look as if you have something more to say."

"Did you know I have a young son named Vintilă?"

Vlad frowned. Why would he be aware of this boy or care about his mention?

Vlậcsan continued without awaiting a reply. "He is in Būrsâ. At the palace school there. One of the twenty hostages submitted to the Ottomans outside Târgovişte. Part of your brother Radu's quest to gain Turkish aid and oust Dan Dăneşti."

Stunned, Vlad shook his head at his brother's folly and the sacrifice the Wolf had made. When would their foes ever stop tearing apart Christian nations and families?

"Vintilă excels, so his teacher permits an indulgence. The boy writes to me each Easter and before winter. No one suspects the coded messages he includes. I taught him the cipher. In his last letter, he shared more about a concern first raised a year ago, after you and I last met. Rumors of missing children around Turkish Būrsâ."

"Why should the Turks' offspring affect me?"

"The stories have thrived for over a decade. Older than my son. Something stalks the Turks' former capital. A revenant, dressed in all white. Furs. The figure has long, red hair. The Turkic people say it steals babies. They are never seen again. Healthy women, grown great with child, suddenly die before they can give birth. They have puncture marks on their bodies. The blood drained away. You know about the tales of night creatures in our land. The evil."

Vlad winced. "You don't think...?" He dared not finish the sentence.

Unbidden, the haunting memory of Arina's voice in his head long after her death returned to him. *Find me, free me.* Was this the unearthly meaning? A monstrous notion.

"Your sister died in Būrsâ. The palace servants buried her in a Turkish tomb. They never summoned a Christian priest to give her last rites. I fear the worst."

A red haze bloomed before Vlad's eyes. He shoved Vlậcsan. "Fool. Get away from me! Arina was a God-fearing woman. He would not let the evil one claim her after death."

The Wolf sighed. "Did not the deceiver of men's souls tempt even our Lord Jesus?"

When Vlad did not answer, Vlậcsan left him.

His chest burned as it rose and fell. He struggled to breathe. It could not be true. His people believed such things about those who possessed red hair and died in Arina's circumstances, unattended by a priest. Denied holy rites. Could she be trapped between the world of the living and the dead after such a time? An unholy blood-drinker?

AFTER IŌANNĒS PALAEOLOGUS announced he would leave Buda at the end of the week, Zsigmond gave a final reception for the Byzantine emperor. Attired in a rich, blue velvet robe embroidered by the double-headed eagle, and rosettes and arabesques of gold, worn with pale yellow leather boots, he sought Vlad.

Still shaken by his unwelcome encounter with Vlậcsan, Vlad struggled to concentrate on the conversation. He caught Zsigmond's eye more than once and forced himself to talk to Constantinople's ruler, albeit in halting Greek.

At least no imperial attendants witnessed how he faltered. A few of the Byzantines were no longer at Buda Castle, including Loukas Notaras. The guard component stayed the same, never far from the sight of their emperor.

"If I did not know otherwise, your fine use of Greek would convince me you are a fellow son of new Rome," he said.

"Your praise is much too generous," Vlad replied.

"It is warranted. I meant what I said to Zsigmond on the day we met, and intend to have you in my service." He laughed as Vlad spluttered, wondering at the emperor's plans. "Don't worry. I won't cause difficulties between you and your king, but I'm a Palaeologus and will always get what I want."

As he went away with his retainers, Vlad frowned in their direction.

Soon his king revealed an artist's portrait featuring the trio of the Danish ruler Eric, Zsigmond, and the Byzantine emperor, to thunderous applause. The latter two with their heads close together conversed for the rest of the evening and often glanced at Vlad.

At night, he went home, still puzzled by his conversation with Iōannēs Palaeologus and worried about Arina's soul. Staico greeted him outside with a frown.

"Why do you seem so perturbed, uncle?"

"I've been waiting for you all day! Călțuna's upset. Go to her now."

Vlad scowled at his uncle as if he needed to be told so, like a child. He raced inside and found his mistress crying on her bed. She revealed her brother came earlier, passing Tobar's test for entry into the townhouse. Their father, bedridden with some illness a doctor claimed would take his life, pleaded for his children to come home to Hermannstadt.

Vlad realized Călţuna wept so much because she wanted to go with her sibling, who would leave in three days, but she also clung to Vlad.

She sobbed. "We vowed never to part again, my love. Yet, how can I ignore the pleas of my father, who may die? I didn't hide the pregnancy from my brother. He wished me well and will share the news with our parent. I want Father to hear about it from me."

Her sorrow dismayed him. He barely slept. Another dawn came too soon. Duty-bound, he left without waking Călţuna. After the morning meal of *prandium*, his king and the emperor met in private before calling Vlad into the royal chamber. He kneeled before them.

"As an act of mercy, at the behest of Our beloved brother in Christ, the emperor Iōannēs, We shall free Friderik of Celje and grant his father Hermann custody. Vlad, you will ride at the head of Our escort and meet Hermann's retainers south of Buda tomorrow."

Although wary of Zsigmond's vagaries, Vlad said, "As my king commands."

"Further, We declare Our consent to Emperor Iōannēs, who has requested your presence along his journey across Europe and back to Constantinople. We will miss your sword in Bohemia, Vlad, but cannot refuse Our Christian brother's fervent wish."

Truly stunned, he stared at both monarchs in silence.

The king bent and rested a hand atop the pauldron on Vlad's shoulder. "Your service is permitted for two years. Surely that is also enough time for you to find an appropriate wife. Iōannēs says there are lovely ladies of stellar repute in the Queen of Cities."

"Far lovelier than the sallow-faced Italian cow my father forced on me," the emperor said with a chuckle, winking at Vlad. "At least, you will make the choice."

The only wife he would ever choose would be Călţuna, whom Zsigmond forbid him from marrying.

VLAD GOT ON THE ROAD early the next morning with Friderik in his custody. Another fitful night occurred, in which his mistress tossed and turned beside him. Her heart was torn in two by love for him and her father, yet she had not decided to leave Buda with her brother the next day. Vlad never slept, his mind tortured by images of Arina in white furs, as he last saw her, but moving in silent stealth. Blood dribbled from her mouth.

Men bearing the banners of the House of Celje met him with the former prisoner Friderik alongside a fork in the Danube. Vlad had not expected the pale, bright-eyed woman in a cloak who waited on horseback. She sprang from her mount with supple agility and raced for Friderik, dark hair streaking behind her.

He dismounted and greeted her with effusive kisses, fisting his hands in her black curls. "My Veronika! You and my men did not fail me!"

Vlad snorted. "What treachery is this?"

Friderik sneered at him. "When my father arrives, tell him not to search for us. I'm going to marry Veronika Deseniška. There's nothing he can do to stop our union. You shouldn't try either! I have twice the forces you've brought, loyal solely to me."

Dismayed, Vlad looked over the score of Celje retainers who could easily outmatch and defeat the escort of eight from Buda. The relatives of Friderik's murdered wife wielded influence equal to his and his sister Borbála's Celje ancestors. Neither family would accept Friderik's flight from justice. Zsigmond could ill afford the discontent when he needed every combatant each side provided in the ongoing Hussite war, where the enemy leader Jan Žižka lately lost his remaining eye, but not his zeal.

"Our king shall hear of this incident," Vlad warned.

"I expect he will." Friderik urged his lover onto her horse and alighted atop another steed before turning to Vlad again. "Tell my sister I'm sorry for causing her trouble with Zsigmond, who may blame her. I can't let Father dictate my future again as he did hers."

He raced away with his woman and deceitful companions.

Hermann, Count of Celje, arrived at the royal bed-chamber moments after Vlad relayed the news about Friderik to Zsigmond and his queen. Borbála sobbed behind her slender hands and collapsed on her husband's bed. In a rare gesture Vlad never thought to see again, Zsigmond patted her shoulder while her father raged.

"The whore has bewitched him! How dare he defy me? Prince Vlad," he shot a dark glance at him, "should've detained them all. However, what is done is done. I shall hunt them down and see Veronika Deseniška tried for witchcraft. How else could the daughter of a lowly knight have so ensnared a son of the illustrious House of Celje?"

Vlad wondered whether Zsigmond believed the same about Călţuna. Was that why his king sought to part them at such a sensitive time?

Borbála pleaded with their parent, "You knew the deepest love for our mother and never remarried. Understand. Forgive your son, Father."

Zsigmond dismissed him. Before Vlad left, he looked at Friderik's sister. "Your Grace, your brother commanded me to say he's sorry for any trouble he causes you."

Though she never stopped weeping, she raised her head and gave him a scant nod.

At home later that evening, he could not find the courage to relay Zsigmond's command for him to join the emperor until his mistress expressed an overwhelming need to see her father. Only then did he speak of the Byzantine ruler's wish. He did not mention his sovereign's added desire that he should marry while abroad.

Nor did he speak of his fears about Arina. He could not. No one else would believe them, not even Staico.

Călţuna drew back in the circle of his arms, pulling him away from those troublesome thoughts as she peered up at him with wet eyes. "This may be a true farewell between us, my Vlad."

"Never!" He hugged her again fiercely in the privacy of his room. "We will be apart for only two years. No more. I'll come for you and our child after I've discharged my duties to Constantinople's ruler."

"Two years is a long time, my Vlad. Anything can happen."

He lifted his head slightly from her trembling form. Did she have some clue about how his king intended him to seek a wife? Did Călţuna imagine Vlad would do so?

"I'm not abandoning you," he swore. "I WILL NOT do it, no matter if a king or emperor should compel me."

"Four years ago, you found me once more in Hermannstadt," she whispered against his neck, "and I told you not to make promises you could not keep."

He reared back. "You doubt me?"

She did not answer, even after he asked her twice more. He hauled her up and crushed her lips with his. While her nails raked his nape and back, he tugged at her clothing. He was not gentle, unlike in the first throes of their love. Anger with Zsigmond and the emperor vied with vexation at Călţuna's uncertainty, and himself. He once swore never to fail her, but perhaps he did at this moment of parting.

After dawn, they lingered beside her brother's waiting carriage, bound for Transilvania. Fruzhin stood next to Vlad and his uncle opposite Călţuna. Despite Staico's initial annoyance over Vlad's upcoming journey with the Byzantines and regret that he would not see the empire himself, Staico agreed not to leave her.

Vlad said, "Călţuna, I will leave soon with the emperor. He hasn't told me about the Christian cities we will visit, but I'll send word to Hermannstadt when I can. Be well, you and our child, and believe in our love."

"My Vlad, I always have," she whispered.

Neither of them uttered the silent truth. Their love could never thwart a king's will.

She kissed him a final time before her brother extended his hand and took hers to help her into the coach. She sat and wept beside him. With an arm draped over her quivering shoulders, he gave a curt nod to Vlad. A third of the older Gypsies and their families, stalwart in their faithfulness to Staico, would not remain behind. At least, Călţuna's sibling accepted the added protection they offered with open gratitude.

Unexpectedly, Vlad felt the same emotion regarding the emperor. On this journey, Vlad intended to uncover the distance between Būrsâ and Constantinople. He would gain imperial consent to travel to Turkic lands, with dual goals in mind.

His king ordered him to give two years of service to the emperor. He would also get permission to seek his sister's grave. Discover if the rumors about the so-called revenant were true. If they were, he would grant Arina's soul eternal peace. There must be a way. Afterward, he would find her lost child and bring the girl home. Neither she nor her mother's spirit would abide among their enemy forever if he could help it.

If, in his time away, he proved himself worthy, perhaps he might also gain imperial favor. Sufficient to press his claim to the crown of Wallachia.

"Thinking about Arina again?" Staico interrupted, resting a meaty fist on his arm.

Vlad forced a smile. "You always assume you know my mind, uncle."

"I know you, my boy." A phrase often repeated over the years. "When you both were little, I watched you and her at play. Sometimes, one of you would smile and the other would nod. As if some silent communication passed between you."

Vlad gave a slight chuckle. "That could never be so." Inside, his heart hammered.

"Even in death, she is never far from your thoughts. I understand."

Although he doubted the possibility, Vlad nodded.

"For all your father's privileges and honors," Staico said as he drew him apart from the others and fingered Vlad's cheek with his mangled hand. "Mircea never attained the highest of them. He did not see how you grew into a fine man. A greater warrior for God than him. The future of the House of Basarab."

Vlad embraced the man who was more of a parent than the one who sired him. Their foreheads pressed together before Staico raised his face and planted a kiss there. He turned and clambered inside the coach. The vehicle swayed beneath his bulk.

As its occupants and their Gypsy escorts raced away, Fruzhin waved alongside Vlad. The horses picked up speed just before Călţuna leaned out of the wooden window and shouted something at him. With the distance between them, he could not hear.

He chased the careening carriage, shouting, "Tell me again, my love!"

"What do I call our...?" The clatter of the wheels and iron-shod hooves extinguished the rest of Călţuna's words.

Later, Vlad sank alone on the bed they had shared just the night before. He realized she had asked what she should name the son whose birth he would never see.

CHAPTER 20

Breathing Fury

"Wickedness and injustice are intentional."-Aristotle (384-322 BC), Greek philosopher and polymath.

IN THE YEAR OF OUR Lord 1424. Kraków, Poland

Vlad slowed the Carpathian pony to a walk and ordered Tobar and Yoska on either side of him to do the same. Their mounts matched the gait of the emperor's horse and the other animals in the small cortege.

They moved ever eastward under Zsigmond's letter of *salvus conductus* in mid-morning along the *Strata Regia.* The Royal Road connected western Europe as far as Santiago de Compostela in the Iberian Peninsula with eastern lands, ending at the Lithuanian Grand Duchy's trade cities, of which Vlad only heard about Vilnius and Kyiv.

Cold, thick mist rose above Polish river tributaries. At a bend in the waterway's embankment on its winding course to the capital, Iōannēs Palaeologus spoke with two of his advisors, rather loudly, about pawning the rest of the gifts Zsigmond gave him before they left Buda almost two months ago. Since then, the journey took them the length of Styria and into Bohemia's east before arriving in southern Poland.

"Eight gilded chalices, the rest of the textiles, and those six excellent horses should fetch us good coin in Kraków," the emperor said with a nod. "We'll add that to the thousand gold florins Zsigmond granted us.

Enough for the return journey. I doubt we will arrive in time for the Chrysostom saint's feast day in mid-November, but soon after, I may relieve my brother of the burden of the crown he accepted in my stead."

As he chuckled, his dual companions joined in while Vlad sighed at the spendthrift ways of the monarchy. He took in the wide vista of his master Stibor's homeland, where crinkled leaves and the crisp breeze warned of a waning autumn season. Stibor should be at his side, introducing him to the sights of Poland rather than lying buried in a crypt at Hungary's royal sepulcher these past ten years.

"Vlad, will you join me, please?"

He looked up and found the Byzantine ruler looking over his shoulder. Vlad urged his pony onward and rode beside Iōannēs Palaeologus. Another of his noblemen served as the 'decoy' ruler, sheltered among the guards ahead of them.

The Byzantine ruler's kind favor to him continued for nearly half a year since their first encounter in the forest outside Buda Castle. Perhaps in their shared disdain and fury against the Turks, some bond became forged. After the latest attack, Iōannēs Palaeologus allowed his advisors to pursue a treaty with them, a negotiating tactic while he traveled Europe seeking allies against the unrelenting menace.

"You've never seen Kraków before, although your king visited in March of this year? I missed his attendance and that of Stefan Lazarević by hours, arriving at Wawel Castle in the evening after their departure that morning," Iōannēs Palaeologus said. "He came for the coronation of King Władysław's fourth bride, Zofia Holszańska as queen. She's a little older than his only daughter and heir, Princess Jadwiga."

"King Zsigmond does not always travel with the same retinue, *basileús,*" Vlad replied in Greek. "I regretted his choice of other household guards, for I would have liked to see Poland then, the birthplace of Zsigmond's great friend and the finest war master I once served, Stibor of Stiboricz. I'm here with you now. An honor."

"You do that very well." Iōannēs Palaeologus smiled broadly. "There is never obsequiousness in your manner, with me or Zsigmond. I observed your dutiful service to him, and you've rendered the same since we left Buda. Your mind is elsewhere. Does it dwell on the mistress you've kept away from the Hungarian court?"

As Vlad gaped at him, the emperor snorted. "No one conceals anything from me for long. I had Loukas follow you to your Buda townhouse. It has a high wall surmounting your back garden. Still, Loukas did not miss a golden-haired beauty with a swollen belly while she plucked vegetables from the ground with the vigor of the Gypsy woman beside her. I assume the beauty was your mistress, carrying your child, and the place where Loukas saw her was what you rented out before we traveled."

Vlad swore under his breath. Had he not warned Călţuna to always keep indoors? His sudden annoyance vied with a breathless ache to hold her against him along with their child. Had the boy she promised him already arrived? When he reached the royal residence of Kraków, he would first write to Staico and inquire.

"You did not like Loukas from your first meeting with him. Have I given you more reason to despise my friend?" The emperor shrugged. "It's for the best that I sent him on to Constantinople ahead of me anyway, where he can ensure my brother Constantine will not lose our father's empire."

"You trust Loukas Notaras more than your sibling, *basileús*?"

"I don't truly rely on anyone in Byzantium." A weary sigh escaped the lips of Iōannēs Palaeologus. "They would sooner secure their futures than risk loss if the Turks attacked and overwhelmed us. Indeed, they would submit to such an enemy before they allowed Rome and the papacy to rule us. Fools!"

He shook his head and scrubbed at his furrowed brow beneath the broad-brimmed red hat he favored. "I have been blessed or cursed with six living brothers, Vlad. Constantine took the place of another with the same name who died in childhood. One night, our Serbian mother left the Blachernae Palace with us and the guards. We went to an old wise woman from Mother's homeland, whom she bade to tell our fortunes."

"What did she say?" Vlad asked after the emperor paused at length.

"For me, the prophecy came true. I wear the crown and rule beside my father and shall do so alone once he is dead. Other predictions followed. The crone also said I would wed three times, but sire no heirs, leaving Constantine to rule Byzantium. And under his aegis, Constantinople will fall to the Ottoman Turks."

Vlad shook his head. "In our time together, I've learned much about you. A man of honor and faith, guided by wisdom. The city will not fall. It cannot."

"After my first wife died, my father remarried me to the ugliest woman in all of Christendom, Sophia of Montferrat. I'll never get a child on her wretched body!" The emperor spat in disgust and stared at the muddied track leading to Kraków's walls. "Never has one of my mistresses or lovers named me the father of any babe. What if the wise woman's words were true, not only about my fate? What about Constantine?"

"You've entrusted him with the duty to serve at the side of your father, *basileús*."

"You still have brothers. You understand the rivalry between those who share blood."

"Better than you may presuppose of me, *basileús*."

"Could you kill your sibling to avoid a potential disaster?"

"Absent your high motives, I've contemplated it enough times." Vlad mused, recalling the death of his deplorable sibling Mihail four years past. "Do you, *basileús*?"

Iōannēs Palaeologus looked up. "You never answered my question about your lady."

"I hoped you had forgotten," Vlad replied, knowing he and the emperor would say no more about Constantine or Byzantium's destiny. "Indeed, my thoughts in part are with her and the child who may be born any day now, if not already. We could not marry because Zsigmond considers her heritage beneath his marital ambitions for me."

"A child of hers to bind you further will not improve his opinion. I can also sense your concern about this journey and what lies ahead."

"I'll admit your plans for me are of great interest."

"You shall have a place at my court. A chamber of Blachernae Palace in the northern section of the city. Loukas ensures preparations. The residence is grand and sprawling, but in disrepair. Some of the reception halls are closed. My family is confined to suites of rooms with better heating. You'll attend court functions, where the unwed sisters and daughters of my dignitaries will try to win you over. As a hereditary prince, you may have your choice of a bride. A shame the Polish heiress, Jadwiga, isn't available."

Vlad concealed his laughter. "Your ambitions for me are truly bold. Whoever she marries would surely become the king of Poland after the death of his father-in-law."

"Anything is possible, dear Vlad, given some ambition and the right circumstances. Jadwiga is younger than you, perhaps by ten years, but already betrothed to a son of the German House of Hohenzollern."

Vlad sat straighter in the saddle at the mention. The dragon knight, accused of fornication alongside Queen Borbála just four years ago, hailed from the same lineage. Now his son would marry the Polish heiress.

The emperor continued, "Hopefully you'll enjoy these two next years. War will come. When the east and west are true allies, you shall fight for me against the Turks."

"You expect they will be ready to attack within the time Zsigmond has allotted me?"

"I am persuasive." The emperor winked. "Didn't I coax you away from your king?"

A ragged sigh whistled between Vlad's lips. His mind fixed on the Turks; a source of persistent anxiety. His hatred for the Turkic people, not solely because of Arina's loss, demanded retribution.

His sister also brought a half-Ottoman child into the world. Her girl posed an unanticipated conundrum. He could not deny her father's heritage. His niece, yes, but also a daughter of his enemies. Without the influence of their father Bedreddin's tolerance, had her adoptive family taught her to fear Christians? What would she make of Vlad once he found her?

"If I wished to travel, *basileús*, and see beyond the empire, would you give consent?"

"Turkic lands impinge upon my eastern borders. A few Venetian strongholds in the south. Beyond the Black Sea lies Crimea and the

Mongol Horde. None of which I would recommend. Why would you leave the Queen of Cities? There will be too much for you to do and see there."

"But would you allow it?"

The emperor frowned at him. "Why so insistent on the question?"

The candor the Byzantine ruler offered about matters in Constantinople inclined Vlad to reveal the truth. He needed to do more than find his half-Turkic niece.

"I must have your word as a Christian believer," he said, pitching his voice lower. "A vow upon your soul that you'll never betray what I shall reveal next."

"You have it. My oath, once given, holds me until death. You may speak."

"Along with brothers, I once had two sisters, the last of whom our father wed to an Ottoman prince. A son of Bāyazīd Hân, Mûsâ Çelebi, became her husband." He paused before saying, "My sister perished in childbirth after bearing him a child. A girl."

The emperor stared at him expectantly. "Go on."

Vlad confided the little he knew about Arina's daughter. He confessed his desire to retrieve her from the family who'd raised her.

"So, this is your true purpose in coming with me to Constantinople?"

The emperor reined in his horse, and Vlad did the same. The retinue surrounding them halted at a discreet distance with their mounts turned toward the broad river.

"That's why you left your mistress behind and never objected to my wish. To discover your sister's child. You hoped I would permit you in these intervening years to pursue her in old Anatolia. But I must ask, in your rush to seek her out, have you considered all the consequences if you uproot her from the only existence she has known? You're a king's knight. How will you raise her while you're on the battlefield?"

"My mistress can do it once we are reunited in Buda." He nodded, certain about their future. Călţuna and their babe belonged at his side. They would return to each other.

"She shall do this for you while she suckles and tends to a babe of her own?"

The emperor's voice drew Vlad from his thoughts and he said, "My uncle can be of aid. He has some years on him, but he is duteous and fierce in his devotion to our family."

"You expect an old man shall take kindly to a young girl foisted off on him?"

"Staico's not so old! You've never met him, *basileús*."

"I've encountered enough of the elderly who know the nurturing of children is best left to the young. You may be sure the girl only speaks Turkish. If you recover her, how will you communicate and convince her to trust you, Vlad?"

He had not completed the details. He must find the child first, and conceded as much.

"Let's suppose you're successful despite the language barrier." The emperor sniggered, revealing his view of the prospect. "By what means will you make her perceive the risks? What will you tell her about the life awaiting her in the north of her birthplace? You know your king better than me. Do you believe he'll undo treaties with the Turks while the Hussites occupy him, for this girl's sake? When, not if the newest sultan, her cousin Murād, learns of her existence, he will want her back!"

Vlad frowned. "She may be sensible enough to understand political dangers. Her mother and I did before she faced a future as a Turk's bride. I'm not so ignorant as to believe finding Arina's daughter alone will end all concerns, *basileús*. The girl and I shall be strangers at first, but we are family. That counts. I'll protect her."

"Like you did your dead sister?" The emperor snapped, "What do you know about raising a girl to womanhood? You say she is at least ten years old. If your niece's first blood comes when your mistress is unavailable, will you help the girl?"

In the red haze of anger, Vlad stared at him in silence for the space of several breaths. "I've misjudged your character. You can be as crass as any commoner."

Iōannēs Palaeologus colored at the insult. "The common people understand reality. From their lives, I've learned patience and adaptability. Skills you haven't mastered."

Vlad could have kicked himself for the foolish outburst. "Forgive my disrespect, *basileús*. Don't dismiss me, I pray. My temper gets the better of me. It's my worst trait."

"I can see that. Do you not see this girl is a Turk of her father's blood? I've admired you since we met, Vlad, and must caution you against foolish behavior. Don't rip that child away from everything she's ever known. She shall reward you with nothing but wrath and betrayal. She may grow to hate you in the end."

"She is my sister's child. The blood of the House of Basarab flows in her. I didn't give up on Arina. I will not do so with her daughter. You wished to know my mind. I've since confided in you and must rely on your assurance of trust, *basileús*."

The emperor nodded curtly and straightened in the saddle. "As you wish, Vlad. I shall forget our disagreement. We move on. The court of King Władysław awaits."

Vlad cursed inwardly. He must do better if he hoped to persuade the emperor to let him travel outside Constantinople and to support his future bid to rule Wallachia.

THEIR COMPANY ARRIVED in relative secrecy as Iōannēs Palaeologus insisted upon in every city they visited. The authority with which the true emperor spoke upon revealing his identity typically compelled even the most recalcitrant guardsman, who allowed his entry into castles and palatial homes. Afterward, one of his Byzantine servants always sought the chamberlain or majordomo.

While this same search occurred in Kraków, Vlad viewed the facade and sun-burnished roofs of Wawel Castle, set on a limestone hill dotted with cave systems. According to legend, a firedrake once nested within the formation, which the Polish monarch had relayed to Iōannēs

Palaeologus on his last visit. A nearby cathedral dwarfed the royal residence. The new arrivals did not enter the quadrangle of the courtyard, proceeding instead to the dank stables to await King Władysław's chief servant.

Vlad's Carpathian pony snorted as he slowed it just outside the stable door, where pungent urine and manure emanated. Inside, a diminutive, hooded figure brushed the coat of a chestnut-hued horse.

"You there! Summon your fellow groomsmen to attend," Vlad called out in Polish.

A petite woman with sea-green eyes turned to him. Startled, Vlad could only gape at her, equally mesmerized and oddly unsettled. The reins slid from his grasp. Her cowl fell just above her black brows. A broad nose flared from smooth, pale olive skin.

"I don't think she can help us, Vlad," the emperor said with a chuckle, tugging off his broad-brimmed hat and brushing at his shoulder-length curls.

While he spoke, groomsmen emerged from the back of the stables, leading more horses. Half of the attendants approached the emperor's entourage, who dismounted.

All except Vlad, who was still struck by an odd silence. The woman gave ministration to her mount, speaking in low murmurs to the animal while she worked. Only then could he release a pent-up breath, as if dragged from the strange stupor.

Half a score of men in black mantles, shorter than the woman's own, blundered into their midst and grasped the reins of the waiting horses from the grooms. Without so much as a look at the emperor or his companions, their corpulent leader slapped red leather gloves against his meaty, pale palm and muttered curses in Latin.

"A waste of time! All of it. King Władysław entreated me with a promise of protection, but I won't let him think of me as a weak simpleton." He reached the woman, who curtsied at his side, revealing a blood-red robe under her mantle. He fingered her fleshy chin and smiled. "I must disappoint you, daughter, as we won't be hunting. We are leaving Poland and going home to Moldavia."

Grunting, he mounted a horse. She managed the same with familiar ease, unaided by any groom, along with the rest of their retinue.

Her father said, "Come Cneajna, I have wasted enough time here in the service of old King Władysław, who can no longer be my overlord. If he won't defend our principality from the Turks, we must secure ourselves against future attacks."

As they departed, the woman urged her horse on. A strong wind raked at her hood and tugged it back around her shoulders. Ravens' wings of hair streaked behind her.

Before the company disappeared, she cast a final glance over her shoulder. Her gaze found Vlad again. His last glimpse of those sea-green eyes conjured the image of turbulent waves on the Black Sea in his mind. He knew next to nothing about her, but hoped she and her father would survive the onslaught of the Turks.

In her wake, he raked a hand over his hair and heaved a sigh.

The emperor laughed and came to him. "Like a whirlwind they were. Alexandru, called the Good of the House of Muşat, the ruler of the Principality of Moldavia, and his daughter Vasilisa Maria. My emissaries have said she's rejected so many suitors, her father must think he will never marry her off. He dotes on her and is loath to see her go from his capital in Suceava. Vasilisa Maria is a beauty, isn't she? She may be a witch too."

Vlad shook his head, still too dazed to think of the lady practicing sorcery. Though that would explain the strange effect she had on him. He recalled her country as the place where he and Arina had once hoped to start another life.

"Her name is Vasilisa Maria? I thought her father called her Cneajna," he mumbled.

The emperor laughed again, before waving over the servant whom he sent earlier in search of the Polish king's chamberlain.

In the evening, after settling into the suite of guest rooms allotted to them, Vlad joined the emperor in the throne room of King Władysław. Since their first encounter at Buda Castle during the royal summit over twelve years past, the Polish monarch aged poorly, with a broad baldpate and deep-set eyes beneath the golden, bejeweled crown.

His gnarled, spotted hand shook as he entreated the pretty young queen Zofia Holszańska, decades younger, to share the kiss of peace with Iōannēs Palaeologus. Despite the march of time, the king's wife's high belly swelled as proof of his potency.

Vlad gave the royal couple scant attention, drawn instead to the pitiable sight of a dour, short-waisted young lady on a cushioned stool beside the king. She wore violet garments trimmed with ermine. Her sun-ripened, wheat-colored hair trailed beneath a linen fillet edged with white pearls. Her expression reminded him of his sullen youth. They could not have been more different in physical appearance.

Could this be the Polish heiress, Princess Jadwiga, whom Queen Borbála's cousin affectionately called Andlein, mothered? Her features barely evoked her kinswoman back in Hungary.

"Is this one any better than her cousin?" He mused in a low tone, catching the interest of the Byzantine noble next to him. Vlad smiled at the man and sipped the wine.

During the evening banquet, the princess sat on her father's left, opposing her stepmother at the king's table. Hardly anyone, including her remaining parent, spoke to her. When the dancing occurred, she fled, stubby fingers covering her mouth. A smirk uglier than that of Borbála twisted the Polish queen's thinned lips as she eyed her stepdaughter's departure. Despite knowing nothing about Jadwiga, her stepmother's behavior stirred Vlad's sympathy for the princess.

Nearing the approach of midnight, with the festivities unabated, he slipped away from the Byzantine entourage. The air, redolent with beeswax, as once perfumed his dining room at the Buda townhouse at Călţuna's insistence, only stirred the desire for escape. The intoxicating wine made his head swim.

He stumbled out into an enclosed garden, surprising a pair of lovers kissing in the bushes before both men hurried away. Stunned, he shook his head and sought to clear his thoughts, before delving deeper between hedgerows. He longed to be far away, at Călţuna's side. In the morning, he must finish the new letter he had already begun for her and compose another intended for Fruzhin.

Myriad stars glittered in the night sky. Discordant noise echoed from the rows of people indoors while loneliness overcame him. Did Călţuna already mourn an ailing or deceased father? Was she resting in anticipation of the birthing or was their son already here? Her image flickered to life in his mind. Florid skin, silky yellow hair, and sea-green eyes.

He rubbed his forehead. No, Călţuna's eyes shone clear and vivid, like emeralds. How could he ever mistake them for the blue-green of storm-driven waves?

Soft weeping intruded on his musing, and he followed the sound, approaching a large fountain. The Polish princess sat on its marble edge. Her hand sluiced through in the water in an absent-minded motion. At her sad sigh, he turned to go.

"My father didn't think to formally introduce me to you either, Prince Vlad," she said. "He believes that the wicked woman he married will give him a son and neglects me. But I won't let her boy replace me on the throne!"

The revelation of her sentiments startled and intrigued him. She possessed a depth of perception that was far beyond her obvious youth.

He turned and bowed before her. "Princess Jadwiga, it is an honor."

She attempted a smile of entreaty and seeing it, he advanced. Only when she waved to a place beside her did he hesitate.

"Believe me, if anyone discovered us here, even my stepmother's spies, they could not besmirch my virtue," she said. "My betrothed and I have declared our love for each other. Everyone knows of our devotion. None can separate us."

Her dulcet tone encouraged Vlad, and he relaxed at her side.

"Are you not cold, princess, even with a fur collar? Should you be alone without ladies-in-waiting or even a pageboy?"

"Jadwiga, if you please." She ignored his concern. "I feel as if I already know so much about you. We must become friends."

Puzzled, he asked after her assumption.

She wiped at her wan, wet cheeks. "Well, Cneajna told me all about you. She promised we would talk with each other and share the sadness of our souls."

His brow throbbed. "Cneajna? Do you mean the daughter of Alexandru of Moldavia? I encountered her for the first today before she and her father left Kraków."

"Oh." A tiny crease formed between Jadwiga's thick honey-brown brows. "But she described you so perfectly before your arrival. Although she is a little older than me, she became a great friend during her father's negotiations with mine. She knew you would come and confided she had seen you many times in her dreams."

Vlad snorted. This Cneajna seemed odder than he imagined at their brief meeting. "It doesn't do well for a good Christian princess to imagine a stranger in her life. I can't explain why she would." He looked down at Jadwiga's plump fingers in the water, pink at their tips. "We should go inside if you please."

"Neither of us wishes it. I've always hated my father's feasts. His nobles are boorish. You're forlorn, as Cneajna said you would be. Are you missing someone too, while I pine for my betrothed? Some among my stepmother's retinue don't want us to marry." She leaned toward him, her voice a conspiratorial hush. "They think we must not reign as king and queen, but we will fight for our right to rule after my father has died."

Refusing to admit his heart's deepest longing to even so affable a lady, he replied, "May God shield you and the one you love. Tell me more about him if it pleases you."

They talked until long after the sentries called the midnight hour. She spoke longingly about her betrothed; the son of the dragon knight, Queen Borbála's paramour.

Zsigmond never brought that matter of her trial to the conclusion everyone else expected. Vlad wondered what his king thought of the match between the dragon knight's heir and the princess of Poland.

Later, Jadwiga consented and let Vlad escort her back to the banquet hall. Inside, she and her stepmother exchanged harsh stares. Władysław's wife whispered something to her husband, who frowned and waved his hand in the air before sipping his wine.

Vlad said, "I met your queenly mother twelve years ago at Buda Castle in Hungary. She aided my lessons in Polish at the side of her cousin, the wife of King Zsigmond."

"I remember little about my other parent, except her retinue called her Queen Andlein." Jadwiga's gray-eyed gaze dropped to the marble floor. "She died eight years ago when I was seven...no, eight years old. Father's third wife, another stepmother, raised me. The dancers are very fine tonight. I wish my betrothed and I could join them. The king's consort would scowl at the sight of our happiness." She giggled.

Somehow, Vlad found himself charmed by her demeanor. Despite the neglect of her stepmother and father, she possessed courage. An admirable trait.

He admitted, "I cannot dance to save my Christian soul, but if you would do me the honor, Jadwiga, I should like to observe the revelers beside you."

He offered his forearm, and she settled her fingertips on the crook, standing at a respectable distance from him. "I hope Cneajna was right, and we shall be friends while you're here with the Byzantine emperor, my prince."

Vlad peered at the queen who eyed them, her small mouth twisted in a sneer. "Please, Jadwiga, you must call me by my Christian name if we are to be friends indeed."

DURING THE THREE WEEKS spent at the court in Kraków, October deepened autumn's chill. Whenever Vlad did not attend the Byzantine ruler's meetings with the Polish king, in a continued attempt to bring about the reunification of Christendom's churches, Jadwiga accompanied him. She rode and hunted as well as a man. Her laughter summoned memories of his two lost sisters.

At the princess' side, along with a few of the curious members of the emperor's entourage, they also explored the nearby limestone caves but found no purported dragon bones. Superstitious, the Gypsy twins Tobar and Yoska waited for Vlad at the cavern entrances through which the party re-emerged. Though naturally spirited, bouts of melancholy overcame Jadwiga when she spoke of her betrothed. The mere sight of her stepmother reignited the fire in her gaze.

The time of the emperor's departure for Constantinople arrived. A day after Poland's queen gave birth to a baby boy. Although eager to begin the hunt for Arina's child, Vlad worried about Jadwiga. In such a short span, the princess became like a cherished sibling to him. He missed having a sister to confide in.

On the morning after the birth of Jadwiga's half-brother, he confessed the source of his misery; the absence of Călțuna and their child.

"And still no word of his arrival from Transilvania?" Jadwiga tapped a plump forefinger against pale lips in the banquet hall garden where they stood. "But you said you wrote seeking news of him the day after you came. Could a message take so long?"

"I hoped it would not. Seasonal weather makes anything possible. I gave my lady instructions to reply here, not Constantinople, expecting to have heard from her by now."

Niggling doubts invaded Vlad's mind. What if something untoward had already happened at Hermannstadt, with his mistress or their baby? Was that the cause of the delay? Not a word from Fruzhin either, though Vlad expected the planning of another Bohemian campaign had absorbed his friend's attention.

At a summons from the emperor, Vlad begged Jadwiga's leave to go.

"We will talk later." She pressed her hand to his shoulder. "All shall be well, Vlad."

She could not have been more wrong. In the guest rooms of the Byzantines, a Hungarian messenger awaited Vlad with a devastating message from his king.

'...Bad as it is that We should be without your sword arm in Our continued conflict with the Bohemians, your wicked behavior before this absence dismays Us. You dared conceal the impending birth of your son, whom the mother named for you! We might have never discovered his existence, had not his grandfather's heirs petitioned for the rights to the old man's estate at death in a writ, naming sons and a daughter holding equal claims of inheritance with their children too.

'We knew the daughter must be the same woman you took from the town of Hermannstadt. Understand Us well. Your bastard matters not one whit. Your deceitful concealment of him offends Us. You shall never see the mother again. That is your punishment. For too long, the woman has distracted you. We separated her from the boy and consigned her to a religious house. Forget her and find a suitable wife. Do not return to the Hungarian kingdom until then. Pray to God Our wrath has abated at such time.'

He collapsed into the chair beside which the emperor stood, while the letter floated to his feet. Călțuna locked away? Their babe, gone from her arms forever? No, it could not be. God would never be so cruel as to separate them permanently, just for loving her.

Uninvited, Iōannēs Palaeologus bent and retrieved Zsigmond's furious decree, reading it before he whistled. "No one keeps secrets from your king for long, either." He dismissed the Hungarian herald and kneeled next to Vlad. "There is no remedy for the trouble now. Grieve if you must, but rouse yourself and prepare to leave for Constantinople. We shall be on the road at dawn."

Vlad gaped at him before yelling, "Have you lost your senses?"

"Have you done so again?" The emperor roared back. "I can forgive the tenor of your question once more because of the clear pain. What do you suppose you can do?"

"Release me from your service. I must go to Hermannstadt." Vlad could not think further of Arina's child, the stories of the revenant in Būrsâ, or even his ambitions. Only the woman he loved and their child, his firstborn son, mattered.

"Do you truly hope to thwart Zsigmond? He warned against your return absent a suitable wife. You cannot enter the Transilvanian lands again."

"There is no bride for me except Călțuna! Don't you understand? Haven't you ever lived for any other's sake? Nothing else matters to me right now, except her and our boy."

He could not let this happen! No one would separate them from each other forever.

The emperor grappled his arm. "Listen, don't be a fool. You'd do better to forget the woman and fulfill your patron's wish for a suitable bride. When we arrive at Constantinople, I'll send word to Suceava in the Principality of Moldavia, offering your suit to the comely daughter of the House of Muşat, Vasilisa Maria. You drew her gaze."

Horrified, Vlad wrenched away and spluttered, "You dare think I can abandon the mother of my firstborn so easily?" He got to his feet and glared down at the Byzantine ruler. "I refuse. I will never let them go. I cannot serve you any longer."

Iōannēs Palaeologus stood. His visage reddened. "You're making a dreadful mistake."

"I'll suffer its consequences. Do you dismiss me from your service?"

"I do," the emperor muttered. "I will not compel you and have only to regret that I've loved no woman so much." He extended his arm, and Vlad clasped it. "Despite your folly, we part as friends. You'll have my writ of safe conduct bearing the imperial seal. I hope you know what you're doing and may find your woman and child."

"Thank you. I must fetch my Gypsies and search for Jadwiga to say goodbye."

Despite the princess' tearful farewell, Vlad hastened to leave her.

She tugged his hand. "Promise you'll write. I want to know about your child. Don't forget about me, Vlad."

"I never could, Jadwiga," he vowed. "We are friends, a rarity at many royal courts."

He mounted his Carpathian pony at the side of the Gypsy twins already atop their horses. He raced away from Wawel Castle, bound for Hermannstadt in Transilvania.

CHAPTER 21

The Red Star of Wallachia

"Look at the stars lighting up the sky: no one of them stays in the same place."-Seneca the Younger (circa 4 BC-65 AD), Roman philosopher, statesman, and dramatist.

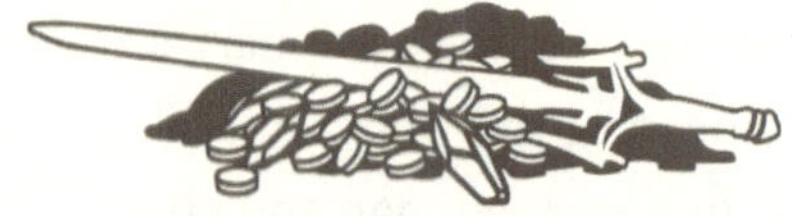

IN THE YEAR OF OUR Lord 1424-1425. Hermannstadt, Transilvania (modern-day Sibiu, Romania)

Frigid winds from the southern Carpathian region chased Vlad and his Gypsies the length of their journey down to Transilvania. He recalled the dangers of his first trip into Hungary, when frost formed on the trailing edge of a beard's beginnings and the cold bit savagely into his gloved hands, and beneath socks, leather boots, layers of clothing, and the ragged old wolf-skin Tobar once gave him.

He never thought to experience such a chill again after those days. The trio found a respite at inns and taverns. The snow slowed their progress and trapped them in the Styrian countryside for two weeks before Christmas.

The delays made Vlad's imagination fraught. Each week brought the possibility that somehow Zsigmond compelled Călţuna to become a nun. How could she ever deny their king? In Vlad's torturous nightmares, their tiny baby screamed and cried for his mother, hour after hour with no one to comfort him.

He woke in a cold sweat one morning and looked around the room, where Tobar and Yoska snored. He rubbed at his bleary eyes.

"My God, am I forsaken? Why, when I've given my life's blood as a Christian?"

More than all his other fears, his son's need for some parent drove Vlad out into the brutal winter weather. But hail and the cold cruelty of air currents turned him aside at the inn's door. His Gypsies came after him.

Kneeling between Tobar and Yoska, he yelled and pounded his fists into the snowdrifts, demanding to know from God why He kept him from those he loved. He cursed his Catholic religion and Eastern Orthodox upbringing, threw his rosary beads away, and swore he would never pray again until Jesus Christ united his mistress and their child.

Even after the weather abated, he did not go back on his word. His faith, only illusory, failed him. Why mutter pleas before the Almighty if He would not listen? Vlad vowed to rely on naught else but himself and his loyal companions.

Sheer will drove him southward through north-eastern Hungary and onward to Várad, Transilvania. The rocky, snow-covered terrain would not permit a direct route from there to his destination. He skirted the most inhospitable landscapes, discovering no other souls daring enough to attempt the same journey.

Bypassing Hunyadvár, he arrived at Hermannstadt on the day before Epiphany. The 'city of eyes' seemed to watch him after he entered the eastern gate, as though its denizens remembered the last time he had appeared here and stole away with Călţuna. An impossibility, of course. He huddled under his wolf-skin all the same. Noonday sunlight filtered through wisps of clouds, but barely warmed the frozen earth, its streets and marketplaces congested.

He came to the house of his mistress' father. The familiar sight of some of his uncle's Gypsies surrounding the residence almost made him weep. He slid down from the horse. Clansmen surrounded him and pulled the pair of their kin into their midst. Vlad pushed through their ranks and mounted the steps. The door opened and Tobar's wife, Dika, stood before him. Her gaze flitted to the husband absent from her for long months, before she hefted the tiny bundle swaddled in her arms.

A tuft of yellow hair peeked out from the cloth, above a rounded face with puckered lips and smooth, pink cheeks. His son slumbered so peacefully; Vlad hated to disturb him. But Dika held the newborn out.

"Support his head and the length of him on your arm, *Domnule*. He came seven weeks ago, faster than your lady expected. Do you know his name?" After Vlad nodded, she added, "He's small, but when he wakes, he's always hungry, and his cries are loud. The wet nurse is my sister. Her husband brings their babe daily to give him suck, too."

"My boy misses his mother." Tears stung the corners of Vlad's eyes. "As I do."

Dika gave the babe a wistful look. "You have each other, *Domnule*."

Vlad accepted his slight weight, holding him the way she'd said. As he hoped, the child barely stirred except to snuggle against him. Fierce protectiveness and infinite love filled his heart, the depths of which he once never imagined. Tobar's woman slipped past him, intent on her spouse, while Vlad stepped inside the home's long corridor.

At its end, Staico did not await him. Rather, his son's youngest uncle.

"You're too late. Do you taste the bitterness of disappointment? I know it well. Călţuna and I never reached our father before his demise," the man spat. "She's gone to some religious house now. I can't uncover her whereabouts. Your king's men dragged her away by her hair."

His head throbbing, Vlad swallowed and asked, "My uncle, where is he?"

"Let your Gypsies take you to him and leave this house. Never come back! Go with your slaves and your bastard. You've ruined his life and my sister's own through your selfishness. Her foolish love for you brought her to an end she never wanted. I shall never forgive you for it." Călţuna's brother turned and walked away.

Tobar entered the house. "*Domnule*, we must flee! Dika says there have been strange men watching the house for over two months. My brethren have counted at least a score of faces they've never seen in this town until now, all of whom have taken an unusual interest in this place."

"They could only be men in the employ of Zsigmond." Vlad clutched his son tighter. "My king knew I would come here, searching for my son. But how can we get away?"

The flight with such a precious bundle in his arms would be even more perilous. Pursuers could mark him by the care with which he held his babe.

"I must find Staico," Vlad said, ignoring how Tobar hung his head at the mention. "Don't delay. Get stones long as your arms from the yard out back and swaddle them, like my child. The men will take them. Each Gypsy rider must wear his wolf-skin over his head, as I do. With the women and their children, we outnumber any potential pursuers. They can't chase us all if we take different directions from Hermannstadt."

Dika rejoined them. Vlad discovered his uncle's whereabouts through her. After a long sigh, he shared the plan he related to Tobar.

"The women will fight and die for you too, *Domnule*," Dika affirmed.

"I would prefer none of you lost your lives because of me," he said. "I owe everyone here that much for ensuring my son's life. Prepare the women and children to leave."

As the couple rushed to do his bidding, Vlad clenched his jaw and looked along the corridor where Călțuna's brother had disappeared. Hopefully, despite lingering anger, the man might not aid those who sought Vlad's capture.

The gates of Hermannstadt might close in four hours, nearing sundown, when the watchmen would also be alert. Vlad guessed if whoever wanted him noticed his arrival, they must gather help within an hour or two before coming. He would be prepared.

Clutching the baby even closer, he whispered in his ear. "I'll keep you safe. No one will take me away from you now."

He remained indoors until Tobar announced the Gypsies' readiness. In bands of only six, they would disperse through the town's five gates, intending to throw off any pursuers and meet in the northern foothills of Stârmina Mountain, Vlad's next destination.

Everyone went to their Carpathian ponies, women herding their young ones and settling them saddled in front of them. All the men, clad in wolf pelts against the bitter cold, carried sizable rocks bundled in the crooks of their arms, the fingers of the other hand grasping reins. When Tobar would have ushered them away, Vlad glimpsed one of two armed bands, each marching up the long street from opposite sides behind a lone figure on horseback. He could not count their number nor wait to find out.

"Go now," he whispered in a vehement hush.

He drove his mount forward, Tobar and Yoska beside him, with Dika, her sister, and that woman's husband with their baby behind them.

"They're trying to get away! Surround them and find the Transalpine prince. Remember, Zsigmond wants him alive," ordered the leader of the company, approaching from the east. Vlad detected a strange accent underlying the Hungarian speech.

His companions did not give the interlopers a chance to stop them. Tobar swung the heavy stone on his arm and bashed the sole rider's head while Yoska stabbed downward with his knife. Dika carried a bow and arrows and proved her talents extended beyond the kitchen. Her sister, the nurse of Vlad's son, fought with a blade too and protected her husband who carried their swaddled baby. When someone tried pulling her down from her pony, Dika fired two arrows straight through his neck.

The clash of metal vied with heavy grunts and cries, filling the length of the road. Likely, the sound attracted unwanted attention through the windows of other houses.

Vlad's gaze swung from those apertures to their assailants repeatedly, ensuring no reinforcements supported them. A flail struck his arm too close to his son who wriggled and cried, stirred from restful sleep. In a fury, he kicked his attacker hard in the chest and urged his horse with gnashing teeth against anyone who approached.

Their foes dwindled, the Carpathian pony trampling a young man who tumbled. Vlad raced away, never looking behind him. Tobar and Yoska's triumphant yells echoed before they and other groups of Gypsies rejoined him. The shouts of pursuers chased them to the gate as they exited and into the woodland beyond Hermannstadt.

The frigid wind struck Vlad's face in a blinding fury. He hunched over his crying child and silently vowed the boy would never know such danger or suffer the bitter cold again. Somehow, he would keep him safe.

IN THE YEAR OF OUR Lord 1425-1427. Tismana Monastery, Oltenia region, Principality of Wallachia (modern-day Tismana Monastery, western Romania)

Vlad found Staico in their homeland at the Orthodox monastery of Tismana in the foothills of Stârmina Mountain. Dense, darkened forests of *tisa* or yew conifers, covered in snow, almost concealed precipitous drops from steep crags. The company arrived in the late afternoon beneath a dull, graying sky and scudding clouds, heralding a tempest.

By the collective permission of the monks, for no abbot lived at Tismana during the last six years, Vlad sank on his knees before the grave, cut into the rock bed and encrusted in rime. His uncle. Dead. The bulwark of his life crumbled to dust beneath ice-covered stones and cold ground. How could it be so?

"My kin all swear it; the lord Staico fought nine of the king's men and killed them before the others took his life. He protected your lady until he could not." Tobar stood behind Vlad while his wife kept the baby on the outskirts of the western entrance.

All but one group of the Gypsies' brethren did not join them on the road to Tismana. Assuming their seizure, Vlad wondered what Zsigmond's men would do once the realization of their quarry's escape hit them. Any captured Gypsies would suffer for his sake. Pangs of guilt almost overwhelmed him, as much as sadness over his uncle.

"This is wrong. He shouldn't be buried here." His gloved fingers clenched in the hoarfrost. The chill did not penetrate leather or flesh. "His body should have rested at Vodița Monastery instead."

"When the spirit is with God, Prince Vlad, concerns of mortal, corruptible flesh are no longer important." The black-robed monk who introduced himself earlier, Pahomie of Tismana, joined them. No hood covered his brown, tonsured head. He stood taller than Vlad, as most men did. "While Vodiţa benefited much from Lord Staico, by the grace of the Holy Spirit and with the help of God, your uncle also gave what he could to Tismana in honor of your father."

"My father?" Vlad repeated, incredulous. "Didn't he quarrel with one of your community's leaders, Abbot Nikodim? My mother told me so in childhood."

"Your parent once greeted Father Nikodim as 'my prayerful father.' But when Prince Mircea offered tenancies belonging to his uncle of the Florea clan, our venerable abbot called it theft and refused the lands until overruled by the Church. Your father's enmity remained unabated until Abbot Nikodim's death nineteen years ago. Lord Staico became our benefactor on behalf of his half-brother during the term of Father Nikodim's successor, Abbot Agaton. The holy brothers say prayers on behalf of both the princes."

"My family has supported the good works you do for over half a century with income from our gold and brass mines," Vlad said. "I shall provide a sizable gift as well, to honor my uncle alone."

The monk's thick brows flared over unusual eyes, one hazel-colored and the other brown with amber flecks.

"In the months before the venerable abbot died," he said, "your father met with King Zsigmond here to begin the alliance of Wallachia and Hungary."

Vlad did not know that, but he simply nodded while wondering why the monk had mentioned his king.

"Upon your arrival," Pahomie added, "you said you'd come from Transilvania, not the court of the sovereign whom you've served from youth, my prince."

"You're well-informed about my life for a member of this secluded monastic order."

"Even monks in a religious house must know about secular life beyond Tismana."

Although Vlad thought to inquire how Pahomie came by his information, he decided against it. Perhaps the monk could help resolve his dilemma, but gaining sympathy required candor. Vlad shared the source of Zsigmond's displeasure with him.

"Ah, so the little babe crying outside the gate is your son." Pahomie spoke in an even tone, no condemnation laced in his voice or regard for Vlad.

"I must do what a father would," he replied, "and protect my child. There is no place for us at the king's court in Buda. I worry my presence at the side of my mother and grandmother at Târgovişte would summon Dan Dăneşti and his warriors from Argeş."

"Then permit me to discuss the matter with my spiritual brothers. We must consider allowing you sanctuary, while your companions live in the village south of here, which depends on this community. You understand no women are allowed here?"

"My son shall live with his wet nurse at the settlement where I will visit him. I hoped you might permit us to at least stay in this land, but I don't mean to invite my sovereign's wrath here either if he should discover my presence."

"Before his death, Father Nikodim served as confessor to King Zsigmond. The sanctity of Tismana is inviolable."

Although Vlad knew his king could and would violate the sanctuary if he so chose, frightening or disagreeing with Pahomie would be a mistake.

"I shall speak with the holy brothers about the offer of sanctuary to you," Pahomie said. "Pray, excuse me."

Vlad lingered at the graveside, despite Tobar's reminder that the baby should not stay outdoors for much longer.

"I miss you, uncle. Your good advice at this perilous time to aid me and my son."

What would they do if the monks denied them sanctuary? Their murderous cousin Dan Dăneşti might discover it if Vlad returned to Wallachia, his only other option. Dan could even assume the two eldest sons of Mircea the Great intended to unite. He might launch a preemptive attack. Vlad would not bring a siege to his mother and grandmother's doorstep, nor expose his newborn son to more danger.

While absorbed in thought, another monk interrupted him, saying Pahomie begged to speak with him at the church. Vlad prayed Pahomie had an answer to avail him. He dismissed Tobar and walked to the ocher-painted wooden structure at the heart of the monastery. There, at the western end of the darkened nave, Pahomie lit a candle at the tomb of Abbot Nikodim before the monk dipped his fingers in a basin of holy water.

"Thank you for joining me," Pahomie began. "The proverbial flame Father Nikodim lit in the hearts of our brotherhood must never go out. We are devoted to his memory and mission. He would want us to offer you sanctuary. We have voted to do so."

Vlad breathed a sigh of relief. The respite would also give him time to consider how he might help his mistress.

"I suppose it may be too much to ask, but could you aid me in the discovery of my son's mother's location in some nunnery?"

With a visage suddenly harder than weathered stone, the monk said, "An impossibility." Clasping his hands at his chest, he added, "Our faith states, 'it is the Lord who directs your life, for each step you take is ordained by God to bring you closer to your destiny.' Have you reasoned how the fate God has led this woman toward is best?"

Zsigmond had decided, not God! Vlad seethed at the unfairness of fate for the women he loved best. Călțuna never wanted the cloistered life Arina once desired before her Turkic marriage. The choice taken from each of them by capricious men, rather than the will of the Almighty, not only infuriated Vlad. He was also worried. Did his lover blame him for her circumstances? The absence of their child from her arms?

As the monk stared at him, Vlad mouthed the words Pahomie surely expected. "You've given me much to consider." He cleared his throat. "Now if you will excuse me, I must see to my son and my Gypsies, directing them to the village."

Before he went away, Pahomie asked, "Would you like me to pray with you after?"

His teeth gritted and hands fisted at his side, Vlad recalled the vow he made, never to embrace religious fervor again. He muttered over his shoulder, "I'd prefer private devotion. I trust you understand."

"As you wish, my prince." Pahomie came to him, those mismatched eyes scouring Vlad's features before the monk made the sign of the cross in the air. "Go with God."

ALMOST A FULL WEEK later, Vlad sat on the small bed of his allotted room in the guest house. A wooden icon watched over him. He sneered at the image and turned away to the large chest at the foot of the bed, draped in his black wolf-skin cloak.

He grabbed the pelt, dragged it on his shoulders, and left the room, and found one of Pahomie's holy brothers awaiting him.

The monk said, "My prince, you have visitors. They wait at the gate with Pahomie."

Vlad smiled, hopeful that Tobar and Yoska had brought the baby for an impromptu visit. The boy's soft down of yellow hair was a persistent, poignant reminder of his mother. Vlad's grin ebbed as he caught sight of Pahomie in a whispered discussion with Vlậcsan the Wolf.

The monk and boyar each stood aside, revealing the Dowager Princess Ana-Călina standing outside of a carriage, attired in widow's black. Fourteen years to the time since Vlad last saw her. The lines on her face were deeper. She remained unbowed by their family's trials. She beckoned him with a gnarled finger. At her feet, he kneeled, and grasped and kissed her proffered hand, the mottled skin dry to the touch.

"Pahomie wrote to my nephew about your arrival. Why didn't you write, my Vlad?"

He bowed his head. "Grandmother, I didn't want you or anyone else imperiled." He cast a stare beside him at the monk, who did not shrink away. "I would have sent a message to you and Mother soon."

"Little good it would do her." The Dowager pulled away from his grasp. "She suffered apoplexy when news of Staico's death reached her from Transilvania."

"Apoplexy?" Vlad's mind could hardly encompass the word.

"She is insensate. A shell of the parent you once knew. Half of her face slackened and her form twisted. But she dreams. At night, she calls to each of you, her children."

"I must see her!" He rose. "Where is she?"

"At my townhouse in Târgoviște." His grandmother placed her palm, fingers curling inward, at the center of his chest. "Since Dan Dăneşti drove your brother Radu from its Princely Court during the last autumn." While Vlad swallowed in acceptance of his sibling's unexpected defeat, she added, "I would spare you the sight of her. Remember Princess Mara of the House of Tolmay, as you last knew her."

Beside them, the monk and boyar mumbled their regrets. Studying both men, Vlad recognized kindred features in the visage and lanky length of the men, but especially in Pahomie's right eye and Vlậcsan's pair, all amber-speckled.

"Is this how you've kept up awareness of me, Pahomie? Through the Wolf, who must be some relation of yours?"

"Yes, my prince," the monk replied. "Our mothers were distant cousins."

"Leave us. I will speak to my grandmother alone."

With slight nods of their heads, the kinsmen withdrew into the monastery.

"Shall we talk inside, Grandmother?" Vlad gestured toward the waiting carriage.

"No. Out here." She looped her slight arm with his and leaned on him. "The cold seeping beneath these brittle bones is a reminder that God still finds use for me."

He led her on the snow-covered path away from the monastery. The wind whistled and rippled through the yew trees, scattering crystalline frost.

"Tell me why you've sought sanctuary," the Dowager said, "and how the body of your grandfather's bastard came to be buried in a rock-cut tomb."

"After death and the years, you won't forgive Staico for the conditions of his birth?"

"You did?" She gave an unladylike snort. "My memory is longer than yours."

"He is at rest. Let peace prevail, Grandmother."

"You must think me ancient and addled with age if I should ever hope for peace in this land or my heart. There is little more than my bitterness left to keep me alive."

"You have my two brothers, me, and... a new great-grandson," Vlad revealed.

At her slight gasp, the words rushed from him. He spoke about the previous year's problems.

"That's why I didn't come to you at Târgoviște, Grandmother, because of Zsigmond's decree. He warned me not to return without a bride he might deem acceptable. If he should strike at me for failing his command, I can't let my family suffer."

"Why did you hide the mother's condition from our king?"

Vlad confessed the one-time miscarriage Călțuna suffered, and admitted, "I never thought about whether anyone except the royal consort might have relished my lover's end and our baby's death. But since then, I've also considered if Zsigmond did not arrange the matter with his queen to remove Călțuna from my side."

"Why would Borbála of Celje be against you?"

He chuckled. "That's an even longer tale than the story of the prior year."

"I grow no younger." She tugged his arm. "I would hear it while we visit the village and see this new great-grandson of mine, the child of your body and blood."

THE GYPSIES ENCAMPED near a small lake on the southern outskirts of the settlement. Each day for three weeks, the Dowager left the inn where she and Vlậcsan each requisitioned a room, and met with Vlad and his son in the Gypsy camp. She delighted in the child, though she saw little of his Basarab heritage as his features formed. The reunited family also celebrated Vlad's thirty-first birthday with wine and song. Tobar's wife outshone all the other female dancers and singers.

Each night, Vlad rode alongside his grandmother's carriage to the inn. He lingered on the night before her planned departure for home, his face partly hidden under a gray hood. The serving wench who brought their food earlier strolled by a third time, ample hips swaying as she hefted two full flagons of ale. She cocked her head and gave Vlad a leer. Dull hanks of mousy brown hair spilled over large breasts. Nothing like his Călţuna.

The village woman reminded him of a man's needs. Perhaps she could attend to them before he retired to the monastery.

His grandmother cleared her throat loudly and pushed away the remnants of a roasted quail dish with the tip of one gnarled finger, its joints swollen.

"How much longer will you remain defiant? Must I return to Târgovişte fearing Zsigmond's coming to Tismana? The thought frightens me more than losing your grandfather or father. Marry as your king wills. Love could follow."

"I don't mean to cause worry." He reached for her spotted, veined hand. "But how can I consider marriage to any other woman when my heart remains with Călţuna?"

"So stubborn you are! I've survived the deaths of a husband, our son, one grandson, and two granddaughters," the Dowager said, heaving a prolonged sigh. "But now I must wonder, shall you be the end of me, my Vlad?"

"Don't say such things, Grandmother!"

"Your mother and father learned to care for each other, like your grandfather and me. Do you think those feelings blossomed overnight? No! They grew in a well-watered garden of love. Your son needs a mother, as you need a wife. A bastard he may be, but he belongs to the

House of Basarab." She squeezed his wrist. "I hope Our Lord will put you on the correct pathway to your future at the right time."

IN THE REFECTORY OF Tismana Monastery, two years later, Vlad sat apart from the monks. He shared their mussels and leek soup. A poorer meal for his birthday than he ever had in thirty-three years. Finished with his bowl, he scanned the next paragraph in a lengthy letter he received that afternoon from Vl̦ăcsan the Wolf.

'...Although matters remain unchanged at Argeş and Târgovişte between your cousin and brother, life alters outside our country's border. Thanks be to God, there is no sign of plague again after it struck Várad in Transilvania almost a year ago....'

When the Wolf first sent such terrible tidings to Vlad, his heart pitched at the revelation of Pipó's personal loss. The Florentine's younger brother and a cousin died of the deadly illness within days of each other. Vlad never offered Pipó condolences, having cut all ties to anyone from Zsigmond's court. Even Fruzhin.

One of two people outside the monastery knew of Vlad's journey from Hermannstadt; Călţuna's brother, and he could no longer speak of it. Plague also took him, his wife, and their children after a visit to Várad last year. Princess Jadwiga of Poland remained Vlad's sole confidant in two years of exile from Buda. Her letter arrived at the same time as the Wolf's did, but Vlad read the latter first, hopeful for information about his mother's state or the whereabouts of Arina's child.

Instead, Vl̦ăcsan's letter continued, *'Mid-year in Buda, King Zsigmond received a papal delegation. Since the death of the Hussite leader Jan Žižka in the previous summer, the sovereign believed the years of conflict must end. The pope in Rome has since called for a new crusade of Catholics to crush the Hussites, but the sole clash resulted in more losses for Zsigmond's adherents against the new Hussite leader.'*

Vlad sighed and wondered whether the specter had returned to that battlefield, presaging the Hungarian army's defeat. His gaze returned to the Wolf's words.

'At the royal court in Buda, King Zsigmond wrote to the Byzantine emperor, demanding to know your intent. The lack of an answer displeased the sovereign. There is even some talk that in your absence, you've sought the Turkic sultan's aid in capturing Wallachia. I'm aware of the truth; your brother Prince Radu did this some years ago.'

'After returning to Constantinople, Iōannēs Palaeologus mourned the death of his father and co-emperor and sent his second wife away. He has been much occupied with finding her replacement. The terms of the treaty his brother negotiated with the Turks have not deterred the emperor's quest to reunify the eastern and western churches.'

'Nor have I stopped seeking your sister's child in Turkic lands. The Dowager insists the girl must be found, as you did. Though you will not wish to hear, tales of the revenant in Būrsâ continue. The people there believe it is a Christian woman who died in childbirth, her vengeful, undead form wreaking havoc on the Turks. That is why she steals their babies and drains the blood of would-be mothers. Who can know the truth?'

Vlad wondered if his tortured dreams, in which the disembodied voice whispered, "*Find me, free me*," had resumed because the matter of the revenant remained unresolved. He had not heard those words in his head while he lived with Călțuna. In her absence, they returned almost every night.

He set the letter aside, as the last line contained Vlậcsan's farewell. Instead, Vlad peered at his namesake son, his only delight. The child sat beside the monk Pahomie, who fed the child. Arina would have adored him.

The spiritual brothers kept a vow of silence during the meal and used hand signals to communicate their needs. A smile tugged at the corner of Vlad's mouth. His boy ate without fuss or mess, and even mimicked the sign for milk perfectly, given Pahomie's nod as he offered the child a wooden cup. Since the wet nurse had weaned him on his second birthday, he lived at the monastery with Vlad.

The boy looked and behaved nothing like him, inheriting the green eyes and golden hair of Călțuna. When their son reached the toddling age and could walk to greet his father as soon as Tobar set him down from horseback, Vlad found his little one also sought Pahomie. Ever indulgent, the monk would set him on his lap and read from the Bible, or share the daily meal with him, as they did now.

Knowing his child remained in good and dutiful hands, Vlad broke the seal of Jadwiga's letter. She wrote about the usual topics; reminiscences of their brief time together in Poland, and the absence and delay of her betrothed.

'To my great shock, Vlad, now King Zsigmond opposes our union too! Although I've asked my father for an explanation, he will not provide it, but I venture he knows.'

Vlad suspected the reason after the emperor had disclosed her espousal. Zsigmond might remain embittered enough about the father of Jadwiga's betrothed, Queen Borbála's dragon knight lover, to thwart the son's marriage into the royal house of Poland. Vlad feared his revelation of the past might dash Jadwiga's future hopes. As her friend, he could never hurt her that way.

Her words expressed equal concern for him. *'What are we to do, dear Vlad? Will we remain bereft of those whom we love? Your misery saddens me as much as my own. At least you have a son to comfort you and remind you of his mother. I cannot understand the cruelty of kings. How can Zsigmond keep you away from her?*

'This letter must end here. I keep the night vigil beside my second brother, although my stepmother disdains my presence. Poor babe; his health has fared poorly for seven months after his birth. From Suceava to our court at Kraków, my friend Cneajna has dispatched a Moldavian healer who once attended her younger brothers. My foolish stepmother disdained him and sent him away. I wonder whether Cneajna thinks of you.'

Shaking his head at the memory of the strange princess of Moldavia, he wondered why Jadwiga believed her friend might recall him two years later.

LONG WINTER NIGHTS stretched unabated for months. Vlad's clandestine visits to the barmaids and prostitutes in Tismana village ceased. He spent more time with his son, reading the Bible, as that was the only book Pahomie offered them. Vlad also taught the boy letters and numbers, which the monks reinforced. They came to rely on Vlad, who chopped logs for the fire and cleared the grounds of heavy snowfall alongside them.

One restless night, he left his bed in the guest chamber and stretched before he went over to the adjacent mattress and placed a gentle kiss on his slumbering son's forehead. The child whispered a vague murmur and his lips curved in a half-smile.

"Sleep well, my blessed boy. May you never know your father's concerns."

With the wolf's pelt over his shoulders, Vlad left the building and entered the yard with its church at the center. Despite his time spent reading the Scriptures, he no longer prayed. While guessing Pahomie must have thought poorly of his absence from services, he vowed no explanation would be forthcoming.

There could never be peace in his heart or reconciliation with his faith, while God kept Călțuna from him and their child. Even if the Lord punished Vlad for years of sin at her side, must the boy also suffer her absence? Did he wonder why Tobar and Dika's little daughter, who was born at the start of winter, had two parents instead of one?

Vlad closed his eyes against the tears stinging their corners, but they still flowed. He missed Călțuna so much! His heart weighed heavy. He heaved a deep sigh and looked up at the starlit heavens. While he would never break the vow against prayer for himself, his son's well-being and future made him contemplate a reversal.

Until a streak in the night sky sent a shudder through him. From the east came a star, glowing red-hot, flames trailing in its wake. He blinked twice, uncertain about what he saw. The image stayed in clear view.

Overawed, he fled indoors. His hurried steps did not falter until he reached the guest room. With a glance at his slumbering son, he closed the door and leaned against it. What was the meaning of that red star over Wallachia? He feared a bad omen.

Within weeks, his anxiety gave way to a real concern. A letter from Jadwiga arrived again with the dawning of spring. Accustomed to her missives at six-month intervals, he immediately sensed the sight of her seal portended some doom.

'My stepmother, in her grief over my second brother's recent death has accused me before my father of having hidden your whereabouts from King Zsigmond! Unknown to me, some servant in the queen's employ found your words. I didn't destroy your last letter, unlike the others. Father is displeased with me and will write to your sovereign at once. His herald leaves for Hungary in the morning. Flee Tismana Monastery with your son!'

His fingers trembled. Where could he go? He looked for the date on the letter; mid-March. Nearly three weeks ago. Enough time for the messenger to travel between Poland and Hungary. What could he do, except warn Pahomie and the other monks, before he rode south to the village with his son and left the Tismana area beside the Gypsies.

He clenched Jadwiga's warning in his fist, recalling the holy brothers prepared for the feast of the Annunciation the next day. The religious community's gates remained locked, barring all visitors, and keeping everyone inside. He would have no chance to take flight until the morning.

After daybreak, when he intended to find Pahomie, another monk directed him toward the monastery's western entrance. There, Fruzhin clambered down from his horse beside Pahomie, who must have opened the gate and now grasped the reins.

The two friends stared at each other in lengthy silence before Fruzhin broke into a run and hauled Vlad against him.

"You utter idiot! You absolute dolt!" He hugged Vlad tightly. "Do you know how I've grieved these past two years, thinking you perhaps rotting in some dank forest?"

Wary, Vlad pulled apart from him. "Zsigmond sent you?"

"I argued with our king against dispatching mercenaries to drag you back to Buda. He's accused you of having withdrawn from his court without permission. He even thought you'd fled to the Ottomans." Fruzhin pawed at Vlad's thick beard. "Have you been here all this time? Others have sworn to Zsigmond that you were serving among the emperor's elite bodyguards in Constantinople."

"That's untrue. I parted with him as soon as our king's angry letter reached me. I came to find Staico's resting place after I learned Zsigmond's men killed him at Hermannstadt before they took Călţuna away from our son in Transilvania."

Fruzhin's hold receded. "A sad happenstance with her and your uncle."

"Were you there?" Vlad grabbed the lacing of his best friend's mantle tied at the throat. "Did you watch them kill him? I want the names of those responsible!"

"Vlad, I was not present, nor did I see who left Buda Castle with Zsigmond's order. You can ask my uncle and János Hunyadi when you see them again. We were with Pipó, defending against a Turkish incursion in Serbia."

"Where are Pipó and János now?" Vlad released his grip. "Do they know I'm alive?"

"That's also why I came." Fruzhin's gaze fell and he pushed back his hood, revealing thick hanks of gray in the hair on his head and face. "János serves my uncle now. Ever since Pipó...since he died at the end of this past December."

Agape Vlad staggered. "Not Pipó!"

"Apoplexy in his fifty-seventh year." Then Fruzhin scowled and he thumped Vlad's shoulder hard. "Had I known where you were earlier, I would have found you so you could visit his burial site among the crypts of Hungary's kings."

"In secret?"

"Yes! If need be...." Fruzhin trailed off and looked away, his cheeks flushing. "János wanted me to find you, too. He never assumed you were dead. He didn't want to serve my uncle, but Stefan accepted him in

Belgrade. He must remain there. The boy swore he would squire only for you, make you accept his service."

"He's not a knight?"

"Pipó might have done it, except in the week before his death, his limbs wouldn't cooperate. Gout. He tumbled down at the dining table. We all laughed and said he had too much wine. He never believed you were dead. Only I did. I should be ashamed."

"I'm still here, old friend." At last, Vlad embraced Fruzhin in full.

As the service of the Annunciation began, they spoke in Vlad's room. He asked Fruzhin about the red star streaking across the sky weeks beforehand, but met with confusion, Vlad ended the discussion. After his son returned from the religious observance, he introduced the child to his best friend.

Fruzhin kneeled and brushed a hand over the boy's curls. "The image of his mother. Anyone who's met her can see it."

"Where is she?" Vlad demanded.

"I don't know!"

"Would you tell me if you did?"

At their raised voices, the toddler exchanged wide-eyed glances with both men before a little sob escaped him and he ran through the open door.

"Aren't you going after him, Vlad?"

"I'm not worried. He'll seek the monks. He prefers them. I've tried to be a dutiful father to him, better than the parent who sired me. When I made him a little wooden sword to play with, he threw it in the dirt and ran to Brother Pahomie, the one who greeted you, to hear the Bible. My son may bear my name, but he is nothing like me."

"He's a child of almost two years."

"Whom I've raised here. I feel as though I'm failing him every day in Călțuna's absence. How can my love ever be enough for him? He needs his mother! I want her back for his sake, not just a selfish whim. If you know where she is, you must tell me."

"Vlad, upon my soul and honor, I do not know. Your misery would test my vows of loyalty to our king if I did. When Zsigmond confirmed your boy's birth, I'm told he raged. Why was he so angry?"

"He knew the child would bind me to my lover always. That I would marry no one else except the mother of my firstborn."

"But you must! He's insisted on it." Fruzhin took up the saddlebag at his feet and fished inside before handing over a sealed roll of parchment. "I don't know the contents of this letter, but our king affirmed; you must find a suitable bride."

"The devil take him!" Vlad tossed the words aside. "He can't move me like a pawn."

"He is our king. Read the missive and stop being so petulant."

The words damned Vlad as he spoke them. *"...The sole emperor of Byzantium says you've encountered the daughter of the Moldavian Prince Alexandru in Kraków. A far better choice of a wife than a boyar's bastard. Love is not for princes and kings! Surely, you must see the merit of proper marital alliances. Prince Alexandru is no longer in the sway of Poland's king. Perhaps he will serve me as a vassal and stop supporting the Hussites if you do as I ask. Wed the daughter and return for Our forgiveness at Buda."*

"You may not wish to hear, but he is not wrong," Fruzhin said. "Remember your greatest ambition. You'll need Zsigmond's support, but a father by marriage who can bolster your claim to the throne with troops would be a great boon too. You'll never rule your homeland without soldiers or mercenaries to aid the conquest."

Vlad cursed and flung the missive again. It ended up in the hall, next to a monk's feet, as he appeared in the doorway. He hesitated to speak.

"What is it?" Vlad demanded of him.

"You...you have more visitors, my prince. The Dowager Princess Ana-Călina and the boyar Vlậcsan await you at the gate."

Vlad took Fruzhin to meet his grandmother. He found his son with a shy grin on his cherubic face, partly hiding his small form behind the full skirt of Pahomie's monastic robe. The Wolf kneeled at the boy's feet. The Dowager looked down at them, her rheumy eyes and mouth beset with crinkles.

Sensing her turmoil, Vlad rushed to her side and gripped the desiccated flesh of her hand. Her fingers shook, thick cords strung across the palm he pressed.

"Your son is a delight." She peered at him while tears glided down her cheek. "I was thinking if only your mother could have seen him just one time before the end."

Vlad shuddered. Fruzhin gripped his shoulder as he bowed his head. Not his mother, too! Would everyone leave him behind?

Bewildered, he asked, "W-w-when did she die? How?"

"Two weeks ago, in her sleep," his grandmother replied. "The last name I heard on her quivering lips was yours. She loved all her children dearly, but she clung to your memory and prayed for you the most. My nephew Vlậcsan and I set out the day after her funeral to bring the news here."

Later, alone with the Dowager, Vlad relayed the contents of Zsigmond's missive.

"God works His will. There can be no future with the mother of your child." The Dowager sighed and palmed Vlad's bearded chin. "You know what you must do. Accept it and wed. Hold Călţuna of Hermannstadt in your heart if you can, but understand this: if she has already taken holy vows, even under duress, she must never forsake them. Her destiny lies along a separate path. A fate already written in the stars, as is yours."

The Dragon Rising

1427-1432

CHAPTER 22

River Princess

"No man ever steps in the same river twice, for it's not the same river and he's not the same man."-Heraclitus (535-circa 475 BC), Greek philosopher.

IN THE YEAR OF OUR Lord 1427. Tismana Monastery, Oltenia region, Principality of Wallachia (modern-day Tismana Monastery, western Romania), and *Suceava, Principality of Moldavia* (modern-day Suceava, north-eastern Romania)

Vlad composed a letter to Jadwiga that same night, trusting that even if the king of Poland or his wife intercepted the communication, they would not thwart his request. Then he stretched out on the bed, unable to sleep. He turned his head and studied the slumbering child beside him. Tiny fingers curled and clasped beneath his son's head. Would the boy ever understand the next steps his father must take?

Within the next two weeks, Vlad also shared farewells with his grandmother and Fruzhin the day before he prepared to leave the Tismana Monastery. Only Tobar and Yoska would accompany him on the journey northwest, bypassing Călţuna's former home of Hermannstadt on their way.

The next morning, he embraced his son and blessed him, kissed his yellow curls, and entrusted him to Pahomie's care.

"You must not worry, my prince," the monk said. "All my spiritual brothers here will care for your son and watch over him. We'll await your return."

"Thank you for your kindness today and for the past two years. I will write upon my arrival." Vlad forced each word from a burning, tightening throat. "Please read the letter to my son and let him know I love him dearly."

"He already understands your feelings, my prince, but I'll remind him."

Vlad nodded and turned away, shaking hands fisted at his sides.

"*Tată*?" His namesake called to him in a soft, plaintive voice.

"Fear not, child. Your father will come back and sing you to sleep at night again," Pahomie said. "You'll be safe with us until then. I promise."

With a nod to Tobar, who held the Carpathian pony's reins, Vlad mounted and led him and his twin brother away. The siblings rode behind him in silence.

"Merciful Father," Vlad whispered a prayer, breaking his long-standing pledge. "Don't forsake me and take me from him for too long. I'll return to worship and accept Your dictates without question until death if you'll only let me hold my son again."

"*Tată*. Come." His child's sweet tone tore at his heart. "*Tată*!"

Tears stung his eyes, and he sniffled, slowing the horse. But he neither dismounted nor looked over his shoulder. His chest hurt terribly; he could barely draw breath. Before his courage failed him entirely, he maneuvered through the opened gate.

"*Tată*!" The boy screamed. "Come!"

THE LAST TIME VLAD made this northbound journey, many things had been different. Back then, winter snow and hoarfrost covered the mountainous landscapes of Wallachia and Transilvania. Now the first buds of springtime flowers greeted him. Whereas he once traveled with sweet Arina and Marko the Gypsy, the man's grown sons accompanied him. Youthful hope for a life free from burdens at Argeş and Târgovişte faded with a man's grasp of how the winds of fate could alter.

Tempered by blood and battle, like his sword, Vlad no longer imagined reaching Moldavia would offer respite. The fourteen-year-old boy had become a man aged thirty-one. He wondered why fate drew him to the place he once sought in desperation.

Did Jadwiga fulfill his request to write to the House of Muşat at their capital in Suceava? Would Prince Alexandru the Good and his daughter Vasilisa Maria acknowledge Vlad's intent and receive him well? What might the pair think of his bold proposal to claim the hand of the Moldavian princess in marriage? Would she accept?

For every prospect of the future swirling in his mind, a castigation followed. What might Călţuna do when she discovered his union with another? Would she assume Vlad abandoned his vows of love, replacing them with lies? Would she fear he left their son in perpetuity, bereft of the care of both parents? Could she hate him almost as much as he despised himself for bowing to Zsigmond's will?

He emerged from rambling woodland tracts onto vibrant carpets of lavender and roses. He crossed the Transilvanian border into the upper country of northern Moldavia. The sun shimmered each day with hints of rain on the approaching horizon.

Dim bleakness ensnared his soul the closer the horse drew to his destination.

A winding river flowed past Suceava, surrounded by verdant greenery. Yet, he hesitated on the outskirts of the lush invitation the town offered. Surely, he would not be leaving everything behind that he cherished, especially his memories and hopes for a life with Călţuna and their boy, as he feared?

"No," he muttered. "I'll never give them up, no matter how my king compels me."

If the Gypsy brothers overheard him, neither said a word.

A wide moat below an earth mound and wooden palisade protected Suceava. Vlad entered the southern gate. The sentinels with their halberds at the hillock of the princely fortress accepted his answers to their brief inquiries. Almost as if they expected him. The gatekeeper sent a guard ahead with a written message. Mutual reliance on the Old Slavonic language, which Eastern Orthodox clergy used for centuries, long united the Wallachian and Moldavian people.

Vlad passed into the rounded courtyard of the prince's home and waited within the confines of yellowed stone. Sprawling trees towered above him. Scant sunlight in the early hours of morning revealed the bleary eyes of guards and servants. Besides Old Slavonic, he overheard the Moldavian native dialect, his Wallachian tongue, Hungarian, Polish, the Germanic language of the Saxons, and even Latin. There were also words he did not know and tradespeople with skin darker than Zawisza's countenance.

He studied his surroundings. Small windows interspersed along the walls of the prince's residence opened onto the area. Vlad wondered if his prospective bride hid behind some shutter, watching his arrival through the wooden slats.

From an arched gateway with the wooden door flung back on its hinges, Jadwiga rushed out at the head of six soldiers to greet him. He slid down from his mount's back, stunned by her presence as much as her effusive embrace. When he asked why she came to Suceava too, her giddy laughter puzzled him even more.

"Did you think I would entrust the important task you gave me to any messenger? Certainly not! I appealed to Father for more than a month. His anger with me relented, and he permitted me to travel here, although with the escort of his archbishop and several men-at-arms. His queen suggested I planned to escape to Germany to wed. As if I would heap shame on my father's head, as she's done."

"What are you saying?" Vlad spluttered, but she hushed him and took his arm.

"I'll tell you of the scandal my stepmother has caused in Kraków later. The prince of Moldavia knows of your coming and purpose. He will greet you this evening at a feast in your honor. The house the archbishop requisitioned has many rooms and it is within walking distance of the fortress. You're staying with me." She looked around, noticing the mounted Tobar and Yoska, who peered at her. "You and your companions."

Jadwiga and her protectors led them across cobblestones to the residence, which proved as accommodating as she promised. Its spacious kitchen had a brick stove. Although Vlad noticed the archbishop's scowl, likely at Jadwiga's perceived impertinence, the prelate offered a kind welcome. Vlad dispersed his men to find their preferred fare; roasted rabbits. Despite their scowling hesitation, he ordered them to see to their needs first rather than his protection. He would be safe with Jadwiga.

"I've already partaken of the morning meal," she said, "but the servants here will bring you something to eat, Vlad."

"I'm not hungry. We rode through the night. A bath and bed would be adequate."

"It shall be as you wish, my friend."

He took his leave of Jadwiga and the archbishop, grateful for the easy acceptance of the lie, and followed a housemaid to the room allocated for him. He was not tired or in need of a wash, having bathed in one of the cool river tributaries before fording the waterway. The dread suffusing his bones was too much for him.

Jadwiga had done all he asked. The Moldavian prince and presumably his daughter knew of his intent directly from the Polish princess. Now, he must convince Vasilisa Maria to marry him, but his courage failed. His heart rebelled against the act and would not let his mind form the words. What could he say to a woman whom he did not know or want?

Informed by Jadwiga's maid that she slept after midday, he found the archbishop and told him he would walk in the river's direction.

"You need not appear nervous, Prince Vlad. Surely, the Moldavian princess' father will accept your offer of marriage and bind the houses of Basarab and Muşat together."

Trying not to sneer at the presumptuous reply, Vlad abandoned the house. His Gypsy twins awaited him and followed from the yard at a short distance.

Vlad simmered inside. He was not anxious like some green boy, as the prelate imagined. But somehow, he needed clarity between him and the woman whose hand he must take. Whatever she imagined or expected or told Jadwiga, he and Vasilisa Maria were strangers and he loved someone else.

Strangers wed each other every day, but Vlad wanted Vasilisa Maria to hold no lofty expectations about their union.

"She should know the truth," he whispered. "Marriage should begin with honesty."

Moving beyond her father's stronghold, he toured the busy marketplace on the opposite street. Traders bartered mostly silk, pepper, and incense. Soon, he reached the riverbank. Earthen elements tinged his nostrils, the brine of algae clumps and the loamy scent of the land. He recalled the brackish taste of mossy water an hour before dawn.

Vessels with billowing sails plied the river headed northward, a sight long familiar to him after years in Buda. He followed the ships' progress until each of them disappeared.

Once, he looked over his shoulder, sighting the prince's home perched on a mound above the other residences. Turning again, he smiled as fowl rose from their hiding places among the thick reeds on the left bank and took flight. He traced their arc across a perfect blue sky. Hours passed in such idle contemplation.

When his stomach growled, he and his men found a waterfront tavern, which sold roasted meat, bread, and beer, but also something the owner called "Greek wine."

Vlad sipped and said to his companions, who grimaced at the taste, "Believe me, this bears no resemblance to the casks of dark-red alcohol the emperor once shared among Zsigmond's closest courtiers."

Some force pulled Vlad to the river again. A fine mist blew inland over the water. Jadwiga might be worried about him and, because of her kindness, he never wanted to cause her distress. Dinner preparation must be near completion at the princely fortress.

His mind had not settled on the words to inform the princess about the circumstances of his offer. After their initial meeting at the feast, would there be a chance for them to speak openly?

The sooner a marital compromise occurred, he could return to Buda and perhaps locate Călțuna. How or when she learned of his union with another woman could not be haphazard fortuity. He must tell her about it. The reason for it. As much as he felt inclined toward an honest beginning with Vasilisa Maria, he owed so much more to the lady who held his heart.

"*Domnule*," Tobar said from nearby, "We should return. Darkness approaches."

The sun began its slow descent, and the mist thickened, becoming fog. An unnatural quiet settled over the land. Absent breezes, sailors grabbed their ships' oars. Dew condensed and cooled Vlad's skin. Shafts of sunlight penetrated the vapor.

An olive-skinned woman came out of the murk. He could not see from afar. She appeared to glide through the grass, though he knew that could not be so. Around her shoulders and diminutive form, a black mantle fell, barely distinguishable from thick locks of raven-colored hair. With her female companion, she drew closer, her sea-green eyes offering a stoic gaze. She moved toward him until they stood a hand span apart. She stood even shorter than he did, the bride he came to Moldavia to claim.

"Prince Vlad of Wallachia." She acknowledged him with a deep curtsy.

Her low tone reminded him of an Italian term Pipó once used to describe János' voice after Vlad first introduced the pair. *Sotto voce* in its quiet pleasantness.

He wanted to ask if the princess remembered their first brief encounter, but as he opened his mouth, no sound came out. When she peered up at him, he experienced the strangest sensation of falling into deep water. He imagined drowning in its wild vastness, although he could swim well.

"At last, you've come to us." She spoke again. "As I knew you must."

"Princess." The tremulous tone of the woman behind her carried a hint of warning.

He blinked and gasped while the shouts of several men intruded on the interlude. They pushed and shoved others, half a score by his count, burdened with short manacles and chains around their wrists and ankles. Hanks of dusty hair sprouted in all directions on the prisoners' heads. Two oared boats bobbed onto which their captors herded them.

"*Tătărași*," the woman before him breathed. "Mongol slaves bound for sale. Their ancestors almost brought mine to the brink of ruin."

Their plight reminded Vlad that, although he respected his Gypsies and treated them well, by Wallachian law, their legal status remained no different. He could not alter their condition until he ruled Wallachia. An impossible task without Zsigmond.

"You'll discover," the princess said with a nod to his men at a scant length away, "we have a few Gypsy slaves here." While he pondered how she could know he considered them, she turned aside and gestured to her companion. "This is Ruxandra Lupu, my former nurse who remained with me after my mother's death."

Both must have thought him a simpleton. He still had not found his voice. But he offered a nod of greeting to Ruxandra and forced himself to utter, "And you're Vasilisa Maria, daughter of Prince Alexandru the Good, whom I first saw in Kraków."

"When you mistook me for the groom before you came to court me as your bride." She gave a slow smile even as warmth crept up his cheeks and his stare lingered on her curved lips. "There is no doubt we will marry. I have foreseen our union."

"Princess Cneajna." The other female again warned, "Please."

Her former charge glanced at her before saying, "You are right, my prince. I am the daughter of Alexandru, but now, I only answer to the name Ruxandra called me."

Recovered from his embarrassment, he asked, "May I know why?"

"You may, but I'll explain another time if it pleases you," she replied, hastening ahead of him. "There's rain on the wind. We must hurry to the fortress."

"Rain? Princess, the sky is still lit...." His voice dwindled as the first fat droplet splattered on his bare head. Followed by more, which fast became a heavy downpour.

He raced with her ahead of their servants up the sloping land. The deluge stung like a thousand prick points. He pointed to the overhang outside an inn, but she moved on despite how the rain doused them. Clothes clung sopping wet and weighed down Vlad. He reached the northern gate before Cneajna did, ushering her and their retainers beneath an archway, where a few guards also huddled.

"We must hurry and change our garments so as not to be late for the evening feast." Although drenched, Cneajna trilled a soft laugh as she looked up at him. "Jadwiga told me you would be her guest at a nobleman's house nearby."

"I am." He palmed back his chin-length hair. A clotted hank rolled and slapped against his temple.

She giggled again, revealing a gap between her front teeth he had never noticed in Poland. Her mouth enticed him. She possessed beauty. He could not deny it even if he tried. Though nothing like Călţuna's fair, golden-locked appearance. Cneajna's eyes and the shade of her hair, her oval face with ample, dimpled cheeks, and her fleshy lips would serve as reminders of the woman he should have claimed for a wife instead. Of the love lost to him in service to his king's commands.

So why the strange impulse to kiss Cneajna and the certainty that if he did, even with spectators, she would not stop him? Was his sentiment only lustful desire?

"You should hurry to the house, Prince Vlad," she said.

"I will go," he replied. "Until we dine, Princess Vasilisa...Princess Cneajna."

She darted through the fog and rain. After a quick curtsy to him, her companion followed. Vlad stared in the direction they went, rooted to the spot for several breaths before he left, too. His thoughts remained focused on the strange princess.

AN HOUR LATER, VLAD waited outside a cavernous, barrel-vaulted, bricked room from which the murmurs of dozens of voices emanated. The herald at the wide doorway had presented a Roman bishop and two cousins of the ruling prince in the wake of Vlad's arrival. Jadwiga had left the rented residence earlier and promised to await him here. Now she stood with the princely family and gave him an encouraging wink. He could not help but smile at her good nature.

"Prince Vlad of Wallachia, son of Prince Mircea of the House of Basarab!"

He stared straight ahead at the announcement of his name. Three plain wooden stairs led up to the ruling prince's throne, with its ornate legs affixed to the uppermost step. Here sat a thick-bearded Prince Alexandru the Good in finer clothes than Vlad recalled in Kraków; a red damask robe and leather shoes with gold bells at the ends of the lacing. Everyone else stood in half-circles on either side of the ruling prince, including Cneajna.

Clad in an indigo-colored dress made of wool and belted underneath her bosom, three pink pearls buttoned the garment up to the turned-down collar. The same small baubles ringed her neck. As an unmarried woman like Jadwiga, no material covered her hair. The length of a single, thick braid curled around one rounded shoulder and fell almost to Cneajna's hip.

She kept a demure gaze on the floor, so unlike earlier, when her stare met his with bold questions in their murky depths.

Before he bowed in deference to her father, Vlad removed his hat with its felt crown and fur brim. For the presentation, he donned a bag-sleeved brocaded robe as black as his and Cneajna's hair. He paired his outermost attire with ankle-length boots of red leather. His narrow belt, with a leather purse tucked under it, cinched the voluminous cloth around his waist. His fingers twitched, but he gripped the hat brim in both hands, rather than pulling at his high, tight collar.

Alexandru welcomed him and introduced three of his sons Iliaş, Ştefan who the family called Stetco, and Petru. The eldest, Iliaş, held the hand of a woman who resembled the young Polish queen. A yellow-haired babe perched on her hip reminded Vlad of his namesake son. How he missed him! Tomorrow, he must write to Pahomie.

The Moldavian prince beckoned him closer. "Greet my honored daughter as well."

At a gesture from her father, she curtsied and might have looked up, except Vlad noted the slight tug of her elbow from the woman Ruxandra beside her.

He and the ruler of the country exchanged pleasantries and gifts. Vlad received fine bolts of Italian silk and furs claimed from Mongol traders. In return, he offered brocaded fabrics from Hungary and a small chest of silver coins out of his personal funds. Other presents remained; the bride price, intended for Cneajna's father once the marital contract concluded, and personal items she alone would claim as the morning gift after the consummation.

Servants took the items away, while Alexandru assured Vlad they would be accounted for and remain safe before leading him to dinner.

THE REST OF SPRING in Suceava passed in much the same way for Vlad, with evening feasts and nightly revelries. He noted a few of Cneajna's preferences. She never tasted meats or fish before having her fill of pottage, nor sampled pastries and pies until she finished the roasted, fried, or boiled fare. She ate with gusto, unlike the habits of the courtly women he previously observed.

His appetite was likewise well-satisfied each night. In sleep, he often dreamed of Călţuna. But over time, sea-green eyes replaced her emerald-tinged ones. In the aftermath of such imaginings, he woke in a cold sweat, his mouth sour with the aftertaste of wine. A deep longing knifed his heart as if some blade had sliced it in two.

The nuptial negotiations began. Alexandru offered a generous dowry on Cneajna's behalf. He would surrender not only coin. Vlad could also claim rights to the rich Danubian port city, Kilia, which Wallachians and Moldavians knew by its original Greek name, 'the mouth of the wolf.'

Cneajna's father also pressed for the same concession of some piece of Wallachian land, which he must have known Vlad could not give. He wondered whether Alexandru guessed at his ambitions.

"I am not the ruling prince of my birthplace! I cannot promise what I do not have. Good Alexandru, I can offer your daughter a comfortable life, with all the honor owed to her as my wife. She will lack for nothing."

Vlad concluded a contentious session with her father, tilted his head, and left to join Cneajna with her constant companion Ruxandra, in the adjacent garden.

He would part with a third of his monies toward the entirety of his bride's dower. The rest belonged to the future; for the expenses of armor, weapons, and his personal livelihood. He could sell the rented house in Buda and grant the proceeds to Cneajna, but always, her father wanted more.

He halted in the passageway leading outdoors. The lie bedeviled him. Cneajna would want more in their union too; his love. He found her picking wildflowers.

"You asked about my name, my prince, when we informally met. Some years ago, a Bosnian lord wished to wed me—"

"If you'll forgive the interruption, he was Serbian." From behind Vlad, Ruxandra corrected Cneajna. "In his land, the rulers of small domains prefer the royal title of *knez*."

Vlad nodded, recalling it as the title Fruzhin's uncle Stefan Lazarević inherited before Constantinople's emperor named him *Despoteses*.

Cneajna stopped and inhaled the unfurled buds before she frowned and asked, "He was from Serbia? Truly?"

"Yes, my princess," Ruxandra replied, her nut-brown brows knitting together. She clenched her fingers around the handle of a willow basket, her frown revealing some exasperation. As if her mistress should have remembered the details.

"Oh. As you say, my dear Ruxandra." Cneajna's mouth twitched.

Although Vlad suspected she perfectly recalled the nationality of her former suitor, he dared not say so.

"I thought well enough of that prince, though not as a marital partner," she said while strolling ahead of him, still gathering her blossoms. "He went away after my initial refusal, delivered by Father, but came again with friends almost a year later. As if he forgot the initial pursuit."

Vlad doubted that. No one could forget Cneajna after having met her.

She continued, "When passing through the hallway just inside, someone in his retinue asked him my name. The prince replied, 'Marina or Maria. Who cares? She's just some *kneaghina*—some *knez*'s daughter.' I dismissed him again, in person, but kept the Moldavian variant of what he called me. Cneajna. So, I would never forget how suitors might view me. As a princess of no value other than an alliance with my father."

The very purpose for which his king sent Vlad to marry her. She represented a means to an end for him; the discovery of Călţuna. He chided himself. How could he tell her so? Wasn't that far worse than what Zsigmond wanted from her parent?

"You won't be like my supposed admirers in the past." She halted and turned to him. "No, you will love me until the end of time, as I will love you."

"Cneajna, that's enough!" Ruxandra stiffened. "Would you frighten Prince Vlad away with such talk?"

"Princess, why do you say things like that?" At a loss, he traded stares between her and Ruxandra before he asked Cneajna, "How can you speak of dreams and our fate when we barely know each other? You told Jadwiga about me before we ever met in Kraków. Now, you say we will love each other. When I am already in love with someone else! I have a child with her. Understand; I wed only at my king's command."

He never meant such a blunt revelation of the circumstances to come out. The strangeness of her implications left him overwrought. As if she imagined he would abandon Călţuna completely in his quest to fulfill a royal demand.

But Cneajna did not deserve his choler. She could not help being someone else other than the woman he loved. He readied an apology and explanation.

Her warm touch forestalled him. The soft pads of her fingertips trailed over his bearded cheek until she cupped his chin.

"One day, you will put aside the past. Banish the sadness I often glimpse in your eyes when you think of your woman and don't realize I'm looking. I know you, as I know the darkest streets of my Suceava birthplace. As I understand the pathways of my heart."

She spoke with such conviction that he could almost believe her.

She added, "Your image first came to me in dreams, months before my father took us to Kraków. I saw this aquiline nose our sons and daughters will have, along with your oval eyes of agate. All will inherit those eyes except one of our children; the fearsome dragon-bane of the Turks. For now, you love another woman and I accept that. But you'll also love me. Don't you think the heart is large enough?"

He could not answer. Even after she smiled in that strange way, as if she comprehended truths which he could only guess. So capable and confident.

Her stroll in the garden resumed. She picked wildflowers until she carried an armful of them.

"Please, my prince. I beg you, don't condemn her as possessed by evil *strigoi* or those in league with the unholy deceiver and thief of men's souls," Ruxandra said. "She is neither. She is a good Catholic, raised so in secret by her Polish mother. Cneajna says her *Pater Noster* every night before going to bed. Her mother was like this. Both blessed and cursed with a strange foreknowledge of what will come. And it always comes. Don't withdraw your proposal. Marry her. Treasure her."

Ruxandra curtsied and rejoined her mistress to offer the woven basket, leaving Vlad still speechless.

HE PONDERED CNEAJNA'S peculiarities while Jadwiga dined with him alone in the evening. No dinner invitation to the palace came for them.

"It's just as well," she said, "for we could never discuss matters in front of the wife of Prince Iliaş. She is my stepmother's younger sibling and Cneajna's sister by marriage. My father wed his queen, hoping the nuptials of the old and young could bring forth many children. The union has brought him naught but grief and shame."

Vlad asked her how.

"A frail little prince born to supplant me and one dead son was bad enough. The doctor Cneajna sent to Kraków would've breathed life into him, but the queen wouldn't let him. She's pregnant again, but also faces accusations of adultery leveled against her this spring season before I left Kraków."

Jadwiga delved into the details, but Vlad paid scant attention. The conversation brought him back seven years to the accusations against Queen Borbála. Despite his personal sentiments about her, he thought her no more deserving of censure than her husband with his many adulterous affairs. Other women Vlad knew suffered in the marriage, too. His mother, his sister Arina, and Fruzhin's aunt Milena Olivera. Would Cneajna also endure a miserable marital life while knowing Vlad loved another?

"Are you even listening to me?" A hard thump on his arm from Jadwiga scattered those thoughts. She glared at him.

He confessed his rambling worries. Afterward, her visage softened.

"If you believe you cannot love my friend because of your lady Călţuna, can you at least promise to be kind to Cneajna?"

"She deserves more than that," he admitted. "My grandmother advised the union, and despite my misgivings, I know she guides me well. Cneajna shouldn't give her heart to me. She shouldn't hope for more than duty in our marriage. Forgive me, but I don't love her, and I never may. Yet, if ever my actions caused her pain, I'd hate myself."

"Tell her in those exact words! She will understand your feelings and decide whether to accept you."

He did so the next morning, in the garden where they had met the day before. Cneajna left him and Ruxandra outside and entered the room where her father sat daily for his negotiations with Vlad.

"Bargain for my dower, my dearest parent." Through the opened window overlooking the garden, her next words drifted to Vlad. "Say you do it solely for my security. But if you cherish me as I know you do, you won't delay the proclamation of my marriage. Vlad has treated me with more courtesy and candor than any other who's come to Suceava, seeking my hand. I will have him as my sole husband."

THE NUPTIAL CONTRACT was sealed with Vlad's offer of a chest of white pearls, amber, and uncut sapphires and opals his grandmother gifted him at Tismana Monastery. The banns appeared on the church doors. He and Cneajna's marriage took place two weeks later. Summer sun streaked into the Catholic church next to the princely fortress.

Cneajna's brothers, along with Jadwiga and Ruxandra attended the wedding ceremony. Alexandru escorted his daughter to the ceremony, but as an Orthodox Christian, he declined to take part in the mass of Catholic rites.

If he gave any thought to the manner of celebration, he must have assumed Vlad merely gave in to Cneajna's wishes. Few, if anyone, outside Hungary, knew about his hasty, and perhaps foolish, conversion to Catholicism. He intended to keep it so for the sake of his quest to rule Wallachia.

Afterward, a raucous feast occurred, lasting for hours. Vlad tapped his fingertips atop the table with impatience. The bedding ceremony approached. He detested the anticipation coursing through him.

Despite his insistent efforts to keep Jadwiga out of the bridal chamber during the ceremony, she took part in unlacing his linen undershirt.

"I remain an unmarried virgin, as you rightly say," she whispered to him, "but I'm no prude. I had kissed and fondled my betrothed before he fled Poland for Germany."

When Vlad scowled at her, she giggled and pulled off the undershirt. "You're just as I imagined an over-protective older brother might be."

Stripped naked, Vlad and Cneajna drew back the white cotton coverlet and settled beneath it on the mattress. The Polish archbishop blessed the marital bed and sprinkled holy oil before Ruxandra whispered in her mistress' ear. Alexandru ushered every person from the room. He smiled at his daughter and pulled the door closed behind him.

"Shall we move a chest there and prevent anyone from coming back in soon?" Cneajna asked. "You know they'll try before Ruxandra must retrieve the bridal sheet."

"You're right, of course." Vlad got up. Although aware his new wife would get more than an eyeful of his battle-scarred body, the movement gave him something to do with his hands that itched to hold her.

He had longed to cover Cneajna's lush mouth with ardent kisses for almost three months. As much as he did not care for Cneajna in the way she wanted him to, a man of flesh and bone could not deny her bounteous beauty. So unlike Călțuna's lithe form.

When he turned again, his bride waited with the coverlet fallen below the curves of her waist. His gaze alighted on the apple-round breasts, ampler than Călțuna's own. Why couldn't this be their wedding night? But it was too late.

While he approached their marital bed again, Cneajna's stare drifted down the length of him and widened. She swallowed and met his regard. A virgin's nervousness was reflected in her wary gaze. Her olive skin glowed, not florid, like his recollections of his lover. He meant the words of his wedding vows, but shame filled him at the thought of wanting Cneajna when he loved another and always would.

"Come, sit." His bride held out her hands. "Let's talk before we fulfill our duty."

"Duty?" He dared not touch her. He stared in wonderment instead. An impossibly lovely woman with bountiful curves.

"To consummate the marriage," she said. "Father told me. Our union does not require love, but we must seal it. Does the sight of me satisfy you, Vlad?"

"Yes!" He gushed. "A blind man would judge you completely perfect." He sat and pulled the coverlet over him. "I will do my...duty, Cneajna." Even if he did not love her, he craved her with every passing moment.

"I want to see all of you and have you look at me. As God fashioned both of us."

He swallowed and nodded, never more self-conscious than even when he clumsily bedded that kitchen maid back in Târgoviște two decades ago.

Cneajna pushed the coverlet past his feet and settled her voluptuous form astride his thighs. Waves of inky hair spilled down her back, the curled tips grazing his skin. He realized he did not know her age and never asked it of her father or brothers.

There would be other, more important things to discover about this wife of his. The thought repeated. *His*. His river princess.

"You have many scars. Brutal memories must trouble you. In my arms, with my comfort, I hope you may forget them. May I touch you, Vlad?"

Mute, he only nodded. She could explore him as she wished, but he vowed to control his impulses, not wishing to frighten or rush her.

She trailed over the hairiness of his skin, vastly different from her smooth flesh, rubbed the calluses on his hands, and fingered the old wounds. She sighed, as if in compassion rather than disgust. He barely kept control of himself while his shapely new wife perused his naked form. Surely, she felt his arousal, seated as she was.

Cneajna grasped and brought his palms to her soft breasts. A jolt ran through him. He inhaled her lavender and cassia scent. Intoxicating.

"Vlad, this bosom is where I shall hold our children, nursing and comforting them myself. Beneath is the beating heart of a woman who can and will love you for all that you are and may ever be. Let me love you, husband."

CHAPTER 23

Confessions

"Love begins with a smile, grows with a kiss, and ends with a teardrop."-Augustine of Hippo (354-430 AD), Roman North African Christian theologian, philosopher, bishop, and Roman Catholic and Eastern Orthodox saint.

IN THE YEAR OF OUR Lord 1427. Suceava, Principality of Moldavia (modern-day Suceava, north-eastern Romania), *Segesvár, Transilvania* (modern-day Sighișoara, Romania), and *Buda, Hungary* (modern-day Budapest, Hungary)

Vlad did his duty to his new bride the morning after their wedding as well. In the dining hall, he stood between her and Ruxandra. He glared at the bloodied sheet stripped from their marital bed, hung on the adjacent wall like some vile tapestry. The evidence of her virtue and the consummation of their marriage.

"Does the custom displease you?" Cneajna asked.

"I accept it as a necessity," he muttered, "but I needed no proof of your virginity. You're not a woman to play a man false. That much is clear."

She cocked her head. "Then you believe I'm discomfited by the display, and that idea offends you for my sake?"

"It does," he acknowledged.

She beamed up at him, the image of serene joy. He scowled in response, not wishing her to believe he cared more than he did. Her smile did not ebb.

"You do not love me, but my feelings are of concern. Your estimation of me grows. That is a fine start to our happiness."

She clasped her hands in front of her. A shaft of light streaking through a window illuminated the simple gold band on her third finger, topped with a ruby like the gift he'd worn for years from Fruzhin.

"There's no embarrassment for me," she continued. "I am your wife. All Suceava must know the truth about it. If your king should ask, we may assure him our union is lawful, fulfilling the terms he required of you."

He gaped at her until his brow throbbed. Earlier, he had watched her in pleasant quietude for an hour, even after sunlight intruded through gaps in the window shutters. She snored lightly, her soft lips twitching in her sleep, hair askew on the pillow.

To his annoyance, he wanted her. She left him satiated the night before. What was the source of the attraction this strange woman willed upon him? It not only made a mockery of his devotion to Călțuna. He barely knew Cneajna. She stirred more than his desire. Something stimulated the urge to protect and comfort her. Had she bewitched him?

He dismissed the errant thought and tilted his head. "I must offer your morning gift. My Gypsies brought them at dawn." He waved to the table, beset with small chests.

She perused the contents of each wooden box. His grandmother sent him to Moldavia with all her heirlooms, the jewels he once foolishly tried stealing to secure a future for himself and his sister. Now they would belong to his bride for life.

Necklaces of cream-colored pearls and gold. Enameled or silver-gilt bracelets festooned with diamonds, opals, smoky quartz, and amethysts. Cneajna admired a gold-tasseled cloak clasp among other smaller pieces, mostly glass or carnelian brooches, before pulling out a pair of filigree earrings with star-shaped agate stones.

"Like your eyes," she murmured to him before turning to Ruxandra. "Hold on to these. I shall wear them every day."

Besides the promised third of the coin he possessed, he gave her twice the piles of fine cloth her father received, along with silk ribbons. High-quality woolens woven in a Flemish city called Ypres, beside glossy linen, and Italian brocade and velvet littered the tables beside the Mongol furs from Suceava's market. Some Hungarian sheepskin hats and cloaks arrived in the waning days of spring. An early, if not a presumptuous, wedding gift from Fruzhin.

Vlad huffed as she dallied. "There is one more chest, Cneajna."

She opened it and withdrew a document, reading in silence before she met his gaze again. "You are giving me the yearly rent from your house in Buda."

"I had contracted with a mercantile family for its use before leaving the city."

"The place where you lived with your lover," she murmured as she replaced the rolled-up paper and closed the chest. "I do not want the rent, Vlad."

"Why not?"

"It belongs to you."

"Not if I choose to give it away."

"I will not have it," she snapped. "You cannot make me accept!"

He shook his head. Where was the tractable woman whom he apparently imagined before making her his bride?

"This is part of your dower. Why are you rejecting the proceeds, Cneajna?"

"Of an abode where you shared a happy existence with your mistress?" She picked up the wooden box and shoved it into his grasp. "We are married, Vlad. She is your past. I am your future. How dare you believe I could ever want the money associated with your life at her side!"

She turned from him and left the dining hall. Ruxandra quickly curtsied to him and chased her fleeing mistress.

He slammed the chest on the table with such force, a servant girl who had entered then dropped her water bucket and rags. One look from him sent her scurrying away.

HE DID NOT SPEAK WITH his ungrateful wife for days, unable to fathom her fury or his resultant displeasure. They shared the same bed in her chamber every night. One of them always rolled away from the other, her typically. Until he could not stand the tension any further and stared at her ink-black strands.

"I know you're not sleeping. Your breathing deepens when you do." He sighed. "You knew I did not love you before we wedded. I've never concealed the truth. Why are you so angry with me when I've offered you all I possess?"

"I do not want the remnants of your life with your mistress!" She turned and glared at him. "Why do you struggle to understand? Did I mistake your ability to reason?"

"You dare question it now? Lower your voice before you speak to me again!" He rose beside her. "I am your husband, and you will honor and respect me. Would you have your father and brothers overhear us from their quarters? Or your constant companion sleeping just outside our door?"

"I am your lawful wife and did not choose to begin our marriage with an insult." She raised her chin. "No matter my visions of our fates, I'm aware of your sentiments now. But clearly, you do not know mine!"

"Then tell me, Cneajna!" He raked his fingers through his hair. "We are still strangers. How can I know your feelings unless you speak about them in full?"

She pushed aside the cotton coverlet and swung her legs off the mattress. Although she said nothing, he joined her on the side of the bed. She bent forward, thick strands spilling over her face and shoulder, hiding his grandmother's earrings. Cneajna's earrings, he corrected himself, while pushing aside her hair.

The light of a low-burning candle in a wall bracket revealed the sparkle of her tears, and the wetness on her cheeks.

"Please, don't cry." Taken aback, he swallowed hard and caressed her chin.

"It's only done when I'm frustrated and any hindrance overwhelms me." She pulled away from him and swiped at her face. "Your mistress can never bother me. But your insistence on offering the rent from your life with her does."

Despite her answer, his uncertainties, and the little he knew about her, he accepted one truth already. Her tears would always unman him.

"I never meant to wrong you with the suggestion," he whispered. "You must believe me." When she hesitated, he leaned closer. "Please, Cneajna."

"I've accepted the truth. Your woman holds a place in your heart. You have a son by her. Had you never told me about your life in Buda, the monies would be no concern."

Her rigid tone and unyielding posture amplified his vexation. Still, he listened.

"I know about her now. Must I allow the specter of her former place at your side to taint us by accepting the rent from the home where you two shared a life? Shall I take from your past to build our new beginnings? No. You were thoughtless to suggest it."

He bowed his head. Where he believed himself exceedingly generous, now her heart's injury made him recognize his folly.

"I'm sorry, Cneajna. You are right. I should have reconsidered the gift. Your father wanted so much for you...." He trailed off as her glare creased the skin between her thick, dark brows. "It's not an excuse. I gave you every possession of mine because I cannot offer what you deserve most of all."

Her gaze softened, and she fondled his bearded chin. "You will."

"You believe so." His sigh filled the room. "I wish your certainty could be mine."

Her fingers slid away. "Until you reconcile past and future, you'll never be at peace and assured of our love. Have you written to your king and your son about our marriage as you intended?"

"No, because I've spent the last few days annoyed with you."

While the tinkling melody of her laughter echoed, the last remnant of his irritation abated. He grazed a thumb over her lip, desiring her again. This terrible wanting overcame him whenever she was near, even in his earlier vexation.

"You should compose your letters." She drew back and stretched out on the bed. "Dawn will come in a few hours. A messenger can take your words to the recipients."

"I regret our quarrel and would make amends to you first." He caressed her wide hip, fingers clenched in the thin cotton cloth covering her skin. After their wedding night, she no longer slept naked although he did.

"Show me the proof of your regret," she said. As he loomed over her, she rolled her head away from him on the pillow and added, "After I've rested until morning."

He stared in disbelief as she closed her eyes. Her faint smile curved plump lips.

A low chuckle filled his throat before he rose from the bed and retrieved the writing materials. He sat on the floor with them. After he removed the wooden cork from the ink bottle, he regarded his slumbering wife again.

An admirable woman. Quiet and tender by nature, but with unpredictable mettle and fierceness. Though he could never imagine their destiny as she foresaw it, he already knew life would never be dreary at her side.

SEVEN WEEKS AFTER VLAD dispatched announcements of his marriage, carried to Buda Castle, Tismana Monastery, and the Princely Court of Târgoviște, Vlad stood with Cneajna next to a small waiting carriage. She embraced Jadwiga.

"One of the truest friends we could ever have," Cneajna said as the women drew apart. "If only there could be a marriage for you as well."

"Father is in no hurry to find another man seeking to claim the Polish crown through me," Jadwiga replied. "He wrote to the archbishop, mentioning some marital offer from the king of Cyprus' son. As if I would wed any other than my betrothed."

"Jadwiga, don't be stubborn," Vlad pleaded. "Learn my lesson. It's hard to thwart a monarch's will. Even unwise."

"I'll die before submitting." When he gasped, she rushed on. "But don't worry about my plight. Be well and happy together. Write to me in Kraków after you've reached Buda Castle." She gripped their hands. The couple exchanged the kiss of peace with her before Jadwiga left them.

Vlad held out his palm to Cneajna. "May I help you into the carriage?"

"As if I am a weakling woman?" She snorted and clambered up on a footstool, seating herself inside the vehicle.

He sighed and closed the door. Six guardsmen from Suceava would accompany them on the journey, protecting the carriage's occupants and their valuables, loaded into the wagon where Ruxandra rode. Before they set out, Vlad spoke with Tobar at the head of their party and Yoska at the rear, leading the mount Vlad brought into Suceava.

On the westerly route through Moldavia's autumnal forests and Transilvanian passes where early snowfall occurred, Cneajna grew irritable, especially if it also rained. She complained about every rut in the road and gripped the seat each time the wheels bumped against some stone or fallen branch.

Vlad soon relished stops along the journey, not only for the crisp air outside the carriage. His bride became more mercurial daily. He could not fathom her shifting moods.

While considering her one morning, he laughed at himself. His mother, Staico, Fruzhin, and Pipó bore his ill humor throughout the years. Did they find themselves equally frustrated? Only one among them remained to whom he might introduce Cneajna.

Would Fruzhin like her as much as he once favored Călţuna? Vlad hoped so, never doubting Cneajna would strive to make a favorable impression even in her ever-changing state. His best friend's good opinion of her mattered.

"Are you laughing at me?" His wife's glower fell on him.

"Never," he vowed. "I would not."

"I'm hungry," she grumbled, scratching at her belly.

"We have some dried meats in the wagon until we rest at an inn for the night."

"I don't want that! I need real food."

He sighed and yelled for the carriage driver to stop. Hopping down, he looked along the length of the forest track, carpeted in gold and russet-colored leaves. He crushed the dried layers of them under his boots as he approached a waiting Tobar.

"Would that the rains never prevailed on the Transilvanian roads into Bistritz. Then we would be well north of here and closer to our destination. Do you know where we are? Cneajna's hungry."

A noisy squirrel interrupted them. It chirped and scrabbled up a tree trunk before Tobar replied, "I think we're close to the small town of Segesvár, *Domnule*. The sun will be high after we arrive."

"Good. We'll rest there for the day."

He returned to the carriage and would have entered, but Cneajna scowled at him. "I want Ruxandra."

"We hardly have room for us," he said.

Her gaze narrowed. "Fetch Ruxandra! It's a fine day and you may ride your horse."

Heaving a sigh, he bowed. Their journey soon resumed with him at Yoska's side.

"If you ever consider the absence of a wife or an opportunity for marriage to be a loss, don't," he advised the Gypsy.

"I will not marry, *Domnule*," Yoska said.

"Why do you say so? Tobar discovered Dika in Hungary."

"I've already found the one I wanted after we first left Wallachia for Hungary in your youth. The girl whose mother tended my wound at Hunyadvár." Yoska fingered the clean linen wrapped around his head, covering the empty eye socket. "When you brought your woman there after taking her from Hermannstadt, I looked for the girl again. Grown and widowed with three sons. She knew me, but as before, she didn't want to go far from her mother or family in Transilvania. And I would never leave your service, *Domnule*. I am Yoska One-Eye. This is my life. I'm contented."

Vlad could not respond at first. Even to the most words Tobar's twin ever uttered in a lifetime of his knowledge of both men.

After some time, he clapped his faithful protector's shoulder. "I swear once my plans for Wallachia come to fruition and I rule there; you, your brother, and all the Gypsies serving me in Tismana village will be free."

"It is enough that you honor us with your trust, *Domnule.* We Roma have shed blood and would give our lives for you because you are worthy."

Resuming the journey through forestland, they emerged outside gray walls where ivy grew in abundance on the muddy banks of the Târnava Mare River. Narrow, winding cobblestone streets of Segesvár's old town greeted them. As did a few wary denizens, most of whom spoke the German of the Saxon people.

Vlad's thoughts flitted to Hermannstadt, sixteen leagues and a day's ride further southwest, and another two days in good weather on to Tismana Monastery. He longed for a glimpse of his son. Even the boy must wait upon Zsigmond's whim, no matter how Vlad resented it.

Cneajna shouted for him. He called for a halt and rushed to the carriage.

Ruxandra flung open the door. "My mistress is weak and needs nourishment."

He hastened for a nearby tavern, and despite the overflowing crowd, soon brought warm bread, cheese with a little mold, and three sweet, small cakes to his wife.

"Not so fast," he chided, as she crammed the first of the confections in her mouth.

She did not regard him, only asked, "No ale?"

Growling low in his throat, he returned to the establishment. He reached the carriage in time to find Cneajna on her knees through the doorway, heaving food onto the cobblestones. Behind her, Ruxandra bore her up around the waist.

The ale jug fell from Vlad's grip, clattered, and broke on the ground, pottery shards scattered. "Cneajna! What afflicts you so?"

"Nothing but your child!" Afterward, she retched again.

He staggered backward, his fingers faltering and failing in the quest for the carriage door. Tobar and Yoska jumped down from their horses and joined him.

"My child?" Vlad repeated.

With a nod, Ruxandra said, "Her mother was...also difficult in the early days, as I recall them. The first sign of pregnancy, followed by...this." She waved a hand at the undigested meal splattered on the road.

"She wasn't difficult, nor am I! Heaven, help me. I'm dying." Cneajna groaned.

"No, princess, you will not die," her companion said. "You have your mother's ways and by the grace of our Lord, her ample hips. You'll survive this child of your prince."

In the old town's central square, a room at an inn offered them relief and meager comfort. Vlad kneeled at Cneajna's side and held her hand, gazing up at her. She sat on a low chair and ate the bread but ordered Ruxandra to take the cheese out of sight.

"I swear, I can still smell it," Cneajna muttered afterward before meeting Vlad's stare. "Can you forgive my loathsome behavior of these last days?"

If she truly carried another babe of his and would be well, he could absolve her of anything. But he did not say so.

She palmed his forehead. "Won't this frown ever fade?"

"I'm worried about you," he acknowledged.

"Were you as concerned about your mistress while she carried your firstborn?"

"She endured no early illness. Are you sure I shouldn't fetch a midwife?"

"I only need Ruxandra, Vlad." Her low laughter did not soothe him.

"Eat some more bread, while I send one of my Gypsies for tarts or pies."

"No, Vlad, no more sweet foods. Bread like this for a start. Ruxandra and I will determine the rest while you go on to Buda and receive your king's forgiveness. Discover where he has sent your lady love."

"What?" He gaped up at her.

"Ruxandra advises rest. I agree with her." She smoothed her fingertips across his brow and leaned forward, landing a soft kiss there. "Less jostling about in the carriage for a time would do me well. But you can't linger in Segesvár, not after King Zsigmond called you to Buda a month ago. My father's guards will protect me."

"I'm not leaving you behind!" The suggestion made him bridle. How could she think he would abandon her now?

"Dearest Vlad." She favored him with the gap-toothed grin he grew accustomed to during his time in Suceava. "Have you grown to care a little for me, or is this a father's concern for his future babe? I can promise, the birth is several months away. Surely, we shall reunite in Buda long before then. Afterward, we will hold our son."

"Our son?"

"He'll be a fighter. Fierce as his father in battle."

Her words, although strange, also tugged at Vlad's heart. He groaned. "How can you know these things, Cneajna, about a child we've never seen?"

"I dreamed about him the night after we left Suceava. I feel him inside me."

"So soon?" He did not recall Călțuna saying so when she carried their firstborn.

"In the way only I can," Cneajna whispered. "He doesn't move, but I know he's there. Thriving. You'll name him for your father, one of his warrior grandfathers."

Scoffing at the suggestion, he tugged her hand. "Please, never repeat the claims from your dreams in front of anyone else you'll eventually encounter at court in Buda, lest they think you're a witch or worse. Superstitions and the Orthodox faith rule this region, and you cannot endanger yourself ever."

"I'll share my dreams only with you, even if you don't understand them. Your concern that I might bring harm to myself is not the only reason you advise caution."

"You are correct. Fate; the will of destiny is often an excuse for inaction. A person must rise to every challenge, no matter how daunting or foolish it may seem to others."

"And you've lived this way?"

"Or tried to. I don't fear the future overmuch, but I'd like to know that any child of mine may be safe and well in it. Beside his mother."

"Can we agree we may part in this town, so I might rest?"

"I don't want to leave you. Not solely because of our baby. I care about your health and safety, Cneajna, but your happiness matters too." He framed her face between his hands and kissed her hard, hoping she would accept his true sentiments.

She laughed into his mouth. "Worry not about my feelings in your quest. I'll wait for you always, secure in the belief that we will love for a lifetime." She raised her head and nuzzled his nose. "Find the answers you seek. Go to your king. He needs you too."

Twice he turned in the night and draped a possessive arm over her waist. Both times she remained awake, trilling a soft song. Her voice lulled him back to sleep. He mumbled a question, wanting to know if she sang for him or their baby.

"Both, my dearest," she whispered in his ear before he drifted off again.

In the morning, he peered at the shuttered window of the inn from horseback, hoping Cneajna slept peaceably in the room at last. Although loath to depart from her, he must. Tobar and Yoska awaited him in watchful silence atop their mounts.

"Protect her, Lord God, and our babe growing inside of her." He prayed for only the second time in two years. "Allow me to return to them soon."

Vlad rode northwestward across Transilvania. He thought of his times there; the initial encounter with spirited Călțuna, finding her again and stealing away with her to Hunyadvár. His later life, among the monks of Tismana Monastery. Sitting with the Gypsies at night around their campfires with his son on his lap, listening to their songs.

His entry into Moldavia, twenty-one years after he first attempted the journey, brought him full circle. He had gained a wife who grew more tolerable every day. In Suceava, its people hailed him as a son of Mircea the Great, a stalwart defender of his country against the Turks, and acclaimed Vlad as the husband of their cherished princess.

Yet, throughout the return to Hungary, Vlad also pondered who he was. Something Călţuna had asked him at their initial meeting in his vain, disdainful youth. A hereditary prince of Wallachia, a son, and a brother. One Christian knight among the Hungarian king's vast army, a battler, and a brutal killer. A tender lover, a devoted father, and a husband now. All parts making up the whole of him.

"Which one will determine my destiny?"

He had never envisaged a home at Tismana Monastery or considered taking holy orders. He would have made a mockery of such sacred vows with the blood of so many dead tainting his hands, using the act solely to escape Zsigmond's decree. The sheltered lives the monks led could not have provided him with a comfortable abode. He'd lodged in Moldavia solely to secure a wife, not intending to remain or return.

Now the familiar hills and grassy plains around Buda greeted him. The wind tugged at the autumn trees and scattered their leaves. Cream-colored sheep bleated and grazed on green fronds while a shepherd kept watch under the noonday skies.

Vlad no longer felt at home here, either. Three years away from the Hungarian capital robbed him of the comfort he had previously found.

He hoped Fruzhin noticed none of his inner turmoil. They shared a hearty embrace in the quadrangle outside the much-altered great keep of István's Tower.

"At last, you've come, but without a pretty princess on your arm." Fruzhin clapped his back hard. "Where is she?"

"I left Cneajna at Segesvár in Transilvania. She is ill."

"Oh? Sick of being married to you already?" Fruzhin teased.

Vlad revealed, "The babe growing inside her body has afflicted her."

"You work fast." His best friend guffawed and hugged him once more.

"The news of my impending fatherhood must please Zsigmond once he hears of it. I've told you because we are blood brothers for life. But it's early and no one else can know, not until Cneajna's pregnancy is further along."

"I understand. You keep saying that name, but I thought in your announcement of the marriage, you called her Princess Vasilisa Maria. Which confused me at first, for our king thought your bride bore the name Marina. His confessor had assumed you meant to marry the Polish heiress instead, although I don't know why."

"I didn't miss the gossip here. Or the spies our king employs in other courts." With a wave to his Gypsies and a tug on Fruzhin's arm, Vlad led him inside the castle's confines.

Courtiers, knights, men-at-arms, and servants gaped at Vlad, who mostly ignored their startled gasps. "Have you heard about János in Serbia? Does he fare well at the side of your uncle Stefan? What about him and your aunt, Princess Milena Olivera?"

"Stefan's dead." Fruzhin halted next to him in the passageway outside the enlarged ceremonial chamber. "My aunt grieves him daily. He died at the height of summer within days of your wedding. My cousin Đurađ Branković rules in his stead now, after Zsigmond duly invested him with the crown."

"I'm sorry. Why didn't you write to me?" Vlad stood stunned by the sudden shock.

"I could not disturb you at your time of marital happiness. I was not with my uncle or here when he perished. The last campaign occupied me instead."

"Against the Bohemians?"

"No, our eternal foes. Raids along the Danube River on the Turkish-held, former Bulgarian cities of Vidin, Oryahovo, and Silistra. I learned your people call the latter Dârstor. Dan Dăneşti told me once we launched our attack there."

"You fought at the side of my cousin the Wallachian usurper?" Vlad shook his head and pulled back from his best friend.

"I drew my sword as our king willed it. No different from in Bohemia." Fruzhin pushed aside a graying forelock of hair. "Zsigmond's eager to meet your Moldavian princess and assess the prospect of an alliance with her father."

"I didn't return to discuss that matter alone. I hoped, if our sovereign has forgiven my absence, he will reveal Călţuna's whereabouts. I want to see her and explain myself."

"You know I've long admired and respected your mistress." Fruzhin drew him into an adjacent alcove, away from any passersby, and lowered his voice as he added, "But I also saw how you smiled when I teased you earlier about your bride. The same smile as the sight of Călţuna once brought to your lips. Give her up, Vlad, and make your happiness with your wife and the children she will provide. Take your joy at her side. God knows you deserve happiness after these years at a monastery without a companion."

"I've had other women before and after Călţuna," Vlad admitted. "But none could compare to her."

"Except perhaps this new bride of yours?"

Vlad turned away, unwilling to consider the possibility. Whatever attraction Cneajna held for him, he could not heed the advice to forget Călţuna. How could he ever, while their son existed? The living image of her, the proof of their enduring love.

ZSIGMOND, WHO RECENTLY returned from Belgrade in Serbia, acknowledged Vlad's return, and publicly announced his recent marriage. The feasting courtiers murmured and peered at each other before joining in the applause. Vlad disregarded their acclamation and bowed before his sovereign.

"When will our king grant me an audience?" He returned to Fruzhin's side.

"Do not trouble yourself. Or are you so eager to get back to your wife?"

Vlad neglected to respond and sipped from his wine chalice instead. Some of his concerns lay with Cneajna. He wanted to know Călţuna's whereabouts, too. He must reach her before the news of his wedding did, a feat which grew more impossible with every passing day.

"In the morning, will you take me to the site of Pipó's grave, Fruzhin?"

"As you wish. Our king shall make an important announcement in the coming days. He's granting me one of Pipó's former Transilvanian holdings. Lipa Castle. From its battlements, he shall allow me to fly flags bearing the Bulgarian coat of arms which my cousin adopted until his death, during our ill-starred uprising against the Turks fifteen years ago. In sable, three lions *passant guardant*. When there's time, I shall visit the fortress and would like you to come with me."

"I will. There's no one more deserving of the castle than you. Pipó would be glad."

"It's hard to believe he's gone. He and our king's most stalwart champions on the battlefield. Stibor and now my uncle Stefan."

Vlad nodded, still mourning the loss of his uncle Staico.

"Yet, we remain." Fruzhin clapped his shoulder. "Our dread purpose must resume."

Vlad set down his drink. "Zsigmond plans for a new Ottoman offensive at last?"

"He does, in Serbia. The Turk wolves want to seize a strategic fortress at Galambóc, a day's ride south of Belgrade. Zsigmond toured the region with his wife and my cousin Đurađ a month after he claimed the throne. If Christendom loses Galambóc, the Ottomans may sail upriver, unimpeded."

The scents of food wafted through the opened doors of the banquet hall. Soon bowls of black sturgeon eggs, crusty white bread, beef goulash, varieties of roasted fowl, candied and jellied fruit slices, pastries, and pies, and tangy, crumbled bryndza cheese from the sheep's milk of Vlad's homeland, covered the tables.

As the dinner service began, he considered the coming campaign. Cneajna knew about it somehow. Before they parted, she told him Zsigmond needed him in battle against the perpetual foes of

Christendom. Twelve years had elapsed since he last faced them in Bosnia.

Although he expected, even relished, the opportunity now, so many changes had occurred since the loss at Doboj. His half-Turkic, half-Wallachian niece lived somewhere, the only child of his beloved lost sister, but also a cousin to the sultan. Someday, she and Vlad must meet. He would ensure it. What would she think of him when they did, the sworn enemy of her father's coreligionists? Without a doubt, he would slaughter each one of the girl's people, if he could.

"Thinking of your Cneajna? Wondering if you will see her before the campaign begins?" Fruzhin interrupted his considerations.

"I am not contemplating her just now." He gripped the wine cup again. "She doesn't occupy my every waking thought, you know."

Fruzhin's low snicker mocked him.

More than a month passed, in which he wrote to his son at Tismana Monastery, his grandmother in Târgoviște, Cneajna at Segesvár, and Jadwiga in Kraków. As expected, his wife's reply came first, wherein she told him not to worry, although her illness persisted. He dared not leave Buda Castle and fetch her. Zsigmond might choose that moment to summon him.

His concern for Cneajna's pregnancy grew. He replied, begging her to seek a midwife's help, despite her reliance on Ruxandra. Her intractable response infuriated him, especially when she ended the letter with, '*Be at peace, dear husband, and know our Mircea will be well, as will I, in Ruxandra's sole care.*'

"As if I would ever honor my wretched father's memory by naming a second son for him!" He crumpled the paper in his fist. Nine years on since the passing of his parent despite that, Vlad's vengeful heart could find no forgiveness for the man.

He left István's Tower and stepped out into the cool, autumnal air. He heaved a weary sigh, his breath evaporating in a wisp of white mist. Near the gatehouse, he spotted Fruzhin. The presence of a woman at his best friend's side forestalled Vlad's approach.

She stood taller than Fruzhin, stabbing the tip of her forefinger into his chest. He held his palms up. Although Vlad could not overhear, clearly an argument ensued between them. Vlad stared hard at her, certain that even with this distance and the hood falling over her brow, somehow, he knew the woman's identity. She withdrew her touch and turned away from Fruzhin. He gaped at her as she strode off.

She joined an older man of lesser height in the skullcap that Jewish men wore by law to identify themselves throughout the Hungarian kingdom. The elderly man's spindly, spotted hand rested on the head of a tall, red-haired boy. Something in the child's features beneath the mop of curls also drew Vlad's attention. At this distance, he could not make any further determination of the boy's identity.

Fruzhin yelled, "Wait, Margit! Don't take him from here again!"

The woman ignored his cries, grasped the child's hand, and led him away, the older Jew shadowing them. Only after Fruzhin stumbled and slipped on the ground, holding his head in his hand did Vlad dare approach, hoping to learn more about the three strangers and why their appearance dazed his best friend.

He helped Fruzhin up, but before either of them could speak, riders on horseback entered the southern gate. János Hunyadi led them. Now Vlad stood stupefied. The youth whom he last saw, aged eighteen, just before joining the emperor on his travels three years ago, became a tall and slender, stalwart man.

An odd scowl hardened János' bearded visage once he met Vlad's gaze. In the next instance, after Vlad blinked, János hailed him with a broad smile. He shook his head. He must have imagined the glare.

"My princes." János dismounted and approached, bowing. "It is an honor to stand before you again as a knight of King Zsigmond. One of the last acts of Prince Stefan in Serbia. Well, that, and teaching me how to hunt wolves in the forest. God rest his soul."

"God rest his soul," Fruzhin echoed.

Vlad enfolded János in his grasp, so proud of the younger man. Not only for his attainment of knighthood but the clear and resolute manner of his speech. His stutter was under better control, as Vlad knew it must be with time and practice.

"You set me on destiny's path. I've never forgotten," János said as they drew apart.

He turned aside and introduced the sole woman among the new arrivals, her face, and form as plump as Jadwiga's in Vlad's recollection.

"My betrothed, the lady Erzsébet Szilágyi. King Zsigmond arranged the match before calling his warriors here to face the Turkish menace together."

She curtsied and greeted them. Dimples and a honeyed voice enhanced her appeal.

"I'm glad you're here among us. With you in our warrior bands, we will defeat our foes." Vlad clapped János' shoulder.

"This battle's been a long time coming. It's an honor to fight at your side, prince."

"Before you do, we'll have some days of sparring," Fruzhin told János. "We need deeds, not words. Show Vlad and me what you've learned from Pipó and my uncle."

"I will," János promised. Rays of sunlight warmed his brown gaze. "Permit me to leave you and seek our king." He bowed and held out his arm for his lady, who smiled at him as they led their retinue into Zsigmond's palace.

"The boy has become a man and a fighter for God." Vlad watched their progress.

"Indeed. Time passes swiftly for us all," Fruzhin replied.

"While it does, the news of my marriage to Cneajna progresses through the kingdom." Vlad returned his attention to his best friend, a renewed sense of urgency gripping and motivating him. "Călţuna doesn't deserve to suffer in ignorance, believing I've abandoned her without cause. When will our sovereign see me, Fruzhin?"

"In his own time. You know the war council meets each day for long hours. Zsigmond has written to King Władysław in Poland, requesting reinforcements. As our sovereign has also demanded from Dan Dăneşti, commanding a Transalpine contingent."

"I've done my duty." Although Vlad bristled at the mention of his murderous cousin, he continued, "Married as Zsigmond willed and returned to Buda by his order. All I want is the name of the sanctuary where he sent Călţuna. Only he can tell me."

"My friend—"

"We are brothers." Vlad gripped Fruzhin's wrist beneath the velvet black mantle. "Bound by sacred blood oath as much as the battles we've shared. I am asking this because of our allegiance: get me a meeting with Zsigmond."

"Vlad, I would if I could—"

"You can! You know how." Vlad released him and waited.

Fruzhin staggered a short distance away, his face no longer visible.

"There are those whom our king regards as more than faithful supporters," Vlad insisted. "But a few who may interrupt the war council's schedule."

"Yes, you're right," Fruzhin said over his shoulder. "A superior member of the Order of the Dragon can do so for any reason." He turned again. His stare met Vlad's own.

In his best friend's steady gaze, Vlad glimpsed the fullness of what others must have seen for years. Quiet, but steely determination and a fierce, indomitable will. Enough to inspire the soldiers who bowed in deference seventeen years ago as he first accompanied Fruzhin into the great keep; and Zsigmond, who gave Fruzhin authority over his forces against the Turks and Bohemians countless times.

Within Fruzhin's eyes, Vlad also saw the warm glimmer of friendship; their shared memories of more than armed conflicts of the past. Strained prior relationships with siblings, long-dead and buried, had first united them. Rare quarrels with each other divided them too over the years. Yet, they would always stand together.

"I gained my induction into the Order of the Dragon at its formation nineteen winters ago," Fruzhin said. "You've remarked in the past on the intimacy Zsigmond and I share. He trusts me, as I rely on him. The rules of the Order require five members to always be present at the side of our master and king to advise him."

Although eager for more from the long-awaited confession, especially the identities of the other members of the Order, Vlad held his tongue.

"I've never asked Zsigmond for anything before," Fruzhin added, "even his aid in the retaking of Bulgaria. But I will call for him to summon you and tell you the truth about Călţuna's circumstances. My standing in the Order will compel him."

"Thank you," Vlad replied. His sigh of relief issued in a blustery breath.

Fruzhin approached and rested a hand on his forearm. "I promise if you are patient and heed Zsigmond's every directive without question from now on, you'll become a Dragon of the Order too. It is our king's wish, but you must prove yourself worthy again. This time, as a captain commanding some of his forces against the Turks in Serbia."

CHAPTER 24

Winter's King

"The world is divided into men who have wit and no religion and men who have religion and no wit."-Avicenna (980-1037 AD), Persian polymath.

IN THE YEAR OF OUR Lord 1427-1428. Buda, Hungary (modern-day Budapest, Hungary)

Early heavy snows blanketed Buda and Pest the next week. Alongside Zsigmond's courtiers, Vlad rushed out of István's Tower in dismay at the sight. He did not consider the weather unusual for the time, given the waning autumn, but his thoughts fled to Cneajna at Segesvár. Would she be warm enough if winter descended early? Had she found a tailor who could fashion suitable clothing from the Ypres wool among her marital gifts?

He chided himself for worrying about such mundane matters. No better than her nursemaid Ruxandra, who would undoubtedly secure his wife's comfort. Although he chafed at the thought, he also realized that despite his preoccupation with Călțuna's life, his concerns for his bride grew. Five months after their wedding, her significance increased daily.

He tried telling himself that their expected child made it so. The lie vied with the inescapable truth budding in his heart. He cared for his wife more than he had expected at the outset. A deepening sentiment in a divided heart. He could neither let Călțuna go nor could he cease his longing for Cneajna. Whatever his wife's assumptions about their futures, his attachment to the two women could never bode well.

His marital vows required him to cling to one woman. He would never live as Prince Mircea and Zsigmond did, seeking the arms of others and sullying his marriage. But how could he ever forget Călțuna or stop his heart from loving her while wedded to Cneajna?

A massive army arriving at the castle gate halted his ruminations. Zawisza rode at the forefront. A gale blew inland and tugged at his cloak, revealing a frosty sheen across the emblazoned eagle, on a breastplate of blackened armor barely shades darker than the man's skin.

As his long-absent friend clambered down from the horse, Vlad pushed through the crowd of courtiers gathered in the snow-banked quadrangle.

They shared a lingering embrace. "The Black Knight returns to Buda at last," Vlad said. "Too much time has passed since we saw each other."

"Over six years, by my count, since you once served under my command," Zawisza replied. As they drew apart, he fingered Vlad's temple. "Is this a spot of gray?"

Vlad batted his hand away. "You should talk. Your hair was graying when we previously saw each other at Hory Kutné."

He lapsed into silence. Zawisza said nothing. The brutality of more than the bloodbath on Bohemian soil must have afflicted him, too. Like Vlad, he might never forget.

Seeking to ease the tension his mention of the past stirred up, Vlad teased, "Are you sure you're fit for the command of an army such as this? You barely got off that mount."

"Take care when you accuse me of frailty and advanced age. Recall, I have more experience on the battlefield than you ever could."

"Yes, and it shows in the lines and crags of your aged face, too." Vlad chuckled and gripped Zawisza's shoulder where the tips of his hair curled, growing overlong. "I'm glad you're here to fight the Turks."

"I've promised them more than combat, my friend. I will give them death." Zawisza waved to the infantry and cavalry units filling the courtyard. "Lithuanians who are loyal to my King Władysław. Much has happened since we last fought together. After paying homage to Zsigmond, I'll share stories with you and Fruzhin over tankards of ale. Where is your closest companion, that old dog?"

"You know Fruzhin, ever faithful, never leaves Zsigmond for longer than required."

While he walked with Zawisza into the palace, Vlad considered whether this friend belonged to their king's Order of the Dragon as well.

Since Fruzhin's promise the previous day, Vlad thought of little else but becoming a Dragon like the men he admired most; his best friend, and Stibor, certainly Stefan and Pipó as well. Would Zsigmond truly command him, as he often did with them, to take charge of a contingent going into Serbia? The prospect thrilled Vlad more than the thought of killing their enemies.

Since the snow did not abate, he accepted the truth; an early winter ensnared Hungary. Still, he sent Tobar and Yoska scouting the passes to the southeast. They returned after two weeks, affirming his suspicions. Blustery weather made the usual routes treacherous. Any attempt at taking them would imperil travelers.

The end of the year approached. Vlad imagined Cneajna, alone with their baby, growing inside her. Although she would never be truly lonely, with Ruxandra as her constant companion, he also wanted his wife beside him.

Zsigmond permitted all his household knights to attend Catholic mass in the king's chapel, the scent of incense heady. On his knees, Vlad returned to daily prayers. He did more than ask God to ensure the well-being of his sons. He prayed for their mothers, too.

Frigid winds rattled the stained-glass windowpanes. Footfalls scuffed the cold stone tiles and drew near to him. He opened his eyes, looking up. Fruzhin stood at his side.

"Our king will see you alone in the gardens below his royal chambers, Vlad. He is already waits for you there. The royal bodyguards are on the outskirts at the sole entrance. He commanded it so you might speak in private."

The breath was almost knocked out of him by Fruzhin's pronouncement. But Vlad stood steadily and offered his heartfelt thanks. At last, he would discover Călţuna.

"Listen to Zsigmond first," Fruzhin advised, "and ask your questions afterward. Be patient, and you'll have the answers you want."

"May we see each other after I've spoken to our king?" Vlad asked. "I would share with you everything he says. Blood brothers should have no secrets."

To his astonishment, Fruzhin looked away and swallowed. Afterward, he nodded.

"Vlad, there's something I must tell you one day soon. But also understand that I cannot explain it in full. Other pertinent truths remain hidden. I'll speak to you when I know them all."

"Once you're ready, Fruzhin," Vlad said, although curious. "I won't pry before then."

They embraced before Vlad left him.

Through whitened trees and hedges where icicles dangled, and with the prevailing winds sculpting curved snowdrifts, Vlad delved into the heart of the garden. He found Zsigmond awaiting him, as Fruzhin promised.

Time had altered their king, only a few months shy of his sixtieth birthday. In the brutal winter, the reddened tips of blunt, gnarled fingers brushed away ice crystals formed on a chest-length beard. He wore his Montauban cap of fur and the hair beneath stuck out at odd angles. Stoop-backed under a thick sheepskin coat, he turned when Vlad's boots crunched the rimed crust formed atop dormant grasses.

"My king." He bowed.

"You must wonder why We chose this place and not the comfort of Our rooms."

"The thought occurred, Your Royal Majesty."

Zsigmond began walking, and as Vlad joined him, said, "We cannot trust anyone within the castle. Certainly not Our queen, who has her maids and pageboys listening outside closed doors, believing We will not guess at their furtive movements."

Vlad wondered if Călțuna, although hidden away, had anything more to fear from Borbála. He resisted the question and stayed silent, as his best friend had advised earlier.

"So many secrets in this place," Zsigmond said. "We keep them all for the security of others, especially those who do not know the danger those confidences pose. Including you. The mistress you had; her younger brother wrote to Us, revealing your arrival in Hermannstadt and the claiming of your bastard. He said We should send Our knights to the place where your Gypsies buried your uncle. We never received a reply to Our letter in response. Do you know what ensued? Did you kill your lover's brother?"

"Never, Your Royal Majesty. The plague took him and his family in Várad."

"Ah." Zsigmond stopped in a clearing, each of his breaths billowing with white smoke. "A fitting end, you must suppose, for one who betrayed you."

"I did not wish his death, my king. I only desired to find Călțuna."

"She holds your heart, even after this marriage to the princess of Moldavia. We understand. Countless others put a claim on Us too, including Wenceslaus' widow Žofie. We thought to wed her to the king of Poland before he chose his young bride instead. Our former lover is perhaps best left where she lives at Pozsony. We still love her."

Zsigmond resumed his ambling. With infinite patience, Vlad rejoined him.

"The heart is strange, is it not, Vlad?"

"It is, Your Royal Majesty."

His marriage to the enthralling Cneajna and his lingering feelings for Călțuna substantiated his king's supposition each day. God gave him the good fortune to win the affection of two honorable women who treated him far better than he deserved. He recalled the unique beauty each lady presented. Slender and supple Călțuna with her golden hair, in stark contrast to Cneajna's voluptuousness and heavy black curls.

His heart thrummed, remembering her eager passion for the first night of their union. The subsequent times when they fulfilled each other's desires. A remarkable lady in her passions and her quiet nobility. Did she miss him, too?

"You're thinking of one of your women, aren't you?" Zsigmond's words intruded on his wandering mind. "Don't dissemble. Which one made you smile so just now?"

Vlad confessed he considered both his wife and mistress before he acknowledged his last thoughts lingered on Cneajna.

"Does your princess know the purpose that drew you here? Does she approve?"

"I would never say so, my king," Vlad said, recalling her tearful fury after he made a gift of the yearly rent from his townhouse below Castle Hill. "She wishes my prior life would never intrude on us, although she would be pleased to meet my first boy someday. She has said I must reconcile my past and present. So, I suppose, I try with her knowledge, if not tacit support."

"She seems a strange, even extraordinary lady, Vlad."

"Again, Your Royal Majesty, your words are truth. I'm concerned for her, especially given this early onset of winter. Soon, I hope we may reunite at Segesvár in Transilvania and welcome the son she believes she will give me."

"We understand and congratulate you on the prospect of a legitimate heir so soon after uniting with your bride. And if We reveal the location of your mistress now, will you leave here and go to her instead?"

Vlad opened his mouth. An intake of frigid air drew the cold inside him. The ready answer he had long assumed would come never did. Because he chose not to let it.

For three years, he had wanted to return to Călţuna. He must explain the reason for his subsequent marriage to Cneajna. What about the aftermath? What would happen if he saw his lover again? Could he walk away from Călţuna once more, this time for good? What about Cneajna, who carried another babe for him? He imagined her awaiting him in Segesvár with patience and dutifulness. A far better wife than he warranted while chasing after a mistress stolen away from him and their child.

Who was he now? Călţuna's lover, or Cneajna's husband? It no longer seemed possible he could be both.

"Before I answer in full, my king, will you at least tell me, has Călţuna already taken holy orders?" Vlad's heart thudded with the realization of what he intended.

"After We learned of your union in the letter from Suceava and sought the news of your mistress' circumstances, the mother superior of the religious house replied as We required. We were told the lady considers taking holy vows, but as of the date on the mother superior's missive, your woman had not pledged herself a bride of Christ."

"But Călţuna thinks of it?"

"Yes. Again, according to the mother superior."

Vlad turned away and exhaled a shaky breath. Deep in his heart, he hoped Călţuna found concordance wherever she lived. As he must do with Cneajna by his side. The union he had never wanted now bound him, as did his bride. Given a chance, at long last to retreat into the past with Călţuna, he found he desired a future with Cneajna more.

He also knew that he could not intrude on his former lover's life again. His grandmother once told him they must walk along separate, different paths toward their destinies. "*Written in the stars,*" the Dowager said. This decision would be final and he would not turn from it.

He could only hope that if Christ gave Călţuna the comfort a life as Vlad's mistress never could have, perhaps she would make her peace with their past, and become a nun. He wished her sincere joy. The only true thing he ever wanted for her.

"What is your answer, Vlad?" The king touched his shoulder.

Tears burned the corners of his eyes. He would never forget Călţuna or cease loving her. He could not, while the living symbol of their ill-fated romance, their tender son thrived at Tismana Monastery. But a shattered heart, wounded by a deliberate choice to sever his important link to the past might heal in time. With Cneajna's care as a balm.

Fifteen years beforehand, when Fruzhin's aunt Milena Olivera revealed details of her marriage to a long-dead Turkic sultan, she spoke to Vlad of a seemingly impossible devotion found within an arranged union. Could he discover the same? For the sake of Cneajna's commitment to their vows, he would seek contentment with her alone.

"Your Royal Majesty." Vlad cleared his aching throat. "Please permit me to...write a letter to my...former mistress. She should know about my marriage and the temporary living our son enjoys at Tismana Monastery in the care of its holy brothers. I ask that you send my message on to her once the weather allows the messenger's travel."

"If you're certain, We will consent and ensure it is done, Vlad."

"Thank you." He exhaled a ragged breath. His heart was still heavy. "May I leave you, my king?"

"You may." But before he could go, Zsigmond gripped his arm with startling vigor. "You've let go of imprudent desire and gained focus. We believe you'll achieve all your aims with such forbearance. In the spring, We will appoint captains of our war bands. You'll number among the leaders."

"You honor me, Your Royal Majesty." Vlad cleared his throat as he added, "My sword is yours, as it has always been and will ever be."

"Very good. We also seek a southern border commander in Transilvania. Show your prowess against the Ottoman Turks, and We shall contemplate whether you may be entrusted with the defense of the frontier region."

Although stunned, Vlad welcomed the test. Transilvania and Wallachia's borders could not encompass his true quest for his homeland's crown. However, if he established his authority along the frontier, the post would grant him greater prestige and show his willingness and ability to learn how to govern a territory. Strengthening his future claim among Wallachia's boyars.

"Again, your consideration is an honor, my king. I'll prove myself worthy."

SPRING'S ARRIVAL THAWED frozen rivulets and tributaries of the Danube during March of the following year. The snowmelt ran down

Castle Hill daily. Vlad hastened from his townhouse, where he collected last year's rent proceeds, and spoke to the leader of the royal guard gathered outside their king's chamber, seeking entry. By consent, soon he kneeled before Zsigmond, dressing for the day amid the royal squires.

"Fruzhin warned Us we should expect your interruption. We had hoped you might allow another full day of the new season to pass before coming to Us."

Mystified, Vlad raised his head. "Fruzhin told you I might arrive?"

"He was certain!" Zsigmond's gruff reply echoed beneath the folds of a linen undershirt he drew over his grizzled head. In a huff, he pushed aside the squires and laced the ribbons at the neckline himself. "During a meeting of Our councilors last night, he reminded Us it's been seven months since you arrived and left your wife at Segesvár."

"Yes, it is, my king." Vlad rubbed at a dull ache in the center of his chest. "A long time, in which the birth of our babe may have occurred. Please, let me go into Transilvania, see Cneajna, and visit my firstborn at Tismana Monastery. I vow I shall meet your army on the road to Serbia after you depart from Buda Castle in two weeks."

"You'd better! Zawisza shall take command of the forces you will lead until then."

"Thank you, great king," Vlad vowed, his heart racing now in anticipation.

"Then go!" Zsigmond ordered before he grinned beneath ginger-hued hair dulled to a pale russet. He still reminded Vlad of a wily fox. "We wish you the joy of your family."

Vlad raced out of the chamber, almost stumbling into the path of Queen Borbála and the maids and pageboys who followed her. Her return to Buda surprised him, as he knew from Zsigmond that she previously lived in her homeland of Styria while her countrymen defended against reckless Hussite incursions near Pozsony.

Before that, he had endured rare glimpses of her. Whenever they chanced a meeting during meals, at *prandium* in the morning, or during evening feasts, Vlad found her actions mimicked his behavior. They rarely exchanged glances and never encountered each other at

Zsigmond's door. Vlad knew why he avoided her wretched sight and believed her disdain for him was unchanged.

Still, he bowed and muttered, "My queen."

"I am not your queen!" She huffed. "In your view, I'm merely the wife of your sovereign. Don't suggest otherwise. You could have knocked me down the stairs. Where are you going in such haste? Has Zsigmond wisely dismissed you from his service?"

"I'm leaving Buda ahead of our king's army to rejoin my wife briefly."

"Oh. I suppose she's birthed this second whelp of yours, whom Zsigmond mentioned. As if I cared. At least it won't be a bastard this time." A grin amplified the prominent lines around her mouth.

He growled low in his throat and leaned closer. "And I may be certain the mother and the child won't come to any harm, either."

Borbála's cruel smile vanished. She lowered her gaze, teeth nibbling on her upper lip. She hid restless hands behind the folds of black velvet skirts. He moved a step closer, and she drew back, gaping at him. He gazed into her eyes of emerald stones and found fear in the widened stare and the flare of her nostrils above quavering lips. At last, he had his answer about her involvement in the loss of his first child with Călţuna.

His glance at the retinue arrayed behind Borbála made one servant girl gasp. The royal guards standing nearby maintained solid grips on the hilts of their swords.

Vlad imagined how it would be if he and Zsigmond's wife stood alone. His fingers clenched around her slender throat. Her pupils reddening and bulging from the sockets. The death rattle filling her throat as he squeezed the breath from her. Taking his revenge in the same cold manner as she once ensured the death of Călţuna's baby. A life for a life.

He knew better than to attempt it. He would never forgive her or forget.

"If I may take my leave of you, Queen Borbála."

"Wait!" Her shrill order echoed against polished marble and stone. "My husband and brother made demands of me last year." She lowered her voice, adding, "They'll be displeased if I don't do what they want. Both say I should thank you."

Vlad sneered. "Why?" What could her words mean now? When she had hurt the woman whom he would always treasure in a part of his heart. Stolen their baby's future.

"You safeguarded Friderik's life when last you saw him. He and his whore Veronika Deseniška wed in Italy, where they hid. Until Father found them and had her tried for witchcraft. The judges did not find her guilty, but God did. She drowned in a bathtub."

Vlad murmured, "A terrible end," while certain that Borbála's parent ordered the woman's death with the same callousness his daughter displayed.

"A deserved one. My brother has said you could have fought those loyal to him, even if you would not have won against superior numbers. I suppose I must show some appreciation to you for letting Friderik go free and not endangering his life, despite his stupidity." A scowl deepened furrows across her brow. "I'm in your debt."

He laughed without mirth. Only her swift end could satisfy him.

"I serve our sovereign alone, Queen Borbála. His gratitude is enough for me. He has my loyalty until the end of days."

"And when he dies?" She cleared her throat and leered at him, her courage returning. "That Habsburg wretch Albrecht will rule in his stead, but my daughter Erzsébet has her husband's ear. Will you be faithful to him and my queenly heir?"

"Long live King Zsigmond," Vlad retorted. He skirted around the hateful wife of his sovereign and left the royal residence. In István's Tower, he found Fruzhin, who helped him pack the scant belongings he had brought into Hungary.

He did not reveal his earlier encounter with the queen. If, as he suspected, she belonged to the Order of the Dragon, Vlad's best friend would never waver in his devoted service to his king's wife.

"You can't leave without saying goodbye to Zawisza or János," Fruzhin said.

Vlad would miss sparring bouts with the latter. Although knighted and accomplished in his use of a blade and crossbow, and having witnessed many skirmishes against the Turks, János had never fought them before. The Serbian conflict would be his first test.

"See that Zawisza and you continue training János in my absence," Vlad said. "I want to witness the proof of all you've taught him when we reunite. Let them know I'm leaving Buda and tell them to meet me outside the great keep."

"As you wish." Before he turned away, Fruzhin added, "Giving orders in command of others comes naturally to you."

His best friend withdrew down the stairs absent Vlad's reply. He continued shoving his garments into two saddlebags. The wolf-skin he draped over his arm. He hoped Tobar and Yoska awaited him with their horses already saddled. He needed the men's aid as he navigated the hillsides and passes, avoiding hidden crevasses still steeped in late snow.

In the quadrangle, the Gypsies stood with their Carpathian ponies at a short distance from the trio of Fruzhin, Zawisza, and János.

To the latter, Vlad gave instructions. "Keep your sword arm up and strengthen the muscles in your daily practice. Remember the importance of a shield against the arrows of Turkish archers. When you fight them, only your life and the lives of your Christian brethren matter." He repeated the words Stibor once told him during training, "Never turn your back on an adversary unless it's a corpse at your feet."

"Be assured I'll train most diligently."

"I expect nothing less of you, János. You will not disappoint me."

He shared brief farewells with Zawisza and Fruzhin, while the former asked, "Have you decided what you'll name your second son?"

"I have not, Zawisza," Vlad murmured while he mounted the horse. "Until we meet again in Serbia, God guard you all."

IN THE YEAR OF OUR Lord 1428. Segesvár, Transilvania (modern-day Sighişoara, Romania)

After a week, slowed by light showers into Transilvania, Vlad arrived at the inn where he left his wife in Segesvár during the previous autumn. He raced for the room where two Moldavian soldiers bowed outside upon his arrival.

He pushed past them and opened the door. "Cneajna?"

"My prince, please lower your voice!" Ruxandra straightened beside the foot of the bed. "Would you upset them?"

"For shame! He could never disturb me," Cneajna whispered. "Or our son."

She sat beneath a coverlet of pristine gray linen, black hair in untidy waves billowing around her bowed, bared shoulders. Above a still engorged belly, she cuddled a large bundle, making loud smacking noises at her swollen breast. Smoky tang rose and ashy residue smoldered in a gilded bowl. A metallic, cloying odor preceded Vlad's brief glimpse of the basin filled with bloodied cloths next to Ruxandra's feet.

He drew closer, but she warded him off. "I demanded fresh bedding for my mistress and herbs to purify this place. Everything that touches the princess must be clean. You are not, my prince. You should cast off those travel garments and bathe."

"I told her you would come in the hours after our boy's birth," Cneajna said. She looked up at her former nursemaid. "Can my husband not remove his attire to join us?"

"That may be permissible, my princess."

Vlad glared at Ruxandra for the presumption of thinking he needed her consent. Nothing could keep him from his wife and son. He began stripping his clothing off.

Ruxandra gasped and hurriedly gathered up the bloodied basin before she fled the shuttered room. Vlad ignored her, focused on the quiet tableau in front of him. A legitimate heir from a wife he barely knew.

Soon he slid into the bed naked and looked down at the delicate curve of his second son's cheek. The babe drew hard on Cneajna's nipple. Rivulets of perspiration ran down the valley between her ample bosom.

"Are you too warm? Shall I open the windows?"

"You must not. Ruxandra warned against it. The evil eye seeks vulnerabilities. No wet nurse shall give him suck either, Vlad. I alone will nurture all our children."

"It is your right to decide," he said, just as Cneajna's visage crinkled and a groan escaped her. "Are you unwell, wife? Shall I call your companion?"

Up close, her pale hands and face appeared splayed. Even her nose. Half-moon circles rimmed the area under her eyes. She grinned broadly.

"No, Vlad, leave Ruxandra be. For many years, she's told me I have good birthing hips. She already warned me the ripples inside my womb would last for days. The sickness that would not leave me throughout the pregnancy and the pains I endured after dawn today were well worth it. See how well he suckles?"

"Indeed, I do. He arrived earlier today?"

"Squalling lustily with the dawn for all the world to hear."

"I wish I had been here to see."

"Ruxandra tells me husbands should not witness a birthing. But you'll be at my side for our dragon-bane, his birth heralded by the star with its hairy tail," Cneajna murmured.

Vlad shook his head at another of her odd, unfathomable predictions before he reached out to their son. He caressed wisps of black, downy hair soft as goose feathers, the dimpled curve of the baby's chin, and the creases in his arm.

"Our first son will be strong, like you and both his warrior grandfathers," Cneajna said, joy suffusing her bright cheeks. "Won't you name him now, husband? I already know what you must call him, but you should whisper it in his ear."

With a glance at her, he sighed and pondered what she had previously told him, to name the boy after Mircea the Great. Nothing about his violent life warranted the honor. Vlad slid his forefinger inside the tiny fist the babe made atop his swaddling clothes. The newborn gripped and tugged with the same strength as the love already suffusing Vlad's heart.

He smiled at Cneajna's beatific beam reserved for their sweet boy, whose eyelids closed as he drifted to sleep. His arrival offered Vlad another chance at a new beginning. Perhaps fate would prove his wife right, allowing him to assuage painful memories about his parent in himself and make a bright future for their small family.

He hovered over their child and in a hushed tone said, "I grant you the name of your Wallachian grandfather. You are Mircea. I'll teach you to be a better fighter, a better man than your namesake. Know you are the treasure of my heart. I'd give my life to safeguard yours. I am your father, Vlad, and you are, like me, an heir to the House of Basarab."

His babe's hold tightened as if the child understood the import of the words.

FRUZHIN ARRIVED THREE days afterward, and Vlad came to him on the inn's outskirts.

"Our sovereign has left Buda this week."

"Did the difference of but a few days matter so much to him, Fruzhin?"

"He's received word of the former castellan's betrayal at Galambóc. It's lost to us, despite the belated efforts of some royal officers, including Pipó's successor in Temes County, to reclaim the stronghold. Turkish skirmishers are also harassing the builders of the new Christian fortress being constructed on the left bank of the Danube by men Pipó had hired just before his death. Zsigmond will use it as a base to drive our enemies beyond the Serbian frontier."

"But he knew I wished to see both of my sons before—"

"Both?" Fruzhin's laughter echoed in the central square. "You have a second boy?"

"Yes. His name is Mircea. Born three mornings ago." Vlad looked at the doorway of his transitory lodging.

He must depart from Cneajna again, earlier than he planned. Without ever explaining that he had returned to her not just because of their child. Perhaps with additional time apart, he might find the words to express himself at another reunion.

"I'd also planned to inform the Dowager of his birth in a letter and visit Tismana Monastery to reunite with his brother before going to Serbia."

"Hmm. Children. Such little things, yet they can alter a father's life in vast, unexpected ways. Give him renewed purpose."

The faraway look in Fruzhin's eyes as he spoke stirred Vlad's curiosity.

Before he could inquire, his best friend rushed on. "I'm sorry you must leave your sons behind, but there's no other choice. Galambóc is so vital to Zsigmond, he's sailing downriver ahead of a fleet of twenty-two ships carrying artillery and gunpowder weapons. You cannot delay further. He is our king."

"I'm well aware!" Vlad huffed and shook his head. Before Fruzhin's arrival, he would have departed Segesvár in days to go south and see his namesake, absent from his sight for almost a full year. Only his first child could have compelled him to leave his wife and their new baby so soon.

"Fruzhin, I must bid Cneajna and the boy farewell."

"Wait, Vlad. There was another reason I rode south in such haste." He retrieved a folded sheet of paper. "A herald arrived in Buda the day after you left."

No seal stamped in the red wax. Vlad unfolded and read the contents of a long-awaited letter from his grandmother. In her usual terse manner, Dowager Princess Ana-Călina delved directly into her purpose.

'Your brother Radu has gone missing. After three years of exile, he brought a Turkish-backed army to meet Dan Dănești the last spring, after we met at Tismana Monastery. You may assume who prevailed in that battle. I ordered Vlậcsan the Wolf to publicly break his ties with me, so he might join your ruthless cousin's court. But Prince Dan is craftier than I believed and still does not trust Vlậcsan enough to end an old woman's torment.

'He also tried to take your younger brother Alex as a hostage in the days after you wrote to me proclaiming your marriage. We have fled my townhouse and found sanctuary elsewhere. It's best if our whereabouts remain concealed until you accomplish the task I set before you now. Vlậcsan's secretly told me your king will go to war against the Turks this coming spring and has demanded Dan Dănești's warriors join the fight. Ask Zsigmond to discover the truth about Radu. Do not fail me, my Vlad.'

He shared the missive with Fruzhin, who asked, "Do you think your cousin holds your elder brother as a prisoner?"

"If so, Radu's not in the cells at Argeş. The Wolf would've determined that much for the Dowager. Zsigmond hasn't spoken about matters in my homeland?"

"I've told you before, Dan Dăneşti went with him and Queen Borbála to Belgrade for my cousin Đurađ's investiture as the *Despoteses* of the Kingdom of Rascia. I know of no communications between our king and his Transalpine vassal before that time."

"Then either he is unaware of what's befallen my elder brother, or our sovereign's keeping secrets from you too, Fruzhin, for my sake. Why would he do that? He must perceive there are no close ties between me and any of my remaining siblings." He peered at his best friend. "Can you swear you've never, even inadvertently, revealed my ambitions to Zsigmond?"

"I've already made that vow and will do so again each time you require it. Vlad, our king is also no fool. He's aware of your enmity for Dan Dăneşti and that there are but three sons of Mircea the Great with legitimate claims to the throne of your country."

"If Radu is dead, two remain. Me and my younger brother. Little Alex."

"The Hungarian army coming from Buda under the palatine's leadership travels into the Transalpine area first. Bound for Argeş to join the forces of Dan Dăneşti. Six thousand archers. Zsigmond will vest Dan Dăneşti and Zawisza with royal authority as captains-general at the siege of Galambóc. All of us in the captaincy of war bands are answerable to them."

"I understand, Fruzhin."

"Do you? You're thirty-four years old. No longer the youth I met in Hungary or a once wayward knight who almost drank himself to death in grief. Can you control your furious impulses when you see Dan Dăneşti? He's not only your homeland's ruling prince. Zsigmond relies on him."

"You may be assured I'll discover what happened to Radu and his right to wear the crown of our forefathers."

Vlad re-entered the inn, found Tobar, and relayed Zsigmond's summons to war. "So, we must part sooner than I had planned. Cneajna and our son are safe here with her Moldavian guards. Go on with your brother to the village at Tismana and see your wife and daughter, the rest of your family."

"Yoska can ride out and tell them we are going with you into Serbia before he catches up with us and the army of your king, *Domnule*."

"No, Tobar. This is not your fight."

"Your fight is ours, *Domnule*." Tobar crossed thick arms over his chest.

A heavy sigh ran through Vlad before he nodded. "You and your twin are the most stubborn men I've ever known. But I'm grateful for your abiding loyalty."

"*Domnule*." Tobar bowed and went away.

The sweet strains of Cneajna's voice came to Vlad through the thin wood of the doorway. He pressed his forehead there. His knightly oath must prevail. One day, would there be no more wars left to fight, no reasons to part from those for whom he cared?

For now, the past called to him, reminding him of what the Turks had stolen. His sister Arina's fragile life. Would he always remain torn between his responsibility to the living and his quest to avenge the dead?

Ruxandra opened the door. He looked beyond her to where Cneajna leaned over the cradle carved of elm, which he, Tobar, and Yoska fashioned the day before. Bundled within, his son rested.

"The little prince sleeps," Ruxandra whispered, as if he could not see for himself.

Despite the baleful look he directed at her, she did not move out of the way. Her over-protective nature would do his boy well at the beginning of life, but Vlad resented her interference and struggled not to find her presence an irritant.

"I don't wish to disturb him, Ruxandra," he muttered.

Cneajna laughed. "Do stand aside and let my dear husband say goodbye to me and our son." She straightened and held out her hands. "We must part now, yes?"

Vlad joined her, grasping her fingers. He looked down at her and the brief farewell he had intended left him. The power of this woman to render him speechless mystified him.

"We do not require words," she whispered. "Your king needs you. Return to us."

The temptation filled him to ask her if he would indeed come back, but he could not give credence to her unusual acts of foretelling. They not only perplexed him. He feared the potential that one day, she might speak truths he would wish he had never heard.

Instead, he said, "Keep yourself and our Mircea safe."

"Do not worry about us, Vlad. God will shield and guide you, great warrior."

He released her hand and gathered his belongings, putting his grandmother's missive with them. He reached for the wolf pelt, one corner of it hanging on the crib.

"Please, leave it near our son." Cneajna stopped him with her fingertips resting on his forearm. "The animal skin has the scent of you and comforts him at night."

"Truly?" He looked down at the ragged, matted fur.

"I'll wrap him in it the first time I take him outdoors and during each day of your absence, husband."

He reached into the crib and laid his palm flat on Mircea's chest, sighing at its rise and fall. The child slumbered in sweet bliss, unaware of his father's leave-taking.

Afterward, Vlad gave a curt nod to Ruxandra, bowed before Cneajna, and left her.

When he closed the door behind him, the sudden clamor of her piteous weeping reverberated through the wood, as did the comfort her former nursemaid offered.

"Don't cry so, sweet princess!" Ruxandra's muffled tone quavered. "He will survive the threat. You foresaw he would return from Serbia and reunite with his family."

"But he goes into darkness and despair, unaware of the deceit he'll encounter at the treacherous hands of his king's warrior! Hatred of the Turks blinds Vlad to all else."

His grip tightened on the door handle while Cneajna sobbed in high-pitched terror. Some dream must have driven her fear that peril might befall him. Perhaps treachery from Dan Dăneşti, who claimed to fight for Zsigmond, but must view Vlad as a potential rival alongside his two brothers.

Although tempted to return and demand an explanation from Cneajna, he refused. Whatever destiny she imagined lay before him, he would not, could not thwart it, if God ordained otherwise. But he would remain mindful of the risks ahead, from both his Ottoman opponents and any Christian fighter prepared to assail and betray him.

CHAPTER 25

The Watcher Made of Stone

"The greatest enemy will hide in the last place you would ever look."-Julius Caesar (100-44 BC), Roman general and statesman.

IN THE YEAR OF OUR Lord 1428. Galambóc, Serbia (modern-day Golubac, Serbia)

After Vlad first glimpsed the frontier stone fortress the Hungarians called Galambóc, perched on a stony promontory, mid-stream of the Danube River, he knew the coming conflict would be unlike any other. Hidden among the foliage, he studied irregular squat towers with conoidal roofs reflected in the waterway.

Situated over twenty leagues and two days' infantry march south of Belgrade, the former ruler's capital, the fort had often changed hands between Hungarian, Turkish, and Serbian garrisons. Long, thick iron links stretched down from the nearest tower into the silvery, shifting water and emerged at a rocky outcrop called Babakaj. Aged pines dangled precariously along the riverbank.

Although Zsigmond's scouts had warned the Turks could raise the chain and prevent the approach of enemy ships, the garrisoned troops never did. Suspecting some other treachery, the scouts reconnoitered as the previous night fell.

Vlad had wanted to see Galambóc for himself. Except for one large catfish leaping up, the buzz of flies and other winged insects, and the creaking groans of wind-twisted trees, relative silence reigned at sunrise over the region. No activity occurred on the walls of the fort. But not for long, Vlad surmised.

At a hand signal to the trio behind him, they scooted backward through the fronds of abundant bushes, undergrowth teeming with pungent animal dung or piss. All kept their silence while finding a path in the thicket. Vlad led their way to the Hungarian encampment. Fingers on their weapons, his companions remained abreast of him.

They cast wary glances through the woods, where shadows flickered and faded. Each man stepped with care. It became impossible to avoid the occasional fallen log or stone hidden under a thick carpet of decomposing leaves with their loamy scent or dead pine needles from the recent winter. Newly budded blackberries often appeared along their route. The thorns snared and snagged their clothes.

No wonder people from Hungary south into Transilvania and Wallachia, and down to Serbia and Fruzhin's Bulgaria called blackberries 'the devil's vines,' Vlad mused.

Although certain of the absence of Turkish patrols on this side of the river, he said in a hushed tone, "A hard fight to take that place."

"I don't know how the former castellan could have surrendered Galambóc to the Turks," János said beside him. "After our king vowed, he would garrison Hungarian fighters there, as he did in Belgrade. The castellan's a traitor. As is Đurađ Branković, for permitting the Turks to remain here. Unlike the man whom I had served after my lord Pipó died."

"Đurađ's predecessor compromised with the enemy too, János, and accepted the yoke of Turkish vassalage. Don't mistake the matter," Vlad advised. "But you are right, in a way. Fruzhin's cousin is a lesser man than their brave uncle Stefan. Fruzhin once praised Đurađ as a bold fighter, worthy of the Serbian throne."

"Hard to believe, captain, when the *Despoteses* favors conciliation."

"In the war council, our spy from his court revealed the castellan accepted twelve thousand of the Turks' gold coinage for relinquishing Galambóc. The price of his so-called honor." Vlad spat in the dirt.

"Fruzhin told me Serbians call this land Golubac. It means 'the place of doves' to them."

János murmured, "The connotation implies peace, but I vow the Turks will never have it. Not with our king's army and ships."

"Indeed, we won't let the enemy sail upriver as they please any longer." Vlad patted the younger man's padded shoulder. He nor János wore armor, lest dawn's light glinted off the metal and revealed their position beside Tobar and Yoska. "Certainly not when I have you among the host I command."

After their king had bivouacked in the woodlands, Vlad requested and accepted János among his war band.

He asked him, "When we crossed the river upstream at Keve in April on Sângiorz's Day, was it the first time seeing your family's ancestral homeland?"

A puzzled frown met his regard before János shook his head. "No. I had visited many times before with my lord Pipó, God rest his soul."

"Your father and uncles must've told you much about your ancestors living on the Wallachian border with Serbia before the remnants of the family moved to Hunyadvár."

"Only that our kin suffered brutal existences too often and too quickly severed by constant Turkish incursions," János muttered with a grim downturn of his mouth and a grave expression before he stiffened. "I'm surprised you recalled me speaking with you about the origins of my family."

"Why should you be? Your life, your destiny, is important to me."

"Because of the oath you once swore to my father?" The younger man's face and cheeks flushed red, as if embarrassed. "To see me enter royal service?"

"My interest should please you, not leave you chagrined. You remind me of myself."

"You'll forgive me if I say we are nothing alike." János chuckled. "You're a prince from a great ruling family. I'm the son of Zsigmond's former household knight, trying to improve my lot in life."

"I became a squire at two years older than the age you did." Vlad halted him on the outskirts of the camp. "No one cared about my past as a hereditary prince, except to tease me about what they imagined was a coddled existence or remind me of inherent defects compared to Mircea the Great. So, each day afterward, I strove to learn from Zsigmond's war masters. To prove myself a better fighter than my parent. I wished to achieve more than he did in life and on the battlefield. As I've said, we are the same."

János cocked his head and nodded, as though accepting the truth of the words.

"Don't dally in thought. Be about your duties." Vlad thumped his shoulder. "Train with any knight who'll fight, no matter his speed or size. You'll be battle-tested soon."

"I look forward to it."

"That's a fool's bravado, and you're no idiot. Brave men shit or piss themselves before their first clash. Brave men perish." Vlad gripped János' forearm. "Your father once said knights rarely die in their beds of old age. After I killed my first man, I told others, including your parent, I felt nothing. It was nearly true.

"But I felt something back then. Fear and worry. My existence would have been cut short unless I learned to kill without remorse. In battle, only survival matters. It's a simple calculation. Your life or that of another. You're newly betrothed and haven't sired a child. There are places you've never seen. Experiences still await you. We'll all die, eventually; here or some other place. When or where doesn't truly matter. What does is how we live while we still breathe! Fight for the promise of your future."

They looked into each other's eyes. Vlad sensed something he could not define passing between them. He hoped the younger man gained a true understanding of what it once took him nearly a decade of warfare to learn.

"I will live, with the help of God and your training, captain. Thank you for everything you've taught me."

"Survive the siege of Galambóc, and you will learn more," Vlad promised.

He parted with János on the outskirts of the camp, built within a wooden palisade in expectation of Ottoman incursions. So far, no scouts, just Turkic ships had intruded. The Christian fleet chased them off three nights in a row, after which they never returned.

Vlad passed beyond the ring of heavy, bronze-barreled guns called *bombarda* near the earth mound's summit, where not a stalk of vegetation remained. Now, two hundred artillery and gunpowder weapons encircled the location, hauled from every ship's hold and overland wagon.

His pair of Gypsies followed Vlad uphill on the muddy knoll. After Fruzhin first reunited with their king onboard his flagship, moored alongside others below the location of the new castle's construction, Vlad told his protectors about what he had overheard from Cneajna back in Segesvár. Tobar and Yoska remained at hand always to safeguard him unless he attended royal war councils.

The castle of Saint László rose, so named for a venerated Hungarian ruler of four centuries past whose chivalrous ideals Zsigmond admired. New stone bastions offered a full view of the river's wide expanse and Galambóc.

Although deathly quiet, some movement began along the enemy ramparts, each connected to the defensive walls, configured for the jagged terrain. Pennons fluttered in the spring breeze. Vlad glared at the Ottoman flags painted bright ox-blood, green or black with silver or gold lettering. Dominant among them was a quartered banner, each section painted with a gold crescent on a red background. A sudden breeze threatened poles topped by horse tails.

Vlad continued up to the construction area. The venerated Sângiorz, whom he revered, once defeated a dragon, an opponent thought insurmountable. He prayed the saint's spirit would give him the same endurance and strength against the Turks during the siege.

A stout man and woman, each clad in a sheepskin cloak, marched in his direction. Their stiff strides and reddened faces warned of an ensuing argument long before he overheard them.

"You're my wife. You will obey. Take that ship and go home before the Turks attack us! I won't lose you to their savagery, my Cecília."

"I am not leaving this place without you. The vessel is mine; a gift from my brothers on the eve of our union. I commanded the pilot to sail it armed with cannons, not just so our king might have another warship. I'm here because of my love for you."

"Will you don armor and sword next? By Christ's blood, you're an ox of a woman!"

"Then we are yoked for life, dearest István. My place is at your side and...."

They bypassed Vlad, both headed down to the riverbank. He waved away his Gypsies and approached a laughing Fruzhin, who looked over his shoulder at the couple. "That's Pipó's successor in Temes County, alongside a very determined wife."

"Heaven, help him!" Vlad exclaimed. "She's a most insistent woman."

"Would that all men were blessed with such devoted companionship."

Vlad smiled, recalling the women in his life. Călțuna would never have been so defiant in front of him, but he imagined his bride could. With her bold displays of temperament, Cneajna might countermand him thus, to protect his life.

"What pleasant contemplation makes the lines around your eyes crinkle so?" Fruzhin asked him. "Your wife again? Her importance to you increases."

"Be quiet," he snapped. "You don't know everything."

"You're right. But contentment shines in your gaze and reveals your thoughts."

Together the friends stared in silence at Zsigmond and his captains-general. Their king gesticulated wildly at the new towers and heavy guns with Zawisza and Dan Dăneşti. Lumber stacks scattered throughout the area stood in piles as high as their heads. Acrid lime-wash mottled scaffolding. Hammers and chisels smashed against stones, and the air tasted of grit and sawdust.

"You left your tent early," Fruzhin said.

"For the river's edge," Vlad replied. "To get a closer look at the enemy." His stare narrowed on his hated cousin.

"Our sovereign did well to place your war band under Zawisza's authority rather than Dan Dăneşti. We can't have him murdered unexpectedly, can we?" Fruzhin warned.

Although certain his wife's fears alluded to Dan Dăneşti's capacity for betrayal, Vlad replied, "He should be cautious when facing our joint foe in battle." He nodded to his best friend. "But I don't believe some traitor's blade in the back will harm him."

Zsigmond waved a hand toward a *bombarda* while he chattered. His captains-general turned in the same direction. Vlad's gaze locked with the Wallachian usurper's own before the latter gave full attention to their monarch again.

After a gesture of dismissal to Zawisza and Dan Dăneşti, Zsigmond summoned Fruzhin. While Zawisza spoke to another captain, Vlad's cousin addressed the subordinates who traveled with him from Wallachia. Vlad turned away, thinking about finding János on the sparring ground.

"Leaving so soon, kinsman?" Dan hailed him with a short barking laugh, mimicked by the usurpers' companions. "Come now. You've barely offered more than a polite address since we met at home. Surely, you'd like to say something else to me."

Vlad subdued a grunt of irritation, swallowed the bitter tang at the back of his throat, and faced his brother's enemy again. Both men kept their distance.

Most of the male descendants of Basarab favored each other in complexion and height. No different, Dan's coif of glossy black hair tumbled beneath a fur hat behind thick shoulders. The length of his broad mustache, the full beard, and the monobrow reminded Vlad of a mural painted on church walls at Argeş of their common ancestor, his grandmother's late husband.

"Where's Radu?" Vlad demanded. His sibling received the name of their grandfather from birth. "Is he a captive? Or did you leave his body rotting somewhere?"

"Do you ask because of the Dowager's concern, or is this some late interest in your brother's welfare?" Dan crossed his well-muscled arms over a wide chest.

"Radu is my blood, was born of the same parents." The absence of closeness between them in childhood did not mean Vlad hardly cared if he lived.

"You have another sibling." Dan tromped through the mud in short leather boots, ordering his companions behind him. "Where's your youngest brother?"

"Safe and far from you." At least, Vlad hoped so. Would their cousin ask otherwise to find out what he knew? He would not give Dan the gratification of unnerving him.

"I'd never harm him," Dan said, although the smirk on his lips belied the words. "He's a man three years younger than you, if memory serves. As the ruling prince, I will defend my homeland and must ensure no... concerns remain in Wallachia. I've seen your devotion to our king and would entrust you with Radu's life under the auspices of Zsigmond. If you gave me the same terms concerning your other sibling."

"Are you asking me to exchange one brother for another?" Vlad's hand went to the hilt of his sword. His guts clenched. "You believe their lives mean so little to me?"

"Each heir to Basarab has ambitions, yourself included." Dan flitted a glance at Vlad's hip before he added, "I hope in Hungary, Radu's political aspirations may be curtailed, while you can ensure I'll keep the youngest of you safe at Argeş."

"As your hostage."

"A guest. Shall we seal this bargain, swear oaths?" Dan barked another laugh, reeking of derision. "There must be some religious foundation with holy relics nearby."

"Guests have free will to come and go as they please." Vlad drew closer, his stare level with his cousin's own. "There can be no trade between us. Not when my siblings' security and freedom hang in the balance. Never assume I'll join you to betray my nearest relations."

"We are also part of a family, although your father once arranged the assassination of mine. A terrible act; brother killing brother. Could you do the same, Vlad?"

"Be glad Zsigmond's siege unites us against a common adversary. Otherwise, you would discover exactly what I can do." Vlad sneered at him and turned and walked away. But he overheard his cousin's muttered curses before Dan spat in the muck.

Vlad should have told him the truth Mircea the Great unknowingly revealed, but what did the past matter in their blood feud? His parent and most of his uncles already lay buried. Their quarrels died with them. Vlad faced uncertainties about his remaining brothers. He vowed to remain guarded in battle here and beyond, lest Cneajna's worries heralded his demise. He must survive at all costs. His growing family needed him.

HEATED IRON BALLS SPOUTED out of the mouth of a *bombarda* and lit up the night sky, just as Vlad led the first wave of his men ashore from an oared galley. Green muck enveloping them up to the thighs, Tobar and Yoska grimaced. At his urging, as one unit, his followers waded through the mossy water on the Danube River's right bank. The warriors edged closer to the westerly base of a rocky promontory, the moon, stars, and torches aboard ships on the water providing their only sources of light.

Four weeks ago, a war band of almost seven hundred infantry, including archers and crossbowmen, followed Vlad from Wallachia into Serbia. Fruzhin's men numbered over twice the same figure. All of them were a part of Zsigmond's forces totaling twenty-five thousand, including Polish cavalry, the Lithuanians under Zawisza's direct command, and a Serbian contingent alongside Dan Dăneşti's six-thousand Wallachian archers.

Since their arrival, skirmishes took place on the shores. Mid-May, the re-taking of Galambóc began with daily bombardment.

Vlad took a cautious, assessing gaze. A steady barrage by Christian ships from daylight until the evening gave him the distraction he needed. The Turks concentrated their answering fire away from him, ignoring all else. They defended breaches of blackened stones along battered walls and gutted towers. They had placed scant numbers on the western approach to the fortress, perhaps thinking no army would be so bold as to attack here. Vlad depended on their ignorant assumption.

A final salvo, the fifth round of simultaneous explosions thundered across the waterway from other warships' guns poised along the north and east, and the completed castle of Saint László. The *bombarda* stationed there fired fewer effective shots at such a distance. Pulverized rocks routinely sprayed Galambóc. Sulfurous smoke stung Vlad's eyes, dispersed on the waning spring winds. Repeated tremors rocked the earth.

Once the blackened night air cleared and the Christian army permitted their guns to cool before overheating, a persistent exaltation from the Turks rose in defiance of the onslaught. "*Allahu Akbar! Allahu Akbar! Allahu Akbar!*"

"What does it mean?" Vlad asked no one in particular. "Why do they repeat that?"

As the last of his three vice-captains came ashore and pressed into the vanguard, the Serbian man said, "They are saying 'God is great,' captain. I heard the same cry each day when they took my home region until I escaped their cruelty."

Vlad grunted in acknowledgment. He would show the Turks his God was greater.

He knew some of his war band well. They had either served at his side or under his vice-captaincy in Bohemia, where they struggled and bled at their sovereign's bidding. Others he did not know, those battle-hardened veterans of Zsigmond's struggles against the Turks as far back as the days of Nicopolis, two years after Vlad's birth.

After assessing them on the practice field, he took the best with him on this dangerous quest. They looked to him now for leadership.

"Zsigmond calls this fortress 'the watcher made of stone.' Scouts claim Ottoman reinforcements are on the way," Vlad said. "Sultan Murād may lead them himself. He knows the strategic value of this place. We will wrest control of Galambóc from the Turks. We must settle it tonight, not with siege guns alone, but in the clash of steel."

As he planned, his men fanned out in the dimness below the palisade of stakes the Turks erected on the western landward side. At Zsigmond's order, Dan Dăneşti's Wallachian archers on galley ships had fired earlier at troops stationed along the defensive walls. The Turks, already mired in the riverine assault, never reinforced those men. Little but corpses and the dying remained for Vlad and his war band as they guardedly approached.

"Ladders and grappling ropes." Vlad passed the edict to his Serbian vice-captain, who waved on the infantry prepared to scale the walls. Foremost among them, János rushed headlong with the attackers. But then, Ottoman archers holding the nearest intact bastion noticed them.

"Shields!" Vlad barely gave the warning before his men defended themselves against a black rain of barbed arrows. Grunts and cries warned a few shots found their targets. He gave the next order. Christian archers at his rear sent their answering volley.

Croaking cries in the dark preceded the tremendous clatter of fallen armored bodies hitting the rough rock face. Just before the ground shook again, behind Vlad's war band. Horns bellowed, summoning the retreat of Zsigmond's forces.

"Whoresons! Their damned reinforcements have arrived," Vlad cursed without turning to see. "We're hemmed in between them and the castle; a hammer and an anvil. Flee for the northern crossing!"

In tight, disciplined ranks, the war band turned. A few screams from the men with ladders rent the air before some of their numbers rejoined Vlad. His glance revealed János with three others. Each fired a Turkish bow retrieved from battered bodies fallen over the defensive wall. Their foes began picking them off, one by one.

"János, to me, now," Vlad commanded. "János!"

Alone, the young man rejoined him among the shielded infantry.

"Did you think you could take on all their archers by yourself? Do nothing so foolish again," Vlad muttered to him.

"When you turned the war band, you were exposed...." János fell silent as Vlad glared at him and then gave the order to keep moving.

Arrowheads thumped against shields and armor, seeking gaps. Where they occurred, Vlad's men filled the space quickly, stepping over their fallen compatriots. While he bent over the first wounded, twitching form in his path, dispatching the unknown Christian with a quick slice across the throat, his Serbian vice-captain gasped.

Vlad said, "Give our dying fighters mercy. The Turks will torture any who breathe."

The vice-captain's throat bobbed before Vlad's command spread through the retreating war band.

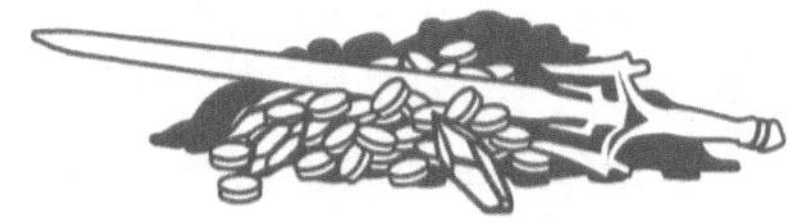

ZSIGMOND CURSED AND raged in the royal tent, pitched at a distance on the same bank where Turks roamed, undefeated. His captains-general and their subordinates stood by.

Their king asked, "How in God's name did those bastards arrive so soon and in such vast numbers to thwart me?"

"They sailed up one of the Danube's tributaries all day," Zawisza muttered. "At least a hundred ships, right, Vlad?"

"By my hasty count during our retreat," he answered. "When can we expect the Teutonic Knights as reinforcements, Your Royal Majesty?"

"I don't know!" Zsigmond paced the tent, rubbing at his reddened, puffy eyes. His hair and clothing were askew, and the acrid scent of gunpowder tainted them. "I've planned this siege for months and built Saint László in less than two years. It's all in disarray. Now Sultan Murād comes in person to ensure my ruin."

"Good king, we are not defeated," Zawisza argued. "When the Teutonic Knights come, they will bolster our numbers."

"Your Royal Majesty, we may not be so certain the sultan brought support," Vlad added what his Serbian vice-captain relayed earlier. "When Murād is in the field, the Turks mount six or seven horses' tails as a standard outside of his tent. But our scouts say there are three tails on display still. If so, this Sinan Bey of Rumelia, who demanded our surrender before the attack on Galambóc, has not deferred control."

"But he is winning against me," Zsigmond murmured. He sighed and sank onto a low, creaking wooden stool. "What losses have we incurred? Give your reports."

Each man did as their king bid.

"Six among my war band fell," Vlad replied in his turn.

His companions gaped at him. Fruzhin clapped his shoulder. "You led them well. Six only? I knew a captain's post would suit your leadership."

Vlad caught the curl of Dan Dăneşti's lips in a sneer before replying, "Tell that to the families of those killed. They won't care for anything but their dead."

"It's a consequence of war and siege, Vlad," Fruzhin said. "Think no more of it."

Zsigmond rubbed his forehead and dismissed them.

As he exited the tent into the coolness of the night, Vlad ignored the eerie specter hanging over the encampment. He felt its presence, rather than saw it, but refused to believe the siege would be a failure. Instead, he thought about his family. A wife and young child left behind at Segesvár, and his eldest son, who must believe himself abandoned to the holy brothers of Tismana.

Vlad lifted his hand, hoping moonlight and torches would set the center of his ruby ring afire. But darkness suffused the gemstone. Warning him about danger.

Fruzhin walked beside him. Flickering flames glowed beneath moonbeams. Crickets chirped and frogs croaked. They vied with the low conversations around crackling campfires and occasional screams from the medical tents set up around the site.

"If I should fall here, Fruzhin, there's something I want you to do for me. Promise me you'll ensure the well-being of my children."

"You will not succumb to any injury at Galambóc, my friend."

"The possibility doesn't frighten me. I do fear leaving such young boys behind. Dan Dăneşti would snuff out their lives and end any threats to his illicit reign. Cneajna's a perfect mother to our Mircea. Her father would protect him in Moldavia, but my eldest is not her child. May I commend his care to you if I should fall?"

"You already know the answer. It would be my privilege to raise any son of yours. There's a boon I want to ask of you too, my blood brother. If I should die here."

"You're the best among Zsigmond's captains. You'll outlive all of us."

"More of my men died than the others combined." Fruzhin sighed. "I've fought innumerable battles and laid siege to countless castles. This time feels different."

Vlad stopped beside him, fronting the riverbank. "What are you trying to say?"

"Something I've longed to tell you, but I needed more information beforehand." Fruzhin raked a hand over his face. "There's a woman I've left behind in Buda. She's no mistress of mine, could never be. She lives with her sole remaining parent and a son—"

"Great God!" Vlad yelled. "They're attacking us."

The infernal glow of reddened balls arced across the night-time sky. A lone Hungarian warship moored in the middle of the waterway shattered. Splintered debris and blackened, ravaged bodies floated on the midnight blue waters of the Danube. Vlad and Fruzhin scrambled down to the river's edge, their conversation forgotten.

It never resumed. Within days, summer arrived. Their king sued for peace.

Vlad stalked the ground outside the royal tent, where a debate ensued. The other officers with him stared at the ground. Fruzhin emerged first, followed by a red-faced Dan Dăneşti, leaving Zawisza to contend with Zsigmond's decision.

"He can't mean to do it!" Vlad grappled Fruzhin's arm. "Even without the Teutonic Knights, we can still take the fortress. Did he say why he wants an armistice?"

"Our king doesn't owe us any explanation," Fruzhin said, shaking off Vlad's hold and turning in a circle of the men. "Your war bands will strike camp soon."

Vlad cursed and slapped his thigh, his scowl mirroring that of Zawisza, who emerged and marched through their midst, stone-faced, without stopping.

Fruzhin's turbulent gaze followed the Polish warrior. "He had vouched for the honor of the Teutonic Knights, having once numbered among them. Now he must disband the Lithuanian companies and tell them they're going home, but not as victors."

"You've said, if we lost Galambóc, the Turks would sail these waters, undeterred."

"We will face them again in some other place. That much is certain." Fruzhin sighed and turned away to his vice-captains, while Vlad pondered their king's choice.

In Zsigmond's rule, from the Battle of Nicopolis two years after Vlad's birth until now, his sovereign notched more losses than wins against Turks. He had killed more Christians. Did those outcomes herald disaster for not only Hungary, but its religion?

ZSIGMOND'S ROYAL COUNSELORS negotiated the terms of the ceasefire and withdrawal. His fleet would ferry the fighters back across the river to the castle of Saint László. Despite their dual protests, Vlad ordered his Gypsies to take the first ships as well. When the orderly retreat began, the palatine with Pipó's successor and others among the royal advisors urged their king's hasty departure. Zsigmond would not go.

"No, not until We have seen to the safety of Our armies. We brought them here to serve Our purpose, and by God, they have tried! We will not depart on our flagship until all the galleys have taken Our brave fighters to safety."

It took hours, but at last, he prepared for the crossing. Night came on and moonlight flooded the Danube. Zawisza, Dan Dăneşti, and their officers would sail on Zsigmond's ship. Their king gave a final look toward the fort his foes had not relinquished, sighed, and strode down to the river's edge, shaking his head at intervals.

Acerbic smoke made Vlad glance heavenward, fearing the sight of fiery balls in the sky again. Something stirred in the woodlands behind him. He stood with Zawisza, who turned from his Lithuanian subordinates and scanned the darkness too.

"Get our sovereign onboard now!" Vlad hollered, as mounted Turkic archers emerged below the tree line. They shot fire-lit arrows through the dimness, catching the Christians unaware.

The Lithuanians withstood Ottoman treachery. Some arrowheads embedded in the hull of Zsigmond's boat set the wood afire. Panicked sailors called out to nearby warships headed for the left bank, while the council members shielded Zsigmond.

As their enemies advanced, Vlad drew back with the others, his sword and shield raised. Except for helmets, none of them wore armor. They never expected the Turks would void the armistice so soon.

"Curse them all! How dare they break terms with me? I'll have their blood." Zsigmond pushed those who shielded him. "Stand aside. Let me fight!"

"They're too many, my king!" Fruzhin shouted. "We won't let them kill you or try to capture you—"

A female's clear voice echoed across the water. "Come aboard, Your Royal Majesty!"

Vlad turned for a brief glimpse of the woman he first encountered below the new castle's construction, arguing with her husband, who waded into the Danube now.

"Cecília, save our king and yourself, my love!" He waved to his wife, carrying a torch on the vessel's bow.

"How many times must I say it, István? I'm never leaving this accursed place without you. Bring our king and climb aboard at once."

As Zsigmond's flagship burned, many sailors dove overboard. With the officers and their sovereign, they swam for the galley as it drew closer. The Turks fired on them. Vlad splashed into the water before he realized Zawisza and the Lithuanians remained on the riverbank. Vlad returned to them.

"What the hell are you doing, Zawisza? Get to the ship."

"There are too many, Vlad, and more of us remain behind. We'll never make it in one vessel," Zawisza replied, whacking at an arrow as it struck his shield.

Vlad peered at the churning water. In the mad dash to clamber aboard, the sailors vied with the royal counselors and officers, all intent on saving their own lives. The lady Cecília's husband urged Zsigmond, who climbed up on the man's shoulders and lurched over the hull. His rescuer fell back into the water while a desperate sailor scrambled atop him. Some of the flagship's crewmen surrounded the pilot and after a vicious argument, one stabbed him and tried to commandeer the galley.

"Perfidious wretch! We're not leaving without István!" The lady drew a dagger.

"Vlad, go from here," Zawisza said. "We'll hold them off."

"You are my friend. I'm not abandoning you," Vlad insisted.

"I gave my word. Before God, I promised death to every Turk I encountered. Zsigmond is a coward for retreating, but I am no such fool. There is no boat big enough to carry my honor. Leave now and return to your family. We will meet again, my Transalpine friend. If not in this life, the next. We'll drink and sing with Stibor."

Zawisza bellowed a war cry, a clamor that rose above all other noises, and rushed headlong with his Lithuanian rearguard against the Turks. They swallowed him up in steel and armor, while more of their reinforcements rode down to the riverbank.

"Vlad! Swim, damn you, for your children's sakes, if nothing else," Fruzhin called out in the blackness.

Searching for a last, desperate sight of Zawisza and finding none, a resigned Vlad threw aside his shield, sheathed his sword, and waded back into the water again. He swam and bumped up against the lady Cecília's husband. Vlad hauled him along despite the heftier man's protests.

"The left riverbank is too far, prince."

"Not for me, my lord István. Hold on now. I'll get you back to your wife."

They reached the boat, where fierce fighting occurred at the wheel. But István's spouse took control of it while waving her dagger in the face of any sailor foolish enough to approach her.

The boom of the cannon preceded splashes in the dark water and Zsigmond's command, "By God, woman, we must flee!"

"Not without my husband! István, answer me, or I swear by Christ and His saints, I'll cut my throat and join you in death right now."

With his grip tight around Vlad's neck, the man spluttered, "Don't be foolish. I'm here, my love! Sail for Saint László before the damnable Turks destroy us all!"

Billowing winds caught the ship's canvas. Vlad and others stranded on the Danube swam in the vessel's wake as the lady Cecília piloted. The craft slowly turned and sluiced across the waterway. Inexperienced, would-be swimmers followed, calling out in desperation before their heads went under. Vlad could save no one else.

Someone unseen shouted, "Christ's blood, they're in the river. Coming after us!"

Vlad struggled, the weight of his companion dragging him, preventing fluid strokes. The shore beckoned, lit by torchlight. If he could just stay at the waterline, he would make it. But after an agonizing, interminable time, his strength flagged. He made out Christian archers on the left bank, firing into the Danube.

As the galley slowed on its approach, István's wife guided the ship's port-side along the dock. Although his chest and arms burned, Vlad swam to the vessel's bow. If the lady Cecília's husband could get himself out of the water, Vlad would be safe, too.

The woman called out, "Ah, I see my dear brave lord! Aim the torches. Get ropes."

Christian archers in smaller river-craft converged on the ship. Others aboard, similarly armed, leaned over the starboard side; all their weapons trained on the Danube. Vlad helped the lady's husband as he grabbed the swinging line. The grunts of men onboard followed as they hauled him out of the murky water first.

Vlad bobbed as the current dragged him astern away from the others. His heart seemed ready to burst. He looked up and caught János' gaze. The younger man grinned as he alone peered over the stern of the ship. A Turkish bow, drawn and prepared to fire. He aimed the arrow's barbed tip straight at Vlad.

In a split second, Cneajna's warning about the betrayal by 'his king's warrior' burst into mind. János! Shocked, Vlad barely ducked under the river. Water rushed and swirled around him. He struck out, his feet tangling with long limbs. A nearby body embedded with a black arrow between the eyes sank through the dank murk and disappeared.

"Vlad! Where are you?"

The waterlogged echo of his name ended the stupor. With a powerful heave, he broke the surface of the Danube. János looked down at him again, the bow withdrawn, before yelling, "Prince Fruzhin, he's here! I see him."

More ropes appeared over the hull. Bewildered and exhausted, Vlad could not raise his arms to catch one. János leaped into the river and pulled him along until they reached the rough sediment encumbered by mosses.

Vlad spluttered. "I glimpsed the weapon and thought you meant to murder me."

János spat out river water. "A Turk swam up right behind you, a dagger between his teeth. He might've killed you with it too, but for this." He laid the short bow across his lap. "I would never have let him claim your life. It was not your time, my prince."

Aboard ship, the lord István embraced his Cecília and kissed her hard on the mouth, to lusty cheers and approval. Vlad laughed at their happiness as the danger receded.

CHAPTER 26

The Knight and the Monk

"Call it Nature, Fate, Fortune; all these are the names of the one and selfsame God."-Lucius Annaeus Seneca (5 BC-65 AD), Roman statesman.

IN THE YEAR OF OUR Lord 1428. Tismana Monastery, Oltenia region, Principality of Wallachia (modern-day Tismana Monastery, western Romania), and *Buda, Hungary* (modern-day Budapest, Hungary)

After parting with Fruzhin and their king, Vlad sat on horseback in his breastplate and pauldrons outside the locked gates of the Tismana Monastery. Despite protests, he left his pair of Gypsy followers on the southern outskirts of the nearby village. He knew they wanted to see their families as much as he desired a long overdue reunion with his firstborn son. He ascended the treacherous landscape of the mountain foothills alone.

The silence stretched. No breeze stirred the yew conifers atop the mountain crags. A faint light shone from inside the ocher-painted church at the heart of the monastery, its silhouette framed by a pink and purple-hued summer sky. A constellation shimmered. Either Sagittarius or Scorpius; he couldn't recall which from his lessons.

Certain the monks would already be at their first daily prayer service, Vlad waited. His patience ebbed with every white wisp as he exhaled. Two of the holy brothers finally emerged. Upon seeing him, the pair rushed and opened the gates.

He clenched the reins hard in his hand, while his other fingers slid away from the pommel of the sword girded at his waist. Otherwise, he might have throttled the men. They stood aside as he rode into the yard where the holy brothers had left the church.

Pahomie, with his mismatched eyes, came out, at last, holding the hand of a yellow-haired boy. Vlad slid down from the horse. The breath caught in his throat at the sight of his son by Călţuna.

She had never replied to his letter from Buda, nor did Vlad expect an answer. She might never know, but her presence lingered in his memory, while their green-eyed child grew in her image.

"My lord prince, you've returned," Pahomie said in a dull monotone. He exchanged wary glances with some of his brethren before shooing them away.

Soon only Vlad, his son, and Pahomie remained.

"I came straight from Serbia once my king ordered an end to the siege of Galambóc. I will take the boy north with me, Pahomie," Vlad replied.

He kneeled at his namesake's feet. Tiny toes in leather sandals stuck out from the hem of a child-sized version of a monk's black robe.

"Why is he wearing this, Pahomie? Didn't the Gypsy women in the village make proper garments for him as he grew?"

"We have them here," the monk replied. "But he prefers these."

"He's nearly three years old. He cannot have fixed preferences already," Vlad snapped as he reached for the boy's cheek.

His son mewled and drew back against the coarse folds of Pahomie's garment.

"Don't be frightened," Vlad whispered. "You must remember me."

"My prince, he is shy of unfamiliar faces—"

"Unfamiliar faces?" Vlad stood, the long leather sheath of his weapon slapping against his thigh. "Did you never read my letters to him, letting him know of my love and intent to return to his side as soon as I could?"

"Of course, I did."

"Yet, you're telling me that in a year, my son has forgotten me?"

"It's been more than a year since you departed through these gates. Another spring came and has turned into summer. You must give him time."

Vlad snorted and crouched low again, holding out his hand for his child to take it. "*Tată.* That's what you called me. Your father. I will take you away to meet your new stepmother and your younger brother. Don't you want to see them?"

The boy buried his reddened cheeks in Pahomie's robe. Vlad reached for the yellow curls, and his child began wailing.

He rose again, fury roused inside of him. "What have you done, monk?" His hand returned to his weapon. "Did you turn my son against me?"

"I could never do that! Would never dare," Pahomie spluttered, his gaze widening as it drifted down to Vlad's sword. He patted the boy's head. "My brethren and I have cared for him. He knows only this place and the village below."

"That's why he's like this?" Vlad pointed at the cowering child. "He is my firstborn. Without him, I would never have learned how to be a father. I'd never harm him."

"He simply doesn't recall you. As I've said, permit him time to do so."

"How long must I wait?" Vlad looked down at his namesake again, tempted to wrest him away. But in the next breath, he decided against it. He would only frighten the boy further. Having already lost Călțuna, would he lose their son next?

"All things occur as the Lord ordains, my prince," Pahomie responded, patting the little one's shaking shoulders. "Believe me, I understand his importance to you—"

"You can't! Because you don't know what I've sacrificed to return to his side. I gave his mother up, putting away my enduring need for her. As my king demanded, I've married a woman who is still a stranger to me.

I've even survived a brutal siege just to come here for him. He and his new baby brother are my life. The reasons I survive."

"Please, my prince, I can feel your ire. Be assured, the boy does as well, and won't understand it. You should go to the village and remove the armor—"

"You would lock the gates and keep me from him?"

"No! I am not some loathsome cur who would steal a child from his parent." Pahomie drew himself up to his full height and raised his voice in a strident tone Vlad had never heard before. "You dishonor yourself, not me, with pernicious thought."

"What else should I think? I've made yearly gifts for my son's sake and my uncle's memory only to suffer this disdain."

"My good prince, even if you withdrew your beneficence now in misplaced anger, the gates of Tismana Monastery would always be open to you. Whether your son lives here or not. He's had enough disquiet for the day, and I believe you have too. Rest in the village and come again tomorrow. Share in our sole meal. Let us have peace and fellowship as we once did."

"I will come back, monk." Vlad marched away and grabbed his horse's reins, the corners of his eyes stinging. "You may be assured of it."

"Go with God, my prince, until we see each other," Pahomie intoned.

"What does He have to do with any of this?" Vlad muttered under his breath. "To hell with you and your platitudes."

At the village inn south of the religious foundation, Vlad decided against returning for his son the next day. Not only because the boy's rejection hurt. Vlad loved him so much. He could not upset him again so soon.

He wished Fruzhin or János remained with him instead of journeying on to Hungary. With the loss of Zawisza at the siege still a heavy blow, the absence of friends who could offer advice left him muddled.

What could he do? His boy no longer knew him. He had abandoned him too easily and far too long in the care of others. Just as he once gave up the child's mother. His heart thudded. When he held his little Mircea again, would the baby also cry and recoil?

On an impulse, Vlad wrote to Cneajna and begged her to join him at Tismana. He needed to hold a child of his. Perhaps his wife could offer counsel about his eldest heir.

Despite their year-long marriage, with more than half of it already spent apart, he scarcely knew her. He also sensed in their brief time together, she gave thought to her opinions before offering them. As a woman with a son, she might have insight.

Her Moldavian guards in tow, she arrived in the carriage at noon on the village's outskirts. He drowned in the sea-green warmth of her gaze before his stare flitted to their son in her arms. Ruxandra and Vlậcsan the Wolf also emerged from the vehicle. He and Cneajna's former nursemaid each extended a hand to aid Vlad's grandmother. Her groan rumbled as she clambered down, while Vlậcsan retrieved her walking stick.

"I never expected to see you!" Vlad rushed to her side.

"I'm not dead." She patted his bearded cheek. "There is still life in these old bones. Greet the rest of your family."

He bowed and straightened at the side of his wife. "You are well, Cneajna?"

"I am now, even more so since I first received your letter. We've missed you. Your Mircea and me." She swallowed. "There is redness in your eyes and swollen folds of skin beneath them. Are you not sleeping at night?"

"I am." He forced himself to hold her regard, despite the lie. "War and duty weighed heavily, but having my nearest relations here eases the burden."

She nodded and held out the small bundle wrapped in swaddling beneath Vlad's wolf-skin. Wide awake, their son stared with eyes Vlad previously recalled as gray-blue just after birth. Now they were a dull green.

"How I've longed for the sight of you." Vlad cradled him close and kissed his black hair before asking, "He still suckles well and sleeps most of the night?"

Cneajna's soft giggle drew his glance. "You may judge by the size of him how well he does at my breasts. But he's kept me and Ruxandra awake almost every night."

"He has, my prince, since you left Segesvár," Ruxandra added.

"I think he wanted you near, Vlad." Cneajna patted the wolf's pelt and smiled.

He nodded, enraptured by the babe. No matter the validity of his reasons, he had left his firstborn son in the care of others for too long. Finally, he could acknowledge that mistake. He must never repeat it with his Mircea.

"Vlậcsan received word of the birth at the end of spring and informed me," the Dowager said, a caustic look flung in Vlad's direction before she too gazed upon her great-grandson. A slight smile deepened the lines around her mouth, but otherwise softened her features. "Two months ago, we set out for Segesvár."

"I didn't know where you were before then," Vlad replied. "Your last missive arrived at Buda and said you'd gone into hiding with my youngest brother."

"If you had thought about it long enough, you would have known we went to the only place where those who keep the Orthodox faith may truly be safe."

When she did not say more, his brow furrowed at the cryptic answer. Then he grasped her meaning.

"Constantinople? You and my little brother made the journey all the way there?"

"I am not so infirm that we could not undertake it." She bridled and sniffed. "As I've learned from Vlậcsan, others believed you also hid there from your king. Your brother Alex is not so little. He's a man of almost thirty years who could be mistaken for you. He served among imperial forces."

"Where is he now? May I see him?"

"No. Your murderous cousin searches for him. We parted on the outskirts of Constantinople. While I journeyed north, Alex went eastward with our loyal boyars."

"My king's siege at Galambóc would not have given me a chance to rescue you."

"You men and your foolish wars!" The Dowager gave one of her typical, unladylike snorts and spat in the dirt. "When will you discover no matter how much you conquer, it will never be enough?" She peered at his child again. "A man's true legacy lies not in lands, riches, or power, but with his family."

"How did you hear about my Mircea's birth, Vlâcsan?" Vlad asked.

"It was well known, my prince," the Wolf replied, "in Segesvár that your new bride settled there for many months and grew great with a child."

"Is Dan Dăneşti aware you've rejoined the Dowager?"

"I doubt. The ruling prince dismissed me from his service before entering Serbia."

"I'm surprised my ruthless cousin didn't have you killed, considering all you had seen of his court at Argeş."

"He tried once...but that is no longer a concern."

"It remains for me so long as you are with my grandmother. You may find the Gypsies encamped beside the lake at a short distance. Join them. I'll speak to my family alone."

"Take the carriage, nephew, you and the companion of Vlad's wife," the Dowager instructed. "We'll walk. The guards will protect us. I shall be well."

Vlâcsan opened his mouth and closed it just as quickly. Ruxandra flicked a glance at her former charge, who dismissed her.

The carriage trundled off. Vlad handed their Mircea back to Cneajna, who hushed the fussing child. Once Vlad offered an arm for his grandmother to lean on him, she gave him a persistent stare and cleared her throat.

He made the same polite gesture to his wife, their baby tucked in the crook of her other forearm. Together they set out across a thick carpet of lush grasses beneath the warming summer sun. The Moldavian guardsmen rode on either side of them.

"You don't trust Vlâcsan," the Dowager said. "I presume you don't want him to hear what you've discovered about your sibling, Radu, my Vlad."

"As it is, there isn't much to tell. He's still missing," he replied. "Dan Dăneşti wanted to trade my youngest brother for Radu."

"Humph. May we be assured the usurper doesn't have him in a dungeon cell?"

"We may not. Maybe Dan tested my knowledge alone. Radu's whereabouts remain uncertain, but after I've rejoined King Zsigmond, I'll seek more information."

"Radu's fate is written in the stars. That wasn't the reason you sent Vlâcsan away?"

"No, Grandmother. There's another, more pressing concern," Vlad confessed. He told the women about his reunion with his namesake son.

"He has not seen you since the spring before you left for Moldavia." The Dowager halted and peered at him. "Are you surprised the boy didn't recall you after such a time?"

"I am his father. I wrote to him, Grandmother."

With a resounding harrumph, she rolled her eyes heavenward. "Letters are no substitute for a parent's comfort. His arms."

Sighing at her response, he turned to his wife. "What say you, Cneajna?"

"He's a little boy, Vlad. Should a grown man resent the whims of a child? If he does, how will it resolve the matter?" Despite her ready answer, her gaze lingered on their baby.

He eyed the pair of indomitable women on either side of him. They represented his past and future. His grandmother's advice had never failed him before. In the time since he and his wife married, his esteem for her only grew.

Yet, he ached to ignore all his troubles, and hold her and kiss her without restraint. Would she think of him as only some ravening beast, driven by bloodlust alone?

He asked her, "What do you believe I should do about the boy?"

"Your path is clear," Cneajna answered. "Give your son time to know you again. Long enough for you both to rediscover each other. Is he not worth patient love?"

When he glanced at the Dowager, she gave a sharp nod to Cneajna. "Listen to the wisdom of the woman you've wed, my Vlad. I doubt she shall ever lead you astray."

At the encampment, Vlad gathered the Gypsy families and introduced his bride. In her turn, she strolled among them with Tobar and Yoska at her side to translate. She asked after the health of newborn babes, as well as the infirm. Vlad studied her casual, relaxed manner and detected no false or forced response in her light, laughing banter. She sat on the cool grass around the main campfire, ate vegetable pottage and fried bread with rabbit, and nursed dear Mircea, nestled in his blanket until early evening.

"It's getting late and your son will wish to sleep," the Dowager said. "We should go to the inn. Vlậcsan stopped there first and arranged for our rooms."

Vlad eyed the boyar, who dunked a wooden spoon in the second bowl of soup Tobar's sister by marriage handed him.

"You wonder why I rely upon him so much, my Vlad," his grandmother remarked.

"Although he is your nephew, your blood, I believe you should be cautious. He strikes me as a man who gives loyalty when he knows he will benefit."

"You are right." As he gasped in surprise, she nodded. "If I had not married into the House of Basarab, the ruling family, that young man would not still be at my side. I know who and what he is. I've always known. On Florea's deathbed, I promised my brother I would protect his son. Even from himself.

"But my Mircea, God rest his soul, wronged Vlậcsan, by taking his holdings in the western villages of Pocruia, Sârbşori, Godineşti, Ohaba, and here at Tismana. My son stole Vlậcsan's future. He will remain aligned with our house to reclaim his lost inheritance." She paused and patted Vlad's hand resting on his leg. "We all do as we must for survival. He acts so for the sake of justice."

"What you call justice, Grandmother, others might easily term a cause for revenge. I hope you'll never know disappointment in Vlậcsan the Wolf."

"Time will tell, my Vlad, as it does in all matters."

Later, at the village inn, Cneajna and Ruxandra struggled with the drowsy and fussy baby. Exasperated with their fruitless endeavors, Vlad took up his black wolf-skin, snuggled his second son inside its warmth, and cradled him against his shoulder.

"My prince, the evil eye!" Ruxandra called out as he made for the chamber door. "He must wear the amulets I have made for him."

"Nothing will harm my child while he's in my care." He never slowed his stride.

Outside the inn, a pair of Cneajna's guards on patrol nodded to him. His Mircea grizzled and wriggled. Vlad patted his back and made a circular path along the street in steady repetition. Soon, his boy settled and slumbered.

The inn's entrance closed behind him with a soft thud. Cneajna and Ruxandra waited for him. Although loath to surrender his child, he let his wife's former nursemaid take the boy to the pallet against the inn wall, where she would sleep beside him. Cneajna stayed, wearing the same blood-red robe as when he first met her in Poland.

He turned from her, knowing what she wanted.

With a sigh, he studied the myriad pin-pricked stars glittering in the night. The monastery's occupants must be resting now to prepare for prayers. Was his eldest son also asleep? What about the boy's mother at her religious house? Was Călțuna awake and able to see the same celestial bodies he did?

"Will you come to bed, Vlad?"

"Soon, Cneajna." Although he rubbed at the burning corners of his weary eyes, he suspected sleep would elude his tortured mind and body tonight. "I promise."

As he feared, she did not leave him, but drew closer with diminutive footfalls crossing the cobblestones.

"Why did you summon me if your only intent is to watch me from a distance?"

He lowered his gaze and turned, glaring at her. His hands fisted at his sides as she closed the remaining gap between them. The temptation of her pursed lips drew his gaze to her lush mouth. He wanted her desperately, but at the sight of her, guilt returned.

Never once did he expect he might have given up Călțuna for Cneajna. His fingertips itched and burned for the feel of his wife.

Something else other than lust also filled him, yet he struggled to define it. No, he did not want to name it.

"Why, Vlad?" She lifted his chin and made him regard her again. She had removed her linen veil. With stray hairs tucked behind her ears and the rest plaited down her back in one long braid, her agate earrings showed.

Weakened by the nearness of her, his limbs quivered and he ached to hold her. But he knew she had questions for him also, more than the outcome of the siege. He could not trust himself to even speak of Galambóc either, the pain of Zawisza's absence was still too fresh. Much less what she surely wanted to know. She gave him the greatest joy with the birth of another heir, their precious son, and asked for little in return. Although he still dismissed her strange, prophetic dreams, they offered hope for the future.

"You don't want to want me. I accept it." She sighed. "But you must stop believing there is some shame in your conflicted heart. You've done me no dishonor."

"You can't understand!" He wrenched away from her. Why must he struggle to explain himself now?

"No, I cannot, because you're still trying to conceal your innermost feelings from me. When I know you as I know myself. After our reunion at Segesvár, I had hoped you might tell me the outcome of your quest for your lady's whereabouts. You never did and you left so soon afterward for war. I feared for your fate in Serbia, seeing the disquiet within you. It has returned because of me." She sniffled.

"No!" Not those damnable tears. The slightest hint of them pierced him to the core, sharper than any blade on the battlefield. He cursed and faced her again. "I'm a blundering idiot, Cneajna. None of...this is your fault!"

"I believe your grandmother would say it is the fault of our stars, Vlad." She forced a wistful smile and looked up at him with shimmering eyes. "If you will not reveal your conversation with King Zsigmond in Buda, at least tell me; have you chosen as regards your past and future?"

"I have," he affirmed. "I'm here with you, am I not?"

"Then I suppose there must be contentment in that fact." Yet, emptiness echoed in her hollow tone. She swiped at her dampened cheek before she fled.

He did not follow, staying outdoors for most of the night. By then, the silvery moon rode high in the heavens and silence hung over the little village.

The climb up the rickety staircase seemed the longest, heaviest steps he had ever undertaken. The wood groaned beneath his short boots, as did the floorboards.

Moldavian guards stationed outside his room yawned before they straightened at his approach. Beyond the door, Ruxandra slept while cradling sweet Mircea against her, tucked in the wolf pelt. Vlad smiled down at the boy who must meet his elder brother.

As he turned toward the bed, Cneajna rose, her shadow moving along the wall in low candlelight. The linen coverlet slid from her exposed shoulders to her curvy waist. Her black hair cascaded, the tips curling around her back.

"You were right." His feet shuffled. He met her stare. "What you said earlier about my desire. The need...shames me because I don't want you to believe I would merely slake a man's lust with you. We're married, but we are still strangers, and Călţuna remains in my heart. I let her go, you see. When Zsigmond could have told me where she was, I chose not to seek the answer. What does that say about me, if I could relinquish her after all that time? Am I more inconstant than I realize?"

"You are likely not the same man she knew." Cneajna clasped her fingers in her lap. "She may not be the same woman. I'm a poor substitute, but—"

"Never say that about yourself!" He approached her but wavered. How could he make her understand? "The pair of you are as different as the day and night. But each day, the past retreats until there is only you."

The admission frightened him more than his candor. Was he in danger of becoming engulfed in their union, losing himself, before he lost her, as he did Călţuna?

Wordlessly, Cneajna extended her arms to him.

He rushed to the bed, kneeling as he framed her lovely face in his hands and kissed her. She gripped his neck, tugging him. He lifted his lips only to nibble and nip at her throat and nuzzle the valley between her engorged breasts. He weighed their ample bounty in his hands and laved the nipples until she cried out. The fluid he tasted was thin and bland.

"Did I hurt you?" He raised his head. "Is it too soon after the birthing?"

She fingered his unkempt beard and mustache, and whispered, "How have you not found the village barber or his counterpart among the Gypsies?"

"Please don't make me seek him out now so that I may have you," he pleaded against her soft lips.

Her husky laugh followed. Then she pushed at his shoulders until he flopped on his back across the bed, stunned further as she clambered atop him.

"You're not leaving my side tonight, Vlad." She tugged at the laces of his shirt. "Or for many nights to come. We have all the time in the world, husband, to know each other as intimately as two people may."

VLAD WAITED ANOTHER three days after Cneajna's arrival with the Dowager before he returned to Tismana Monastery. This time, he took the women with him, while Ruxandra, little Mircea, and Vlậcsan stayed behind at the inn.

Pahomie greeted them at the gates. As they swung open beneath the dawn sky and the family entered, he displayed his usual deference and invited them to the impending service of worship at Matins. Biting back the groan inspired as much by his resentment of religious rites as concern for Cneajna's religious beliefs, he glanced at her.

"My mother raised me as a Catholic in secret," she said, to the Dowager and the monk's clear surprise, "but my father observed Eastern Orthodox customs. Lead on."

Soon they stood in the recesses of the church. Wooden icons of the Lord Jesus Christ and Orthodox saints hung in the sanctuary, affixed to walls around the altar. Heady incense preceded the monks' procession through the doors as they chanted a hymn.

Vlad stared in shock as his son stood at the forefront of the holy brothers, carrying a small candle in a silver holder. Although nearing three years old, he showed devotion and patience throughout the prayers, various readings, and homilies. The little boy even mouthed parts of the Nicene Creed and Lord's Prayer while the monks chanted them.

During the Divine Liturgy, as the brothers took wine and bread and offered the same to Vlad and his family, Pahomie also gave his son the latter. When the monks withdrew into the nave, Vlad watched from the doorway. His namesake, with Pahomie's attentive guidance, lit the flame at the revered Abbot Nikodim's tomb.

Pahomie dismissed the holy brothers, took the candle from the child, and invited his small family to greet him. While the monk hovered nearby, Vlad crouched before his firstborn, hard-pressed to restrain tears of pride.

"I was watching you today at Matins. You were quiet and did your duty well."

"Thank...you." His child looked at Pahomie, who gave him an approving nod.

"This is your father, Prince Vlad. He came to visit in recent days," the monk said.

The boy questioned, "His name is Vlad? Like me."

Pahomie nodded. "Will you be well with him if I wait outside the church?"

Vlad's son peered up at the holy brother, wide-eyed before replying, "Yes."

Pahomie tilted his head and left them. Vlad summoned his grandmother and Cneajna, the latter of whom kneeled at eye-level with his son as she greeted him.

"What a fine child! Your father's very pleased with you. As I am to meet you at last."

The boy's gaze flitted between her and the Dowager, who leaned on her walking stick. When she winked at him, he giggled softly before casting a furtive look beyond the nave door, where the edge of Pahomie's robe remained in view.

"I am indeed your father," Vlad said, drawing his attention. "You also have a brother of my blood. His name is Mircea. Can I come back another day and bring him?"

His eldest son seemed to mull over the words before nodding. "Yes. Come back."

"Until then, my sweet boy." Although reluctant to leave him so soon again, Vlad ended the conversation there. "Now go to Brother Pahomie. Be well, always."

"Thank you," his child whispered, darting outside.

Vlad heaved a long sigh. Cneajna and his grandmother pressed one hand each to his shoulders at the same time. Their mutual touch imbued him with warmth, renewed strength, and comfort. A sentiment only close and valued family could impart. Clearing his throat, he stood and offered his forearms, leading them away.

He arrived again in another three days at the Matins service, as his grandmother insisted. Comfortable in Cneajna's lap, tiny Mircea slept through the ride up Stârmina Mountain and never stirred during the chanted prayers.

If Vlad found himself surprised by his eldest heir's attentiveness during the rituals, he stunned him further. With Pahomie's aid in sounding out the Slavic words, the boy read a few lines of the Epistle and chanted the canticle that followed.

Later, while Cneajna and the Dowager sat inside the carriage and introduced Vlad's children to each other, he strolled near the gates beside Pahomie.

"My firstborn can read already, and so well. You've done wonders with him."

Pahomie gave a sage nod. "Any child given attention and encouragement can do the same at his age. Your son is precocious and humble. He brings honor to your name."

They halted together and watched him playing with his half-brother, who chortled.

"I only wish his dear mother could know about his talents and see him grow.," Vlad said. "But the last I heard of her from my king, she considered taking holy orders."

"Ah. Well, God guides each one of us along the path of our destiny," Pahomie intoned. "I grow more certain of the fact each day, especially while observing your son. Our Lord led him here and perhaps intends him to stay forever."

"What are you telling me?" Vlad's raucous tone drew the attention of his wife, grandmother, and firstborn through the opened carriage door. Even little Mircea cried before Cneajna soothed him.

"He is an heir to the House of Basarab." Vlad tamped down his burst of temper. "What do you mean by suggesting he should live here?"

"This monastery and the village." Pahomie turned in a half-circle, his eyes lit at their centers by the newly risen sun. "They're all he's ever known after his birth at Hermannstadt. You came for respite and left him in the care of the holy brothers. You've endowed this place with yearly gifts, but what if Our Lord requires a sacrifice of you as He did when testing the patriarch, Abraham? The life of your son, in His service."

The matter became Vlad's only consideration in the coming days.

"Your heart thrums faster when you are deep in muddled thoughts." His wife rested her head on his chest one night.

"You are learning my moods all too well." He tightened the hold of his arm, previously languid across her shoulders. "But I don't want to trouble you. Sleep."

"I'm your bride." Her chin rose. She looked at him. "Your concerns are mine."

He conveyed the monk's earlier words. She sighed and shook her head.

"Will you do nothing else," he asked, "and remain silent now that you know?"

"I should not offer any opinion," she murmured against his skin.

"Why?"

"Because I'm not only your wife, but the mother of your second son as well. If I speak now, you may think the words come from a woman partial to her child alone. What did the Dowager advise after you revealed Pahomie's words to her?"

"I haven't told her. Although I'll always trust Grandmother implicitly, I rely upon your opinion, too. She said you would never lead me astray. Tell me what is in your head and heart, Cneajna. You are fair, in form, and thought."

And, these days, he found quiet relief in her presence.

"Your trust is an honor, Vlad." She peered at him in the dimness.

"You've earned it." He fingered the dimpled curve of her cheek.

She swallowed audibly and whispered, "I love you." Although he gasped and opened his mouth, she pressed a finger to his lips. "I don't expect any declaration of the same. You should understand that what I shall say next comes out of that love."

She gripped his hand and held it against her skin. "Your namesake nears his third birthday, while our child is still a swaddling babe. What if Wallachia's ambitious boyars seeking power through a willing recruit found your namesake son and offered him support, thwarting our child's future? If your eldest boy remains at Tismana Monastery, where a monkish life shall cure him of any latent aspirations, no one else may use him as a threat against our child's future fortunes. I have a mother's fear about Mircea's fate."

"You're more than his parent." He perceived her sound rationale alongside her priorities as a mother. "You would be an insightful advisor to his future rule."

"Is power your goal also? We've never spoken of it, but I sensed more underlay your concerns about your elder brother, Radu. You want to ensure a path to the crown in your homeland as well."

His thumb stroked her cheek. She loved him without expectation. How could he ever withhold any truth from her, especially as important as this?

"Yes. Since boyhood, I've coveted the throne at Târgoviște." A long sigh escaped him afterward, as did the sense of a burden lifted from his shoulders. He had never even spoken about his ambitions to Călțuna.

He continued, "When my eldest brother Mihail sat there, I hated the sight of him because he didn't deserve to wear the crown. I expected and accepted that Radu would follow him, guiding both Princely Courts. Dan Dăneşti interfered. He took Argeş and may have killed Radu. I want the crown, Cneajna, for myself and my heirs. It should be mine."

Only the strongest and smartest of the sons of Mircea the Great should rule. He would show his king, his wife, his friends, and the world that he could guide Wallachia's future better than any of his siblings.

"Then you shall take the throne by your will alone and decide whether your firstborn or second son shall succeed you." Cneajna stretched. "They must never fight. Brothers should not kill each other! If you wish to avoid that calamity, the choice before you regarding your namesake is of even greater consequence." She yawned, wriggled, and snuggled against him. "Speak to the Dowager. Hear what she shall say."

"IT'S A GOOD SOLUTION, my Vlad," his grandmother told him the next day. They rode to the religious foundation, leaving Cneajna and the baby guarded at the inn. "You'll miss your oldest boy terribly, but the monks of the Tismana Monastery will not deny you access to him. They value him as much as your bequests of coin. You can visit often."

"If he stays, I can't intrude on his life without warning, as I please." Vlad leaned back and closed his eyes as their conveyance rocked back and forth. The harness jangled. "Just as I could not do that to his mother."

"You've learned so much along the road of sacrifice, more than your father ever did." The Dowager touched his shoulder. "The battle against self-serving desires is rarely won. I'm proud of how far you've come. My dear Mircea would be too."

"His good opinion never mattered in life, Grandmother," Vlad muttered. "Why you think it should concern me after his death is a wonder."

She snorted and stared out of the window as the carriage ascended to the monastery. In the quietude that followed, Vlad sensed he still had so much further to go along a painful journey, as he veered toward relinquishing his eldest son. He also prayed wherever Călţuna might be, she would understand and accept the second-most difficult choice he would ever make.

He and Cneajna lay awake that night, their heads on pillows. Both naked under the coverlet and satiated by their passion, they chattered. Until she thumbed his forehead.

"Too many lines?" He chuckled. "Am I growing too old for you?"

"Don't make sport of your concerns. They are grave. We've talked about a great deal since our reunion, including the loss of your Polish friend at Galambóc. There is one thing you've never told me. Why do you hate the Turks so much?"

"They are the natural enemies of Christendom."

"Yes, but I sense a deeper, personal grievance against them. Will you tell me why?"

He nodded. "I have never spoken with you about my sister Arina, bartered in marriage by our father to a Turk, so Wallachia might have peace while her husband lived."

As she gasped, he sighed. How did this bewitching beauty break down the defenses he had built up over the years with her simple questions?

"Arina and I were twins..." he began. He told Cneajna about their happy childhood, their father's plans for her, and the sad, final farewell, not intending at the outset to reveal the entirety of their years together. Yet somehow, he knew Cneajna, with her prophetic dreams would understand.

"Our parents and our uncle Staico always wondered why we were so close and never spoke openly to each other until we were four. We could hear each other's thoughts and feel each other's emotions. As vivid and real as when you look at me with love in your beautiful eyes."

She smiled. "Go on."

He exhaled a sigh of relief at having guessed right about her.

"Arina lost one child and became pregnant again. She perished in childbirth and I thought the baby, a girl, died with her. My worst fears came true. Her life had ended like our eldest sister's did, but alone, except for her servants. Her husband was already dead. After I heard the news, I swore to avenge her loss. That is why I hate the Turks. They took her from me."

"Oh, Vlad, I'm so sorry for your pain."

"You must hear the rest. I will keep nothing from you."

"Your candor honors me."

"Arina's second child survived. A man loyal to her Ottoman father has raised the girl as his. She is somewhere in Turkic lands. Vlậcsan's son is a hostage among their people. His father has promised to help me locate my niece." He breathed deeply. "Some years ago, the Wolf told me something else. About a revenant stalking the city where my sister died. Though I cannot be certain, Arina may have returned from her grave as an unholy blood-drinker. If so, I must give her spirit eternal peace and rescue her child."

His wife gaped at him. When she said nothing, he feared the shock might have overcome her.

Instead, she began sobbing. "You mean to enter Turkic lands? Oh please, do not go!"

He pulled her close and hugged her. "I don't want to leave you or our son, but I must do this for Arina. Please tell me you understand why, Cneajna."

"I do," she wailed. "But Vlậcsan or some other must go in your place. Please don't attempt it. If you journey into your sister's past, it will rob you of your future, Vlad."

He did not understand what she meant, but guessed some vision of hers warned against the plan. He comforted her, making no promise never to undertake the journey. Though it would put him at odds with his wife, he owed his sister that much.

THROUGHOUT THE SUMMER, Vlad spent almost every day at Tismana's religious house. He watched and listened to his eldest heir and saw his reading abilities and knowledge grow. As did his dutifulness to prayers and a life in God's service.

Often, Vlad blinked back tears but never turned away from the sight. Sometimes, he brought the rest of his family. Little Mircea's elder brother drew the babe's fascination and always elicited a smile or chortle.

At other times, Vlad rode his Carpathian pony up Stârmina Mountain alone. As he did on the day before his planned departure to Hungary. Ahead of Vespers, he walked beside his namesake in the herbal garden until they sat on a wooden bench.

"You're happy here, little one?" Vlad asked.

"Yes, *Tată*." The child swung his short legs back and forth with exuberance. He peeked up at Vlad and fingered his bearded cheek. "But *Tată* is sad."

"No, never!" Vlad swiped the wetness on his face he had not realized was there. "I'm always happiest with you. But I'm taking your stepmother and brother away. I'll miss you very much. You'll live with Pahomie and the holy brothers. Do you like the monks?"

"Yes, *Tată*. I like them."

"That's very good to know. I'm glad. While you are living here, I will be in a place called Buda. It's where the king whom I serve has his castle."

"Buda," the child echoed. Then he asked, "You will come back?"

"Always!" His heart nearly bursting, Vlad hugged his child and kissed the curls so like the boy's mother's own. "I will come back to you."

"Don't be sad, *Tată*." His son returned the fervent embrace.

After the evening prayer service, Pahomie carried a torch and escorted Vlad to the gates. "You're leaving tomorrow, my prince. Have you decided your child's future?"

"I am giving him over to God. I accept that the boy's life is here."

"He will excel," the monk replied, his cheeks suffused with happiness. "I'll ensure it. You may visit him whenever you wish, my prince."

"I shall write often, but I want him focused on his duties. Not wondering when his parent's sudden appearance will disrupt monastic life again."

At last, he grasped the harsh lesson both his parents imparted when they stayed away and let him find his path in Hungary. He must do the same for his firstborn.

'You'll come again in the morning before going northward?" Pahomie asked.

"No, we must be on the road from the village after dawn." Vlad stopped and looked back at the monastery's buildings framed by dark gray skies. The rising moon loomed. "The Dowager and my princess already said their farewells the last time they were here, knowing of my intent. Brother Pahomie, if my son should ever need me..." The words caught in Vlad's throat and he looked away, unable to speak further.

"Know that I shall send prompt word," the monk promised. "You've made the right choice for him, my prince, although I know it is hard for you. Take consolation in knowing that the holy brothers and I shall keep him safe and nurtured. A sacred duty."

Vlad sniffled and coughed. "Don't let him forget me again."

"Never," Pahomie swore. "He shall hear about his brave father and read your letters. You will be reunited. I'm sure of it."

AUTUMN LEAVES BLANKETED Buda as Vlad returned to the city, having parted with his grandmother and Vlậcsan outside Tismana village. In the carriage next to his horse, Cneajna chattered with Vlad, pointing out all the sights that drew her interest to Ruxandra, including the wide, glittering swath of the Danube River at noon, and held their Mircea up the window so he might see.

"Buda's so much larger than Suceava! Does your king expect our arrival, husband?"

"He does, Cneajna," Vlad replied. "The Gypsy rider I sent ahead of us before we left Transilvania carried three letters, for Zsigmond, Fruzhin, and János."

"Then I'm glad for the good sense to don fresh garments before we resumed our journey this morning and make our presentation at court."

Vlad smiled at her. The velvet brocade with floral motifs in the olive-green robe suited her well and complemented her complexion and agate earrings. Small, pink-tinged pearls, Cneajna's clear favorite among jewels, embellished the silver neckband and wrists. Earlier, Ruxandra braided her hip-length hair into two plaits, and coiled and pinned them to a silk fillet covered by a linen veil. The baby tugged at its folds.

Vlad wished Mircea's elder brother could be with them in the carriage, but what use could he find in desiring the impossible? The boy deserved contentment in a life devoted to God, as did Cneajna and Vlad in their quest for marital happiness.

They arrived in the quadrangle outside István's Tower. He had assumed Fruzhin might await him. But his best friend made no appearance. Vlad accepted the courteous greetings and well-wishes of courtiers, most of whom cast admiring glances of interest at his wife. He led her and their son, with Ruxandra in tow into the royal palace.

"My prince!" János hailed him as soon as he crossed the threshold.

János released the hand of his betrothed, Erzsébet Szilágyi, and left her behind him, bowing before Vlad.

"I keep telling you, I'm not your prince. I'd like to think after Galambóc, we are friends. You don't owe this deference to me. You are well, I trust." With a pat on his shoulder, Vlad gestured for the younger man to rise.

"Very well and glad to...to see...you again." János faltered for some unknown reason until Vlad realized his taller counterpart looked beyond him to Cneajna.

He smiled, for his wife's quiet beauty occasionally left him speechless too.

"I present my lady, Princess Vasilisa Maria, called Cneajna by her acquaintances. The daughter of Alexandru the Good of Moldavia and mother of my son, Prince Mircea. Cneajna, this is János Hunyadi, a knight of the court from Transilvania."

"An honor." Cneajna dipped into a curtsy and offered a tight-lipped smile.

"It is a greater privilege to meet you." János bowed with his thin hand pressed to his chest over his heart. "My family came originally from Keve to Hunyadvár, where our king granted rights to an odd thirty villages, and the management of nearby mines, producing salt, gold, silver, and iron...."

"Damnation, Vlad! You made it here before I could."

With a frown, János fell silent as the interruption of a familiar voice echoed behind Vlad. He turned before Fruzhin enveloped him in a hug.

"I thought you'd be outside the great keep awaiting me," Vlad said.

"The original plan, but I took overlong in town to attend another matter," Fruzhin replied, drawn as János had been to the sight of Cneajna.

At their introduction, she grinned broadly. "My husband has told me you've saved his life often. I must be exceedingly grateful to you, my prince."

"And I, you, princess. Vlad has found renewed purpose with a wife and child. I hope he'll have less occasion to risk his life or require my defense of it."

"He's also said you taught him how to fight Turks."

"Alongside others. A duty, my princess. Someone had to make sure he wouldn't get killed the first time he faced them. Please, I hope we may be friends. You must call me by my Christian name."

"If you will call me Cneajna. If I may, Fruzhin, permit me to introduce my former nursemaid and confidant, Ruxandra Lupu. Like me, she is from Suceava...."

Their easy banter pleased Vlad. He wanted his companions, especially his best friend to accept her. If Cneajna seemed reticent with János, Vlad reasoned she had not learned enough from him about the younger man's virtues. The knight and Cneajna would have other opportunities for the conversation Fruzhin interrupted. Vlad noticed the scowl Erzsébet Szilágyi directed their way.

"Your lady." He leaned close to János and whispered, "You're neglecting her. That won't ensure a happy marriage."

János blinked and turned away from her. Vlad attended to his wife and best friend, aware of the furious whisper from the betrothed young lady behind him.

"You couldn't stop looking at her! You think she's more beautiful than me?"

"Don't be ridiculous," János said. "Come meet the princess for yourself."

At his entreaty, Cneajna greeted his betrothed in the same polite, yet crisp manner. Their Mircea fussed, although nestled in Vlad's wolf pelt.

"Our son's inherited his father's lusty appetites," she said, to the guffaws of Fruzhin and János, and the pretty blush of Erzsébet Szilágyi at the innuendo. "My husband, permit me to nurse him in the carriage. I shall rejoin you when he's had his fill."

"Do as you see fit, Cneajna," Vlad replied. "I'll await your return."

Her devotion to their child drew a smile from him. No matter the hour or how exhaustion weighed upon her, often evidenced in her red-rimmed eyes each morning, her attention to their son never wavered.

"Forgive my curiosity. You are a princess, but employ no wet nurse in your retinue?" Erzsébet Szilágyi cocked her head. "Only the poor nurse their children."

With another close-lipped smile, Cneajna replied, "Dear lady, I do not need a retinue beyond my Moldavian guards and my Ruxandra. I provide for my son's wants." She turned away. "Come, Ruxandra, before he screams down the walls of this castle."

János waited until she left to chide his betrothed in a low tone. Before she could argue, he bowed to Vlad and Fruzhin and took her away.

"Your princess is quite a steadfast woman. Like the lady Cecilia at Galambóc. Since you were away, our king has rewarded her and her brothers, who provided the vessel that helped save his life." Fruzhin smiled at Vlad.

He nodded. "They deserve the acclaim. I hope Cneajna never has to pilot a ship away from vicious Turks."

At the dinner feast that night, Vlad presented his bride before King Zsigmond, Queen Borbála, and their courtiers.

Cneajna addressed the monarchs entirely in Latin. Vlad gripped the tips of her fingers. She stood resplendent in the same robe now paired with a caul of lattice silver braid for her hair, decorated with lustrous pink pearls. A strand of rosary glass beads tucked beneath her narrow leather belt completed her attire.

"*Principesa*, have you seen much of Our fair city?" Zsigmond asked.

"Not as much as I would wish, Your Royal Majesty, but it is only my first day," Cneajna replied, eliciting some approving titters from the ladies of the court, although not the queen. "If you will grant him the opportunity outside of his duties, I'm sure my husband may escort me around Buda, Pest, and Óbuda. In Moldavia, my honored father saw to the education of his children, including the history of Hungary. The *Chronicon pictum* with its gold miniatures, as our tutors described, must be wondrous to behold."

The queen asked, "You know about the codex, the *Illustrated Chronicle? Kalt's Chronicle About the Deeds of the great Hungarians*?"

"Yes, Your Grace. Is it still in French hands?"

"A pity We have never seen it either," Zsigmond commented. "If you wish to learn more, We would be delighted to educate you while Vlad attends to his duties to Us."

Vlad's guts roiled. His grip closed on Cneajna's hand. Her cheeks colored.

"Our sovereign and I know much about the kingdom he rules," Borbála added, sliding her fingers across the white linen tablecloth to grasp her husband's gnarled fingers. "We shall be pleased to discuss the history or show you the best sites to visit together."

While Zsigmond glared at his wife, her brow likewise furrowed, Cneajna sneaked a furtive look at Vlad. He gave her hand a reassuring squeeze and grinned. Their mutual gazes lingered even for a few breaths after Zsigmond cleared his throat.

"We trust you may enjoy Our banquet and expect you will like the Malvasia wine; Borbála's favorite, and the German musicians tonight."

"We're grateful, my king," Vlad said, although he despised the sweet, heavy taste of the white wine. He spared the queen a courteous glance. "Your Grace."

"Your Royal Majesty, Your Grace, thank you. *Vinum bonum laetificat cor*." Cneajna smiled and curtsied.

"Indeed, wine and music gladden the heart." Borbála signaled someone outside of their periphery with a crook of her forefinger.

"You may leave Us and be seated," Zsigmond said, waving his hand before he hissed and clutched at the joints, rubbing them.

Vlad and Cneajna turned as one at the dismissal, taking their places among Fruzhin, János, and his betrothed. The men offered welcomes, but Erzsébet Szilágyi gave a stiff nod and a thin-lipped smile to Cneajna. Disliking even the smallest slight against his bride, Vlad ignored János' petty companion.

His wife and Fruzhin kept up the rest of the conversation at dinner in Latin. Vlad noted János barely took part. After the meal came music and dancing. With nods of assent to Cneajna and his best friend, Vlad watched as they joined the revelry. While János' betrothed sulked, Vlad slid closer to him along the bench.

"You were quiet while we talked, János."

"My Latin isn't so good. I didn't want to embarrass myself before you and the princess. I barely took in the full exchange you had with Zsigmond."

"Since you came to Buda, I've heard your easy use of Hungarian, Old Slavonic, German, Italian, and the Wallachian of your family's heritage."

"I'll be forever grateful to my lord Pipó for offering the lessons in Italian and encouraging my studies. But I'm older now and well past the days of relying on tutors."

"No one's ever too young or old to learn," Vlad advised. "The lesson of our survival at Galambóc is true of ordinary life. Keep thriving and moving toward your goals, no matter their magnitude. Don't limit your ambitions. It means stagnation and death."

He turned away and watched Cneajna while she danced. Ever impressed with her ease and adaptability, he reflected on how comfortable she was in royal courts as she was in a Gypsy camp. She never questioned whether she belonged in either place. Although she was not the wife he might have otherwise chosen to marry, he acknowledged she suited her role as his lifelong companion. The perfect woman for him.

CHAPTER 27

The Abode of the Heart

"The stars incline us; they do not bind us."-Ancient Latin proverb.

IN THE YEAR OF OUR Lord 1429. Northeast of Buda, Hungary (modern-day Budapest, Hungary), and *Tismana Monastery, Oltenia region, Principality of Wallachia* (modern-day Tismana Monastery, western Romania)

The Hungarian royal family came to Pozsony in the country's north. A smaller company of courtiers, including Vlad, continued south to the capital. In the vanguard beside him, Fruzhin rode a prime stallion with a long, arched neck like their warhorses, its coat blacker than his favored long mantle. On Vlad's right, Cneajna sat high in her saddle, her face tilted up to the noonday sun while the horses cantered.

Eyes closed, she reveled in the light and the cool spring breeze wafting over the hills and meadows of Buda, where newborn lambs frolicked. Vlad turned for a view of the carriage. Ruxandra leaned out of the aperture, pointing out the sights of the oncoming city and gesturing to Mircea, seated on her lap. Hard to believe a year had already flown by since his birth. A spirited boy. Vlad's heart swelled impossibly larger with love for him.

As for Mircea's mother, Vlad's deepening feelings remained unspoken.

He asked her, "You're glad we've returned home after our journey to Lithuania?"

"I could never call Buda home. A part of my heart will always miss the familiar streets of Suceava in my Moldavian birthplace." She leaned forward and directed a nod to Fruzhin. "Even with the comforts of your townhouse, which you've rented to us for these past eight months. I wouldn't want you to think me ungrateful."

"You are the very opposite, Cneajna," Fruzhin replied. "The capital can become your home. I've lived more of my life in Hungary than in Bulgaria. Though less of it in the house than I might've liked. I'm glad to know the property is in use. Your child, whom I'm blessed to call my godson, plays in the shadows of the garden wall. Laughter and music fill the dining hall each night."

"Will you join us for this evening's meal?"

"No. There's a task I must attend to. If you allow, I'll dine with you all tomorrow."

Vlad wondered at the matter Fruzhin meant to undertake. Of late, his best friend disappeared for hours to parts unknown outside Buda Castle. Was it the secret that Fruzhin still hesitated to reveal, or something to do with the Order of the Dragon? Perhaps he finished some business left incomplete before the king and court departed Hungary the day after Vlad's thirty-third birthday for Luchesk in Lithuania.

There Zsigmond had conferred with his counterparts, including his Danish cousin King Eric, and the Polish ruler and his wife. Other attendees included the Grand Prince of Moscow, and the ruler of Lithuania, who had founded Luchesk. Unfortunately for Vlad, he and Cneajna found Jadwiga did not number among the guests. His usurping cousin Dan Dăneşti did.

"You'll always be welcome among us, dear Fruzhin," Cneajna said, drawing Vlad's attention back to the conversation. "If only I could find you a wife to share in this life you've built for yourself and see you sire children. Surely, our king must have plans for your marriage, as he did with my husband. You must find a lady to wed."

"Who'd have me?" Fruzhin laughed. A bitter, hollow sound. "A graying warrior with too much time in the saddle at forty-one? Don't wish that fate on any woman."

"You're too cruel to yourself, my friend," Vlad said.

"Not everyone can find the happiness you've achieved. I may not have your luck."

Vlad peered at Cneajna. She blushed in that pretty way, which often left him mesmerized. A great beauty in appearance and within her soul, she brought peace and domestic bliss into his life, as he might never have imagined possible two years ago after they had first united.

"Look at the way the pair of you admire each other." Fruzhin interrupted their mutual stares. "I don't deserve contentment like that." As Vlad turned his way again and would have argued, Fruzhin shook his head. "I've killed too many husbands to merit the honor of a wife. I can never wash away the blood of other men's sons from my hands. Fair punishment for a life of sin, spent meting out death."

The discussion fell to a lull, until Cneajna said, "You are a knight and a warrior for God, whom you dutifully serve. If you believe He is just, you must also believe Him merciful. And you must hope He sees into your true heart and seek your forgiveness with Him. You may find He hasn't forsaken you, Fruzhin."

"Don't dwell on the violent past," Vlad advised. "With any luck, Brother Pahomie has already received my letter. I want to visit my namesake for his fourth birthday this year. Once I've had the monk's reply, why don't you plan to come with me to the Tismana Monastery in the autumn?"

"I cannot, Vlad. Recall Borbála's mention of her nephew Ulrich, Friderik's son, with the wife he murdered. The Celje heir is twenty-three years of age. The queen would have me accompany him on his travels this year. I won't return in time to join you."

"Ah yes, that grand tour the young man wishes to make, beginning in Moorish Granada in Spain, then Prussia, and finally Novgorod in Russia."

"Will King Zsigmond make that incredible trip as well?" Cneajna asked. "He's so well-traveled. I couldn't believe the time we took to reach Luchesk. It felt as if we went half the length of Europe."

"The sovereign can't undertake another such journey," Fruzhin replied. "Gout pained him from Lithuania, which is why he took a respite at Pozsony. He's summoned his German doctor there. He plans to enter Vienna next year."

From behind them came Mircea's wails.

"You must both forgive me, but a hungry young prince reminds me of my foremost duty." His mother turned aside her mount and drew apart from the column.

"A tolerant woman. May your union with her always be blessed, Vlad," Fruzhin commented as her horse trotted away from them.

"I believe it already is," he replied, looking over his shoulder briefly to where Cneajna dismounted and handed the reins to one of her Moldavian guards protecting the slowed carriage. She darted inside and cloth flaps came down over the apertures.

"Does she know you think so?"

"Cneajna is aware of my admiration for her and dutifulness to our marriage. She doesn't doubt my commitment, nor has she worried about my feelings for Călțuna or that I shall stray with another woman. She never has."

"I'm asking if you've told her how you feel?" Fruzhin leaned toward Vlad.

He lifted his chin. "I've said she knows, Fruzhin."

"Christ's blood, man! Still stubborn, I see, but you're also cleverer than this. Women always want the words, no matter how devoted they are. Why haven't you told her what is plain to see for anyone who knows you, or has spent time with both of you? Vlad, you're in love with her."

He knew it too, yet whenever he wanted to tell her the undeniable truth, he faltered. No, that was untrue; he simply refused. It should be the easiest thing in the world to do.

He never even knew how love first shattered the defenses he had erected around his heart. Perhaps on the night after Cneajna arrived in Buda, while he watched her dancing among Zsigmond's courtiers.

Whenever they were apart during his duties with the royal guard, her sweet visage came to mind. She had won him over, in the only battle where he found himself helpless and on the cusp of surrender. So why could he not submit?

Fruzhin asked him the same question.

As he knew the truth of his changed sentiments toward Cneajna, so too did he perceive the source of his struggle. He also feared she might not appreciate the reason.

"Fruzhin, it's not that I don't want to be in love with her. She fills me with such joy, but...I falter still."

"Talk with me. I'll help if I can. We are friends and blood brothers. Try, Vlad."

He heaved a long sigh. "Have you ever known an all-consuming love, my friend?"

"No. I've never been so fortunate. You would know if I had."

"I've loved Călţuna like that. She still occupies my heart, as Cneajna does. Those feelings can overwhelm and make men reckless. When I first lost Călţuna, I spent the next two years lavishing all my adoration of her on our son. Yet, what I felt for his mother would not abate. It lingered and pained me."

Only in time did the searing agony of letting her live without him ebb and flow until it dulled. It no longer caused physical hurt to think of Călţuna. His wife's love and his feelings for her proved the right balm for his heart and soul. Cneajna had healed him.

The household guards announced their arrival on the city's outskirts. Vlad slowed his horse to a walk alongside Fruzhin and the others.

"Once, I overheard a conversation between my parents. They talked about their firstborn, who died in a tragic accident, the twin of my eldest brother. Prince Mircea said he couldn't let himself show love for any of his subsequent children, because he didn't want to experience the deepest pain again if he ever lost them.

"That's what makes me hold back the truth from Cneajna. People die every day. Senselessly. Women, in childbirth, as my sweet sister Arina did. What if I lose Cneajna? I've already been ripped apart from one great love, at more than a cost to me. Our son lost too. Losses are all I've ever endured."

He sighed and bowed his head. An end would always come. A time when he must part from Cneajna.

"Oh, my friend." Fruzhin shook his head and pressed his hand to Vlad's steel pauldron. "All life is an experience, some of it good and bad. What matters most is not what we lose, but what we gain in the time spent with those whom we treasure. We, too, must leave our friendship behind. Memories shall sustain me. To love is to lose ourselves. Wouldn't you rather enjoy the fullness of the feeling than never drown in its richness? Unburden yourself and let Cneajna into your whole heart. It's where she belongs."

Vlad could not imagine living without her. At last, he felt ready to do as she advised in the days after their wedding. To reconcile his personal history and present circumstances, and accept their love. His feelings for Călţuna might never fade. They posed no threat to a future with Cneajna. He would, as she once suggested, love her until the end of time. Beyond death.

He and Fruzhin entered the northern fortified gateway, still walking the horses.

"You offer good advice, my blood brother. Take the same. A pained look fills your gaze whenever you hold my Mircea. Seek God's forgiveness for the years of wars and bloodshed. Build a family. There's great love in your heart. Share it with someone."

Fruzhin sighed. "Have you ever done something so unforgivable, you couldn't imagine how to atone for it? A disgraceful memory that condemns and tortures you?"

"Weeks before my sixteenth birthday, I fought with my parent after accusing him of fratricide. Immense shame filled me once I learned the claim was false. I can't undo that history. If you can make amends, do so and let the past die. What we've done is not nearly as important as what we might do. The things we can make right in the end."

Fruzhin nodded. "Can it truly be that we both grow wiser as we get older?"

"One of us is definitely older." Vlad punched his arm. "All the mixture of nuts, iron shavings, and alum won't hide every gray thread on your head and in the beard. Nor the pungency of vinegar mixed with the alum. It's made my eyes water along the journey."

"I should bash your skull in for that! Except, I hope you'll live to confess your love to Cneajna," Fruzhin muttered. Then he looked at Vlad. "Does my dyed hair really have an odor? Could your wife smell it? Can others?"

Vlad sniggered. His best friend erupted in laughter. They held their bellies and each other's warm gazes.

VLAD SETTLED WITH HIS family in the rented townhouse again and resumed their lives. Whenever he did not attend court because of Zsigmond's absence, he trained with the sword. Tobar and Yoska hammered his blade with ferocious blows. Once, Cneajna, with her constant companion brought a toddling Mircea to see the clamor. Distracted by her charming smile, Vlad sustained a deep cut across his hand.

"Oh, my dearest husband! Are you hurt badly?" She rushed to his side.

"It stings by Christ's blood," he growled, as crimson rivulets pelted the cobblestones.

"Don't roar at me! I'm not the cause of your hurt." She released his bloodied limb and drew back. A frown crisscrossed her pale, olive-skinned brow.

He swallowed. "Forgive my harsh tone, Cneajna. Just a lucky blow Yoska landed."

"He's fierce with a weapon despite having one eye." She nodded to the Gypsy. "Yoska; have a care for my lord husband. His life is most precious to me."

"I will be more careful in the future, *Doamnă*," Yoska replied, bowing before her.

Tobar mocked his twin's fine display of manners. His brother shoved him and they traded blows. Vlad and Cneajna shook their heads.

"Princess, we should go inside." Ruxandra balanced the tiny Mircea on her slim hip.

"You're right. Let's return to our work in my private chamber." She looked at Vlad again. "Please, attend to that injury in haste."

"It won't fester. I promise."

Later, Vlad stood outside the bedroom Cneajna chose for her use. Invariably, at night, one of them would seek the other in their rooms. He rapped at the door and entered at her entreaty.

She sat by the window, Mircea's crib of elm between Ruxandra and her. Skeins of wool covered half of her bed, with socks and mittens littering the rest of the coverlet.

"Do you expect we will need so much this winter?" He grinned at her.

She rose and came to him. "Not just us. You found the monk's answer awaiting you upon our return. Some of these are gifts intended for the holy brothers and your son."

"You're very considerate. I'm sure they will be grateful." He took her hand. "You and our Mircea should come with me later in the year. We'll depart Tismana long before winter can descend in full. I don't want to be trapped there while Dan Dăneşti rules."

"Are you asking me to join you because Fruzhin declined your invitation?"

"I want you and our son near." He lifted her fingertips to his lips and kissed them. "I would miss you too much if you were not at my side."

A faint blush colored her cheeks. "Then we shall come."

HOW DID A MAN WOO A woman? Especially if he had already married her?

Vlad pondered the question while he crossed the Transilvanian-Wallachian frontier with his small family, under the twin

Gypsies' protection and that of Cneajna's Moldavian guards. He could not just blurt out his love. That would be no better than when he bungled their first meeting and curtly revealed his reason for marrying.

Moments when they stopped at inns or found shelter from late summer rains in a copse of trees seemed inopportune. They were never truly alone, even at night, with either Ruxandra or their guardians always at hand. He never had such difficulties in revealing his heart to Călțuna. They came together in a way that felt perfectly natural. Almost as simple as breathing.

However, with his wife, Vlad desired the perfect moment to reveal his feelings.

"Husband, may we stop, eat, and enjoy the fresh air for a little?" She called to him from the carriage window. "Or do you have concerns about wolves?"

He looked around at the lush meadows of the Jiu Valley. Sparse huts dotted the mountainous terrain, where cool winds enveloped the landscape, and clouds almost obscured the eastern peaks. The dominion of shepherds and their flocks. A wild place where any daring predators would go after the grazing sheep, not mounted fighters armed with swords and lances.

Spruce and silver fir trees bordered clusters of white flowers, which Vlad's people called *floare de colț*. The Germanic Saxons knew them as edelweiss. Tismana Monastery lay ahead. They were directly south of Hunyadvár, where Vlad had stopped over for one night and visited with János.

Cneajna never warmed to the young knight. She had insisted they must push on for the monastery the next day. Perhaps she did not like János because he once boasted about his family's holdings upon greeting her. Vlad knew she must have a good reason. He respected her decisions, even when he could not comprehend them.

"If you wish, we may linger here a bit." He dismounted and led his horse to the tree line. "Your men and the Gypsies shall keep watch." No use in telling her more than wolves roamed the mountainside; brown bears and lynxes, too.

They sat on a dampened carpet of grass and ate day-old bread with the dried meat of roe deer hunted one morning ago. An ale skin passed between them. Little Mircea reached out with eager hands for every piece of food his parents took while seated beside him, and whined when they wouldn't share.

Vlad kissed his curls while he fussed. "You only have two teeth, my son."

"He doesn't know that." Cneajna picked him up, pushed aside her green mantle, and unbuttoned the collar of her broadcloth traveling gown to the breastbone. With her back to the soldiers and Gypsy twins, she nursed their child while Vlad looked on. Ruxandra ate beside them.

After they finished their portion, half the Moldavians and Yoska took some food. His brother and the other men scanned their horizons, as did Vlad. But all he saw were men and dogs guarding animals, the occasional chamois, and two or three elk herds.

Ruxandra excused herself and headed out of sight into a thicket, leaving Vlad and his wife alone with their child.

"Your homeland is perfect. I see why you wish to live and rule here," Cneajna said.

"With you and our son at my side." He reclined on the cool grass next to her and watched while the wind stirred the trailing ends of her braid, worn beneath a linen veil.

"Your family never knew about your ambition?" She rocked a little from side to side as sweet Mircea palmed her exposed breast.

"My dear mother, God rest her soul, suspected." He recalled Princess Mara's rebuke at Târgoviște before Arina's marriage. "She told me not to covet the throne. My other brothers likely never imagined I held such an interest as a third son."

"They disdained it because of your age and their intent. It's hard being a younger child in a mighty family. I know. Others do not see you in the way you see yourself."

He nodded. They had more in common than he realized.

"How will you do it, Vlad? Capture the crown?"

"The true power of my homeland lies not in the strength of its ruling prince, but the boyars." He snorted in disgust, thinking of those few slavering sycophants during Prince Mircea's reign. "I must have their support, as well as an army."

For some time, he had considered whether Vlậcsan the Wolf could aid him among the noblemen. Of the boyar class and a kinsman, would the Dowager's nephew wield enough influence? Vlad did not trust the man's motivations entirely. The surest way to forge a mutual understanding with the Wolf would be a promise of Wallachian lands Vlad could not hold until he took over the country.

"Moldavian men will fight for you because of my father." Cneajna lifted a sleeping Mircea from her bosom and handed him to Vlad before she laced up her garment.

He grinned at the child, whose cherubic lips curved in a half-smile. "Because of you and our heir. Whatever I gain in my country will become part of his legacy."

"A proud inheritance," she murmured.

He glanced at her, realizing he required no grand plan or a magnanimous gesture of love. Their relationship began with candor. He only needed to tell her the truth.

"You must know," he said, "no matter the reason for my proposal of marriage, I did not see you as those old suitors did. You were never just some '*knez*'s daughter' for me."

Her mouth quivered. He balanced their boy on his other forearm and reached for her fingers. "You've long enchanted me and I have been under your spell since, dearest Cneajna. Your prophetic dreams mystified and frightened me. Unlike you, I'd never held certainty about fate. Until now, in the life we share. It is you alone whom I shall treasure and comfort, whom I shall hold in my heart until the end of days."

Her eyes watered. When she opened her mouth as if to speak, but could not, he grinned. She still had much the same effect on him.

"I love you, my Cneajna," he vowed.

"I love you too, my Vlad." She squeezed his hand.

They held each other's rapt gazes, even after Ruxandra returned and cleared her throat. "Shall I take the little prince into the carriage?"

Vlad nodded, handing his Mircea over. Then he stood and tugged Cneajna up with him. His palms resting on her wide hips, he gazed into the depths of her stare. No longer drowning in the sea-green color, he saw himself reflected there as the man to whom she had surrendered her heart. He would never give her cause for regret.

"My Cneajna," he whispered again as he kissed her forehead and lips. "You are the contentment of my life. With you, there is only peace and delight."

"I can scarce believe there was a time when I did not call you my own, my Vlad."

"But I am your own and always will be."

Her eyes sparkled. He silently swore she would only shed tears of joy as his wife.

Hand in hand, they strolled, Yoska following at a discreet distance. His sibling finally ate with the rest of the Moldavian men. The landscape rose, and Vlad and Cneajna made their ascent. He stopped near a windswept patch of edelweiss, which the Germanic Saxon people admired as a symbol of devotion and deep love, for the courage required to fetch it from the mountain heights.

Vlad cradled Cneajna close. Blustery cold surrounded them. They kept each other warm against the wind's onslaught. One arm curled around her waist under her mantle. She rested the crown of her head beneath his chin. Both sighed and breathed deeply.

He described the features of the southeastern vista she could not see, but would one day, as the princess of Wallachia and the lady of these lands. Beyond the rugged terrain lay his birthplace at Argeş and the Princely Court of Târgovişte, where they would nurture and cherish a family he intended to protect with his life.

"By God's grace and my will, all this shall be the birthright of our lineage for generations to come, my Cneajna," he murmured while nuzzling her forehead.

She hugged him and sighed again. "May it be, my Vlad."

UPON THEIR ARRIVAL at Tismana Monastery, they left the carriage and waited outside the locked gates for Brother Pahomie. He came to them soon afterward. Vlad's heart churned like the vast depths of an ocean, swelling with fatherly pride in the boy who walked beside the monk. No taller than he appeared over a year ago and perhaps still as thin, the child gripped the stems of delicate pink roses. As Pahomie allowed him outside, he offered the flowers to Cneajna before he gave Vlad a tentative smile.

"*Tată.* Welcome."

Vlad grinned, picked up his firstborn, and squeezed him. He sighed as his son's arms came around his neck for a furtive hug at first, then a whole-hearted embrace.

"You did not let him forget me," Vlad said to Pahomie.

The monk nodded. "I could not, my lord prince."

Although received with great warmth, Vlad respected the convention against female intrusion into the holy order's sacred spaces. He limited subsequent daily visits to himself and a few times brought little Mircea.

Cneajna consented, preferring to spend those occasions outdoors in the small village. She made further gifts of the ample woolens she and Ruxandra had knitted to the mothers of Tismana. They cheered and hailed her whenever she appeared in the streets, and she greeted and conversed with them to Vlad's delight.

Oddly enough, although the denizens of Tismana were as courteous to Vlad, a strange undercurrent rippled through the village when anyone saw him. A hushed conversation or sly look made him want to confront several people. But he avoided causing any offense.

While his wife held Mircea on her lap and gathered with a gaggle of mostly women seated around the largest well, Vlad marked the unexpected entry of Brother Pahomie into the village. The monks rarely left their sanctuary, except for important business.

"Are you well? And my son?" While Pahomie alighted from a mule-driven cart, Vlad patted the leading animal's head and nodded to the younger monk holding the reins.

"My lord prince, there is no trouble. Thanks be to God. The child is at his lessons in Scripture. Shall you visit him again tomorrow?" Pahomie asked.

"If that is acceptable."

"It is." Pahomie turned and directed his fellow holy brother to the next street. "Be sure to fetch the two sacks of flour we were promised as well," he added.

Once they stood alone together, Vlad walked with him in companionable silence, circling the central square in the space between market stalls left empty until next week and the facades of buildings.

"I am pleased with the progress my namesake has made, Brother Pahomie."

"You should be, my lord prince. He will make an excellent monk if he so chooses."

"Can he decide otherwise, eventually?"

"It would be unusual, but also not unheard of, even for one singled out by our Lord God at such a young age."

Vlad swallowed a derisive chuckle. He did not believe God had anything to do with the path Pahomie suggested best suited the boy.

Instead, Vlad said, "My lady wife and I shall leave this area in two weeks to avoid the onset of a changing season."

'That is wise, but before you go, I believe there is a matter of which you should be aware. There has been some talk here for years that only recently reached me in recent days. Two women in the village; each claimed to have borne a daughter for you."

Vlad halted. Could it be true? He had left bastards behind at Tismana?

"My lord prince, I do not tell you to cast blame or suggest I believe the rumors. But if the possibility exists...well, I have learned enough about you in your time among us at the monastery and your interest in your firstborn, not to keep silent. Though you may think me impertinent."

"I do not." Vlad leaned against a boundary wall shared between a tavern and the house next door. Did he have daughters also? His gaze flitted to Cneajna, engrossed with the women at her side. Someone said something. Her laughter pealed around the square. The gossip could not have reached her ears. She would have told him.

"What do you know about these women, Brother Pahomie?"

"Little. One was a maid who served at the village inn. The owner ran her off when he discovered her unwed and growing great with child. Another was the blacksmith's wife until she and her husband perished in a rockslide from Stârmina Mountain. Her child was not with them during the incident, by God's grace."

Vlad recalled bedding a serving wench at the inn where his grandmother stayed during one of her visits. But in two subsequent years at Tismana, the same woman never accused him of fathering any babe. Could he have gotten her pregnant just before he left the monastery to seek Cneajna's hand in marriage? He did not remember the blacksmith's wife at all.

"I've seen both children, each at most two years younger than your namesake," Pahomie added. "The maid's daughter looks nothing like you, has her mother's mousy brown hair. The orphaned girl; her uncle, the blacksmith's brother is raising her. She has dark russet hair and large brown eyes. They remind me of chestnuts."

Vlad nodded. Like his grandmother's features in her younger years.

"Are those the only women who believe I've sired their children?"

"I've heard of no others, my lord prince."

"I won't deny having enjoyed the pleasures of the flesh while here some years ago." Vlad pushed away from the wall and resumed walking while the monk fell into step beside him. "Resemblance counts for nothing. My namesake does not look like me. He favors his mother. Both the girls are still being raised in this village?"

"Yes, they are."

"Then, as a prince of their country, I shall provide money for their well-being if they will enter religious foundations and take vows as nuns." Although Pahomie gasped, Vlad went on. "I trust you can ensure it without rousing further suspicions or causing concern."

"Oh, of course. You're an extraordinary man to take an interest in bastards, even when you cannot verify their paternity. My father, the nobleman from whom I inherited these two mismatched eyes, did not claim me for his own back then. But Vlậcsan the Wolf's father took pity and offered me to the Church."

Vlad sighed. "Relationships between a father and his child are not always what either would wish. Our parents create us, but the act alone does not dictate our circumstances. Fate is not always written in the stars; our choices govern outcomes too. I choose to be a better father to my children than I knew in my boyhood. A better man. One whom any offspring might be proud to call a parent."

The monk gave him a rare smile. "Perhaps, by the will of God, a wiser ruling prince? I may indeed be insolent, but you have the traits of a just and brave leader of this country. Wallachia would prosper under you. As would the progeny you've acknowledged."

"Time shall tell, Brother Pahomie. It does all things," Vlad replied, looking to where Mircea squealed and giggled as Cneajna tickled him.

Vlad sighed. Having promised her full honesty in their marriage, he could not conceal the news from Cneajna. Would she be angry about his bastards or accept them? Whatever her response, he would always do right by those children who claimed him as a father. He told her the truth that same night.

"You were right not to hide these girls from me. They were conceived before we met. You've done well by them if they are the siblings of our Mircea and Vlad Călugărul."

"Vlad the Monk? Is that the name you've given my firstborn?"

"It's his destiny."

When the time arrived for them to depart from Tismana, he took her hand in his at night, snuggled closer to her, and whispered against her hair, "It's grown colder, my love. Shall we visit the monastery tomorrow and go home afterward?"

"I'm already at home, my Vlad." She rested her head on his shoulder and palmed his chest. "Whenever we are together, my abode is in your heart."

CHAPTER 28

The Order of the Dragon

"Thou shalt tread upon the lion and adder: the young lion and the dragon shalt thou trample under thy feet."-The Bible, Psalm 91, verse 31.

IN THE YEAR OF OUR Lord 1431. Buda and Óbuda, Hungary (modern-day Budapest, Hungary), and *Nürnberg* (modern-day Nuremberg, Bavaria, Germany)

In the night, over two weeks after Vlad's thirty-seventh birthday, an unexpected message came to Fruzhin's Buda townhouse. Vlad had occupied its rooms with his small family for the last three years. The letter in Fruzhin's distinct handwriting dismayed him.

'Our queen wishes to see you at once. Come to her alone in the royal residence of Óbuda. This is important, Vlad. You cannot ignore or disdain her royal command.'

"Why does the bitch seek me out now?" He crushed the paper.

Moving quickly and quietly, he went from the dining area where the herald waited. He returned to the bedroom Cneajna occupied beside their son, who favored nestling between his parents at night, and Ruxandra sleeping opposite the chamber door. Not one of them stirred as Vlad dressed.

On an impulse, he reached for his sword belt but hesitated. If Fruzhin waited with the queen, Vlad faced no danger from her. Still, a natural suspicion of Borbála vied with the urge to protect himself. He opened the lid of a wooden chest at the foot of the bed.

He retrieved the Turkish-style dagger Zsigmond gave him twenty years past and pulled the blade from the jade stone scabbard. Pipó once said the weapon must have a fitting use against his enemies. Vlad sheathed and tucked it into his sword belt. No one else would know it was solely ornamental.

He turned for another view of the bed's occupants and approached them. He touched the cool curve of his wife's fleshy cheek and kissed the black curls atop Mircea the Younger's head. Everlasting love for the son they created filled his heart. Four years into their marriage, a fierce passion for Cneajna grew deeper and richer. She belonged to him, and he, well and truly, belonged to her.

Her long, black lashes fluttered and she stirred, staring at him. "Why have you dressed already? What's happened?" She rubbed her eyes. A frown crinkled her brow. "What hour is it? Where are you going?"

"Be at ease." He kneeled at the bedside and fingered a lock of her hair. "It is the hour of the wolf. There's an urgent summons from the queen in Óbuda. I must attend to her."

"Oh, so late? Heavens!" She clutched his shoulder and drew him close. "But you'll return as soon as you can?"

"For you, I always will," he whispered in the crook of her neck.

They stood together and embraced each other in full. As they kissed, he pressed her lush body to his, wishing only to hold her forever. But Borbála awaited him.

Beneath the midnight-blue skies, Vlad left the residence alone. He waved away his Gypsies Tobar and Yoska, who would have followed but for his dictate. For the first time in twenty-one winters since his arrival in Hungary, Vlad headed directly north to Óbuda, the dower land of Queen Borbála. The messenger from Fruzhin guided him.

Although he had no cause to distrust someone in the employ of his best friend, the oddness of the royal command at such a late hour made Vlad suspicious. He also had more than enough reason to despise the royal consort. Especially for her role in robbing him of the first child he and Călţuna should have had nine years ago.

He rode north, past Castle Hill, overlooking the Danube River's right bank. Snow blanketed the ground and gray mist obscured the water. A torch and moonbeams lit his way. Town patrols acknowledged and eyed him with his escort as they rode by. Wintry air rustled the mantle on his shoulders. He wished his wolf-skin offered protection against the night chill, but three-year-old Mircea favored the pelt and slumbered atop it, much the same as he did while he was a baby.

"How much further?" Vlad demanded of Fruzhin's herald.

"Not too far now, my lord prince," the man answered.

Atop the hills rose Roman ruins. The old bathhouse, amphitheaters, crumbling aqueduct, and brick walls hearkened back to Hungary's past. A nunnery, the foundation of the Poor Clares, existed in Óbuda. Vlad wondered whether Călţuna lived among its holy sisters. He also accepted the choice he made to never know where she made her home. Wherever she was, he wished her peace.

Westward stood the centuries-old site of the queen's dower castle. Whenever she did not travel outside of the country with her husband, she preferred the location here, though Vlad could not guess why. Nor could he imagine why she returned to Óbuda.

Zsigmond could not be with her, for the royal summons would have come in his name. The couple spent a significant part of the previous year at Pozsony and defended the kingdom against more Hussite infiltrations during the spring. They enjoyed some of the summer in Vienna before summoning the most prominent physician in Nürnberg to treat Zsigmond's gout. At least Fruzhin's prior letters said so.

With the permission of the castellan, Vlad crossed the wide ditch via the drawbridge. He passed underneath the ribbed vaults of the gatehouse, constructed within a massive tower of ashlar blocks. Sentinels kept guarded glances fixed on him as he entered the precincts of a rectangular building set inside a small courtyard.

Shuttered windows pierced two stories of the structure. Scant light emanated through gaps in the wood. A tall, hooded figure clothed entirely in black cloth and armor awaited him at the entry with a torch in hand.

He dismounted and a groom approached, taking the reins at his gesture. He approached the cloaked form. "I came at the summons of Her Grace the Queen."

No audible answer followed. Instead, at a beckoning wave, he crossed the threshold into an antechamber. They went through an ornate portal into another much larger room. Red marble slabs beneath his feet emanated heat, like the embers of dragon fire. Benches stacked atop tables lined the expansive space. Flames flickered at odd intervals in iron sconces along the walls in what must be a ground-floor banquet hall. At the opposite end of the entrance, a lone door stood ajar.

"Where is Zsigmond's wife?" Vlad asked. "She sent for me. How long must I wait?"

Still, no response before his unidentified escort left him. Puzzled, he turned and stared at a heraldic symbol painted on the black length of the stranger's long, voluminous mantle; the red cross of Saint Gheorghe on a silver field.

The entryway closed with a heavy thud. He stood alone. Leery now, his hand went to the sword belt. His loud groan echoed as he recalled only bringing the dagger.

"You'll have no need of a weapon with me, Prince Vlad. If you can follow commands." Borbála came through the opened door beside a hooded companion of similar height, who carried a lit torch. Both wore the same black robe and mantle as the one who brought Vlad inside the castle's confines.

His fingers twitched. He did not remove them from the Turkish hilt. The queen and her cohort halted in the center of the shuttered chamber.

Vlad's stare flicked from her sallow, lined features to her associate. Where was Fruzhin and why had his best friend not joined him in this hall?

"You still don't trust me," she mused.

"I've had no cause," Vlad said. "The enmity you've shown over the years gives all the proof of your contempt for me. It's been so long; I don't even know why you hate me."

She spat, "Your arrogance offends me! You're no better than your sire, who swayed Zsigmond with oaths of loyalty too easily broken. Then there's the mother who whelped you. Do you think I was ever ignorant of my husband's longstanding desire for her?"

"Our king has always wanted other women." And had them at a whim. But he would not offer the reminder, knowing of her unfaithfulness years ago. "But he never had my mother. She told me so."

"And you believed her?" Borbála's husky laughter filled the cavernous room, laced with bitterness and derision. "Zsigmond always looked to bind his whores' hearts to him, just as he demanded the loyalty of their foolish husbands, fathers, brothers, and sons. He required the same of you, too. You offered it so willingly. Turning your back on the religion of your youth."

"Whether Roman Catholics or Eastern Orthodox, we all believe in a Christian God."

"We live in an age of faith and blood. To shed the latter for the sake of the former makes believers and martyrs. But what should I expect of someone like you, who casts aside his religious upbringing with such ease? How can anyone trust someone like that? You adhere to my husband because you want something from him. Power? Do you think Zsigmond is the only one who can grant your wishes?"

What was this? Some poor attempt to seduce him. If the whore thought she could ply her tricks with him, she did not know the extent to which he despised her.

"Did you get me out of a comfortable bed next to my wife to uncover my desires?"

"No!" She scoffed at the innuendo underlying his voice. "I must repay an old debt."

The door behind him creaked. He turned to the sight of men bursting into the chamber. They rushed at him and sought to drag him down. He fought back against every person who grappled with his limbs. His powerful kicks, hard punches, and elbow strikes threw off the first set of attackers. More men entered the room.

He became the boy who faced off against his eldest brother and the bullies who tormented him at Târgoviște. Knighthood taught him about survival against the odds.

The chokehold of a massive forearm made him wheeze and left him gasping. A hand lunged for his dagger and took it away.

Tugged to the heated floor, he wrenched his hand free and clobbered the limb around his throat, but it did no good. Through floating stars in his vision, he glimpsed the queen hovering close, her companion's torch illuminating her lined face.

"Release his neck only," she commanded. "Where are the ropes I demanded? He's stronger than an ox." She tittered. "Amazing for such a little man."

Was this her repayment for the proof he once offered of her adultery?

The chokehold withdrew and he coughed, spluttering. "You think your fire can harm me? I'm a son of the House of Basarab! My fury is the dragon's flame! No matter the form of your treachery, I will rise again to burn you to ashes."

"Brave words. We'll see the truth of your fire soon enough." Borbála turned to her silent aide. "We are ready. Do it."

Vlad wrestled and lunged a kick at her, but she scuttled off like one of the Danube River's crabs. The person next to her handed the light source to someone else and with blunt fingers, reached beneath a black mantle to retrieve a stained cloth. A scent headier than vinegar emitted from the material, its ends gripped tight in both sets of fingers.

Vlad stared up at one palm of the stranger's hand. A deep slash across healed skin. Mirroring the same cut he had, over two decades old, born of a blood oath. He would know that distinctive scar anywhere.

"Fruzhin!" He yelled before the cloth covered his nose and mouth. He tried to turn away from the foul odor. Someone else wrenched his head to the floor. He twisted away but could not escape. The blood roared in his veins and his vision blurred.

As his lids fluttered and blackness encroached, his attacker loomed above him with a face still concealed beneath the hood.

"He is finished, my queen."

Vlad let the malodorous stench take him where it willed, far away from Borbála's smirk and the disembodied voice of his best friend. Fruzhin had betrayed him.

HE ROSE FROM THE DANK depths to the baleful glare of the sun high in the sky. A spotted eagle with white patches on its wings soared and screeched somewhere aloft. He shuttered his gaze against the brilliant light. Wheels rumbled and wooden slats creaked beneath him. Metal jangled. A cart. They had put him in a cart. To go where?

Away from Óbuda, he guessed. Why leave? When they could have disposed of his body in the Danube if they wished? Such questions made his head hurt. The vehicle bumped against a rut in the road, worsening the ache. Better not to think. To rest instead. Gain his bearings and plan for an escape. He drifted into oblivion again.

Sometime later, he blinked. Above him, a myriad of stars. A moonless night. Had he slept the entire day? His tongue felt heavy and swollen, and the center of his brow still throbbed. As did the arm he lay on. Both were manacled behind his back, he realized. Pinpricks coursed along his reawakened body. The apex of his hose clung to him, fetid and rank. How many times had he pissed himself?

He focused on the direction he faced. A dun-colored horse came into view. A strong and stocky build with a small head. The animal stirred memories of the mount Jadwiga raced against him on the outskirts of Kraków. Was that where Borbála and the perfidious Fruzhin were taking him? Poland? He tried to envisage the rider, who carried a torch. Its orange flames almost blinded Vlad, like the sun. His concentration ebbed before a loud groan escaped him.

"He's awake!" The man atop the horse gave the alert and pushed back his hood, peering inside the cart.

Although thick hair curled away from a face creased by time, Vlad recognized the namesake son of his old master Stibor. Who once watched while the father trained Vlad to withstand the Turks. If Stibor had lived, his heart would have cleaved in two at the sight of how his heir and Fruzhin abandoned Vlad. Certainty filled him that as a man of honor, Stibor would never have condoned their actions. Vlad wondered about Zsigmond and what the king knew, too.

He spat against the side of the wagon, glaring at Stibor's heir as he wriggled his bound wrists. A cascade of tingles thrummed through his fingers.

"It's useless to struggle, Vlad. Rest now. We'll stop soon enough."

He closed his eyes again as if by doing so, he could blot out Fruzhin's voice coming from the other side of the vehicle. How could his best friend have deceived him? Was this why Fruzhin spent most of the previous year away with the queen? Plotting Vlad's end? He still could not believe it, even as the stink of that cloth tinged his lips still.

"Traitor," he muttered. "You were a vile rapist at Kutné Hora. But this is the ultimate betrayal of yourself and me."

"You believe that so easily," Fruzhin replied. "And wonder whether we knew each other at all, hmm?"

"Don't speak to me!" Although his throat burned with the reply, Vlad ignored the pain. "God damn you as a deceiver until the end of your days."

"It's true. I have lied to you. But we'll see if God offers punishment or reward," Fruzhin said. With one hand, he gestured to Stibor's son. "Give him some water. Splash it over his lips and face. Too dangerous to stop the cart and raise him for a drink."

"I'm glad you realize how close I am to killing you." For if the man he loved as a blood brother came near him, Vlad would strangle Fruzhin with his feet.

Warm water from an animal skin spouted and sloshed over him. He opened his mouth and some dregs dripped in. The rest trickled over his cheek, which stung with sunburn. During winter. How many days had he traveled in the cart? It clattered up an incline before stopping.

"Open this gate in the name of Her Grace the Queen," some unseen man ordered.

Within moments, Vlad passed beyond red brick walls, interspersed with rounded and rectangular towers. The wagon rumbled across cobblestone streets. The wheels bumped against every groove and banged Vlad's head on wooden planks. He became dazed.

The cart finally stopped on a more gradual slope. A multitude of torches revealed the escarpment of a pink-gray sandstone ridge disappearing beneath stout walls and behind trees, whose lobed leaves recalled rowans Vlad saw during his king's travels in Germany.

The riders lunged for him again. Wild wraiths cloaked in black clambered over the vehicle's sides. Least among them, Fruzhin with that damnable cloth again, saturated in the same vile stench. Vlad fought and knew some satisfaction, as he butted one man and sent him sprawling against the wood. But the result stayed the same. He succumbed.

Sometime later, when he roused himself again, he found his arms shackled in front of him to the slick, black stone floor of a large, rounded room. A tower, perhaps, with no windows. Hair clung to his brow, temples, and neck. He kneeled in his shirt, many stains sullying the once white material, and his dampened hose, manacled to the ground by his ankles above his shoes and just behind his knees. What new hell was this?

He stared at his restraints. Iron links extended from the bands on his wrist and looped through a pair of rings affixed to the floor. The chains disappeared into a crevice. Although his arms throbbed, he hauled them up. He stretched his limbs above his head. Muscles burned, and he grunted.

A door behind him opened. He scowled at several hooded, green-mantled figures. They came into view, all dressed in blood-red garments and shoes.

"Too cowardly to reveal your faces?"

None replied. Half a score by his count spread out, aligned along the wall, hands clasped in front of them, facing him with their heads bowed. Fruzhin entered, dressed like them, and carrying two wooden buckets. Water sloshed over the side of one.

"I'll kill you myself!" Vlad raged as he wrenched one arm and swung at Fruzhin.

"You won't, so be quiet. Stop wasting your energy." Fruzhin signaled others beyond Vlad's peripheral view, four of whom kneeled and unlocked the bond around his lower limbs. He would have aimed a kick. But each pair secured his feet.

"Don't do it. Stop resisting." Fruzhin approached.

Vlad reared back and smashed his forehead into Fruzhin's mouth.

Yelping, the cunning wretch backed off, cupping his lips. Blood sluiced between his fingers. He drew a fist. But for the sudden grip on his elbow, he might have lashed out.

"You can't!" Stibor's heir said, his face only partly obscured. "The king will see."

Vlad reeled. Zsigmond knew!

Although the extent of the betrayal stunned him, Vlad could not absorb it. He could not react as the men at his feet tugged off his shoes and hose. Someone cut away the ruined shirt that clung to his back. Fruzhin opened the laces and sliced the material along the front, ripping it by the sleeves down the length of the chains.

Frigid water doused him from each of the buckets. A new shock. Pain needled and knifed him. The liquid seeped into and settled in small fissures between the stone flooring. His teeth chattered as, naked, Vlad shook off droplets like a rain-soaked dog.

He lunged at Fruzhin again. Their aquiline noses barely touched. "Lying whoreson! I'll cleave your beating heart and rip it from your chest while you still breathe. No different from what you've done to me by your disloyalty."

"You never know when you should submit, do you, Vlad?"

"To someone like you, who must face me in the company of half a score of men while I stand with my arms chained? I won't do it. Ever."

"No wonder the queen had to take you this way." Fruzhin shook his head and drew back. "She swore you would never yield easily at her command alone."

"So, you devised a way to ensure my compliance in Óbuda."

"I did."

"After everything we've survived. And all the blood we've shed! How could you?"

"You'll soon discover some things are more important than blood, Vlad." He looked down at the men on the ground. "Hold him, brethren!"

Vlad readied to fight again. Some mechanism below the floor dragged his arms down while his assailants secured his lower limbs. Fruzhin brought another bucket. With a harsh gulp of air, Vlad steeled himself against the torture of ice-cold water.

But Fruzhin drew out a brush and soap. He scrubbed Vlad's skin.

"What is this?" Vlad demanded. "The king and queen care whether they murder a dirty prisoner."

"You've surrendered your stubborn will before Zsigmond countless times." Fruzhin came around and soaped his neck and back. "Here, when the darkness retreats and all the revelations you've long sought must come into the light, you question everything. Here, trust eludes you."

"Because I see you for who you are! How did you fool me for so long? Or did the queen tempt you to betray me only recently? That vengeful bitch has finally caught me in her trap and even persuaded our king to side with her. And you helped."

"I'd sooner cut off my sword arm than turn against you, friend." Fruzhin's ministrations with the bristles ceased. "You aren't listening or observing."

"For what? What more could I learn?" Vlad peered behind him, but barely caught a brief glimpse of Fruzhin's profile. "How to betray a friendship? I never would."

"Bring them!" Fruzhin's command filled the tower room.

Bring what? Vlad wondered if some new torture awaited him.

Another pair of cloaked figures came into view. The first carried folded vestments of shining scarlet silk, woven socks, and a clean linen shirt in one hand and a pair of short, red leather boots in the other. The second with palms upturned supported voluminous folds of green velvet. Luxurious like the mantle Fruzhin and the others wore.

Draped across the material, a double necklace of gold joined by the sign of a red Hungarian cross. Two Latin phrases ran the length and width.

His eyes still stinging from the buckets of water thrown at him, Vlad made out the words and mumbled them. "*O quam misericors est Deus. Justus et paciens.*" Aghast, he looked at Fruzhin again. "What is the meaning of all this?"

"This is the last time I shall ask, my friend. Please, be quiet and let me aid you. We didn't bring you here to harm you. Your mistrust of Queen Borbála, though warranted in your view, blinds you. All the answers shall come in the fullness of time."

Vlad's arms hung listlessly at his sides. The struggle had not gone out of him. He did not know what to think anymore. The violence of his capture and Fruzhin's obvious unfaithfulness coupled with sudden mercy? What did any of it mean?

Without another word, Fruzhin gestured to someone else, who finally unlocked the shackles on Vlad's wrists before the washing continued.

Afterward, Vlad dried off and dressed. First in the hip-length, laced-up shirt. Followed by the red silk tunic and the hose, tucked into the socks and boots. The hooded velvet cape came last. Fruzhin brushed away Vlad's damp hair from his forehead and did not draw up the emerald-hued hood or close the mantle with its strings. Instead, he took the necklace and held it up.

Beneath the crucifix, a coiled dragon sat on its belly. Wings flared from the body. The tip of its tail wrapped around its neck. The cross of Christ shimmered on its back.

"Oh, how merciful God is. Just and patient." Fruzhin offered the Hungarian translation of the crucifix's inscription. He draped the necklace over Vlad's head and pressed the pendant to his chest. "Be glad Our Lord God is especially tolerant of you."

At his hand signal, those he called brethren left the room in a single column.

"Follow us, now," Fruzhin said before he drew his hood on again.

Although Vlad wanted to ask where they were going, he walked in stunned silence. Along the corridor, a few of the men retrieved torches from the wall.

Vlad trailed behind them, aware that they had descended into a slowly sloping dimness. He peered through a long passageway dug out of sandstone. The labyrinthine tunnel narrowed so much that the width of his shoulders scraped against the rough-hewn rock. The men ahead ascended some carved stairs, setting aside their torches in wall brackets as they exited an opened door.

Their torches gave the space beyond an eerie glow. Vlad took a deep breath and at last emerged at the end of the line in a pillared basilica with three wide aisles. His gaze flitted over the array of Catholic icons to a slivery shrine with small round openings, a leather cover set beside it at the forefront of low stalls intended for prayer.

No congregation gathered in the basilica, only the silent, green-robed band who ushered him here. The glimmer of early morning light streamed through stained-glass windows. Thick snow flurries swirled outside.

The others in red garb had doubled in number. They encircled the sanctuary where only a pair of candles lit the space. Before the high altar, King Zsigmond stood dressed in the same crimson and green finery. The Hungarian crown gleamed atop his bared, grizzled head. Vlad gaped before Fruzhin waved him forward and drew back to the sole space left beside their sovereign.

Zsigmond approached Vlad with hands clasped. "Who are you to come before the master of the Order of the Dragon? Tell Us of your name and lineage."

"I am Vlad, a prince of Wallachia." With an audible swallow, he continued, "A son of Prince Mircea the Great of the House of Basarab."

His king returned to the previous position. "Brethren, recite the creed of the *Societas Ordo Draconistellarum Secretum*."

His heart pounding so wildly, Vlad scarcely believed he stood among the members of the Order of the Dragon. Finally, the second greatest prize he coveted throughout two decades of his service would be his.

As one, the occupants of the room recited a sacred oath in Latin, "...to crush the pernicious deeds of the perfidious enemy of Christendom, the Ottoman Turks, and of the followers of the ancient Dragon, and of the pagan knights, schismatics, and those envious of the Cross of Christ, and of our kingdoms, and of Jesus Christ's holy and saving religion of faith, under the banner of the triumphant Cross of Christ. Amen."

They fell silent. Zsigmond approached again. "Now comes Vlad, a prince of Wallachia, and the son of Prince Mircea the Great of the House of Basarab to join us. Do we permit him to enter the mysteries of the *Societas Ordo Draconistellarum Secretum*?"

"Yes, yes, yes!" The trebled chorus from the members filled the church.

"Kneel before us, Vlad of Wallachia," Zsigmond ordered.

As Vlad did so, his king held out a symbol. A seal shaped like an ouroboros. A primeval dragon swallowing its tail.

"Vlad of Wallachia, all life remains bound in a cycle of renewal," Zsigmond said. "Always, we are born, and always, we are dying. The circle remains unbroken, and thus, we who live within it are everlasting. Take this emblem as a sign of the covenant you share with your brethren. Your pledge to remain devoted to our cause, no matter the sacrifice."

At a gesture from their sovereign, Fruzhin asked Vlad, "Will you keep it secure, treasure it as you do your life and eternal soul? Will you honor the creed of the *Societas Ordo Draconistellarum Secretum?* Will you remain faithful to the commands of your master and king, and the duties of the brethren to protect Christendom? Swear by the blood of our Lord Jesus and the cross you wear."

Vlad looked at Zsigmond and replied. "I will, by the blood of our Lord God and the cross I wear."

"Let all present here," Zsigmond lifted his head and addressed the room's occupants, "witness and attest that Vlad of Wallachia, having sworn by the blood of our Lord God and His holy cross to guard the realms of Christian faith, is accepted as a member of the Order of the Dragon. In acknowledgment of his commitment, he shall receive a knighthood within the *Societas Ordo Draconistellarum Secretum*."

Fruzhin brought their king a long sword and a vial of oil. With the ouroboros clasped in his hands, Vlad bowed his head while Zsigmond anointed his brow with the fragrant olive lipid in the sign of a crucifix.

"By the Grace of our Lord God, Jesus Christ His Everlasting Son, and the Holy Spirit," their sovereign took the weapon afterward and tapped each of Vlad's shoulders. "I grant the honor of knighthood in the *Societas Ordo Draconistellarum Secretum*." Once he handed the blade back to Fruzhin, Zsigmond touched the crown of Vlad's head. "Rise a knight of the Order and be recognized by your brethren."

Their master and king with Fruzhin went away. Afterward, the latter returned, took the ouroboros away and set it on the altar, before he removed his hood. Pushing aside the folds of the velvet mantle on his shoulders, he revealed the same type of cross with the dragon on its reverse nestled against his chest.

Fruzhin grinned and cupped Vlad's fingers, enclosing them within his palms. "I welcome you as my brother Draconist. I invite you to recite the Order's creed with me and exchange the holy kiss of peace, a token of Christian love and unity."

Although overwhelmed, Vlad repeated the words with Fruzhin, who spoke slowly and aided him. Once they finished the credo, they shared the kiss of peace, each murmuring the Latin phrase, "*Pax tecum*," or "peace be with you" before drawing apart.

The man next to Fruzhin approached, took off his hood, and flung his mantle back over slightly bowed shoulders. With a wizened gaze, the old count of Celje, Queen Borbála's father looked into Vlad's eyes. He uttered the same phrases Fruzhin had said and gave Vlad the kiss of peace. Next came his son, the lord Friderik, who offered Vlad another long, incisive stare before repeating his father's deeds and words.

Afterward, the foremost minister of Hungary, the palatine Miklós Garai stepped forward. Followed by his son, another court official. Ernest, the so-called Iron Duke of Austria, whom Vlad recalled with the apt description from Stibor as, 'a cow-faced Habsburg idiot,' preceded his nephew, the sallow and dour heir Albrecht who expected to ascend Zsigmond's throne after his death. Stibor's namesake followed. As did others, a few of whom Vlad had never encountered before today. Over twenty men in total.

After each revealed his face, including those whom Vlad long suspected were members of the Order by their rank at court, he could not help but recall people who were not there. The great Stibor, Fruzhin's uncle Stefan Lazarević, and Pipó and Zawisza. In the days ahead, Vlad would seek the truth about their association with the Order.

At last, a sole hooded figure remained beside their master and king with whom Vlad must perform the ritual recitation. Slender, gemstone-ringed fingers reaching up, Queen Borbála drew her hood down from her unbound, crinkled golden hair. Her brow creased. She met Vlad's stare with a glittering green gaze. She brushed back the folds of her mantle, too. The dragon-cross pendant hung between her breasts.

Although he had known she belonged to the Order for some time, when faced with the moment in which they would acknowledge each other as fellow Draconists, Vlad only considered the years of hostility between them. Yet, the Order bound them together in the defense of Christianity.

She held out her cupped hands. "I welcome you as my brother Draconist. I invite you to recite the creed with me and exchange the holy kiss of peace, a token of Christian love and unity."

Vlad stared into her eyes. How could he ever have any harmony with her? She had robbed him of the bride he once preferred but bore responsibility for the death of their first child. He drew closer, remembering when he gained proof of Borbála's guilt.

Although he could never forgive or forget all she had done, he acknowledged a higher purpose than revenge must govern him now. The precepts of the Order.

He placed his clasped fingers within her hold and did as he had done with all the others present. Afterward, he and the queen bussed each other's cheeks.

She whispered against his skin, "The old debt between us is repaid."

He drew back and held her in silent regard. They would never relinquish the past.

Fruzhin brought Borbála a velvet-wrapped bundle tied with a gold cord. She opened it and showed Vlad the set of black garments inside.

"For everyday wear. What you are dressed in now only befits important occasions, such as this induction or the Catholic feast day of Saint Gheorghe," she instructed.

"I understand, Your Grace," Vlad replied, accepting the materials.

Taking her hand, their king and master preceded everyone else down the central aisle into the nave.

Friderik lingered among a few others who congratulated Vlad again. Soon, he and Fruzhin stood alone in the silent basilica. The blare of fifes and trumpets intruded.

His best friend explained, "The royal progress will begin soon. Zsigmond has summoned the members of the Imperial Diet here to the Bavarian city of Nürnberg."

"That's where we are? May I ask why?"

"Of course. As titular Holy Roman Emperor, grave matters weigh upon our king and require consideration. The end of the Great Schism at the Council of Konstanz thirteen years ago has not united Catholics. The English captured the Maid of French Orleans late last spring and mean to burn her as a witch. Hussite incursions continue. Turks still threaten our borders and the heart of Eastern Christendom."

Vlad nodded, perceiving the heavy burdens Zsigmond bore.

Fruzhin continued, "To others who may glimpse you in the procession, your presence must raise no questions. Like all your fellow Draconists, you'll remove the green mantle and don the black in its place before we exit. How do you feel?"

"I hardly know," Vlad replied, looking down in wonderment at the dragon-cross pendant suspended from his necklace. "I've wanted this for so long, from the moment I knew about it. My sentiments are in a muddle."

"A few questions are permissible in the time we have. Your education in your responsibilities to the Order begins now."

"Am I allowed to speak of this day with my wife?"

"No. The Order and its activities must remain a secret from the uninitiated, Vlad."

With a sigh, he nodded. "I accept. I understand."

"As I perceive the reason for your inquiry." Fruzhin patted his shoulder. "The union and the love you share with your wife make it difficult to hold secrets. Yet, you must. For now, be assured she is not mystified by your absence. She knows you're here. By now, she and your young prince should be well on their way. If she followed my written instruction to depart last week Thursday, the first day in February."

Vlad pondered what he could say when Cneajna arrived. He despised the thought of lying about anything to her. They would never have the harmony both strove for if he kept truths hidden throughout the marriage. When she asked why he left without returning to the townhouse, she would expect the usual candor.

"The Order requires secrecy because our duties often involve actions the Church would abhor." Fruzhin interrupted his thoughts. "We do more than try to keep the borders of Christendom intact. Prelates frown upon treaties with enemies and necessary bribes. We do as we must for our faith. That includes withholding the truth about our membership from our loved ones. What they do not know, they cannot speak of in the confessional. Sacrifice for the security of others is a sacred duty of the Order."

"So, I will keep the secret from Cneajna to protect her and my family." Vlad nodded and held up the velvet bundle and the ouroboros. "Must I hide these from her, too?"

"Oh, never. You should don them. Just as I have worn my mantle in Buda." He fingered its folds. "Wear yours as you like, but always on Fridays. Display the seal too. Only a fellow Draconist will know its significance."

"Were Pipó and Zawisza also Dragons of our Order?"

"Yes, Pipó was, but never Zawisza." A slight smile broke the crags of Fruzhin's face. "He declined the honor. There was a time he would have set aside his wife for the hand of Zsigmond's former sister by marriage, Queen Žofie of Bavaria. As her lover, our king would not permit it. He thought to mollify Zawisza by having him join. The Black Knight's rebuff cooled relations between the pair for some time, especially after the siege at Kutné Hora."

A time Vlad wished to forget, as much as Fruzhin, who swallowed and looked toward a window. Vlad followed his gaze to where the snow flurries still swirled.

"There are other Dragons of the Order who could not be present. For one, the old Grand Duke of Lithuania, whom you met two years past at Luchesk. He's in his seventy-ninth or eightieth year, but no one can deny his defense of Christendom. The king of Poland as well. I'll tell you about the rest. All the truths of the Order must be yours."

Vlad still marveled at his admittance before horror overcame him again. "Christ's blood. I've thought the worst about you and said it during these fraught hours." A long sigh escaped him. "Can you ever forgive me?"

"You are my blood brother." Fruzhin reached out and clasped his shoulder. "There's no need to seek forgiveness. We're bound as friends and Draconists till death."

THE MOON WAXED GIBBOUS later that night over Bavaria. Alone with his master and king, a black-cloaked Vlad ambled along the imperial castle walls. He took it as an ultimate sign of trust that no royal bodyguards accompanied them.

"In a few weeks, Vlad, I'll leave for Italy," Zsigmond announced. "I will take its Iron Crown for my own."

Another kingdom and another throne fell under his dominion while Vlad desired one prize. Wallachia.

Dutifully, he asked, "Shall I be accompanying my master and king?" Would he always leave Cneajna and their Mircea behind, awaiting his return?

"No, but when I depart from here, you'll also travel. To Segesvár, where you will serve as my border commander. Protecting the mountain passes between Transilvania and the Transalpine region."

"Thank you for your trust in me." Hard-pressed to hide his grin, Vlad bowed. "It is an honor. I'll defend the frontier as you wish. You have my oath as your knight and a member of the Order."

"I'd expect nothing less of you." Zsigmond stopped along the rampart and gazed out at the city. "The new role is but a necessary step in gaining influence over the region's boyars, in pursuit of your goal."

Vlad gripped the parapet and held back any words he could have said.

"You're an ambitious man," his sovereign continued. "I never realized how much until you returned to court three years ago and asked after your brother, Radu. Yet, you expressed only simple sorrow at the confirmation of his death. You wanted his seat at Târgoviște. You wouldn't have killed him for it. Unlike your eldest brother Mihail or Dan Dăneşti. But you desire to become the ruling prince of your country."

"I won't deny that." Vlad sighed. "Besides, it's useless to try keeping anything a secret from you. A hard lesson I've learned over twenty years."

Both men shared rueful chuckles.

"You understand now why I once insisted you must marry well," Zsigmond said. "Not to be cruel or ignorant of your feelings. I know how they can bind the heart. The right marriage seemed the best way to ensure your continued path to success. You've trod it for several years; as a royal squire, my knight, my valiant warrior. If you want to rule as my vassal, you'll need a strong army to defeat Dan Dăneşti. He remains in full control of your homeland with my outward support. For now."

"And when the time comes and I have the fighting men needed to vanquish him, will you thwart my moves and my ascension at home?" Vlad asked.

"I'll never go against the principles of the Order and good judgment. You've proven your fortitude and learned patience. You can gain loyal men and secure the desired outcome. Fruzhin supports you. Marriage to the Moldavian princess ensures her father's protection of you and his grandchild's future interests. You have my trust. You're a part of the Order."

Although pleased to have his king's answer, Vlad also noted what went unsaid. No direct offer of Hungarian fighters to take Wallachia from the usurper. The post as a border commander would be but another of Zsigmond's tests. To determine whether Vlad could manage a small territory effectively and bind the hearts of men in his service.

He smiled and nodded to himself. He had faced so many trials, from boyhood to manhood. What was life and a man's existence, except a test of his faith and resolve?

The future lay ahead at Segesvár and beyond. More battles with the Turks, the conquest of Wallachia, and the retrieval of his beloved sister Arina's long-lost daughter. Discovery of the truth about the revenant. He would meet each challenge with determination and the will to survive.

And, he recognized, he would never have to do so alone. Fruzhin approached, and with an acknowledgment from Zsigmond, stood beside them. He returned the Turkic blade Vlad had lost in Óbuda. With his Draconist brethren beside him, he surveyed the night-time Bavarian countryside in silence.

VLAD REMAINED AT THE Kaiserburg. Other initiates joined the Order. Vlad took part in the ceremonial duties. The novelty of his inclusion left him as awed as the newest members.

When he was not with Fruzhin or their master and king, learning more about the duties of a Draconist, he contemplated destiny. Specifically, the support he might seek among the boyars of Wallachia. Who knew them better than Vlậcsan the Wolf? Vlad wrote to the man and asked to meet him in Segesvár during the spring.

A few surprises remained. Not only did he encounter the leader of the Teutonic Knights, whom Zsigmond scorned after losing Galambóc in Serbia. The head of the German House of Hohenzollern, whose son's betrothal to Jadwiga in Poland remained outstanding, also appeared despite his quarrels with their king. But Vlad's most pleasant shock came when he found János on duty at Zsigmond's door one early morning after their sovereign sent a summons.

"You've joined the royal bodyguards already? A great honor!" Vlad exclaimed.

"It is, and I'm pleased Zsigmond singled me out." János' gaze traipsed over the length of him. "Your mantle, it's like that of Prince Fruzhin. A gift from our sovereign?"

Vlad nodded. The younger man's stare flitted back to his face. They shared each other's regard in silence until Vlad tilted his head.

János opened the portal into their king's chamber for him, murmuring, "My prince."

Three days after his investiture, Vlad shared a joyous reunion with Cneajna and their Mircea with Ruxandra, Tobar, and Yoska at their side. The next day, in the paneled guest room allotted to them, Cneajna fingered Vlad's chin-length hair and the beard and mustache that a castle barber had trimmed earlier in the morning.

"Why won't you wear your hair a little longer, my Vlad? It would suit you."

"Not on the battlefield, my Cneajna. There will always be warfare."

He nuzzled her nose. They shared a kiss.

"Especially in this border commander's post, my Vlad." She ran her fingers down the length of his black mantle. "You favor this velvet cloth for everyday wear now."

"I do." He would say no more.

Her gaze assessing, she said nothing. As if a veil of reticence fell between them.

Through it, he glimpsed the questions reflected in her eyes of late and knew he could never provide an answer.

"I have something for you," he said to distract her.

He turned away and retrieved a small jewelry box of birch wood hidden under the bed. Brushing aside a light coating of gray dust, he lifted the lid. Flattened inside, a necklace of translucent, perfectly spherical white pearls, paired with an agate pendant.

"From the forest currents of Bavaria, for you, my Cneajna."

"It's too early in the year to be my birthday." She fingered the smooth gems while he appreciated their deep brilliance. "Why offer a present now?"

"Do I need a specific occasion to be generous?"

She flicked a glance at him. He swallowed. She knew him at his core. Keeping her ignorant of his involvement in the Order would test their bond.

"Thank you, my Vlad." She kissed his cheek. "Help me put it on, please."

After he did so, she lifted the agate pendant. "Like my earrings."

He admired her. She demanded so little from him. If he could, he would give her all the riches of the world. Their value paled compared to wisdom from her or a tender kiss. He hated concealing the Order from her.

Clearing his throat, he said, "I can only hope our Mircea does not tug the necklace too hard when he hugs you. Our boy doesn't recognize his growing strength."

"Where is he? He kissed me this morning after mass," she said, turning to face him, "but would not let me nurse him. He should be weaned. I must do so if we are to have more heirs. Ruxandra says that's why I haven't conceived our dragon-bane."

"Come with me and let's fetch our rambunctious son." With another lingering kiss, he sought to subdue her concern and those pronouncements about a future he could not fathom. "It's the only way we'll ensure he consumes anything this afternoon."

"Mircea disappeared before Ruxandra could catch him."

"You should both know where he is by now."

She groaned and massaged her temples. He chuckled, grasped her hand, and led her from the chamber. They went through the passageways where dull light filtered through half-timbered windows. Arriving at the outskirts of the inner castle courtyard, a spire atop the Sinwellturm round tower pierced steel-gray skies.

At the center of the courtyard, under a broad, frost-covered linden tree, a small gathering occurred. Tobar and Yoska trained in daily practice with their long knives. Among the spectators stood Ruxandra, with a firm grip on Mircea's slim shoulders. He wore a full-length robe dyed indigo blue and buttoned up to the high collar under his mantle. A simple style that mimicked his father's own.

The boy's agate-green eyes followed the sinuous movements of the Gypsy men. They thrust, parried, and blocked each other. A chill rustled the lustrous black, shoulder-length curls inherited from his mother. In the boy's visage, Vlad recognized the characteristic lineage of the House of Basarab. Same long aquiline nose as his, the wide gaze framed by long lashes and thick brows, and thin lips set in a long face. Mircea cheered the Gypsies, imitating the fervor of the older onlookers.

"Our son's martial interest is clear," Vlad observed, before he offered Cneajna a smile. She did not return the gesture. "You believed he would grow into a fierce fighter."

"A fact. Not only a belief." She lifted her chin and her sea-green gaze narrowed. "One that can bring no mother joy."

"Don't worry so soon." He squeezed her fingers and brought them to his lips. "It will be another three or four years before I allow Tobar and Yoska to train him."

Perhaps their son would even become a dragon knight like his father one day.

His wife murmured, "You mean to turn him into a brutal killer?"

"Yes, my Cneajna. Like me. It's the only way he can survive this savage world with the Turks at our borders and Dan Dăneşti, who will undermine every effort I undertake to secure Mircea's rightful inheritance. But for now, we can let him be our little boy."

As he spoke, Vlad looked at their child again. He wondered when his Mircea would discover war was not a game.

Shimmering bands drifted across the courtyard outside the Sinwellturm. The shadow of the round tower appeared elongated the more Vlad stared.

Cneajna gripped his hand. "What is it, husband?"

He could feel it, too. A strange stillness in the air. The castle's dogs had gone silent.

Vlad looked up, shading his eyes. Gloom crept across the darkening afternoon sky, casting the sun into a silhouette. He quivered. The return of the celestial dragon.

People pointed and cried out, Cneajna along with them. Vlad held her against his shoulder and called for Ruxandra and his son, who ran to them. Others scattered from beneath the linden tree, including Tobar and Yoska.

Vlad took another look at the sun. A golden crescent shape, it resembled the symbol he saw on most Ottoman flags at Galambóc. He took his family indoors but did not remain with them. Cneajna pleaded with him to stay.

"I've witnessed two such events in my life. Each preceded some tumult. The first time in Germany, followed by the Christian defeat in Bosnia and the Hussite wars that embroiled me. The second time was nine years later. An eclipse occurred over Buda and other Hungarian cities. Before the Byzantine emperor demanded my service and I separated from Călţuna. Whatever changes may come now, I am still unafraid."

Alone in the shadow of the Sinwellturm, Vlad studied the appearance of bright stars. Where the sun should have shone, a strange, fiery halo surrounded a black shadow. Flames leaped around the edges. A most terrifying and beautiful sight.

He murmured, "How will you alter my fate again, celestial dragon?"

CHAPTER 29

The Dragon and the Devil

"The devil tempts that he may ruin; God tests that He may crown."-Ambrose of Milan (circa 340-397 AD), Christian theologian, bishop, and Roman Catholic and Eastern Orthodox saint.

IN THE YEAR OF OUR Lord 1431-1432. Nürnberg (modern-day Nuremberg, Bavaria, Germany), and *Segesvár, Transilvania* (modern-day Sighișoara, Romania)

Spring arrived in full, and with it, King Zsigmond's departure for Italy. Queen Borbála made no plans to attend the imperial coronation. Her father and the palatine would aid in her governance of Hungary while ensuring the defenses against Hussite attacks. Vlad witnessed their parting from Zsigmond after dawn in the courtyard of the Kaiserburg. Although still unsure what to make of the bond he and Zsigmond's wife now shared, Vlad resolved never to forgive her for hurting Călțuna. An inexcusable act.

Afterward, he walked alongside Fruzhin and their master and king, whose entourage prepared to ride out in a few hours at midday.

"The truce of Galambóc with the Turks will expire this year," Zsigmond said. "That is why We are sending you, Vlad, to Segesvár. You shall mint silver coins, a sign of prestige and Our faith in you. We've summoned an experienced engraver to help you begin the operation.

He'll find you. If there are Turkish raids into the northern Transalpine land and southern Transilvania, We expect you to stop them. Call up the levies in the region and recruit mercenaries."

"The Székelys, those fierce warriors who live in the shadows of Transilvania's Eastern Carpathian Mountain range, would make excellent fighters," Vlad replied. "After I've settled in Segesvár, I'll ride out to enlist them."

"You will not fail Us. We'll muster all our vassals, Moldavia included. They are new to Our alliance, thanks to your marital union, but must learn what is required of them."

"My loyal wife's father and brothers are committed to the cause of vanquishing our foes. The Moldavians won't disappoint you, either."

"What about the Venetians, Your Royal Majesty?" Fruzhin asked. "Will they stand in our way with the Turks? Or will we have peace at last concerning Dalmatia?"

"We must, it seems. We'll give Doge Francesco Foscari of Venice full consideration in due time...." Their sovereign trailed off. The trio stared as men in rich robes and felt hats approached and bowed. Among them, Vlậcsan the Wolf stood out, for he had paired his damask robe with the animal pelt he favored.

With Zsigmond's consent, Fruzhin spoke with the new arrivals at a short distance from their king and Vlad. He reasoned; nothing could be wrong with his grandmother. If so, her nephew would have come alone, not as part of a delegation. Too early for the meeting that Vlad planned with Vlậcsan as well. No, some other need brought him and his cohorts to Nürnberg.

Fruzhin returned. "Discontented boyars from the Transalpine area, some who've defected from Dan Dăneşti's court at Argeş and others who tire of his rule."

"So, my treacherous cousin still lives?" Vlad interjected.

Fruzhin nodded to him before continuing, "They wish to speak with you, my king. Their leader is named Albu Tocsaba. Do you recall him, Vlad, from your father's court?"

He glanced at the broad-chested boyar. Although certain they had made no earlier acquaintance, Albu frowned at him, and he wondered why.

"I've never encountered the man before, but the name Tocsaba is familiar. Comes from the western region of my land. I know one other man with him who wears the pale gray wolf-skin," Vlad said. "He is called Vlậcsan, the son of Florea. He is my grandmother's nephew, the child of her brother."

"Then We will listen to the companions. Both of you will attend Us with the royal guards," Zsigmond replied. "See that they remove the noblemen's weapons."

The meeting occurred in the Kaiserburg's Imperial Hall, where delegations received a royal audience. Divided into two aisles by five oak columns, the room flooded with light from large windows overlooking the southern environs of Nürnberg.

During the assembly, Vlad kept a watchful gaze on the Wolf. Yet, the boyar would not meet his stare and stayed silent while the stout head of his delegation or others spoke. An ill feeling of foreboding came over Vlad as he listened. Even if nothing had occurred with his grandmother, Vlậcsan's behavior could not bode well.

The long list of the nobles' grievances drew ever louder sighs from Zsigmond, who alone sat along the western wall, until he demanded, "Say what you want, Albu Tocsaba! You and your compatriots no longer desire the rule of Dan Dăneşti. He has three sons, but their youth makes all of them undesirable candidates whom We could never support! We must have a leader with the experience to field armies against the Turks. Is there some other acceptable member of the House of Basarab whom you have in mind?"

Vlad held his breath. A steady pulse surged to life at his temple. This might be his moment. The noblemen could choose him. Although only Vlậcsan knew him, given their kinship, the Wolf might persuade the others to support him. With Radu dead, only Vlad and their younger brother, whom he affectionately called little Alex in their boyhood, remained as the legitimate heirs of their father. The boyars would not throw in their lot with one of the innumerable bastards he had sired.

"There is a sole person," the chief nobleman said. "Once a boy, now risen from the long shadows that his elder brothers cast." Albu Tocsaba raised his prominent chin and turned his bulbous head. Shaggy brows flared as he eyed Vlad, whose heart hammered. "The only man whom we will support. Alexandru Aldea, the last son of Mircea the Great."

A tremor ran through Vlad. Little Alex? No longer so small, surely as in their youth. A man, full-grown at thirty-four. Three years younger than Vlad.

When he would have surged forward, Fruzhin, who stood beside him, grappled his elbow. "No! Wait and listen," he hissed in Vlad's ear.

"And what is this Alexandru Aldea's claim to being a successful leader of men in battle?" Zsigmond asked. "Why should We believe he is most suited to rule the land beyond the mountains with Our support? We've never heard of him taking the field with his sibling Radu or his cousin Dan Dăneşti against the Turks."

"The prince has been dutiful in service to his brother's principality. When Radu ruled our land some ten years ago, Alexandru Aldea administered the region around Rucăr. He will keep the Turks at bay. So long as Alexandru Aldea is the official prince of Wallachia, they won't attack." Albu Tocsaba smiled as if he truly believed that knavery.

Vlad had heard enough. He shook off Fruzhin's hold and approached and bowed before Zsigmond. "Your Royal Majesty, you cannot believe it! If my younger brother was so...foolish as to trust the promises of Christendom's enemies, he deserves to discover the truth of their intent when they renege on a false oath of support."

"Your sibling may buy the time We'll need to prepare for the future," the king said.

"The price is too grave, the blood of our people. They shouldn't suffer under the yoke of Turkish peace. You know what it would mean for them; the blood tax. The taking of Wallachian boys to fight in Sultan Murād's army. His janissaries. He's imposed conscription on every Christian land he considers a Turkic vassal. Don't let Alex...Alexandru Aldea rule. His reign shall destroy my country."

Although he moderated his tone, the dragon's blood seethed inside him with such fury that he could have burst into flames. Alex, held in the sway of the Turks! How could he have done it? Betrayed their countrymen?

"I am aware of Prince Vlad's presence among your courtiers, my good king," Albu Tocsaba said, "including the time in which he has spent at your side. Away from Wallachia. He doesn't know the land like his brother, Prince Alexandru Aldea. The people have changed. They desire only peace."

"Impossible with the Turks!" Vlad turned and glared at the boyar. "Only an idiot could think so! Or a coward."

"How dare you!" Spittle flew from Albu's mouth. "I don't care who you are, prince or not. You'll never call me craven."

"I'll name any man thus who willingly submits to the eternal adversaries of Christ."

As he said so, Vlad turned for a view of Vlậcsan beside one of the oaken pillars. The man's throat bobbed, but he did not look away.

"Leave Us with Our royal guard, all of you," Zsigmond commanded with a wave of his hand. "Shut the doors behind you."

As the Wallachian delegation withdrew, Vlad stalked behind them.

"Do nothing rash," Fruzhin warned from beside him.

Vlad waited until they all stood within the inner courtyard again. The boyars huddled together, speaking in low tones. He shoved the nearest pair aside and hauled Vlậcsan by the high collar of his garb from their midst. The other nobleman looked on in horror. Vlad dragged his kinsman under the lone linden tree at the center of the yard.

"Does the Dowager know what you've done?" He shoved Vlậcsan against the rough bark. "Did she support your choice?"

"She understands me very well. Unfortunately, you do not, my prince."

"Ten years ago, you came to me at Pozsony. I told you then that I wanted to know the moment either my brother Radu or Dan Dăneşti lost their thrones. You've arrived at Nürnberg to support Alex."

"He is the same as you. Of the old blood of Basarab. He lives in Wallachia. You were not there. Mine was not a difficult choice to make, my prince."

"Slavering cur! I could kill you where you stand." Vlad rammed him harder against the tree, making him cry out as his head thumped the wood. "You've betrayed me!"

"How so, my prince? I never agreed to back your pursuit of the crown."

"In Pozsony. You said Wallachia required a strong and cunning prince as a worthy successor to my father. I asked you if you thought this prince would ever exist again. And you told me he already does. You looked into my eyes as you spoke the words."

Vlậcsan returned his gaze, unwavering. "I said so, but you mistakenly believed I meant you. Prince Alexandru Aldea had vowed beforehand to aid in the recovery of all the lands belonging to my father, which your father stole from us! Thrice, under different Wallachian ruling princes, your king has affirmed my family's rights to the lands held by Tismana Monastery. Do I control them outright? No. Am I wrong to want what is mine?"

"No." Vlad released his grip. "Even I desire the same. Now, I have only to berate myself for hoping you would be first among the boyars to assist me."

"My prince...."

"No, Vlậcsan. The fault is mine. Believe me, I'll never repeat the error. You've taught me a valuable lesson about my expectations. The will and whim of nobles. My countrymen. As inconstant as the winds. I'll never rely on you or any boyar again."

Vlad turned away and rejoined Fruzhin.

"What happened?" His best friend tugged his arm. "Why did you argue with him?"

"It doesn't matter." He raked a hand across his brow and pushed the black hair away from his face. "I must find my family. We're leaving for Segesvár in the wake of our king's departure today."

"Will you not wait and hear Zsigmond? Whether he'll support your brother?"

"I already know the answer." Vlad patted Fruzhin's arm and walked away.

Indoors and away from the view of all others, he slammed a fist against the cool masonry. Wallachia would be his. No one; not his sovereign, his cowardly little sibling, or duplicitous noblemen could stand in his way.

THE ROADS DOWN TO SEGESVÁR were muddied and slick with rain. From the imperial city, Vlad led the way, with Cneajna, their Mircea, and Ruxandra bundled inside the carriage. They undertook a month-long journey, stopping in Vienna and Pozsony before reaching the Hungarian capital. The Moldavian guards protected them and the wagons that they retrieved in Buda before parting with Fruzhin there at his townhouse.

Tobar, Yoska, and their Gypsy kin brought up the rear of their large company. From there, they went to Várad before crossing the border and heading for Segesvár.

Approaching the town's gray walls, covered in ivy once again, an unexpected sense of familiarity overcame Vlad. The calm waters of the Târnava Mare River soothed him. He had spent so little time in his second son's birth country.

Somehow, when he entered the gates of Segesvár in the early morning, it felt like a homecoming. Good, he reasoned, for it would be his domicile until he ruled his country. He paused and looked to the south over his shoulder. Within a week's ride through the Bran Pass lay the border his homeland shared with Transilvania. One day, he would cross it as a conqueror.

As he approached, the townspeople eyed him warily. A few eventually recognized him. "Look, it's the prince from across the mountains. Prince Vlad!"

He hailed them as he rode toward the central square, where Cneajna spent her long sojourn before and after their Mircea's birth.

Nearing the site, Vlad called out, "Where is the lord of Segesvár? I must greet him!"

"He's not here," one man answered. "Went south to Kronstadt."

"Yes, to his mistress' bed while leaving his wife and children behind," another offered, to the laughter and derision of others.

"Then who is your headman?" Vlad asked. "Who puts an end to all of your troubles when the lord or his magistrate cannot?"

"That's *Tată*. His name's Dragomir."

Vlad slowed his horse and looked down at a mousy-brown-haired boy, who stood no taller than his Carpathian pony's foreleg. "And who are you, little one?"

"My name's Petru."

"And I'm his father, Dragomir." A behemoth of a man, in the company of an elderly woman, pushed through the gathering crowd and hoisted up the boy on massive shoulders. "My lord prince, welcome again to Segesvár."

"Thank you," Vlad said. "By the grace of His Royal Majesty, King Zsigmond of the House of Luxembourg in Hungary, I shall serve as the border commander of this town and the southern territories westward to Hermannstadt and Kronstadt in the east." Vlad gestured to the carriage. "But first, Dragomir, my family and I need somewhere to live."

He slid down from his saddle and pushed the folds of his black mantle behind him. Gasps and muted conversations followed among the denizens.

"Look, *Tată*," Petru pointed to Vlad's chest. "Like in your stories. It's a dragon."

Vlad looked down and saw the pendant on his necklace spun around to its obverse side. "You're right. You have keen eyesight, Petru. How old are you?"

The boy held up five fingers, which made his father laugh.

"No, son, both your grandmother and I have told you before. You're six years old now," Dragomir said. "Forgive him, my lord prince. He's still grasping his numbers."

"My eldest son will soon be six years of age later this year. Petru's blessed with a patient father and a good family."

Vlad looked over Dragomir's meaty shoulder and nodded to the hovering old woman behind him. Deep creases lined her time-worn face.

"Dracul," she whispered, recoiling from him. She backed away through the crowd.

Vlad stared in her wake and wondered at the strange reaction.

"Ignore my late wife's mother, my lord prince," Dragomir said. "She's superstitious. Come with me. I'll take you into the upper town. I know a place for you and your family. It's the only former residence that's available straight away."

Vlad mounted again. The headman and his son led the path from the central square. Some of the more curious and idle citizens followed them. After climbing a slow but steady incline, they entered the precincts of jumbled, even narrower streets. The faded facades of buildings tightly juxtaposed with others, freshly coated in lime-wash, gave a sense of the old and the new. A nearby clock tower chimed the hour.

Dragomir took them along an alley beneath a rounded arch, which dwarfed them. The archway connected two buildings. As Vlad feared, the headman turned left to the more dilapidated structure. Two men sat outside the adjacent house, sorting through a barrel of tin ore. They stopped working and joined the spectators who had followed Vlad to the upper town.

"Before our new lord ascended here," Dragomir said, "the guards who served the old lord lived in this place. Built with mortar and good, strong river stones. It's somewhat dark inside. Even when candles are lit and with the narrow windows. There are enough rooms for the comfort of your immediate household, my lord prince."

"You have the keys to this place?" Vlad asked.

"I can fetch them."

"Do so. My lady wife will wish to see inside."

As Dragomir nodded and went away with his son, Vlad approached the carriage. He found Cneajna and Ruxandra with a sleeping Mircea's head resting in the latter's lap. Both women gaped in silence at each other.

"My Cneajna, what is it?" Vlad inquired. "Does something trouble you or our son?"

"No...no, my...Vlad," she sputtered. Her visage pale, she took the hand he extended and clambered down the step to join him on the smooth cobblestone street.

Although he did not believe her, he never inquired further as she spun in a circle, taking in a view of the other houses lining the square. Vlad gazed alongside her. Sharp-sloped roofs with tiny apertures reminded him of Hermannstadt's homes.

"This is where we shall live?" She peered at the narrow door in front of them.

"If you find it agreeable. Ah, Dragomir returns."

The large man skidded on a few cobblestones as he caught sight of Cneajna and rushed to bow. His son yelped and tried to prevent his fall.

"Be careful, man!" Vlad took Cneajna's arm. "My lady wife and I depend on your good health. This is Princess Cneajna, the mother of our heir, Prince Mircea."

She greeted Dragomir and a few of the spectators before the headman approached the house. With a groan, he turned the key in the lock. The door would not budge. He rammed his massive shoulder into the oak wood. It flung open; the hinges creaking and dust billowing. Red-faced, he gestured to Vlad, who took his wife's hand. Together, they entered the narrow doorway and stared into the darkness.

A vaulted ceiling became visible. Cracks crisscrossed and ruined the paint. Tables and chairs lined the wall, stacked haphazardly. Dead, winged insects, cobwebs, mouse droppings, and fine dust coated nearly every surface. A musty scent pervaded the house. Vlad looked down two corridors, each leading to other rooms with closed doors.

"The guards used to eat here." Dragomir pushed inside, joining them with Petru. "Through the hallway on the left, another door leads out back to an old vegetable garden within the high walls. Our women can clean and make this place comfortable."

"Shall I have them come?" Vlad asked Cneajna.

"Certainly not." Her nose crinkled. She returned his look with fierce regard.

He groaned. She deserved far finer accommodations in which to raise their son. He would do better and provide a more suitable home.

"It is the responsibility of the lady of the house to ensure its readiness and comfort." She squeezed his hand, smiled down at Petru, and faced Dragomir. "Tell the women to bring buckets of water from the wells, and as many rags and cloths as they can. My husband shall determine whether we need masons and carpenters. We will pay any workers a just wage when all is ready. Also, send word to the lord of Segesvár. We'll be renting this house at a fair price. Not one more coin than merited!"

"Yes, as you say. At once, princess." The headman nodded and withdrew, taking his son. He bellowed the instructions Cneajna provided to the excited onlookers.

"I thought you would refuse." Vlad framed her trim waist in his hands. "Dragomir said this is the only house available to us right now. Are you certain you can live here?"

"Yes, we will make it a home for us." She moved his fingers to her belly. "And our little princes. Our second son will be born in this place during the coming winter."

"Are you carrying another child now?"

She nodded, beaming up at him.

"But you haven't been ill, as with our Mircea. There have been no signs."

"While we spoke in the carriage, Ruxandra and I realized the truth at the same time. I have not bled in two months. Not since we reunited in Nürnberg, my Vlad."

"Oh, my Cneajna." He palmed her abdomen and kissed her deeply. "Another baby."

"And we will be happy together," she promised.

WHILE SHE PATIENTLY and dutifully oversaw the restoration of their home, he assessed Transilvania's regional defenses under his dominion, from Călțuna's former home of Hermannstadt in the west and eastward to Kronstadt. After, he took Tobar, Yoska, and Dragomir northeast to the land of the Székelys, traveling the breadth of their domain. He extracted their promise to fight the Turkish menace despite their count's resentment of Vlad's new role.

At intervals, he returned to Cneajna's side and marveled as her belly swelled with their child. Her olive skin browned in the sun as she revitalized the vegetable garden with Ruxandra's aid. Under Cneajna's direction and steadfast attention, their home became inviting, urging Vlad's eager return each time.

Across from the clock tower, two Catholic religious foundations existed; a monastery for Dominican monks and a Franciscan nunnery. Whenever Vlad rode by on his way home, he considered Călțuna and their son.

Each Friday he shaved his beard, left the mustache, and went outdoors garbed in his black mantle, his chest, and belly much broader than in his youth. He always carried the ouroboros seal on a chain in one hand. He gave alms for the benefit of the poor and donated to the monastery and nunnery. He became the benefactor of local churches and religious houses devoted to the saints Gheorghe, who defended against the dragon, and Margit, martyred by it. Both were patron saints of the Order.

In the first chamber of the house, benches lined the wall. Cneajna placed a large comfortable chair with a cushion opposite the doorway, where Vlad intended to conduct meetings or discuss war strategies with Segesvár's lord and noblemen.

"Thank you, my Cneajna," he said as she patted his shoulder while he relaxed in the seat and stretched his legs out. "This shall do nicely."

The other chambers served as areas for the family to dine and sleep. Cneajna's Moldavian guards would take their rest in the largest room, closest to the door at night. Tobar and Yoska planned to stay there as well, but their families had already made camp alongside the river.

On the right side of the house, Vlad reopened the bricked-up former entrance near the connecting arch, making the alley and Tin-Makers Street accessible to the new servants. They retrieved deliveries of requisitioned goods from the back road.

A cellar ran the entire length. The hearth stood here, and the cook and maids prepared food. Vlad re-established the mint in an adjacent room. When Zsigmond's engraver arrived from Buda, Vlad ordered the production of silver coins. Dragomir volunteered that his elder brother, for whom he had named Petru, also worked as an engraver in Hermannstadt's guild. Vlad planned to lure Dragomir's sibling to continue the minting at Segesvár before Zsigmond's engraver departed.

Once introduced, the skilled men worked well together and created the coin dies to Vlad's specifications by summer's end. At a tiny window built low to the ground on the upper floor, he stood in the faint light and examined his first coinage. The heat of the house would have stifled him any other day, but not while he studied the metalwork.

On the head of the silver coin, an eagle stood beneath a cross, incorporating a traditional symbol of Wallachia. On the reverse, a dragon with outstretched wings, the same symbol being stitched in red dye on his banners by Gypsy women.

"My Vlad, you must come up!" Cneajna called to him from the stairs on the opposite side of their home.

He knew it could not be the birthing time of their child so soon, but he hurried and entered the back garden. Fruzhin and János awaited him on either side of Cneajna.

"I thought you would both be with our king in the Italian countryside, but I'm glad to see you here." With a hearty embrace for each of his friends, he welcomed them.

"As I am, to greet you," Fruzhin replied. He grinned at Cneajna. "Your family grows."

"Where is Prince Mircea the Younger?" János asked.

Vlad replied, "In the square at the front of the house, watching Tobar and Yoska sparring with two of the Moldavian guards. I'm surprised you did not encounter them."

"They entered the side gate, my Vlad, after Ruxandra and I visited the nunnery with our weekly donation." Cneajna curtsied, despite her growing bulk, and withdrew.

Vlad showed off the newly minted coin. "The first of many. They will be used throughout Transilvania and shall help pay the mercenaries."

"That's why we've come, my friend," Fruzhin said. "I've brought fifty Bulgarians. János summoned another fifty men from his home at Hunyadvár and the surrounding areas. You cannot train the levies alone."

János added, "When I leave with Prince Fruzhin for Italy six weeks from now, the bulk of my mercenaries shall stay to help defend against an Ottoman attack."

"As will mine," Fruzhin promised.

Warmed by their generosity, Vlad thanked them and embraced them again. He led them inside the house, where the trio sat and enjoyed cups of wine.

"What do you have to say about the news from your home?" Fruzhin asked Vlad.

He knew what his best friend meant, but what could he offer as a comment?

"I hold no ill will against my brother Alex in his quest to claim the country. He didn't steal my birthright; we had an equal claim. Let's see if he can hold on to Wallachia or if the Turks shall desert him. For now, I am concerned with safeguarding from him our father's hereditary lands at nearby Făgăraş and Amlaş. I may send your fighters there if there is no Turkish attack elsewhere in southern Transilvania."

A long look passed between Fruzhin and János before the latter said, "You must have heard about the Moldavian forces who are aiding your sibling to secure his crown."

"Moldavian forces?" Vlad jerked from his seat. "At the side of my little brother?"

"That's a lie!" Cneajna flung open the front door and came into their midst. "It can't be. My father would never have approved of that. Let his men fight for the one who usurped your rights. It can't be, my Vlad. You must not believe it."

He drew her to his side, rested his chin on her covered hair, and hushed her.

"My father by marriage is ill," he explained to his friends. "He has ceded responsibilities to his son Iliaş, or so Cneajna's youngest brother Stetco, whom she favors, has said. If the Moldavians went into Wallachia to support Alex, Cneajna's parent did not order it."

"The last official act of my father was the gift of thirty-one Gypsy families and some cattle to the monastery in Bistritz." Cneajna raised her head and exchanged terse looks with each man. "I know him. He could not have sided with anyone against my husband." She left them and slammed the door behind her.

"Whoever gave the order," János pitched his voice lower, "we can attest those Moldavian forces came at Zsigmond's command."

Vlad's fingers tightened into fists at his side. His king swore he would not interfere in any overt move Vlad undertook against Dan Dănești. But Vlad never imagined he should have asked Zsigmond not to send the Moldavians needed against the Turks, to bolster Alex's fight for the throne instead.

He uncurled his hands. "Come, we must meet with the lord of Segesvár and summon the first levy if they are to train effectively against our enemies."

DURING THE SUBSEQUENT weeks, as a warm summer gave way to the coolness of autumn, Vlad and his friends oversaw the instruction of boys and men between the ages of fourteen and sixty; anyone deemed fit and useful enough in the expected fight. Their lessons occurred in the public squares and on the riverine edges of the town.

While a training exercise ensued, Cneajna lingered in the doorway of their home with their Mircea. They ate sliced pears and apples, while Vlad taught tactics with a peasant flail, which he learned while fighting Bohemian Hussites.

His wife called out, "What about the women of Segesvár, dear husband?"

He lowered the wooden staff. "What about them, Cneajna?"

"Why are you not training them as well?"

When János laughed, she scowled at him.

Vlad approached her. "The men will defend the town when necessary."

"And if they should fall in battle? What then?" She rolled her eyes heavenward. "The women may not number among your would-be fighters, but they can still die if there is no one left to protect them." She looked down at their son, crouched in front of a nearly empty bowl. "Come, my Mircea. You have quite the appetite today."

They left Vlad and closed the door. He turned around and with an exasperated sigh, looked at Fruzhin, who shrugged. That evening, Vlad discussed the matter with the lord, who agreed the women could train with the peasant flail and similar tools.

One night after a grueling late autumn drill had ended, a week after the departure of János and his best friend, Vlad rode the sloping cobblestone streets, bound for home. Tobar and Yoska accompanied him.

He found Cneajna outside in the center of the public square. A pair of her guards with torches watched her from the house's entrance. Her face upturned toward the heavens, a smile curved her lush lips and highlighted dimples.

"Why are you out here?" Vlad asked.

"Look. It's arrived." She came to him and pointed at the sky. "Our dragon-bane's star. It heralds his birth. This child will be different, unlike any of his siblings. You'll see."

Alongside the Gypsies, he stared in the direction she indicated. A yellow ball with a strange halo around it streaked among the stars. The twins gaped and whispered in the Roma tongue about the evil eye.

Vlad dismounted and drew Cneajna inside against her protests. During the following days, he would not speak of the fiery orb that remained visible over Segesvár, even perceptible during a cloudless day.

"The townspeople associate the sighting with malevolence." Cneajna sewed felt foot coverings for their baby, expected in a month by Ruxandra's estimation. "They're a superstitious lot. Did you know when they call you 'Dracul' in the streets, it has dual meanings? The dragon or the devil."

"More than Dragomir's mother by marriage believes in the latter association," Vlad muttered as he stared into his cup of ale. "I don't care what they say about me, so long as they heed my orders to defend against our foes."

THE TIME OF THE BIRTHING arrived on a wintry night, one of the last in December. Fierce winds howled and clawed at the shutters. Cneajna awoke a startled Vlad in their bed with her screams. Ruxandra, who left a sleeping Mircea, bolted into the room. Cneajna gripped and clawed at her belly. As if a monster struggled to emerge. Her close companion dragged off the coverlet and revealed the sheet half-soaked in watery blood.

"He's fighting me, Vlad!" Cneajna scrabbled for his fingers.

"My prince, I'll go downstairs to the kitchen and inform the housemaids. Stay by her side, please," Ruxandra pleaded.

"I'm never leaving her unless she wishes it." He kissed his love's hand.

Everything happened so fast. The gaggle of women urged him to the recesses of the room. Cneajna's labor pains stopped and then returned with terrifying intensity. Freezing rainfall pattered. Mircea scrambled into the room for the safety of Vlad's arms.

"I beg you, my prince, to take him back to the nursery. He shouldn't see this." Ruxandra maneuvered a weakened Cneajna into a sitting position. "Come, my lamb, my sweet princess. You must try to push now with every pain."

"*Tată*, what's wrong with my mother?" Mircea asked, tugging Vlad's hand.

"She will be well. Don't worry." He scooped up his son and left the bedroom, carrying him into the adjacent nursery.

Raindrops splattered on the roof. For a long time, Vlad lay on the ground next to Mircea's bed, covered in Vlad's black wolf-skin, and talked with or sang loudly to his child. Anything to distract them both from the frenzied shrieks across the hall. They grew louder, vying with the windy, wet weather. Then a bleak silence fell over the house.

Vlad listened for the distinct cries of a newborn. But no sound followed. Except for muffled tones amid the rain splatter. Followed by weeping.

A scream echoed, "No! My Vlad!"

He jerked to his feet. Cneajna! He made it almost to the door before Ruxandra opened it. He would have fled past her tear-stricken form, but he needed to remain calm for his wife's sake.

"What happened to her and our baby, Ruxandra? Do they live?"

"She does. The little prince came, but he was not breathing. Stillborn."

"It cannot be!" He had already lost one babe, who never drew breath outside of Călţuna's body. He would not lose another with dear Cneajna. "Stay here with Mircea."

He rushed into his bedroom. His wife curled up, sobbing. She reached for his hand, but he went to the opposite side of the bed. The maids gathered beside a small, motionless bundle. He picked it up and tugged aside the folds of lightly bloodied linen.

Inside, a tiny hairless child rested with eyes sealed shut in a crinkled face. Tears threatened. Vlad would not give in. His mind raced, recalling something Jadwiga said, about a doctor who could have breathed life into her little stepbrother before he died.

Vlad inhaled, opened, and covered his baby's mouth. He sent a rush of air into the tiny chest. All the maids screamed and backed away. Desperate, Vlad ignored them. He tried twice more. Nothing occurred. Cneajna wailed, but he did not look at her.

Instead, he went to the windows and flung open their shutters. Frigid air intruded, as did frozen droplets and icicles clustered on the windowsill. Through it all, the hairy star continued its nightly progress, although it seemed fainter than before. Vlad held his son against his body, lifted his dimpled chin, and patted his back.

"Breathe, my child. Breathe!" Bewildered by the lack of movement, he raised the bundle, this time pinching the small nostrils closed before he exhaled into the gaping mouth. A foot kicked his forearm before the newborn squalled.

Vlad wrapped him up again as Cneajna sobbed anew. He closed the aperture and brought their second son, third son of his, to the bed and placed him in her arms. She kissed the baby's forehead, her tears trickling into the cloth folds.

"I thought we'd lost him forever," she whispered, "but he is truly here."

"Yes." Vlad touched the black curls, relieved that although they were not the lusty screams of either of his earlier children, at least this boy cried out. "He's a blessing. A miracle. What shall we call him, my Cneajna?"

"A fitting name. The only one he should have. In thanks to the father who created him, gave him the breath of life, and held on to hope while I forsook it."

"You want me to call him Vlad?" He chuckled. "His eldest brother is Vlad Călugărul."

"Christian families throughout Europe make a practice of such naming. Besides, can you think of a personal name he deserves more?" She fitted their new son to her body while he wriggled and turned, seeking her breast.

Mircea and Ruxandra reappeared in the open portal. She ushered the maids away and closed the door. Mircea edged close to the bed.

"Come," Cneajna beckoned him, patting the clean half of the mattress beside her. "Meet your new little brother. Our family's future dragon-bane."

As Mircea clambered beside them, he asked, "Why's he so small?"

"All newborns are," Vlad said. "Even you were this tiny."

Mircea scrunched up his cherubic face as if he could not believe it so.

Cneajna helped the baby find her nipple and sighed as his small mouth closed on the swollen bud. She winced but soon relaxed. Their child drew hard on her breast until he fell asleep.

Afterward, Vlad took him, although Ruxandra would have wiped him clean and swaddled him. "Wait. There's something I must do. My sacred duty and honor as a father."

He lifted his boy and returned to the window, pulling open a shutter. He protected the child and held him flush against his body, protecting him from wind and rain. The distant heavenly orb gave off an incandescent glow, like the embers of dying light.

"You are little Vlad, the son of Vlad." He bent close to his new child's ear. "You were born under the sign of the fiery star, as a new year arrives. Some bright destiny must await you. I shall ensure it and keep you safe. Your mother, your brothers, and you are my life! Never doubt my love. You are also my heir and, like your siblings and father, a prince of the House of Basarab."

Little Vlad slumbered on, but his lips twitched. Vlad latched the shutter again.

THE NEXT MONTH, CNEAJNA wept bitterly. Hearing her cries from outside on Tin-Makers Street, Vlad rushed inside the house and found her in the nursery. Ruxandra rocked little Vlad in her arms while Mircea looked on. A sense of foreboding returned to Vlad, which hadn't happened since the third night after his youngest son's birth when the strange star finally faded from view. Unable to speak, Cneajna handed him a missive.

"From her favorite brother, Prince Stetco, in Suceava," Ruxandra revealed.

Vlad comforted his wife while he read. His heart pitched. He shared her sorrow.

"Christ's blood. Not only is your father gone to glory this month, but Jadwiga, dead at the start of last December! She was only twenty-three years of age." Sadness overwhelmed him at the memory of the charismatic Polish princess with her wheat-colored hair, warm smile, and good advice. "Your sibling doesn't say how she died."

"You know and I know!" Cneajna wrenched away from him. "Her stepmother poisoned her. Is there another reasonable explanation for this sudden death?"

"That's a grave accusation, my love. You're overwrought because of this twofold loss." He took her hand. "Did you see Jadwiga or your father in some...dream of yours?"

"No. I've had no fitful nights. Little Vlad sleeps peaceably, so I do as well. You know he never cries unless he's hungry. Just as you know that evil woman had a hand in Jadwiga's end. I can accept Father's loss, but not hers. The Polish prince has reached his seventh year and his surviving brother is three. Jadwiga was a threat to Poland's queen from the moment she birthed one son for King Władysław. He grows weaker. Jadwiga would have been a good queen in his stead. As she was an excellent friend to us."

Later in the night, thirty-eight-year-old Vlad lit a lone candle on a table set below the bedroom window. He whispered prayers for sweet Jadwiga's soul.

THE FOLLOWING SPRING brought word of an Ottoman offensive into Transilvania. From Hungary came a warning of two simultaneous campaigns. Despite the news of almost seventy-five thousand seasoned warriors combined, who would soon invade, Vlad remained unperturbed. The Turks always attacked between April and October each year. He ordered the defenses prepared across the southern border. But enemy soldiers struck quickly in eastern Transilvania and devastated the Moldavian countryside.

Vlad revealed to the lord of Segesvár, "The Albanian-born commander, Hamza Bey, comes up from Anatolia to attack southern Transilvania, while the Balkan governor Ali Bey will cross the Danube at Nicopolis. My brother Alex sent a warning from Târgoviște, but he will not deter the Turkish march. Dan Dăneşti rides with them. Vengeful, he's aligned with the Turks, hoping to kill Alex."

"What will you do, my prince?"

"What else, except thwart the Ottomans?" Vlad grinned. "The murderous Dan and my traitor brother shall deal with each other. It's not my concern."

During two subsequent summer days, Vlad summoned the Székelys. Less than half the expected number appeared. He also readied Fruzhin's and János' mercenaries, gathered his Gypsy fighters, and organized the peasant levies. Everyone prepared to ride from Segesvár on the third day.

That morning, Vlad's kiss lingered on his wife's tender lips. He hugged Mircea and held little Vlad up to the narrow window, pointing out the banners until the baby fussed.

"Let me have him," Cneajna said behind him. "He's always ready to drink."

"He's greedy for life," Vlad said, giving him over. "Will he desire war games like our Mircea when he grows up?"

"It's bad enough that our eldest pleads with Tobar or Yoska for a wooden sword. He's barely approaching his fourth birthday. Shall each of our sons follow you into battle?"

He wondered if she had envisioned it so in her dreams. Heavens forbid!

Still, he acknowledged, "It's the age in which we live. Would that they were born in simpler times. Knowing men's warlike nature, I doubt such a period has ever existed."

He parted from his family, promising to come back. He tromped outdoors in the armor Tobar and Yoska had helped him with earlier that morning. The black mantle of the Order of the Dragon hung from the pauldrons on his shoulders. Mounting the war stallion, with a wave of his hand, he directed his forces southward with him.

Székely horsemen and the mercenaries preceded the Gypsies and peasant levies. Women, children, and the infirm who could walk came out to wish them well. The more superstitious locals pointed to Vlad's banners. His coat-of-arms sewn or painted on blue, yellow, or black flags featured the red dragon vanquishing a lion.

"Dracul! Dracul!" The cries filled the streets and made him smile. In his Wallachian tongue, it meant dragon. Transilvanians viewed such creatures as minions of the devil.

After Vlad survived the Turks and returned to his Segesvár home and family, he vowed he would adopt the sobriquet. Friends and foes alike would know him as Vlad Dracul. His heirs would bear the cognomen Dracula for the 'sons of Dracul.'

A ferocious midsummer breeze, the dragon's breath, whipped his banners. To him, the flurry imitated what must be the flight of hundreds of winged beasts, heralding fiery deaths for their enemies. Then the wind tore one of the flags from a warrior's spear.

Vlad grinned as the fabric flew aloft, and whirled and glided, never touching the ground. The red dragon stitched on yellow cloth soared on, as if in triumph.

THE END

CHARACTERS

The Christians and their retainers
-Wallachians, Moldavians, & Transilvanians-

VLAD II DRACUL OF THE House of Basarab, the third son of Mircea the Great of the House of Basarab and Mara of the House of Tolmay, born circa 1394.

Cneajna (Vasilisa Maria) of the House of Muşat, daughter of Alexandru the Good of the House of Muşat in Moldavia. Wife of Vlad II Dracul of the House of Basarab.

Mircea Dracula (Drăculeşti) of the House of Basarab, eldest son of Vlad II Dracul of the House of Basarab and Cneajna (Vasilisa Maria) of the House of Muşat, born in 1428 at Segesvár, Transilvania.

Vlad Dracula (Drăculeşti) of the House of Basarab, the second son of Vlad II Dracul of the House of Basarab, and Cneajna (Vasilisa Maria) of the House of Muşat, born December 1431 at Segesvár, Transilvania.

Călţuna, a Transilvanian nobleman's bastard daughter from Hermannstadt. Lover of Vlad II Dracul of the House of Basarab. Mother of Vlad Călugărul.

Vlad Călugărul, only son of Vlad II Dracul of the House of Basarab and Călţuna, born circa 1425.

Ana-Călina, born circa 1340. Widow of Radu of Wallachia. Mother of Mircea the Great of the House of Basarab. Dowager Princess of Wallachia. Paternal aunt of Vlâcsan Florescu.

Mircea the Great of the House of Basarab, son of Radu of the House of Basarab and Ana-Călina, born circa 1355. Husband of Mara of the House of Tolmay, married circa 1377. Elected as hereditary prince (*Voivode*) of Wallachia 1386-November 1394 and January 1397-January 1418. Duke of Făgăraş and Amlaş in Transilvania. Vassal of King Zsigmond of Luxembourg 1405-1418. Died 31 January 1418 at Curtea de Argeş and buried at Cozia Monastery.

Mara of the House of Tolmay, Hungarian-born wife of Mircea the Great of the House of Basarab, born circa 1363. Princess of Wallachia circa 1377. Duchess of Făgăraş and Amlaş in Transilvania.

Mihail of the House of Basarab, eldest son of Mircea the Great of the House of Basarab and Mara of the House of Tolmay, born circa January 1382. Elected as co-ruler of Wallachia at Târgovişte 1415-1418. Elected as sole hereditary prince (*Voivode*) of Wallachia 1418-1420. Duke of Făgăraş and Amlaş in Transilvania 1418-1420. Vassal of King Zsigmond of Luxembourg 1418-1420. Died August 1420.

Radu and **Mihail of the House of Basarab**, sons of Mihail of the House of Basarab. Hostages of Mehmed I Hân after autumn 1419.

Radu II Praznaglava of the House of Basarab, second son of Mircea the Great of the House of Basarab and Mara of the House of Tolmay, born circa 1386. Elected as hereditary prince (*Voivode*) of Wallachia at Târgovişte August 1421-1422, summer of 1423, autumn of 1424, January-spring of 1427. Vassal of King Zsigmond of Luxembourg. Died after spring 1427.

Alexandru Aldea of the House of Basarab, fourth son of Mircea the Great of the House of Basarab and Mara of the House of Tolmay, born circa 1397. Elected as hereditary prince (*Voivode*) of Wallachia March 1432. Vassal of King Zsigmond of Luxembourg and Sultan Murād II Hân.

Arina of the House of Basarab, second daughter of Mircea the Great of the House of Basarab and Mara of the House of Tolmay. Elder twin sister of Vlad II Dracul of the House of Basarab. First wife of Mûsâ Çelebi, married 1409-1413.

Staico, bastard son of Radu of the House of Basarab. Half-brother of Mircea the Great of the House of Basarab.

Dan II Dăneşti of the House of Basarab, son of Dan I of the House of Basarab, and Mara Branković of Serbia. Paternal nephew of Mircea the Great of the House of Basarab. Elected hereditary prince (*Voivode*) of Wallachia at Curtea de Argeş August 1420-May 1421, November 1421-summer 1423, summer 1423-December 1424, May 1426-January 1427, and spring 1427-March 1431. Disputed Duke of Făgăraş and

Amlaş in Transilvania until 1427. Vassal of King Zsigmond of Luxembourg and Sultan Murād II Hân.

Alexandru the Good of the House of Muşat, son of Roman I of the House of Muşat, born circa 1375. Father of Iliaş, Ştefan, Petru, and Cneajna (Vasilisa Maria) of the House of Muşat. Hereditary prince (*Voivode*) of Moldavia 23 April 1400-January 1432. Vassal of King Władysław II Jagiełło 1402-1431 and Zsigmond of Luxembourg. Died January 1432 at Suceava, Moldavia.

Iliaş of the House of Muşat, son of Alexandru the Good of the House of Muşat and his wife Anna (Neaksha), born 20 July 1409. Sole hereditary prince (*Voivode*) of Moldavia January 1432. Co-ruler of Moldavia 1414-1432. Vassal of King Władysław II Jagiełło.

Maria Holszańska, sister of Zofia Holszańska, Lithuanian-born wife of Iliaş of the House of Muşat. Princess of Moldavia 1425.

Roman II of the House of Muşat, son of Iliaş of the House of Muşat and Maria Holszańska, born circa 1426.

Ştefan II (Stetco) of the House of Muşat, son of Alexandru the Good of the House of Muşat and his mistress Stanca, born circa 1410-1411.

Petru III of the House of Muşat, son of Alexandru the Good of the House of Muşat, born circa 1422.

Vajk Hunyadi, a Wallachian-born knight. Vassal of King Zsigmond of Luxembourg 1395-1419. Died before 12 February 1419.

János Hunyadi, Hungarian-born son of Vajk Hunyadi, born circa 1406 at Castle Hunyadvár. Vassal of King Zsigmond of Luxembourg 1419.

Erzsébet Szilágyi, daughter of László Szilágyi, born circa 1410. Fiancée of János Hunyadi.

Albu Tocsaba, son of Albu Tocsaba, a Chief Magistrate of the Princely Court in the service of Alexandru Aldea of the House of Basarab. The highest official among the council of boyars.

Vlậcsan Florescu, son of Florea, called the Wolf. Paternal nephew of Ana-Călina, cousin of Mircea the Great of the House of Basarab.

Vintilă Florescu, only son of Vlậcsan Florescu.

Pahomie of Tismana, cousin of Vlắcsan Florescu. A monk at Tismana Monastery.

Ruxandra Lupu, the Moldavian noble maidservant of Cneajna (Vasilisa Maria) of the House of Muşat.

Dragomir, a minor official at Segesvár, Transilvania.

Petru, only son of Dragomir.

Marko (kennel master), a Gypsy slave in the service of Mircea the Great of the House of Basarab.

Tobar (chief huntsman) and **Yoska One-Eye** (kennel master), twin sons of Marko the Gypsy kennel master. Former Gypsy slaves loyal to Prince Vlad II Dracul of the House of Basarab.

The Order of The Dragon, their relations, overlords & vassals

- Hungarians -

ZSIGMOND OF LUXEMBOURG, son of Holy Roman Emperor Charles IV (Wenceslaus of Luxembourg) and Elisabeth of Pomerania, born on 15 February 1368. Prince-elector of Brandenburg 1378-1388 and 1411-1415. King of Hungary and Croatia 1387, and Germany 1411, and Bohemia 1419, and Italy 1431. Founder of the Order of the Dragon (*Societas Draconistarum*) on 12 December 1408.

Borbála of Celje, Slovenian-born, youngest daughter of Hermann II, Count of Celje (Styria) and Countess Anna of Schaunberg, born 1392. Second wife of Zsigmond of Luxembourg, married 1405. Queen of Hungary and Croatia. Regent of Hungary in 1412, 1414, 1416 and 1418. Queen of Germany 1411, and Bohemia 1419, and Italy 1431. Founder of the Order of the Dragon (*Societas Draconistarum*) on 12 December 1408.

Erzsébet of Luxembourg, daughter of Zsigmond of Luxembourg and Borbála of Celje, was born on 4 October 1409. Wife of Albrecht the Magnanimous, married 1422

Albrecht the Magnanimous, born 10 August 1397. Husband of Erzsébet of Luxembourg, married 1422.

Miklós II Garai, son of Miklós I Garai, born circa 1367. Palatine of Hungary 1402; the highest great officer of state in the Kingdom of Hungary. Former Banate of Croatia, Dalmatia, and Slavonia. A superior within the Order of the Dragon from 12 December 1408. Vassal and ally of Zsigmond of Luxembourg 1387. Brother-in-law of Borbála of Celje. Former brother-in-law of Stefan Lazarević and Milena Olivera Lazarević through marriage to their sister Theodora Lazarević.

- Serbs -

Stefan Lazarević, son of Lazar Hrebeljanović and Milica Nemanjić of Serbia, born circa 1377. *Despoteses* of the Kingdom of Rascia (northern Serbia) 1389-1427. Former Turkic vassal 1389-1402 and brother-in-law to Sultan Bāyazīd Hân. Vassal and ally of Zsigmond of Luxembourg 1404-1427. A superior within the Order of the Dragon from 12 December 1408. Died 1427.

Milena Olivera Lazarević (Despina Hatun), the youngest daughter of Lazar Hrebeljanović and Milica Nemanjić of Serbia, born circa 1372. The eldest sister of Stefan Lazarević. Widow of Sultan Bāyazīd Hân (married 1389/1390) and mother of his daughters, Beyhan (born 1391), Melek (born 1392), and Oruz.

Đurađ Branković, son of Vuk Branković and Mara Lazarević, born 1377. Despoteses of the Kingdom of Rascia (northern Serbia) from 1427. Vassal of King Zsigmond of Luxembourg 1427. Maternal nephew of Stefan Lazarević and Milena Olivera Lazarević. Maternal cousin of Fruzhin of Bulgaria.

Radič Postupović, born circa 1372. Count Palatine of Serbia; the highest great officer of state in Serbia. Vassal of Prince Stefan Lazarević 1405-1427 and Prince Đurađ Branković from 1427. Widower of Anna of the House of Basarab and father of their son Misailo.

- Bulgarians -

Fruzhin of Bulgaria, son of Ivan Shishman of Bulgaria and Dragana Lazarević of Serbia, born circa 1386. Maternal nephew of Stefan Lazarević and Milena Olivera Lazarević (Despina Hatun). Maternal cousin of Đurađ Branković. A superior within the Order of the Dragon from 12 December 1408. Vassal and ally of Zsigmond of Luxembourg 1397.

- Polish -

Władysław II Jagiełło, son of Algirdas, Grand Duke of Lithuania, and Uliana of Tver, born between 1352 and 1362. Grand Duke of Lithuania May 1377-August 1381, August 1382. King of Poland 1386.

Zofia Holszańska, born circa 1405 in Lithuania. Fourth wife of Władysław II Jagiełło. Queen consort of Poland February 1422.

Władysław III Jagiełło, eldest son of Władysław II Jagiełło and Zofia Holszańska, born 23/31 October 1424.

Anna of Celje (Andlein), daughter of Viljem of Celje and Anna of Poland, born 1386. Second wife of Władysław II Jagiełło. Queen consort of Poland 29 January 1402-21 May 1416. Maternal first cousin of Borbála of Celje. Died 21 May 1416.

Jadwiga Jagiełłonka, daughter of Władysław II Jagiełło and Anna of Celje, born 8 April 1408. Maternal second cousin of Borbála of Celje. Died 8 December 1431.

Stibor of Stiboricz of the House of Ostaya, Polish-born son of Mościc, *Voivode* of Gniewkowo, born circa 1348. Governor (*Voivode*) of Transilvania 1395-1401 and 1409-1414. A great officer of state in the Kingdom of Hungary. Ally of Zsigmond of Luxembourg. A superior within the Order of the Dragon from 12 December 1408. Died February 1414.

Stibor II of Beckov of the House of Ostaya, son of Stibor of Stiboricz of the House of Ostaya. A superior within the Order of the Dragon from 12 December 1408. Vassal of King Zsigmond of Luxembourg 1408.

- Styrians -

Hermann II, Count of Celje, father of Borbála of Celje and Friderik of Celje, paternal uncle of Anna of Celje, born circa 1365. Formerly of Banate of Croatia, Dalmatia, and Slavonia April 1406-January 1408. Ally of Zsigmond of Luxembourg. A superior within the Order of the Dragon from 12 December 1408.

Friderik of Celje, eldest son of Hermann II, Count of Celje and Countess Anna of Schaunberg. A superior within the Order of the Dragon from 12 December 1408.

Veronika Deseniška, second wife of Friderik of Celje. Murdered 17 October 1425.

Other royals & nobles, their relations, overlords & vassals

- Byzantines -

IŌANNĒS VIII PALAEOLOGUS, eldest son of Manouēl Palaeologus and Helena Dragaš of Serbia, born 18 December 1392. Co-emperor of Byzantium at Constantinople from 1416 and sole emperor from 1425.

- Germans -

Friedrich of the House of Hohenzollern, born on 21 September 1371. Burgrave of Nürnberg (1397-1427) and Prince-elector of Brandenburg 1415. Reputed lover of Queen Borbála of Celje.

The Muslims and their retainers

MÛSÂ ÇELEBI, third son of Bāyazīd Hân, born circa 1388. Ottoman Sultan of Rumelia (the Turkish Balkans) at Edirnê (Turkish Adrianople) 17/18 February 1411-5 July 1413. Husband of Arina of the House of Basarab, married 1409. Murdered 5 July 1413 by the soldiers of his brother Sultan Mehmed I Hân.

Şeyh Bedreddin, son of Israil Ghazi and Melek of Simavna, born 1359. Chief Ottoman military judge. Vassal of Sultan Mûsâ Çelebi. Murdered 1418 or 1420 in Sérres, Turkish Macedonia.

AUTHOR'S NOTE

About this Novel

ORDER OF THE DRAGON – Book One is a highly fictionalized novel, exploring the life and times of Vlad Dracul, a prince of Wallachia; a country that would emerge in the nineteenth century, after Turkish domination, as Romania. Several events, including Vlad's time in the Hungarian court of Zsigmond of Luxembourg and his sister Arina's marriage to Prince Mûsâ Çelebi, the battles and diverse relationships between European Christians and Turks, Vlad's unions and children with the women called Călţuna and Cneajna, as well most historical figures are representations based on varied historical accounts. However, this could never be a purely biographical, historical novel, because intimate details the true ties or discord between Vlad and any of the historical figures are uncertain. I took my "best guess" from academic sources to create a narrative where certain interactions are plausible. The dates of historical events referenced in the novel are based on the Julian calendar; usage of the more modern Gregorian calendar by Catholics did not occur until 1582.

- The Wallachians -

THE PEOPLE OF ROMANIA once lived as the Wallachians. Romania did not legally exist as the name of a country until 1866. A prince ruled the Wallachian people with the support of the nobility of their land, called boyars. There were typically ten to fourteen boyars who served as members of the Princely Court in Wallachia. Boyars elected their princes and they could destroy their political power. Typically, the Wallachian royals, nobles, and dignitaries signed their first names and perhaps a sobriquet (e.g., Dracul) or nickname (e.g., the Wolf) to documents. They did not use family names until the 17th century.

- The Ottoman Turks -

THE TURKS EMERGED FROM their small villages to conquer the cities and regions of Anatolia that were previously under the rule of the Eastern Holy Roman Empire, set in Byzantium or Constantinople. The Ottoman Turks descended from Osman Bey, known to his people as the son of the tribal chieftain and conqueror Ertuğrul Bey, and the grandson of Suleyman Shah. Osman Bey had a dream that a tree grew to encompass the world, which he believed symbolized the great empire his sons and descendants would rule. Throughout the Turkic conquests across Anatolia, Constantinople remained one of the chief targets of the Ottomans.

- Other Medieval States -

THE BYZANTINE TITLE of the *Despoteses* of the Kingdom of Rascia was the official name for the ruler of Serbia at the time, e.g., Stefan Lazarević and Đurađ Branković. Historically in Byzantium, the title, which ranked just below that of an emperor, was a personal court title, typically assigned to members of the imperial family. In the summer of 1402 Stefan Lazarević received the title in Constantinople from the imperial co-ruler Iōannēs VII Palaeologus. The Christian rulers of Serbia after Stefan's death retained the title.

A BRIEF FACTUAL ACCOUNT of the historical figures featured or mentioned in the novel will appear on my website, www.lisajyarde.com[1] at the conclusion of the series of novels and novellas about Vlad Dracul and his family. Unless noted otherwise, all battles and sieges, and celestial phenomena took place on the dates indicated in the narrative.

About Vlad Dracul

BEFORE WRITING THIS novel and embarking on an obsession with Vlad Dracul and his family, I asked myself, "Why choose this historical figure? What might make him a fascinating character for readers?" History cares about Vlad Dracul insofar as he became the father of Vlad Dracula in 1431; the inspiration for author Bram Stoker's Count Dracula, the vampire.

Vlad Dracula is so mired in vampiric mythology; I hesitated to explore his lineage for several years before setting down this tale. There's been more written about Count Dracula than the real-life Prince Vlad Dracula; a perpetual annoyance for anyone trying to research the true origins and experiences of his family. Yet, the historical figure of Vlad Dracula is even more complex and cruel than any portrayal of him as a vampire.

You may well be asking at this point, why am I reading about Vlad Dracula if his father is the focus of this novel? Every story has a beginning. Quite literally, there is no Vlad Dracula; monstrous tyrant, or vampiric myth, without his father Vlad Dracul.

While contemplating whether to write about Vlad Dracul, good fortune or sheer luck brought me to Dr. Peter Dan's paper *Psycho-biographical considerations about Vlad the Impaler also known as Dracula*. A key phrase from Dr. Dan's work, "... early childhood data suggests that Vlad (Dracula) may have suffered a certain degree of emotional neglect, and may have shown a propensity to at least watch violence..." set my imagination on fire.

1. http://www.lisajyarde.com

What sort of man could Vlad Dracula's father have been to allow him the experience of emotional neglect and violence? The conceptualization of this novel came to life in that moment and I set off to uncover facts about Vlad Dracul. What did I discover? The facts were sparse at best.

As with everything I have ever written or while ever write, this novel is not a factual account of Vlad Dracul's life. I suggest what may have been possible only. Much of the research into historical events portrayed in this novel were timely discoveries incorporated in the narrative; to paraphrase one of my favorite characters, very little in life is coincidence.

It's verifiable that Vlad Dracul was a child of Prince Mircea the Great of the Elder. Vlad Dracul has been called a legitimate heir of his father and a bastard in varying sources. Whether he was born in or before 1394, as a legitimate son of Mircea and his wife, Mara of the House of Tolmay or Toma is unclear. He may have been the bastard of another woman as his father purportedly had several mistresses.

As I've mentioned, all Wallachian princes, regardless of their mothers' heritage, were viable candidates for election as ruler of the country in the view of the nobles or boyars. Vlad Dracul had at least five siblings; Mihail, Radu, and Alexander, brothers who each ruled Wallachia, and two sisters; Anna, who married the Serbian magnate, Radič Postupović and Arina, who wed Mûsâ Çelebi, the Turkic prince whom their father Mircea tried to keep on the Ottoman throne for reasons explored in the novel.

The length of time in which Vlad Dracul spent his formative years in Wallachia or Budapest, Hungary at the dazzling court of Zsigmond of Luxembourg is also debatable. One history suggested he lived in Constantinople during his formative years. The historical figures of Zsigmond and his queen Borbála, Prince Fruzhin of Bulgaria, Stibor of Stiboricz and his namesake son Stibor of Beckov, the Serbian despot Stefan Lazarević, Pipo of Ozora, and the father-son duo of Vajk and János Hunyadi, along with many others, inhabited the social circles in which Vlad Dracul would have resided in Hungary. What is lost to history is how he interacted with them. Well, much more is certain about the relationship of Vlad Dracul and János Hunyadi. More about that association will unfold in the next novel.

History provides light details about Vlad Dracul's time in Hungary, except a brief mention of his encounter and subsequent travel with the Byzantine emperor Iōannēs VIII Palaeologus in 1424. King Zsigmond played host to the emperor who advocated the reunification of the Catholic and Orthodox churches, in the face of the persistent threat from the Ottoman Turks.

There are two theories on Vlad Dracul's interaction with the emperor. Both find their origins in the idea that, frustrated with Zsigmond 's refusal to help him gain the throne of Wallachia, Vlad Dracul sought the emperor's support and may have enlisted with him as a soldier. In doing so, he left the Hungarian court in 1425 alongside the emperor with Zsigmond 's permission, or Vlad Dracul did not have consent and thus, earned his king's ire.

Other sources indicate the Wallachian prince appeared at the court of the Turkish sultan Murad II Hân in 1422, during a siege of Constantinople. Thereafter Vlad Dracul allegedly entered the Byzantine capital of the emperor Iōannēs VIII Palaeologus, who put him on a galley bound for his homeland, where he could not persuade its people to support him.

Whatever the truth, by such time Vlad Dracul had already met the woman often called his mistress, Călţuna. History hardly notes her except the later change in her circumstances, when she lived as a nun. Before then, Călţuna mothered Vlad Dracul's first namesake son, called Vlad Călugărul or Vlad the Monk, born in 1425. For whatever reason, including the one I speculated about in the novel, Vlad Dracul never married Călţuna; except one recent source says she became his third wife, which I believe is inaccurate. Others have posited that he had a Polish wife, who died early.

More common is the theory that he wed Vasilisa Maria, alternatively called, or conflated with Marina of the House of Muşat in Moldavia, the princess Cneajna in the story. I've explained her use of the name Cneajna; the most logical reasoning for the word, '*kneaghina*—a *knez*'s or prince's daughter' as the source of the name often recorded for Vlad

Dracul's wife. Like his father Mircea the Great, Vlad Dracul's assumed to have had many mistresses, so Călţuna and Cneajna were not the sole mothers of his children.

In 1431 he became a member of the Order of the Dragon at Nuremberg in Bavaria. Founded on 12 December 1408 by King Zsigmond and Queen Borbála—one of the rarest instances in the medieval period where a woman formed and held high rank in a knightly order, a unique mission bound its members: the protection of the Hungarian monarchs and the destruction of the Turks. During the first initiation ceremony, Prince Fruzhin of Bulgaria, Stibor of Stiboricz and his namesake son Stibor of Beckov, the Serbian despot Stefan Lazarević, and Pipo of Ozora among an odd-twenty others joined the Order. When Vlad Dracul gained admission, I wonder if he guessed at how his oath would be tested.

Zsigmond dispatched him to modern-day Sighişoara to a new post as a border commander. Vlad Dracul's banners and later coinage bore the dragon heraldry associated with the Order. When superstitious medieval people saw the symbol, they called it 'Dracul,' meaning the dragon or the devil. That's why the epithet remained attached to Vlad Dracul and his descendants, surnamed Dracula, literally the 'son of the dragon or devil.' Although the Dracula family did not consistently use the name as identification of their line of descent from Vlad Dracul, I did so to distinguish them from their other relations who vied for the throne.

Vlad Dracul's story deserves to be known, as does a full examination of the role he played with AND against the Ottoman Turks. That's why I wrote this novel. Learn more about Vlad's fate after he reached Sighişoara in the final installment about his life.

GLOSSARY

About transliteration, spellings and pronunciation in Order of the Dragon

THE SPELLINGS OF PERSONAL names for European and Turkish historical figures, and most medieval place names are as Prince Vlad Dracul would have known them, rather than their Westernized or modern equivalent, as they would have been anachronistic in the Middle Ages. For readers' comprehension, the modern variants of cities, towns, and countries occur in brackets at most chapter headings. Thus, Wallachia rather than Romania, which did not exist as a nation until 1866. Transilvania, rather than Transilvania, was the preferred usage during Vlad Dracul's time. The prince would have known the cities and townships of the Czech Republic as parts of Bohemia, and sites in the country of Bosnia and Herzegovina, as being in Bosnia. In his interactions with the eastern imperial adherents of Orthodox Christianity, its last emperor considered his people the 'descendants of Greeks and Romans' but for readers' comfort and familiarity, this novel describes them as members of the Byzantine Empire.

There are exceptions where modern or common names are used, such as rivers like the Danube, known in Hungarian as the Duna. Other areas mentioned with modern names include the regions of Germany and Poland, and place names in Serbia, like Belgrade; its erstwhile medieval capital. Vlad Dracul traveled across Europe in the service of Hungary's king, Zsigmond of Luxembourg.

The title of *Despoteses* for some European historical figures, including the rulers of Serbia, derives from the Byzantine Empire where in ancient Greek it meant "the master."

For over two centuries before Vlad Dracul's birth, the Ottoman Turks had coveted Constantinople, which they referred to as Konstantiniyye, rather than Istanbul. As some Turkish words and their meanings have become common for English readers, I have relied on the commonly accepted Anglicized version of such terms, e.g., Pasha, rather than the Turkish form, Paşa. Some terms that have appeared or will appear in this series of novels and novellas include:

- Bey: in the Turkic language, a title junior to Pasha and conferred on civil and military officers on a personal basis; also borne as a courtesy title for the sons of a Pasha.
- Çelebi: in the Turkic language, meaning a gentleman. An honorific term for the sons of Ottoman Turkish sultans in the 14th century.
- Devşirme: in the Turkish language, the blood tax or blood tribute. A forfeiture of Christian boys between the ages 7 to 14 or 18 in the Anatolian and Balkan regions, with the purpose of converting them to Islam and educating them as Turkish Janissaries, or elite infantrymen. Exemptions occurred with orphaned boys or the sole son in a family.
- Doamna: Princess in the Romanian language.
- Domnul: Prince in the Romanian language.
- Io: an abbreviation of the theophoric name, Ioan or John. A title used mainly by the royalty in Moldavia and Wallachia, preceding their names and honors.
- Janissary: in the Turkic language, from *yeni-ceri*, for 'new troops.'
- Pasha: in the Turkic language, a very high official or Lord, a title senior to that of Bey and conferred on a personal basis on senior civil officials and military officers. Awarded in several grades, signified by a whip, the highest rank being a whip of three yak or horsetails.
- Pashalik: in the Turkic language, a vassal state.
- Sanjak: in the Turkic language, meaning distract, flag, banner, or standard. An administrative division within the Ottoman Empire.
- Sanjak-bey: in the Turkic language, a high officer of the cavalry who governs an administrative division within the Ottoman Empire.
- Voivode: one of several Slavonic terms for Romanian and

Moldavian rulers, meaning warlord, hereditary prince, or governor.

ORDER OF THE DRAGON-BOOK ONE

Lisa J. Yarde

LISA J. YARDE is the author of a six-part series set in Moorish Spain, *Sultana*[2], *Sultana's Legacy*,[3] *Sultana: Two Sisters*[4], *Sultana: The Bride Price*[5], *Sultana: The Pomegranate Tree*[6], and *Sultana: The White Mountains*[7], where rivalries and ambitions threaten the fragile bonds between members of the last Muslim dynasty to rule in Europe. The first title in the series is available in multiple languages. She has also written *The Order of the Dragon – Book One*, the first novel in a series about the family of the real Dracula.

Lisa has also published two historical novels set in medieval England and Normandy, *On Falcon's Wings*[8], featuring a star-crossed romance between Norman and Saxon lovers before the Battle of Hastings in 1066, and *The Burning Candle*[9], based on the life of the first Countess of Leicester and Surrey, Isabel de Vermandois, progenitor of modern royal and non-noble families. Lisa's short stories include *The Legend Rises*[10], in the **HerStory** anthology, which chronicles the Welsh princess Gwenllian of Gwynedd's fight against twelfth-century English invaders, and *The Heretic*[11], in the anthology **We All Fall Down**, wherein the Hispano-Muslim doctor Ibn al-Khatib struggles to survive the Black Death.

---

2. *http://www.lisajyarde.com/p/buy-books.html*
3. *http://www.lisajyarde.com/p/buy-books.html*
4. *http://www.lisajyarde.com/p/buy-books.html*
5. *http://www.lisajyarde.com/p/buy-books.html*
6. *http://www.lisajyarde.com/p/buy-books.html*
7. *http://www.lisajyarde.com/p/buy-books.html*
8. *http://www.lisajyarde.com/p/buy-books.html*
9. *http://www.lisajyarde.com/p/buy-books.html*
10. *http://www.lisajyarde.com/p/buy-books.html*
11. *https://books2read.com/falldown/#_blank*

Born in Barbados, Lisa lived abroad for 33 years until a recent, permanent return to her island home. For more than a decade, she has been affiliated with the Historical Novel Society[12], presented at its 2015 Denver conference, and served as the co-chair of the Historical Novel Society – New York City chapter[13] (2015-2017) and social media manager (2017-2022). She remains involved as the current program chair. An avid techie, she has presented to varied audiences on the topics of historical fiction, self-publishing, and website and social media management. She has moderated and contributed to Unusual Historicals[14], Great Historicals[15], and History & Women[16], and previously reviewed historical fiction for the History & Women[17] blog, Washington Independent Review of Books, and through NetGalley. Her personal blog is The Bajan Scribbler[18].

Learn more about Lisa and her writing at the website www.lisajyarde.com[19].

---

12. https://historicalnovelsociety.org/#_blank
13. https://www.facebook.com/groups/631473066981339/#_blank
14. http://unusualhistoricals.blogspot.com/
15. http://greathistoricals.blogspot.com/
16. http://www.historyandwomen.com/
17. http://www.historyandwomen.com/
18. https://thebajanscribbler.blogspot.com/
19. http://www.lisajyarde.com/

Dear Reader

THANK YOU FOR READING this novel. If you care to share your thoughts about it, consider leaving a review at the site where you made your purchase. You can always contact me at lisa@lisajyarde.com if you have any questions about the story, including the historical figures and events detailed in these pages.

Sincerely,

Lisa J. Yarde

www.ingramcontent.com/pod-product-compliance
Lightning Source LLC
Chambersburg PA
CBHW030741030726
47497CB00001B/85

* 9 7 8 1 9 3 9 1 3 8 2 4 8 *